"The ideas expressed here are both exhilarating and cathartic. This is speech at its most theatrically extreme. One leaves Theater For The New City not knowing whether to go home, or out for a stiff drink." **BACK WHEN-BACK THEN, Ricky Spears, In Theater, New York City, November 28, 1997.**

"Barry's artistry is definite. Form and content are inseparable in **ONCE IN DOUBT** adding up to a statement that is coherent, evocative and richly entertaining. The short play is wonderfully full and despite its serious themes - delightfully funny. The dialogue is sharp and witty. The man's mental journeys are full of powerful images and strong, elastic rhythms. The play suggests reality with deep thought and imagination." **Eric Suben, Villager Downtown, New York City, November 27, 1984.**

"This brief, surrealistic one-act explores a grown man's conflicting feelings about his domineering mother with an intensity that borders on savagery." **MOTHER'SON, Tom Jacobs, Daily Variety, March 16, 1994. Los Angeles.**

"Barry's... **ONCE IN DOUBT**, an alternately harrowing and hilarious study of the obsessive relationship between an artist and his live-in lover... This is a fabulous show – electrifying and thought-provoking." **Albert Williams, Chicago Reader, August 7, 1992.**

"This disturbing, ritualized, *pas de deux* is written by Barry, who seems to have taken lessons in domestic nightmare from Edward Albee." **Helen Meany, BACK WHEN-BACK THEN, The Irish Times, October 12, 2000, Dublin, Ireland.**

"Dark, hilarious, menacing and brilliantly performed, **MOTHER'SON** is an exaggerated theatrical rendering of a hundred stifling mother/son relationships." **Stella Goormay, The Stage, September 21, 1995, Edinburgh Festival, Scotland.**

"Barry's fine surreal psychodrama, **MOTHER'SON**, pulls no punches in making the point that this kind of relationship is not funny, or cozy, or harmless, but deeply life-denying, implicitly violent, and a breeder of free-floating aggression on a horrific scale." **Scotland On Sunday, Edinburgh Festival, August 13, 1995.**

"Barry writes hilarious Joycean soliloquies and solipsistic arguments." **MOTHER'SON, Richard Stayton, Los Angeles Times, March 16, 1994.**

"A brittle, brilliant script by Raymond J. Barry careens through a myriad of themes, constantly hurling disparate and distressing images at the audience." **MOTHER'SON, The Herald, Edinburgh Festival, August 30, 1995.**

"The dueling dialogue, with its non-sequitor asides and conflicted characters crossing words in terminal non-communication, makes for absurdist comedy with inspired reverberations." **ONCE IN DOUBT, Sylvie Drake, Los Angeles Times, November 13, 1989.**

"**ONCE IN DOUBT** is quite an accomplishment. Barry's play is a bizarre experience. It is very powerful theatrically." **Carol Burbank, Philadelphia City Paper, July 21, 1989.**

"Raymond J. Barry's **ONCE IN DOUBT** at the Remains Theatre puts its three actors way out on a limb, which it constantly threatens to saw off. The play's first half is a ferocious – and hilarious – battle of the sexes..." **Richard Christiansen, Chicago Tribune, June 30, 1992.**

"New York stage actor Raymond J. Barry, who both wrote this seriocomic collage of love and hate, has fashioned an insidious drama of a human relationship that sticks like blood on a white canvas." **ONCE IN DOUBT, Ray Loynd, Los Angeles Times, January 1989.**

"Unusually sophisticated... so disturbing I had to avert my eyes and cover my ears." **ONCE IN DOUBT, Hedy Weiss, Chicago Sun-Times, July 5, 1992.**

"There are times during **ONCE IN DOUBT** when you just have to smile. Rarely does a playwright – in this case, Raymond J. Barry – capture exactly how comically difficult, how nearly impossible, it is for two people to love one another. It's rarer still for a playwright to capture that frustration while remaining keenly aware of how much we need love." **Scott Collins, Southtown Economist, Chicago, June 29, 1992.**

"The experimentalism is the playwright's scraping away of all the polite conversation and rational self-deceptions. He shows us bloody bone and marrow being exercised in the pursuit of happiness." **ONCE IN DOUBT, Jimmy Fowler, Dallas Observer, October 7, 1998.**

"BACK WHEN-BACK THEN is an astonishing play. It is imbued with a lyricism all but banished from an American stage frozen in naturalism." **Stephan Silvis, Willamette Weekly, Portland, Oregon, February 11, 1997.**

ONCE IN DOUBT is a savagely funny, unsettling work, and is recommended for its intelligent exploration of personal and artistic passions and the risks associated with them." **Greg Aaron, University City Review, Philadelphia, July 1989.**

"ONCE IN DOUBT" is a vivid, vibrant roller-coaster of a play." **Daily Variety, November 14, 1989, Los Angeles.**

"The tension ... bounces between a soft, ethereal self-awareness, and a harsh verbal violence... The language is rich and elliptical." **BACK WHEN-BACK THEN, Barry Johnson, The Oregonian, Portland, Oregon, February 11, 1997.**

"MOTHER'SON has a rough energy and a dramatic punch that is undeniable, sort of a scream (sic) of consciousness unleashed, a study in contrived and deliberate terms – but fascinating, sweeping, and at once repulsive and erotic." **James Metropole, The Movie Gazette, April 1994, Los Angeles.**

"ONCE IN DOUBT is a gem of a play that is its own reason for being." **Madeleine Shaner, Back Stage West Dramalogue, May 27, 1999, Los Angeles.**

"MOTHER'SON is one of the most delicious, if guilty, pleasures on a local stage." **Rob Kendt, Back Stage West, March 17, 1994, Los Angeles.**

"The play is a Joycean flight of words, full of free associations, abrupt turns, unexpected lulls, explosive humor." **MOTHER'SON, Jim Delmont, Omaha World - Herald, September 10, 1993.**

"MOTHER'SON is a terrific play containing verbal gymnastics that are absolutely fantastic." **BBC Radio, Edinburgh Festival, October 12, 1995.**

"Raymond J. Barry's soliloquies are poetic, conscious, and aware." **MOTHER'SON, Daniel Goldman, Independent, May 1994, Colorado Springs.**

"If a full-bodied play can be considered a symphony, then Raymond J. Barry's **ONCE IN DOUBT** at the Los Angeles Theater Center is a very bitter suite, a deadly divertimento, jaunty Jacques Ibert with karate chops, a stinging jazz riff-the theatrical equivalent of a heavy metal power chord." **John C. Mohoney, Downtown News, Los Angeles, November 20, 1989.**

"People's Light and Theater's premiere of **ONCE IN DOUBT** is an explosive, shocking comedy-drama which leaves the audience in almost breathless anticipation." **Michael Byrne, Main Line Times, Philadelphia, July 20, 1989.**

"Its language is as arch as Pinter, as bewildering as Ionesco, and (at times) as visceral as Mamet." **ONCE IN DOUBT, Elizabeth A. Finkler, Welcomat - After Dark, Philadelphia, July 12, 1989.**

"Barry has a terrific ear for dialogue, and some of the writing is more poetry than prose." **BACK WHEN – BACK THEN, Mark Arnest, Gazette Tele-graph, Colorado Springs, May 20, 1994.**

"**FOUL SHOTS** is a fierce collision of wills that threatens to destroy the fragile present, the despised past and the threatened future of lives almost lived, memories, regrets, fears, despair and ineffable yearnings." **Madeleine Shaner, Park LaBrea News, Los Angeles, July 17, 2003.**

"**FOUL SHOTS** is a play every man should see, as we, in our own various ways, live it. Here's a theater artist to seek out so as to say later in life, 'Yes, I saw him.'" **Stephan Silvis, Willamette Week, January 29, 2003, Portland, Oregon.**

"**BACK WHEN BACK THEN** shifts effortlessly from black humor to lyricism, from skittishness to menace, a disturbing, ritualized, pas de deux, deserving of four stars." **Helen Meany, The Irish Times, Dublin, Ireland, October 12, 2000.**

"The frankness of Raymond Barry's play, **BACK WHEN - BACK THEN**, both in presentation and message is most refreshing compared to the touchy-feely psychodrama we often see in our theaters today - Critics' Choice" **Chad Jones, The Oakland Tribune, Magic Theater, San Francisco, September 28, 1997.**

"**BACK WHEN - BACK THEN** is a study of rage, and Barry does his best writing when he puts you inside the mind of someone who's out of control. It's an evening of theater you won't forget." **Mark Arnest, Gazette Telegraph, Colorado Springs, May 20, 1996.**

"I went to see **ONCE IN DOUBT**... and it was the best thing I had seen. And what struck me was the total experience of it - that you got hit with this wave of emotional words, which kept coming in a barrage, and then it would stop on a dime, and it was very precise. You could see the work and it was beautiful, and it's something that was kind of shocking to see." **Interview with Jack Black, Back Stage West, February 22, 1996.**

"I read a review of the play, **ONCE IN DOUBT** that was being performed at the Los Angeles Theater Center. I was blown away by it..." **William Petersen of CSI in an interview for Back Stage West; February 17, 1994.**

"Barry's dystopian comedy of a world where the safety of cake has replaced the dangers of sex is a fast-paced, tough-talking saga... an excellent playwright is perfecting his work before our eyes." **A PIECE OF CAKE, Stephan Silvis, Willamette Weekly, Portland, Oregon, July 26, 2000.**

"**PORNOGRAPHIC PANORAMA** is a pitch-black comedy that dares to pry back the rock and shine light on our empty, artificial culture, which has been reduced to distraction and the simulacra of real experiences. This is surreal satire as potent as Albee's 'The American Dream' and just as much a picture of our time." **Steffen Silvis, Willamette Weekly, Portland, Oregon, May 12, 1999.**

"The audience stumbles off this roller-coaster dizzy with horror over what it's seen but also having some dark chuckles along the way. This is the kind of show that should help Stark Raving Theatre re-establish itself with its hard-core experimental-loving audience." **PORNOGRAPHIC PANORAMA, Barry Johnson, The Oregonian, May 12, 1999, Portland, Oregon.**

"**A PIECE OF CAKE** is Barry's dystopian comedy of a world where the safety of cake has replaced the dangers of sex. It is a fast-paced, tough-talking saga where an excellent playwright is perfecting his work before our eyes." **Oregonian, July 26, 2000.**

Mother'Son
and
Other Plays

Raymond J. Barry

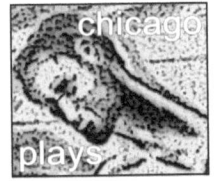

Mother'Son and Other Plays
by Raymond J. Barry
© 2009
ALL RIGHTS RESERVED
Printed in U.S.A.

ISBN 978-0-578-01787-7

For information regarding amateur and stock royalties for any of these plays, contact: Fifi Oscard Agency, 110 W. 40th St. 16th floor, New York, New York, 10018 (212) 764-1100

For any other information regarding these plays, contact: Raymond J. Barry, c/o Fifi Oscard Agency, 110 W. 40th St. 16th floor, New York, New York, 10018.

Raymond J. Barry's website:
www.raymondjbarry.org

*For performance of such songs and recordings mentioned in these plays as are in copyright, the permission of the copyright owners must be obtained; or other songs and recordings in the public domain substituted.

Cover Art by Raymond J. Barry

This book is dedicated to my wife
and closest friend,
Robyn Leslie Mundell.

Performers' Note:

Throughout these plays, when the action calls for simultaneous dialogue, the actors can be heard best when both people modulate their voices instead of following the impulse to increase volume.

Mother'Son and Other Plays

By

Raymond J. Barry

Contents

Playwright's Foreword

The first stages of *Mother'Son and Other Plays* dates back to a period in the mid-seventies when I was directing at the Theatre For The New City, Theatre Genesis and The Nuyorican Poets' Cafe in New York City, as well as workshops at Sing Sing, Attica, and Grasslands Penitentiaries.

In order to deal with essential questions in the manner with which they must be dealt, I have selected themes that come from the depths of my own daily crisis. Until I began to write *Once In Doubt* in 1980 my capacity to take notice of such crisis had been either dulled or habitually avoided, and subsequently I'd permitted myself to develop only so far as a writer. After many false starts I have become aware of the incumbent traps that will no doubt come my way in the future, but at the very least, thanks to the growth that has come with creating this body of work, my eyes have been opened to the crisis of my daily experience. By admitting such a crisis exists, I hope to have discovered a more private, more political, and, above all, a more human exploration.

While these plays were being written, I found myself dealing with the question of what I was willing to reveal. That question coerced me to set aside my defenses in order to delve into recurring themes that appear in the plays. These themes were personal to me and therefore necessary, leaving me with the choice of whether or not to lower my various protective masks in order to bring my involvement away from the pleasant amusement often offered as acceptable subject matter for the theater. The mask often did fall; first once and then again and again, until, as years went by, I developed the habit of trusting the truth.

Poetry has been most useful for me, not so much to define elaborate thoughts but rather to cause thinking, aiming first at the senses and later at the intellect. The verbal metaphor is a powerful tool when describing something so abstract as one's private internal experience. The use of metaphor "suggests to" rather than "dictates to" the audience. Poetry's combined ambiguity and clarity leaves enough space for people to suggest to themselves what the words mean without being mandated to think one way or the other. Also poetry doesn't necessarily have to be spoken the way we speak in real life at the functionary level of revealing information.

Inner life brought to the surface is characteristic of all of these plays. Particularly in *Mother'Son, Back When - Back Then* and *Once In Doubt,* I have attempted to develop a distilled language describing the subtext of each character, the meaning of which is not directed so much towards introspection as towards direct expression. Henceforth, the manner in which they speak is not socialized in the usual sense of the word. The characters' choice of language does not hide but rather displays what ordinarily would not be spoken in real life. The characters do not hint at what they are feeling and thinking but rather specifically say it.

During the fifties theater offered variations of generally one approach, a linear one based upon plot that favored one style of acting, "The Method," or what was commonly known as naturalism. Generally, that technique encouraged behavior to be as "real" as possible on stage with the limited understanding that "real" could only be that which was visible on the street, in the office, and so on. Subsequently playwrights were encouraged to approach all levels of consciousness from this point of view, including those realities that exist within the private realms of fantasy and dream. If a writer dared to disagree with that approach, he most likely would be labeled unacceptable to those who produced plays. Nothing can be more paralyzing both to the writer and to the theater. Unlike the painter who works and paints for himself, the playwright is often put under pressures having to do with entertainment considerations and ticket sales of our bankrupt theaters at the sacrifice of his personal voice.

Naturalism, in its attempt to train actors to talk the way people really talk, has done exactly that, but theater can have its own language in the same way music, dance and painting has, and that language can describe more than what we experience around us in real life. People generally choose words only within a certain limited, informational range that suits standard socialization, often leaving an individual's ability to communicate out of touch with what is happening internally. Generally, as speech becomes more sophisticated, talk becomes a means of transferring information at the expense of expressiveness. The possibilities for expression of a character while being "real" is not nearly as direct as revealing the mind inside its own reality, stripped of the bonds dictated by preconceived notions of what communication should be. I have written the characters in these works to speak as imaginatively as possible, making vivid the secret, inner worlds in which they live. A stage, thundering with the lyricism of poetry and suggested physical images that express what is hidden beneath conversation, together with carefully chosen resting points that change the dynamic to relative immobility is much more exciting to me than seeing the characters lounging on sofas or walking like sticks as they reveal psychological bits of information about themselves that are considered to be "real" or conversational.

Raymond J. Barry
October, 15, 2008

Once in Doubt

Notes on "Once In Doubt"
by Albert Williams
Chicago Reader, July 1992

"Once In Doubt" deals with the self-destructive anguish of a dying romance - that point at which couples humiliate themselves in order to hurt the other. Harry, an artist, creates a painting/collage on the fourth wall using blood (invisible) from his slashed wrist and the objects (also invisible) that surround him and his wife, Flo, in a tiny white "Skinner Box" room. The collage is his legacy to his wife, his cynical, final statement about the absurdity of the human condition. Their mutual dependency is a sore point between them; they resent it just as they resent any suggestion that they put some distance between them. They resent it when they don't flatter each other's looks and when they do. They resent the isolated exclusivity of their relationship and they resent it when another person enters the scene. And they express their resentment, their fear, their passion, their anxiety, their distrust and their undying love in a scathing torrent of in-jokes and insults.

As Harry makes his "death creation," adding to the smeared blood such objects as Brillo pads and cat food cans to symbolize the detested and desired domesticity of his life with Flo, the couple tease and taunt each other, laughing in lusty memory of a famous bath they once shared, sarcastically trading happy, home-maker clichés, declaring their love and loathing in a crossfire of confessions and complaints. "I wish something exciting would happen... that someone exciting would drop by," says Flo. And someone does: Mr. Wagner, a neighbor curious about the noise. Mr. Wagner may not know art but he knows what he likes, and he likes Flo. Just what the relationship needs, new blood. Blood is the central metaphor in this reflection on the anguish, risk, and endless dissatisfaction of making art that comes from the heart and in this case transcends from the imagery on the fourth wall to a "work of art consisting of three people, namely ourselves," in Harry's words. After manipulating Mr. Wagner and his mate to have sex, Harry succeeds in making Mr. Wagner "part of the family so to speak," and transforms Mr. Wagner's sensibility from that of a simple common-man worker to a full-blown artist, who paints with red paint an abstract painting of his own upon the back wall of the set. Behind

Raymond J. Barry

the sadistic fun and games of the principals, the play sanctions any artistic impulse, the integrity of self-expression. Art is not presented as an object of worship. Instead it emerges as a means of expressing the inexpressible, a conduit to the soul through which the demons that plague all of us can be exorcised.

Production Notes

When actors speak simultaneously they can be heard best by both people modulating their voices instead of following the natural impulse to increase volume. Harry's attempted suicide shouldn't be commented upon by Flo, who simply reads her book as if it is an everyday occurrence. The play's natural rhythm can be established by insisting upon seamless cueing. However, during the seduction scene between Mr. Wagner and Flo, the actors can take as much time as they please. Until that point the play works best set at a brisk pace.

Characters

HARRY: An artist in his early forties to early fifties
FLO: His live-in lover; mid-thirties to early-forties
MR. WAGNER: A working class man in his late forties to mid-fifties

History

Once In Doubt was first performed as a one act at **La Mama ETC**, New York City, New York; Ellen Stewart, Artistic Director, November 1984. The part of Mr. Wagner had not been written.

CAST:

HARRY ....Raymond J. Barry
FLO .... Jean Reynolds

DIRECTOR ....David Saint
SET DESIGN...................................Raymond J. Barry
MUSIC............................ Ellen Maddow & Harry Mann

Once In Doubt was performed at the **Cast Theatre**, Los Angeles, California, Ted Schmidt, Artistic Director, January thru April 1989.

CAST:

HARRY ....Raymond J. Barry
FLO .... Kim O'Kelley

DIRECTOR ....David Saint
LIGHTING..Erika Bradberry
SET DESIGN................Raymond J. Barry/David Saint

Once In Doubt was given a production at **The Peoples Light and Theatre Company** Danny Fruchter, Artistic Director, June/July, 1989.

CAST:

HARRY ....Raymond J. Barry
FLO .... Kim O'Kelley
MR. WAGNER...John Nesci

DIRECTOR ....David Saint
DESIGN..................... Raymond J. Barry & David Saint
LIGHTING...F. Pyne Jr.

Raymond J. Barry

Once In Doubt was given its first completed production at the **Los Angeles Theatre Center**, Bill Bushnell and Diane White, Artistic Directors, November 1989 - January 1990.

CAST:

HARRY .... Raymond J. Barry
FLO .... Kim O'Kelley
MR. WAGNER .... Howard Schechter

DIRECTOR .... David Saint
DESIGN .... Raymond J. Barry & David Saint
LIGHTING/SOUND .... Douglas Smith/Jon Gottlieb

The **Los Angeles Theatre Center** production received a **Los Angeles Drama Critics Circle Award** and five **Dramalogue Awards**, including a **Dramalogue Award For Writing, 1990.**

Once In Doubt was performed at the **Remains Theatre** in Chicago, Illinois, Artistic Director, Larry Sloan, July-August 1992.

CAST:

HARRY .... William Petersen
FLO .... Amy Morton
MR. WAGNER .... Gerry Becker

SCENERY AND LIGHTING .... Kevin Snow
COSTUMES .... Laura Cunningham
SOUND .... Christian Petersen

Once In Doubt was chosen **Outstanding Play of 1992** by both the **Chicago Tribune** and the **Chicago Sun-Times** when it was performed at the Remains Theater.

Once In Doubt was performed at the **New Theatre Company** in Dallas, Texas, October-November 1998.

CAST:

HARRY .... Jim Jorgensen
FLO .... Charlotte Akin
MR. WAGNER .... Carl Savering

DIRECTOR .... T. A. Taylor

Once In Doubt was performed at the **Odyssey Theatre Ensemble** in Los Angeles, California, Artistic Director, Ron Sossi, June-July 1999. The production won a **Maddie Award** for Best Play 1999.

CAST:

HARRY ....Raymond J. Barry
FLO .... Kim O'Kelley
MR. WAGNER.. Biff Yeager

DIRECTOR .... Bernard White
DESIGN... Markus Maurette

College and Workshop Productions

1993, **University of South Dakota,**, Student Production.
1990, **Yale University**, New Haven, Connecticut, Student Production.
1983, **New Paltz State Teacher's College**, Workshop Production.
1983, **Open Eye Theatre**, New York City, Workshop Production

Raymond J. Barry

Raymond J. Barry, Kim O'Kelley, **Once in Doubt**
Los Angeles Theater Center, 1989-1990

Once in Doubt

Raymond J. Barry, Kim O'Kelley, **Once in Doubt**
People's Light and Theatre Company, Philadelphia, June-July 1989

William Peterson, Amy Morton, Jerry Becker, **Once in Doubt**
Remains Theatre, Chicago, 1992

Raymond J. Barry

Raymond J. Barry, **Once in Doubt**
La Mama ETC, New York City, November 1984

Once in Doubt

Raymond J. Barry, Kim O'Kelley, **Once in Doubt**
Odyssey Theatre, Los Angeles, 1999

David Saint, director of **Once in Doubt, Mother'Son**
New York City, Los Angeles, Edinburgh (Scotland),
Philadelphia and Chicago

Raymond J. Barry

Amy Morton, **Once in Doubt**
Remains Theatre, Chicago, 1992

Once in Doubt

Once In Doubt

Act One

[Interior. Manhattan loft - late day. The stage is empty except for two chairs on both sides, one slightly forward from the other. The chair in front belongs to Harry; it is simpler and smaller. Flo's chair, which is larger, is stage right. It is ornately carved, grand like a throne. Placed next to stage right of it is a small table where she keeps her tea and her book. There is only one exit, up center stage. Against the back wall, fourteen feet in the air, is a shelf where paintings are stored. The shelf should be wide enough for Harry to walk out on it. The paintings should be abstract and partially visible, overlapping each other. Harry enters up center stage in the dark, sits on his chair stage left, lights a cigarette, smokes, and stares at the fourth wall. Lights come up gradually. He can be anywhere from late thirties to his early forties, ruggedly built and lean. He could be mistaken for a construction worker, dressed in a black T-shirt and faded, patched dungarees. Flo enters studio with a silver tray carrying a silver teapot, two teacups, one spoon, two saucers, and a honey bear. There is also a book, nondescript, which she shall read from time to time. Harry looks up briefly when she enters, returning immediately to his study of the fourth wall while he smokes his cigarette. Flo is mid-thirties to early forties. She is pretty, somewhat all-American in an oddball way. Her dress and high heels are black. She places the tray upon the table and sits down, simultaneously pouring herself a cup of tea and watching Harry. Harry pays little attention.

He clearly doesn't want to be interrupted. There is silence, tension between them. He smokes, she makes tea — one cup only, though there are two on the tray. Flo takes two slow sips of tea from her cup and looks straight out to the audience after each sip. She moves deliberately, slowly as she places her cup and saucer down upon her table. Very slowly, she reaches for her book. She opens the book to the place that has been marked. She begins reading for four seconds. She looks up from her book to Harry. She speaks. The following scene should be tightly cued.]

FLO. Good morning.
HARRY. Good morning.
FLO. You shouldn't smoke.
HARRY. It's none of your business.
FLO. No, seriously, you shouldn't smoke.
HARRY. It's none of your goddamned business.

Raymond J. Barry

FLO. I wish you would listen to me sometimes. You can learn from me.

HARRY. I've learned all I have to learn from you, my dear. I've had enough of your advice.

FLO. Your hostility simply gets in the way.

HARRY. Call it what you will. I'm free of your advice.

FLO. Why are you so hostile?

HARRY. Don't tell me what to do. If I want to smoke, I'll smoke.

FLO. It's bad for your lungs.

HARRY. So what?

FLO. You shouldn't do it.

HARRY. Living is bad for my lungs.

FLO. Not necessarily.

HARRY. Just leave me alone.

FLO. I can't.

HARRY. Obviously that's true.

FLO. I just can't. I'm trapped.

HARRY. We're both trapped, aren't we?

FLO. Yes. We're both trapped. *[Pause; count of five]* Smoke if you wish.

HARRY. Don't give me permission.

FLO. I'm trying to be nice.

HARRY. It's too late.

FLO. Why do you say that?

HARRY. It's too late.

FLO. I don't think it's too late.

HARRY. Well, it is.

FLO. What do you like about smoking?

HARRY. I don't like it. I need it.

FLO. Just like me.

HARRY. Yes, just like you.

[Harry continues to look at her for half a moment and then puts his cigarette out in the bronze ashtray at his feet. After this he looks straight out to the audience for the following speech. Flo again opens her book to a book-marked page and reads.

It should be mentioned that there are times when the actors will break the "reality" of the fourth wall and speak directly to the audience. At other times, depending upon the needs of the play, the invisible fourth wall will exist and will be played accordingly.]

HARRY. *[to audience]* My enthusiastic suicidal plunge, seeking a new birth, a bowel elimination, an intestinal shitting, shedding "out," I say and I die. I sit here transfixed, planted for a moment, silent, and slowly I recoil as if to attack with my fangs any slight move... *[Flo, who has been absolutely still up to this point, moves her foot. Harry stops, distracted by the movement, fixes his gaze upon Flo and then turns back to the audience and continues.]*

Once in Doubt

HARRY. ... movement in my immediate surroundings.

[Turns to Flo, who looks up from her book at Harry.] You will hear from me no more, my love. My seasonal skin has been shed. The snake is squirming out of its scaly covering, hissing goodbye on this rainy morning before I take my last breath.

[To audience while Flo reads] If I do it with a gun, will it hurt? If I do it with a gun and spray the wall with my brain cells as a genius painter would do, will it hurt? Will there be a buyer for my aching cry for help, a collector of wall murals who will pay a fantastic price for it? I, the devotee of abstract expressionism, will pull the trigger in my own art gallery, flinging pieces of my brain onto the wall and with line, form and color create an abstract celebration of the moment. *[Harry turns to Flo]* I will wave to you goodbye, my love, *[Flo looks at Harry]* blowing soft kisses for your blue eyes to catch as I die. My lips will touch your eyelashes as I wave again to the 'other side' where bodiless souls bounce upon one another, an entire community of suicidal souls, their brains shot out, spewed onto walls by the beings who owned them. And I knew that when I ask, "Should I do it? Is it all right to take a chance? Will there be some relief from this, each complex walk-a-day, talk-a-day, eat-a-day I see before me everyday?" Walk, talk, eat, walk, talk, eat, chew your food, swallow, you shouldn't smoke, be political, avoid manipulation, certain someone, meaning in your life, find it!

FLO. *[Looking up from her book]* I hate you.

HARRY. Why?

FLO. Because I do.

HARRY. That's not a reason.

FLO. I just hate you.

HARRY. Well, tell me why.

FLO. Because when I'm around you I hate you.

HARRY. That's not a reason.

FLO. Well, it's a reason to me.

HARRY. Look, if you want to talk about this then talk. But don't just tell me you hate me.

FLO. I can't talk right now.

HARRY. Why?

FLO. I keep reaching out for help, but there isn't any from anyone.

HARRY. I don't understand you. What do you expect from me? You keep reaching out for help. Help yourself first. Don't make yourself feel bad. You not only affect yourself when you do that, you affect the people around you; including me.

FLO. I know, I'm sorry for saying that.

HARRY. Well I'm sorry, too, but I can't let you get away with that. I really can't.

FLO. My mind isn't working right now.

Raymond J. Barry

HARRY. It isn't?

FLO. No. You know that.

HARRY. Yes, I know what you mean.

FLO. So let me say things like that once in a while, okay?

HARRY. No, I won't. You don't how it affects me. I internalize it when you tell me you hate me.

FLO. I know.

HARRY. I'm tired of people telling me they hate me. I'm really very tired of it. I can't let anyone say that to me anymore. It's not good for me.

FLO. I don't say much. Let me say something.

HARRY. But why did you say that?

FLO. I said that because I wanted to talk to you.

HARRY. Why didn't you just talk?

FLO. I didn't think I could.

HARRY. What did you think I would do if you talked?

FLO. Nothing.

HARRY. Oh.

[Flo returns to her book. Harry rises from his chair, crosses upstage left and then to up center stage entrance and stares at Flo, who is stage right. Flo is reading. She is focused on her book. Harry continues staring at Flo. He reaches into his pocket and pulls out a small piece of glass with a sharp edge; he studies it for a long moment. Flo reads. Harry stares at the piece of glass, then looks to the audience.]

HARRY. This is the way, not a gun. This is better; more process involved, more process. After all is said and done, I'll still be conscious. I'll see what is happening.

[He is holding the glass, trembling. He studies the glass.] But it takes courage, it does; that is, to take the glass and cut. I am trembling. I am. It will hurt. I know it will hurt. A piece of glass will cut into my wrist. It will bleed. Floating ghosts will pass out of me. *[Flo looks up from her book. Her eyes meet his, alert, matter of fact. She is not alarmed; it is part of their everyday routine. She continues to look at him. Harry turns back to the audience. Flo resumes reading.]*

HARRY. She is watching, but this event has nothing to do with her. Nothing at all to do with her. This is I and only I.

[PANTOMIME: The glass penetrates his wrist, cutting across the tendons. The veins in his neck protrude as he slashes. Beads of sweat on his brow, his jaw muscles clenching as he cuts. Flo is calm, alert, reading her book. Harry holds up his hand. Imaginary blood oozes slowly out of his wrist. He studies it. He looks at the empty fourth wall before him, walks toward it. He holds his wrist above his head, chooses an exact spot on the wall and flicks his arm at it, spattering imaginary, oozing blood onto the wall. He does this repeatedly at different strategic points on the wall as though it is a canvas. He applies the bleeding wound directly to the fourth wall,

moving his arm across its imaginary surface, creating strokes of red both up and down and across. He steps back, evaluating his work, and again approaches his painting and places one dab of blood onto a lower section, somewhat off center stage left. The imaginary result, if it could be seen, gradually takes on the appearance of a Willem de Kooning painting: broad strokes, sprays of color, varied smatterings throughout, reminiscent of the abstract expressionist period of the fifties. Finally he stands back and observes his imaginary creation. Flo is reading without expression. Harry stands, imaginary blood dripping from his wrist. For the remainder of the play, he will hold his arm up as if its wrist has been slashed. No stage blood should ever be used. The actor can create the illusion with his extended arm. He stares happily at his work on the fourth wall.]

HARRY. Ecstasy of creation, painting, I am an artist again. My first wrist stroke upon the wall confirms the moment. I exist, I feel, seeing the sparkling wet crimson upon the white. If only I had a blue, blue and crimson next to next, a composition being born, but no, only crimson to be had...

[Harry holds up his wrist, the wound facing the wall. Flo reads. Harry is looking at his painting.]

HARRY. ...and then it comes upon me, a thought to my brain, having not been blown out as yet. Perhaps a collage; textured to my own liking, textured, yes, perhaps that is it!

[Flo looks up, sitting quietly, stage right, calmly.]

FLO. Yes, perhaps that is it.

[Harry turns towards Flo, then abruptly turns away, surveying the studio.]

HARRY. I turn away from the crimson stroke and send a glazed-eyed look to the floor.

[Harry moves throughout his studio, pointing out different imagined objects. Flo reads.]

HARRY. Crumbs of stale cookies, old socks, shoes, books, even cans of cat food, plants with leaves, all for me to play. A broken pencil! What delight. A mashed jelly bean there, pieces of paper crumpled or ripped, shirts wrinkled from not being ironed, those good pants I'll not be wearing anymore, a bicycle wheel, dishes, a clock. I imagine I can compose a symphony of objects, arranged to my own pleasure, arranged to my own desire. But I must hurry. The blood is dripping. The glass has done its chore. I am dying, but still there is art to make. *[Harry turns to Flo. She remains calm, staring at him.]*

HARRY. She is looking, but this event has nothing to do with her, nothing at all to do with her. This is I and only I.

[He hastens downstage left to his chair, sits.]

HARRY. In my reverie, I dream I am a fish exposed belly upward, white belly skin upward to the sky. A long pike drives itself into me, harpooning me...

Raymond J. Barry

[Harry pantomimes pulling a harpoon into himself.]

FLO. I'm attracted to you.

HARRY. *[turns head to her]* I know. *[turns head to audience and pulls imaginary pike into himself]* Harpooning...

FLO. I'm uncontrollably attracted to you. *Flo rises from her chair and runs to Harry's chair. She goes down on her knees at his side. He stays seated in his chair, focused on the painted wall, attempting to continue. When she interrupts, he will turn his head briefly to answer her and turn back to the wall. He pulls the imaginary pike into himself throughout.]*

HARRY. *[turns head to her]* I know. *[turns head to audience and pulls the imaginary pike into himself]* Harpooning me to...

FLO. I wish I could be inside your body.

HARRY. *[turns head to her]* I know. *[turns head to audience and pulls the imaginary pike into himself]* Harpooning me to...

FLO. I wish I could be welded to you forever.

HARRY. *[turns to her]* I know. *[turns head to audience and pulls imaginary pike into himself]* Harpooning me to the sand...

FLO. I wish you loved me the way I love you.

HARRY. *[turns head to her]* I know. *[turns head to audience and pulls imaginary pike into himself]* Harpooning me to the sand, capturing...

FLO. But you don't.

HARRY. *[turns head to her]* Yes, I do. *[turns head to audience and pulls imaginary pike into himself]* Harpooning me to the sand, capturing me...

FLO. No. You don't.

HARRY. *[turns head to her]* Yes, I do. *[turns head to audience and pulls imaginary pike into himself]* Harpooning me to the sand, capturing me, sticking...

FLO. No. I don't think so.

HARRY. *[to her]* I just keep it in.

[Harry turns to the audience and continues his speech and Flo speaks simultaneously to Harry:]

HARRY.	**FLO.**
Harpooning me to the sand, capturing me, sticking me to the sand of the white beach. I flop around a bit. Fish do that when they are stuck. Humans, too. I bleed. Gathering my collage materials, I flop. Now my mind is totally engrossed in puzzle-making construction.	What do you mean you just keep it in? You mean I'm being totally honest with you and you have the nerve to say you don't want to say what you're feeling towards me. You're exciting to me. I'm excited by you. How can I not be excited by you? You're exciting to me.

FLO. Why don't you love me?

HARRY. *[to Flo]* I do. I really do.

[They kiss. Harry abruptly pulls away from the kiss and goes back into his speech to the audience. He rises, extending his cut wrist to the fourth wall as he speaks. Flo, on her knees, grabs his legs.]

HARRY. My hammer is found with a nail with which I hang a lovely wrinkled pair of pants upon the wall.

FLO. Why can't you...

[simultaneous]

HARRY.	**FLO.**
They are blue.	show me.

HARRY. I rub my crimson...

[simultaneous]

HARRY.	**FLO.**
... red into them from my wrist.	Please show me for a change.

[simultaneous]

HARRY.	**FLO.**
It shines...	Show me...

HARRY. ...crimson red, blood blue.

[simultaneous]

HARRY.	**Flo.**
It shines crimson red. It shines.	Show me.
It shines blood blue. It shines.	Show me.
[pause]	Show me.

HARRY. And I'm going about my business, and she's going about her business, and we're both going about our businesses in our own way. In the only way we know how.

FLO. *[Returns to the stage right chair. To Harry:]* I didn't mean for things to turn out the way they did.

HARRY. *[to audience]* And our lives continue in the same old way...

FLO. *[to Harry]* I guess I didn't know what I was doing.

HARRY. *[to audience]* In the same way that we are used to...

FLO. *[to Harry]* I was mad.

HARRY. *[to audience]* In the same way that has repeated itself one hundred times before.

FLO. *[to Harry]* You shouldn't talk to me the way you did.

HARRY. *[to audience]* Maybe a thousand times without explanation.

FLO. *[to Harry]* I was scared.

Raymond J. Barry

HARRY. *[to audience]* Without any need for an explanation, ever.

FLO. *[to Harry]* I thought you were going to get violent with me again.

HARRY. *[to audience]* Just repeating the same tasks, the same repetitive motion, from one moment to another, over and over...

FLO. *[to Harry]* If there's one thing I can't stand, it's violence.

HARRY. *[to audience]* From one hour after another, over and over.

FLO. *[to Harry]* I get so afraid sometimes.

HARRY. *[to audience]* Day after day, every day.

FLO. *[to Harry]* Because I think you're going to hit me.

HARRY. I wasn't going to hit you. I didn't hit you, did I? Tell me I didn't hit you. You know I didn't. That was the last thing in my mind, to hit anyone. You know that only happened one time ever and you remember the circumstance. *[He rises from his chair and crosses to her, stage right. He circles her as he speaks.]* Goddamn it, turn around and listen to me. Don't turn your head away from me. You know you're playing a game with me. What are you trying to prove anyway? You want some kind of power or what? That's it. You want power. The power to control me.

FLO. No, that's not true.

HARRY. *[crosses stage left center]* Yes it is. You're just interested in tearing me apart with your little power games, trying to fuck me up with some kind of sick bullshit.

FLO. Just because I'm upset you automatically think I'm playing a game. Well, I'm not. I'm not playing a game. I just don't feel right, that's all. I don't feel right about anything. There is something blocking me, preventing me from functioning. I try to do more, but I've lost hope. Things just don't make sense to me anymore. *[crosses to stage left]*

HARRY. What do you mean, make sense? Why does anything have to make sense? What is this, "Change the World Week?" Things generally don't make sense. Get used to it. It's real.

FLO. Sometimes, I feel clear.

HARRY. Sure you do. But how long does that last? One hour? Two hours?

FLO. I remember a time in my life when things made absolute sense to me.

[Flo remains seated in her stage right chair. Harry crosses to his chair, stage left, sits. Pause.]

HARRY. What happened to us? Remember in the beginning? How you were with me? When I met you, you seemed to care about how I felt. You made a bath for me. Remember?

FLO. Yes, I remember.

HARRY. It was nice.

FLO. I know. I remember. It was nice.

HARRY. We were making an effort then.

FLO. Yes, I guess we were.

Once in Doubt

HARRY. I got into the tub and you shaved me. Remember?

FLO. Yes, I do.

HARRY. You did a perfect job. Not a hair was left on my chinny-chin-chin. You always did everything with a sense of perfection.

FLO. I know. You're like that, too.

HARRY. I know. Then you washed my hair. Do you remember that?

FLO. Yes.

HARRY. You washed my hair and my back with care and tenderness. It was as if you were making love to me.

FLO. I was.

HARRY. Did you know you were?

FLO. Yes, I knew. How could I not know?

HARRY. I don't know. I thought it might have all been subconscious or something.

FLO. No. I knew.

HARRY. Then you took your clothes off and climbed into the tub with me. Remember?

FLO. Yes, I do.

HARRY. You were beautiful, slightly overweight, luscious.

FLO. I've lost my baby fat since.

HARRY. You got a perfect body now.

FLO. I know.

HARRY. What do you mean, "you know?"

FLO. I mean, "I know," that's all.

HARRY. I can't stand that about you. How can you tell me you have a perfect body? What a conceited thing to say. Totally conceited.

FLO. You said it initially, I didn't.

HARRY. Yeah, but you picked up on it. It was an automatic response.

FLO. Fuck you! You dumb jock! You're nothing but a Goddamned dumb jock and I hate your guts! You make me absolutely sick to my stomach! I'm leaving this fucking place, understand? I'm tired of playing out this fucking role, understand? You don't show me nothing. Fuck! Fuck you! You Goddamned moron.

[Flo runs out through upstage entrance, still shouting at the top of her lungs and Harry follows her to the entrance. Flo slams the door back stage. There is silence. Then her shouting starts up again when she yells from behind a closed door, "Suck my dick!" and more muffled shouts until again silence.

Harry upstage, looking at the fourth wall he has painted with his blood. He stares at it and then walks toward it. Puts another imaginary object onto the fourth wall. Finally, he speaks.]

HARRY. Art is in the making, it is: the pants, the can, the strokes of crimson are expecting creative decision, explored possibility, probed inward position. Probe it, find it, fetch it out, make that ultimate

Raymond J. Barry

statement, the final balance, the teetering seesaw, the inward motion, inward, hidden, beyond perception, beyond logical. Time is pressing. I hurry, stumble around the room looking for some other addition to my collage. I bleed. *[He holds up his arm, pantomimes imaginary blood falling to the floor.]* My heart is pumping. I think of her. Two cheeks cleft neatly, meeting gently at a tuft of hair, brownish-black, unseen by most, visible perhaps to one, maybe two. I need that for my painting, my wall mural; I need that, I do. I run to the sink where there stands an idle box of Brillo pads and brutishly rip the thin cardboard apart, releasing the light gray balls of wire mesh puffs, bouncing and flying onto the floor. *[He grabs for the imaginary Brillo pads.]* Like a killer, I swoop down upon them, gobble them up with my hands, gobble them up, grab them, grabbing at them, dousing them with my own blood, clawing at them, finally holding a few, holding a few. I think of her again for one isolated needle-sharp second. I think of her, I do. I can think, I think. I can think, I think. I can think!

[He dances around the room, throwing imaginary Brillo pads onto the wall, all done in pantomime, and movement inspired by the actor.] Pouncing upon the wall, punching Brillo pads to its surface, little vagina cunts, my symbolic creation, nailing them again like that fish, arranging them to suit some vague configuration, conceived by myself, sticking them to the wall. Breathing Brillos, popping at the surface, breathing Brillos, bulging outward... *[pause]* If only there were an art dealer here to look, to see my death creation. *[We hear footsteps. Harry comes to his senses. He stands, center stage, frozen, afraid to look, knowing what is coming... it has all happened before. He is like a block of stone. Finally Harry turns to see Flo coming. She stands before him as if she is going to slap him, but suddenly she kisses him passionately on the mouth. He gradually returns the kiss, embracing her, careful not to touch her dress with his imaginary blood. Flo abruptly breaks the kiss. Flo walks proudly away. She stands quietly, stops for a moment, glares at him with knives in her eyes. Then she sits stage right, and opens her book. She reads with Harry standing stage center left. Finally, she looks up from her book.]*

FLO. I'm not talking to you. I said I'm not talking to you. Can't you hear me? I'm not talking to you. Don't you care?

HARRY. No, I don't care.

FLO. Don't you care at all? I'm asking you a question. Can't you hear me? I know you can.

HARRY. No, I can't.

FLO. You're hearing me. You know, somehow you're saying more to me now than you ever have. You don't like me, do you?

HARRY. No, I don't like you.

FLO. Why?

HARRY. You're non-communicative.

FLO. But it's you who's not talking.
HARRY. You know what I mean.
FLO. No, I don't.
HARRY. Oh, come on.
FLO. I don't know what you mean. I don't think you're direct about your feelings.
HARRY. I'm direct about my feelings.
FLO. You are?
HARRY. I'm expressing myself all the time.
FLO. Who do you think you are? The boss or something?
HARRY. Yes, I'm the boss. So what? *[crosses upstage left away from Flo sitting in her chair stage right]*
FLO. So what makes you the boss?
HARRY. I'm bigger'n you are.
FLO. So what? That doesn't mean you're the boss.
HARRY. I say it does.
FLO. Well, it doesn't.
HARRY. What do you think makes a boss?
FLO. It's not size.
HARRY. *[crosses from stage left to Flo's chair stage right where she is sitting]* Are you sure of that?
FLO. Yes, I'm sure. There are plenty of people who are small, who are bosses.
HARRY. Name one.
FLO. Napoleon.
HARRY. He wasn't small.
FLO. He was too.
HARRY. *[crosses to his chair stage left]* No, he wasn't either. I've seen pictures of him. He looked big. He had medals all over him.
FLO. How can you tell how big he was from his pictures?
HARRY. He looked big.
FLO. He probably was on a horse.
HARRY. No, he wasn't either. I've seen pictures of him. He looked big. He had medals all over him. *[He becomes confused.]* No, he wasn't either... He looked... big. He had a hat. He was fucking big!
HARRY AND FLO. *[to audience]* The point is not the point.
HARRY. AND FLO. *[to audience]* The issue is not the issue.
HARRY. AND FLO. *[to audience]* The point is not the issue.

[simultaneous]

HARRY. *[to Flo]*　　　　**FLO.** *[to Harry]*
I hide from her noise.　　I hide from his noise.

HARRY. *[to audience]* It assaults me.

Raymond J. Barry

FLO. *[to Harry, whispered]* Listen to me!

HARRY. I cannot fight back...

FLO. *[to Harry. Whispered.]* Listen to me.

HARRY. ... but hide in my own self-doubt.

FLO. *[to Harry. Whispered.]*

HARRY. AND FLO. *[to audience]* It attacks me.

HARRY. *[[to audience]* Verbal spears...

FLO. *[to Harry]* Listen to me!

HARRY. *[to audience]* Sound that brags and swaggers...

FLO. *[to Harry]* Listen to me!

HARRY. *[to Flo]* Insisting upon its own correctness by bashing all in its way.

FLO. *[to Harry. Whispered.]*

HARRY. *[to Flo]* The point has been lost...

HARRY & FLO. *[to audience]* The issue has been forgotten, stepped upon...

FLO. *[to Harry]* You need all the attention, don't you? You don't permit any breathing space for me!

HARRY. *[sitting stage left]* You can breathe.

FLO. Because you say so I can breathe? You are giving me permission to breathe? Well, thank you. Thank you. That's kind of you. I appreciate that. How much air do you think I can have? Exactly how many cubic inches of air do you think I can have today?

HARRY. Why are you talking to me like this? I don't want to make war with you. I really don't.

FLO. How innocent you pretend to be when you have done this to me.

HARRY. I have done what to you? I haven't done anything to you.

FLO. Oh, no, you haven't done anything to me. You rapist. You usurper, you. You have usurped my power. You have taken my strength. You have robbed me of my drive. You have taken my vitality. Well, I will take myself away from you. I will steal away from you. *[She gets up from her chair.]* I will fly. I will sing. I will race. I will run. I will experience joy. I will. I will. I will get away from you. *[sits]* Can you hear me?

HARRY. *[menacing]* No, I can't. My ears are hard-caked with wax, thinking to quick-stick it out with little Q-sticks, remaining there always and certainly impairing my hearing ability, certainly impairing that, making hearing difficult. *[rises from chair, crosses to her]* But I hear all right. I do. I hear all right. I do. Why, right now there's a sound of an ax pounding on some wooden log, making a comfortable sound, a familiar sound. *[Crosses to upstage right in back of Flo sitting.]*

FLO. *[To audience.]* I want to be honest.

HARRY. I've heard it before, when I was a waddling of a boy with an ax in my hand...

FLO. *[To audience.]* I want to express myself freely.

Once in Doubt

HARRY. *[Chopping move at Flo's neck.]*... chop, chopping for the sake of seeing the wood chips fly, for the sake of seeing them fly into the air, for the sake of seeing them fly.

FLO. *[To audience.]* I want to give in to impulse.

HARRY. *[To FLO]* There was a power in that, a real living power that I liked.

FLO. *[To audience.]* I want to laugh.

[Harry, stage right directly behind Flo, who is sitting in her chair.]

HARRY....and I could hear them too, those chips rocketing skyward from my ax, chop, *[Pantomimes chopping with hand at Flo's neck from behind her.]* dying to chop *[Chopping at her neck.]* with my arms, signaling to me from my arms.

FLO. *[to audience]* I want to cry.

HARRY. *[to Flo]* There was something so gratifying about that.

FLO. *[to audience]* I want to move openly.

HARRY. *[to Flo]* I didn't care what I chopped with the ax either. *[Pantomime chop at Flo's neck.]* I'd chop at anything just to see that. *[He chops at her neck.]*

FLO. *[to audience]* I want to be myself.

HARRY. *[to Flo]* I liked to chop live trees with the ax... *[chops at Flo's neck]*

FLO. *[to audience]* I want to say what I mean.

HARRY. *[to Flo]*... pulpwood that felt so succulent and good...

FLO. *[to audience]* I want to be my own woman for a change.

[Harry crosses away from Flo's chair, downstage left corner.]

HARRY. ...chopping new things eventually, new things in future times...

FLO. *[to audience]* I want to be loved.

HARRY. *[to audience]*... and then the chain saw was invented and there wasn't much chopping left to do anymore.

[Harry is looking at his slashed wrist as he crosses to downstage left. The separation between them is best for the next section.]

FLO. It has occurred to me to sleep with another man.

HARRY. Who?

FLO. What do you mean who?

HARRY. Just who do you mean?

FLO. What do you mean who do I mean? You know who I mean. You know.

HARRY. Why do you assume I know all of a sudden?

FLO. C'mon, stop pretending.

HARRY. I'm not pretending.

FLO. You're pretending.

HARRY. Okay, I'm pretending.

FLO. So getting back to the point. Who?

HARRY. What do you mean who?

FLO. You know what I mean by who.

Raymond J. Barry

HARRY. I do?

FLO. You were just asking who.

HARRY. I was?

FLO. You know you were.

HARRY. I do.

FLO. C'mon, don't play games with me.

HARRY. I'm not playing games as far as I can see.

FLO. You're not?

HARRY. No, I'm not.

FLO. Well what are you doing then?

HARRY. I'm simply asking who.

FLO. This is bordering on the ridiculous.

HARRY. This isn't getting us anywhere.

FLO. It isn't?

HARRY. No, it isn't.

FLO. Who says so?

HARRY. Why do you insist upon referring to "who?"

FLO. What's the difference?

HARRY. The difference is that it confuses me.

FLO. So what's wrong with confusion?

HARRY. I guess nothing's wrong with it.

FLO. Why don't you have some tea?

HARRY. Some tea? Why don't I have some tea? Some tea for me? All right, I'll have some tea. *[As he speaks, Harry crosses from stage left to the table stage right upon which sits the tray with teapot and teacups.]* I will have a little spot of tea, a little bit of tea, some tea for me. *[He lifts the teapot two or three feet above the saucer and empty cup in his cut hand and pours the tea into it.}* I'll have a little fucking tea, a little bit of tea for me. I'll have some tea. I'll have a smidgen of tea, a little smidgen of tea – for me. *[When the cup is full, he continues to pour, the tea flowing out of the cup and onto the floor]*

HARRY. I'll have some goddammed motherfucking tea!

[Harry smiles an exaggerated smile to Flo when the tea pot is empty. He sips the tea, the saucer and cup in his cut hand and the tea pot in his right hand. Tea spills from the saucer as he sips. He dumps the remainder of tea into the overflowed cup.]

HARRY. Pass the honey, please, dear. *[Flo doesn't move; Harry reaches for the honey himself after setting down the teapot.]*

HARRY. Thank you.

FLO. You're welcome.

HARRY. *[crosses in back of Flo to center left]* Beautiful collage I am making. Don't you think so?

FLO. Hmm, yes.

HARRY. *[crosses down center stage left]* Whenever something comes up that may upset me I always turn to my work.

FLO. You're a lucky person to be able to do that.

HARRY. It's better all around.

FLO. Yes.

HARRY. My work activities make me a better person all around.

FLO. Yes, of course.

HARRY. *[sips tea loudly]* I have something with which I can identify.

FLO. Yes, of course.

HARRY. I am my work.

FLO. Yes, you are.

HARRY. *[crosses to downstage left]* I had a thought.

FLO. You had a thought?

HARRY. Yes, I had a thought.

FLO. You did?

HARRY. What was it now?

FLO. I don't know. What was it?

HARRY. It was on my mind just a short time ago.

FLO. It was?

HARRY. Yes it was.

FLO. Just a short time ago? Well, fetch it up, my dear.

HARRY. Yes, I am fetching it.

FLO. Has it come?

HARRY. No, not yet.

FLO. Can you try harder?

HARRY. I don't know.

FLO. Well, enjoy your tea. Perhaps it will come.

HARRY. *[Crosses upstage left to his chair. During the speech, Harry cross upstage and downstage and around the chair.]* Yes, I'll enjoy my tea... Perhaps it will come. I'm having trouble remembering. Seems ridiculous doesn't it, but I'm having trouble remembering. Every time I try to remember, I realize I am trying to remember, which makes it difficult to simply remember, as opposed to trying to remember. I'm trying much too much. I'm whipping myself for not remembering. I'm angry at myself for not remembering. I'm checking myself out, not just once, but all the time, checking myself, checking myself. There is a policeman constantly watching me.

FLO. The policeman is you!

HARRY. Yes, watching myself. The policeman is me watching me. I want not to watch myself but I am obsessed with watching myself. As soon as I imagine myself not watching myself I'm watching myself not watching myself. Now I'm watching myself forget, hoping I have control over myself so I won't forget. I need some control over myself so I won't forget.

FLO. You're controlling yourself too much, just relax!

Raymond J. Barry

HARRY. I do for a moment but I'm still watching myself, goddammit! As long as I'm watching myself I know there is expectation that something is wrong. "Something is wrong" is the reason for my watching myself to begin with. If something hadn't gone wrong a long time ago I never would have started watching myself.

FLO. How's the tea?

HARRY. Fine, my dear, just the way I like it. A touch of honey and just plain old tea. Nothing like it. *[sits stage left]*

FLO. *[to audience]* I like taking breaks like this in the middle of the afternoon. *[Flo is sitting at the table stage right. Harry is sitting stage left.]*

HARRY. *[to audience]* I hear a faint scream penetrating the echoing chambers of my mind...

FLO. *[to audience]* A shift from work to play keeps the doctor away, I always say.

HARRY. *[to audience]*... a human scream, sounding much like the voice of my own...

FLO. *[to audience]* I need these moments.

HARRY. *[to audience]*... coming from the deepest center of my brain...

FLO. *[to audience]* They help keep everything in perspective.

HARRY. *[to audience]*... a familiar scream between my ears.

FLO. *[to audience]* Gives me time to gather my thoughts.

HARRY. *[to audience]* I hear it every day.

FLO. *[to audience]* Keeps my mind away from things.

HARRY. *[to audience]* It won't let go of me, an imaginary scream.

FLO. *[to Harry]* Speaking of thoughts, do you remember what it was you couldn't remember?

HARRY. *[to Flo]* You know I can't yet. It all escapes me somehow.

FLO. Don't worry. It'll come back to you.

HARRY. *[to audience]* Sometimes, I take my scream to the movies, alone, away from the "other" people.

FLO. *[to Harry]* Have some more tea.

HARRY. *[to audience]* My scream makes me impatient with the "other" people...

FLO. *[to Harry]* I think I'll have some more tea.

HARRY. *[to audience]*... especially when they eat candy and popcorn and whisper to each other. I imagine they are whispering about me.

FLO. *[to Harry]* Should I make another pot?

HARRY. *[to Flo]* I don't know. It's up to you.

FLO. No, it's up to you.

HARRY. No, it's up to you.

FLO. No, it's actually up to you.

HARRY. No, it's really up to you.

[simultaneous]

Once in Doubt

FLO. *[to herself]*
It'll only take a minute. Two tea bags and boiling water and we'll have it ready. And a little spot of honey just for you.

HARRY. *[to audience]*
I hate the habits of people in crowds. Their snortling, cackling, coughing, cacking, cuffing, tapping, finger-licking, sucking noises

HARRY. ...make me want to kill them.

HARRY & FLO. *[to each other]* It's as simple as that!

FLO. What do you think? Do you want some more tea?

HARRY. I don't know.

FLO. Well, I don't know either.

HARRY. Well, somebody's got to make a goddammed decision.

FLO. Yes, that's true. Somebody's got to. It might as well be me. *[She rises from her chair.]*

HARRY. Are you going to make some more tea?

FLO. Yes, darling, I'll make some more.

[Flo takes the silver teapot and leaves through the upstage Exit. While Flo prepares another pot of tea offstage, Harry gets up from his downstage left chair. Then he paces in a circle at the entrance.]

HARRY. Good. Then I'll have some. With a little spot of honey.

FLO. *[offstage]* All right. Now first I'll fill the teapot with hot water so it'll come to a boil that much faster.

HARRY. *[pacing up center stage]* Good thinking, dear.

FLO. *[offstage]* Then I'll lay aside two tea bags to put in the water when it does come to a boil.

HARRY. *[pacing up center stage]* Very good indeed.

[Flo is supposedly heating water offstage. Water should never be hot.]

FLO. *[offstage]* Now we can wait until everything takes care of itself.

HARRY. *[pacing up center stage]* Everything can't really take care of itself. You know that. You are doing it.

FLO. *[offstage]* Yes, I am doing it. I know.

HARRY. *[pacing up center stage]* Just to keep the record straight, it is we ourselves who are keeping everything on the move so to speak.

FLO. *[offstage]* Yes, that is true.

HARRY. *[pacing]* Just to keep the record straight, it is we who are living our lives and not anyone else. We are taking the initiative.

FLO. *[offstage]* Yes.

HARRY. *[pacing]* Just to keep the record straight.

FLO. *[offstage]* Yes, darling.

HARRY. *[To audience; he sits in his chair stage left.]* She thinks I am normal. I pretend to be normal. I scream. I smile. My smile I'm told is pleasing to the eye. I don't know. I'm not aware of my smile. My smile doesn't appear when I look at myself in the mirror. I don't smile at

Raymond J. Barry

myself in the mirror. Oh yes, occasionally I have smiled at myself in the mirror but I can never tell much from it, whether it is appealing or not. Other people have told me about my smile. They know not of my scream. There are some who know. They have it too. They know from my eyes that I have a scream. They know; they do. They smile and nod approvingly when I walk-scream on busy streets and eat-scream in luminescent cafeterias. We are a family, the scream family; we are all screamers; we all scream.

[Flo enters with the silver teapot, crosses to her table, sets it down on the tray, stage right.]

FLO. Do you remember what it was you wanted to tell me before?

HARRY. This is becoming a goddammed nuisance! I can't remember yet. But it'll come. It'll come.

FLO. I certainly hope so. I'm becoming curious.

HARRY. I know what you mean by that. I'm becoming curious too.

[Flo prepares two cups of tea as she talks with Harry who talks to the audience while Flo speaks to him. Harry's attention is split between his inner monologue and their conversation. Simultaneous:]

HARRY.

[soft]
She knows not of my scream, my silent partner. She knows only of my intensity and of my smile. She knows I am intense not because of my smile. She knows I am intense because of the furrows in my face when I think. She knows of my furrows but not of my scream. Scream is something else. Scream is like white heat, separating people, beyond pain, unspeakable, beyond hurt, not to function, a kind of giving in. I am still resisting. I am still resisting.

FLO.

All right, I'll make the tea. There now, I'll pour the water into the cup. Give me your cup. *[Harry hands her the cup as she crosses to him and she returns to her chair stage right.]* Thank you, my dear. Now just one little tea bag... and there we are. Water over and into the cup, and just take a moment for the honey the way you like it. A big steaming cup of hot tea just for you, my dear.

[crosses to him stage left with the tea in her hand]

[Flo hands Harry the cup which he takes. He sits calmly.]

FLO. *[crosses to her chair stage right]* And now the same for me but without the honey.

HARRY. You're sweet enough.

FLO. Yes, do you think so, darling?

HARRY. Yes, I do. After all these years I still think you are very sweet.

Once in Doubt

[Flo is sweetened by his flattery, brimming with happiness over this attention being paid to her.]

FLO. Why, thank you, my darling.

HARRY. I mean it.

FLO. I know you do and I appreciate it.

HARRY. You're my gal.

FLO. You are sweet.

[Harry leaps from his chair, spilling some of his tea.]

HARRY. I'm beginning to remember my thought!

[Flo attempts to speak.]

Don't say anything! I'm beginning to remember what it was I was thinking.

FLO. I won't say anything.

HARRY. Don't talk! *[tries to remember]* It went away. Boy, that's frustrating. *[He begins again to pace around his chair stage left.]*

FLO. *[sits stage right chair]* That is frustrating. I know exactly how you feel.

HARRY. *[pacing]* I had it right on the tip of my tongue but it went away. My mind must be failing me.

FLO. Don't talk that way, dear. Your mind isn't failing you.

HARRY. *[pacing]* I know it isn't. It's just a way of speaking.

FLO. Well, you shouldn't be talking that way.

HARRY. Why? What's the difference. We both know the truth.

FLO. The truth? *[Her face is expectant, waiting, listening, watching.]*

HARRY. Yes. I mean really the truth.

FLO. Tell me the truth.

HARRY. All right, just the truth? Are you ready?

FLO. *[Looking at Harry. She is sitting stage right.]* Yes, I'm ready.

HARRY. *[sits in his chair stage left]* Okay, here goes. *[He readies himself, clears his mind to line up his thoughts. This speech can be whispered to Flo without the audience hearing it, if necessary]* I want to stick the head of my dick into your pussy, only about three quarters of an inch deep, ever so gentle, see? I want to work my cock in there little by little so you barely notice I'm fucking you and yet you'll think about nothing else. As a matter of fact, you won't be able to think about anything else. And the lips of your cunt will contract on my dick. They will hold on to it, oh so tight, a little tightness, just a little tightness, ever so little and ever so tight, nice and sweet.

FLO. *[She turns her head to audience, sitting.]* That's filthy.

HARRY. No, it isn't.

FLO. Yes, it is. It's filthy.

HARRY. But you liked it, didn't you?

FLO. No, I didn't.

HARRY. Yes, you did. You liked it.

Raymond J. Barry

FLO. But I really didn't.

HARRY. Yes, you did.

FLO. Don't do that again.

HARRY. Why not if you liked it?

FLO. I don't want any of that stuff.

HARRY. Yes you do.

FLO. No, I don't. I don't want any of that business.

HARRY. Are you lonely?

FLO. No. I'm not lonely.

HARRY. Yes, you are.

FLO. No, I'm not.

HARRY. You're lonely.

FLO. I'm not lonely.

HARRY. But you like it when I talk like that, don't you?

FLO. *[turns to Harry]* Yes, I like it. *[Pause. Turns away from Harry directly to the audience.]* But I really don't. *[Harry waits, looks at Flo. He sips his tea loudly, eventually filling his mouth and comically squishing it around in his mouth until he gets a rise from her. He then gurgles his tea. When she reacts with a smile, he gulps the tea down.]*

HARRY. Well, time to get back to my old routine. My collage is waiting. *[He leaps from his chair and runs upstage searching for the piece of glass he dropped on the floor in the beginning of the play.]* My blood is coagulating. *[He reopens his wrist with a few swift slashes from the piece of glass and adds some imaginary blood to the fourth wall collage, moving his chair close to the fourth wall, stepping up on it downstage left.]* Objects are mounting high upon my bleeding wall, my wall of blood.

FLO. I have needs, you know.

HARRY. *[back to wall]* Oh, yes. *[to her]* The Brillo pads, cat food cans, pants sprinkled with my own blood...

FLO. One of them is you.

HARRY. *[to her]* Yes, thank you. *[back to the fourth wall.]* A pretty sight, textured altar of my belongings...

FLO. I need you or... someone to hug me once in a while.

HARRY. *[to her]* I understand. *[back to the fourth wall]* I'm like that, too. The crumpled paper is stuck to the wall by coagulated blood...

FLO. Of course, if I don't get a hug I'll survive.

[Harry grabs chair stage left and places it next to the fourth wall. Then he steps up onto the chair so he can flick his blood higher on the painting.]

HARRY. *[to her]* No question about that. You're a tough person...

[simultaneous]

FLO.	**HARRY.**
But in terms of the most ideal situation possible it would be	*[back to the fourth wall]* Sitting idly above the streaks of

Once in Doubt

best for me to be with someone who was somewhat familiar with my needs.

crimson, just below the searching hand print, my handprint, carelessly placed beside an old shirt...

HARRY. I'm familiar with your needs.

FLO. No, you're not!

HARRY. Please don't raise your voice! We'll have no raising of voices here! We can discuss without the raising of voices!

FLO. Even though I needed to do it?

HARRY. What? What do you mean by that?

FLO. Even though I needed to raise my voice?

[Flo crosses from her upstage right chair to Harry, who is standing on his chair downstage left. As she approaches him, he steps down from his chair and confronts her.]

HARRY. I need you not to raise your voice. It is rude and unnerving. I'm afraid the raising of voices will turn eventually into some sort of physical violence.

FLO. Now you're making things up.

HARRY. You never know. You raised your voice pretty easily just now. Just a little too easily.

[Flo bashes Harry on the shoulder and, as he tries to escape her blows, she kicks him in the ass. During the following speech, Harry slides his smaller chair from stage left to stage right, back and forth, while Flo chases him. He should move across the stage twice. Eventually, she retreats upstage right to the corner, which traps her. Harry ends up downstage left hiding behind the chair, popping his head out occasionally to make sure she is not attacking him again.]

FLO. You fucking egomaniac. What do you think, you're the only person in the world, you fucking bastard? Well, you're not. There are other people too, like me. I count, too. I have needs too, just like anyone else, you selfish fuck. You and your work. Take your work and shove it up your ass. *[crosses upstage left corner]* I've had enough of listening to your demands. I hate you. I hate you. No... I don't hate you. I love you. I love you very much but there is something about this relationship I don't want anymore. I don't want to hit you anymore. I don't want the ugliness. I don't want this "thing" we're tied up in. It won't come loose. It won't come apart... this knot... tied up so tight. It's no good anymore. It's just no good. You don't pay attention to my needs.

HARRY. *[He pops up from chair.]* No, that's not true.

FLO. *[She throws herself against the wall]* It is true. *[Harry pops down.]* You don't pay any attention to my needs. All you think about is your work. Never do I fit into your list of priorities. I can't stand it anymore.

HARRY. *[He pops up from the chair.]* Calm yourself!

Raymond J. Barry

FLO. *[She throws herself at the upstage wall violently]* Calm myself! *[Harry pops down again]* Calm myself! Why calm myself? What do you mean, "Calm myself"? I can't calm myself. It is impossible to calm myself. *[crosses to center stage]* Darling, I need a hug and a kiss. Come here and give me a hug and a kiss.

[Harry cautiously peeks from behind the chair where he has been hiding. He approaches her, standing with her arms extended, waiting for him right center stage. He finally runs to her, grabs her and twirls her in a circle using his good arm.]

HARRY. I love you! I love you! I love you!

FLO. I love you!

HARRY. I really love you!

FLO. Me too!

HARRY. Isn't it wonderful? Isn't it all wonderful?

FLO. Isn't what wonderful?

HARRY. *[stops twirling her, but holds her in his arms]* This "thing" we have together. This marvelous "thing" that rebounds between us even when we are apart! I'm emotionally glued to you! It's both wonderful and difficult at the same time! I love you.

FLO. You're my too-too.

HARRY. Darling, you are radiantly beautiful. I've never seen such beauty. Your eyes, your lips, it all overwhelms me. *[He looks to an imaginary bicycle wheel in the stage left corner.]* Why, in your honor I will place that bicycle wheel in the middle composition, smack in the middle.

[Harry dances to the imaginary bicycle wheel lying in the corner, downstage left, picks it up, pantomimes placing it in the composition. He flicks a little blood on it. Flo crosses upstage left and looks up at the painting.]

HARRY. Look at my configuration. "Perfect sense... perfect logic," bending at the exact moment, surging downward, upward, sideways with a precision that feels right. *[crosses downstage right and then left]* Sprinkled splashes of my own blood enhance the integration of its components. We are partners now, all part of a whole. We are equal with the bicycle wheel. We are all part of a creation. *[He kneels down center stage right]* I am a maker of beauty. I bleed. No turning back now.

FLO. No turning back now.

HARRY. You bitch! I love you, but you are not part of this. This is me and me alone.

FLO. Will you stop this?

HARRY. Yes, I will stop, as soon as I finish what I started out to do. *Harry's face turns up to the ceiling, from which there hangs an imaginary bare light bulb by a loose wire]* The light bulb, should I smash it into little pieces, break it into smithereens? But if I do that will we be able to see my work? I will do it. I'll break up the light, hit it with my fist.

[He crosses to the chair stage left turning away from Flo. Flo steps over the objects placed around her and bolts for the exit. Harry turns, shouts abruptly while blocking her exit. Flo crosses back downstage right into her corner. Harry crosses with the chair down center stage and steps up onto it. He looks at the imaginary light bulb but steps down, moves the chair only one inch to the right, then steps up onto the chair again. He punches the imaginary bulb after which he brushes imaginary glass out of his hair. Flo reacts to the punch also]

HARRY. Little bits of glass reflecting a myriad of colors, sparkling all about, sending their own source of light to the far regions of the room, all honoring my work, paying homage to my work. I will step on them. I will bleed from my feet. I will give my last drop of blood to my creation here before me.

[Harry pulls off his shoes and socks, and jumps onto the imaginary broken pieces of glass. He screams excruciatingly from the pain. He crawls away with imaginary bloodied feet from the broken glass, in great pain, screaming in pain. He is faking it to gain her sympathy.

Harry should scream with less and less conviction after each time that he looks at her. He wants her sympathy. She ignores him. At one point, he says "Ouch" and continues a soft, fake moan. Flo watches Harry on his hands and knees, crawling away from the glass. Flo takes her time picking up the mess; she's particularly concerned about one favorite broken cup downstage left. She utters a soft expression of concern for the cup and crosses downstage left towards it. Harry responds, expecting to be embraced. Flo walks past him. He moans some more. Flo returns upstage right with the precious cup. She continues picking up things and putting them in their proper place. He stops intermittently to see if she is noticing him. On the third long series of moans, he stops.]

FLO. I wish something exciting would happen.

HARRY. What do you wish would happen?

FLO. Oh, I don't know, something exciting. I wish, for example, that someone exciting would drop by.

HARRY. Yes, that would be exciting if someone exciting would drop by.

FLO. Yes, that would be exciting.

HARRY. Yes, if someone exciting would drop by it would be exciting.

FLO. Perhaps if we stared at the door for a long time, for a very long time, and just concentrated upon that event of someone exciting dropping by, then someone exciting would drop by.

HARRY. Yes, perhaps if we did that, someone exciting would drop by.

FLO. Yes, let's do that.

HARRY. Yes, let's do that.

[Flo goes to her chair and turns it towards the upstage exit door after which she sits upon it, staring at the exit. Harry observes her, and when Flo has been seated for a moment, he crawls with his feigned hurting feet

Raymond J. Barry

to his chair, places it downstage left also facing the exit, and pulls himself onto it. Harry looks again at Flo who is totally concentrated upon the exit door. Harry then faces the exit door and also waits for "someone exciting" to come. They both sit quietly, backs to the audience with lights dimming to two pools of luminescence surrounding each individual. Suddenly, a man appears in the exit door. This is Mr. Wagner.]

[BLACKOUT.]

End Act One

[During the act break the stage manager places the downstage left chair against the upstage left wall. He then goes to downstage right and wipes up the spilled tea from the floor. When Harry built the fence of teapot, cups, honey bear and saucers around Flo, these same objects were left on the floor. All should be left where they have fallen.
It should be noted that Once In Doubt works best without an act break which interrupts both the intensity and the rhythm of the play but this is strongly dependent upon the director's judgment.]

[If there is not an act break...
Blackout
In the darkness the stage manager hands Harry a towel and a bottle of whisky from the upstage center door. Harry finds his way in the dark to the chair downstage left and places it against the upstage left wall. He then goes to downstage Right and begins wiping up the spilled tea from the floor as the lights come up. Mr. Wagner is sitting center stage and Flo is standing stage left.]

Act Two

[Mr. Wagner is sitting center stage and Flo is standing stage left.
All three are feeling their liquor, having a good time. The general mood is
festive. The threesome are well on their way by now. Semi-loud music
plays. The name of the song is "Dark and Lovely" from the "Characters"
album by Stevie Wonder.*]

MR. WAGNER. I just came here to check up on things. I don't do that
often, mind you. Figure they got a handle on their own lives without me
"butting-in" my two cents. To tell you the truth, you had me worried
there for a while. I heard all the shouting from out the windows, and I
didn't know what was the matter here. There was something alarming
about it. I had to come over to make sure everything was all right.
FLO. I understand. We were having a discussion, weren't we, dear? We
were having a routine discussion about, er... things. I'm so embarrassed
we disturbed you. Aren't you embarrassed, dear?
HARRY. *[stage right]* Yeah, I'm embarrassed.
MR. WAGNER. You folks needn't be embarrassed. Hell, I'm embarrassed
for bringing it up in the first place. I'm really embarrassed.
FLO. You don't have to be embarrassed. Come on, let's dance! Harry,
turn up the music!
[Harry runs upstage and pantomimes turning up the volume of the music
by putting his hand behind the back wall at the entrance. He runs down
center stage and clears the chair away to the stage right table and begins
to dance himself.]
MR. WAGNER. *[dancing with Flo stage left]* Whoops! I think I stepped on
your big toe. I'm not the best dancer in the world but I try hard.
FLO. Oh, go on, you're doing fine.
HARRY. *[dancing by himself]* You're expressing yourself, man. Move with
the music. Get your ass into it and move with the music. You're doin'
great.
MR. WAGNER. Watch this one.
[Mr. Wagner tries an elaborate step that proves too complicated for him to
maintain his equilibrium... he stumbles, and Flo catches him, preventing
him from falling.]
MR. WAGNER. Thanks, I almost tripped.
FLO. Ha-ha, you did trip. I saved your life.
HARRY. *[dancing]* She saved your life. You threw yourself so far into your
expressiveness that it almost cost you your life, but she saved you, just
like she saved me. We're both lucky.
MR. WAGNER. You think that? You think we're both lucky?
HARRY. Oh, yeah. We're having a good time, aren't we? That makes us

Raymond J. Barry

very lucky. We're very lucky to be having such a good time. We are the lucky ones.

FLO. *[dancing stage right]* Yes, we are the lucky ones.

MR. WAGNER. I want to be a model for your next picture. I got muscles, see? *[Mr. Wagner takes off his shirt, flexing his aging muscles. He exhibits himself proudly.]* See what I look like? I'm a big, strong son of a bitch. I want to be in your next picture. I want to model for your next picture. How 'bout it? *[He crosses to Harry and punches him lightly on the shoulder downstage right.]*

HARRY. All right, but I got a better idea. *[refers to fourth wall]* Why don't you be in my next picture? Why don't you actually be in it?

MR. WAGNER. I think you're sayin' something weird to me, but I can't figure it out. I can't think straight right now. Everything is too weird.

FLO. *[crosses to Wagner, pulls him back downstage left]* You don't have to think straight. Just keep dancing the way you are. You know, you're cute... you know that? *[Flo dances with Mr. Wagner flirtatiously.]*

MR. WAGNER. You think so?

HARRY. *[pulls him away from Flo to downstage right]* Yeah, we should put you into it. Along with your shirt. I like the way you look with your shirt off. Don't you, honey? He's got some real muscles.

FLO. *[Crosses to Wagner, pulls him back to stage left to dance as Harry holds onto Wagner's other arm this time creating a tug of war between the two of them with Wagner in the middle.]* Don't let him kid you. He's just having a good time. That's the fun of it. We're all having a real good time. *[Tug of war ends with Flo winning, thereby pulling Wagner too far stage left, propelling him out of her hands with her dancing up center stage and drifting stage left. Simultaneously, Wagner hurriedly runs to Harry downstage right.]*

MR. WAGNER. Yeah, but I still wanna model for your next picture.

HARRY. My next painting is about you and you're gonna be in it. You're gonna be right inside of it with your hands stretched out like Christ. *[As he is saying this, Harry grabs Mr. Wagner and spreads his arms out with Mr. Wagner facing the audience as if he were on a cross.]*

HARRY. *[pretends he is hammering him]* In fact I'm gonna nail you to the goddammed thing, that's what.

FLO. *[Pushes Harry away and takes Mr. Wagner back to stage left.]* Harry, don't get any of your weird ideas. Let the man dance. Come on, let's dance. Let's have a good time and dance.

[Mr. Wagner and Flo continue dancing. Harry watches.]

HARRY. *[dancing towards them]* You two look beautiful.

FLO. Do we, Harry? I feel beautiful.

MR. WAGNER. You feel beautiful to me. That's for sure. *[Mr. Wagner and Flo are dancing close. Harry dances wildly around them stage left.]*

HARRY. Ah, I wish I could capture the both of you now like this...

Once in Doubt

somehow capture you. But, wait a minute, maybe you should be sculptures. That would be even better. The two of you would be great sculptures.

MR. WAGNER. That's me, a big statue. Ha-ha. *[He steps onto Flo's chair stage right and goes into an exaggerated pose, flexing his aging muscles.]*

FLO. *[crosses stage right of Wagner posing on chair]* Oh, you silly thing, you.

MR. WAGNER. What, me silly? You think I'm silly?

FLO. Yes, I do. I think you're silly, a big, silly man.

HARRY. *[dancing wildly stage left]* He's not silly. He's just responding to the moment in the here and now. We all are. We all are in the moment, ravishing life.

FLO. *[dancing wildly stage right]* Yes, that's what we are doing. We are ravishing life.

MR. WAGNER. So how 'bout it? You think I can pose for your next picture?

HARRY. *[dancing wildly stage left]* You'd have to stay very still for a long period of time. Are you up to it?

MR. WAGNER. Oh yeah. You bet I am.

HARRY. But would you be willing to give all of yourself?

MR. WAGNER. Oh yeah. I'll tell you one thing though, my wife is gonna wonder where I am. She's a worrywart and she's gonna wonder what's going on if I'm not home pretty soon. *[Harry throws him his shirt and puts hand behind exit to turn off music. Harry crosses downstage left, sits. Whisky bottle should be with him. Mr. Wagner catches shirt thrown to him, stops dancing and steps down from the chair, crosses downstage left to put it on.]*

HARRY. Oh well then, maybe we should just have a nightcap and call it quits.

MR. WAGNER. That's what I was thinkin'.

HARRY. Maybe it would be better not to include you in my next work after all. *[Flo crosses to her chair stage right and sits.]*

MR. WAGNER. Yes, maybe you're right.

HARRY. Only a few chosen ones are suited for this work, you know. Only a few people can be artists.

MR. WAGNER. I guess so. I feel like I'm copping out or something.

HARRY. Don't look at it that way. You're just not built for it, that's all.

MR. WAGNER. Yeah, but I really want to be built for it. I just feel there's something weird about it, that's all.

HARRY. Art can be weird to the onlooker. *[refers to the fourth wall]* Art can be like nothing else.

MR. WAGNER. *[He notices Harry's wrist.]* You cut yourself or something?

HARRY. It's nothing really; just a lot of blood.

MR. WAGNER. How'd you do that?

Raymond J. Barry

52

HARRY. Attempted suicide, slit my wrist. It's nothing. Don't worry about it. Had to be done.

MR. WAGNER. I see... you really take things pretty far, don't you?

HARRY. How do you mean?

MR. WAGNER. Well, it seems a little extreme...

HARRY. How do you figure?

MR. WAGNER. Well, you know...

HARRY. I'm not sure I do.

MR. WAGNER. Well, to do something so extreme. It's a little extreme, isn't it?

HARRY. I'm still not sure what you mean.

MR. WAGNER. Well, I mean... It must have hurt, didn't it?

HARRY. Hurt?

MR. WAGNER. Yeah, cutting into yourself like that. It must have really hurt. Didn't it?

HARRY. I don't know.

FLO. *[sits stage right]* I'm frightened to death.

HARRY. *[turns to her]* I'm frightened, too.

MR. WAGNER. You don't know?

HARRY. *[turns back to Wagner downstage left]* No, I don't know exactly.

FLO. I don't know what to do with myself.

HARRY. *[turns to Flo]* There, there, don't let it run away with you. I'm here.

MR. WAGNER. Oh, I get it. You were sleepwalking or something.

HARRY. *[turns back to Wagner]* No, I was wide awake.

FLO. I know it's silly, but my emotions are running away with me.

HARRY. *[turns to Flo]* Just don't let them.

FLO. I'm trying not to.

MR. WAGNER. You mean you knew what you were doing to yourself?

HARRY. *[turns back to Wagner]* Yes, I knew.

FLO. I feel so silly.

HARRY. *[turns to Flo]* You're not silly.

MR. WAGNER. Boy, that's something.

HARRY. *[to Flo]* Anyone can be frightened, anyone.

MR. WAGNER. You must have been really nervous, huh?

HARRY. *[turns to Wagner]* Nervous? I suppose. *[to Flo]* I told you before I get frightened.

FLO. I know, but you handle it so much better than I.

HARRY. *[turns to Flo]* That's what you think.

FLO. That's how it seems to me.

MR. WAGNER. I get really nervous.

FLO. You're more balanced than I.

HARRY. No I'm not.

MR. WAGNER. Not that nervous, but pretty nervous.

Once in Doubt

FLO. Yes you are.

HARRY. *[crosses center stage to Flo sitting]* We're in this together.

MR. WAGNER. I usually bite my nails or have a drink of whiskey when I get like that.

HARRY & FLO. *[both turn to Wagner]* I don't bite my nails.

MR. WAGNER. *[pause]* Yeah, I wish I didn't. Sometimes I nibble them right down to the skin and I keep chewing, you know. I oughtta stop doing that. I really oughtta stop doing that.

HARRY. If you did you might slit your wrist.

MR. WAGNER. Ha, ha, that's really funny. You got some sense of humor. You really do.

HARRY. I didn't mean it to be funny, goddammit. I meant every word of it.

MR. WAGNER. *[downstage left]* That's not so funny.

FLO. I'm aware of what's happening to my face.

MR. WAGNER. You want me to go, I'll go.

FLO. My lines are getting deeper every day.

MR. WAGNER. But I'm not trying to be a wise guy, you know?

FLO. *[sitting stage right]* I can see the difference every morning when I wake up and look into the mirror.

HARRY. *[next to Flo, stage right]* There isn't a thing that can happen to you while I'm here.

FLO. *[rises from her chair]* Are you serious?

MR. WAGNER. *[crosses to Harry center stage]* You and the missus had a little trouble, all right... I can understand that.

FLO. *[stage right of Harry]* Are you serious?

MR. WAGNER. *[stage left of Harry]* I had trouble in my time and lots of it.

FLO. Are you serious?

MR. WAGNER. You don't have the market on trouble, believe me. You don't own it.

FLO. Are you serious? It's happening every second. I'm rotting away.

HARRY. Well, you're not. You're exaggerating.

MR. WAGNER. I came here as a friend.

HARRY. Now calm down.

MR. WAGNER. If you don't respect that, then I'll go. No sweat off my back. *[He starts to exit. Harry and Flo race upstage and block him at the entrance.]*

[simultaneous]

HARRY.	**FLO.**
I apologize. Please forgive me. I didn't mean to be rude. It's been a trying day. We appreciate you took the risk to	Don't take everything he says so seriously. Actually, we were hoping for someone exciting to drop by, and you did, so please

Raymond J. Barry

come. So please stay and relax.   stay and relax.

[Harry and Flo step into Wagner's face.]
MR. WAGNER. I won't overstay my welcome.
FLO & HARRY. Don't worry about that.
[Harry and Flo lead Mr. Wagner down center stage. Harry places a chair under him and pushes him down on it. Flo gets a glass and Harry pours whiskey into it. Mr. Wagner drinks and stares at the fourth wall collage. Harry stands stage left over Wagner. Flo stands stage right over Wagner. Pause.]
MR. WAGNER. You do this?
HARRY. Yes.
MR. WAGNER. What's it supposed to be?
HARRY. *[All look at specific spots on the fourth wall.]* It's a bicycle wheel, a pair of pants, a blue shirt, Brillo pads, strokes of crimson red, pieces of paper crumpled or ripped, cat food cans, dishes and a clock, all put together to celebrate the moment.
MR. WAGNER. Celebrate what moment?
HARRY. The time span during which I composed it.
MR. WAGNER. Okay. It's pretty wild.
HARRY. Yes.
MR. WAGNER. I never understood this stuff too much. I like the green.
FLO. I did that. *[Harry gives her a dirty look. Flo reacts.]*
MR. WAGNER. You did? The red reminds me of blood.
HARRY. It is blood.
MR. WAGNER. What do you mean? Real blood?
HARRY. Yes.
MR. WAGNER. What are you talkin' about? You didn't use real blood for that, did you?
HARRY. Yes, I did.
FLO. *[to Harry]* I need a kiss.
MR. WAGNER. Boy, you artists are really something.
HARRY. *[to Flo]* How can you think of sex at a time like this?
MR. WAGNER. I'd hate to ask you what the other pictures are made of.
FLO. *[to Harry]* What?
MR. WAGNER. Just kidding.
FLO. *[to Harry]* What are you talking about?
MR. WAGNER. You really take yourself pretty serious, don't you?
FLO. *[to Harry]* I asked for a kiss, that's all.
MR. WAGNER. I can't get over it. To use your own blood for a picture.
FLO. *[to Harry]* A kiss is a gentle thing.
MR. WAGNER. Who was that guy who cut off his ear or somethin'?
HARRY. Van Gogh.
MR. WAGNER. Yeah, that was him. He reminds me of you.

FLO. *[to Harry]* Why won't you give me a kiss?

MR. WAGNER. Didn't he send it in a package to his girlfriend?

HARRY. Yes.

MR. WAGNER. Boy, what a guy. What a guy. Can you imagine what she musta said when she opened the box. What a pisser. I bet she never went out with him again after that, did she? *[Flo steps up to Wagner and kisses him on the lips while he is sitting. Then Flo crosses upstage right. Harry crosses upstage center right, next to Flo who sits.]*

MR. WAGNER. Oh, my. *[pause]* What did your wife say when you started that blood painting?

HARRY. She understands me.

FLO. I'm frightened to death.

HARRY. I'm frightened too. *[crosses downstage right to Flo]*

MR. WAGNER. You mean this is a pretty common thing around here.

HARRY. We argue. The arguing is common.

FLO. I don't know what to do with myself.

HARRY. We might as well make the best of everything, just make the best of it all.

MR. WAGNER. Just a normal marriage, huh?

HARRY. *[Explodes. Wagner falls off his chair.]* I didn't say normal! God, I hate that word normal! I hate it! I did not mean that! *[Harry crosses to stage left.]*

[Flo attacks Harry with blows and kicks; she chases him. They end up downstage left corner.]

FLO. Did you raise your voice? Did you? Did you? Don't raise your voice in this house when we have a guest. I'm so embarrassed. This is so embarrassing. Aren't you embarrassed, dear? Don't you feel embarrassed?

MR. WAGNER. Don't be embarrassed, lady. *[sits in center stage chair. Flo beating Harry. Flo immediately stops, switches her mood abruptly and crosses to the chair at the upstage left wall. She brings the chair next to Wagner's center stage chair to the right of it. She sits and Wagner sits. Harry crosses upstage left corner.]*

MR. WAGNER. Your husband is a little excitable, that's all. I used the wrong word and he got excited. Nothing to worry about. You know, I used to be pretty good at art when I was a kid in school. I did some pretty good winter scenes in my day. Snow was easy. Just use white crayon all over. I had the most trouble with the Fall scenes. The leaves were tough to make. I never did get it right. But I was pretty good doin' planes flying around and shootin' at each other. I did the details really good with wings flyin' off and everything. I got excited when I did those scenes, like I was shootin' the guns myself. I did water good too...waves with sail ships floating on top. They were good. I don't call myself an artist but I did have a talent for it when I was a kid.

Raymond J. Barry

FLO. You ought to pick it up again.

MR. WAGNER. I don't know. It seems a little out there to me.

FLO. Harry would give you materials. You ought to try it.

MR. WAGNER. What materials? A pint of blood? *[Both Wagner and Flo laugh uproariously. They turn to Harry who glowers at them.]*

FLO. Harry doesn't always use his own blood. He just tried that today... an experiment.

MR. WAGNER. Oh, an experiment. It could have been his last picture. *[Flo and Mr. Wagner laugh as Flo's mouth is full of drink. Her laughter makes her spit the drink into Wagner's face.]*

MR. WAGNER. *[while dealing with whiskey in his face]* The idea of using your own blood. Now that's real smart. It's so out there it's intelligent. It takes guts too.

HARRY. I'll say. Lots of courage to cut. *[cross stage left]* Not an easy thing to do.

FLO. I wish we didn't have to refer to that attention-getting gimmick every time you need some affirmation of your ego.

HARRY. What? What did you say, you bitch! You unappreciative little bitch!

[Crosses to Flo who gets up from her chair. They argue over Wagner who gazes up at them.]

[simultaneous]

FLO.	**HARRY.**
There you go again, flying out into space somewhere... anytime someone doesn't agree with you. Just because you are angry, or passionate, or whatever, does not mean you are correct. Anger never has and never will make anyone right.	Do you have any idea how much it took out of me to create that masterpiece, and I did it for you, you ungrateful little bitch... You bitch! You little bitch! Why you rotten little bitch! What did you say, you goddammed bitch? What Did you say, you little bitch?

FLO. You may bully me with anger 'till the day I die, but I'm not convinced you're right in what you're saying. I'm not convinced.

MR. WAGNER. Wait a minute! That's something there. He's mad, but that don't make him right. Is that what you're saying?

HARRY. *[hits Wagner on his shoulder]* You keep out of this!

FLO. Harry!

MR. WAGNER. *[runs away from him upstage left]* Hey, wait a minute, buddy. Don't you talk to me like that. I ain't your wife, get me? I'll knock your block off if you try that shit with me.

FLO. No, please, let's not get hostile with each other, please.

MR. WAGNER. *[crosses center stage left]* To hell with that. If he wants to

Once in Doubt

throw his weight around with me, I'll throw it right back. I don't have to put up with this kind of bullshit. Not me.

HARRY. *[crosses down center stage right]* Oh, please.

FLO. *[upstage center]* Don't aggravate the situation, Harry.

HARRY. I can't deal with this macho bullshit.

MR. WAGNER. I'm not gonna be yelled at like that.

HARRY. *[crosses toward Wagner]* Maybe you're forgetting whose studio you're in. Did you ever think for a moment about that?

FLO. Harry, don't you treat our guest like that.

HARRY. *[crosses downstage right]* You keep out of this! He's out of line here. I got my rights. I got my rights.

FLO. *[cross down center stage between them]* All right! Let's everyone settle down now. This is getting out of hand. This is getting way out of hand.

MR. WAGNER. *[attempting to exit]* I think I should be going.

FLO. *[stops him]* No, wait, don't go. Finish your drink. Don't go. *[She hits Harry on the head.]* Harry, apologize. Shake hands and apologize.

HARRY. *[Stops him. Extends his hand while crossing to Wagner upstage left.]* Look, maybe I was a little out of line.

MR. WAGNER. *[shakes his hand]* It was my fault as much as yours. I was partly to blame.

FLO. *[assists Wagner to center stage chair]* Never mind. He shouldn't be talking to you like that. It's not nice.

MR. WAGNER. *[sits]* It's all right. I didn't mean nothing by my behavior. I got a little excited.

HARRY. *[fills his drink center stage left of Wagner]* You were simply expressing yourself, that's all.

MR. WAGNER. Yeah, I guess I was. That's one way to put it. That's the artistic way to put it. I'm not used to dealing with the artistic temperament.

FLO. It's okay. You didn't come over here to get involved with Harry.

MR. WAGNER. I just came here to check up on things.

FLO. Right. And you did that, didn't you?

MR. WAGNER. Yes, I did. I didn't plan on staying for such a long time. I didn't expect to start drinking and carrying on quite the way I did.

HARRY. *[downstage left]* What did you expect?

MR. WAGNER. I guess I just expected to talk a little and go.

HARRY. But you didn't, did you? You stayed.

MR. WAGNER. Yeah, I stayed.

HARRY. *[stage left]* I wonder why you stayed. I wonder what happened to make you stay.

MR. WAGNER. I dunno. I like the picture with the Brillo pads and the bicycle wheel.

HARRY. *[crosses stage left center of Wagner's chair]* You liked the

Raymond J. Barry

painting, did you? The one I painted with my blood?

MR. WAGNER. Yeah, I like it. It's weird, but I like it. I didn't know you painted it with blood, your own blood. I didn't know that.

HARRY. But you found that out, didn't you? After I told you, you found that out.

MR. WAGNER. Yeah, I did.

HARRY. [circles Wagner who is sitting center stage] And still you stayed. You even drank our whiskey, didn't you? After you found out about the blood, you began to settle in for the evening, didn't you?

MR. WAGNER. Yeah, I guess. What are we talking about here?

FLO. What are you driving at, Harry?

HARRY. I'm just pointing out that whatever he found here couldn't have been that offensive, since he stayed. You even got drunk and laughed and danced with Flo. You had a good old time, didn't you?

MR. WAGNER. Yeah, it was a good time.

HARRY. [crosses to stage left corner] So I can assume that there was some aspect of our life here that made some sense to you, some attraction here that kept you interested. Maybe it was the creativity of my work that you liked or maybe it was Flo.

FLO. [crosses to downstage right] Harry!

HARRY. [slides on his knees to Flo downstage right] No, really, maybe, just maybe, he was enraptured by your beauty, your sexuality, if you please... just maybe.

FLO. All right, this is getting way out of hand. What the hell are you driving at?

HARRY. [in front of Flo, stage right] What I am driving at, my dearest one, is that we have here a concerned citizen who is attracted to life as it exists within these four walls. [crosses to Wagner sitting center stage] In a sense, he has in this short period of time, become one of us, almost part of the family so to speak, and being part of the family, he should be included in all of the advantages that go along with that.

MR. WAGNER. Thanks, thanks a lot.

HARRY. [places arm around Wagner's shoulder] Oh, you're welcome, brother! That's what you are to me now. You are my brother. How do you feel about that?

FLO. Don't let him take advantage of you.

HARRY. [crosses downstage right corner to Flo] Take advantage of him? Why, I'm making an offering. I'm not taking advantage. This is a gift from us to him.

FLO. What about me? Don't I have a say-so here? What about what I feel? He's not my brother.

HARRY. No, he's not, but perhaps he could be something else.

FLO. Like what?

HARRY. Well, if there were two of us, maybe all of your needs could be fulfilled and you would learn to appreciate me a little bit more. What do you think?

[He backs away from Flo in front of Wagner and slightly past him down left center.]

HARRY. What do you think, brother?

MR. WAGNER. Well, I don't know exactly.

HARRY. You don't have to know.

MR. WAGNER. *[sitting center stage as he is embraced by Harry]* I don't follow everything here.

HARRY. Nobody knows anything anyway.

MR. WAGNER. But you sure sound like you're trying to be friendly, and that's all I'm concerned about.

HARRY. Nobody knows a thing.

MR. WAGNER. I don't want to make enemies with you folks.

HARRY. Everybody's guessing.

MR. WAGNER. You're good people.

HARRY. Everybody's playing a guessing game out there. *[He crosses down center stage to the chair upon which Wagner is sitting. He puts his arm around Wagner as if he were his buddy.]* Don't require yourself to know. You'll be much better off.

MR. WAGNER. It's really nice of you to make me part of your family like you are. I kinda like that.

FLO. We were calmly living out our lives when this man came here. Now suddenly you're calling him "brother" and making him one of the family? I don't get it. *[attempts to leave]*

HARRY. *[crosses to downstage right, blocking and confronting Flo]* Live creatively, that's all. Don't allow your life to be what it is. Make it what you wish it to be. *[crosses to Wagner sitting]* How do you wish your life to be, buddy?

MR. WAGNER. Me? Oh, I don't know exactly.

HARRY. Well, you want it to be special, don't you?

MR. WAGNER. Yeah, I guess so.

HARRY. *[referring to collage]* You like my art work, don't you? You said so before.

MR. WAGNER. Yeah, I like it. It's pretty interesting, I think.

HARRY. *[crosses downstage left]* There now, "pretty interesting, I think." That's a "pretty interesting" way to put it. It took "risk" to become an artist, you know. I had to go against the "Flo" in order to accomplish that. Do you know what that means?

MR. WAGNER. Against the flow?

HARRY. *[crosses to Wagner center stage]* Yes, I had to resist the pressures of society in order to know who I am. I couldn't make paintings unless I knew who I was.

MR. WAGNER. Yeah?

Raymond J. Barry

FLO. He's talking in riddles.

HARRY. [cross to Flo stage right] But how was I to accomplish such a thing? Why, it took risk, that's how. I had to watch myself under fire when the chips were down.

MR. WAGNER. Yeah?

HARRY. Do you know what that means?

MR. WAGNER. Not exactly.

FLO. Don't listen to his nonsense.

HARRY. Do you know, buddy, what risk is, what real risk entails?

MR. WAGNER. Maybe like bettin' on a football game?

HARRY. [crosses center stage to Wagner] Yes, something like that. It has a lot to do with the natural fear we experience when we don't know what the outcome of our actions will be.

MR. WAGNER. Like if I bet on the Giants and I don't know if they're gonna win or not.

HARRY. Yes, but there are more profound examples.

MR. WAGNER. There are? [Flo attempts to leave.]

HARRY. [blocks Flo] There sure are. What if, for example, you fucked Flo.

FLO. Harry!

HARRY. Would you know what the outcome of that action would be?

FLO. Harry!

HARRY. I bet you wouldn't, would you?

MR. WAGNER. [prepares to leave] Hey, wait a minute, Bud, I ain't thinking about doin' that, you know, so you can get off it right now. What the hell are you trying to encourage here? You're not gettin' me involved in this kind of bullshit. [Wagner crosses to exit.]

HARRY. [blocks exit] See how you react? You're reacting so violently against it that there has to be some nerve that has been touched here. That's what risk is, buddy; when you can deal with what you're afraid of. You're afraid of fucking her so there must be something to that. There's got to be.

FLO. [crosses to exit blocked by Harry] Oh, brother, what a con man. What a fucking con man!

HARRY. [faces Flo] What?! You're denying that such a risk might be properly taken?

FLO. I don't want to fuck this ape!

HARRY. You said he was cute before.

FLO. That was before. I don't want to fuck this guy.

MR. WAGNER. We don't want to do it, mister!

HARRY. No risk... no joy. I rest my case. I'll leave you alone now so you can discuss whatever it is you want to discuss. I shall come back at the appropriate time. [Harry goes to the exit door, leaves. Wagner and Flo stand in place for a while without saying a word. Finally, they begin to giggle. She first and he after. The giggle swells into a guffaw which *continues for some time. Finally, it subsides, followed by silence.]*

MR. WAGNER. *[downstage left]* What are ya' laughing at?

FLO. *[upstage right]* I don't know. What are you laughing at?

MR. WAGNER. That guy is really amusing.

FLO. Yes, he is amusing, isn't he? He's very amusing. I've been amused by him for years. Very amused.

MR. WAGNER. *[crosses downstage right to put his drink on the table]* Well, it's time for me to go.

FLO. No, wait, don't go.

MR. WAGNER. *[crosses toward exit]* I really can't stay any longer. My wife...

FLO. *[blocks his way]* Your wife won't mind if you stay just a bit longer.

MR. WAGNER. She won't?

FLO. No, she won't. I wouldn't, as long as you're safe. You are safe and you've had a good time, haven't you?

MR. WAGNER. Well, an unusual time anyway.

FLO. Yes, it has been unusual.

MR. WAGNER. I can only stay a little longer.

[Wagner sips a drink. There is silence. Finally Wagner sits on chair center stage] This stuff is beginning to get to me.

FLO. I feel like we've been thrown together.

MR. WAGNER. Yes, well...

FLO. So... what shall we do? Shall we do it? Shall you lay me right here on the floor?

MR. WAGNER. You want to? I thought you didn't want to.

FLO. No, I wanted to. I didn't want him to know...

MR. WAGNER. He knew. He knew for sure.

FLO. You're probably right. He has an uncanny perception.

MR. WAGNER. I sense that. Yeah. He's an artist so he's trained to look at the world differently from guys like me.

FLO. I wouldn't put yourself down so easily.

MR. WAGNER. Okay. I won't. He's still a very unusual man. I envy him in a way.

FLO. You needn't. He is tormented in ways you wouldn't believe.

MR. WAGNER. No. I would believe it. I've heard him talk. He's not like other people. This guy sees the world different.

FLO. Yes, he does. Maybe that's why I stay with him. I'm mesmerized by his power. *[Harry appears up above on the level where the paintings are stored. Harry watches Flo and Wagner silently.]*

MR. WAGNER. How did he get that way?

FLO. Risk. Which, by the way, in case you don't remember, is why we are together now, isn't it? You want me to take my clothes off? Shall we do it?

MR. WAGNER. I want to very much, but I'm not sure we should.

Raymond J. Barry

FLO. [*crosses to Wagner*] We have permission.

MR. WAGNER. Yes, we have permission.

FLO. He'll stay out of here for a long enough time for us to finish.

MR. WAGNER. He will?

FLO. I think he will. He would want us to enjoy it, I would think, since it's so important to him.

MR. WAGNER. It is important for him, isn't it? He wants me to do it, doesn't he?

FLO. [*crosses away from Wagner to stage left*] Yes, I'm afraid he does. I want you to do it to me, too, if that's a help. I know it's not easy for you.

MR. WAGNER. [*sitting center stage*] No, it isn't. I've been married for years. I look at women all the time, but I never do anything about it. I'm in love with my wife. It's good with me and her.

FLO. [*downstage left*] Now I'm going to reach under my dress and take down my panties like this and I want you to watch me do that. [*She does that; looks directly at Wagner.*] There now. I'll leave my dress on because I don't want to be too fast. I think we should take our time with this. [*She lies center stage on the floor.*]

MR. WAGNER. Yes, I would like to take our time too. I keep worrying about him though. I don't want him to walk in while we're doing it.

FLO. Now I'm going to lay my panties on the floor beside me like this. [*She does so.*]

MR. WAGNER. Yes, do that. I think I'll make myself more comfortable. I'll take my shoes off... stretch out my feet a little. [*He takes off his shoes and wiggles his toes.*]

FLO. Yes, do that.

MR. WAGNER. Well, what'll we do now?

FLO. Just relax. Everything will happen in its own time.

MR. WAGNER. Yes, I'll relax. I want you to relax too.

FLO. Yes, I'll relax. I'm naked under my dress. I just wanted to remind you of that.

MR. WAGNER. I'm glad you did. I was forgetting for a brief moment.

FLO. You were forgetting I was naked? How could you forget that?

MR. WAGNER. I was only kidding.

FLO. Oh, you.

MR. WAGNER. I want to touch you between the legs, but I'm afraid he'll walk in.

FLO. Take the risk or don't take the risk.

MR. WAGNER. I want to take it.

FLO. Then do. [*Wagner slowly leaves his chair and sinks down upon his hands and knees. He slowly crawls to her open legs, stage left.*] [*BLACKOUT.*]

Once in Doubt

[*Lights up on Harry in the doorway up center stage. A faint, high pitched sound begins softly and gradually builds in volume during the following speech by Harry.*]

HARRY. I hear it now as I always do, that sound.

I hear that sound between my ears, that sound.

It drowns my thoughts, that sound. I'm drowning in my
  thoughts.

That sound is drowning me in my own sound, drowning me.

Maybe the little white heat monster will leave me
  someday.

Maybe it will at least become more quiet.

Don't think about it.

Don't think about it.

Think about something else.

Think about something pretty like a flower.

A flower is nice.

My first painting was of an azalea.

My very first painting was of that flower.

[*High pitched sound cuts off. Full stage lights come up. He crosses downstage right to Flo sitting in her chair.*]

HARRY. So how was it? Was it a good fuck?

FLO. Yes.

MR. WAGNER. [*Lying on the floor stage left. He hurriedly gets up and tucks in his shirt, zips up his fly, and fastens his belt.*] Yes.

HARRY. And did she cry out into the night as she does for me?

FLO. I made a few sounds.

HARRY. A few sounds?

FLO. Yes, a few expressions of pleasure.

HARRY. Care to repeat them for me?

FLO. Definitely not. It's too personal. It's between him and me.

MR. WAGNER. I made a few sounds, too. I cried out, "Oh, God!" when I reached my climax.

HARRY. You did?

FLO. Yes, he did.

HARRY. Are you answering for him now?

MR. WAGNER. [*crosses stage right to fetch his shoes*] I can speak for myself.

HARRY. You certainly can. You've been speaking for yourself all night and I like what you've been saying. You're one of the family now. You're part of us.

MR. WAGNER. [*crosses with shoes stage left*] Thanks.

HARRY. How does it feel to take risk?

MR. WAGNER. [*puts on shoes stage left*] I was pretty scared but I got to like it after a while. I'm glad I stayed.

Raymond J. Barry

HARRY. I am too. Aren't you glad he stayed, honey?

FLO. Yes, I'm glad he stayed.

HARRY. Oh, by the way, I found these on the floor. They're yours... *[He gives Flo a pair of panties he's been holding in his hand behind his back.]*

FLO. Thank you.

MR. WAGNER. *[gets up and crosses to upstage center exit]* Well, it's time for me to be going.

HARRY. *[Blocks Wagner's exit. Brings him downstage left.]* Wait a minute. We're not finished yet. You can't just eat and run. You can't just come in, get laid and leave. That's not the whole of it. You've taken a risk in your life and now you've got to see what that leads to.

MR. WAGNER. What it leads to?

HARRY. Yes, we have to find out. It isn't enough to just stick Flo.

FLO. I don't want you to go either. I can't take him anymore. Don't forget how it was with us just a short time ago. It was good, wasn't it?

MR. WAGNER. I hate to say it in front of your husband, but, yes, it was the best. You were great, more than great – stupendous.

FLO. Don't leave me, please. You mustn't leave me.

HARRY. You see? She wants you to stick around, too. *[crosses center stage, stands on chair]* What we are creating here is a work of art consisting of three people, namely ourselves. This is getting interesting, isn't it?

MR. WAGNER. Things haven't been this interesting in my life for years. I thought I was gettin' old.

HARRY. *[steps down from chair, crosses stage left to Wagner]* You are getting old. We all are. We have to find out things before it is too late. Might as well take a chance.

FLO. He's got a point there.

HARRY. Put your panties on.

FLO. *[rises from her chair stage right]* Who the fuck are you to tell me to put my panties on? I took them off when I wanted. I'll put them on when I want.

HARRY. *[crosses to Flo]* Have it your own way. Maybe I was talking out of place. I apologize for that.

MR. WAGNER. Where do we go from here?

HARRY. *[crosses to Wagner stage left]* That's the stuff. Where do we go? You are feeling things, aren't you? An artist must listen to his feelings at all times. They are his life, his reason for making art. An artist is born, not made. I believe you were born an artist but you never realized it.

MR. WAGNER. Yeah?

HARRY. You emanated a creative spark from the very first moment you entered my studio.

MR. WAGNER. Yeah?

HARRY. I and I alone saw that.

FLO. What about me? What am I, chopped liver or something?

HARRY. Are your panties on?

FLO. You sarcastic son of a bitch.

HARRY. Your names can be directed elsewhere now. There are two of us now.

FLO. I'm directing them towards you.

HARRY. I wish you wouldn't, but if you must, give it a form. Give your frustrations a definite form. *[Drops to his knees downstage right, looking at the fourth wall collage. Flo crosses to Harry who is kneeling toward the collage. She dumps a full pot of tea on his head. Harry kneels, frozen. She runs to a bucket that contains, let us say, green paint, imaginary, of course. She throws the paint upon the fourth wall. Although the bucket is really empty, it will be understood that a huge splash of green paint has devastated Harry's masterpiece. Flo, standing before him, imaginary paint on her clothes and hands, holding an empty bucket. She throws the bucket down and sits stage left.]*

MR. WAGNER. Jesus, lady, you shouldn't have done that!

FLO. You're so locked up and repressed.

[Flo breathing hard. Harry, on his knees, is dumbfounded by his ruined collage.]

HARRY. I damn well better be repressed for your sake.

FLO. Why do you say that?

HARRY. I think it would be better for me to be quiet... about some of the things I have been experiencing with regard to you.

FLO. Don't be quiet. I want you to be totally honest.

[Harry seems mesmerized by the color of the paint that has been thrown onto the collage.]

FLO. What are you doing?

HARRY. Thinking.

FLO. About what?

HARRY. *[on his knees, staring at the ruined collage]* Do I have to tell you everything going on in my mind?

FLO. All right, drop it. Keep it to yourself.

HARRY. *[staring at the ruined collage]* I don't want to tell you everything going on in my mind. You wouldn't like it all. If I were to act out my innermost feelings, I would become a different person altogether. If I were to become a different person altogether, it would give you more reason to badger me.

FLO. Badger you? *[Flo sits on Harry's stage left chair. He turns to face her from his knees.]*

HARRY. Yes. Badger me. That's what you do, you know. You badger me all the time. *[He approaches her on his knees, crossing to stage left.]* Badger! Badger! Badger! Here, I'll give you something real to badger me about. *[Harry grabs Flo's foot and bites the toe of her shoe. She struggles*

Raymond J. Barry

to get away from him.]

FLO. Ouch! Let me go, please. Let me go! What are you doing, you madman? You're hurting me. *[She breaks away from him, crosses downstage left corner.]* You hurt me.

HARRY. *[Soft. Apologetic.]* I'm sorry. I didn't know what I was doing.

FLO. You did too know what you were doing.

HARRY. I know but I lost my head.

FLO. You hurt me.

HARRY. *[on his knees, center stage left]* I knew you wouldn't like it if I expressed myself.

FLO. You call that expressing yourself?

HARRY. You mean I'm supposed to express myself in a specific way, a nice way?

FLO. No, that's not what I'm saying.

HARRY. Then what is it you're saying.

FLO. I'm saying you hurt me and there's no reason for that.

HARRY. Oh, really?

FLO. Yes, really. I'll have the police on you, you motherfucker!

HARRY. What do you mean you'll have the police on me? I cut my wrist for you! I made a collage for you! You ruined my fucking collage!

FLO. That was different.

HARRY. I'll say it's different.

FLO. I was making an honest effort to communicate with you, an effort to open things up between us. Now you pull this kind of shit. I love you and I want to preserve what we have between us. You don't seem to want that. Now stop it. You're scaring me.

[Flo is slowly backing away from him downstage left corner as he approaches her on his knees. He rises to his feet and gently slides the ashtray and a saucer in her direction. She crosses to stage right corner and he follows, thereby trapping her at the downstage right corner. Mr. Wagner is petrified he grabs the whisky bottle and guzzels a drink.]

HARRY. *[gently tips over Flo's chair]* I can't stop now. It wouldn't make sense to stop. That is, if you mean what you're saying about my expressing myself. That's what I'm doing, my darling. I'm simply being honest about everything.

[As he speaks he gathers in his hands all of the objects on Flo's table, a cup, a saucer, the honey bear, the teapot, the tray. Throughout the dialogue he gradually builds on the floor with the crockery, a fence of sorts, that traps Flo in her stage right corner. The fence will be made of the saucer, a cup, a honey bear and the tray, as well as anything else he has gathered from the tea table, all placed in strategic positions with the intention of making clear that Flo is not to step beyond that point. The fence should be designed spontaneously, according to Harry's imagination for each performance.]

Once in Doubt

HARRY. You see, just now, when I bit your toe, I somehow knew it would be far better for both of us if your toe hurt rather than my head. My head has been hurting, my darling. Did you know that? *[Harry places on the floor, perhaps, the teapot, a saucer and a cup in front of Flo to establish the beginnings of his fence around Flo.]*

FLO. No. I did not.

HARRY. Well, it's true. My head has been hurting.

FLO. I didn't know that.

HARRY. No, you didn't, did you?

FLO. No, I didn't.

HARRY. Maybe you should have known.

[Flo is backed to the tip end of the downstage right corner. This scene works best when Harry speaks with quiet intensity, ready to explode. Shouting will diminish his power. Perhaps now he would place a saucer on the floor in line with the teapot and other articles to complete his fence even more.]

FLO. How could I? You never told me.

HARRY. Do you always have to be told? Then again, I suppose you do. You're so insensitive you can't see things on your own. You can't feel what is happening before your eyes. You always have to be told. What a pity...

FLO. What does that mean?

HARRY. It's a pity you can't feel what is happening.

FLO. I had no way of knowing.

HARRY. You did though!

FLO. No, I didn't. You must believe me. I'll try to make it up to you.

HARRY. You're frightened, aren't you? *[placing a cup and honey bear on floor to complete the fence enclosing Flo.]*

FLO. Yes, I am frightened. I'm afraid of you. I'm afraid of your violence. I'm afraid to say I love you, and that I'm hungry for you, and I need you and I need to be held and all those other things people need because we are what we are... hungry.

[Harry and Flo are standing, downstage right looking at each other.]

HARRY. I'm not violent.

FLO. I just want you to care for me.

HARRY. I don't care enough to be violent.

[simultaneous]

FLO. *[gentle]*	**HARRY.** *[gentle]*
I need care. I feel insecure sometimes. You're not always there when I need you.	I really don't care enough. I would do harm to myself rather than be violent to someone.

Raymond J. Barry

HARRY. I like you. No, I take that back.

[simultaneous]

FLO.	**HARRY.**
I hope you understand what I'm talking about. I don't mean to complain. I really don't mean to complain.	I just don't want to be violent. I wouldn't even know how to begin to be violent.

FLO. The problem is us, not me.

[simultaneous]

FLO.	**HARRY.**
Are you not responsible at all? Are you not to be held accountable?	I would probably burst out laughing if I were violent to you. I would put my hands around your throat and burst out laughing.

FLO. Will you stop this?

HARRY. Yes, I will stop, my darling. Yes, I'll stop. *[crosses downstage left to Wagner]* Now what do we do about your pent-up emotions?

MR. WAGNER. I don't know.

HARRY. *[takes Wagner up to back wall]* I say we release them, that's what we do. We allow them to take form.

MR. WAGNER. This is confusing to me.

HARRY. Don't be confused in your confusion. Let it all unravel itself on its own. Don't be afraid of not knowing what the next moment will be. It will happen by itself... Take your time. Take your time. *[He takes the wide four inch brush from the paint can adjacent and stage left of the entrance and places it in Wagner's hand. The can has been there from the beginning of the play along with the wide brush placed in the acrylic red paint. The paint can be washed off after each performance before re-coating the wall with white. To facilitate this it should be mixed with Dove liquid dishwashing soap to weaken its tensile strength.]*

MR. WAGNER. *[paints on the wall with bright red paint]* Yeah, okay. I'm takin' my time.

HARRY. *[He works on his collage on the fourth wall by flicking his wrist with imaginary blood.]* Atta boy!

MR. WAGNER. *[He continues painting throughout the remaining scene.]* I don't know which end is up anymore.

HARRY. *[moving stage left to right on the fourth wall]* A divine state of mind... not knowing. Enjoy that condition... It is a highly developed state. Shift into cruise and ride it out.

FLO. This can't go on.

MR. WAGNER. Do you feel like I do?

HARRY. *[stands on the chair center stage]* Yes, I must. We're connected, aren't we?

MR. WAGNER. Connected... yes! I'm connected to you... to something!

HARRY. Art is in the making it is...

[Wagner paints with red paint upon the stage left back wall. His work resembles the abstract expressionist style of the fifties, Willem de Kooning or Franz Kline. He wildly applies the paintbrush onto the wall.]

MR. WAGNER. You know, I used to be pretty good at art when I was a kid in school.

HARRY. I want to lean upon my work with all my weight...

MR. WAGNER. I remember drawing pictures of naked women and guys too.

HARRY. ...so that at the last moment...

MR. WAGNER. But I always ripped those up before my mother saw them.

[Harry takes the center stage chair, places it downstage right, steps up onto it and flicks imaginary blood onto the upper part of the fourth wall as he speaks. Wagner paints with real paint the upper left stage wall with his back to the audience as he speaks.]

HARRY. ...during my very last gasping breath...

FLO. *[crosses to Harry]* There's something about this relationship I don't want anymore!

HARRY & MR. WAGNER. I know.

MR. WAGNER. I don't remember how I got rid of them...

HARRY. I myself, the creator, will be part of the visual composition.

FLO. Would you like some tea.

MR. WAGNER. ...but I think I threw them into the wastepaper basket.

HARRY. My composition needs a human figure!

FLO. I think I'll have some more tea.

MR. WAGNER. I hope nobody ever pulled those drawings out.

HARRY. I am imagining the position that would look best.

FLO AND MR. WAGNER. Handstand position!

HARRY. Yes! Legs upward!

MR. WAGNER. Those were my secret drawings with people doin' it and everything.

[simultaneous]

HARRY.	**FLO.**	**MR. WAGNER.**
Sixty degree angle to that old shirt, that same shirt I wore some months ago as we ambled, arguing through an abandoned street. It was in the air	I'm uncontrollably attracted to you! I want to be inside your body! I don't want this "thing" we're tied up in! It won't come loose!	I hope nobody ever saw them. It would really be embarrassing. I don't call myself an artist but I did have a talent for it when I

Raymond J. Barry

then.   was a kid!
[pause.]

FLO. [down center stage] How difficult it is to love each other.
HARRY. [steps down from the stage right chair] Yes, it is difficult, but worth it.
FLO. Yes, it is worth it.
HARRY. You do think it is worth it, don't you, dear?
FLO. Yes, I think it's worth it. Of course I do.
HARRY. Because if you didn't think it was worth it, I don't know if I could go on.
FLO. But I do think it's worth it. Really, I do. I know it is worth it.
HARRY. After all, what else is there?
FLO. Yes, after all, what else is there?
FLO. Yes, just more of the same.
HARRY. Yes, just more of the same. Maybe a different arena but more of the same basically.
[Wagner continues painting with real paint on the back wall. Flo stands motionless center stage facing Harry downstage right.]
FLO. You always seem so difficult to talk to... even when I need to speak; I mean really speak from my heart.
HARRY. Can you speak now? From your heart? I mean now.
FLO. I don't know.
HARRY. But you must. You absolutely must. It's not fair for you not to speak. I need you to speak, at once, now. You must speak. Open your mouth. Out with it. On with it. Speak, speak, from your heart, speak, speak.
FLO. I hate your guts! [pause] No, I didn't mean that. Really, I didn't mean that. It just slipped out. I swear to you, I didn't mean that. Really, you must believe me. I didn't mean that. [Harry is stunned, stares at the fourth wall. He walks down to the painting. Wagner dips his brush into the paint can and begins, once again, to paint. Harry raises his arm and flicks his blood on his painting. The stage lights turn blood red. Flo sinks to the floor.]
MR. WAGNER. [back to audience, working on collage] I'm in love with my wife. It's good with me and her. [The stage lights fade gradually to black.]

End of Play

Back Home

Characters

Henry: age sixty-five, a retired bricklayer by trade. He's in good physical shape and married to Constance, the father of Pete.

Constance: in her mid-fifties, is a home-maker with a pleasant face and a generally optimistic outlook of the world. She is a plump woman, who at one time was very pretty; wife of Henry and mother of Pete.

Pete: return Iraq War vet, twenty-four years old, son of Henry and Constance; paralyzed from the waist down.

Mel: sixty-seven, overweight and sportily dressed. The man has the look of being beaten by life with bags under his eyes and generally unhealthy in appearance. He likes to joke, smile and laugh, possibly to cover up what's really going on.

Karen: twenty-four and pretty, dressed simply in a skirt and blouse; Pete's love interest.

Back Home

Act One

-

Scene One

[HENRY and CONSTANCE sit in their living room. HENRY is age sixty-five, a retired bricklayer by trade in good physical shape. CONSTANCE, in her mid-fifties, is a home-maker with a pleasant face and a generally optimistic outlook of the world. she is a plump woman, who at one time was very pretty. Indulgence of food and drink has worn away her good looks. Placed on one wall is a large, abstract oil painting with brilliant colors and swirling brush strokes. The rest of the living room is decorated in the usual middle-class manner that befits the suburbs. There is a crucifix hanging on one wall, and, of course, a television. An exaggerated silence pervades, as HENRY reads the paper and CONSTANCE putters about the living room, cleaning and dusting the floor and furniture.]

CONSTANCE. You came home late for just lunch.
HENRY. What time is it?
CONSTANCE. Five-thirty.
HENRY. You're right. It's a bit late for a lunch.
CONSTANCE. A long time for eating a lunch, just one lunch. What did she eat?
HENRY. Salmon.
CONSTANCE. Oh, yes, salmon. I like salmon.
HENRY. And a salad.
CONSTANCE. Oh, yes, and a salad.
HENRY. Then dessert, peach pie.
CONSTANCE. Peach pie?
HENRY. Yep, peach pie.
CONSTANCE. Fattening.
HENRY. I get away with it up to a point.
CONSTANCE. Up to a point?
HENRY. I would get heavy if I ate peach pie every day.
CONSTANCE. Where did you have lunch?
HENRY. Pangea.
CONSTANCE. What is Pangea?
HENRY. *[reads newspaper.]* The name of the restaurant.
[pause]
CONSTANCE. We should paint the living room.

HENRY. You think so?

CONSTANCE. Yes, we need a fresher color.

HENRY. Fresher?

CONSTANCE. Yes, something fresh.

HENRY. I'd like that – something fresh.

CONSTANCE. I can't tolerate drabness anymore.

HENRY. Gets you down, does it?

CONSTANCE. I'd like something fresh.

HENRY. I heard you.

CONSTANCE. Freshness makes one's life fresh.

HENRY. I get it.

CONSTANCE. Fresh, fresh.

HENRY. Yep, that word again. What's the point?

CONSTANCE. Just thinking out loud, making conversation.

HENRY. I'll paint the wall sometime.

CONSTANCE. Thank you.

HENRY. *[reading newspaper]* Don't mention it.

[pause]

CONSTANCE. Who picked the restaurant?

HENRY. She did.

CONSTANCE. She must've had a plan.

HENRY. Neither one of us had a plan.

CONSTANCE. How much was the check?

HENRY. I think around forty dollars with the tip.

CONSTANCE. Not that expensive really.

HENRY. It was a quiet restaurant with very few customers.

CONSTANCE. No one noticed you?

HENRY. No one noticed. We were in the corner of the room.

CONSTANCE. You know how long it's been with us?

HENRY. Yes, I know. I'm sorry.

[pause]

CONSTANCE. I love that painting. Don't you?

HENRY. Yes, I love it.

CONSTANCE. It describes chaos so eloquently.

HENRY. Yes, it does, doesn't it?

CONSTANCE. Our son is a talent. He should take it up again. If only he would he'd try. He has to try.

HENRY. Let's talk about other things.

CONSTANCE. Oh, all right. *[pause]* We're very lucky really. To have such memories of him.

HENRY. You talk as if he's dead for goodness sake.

CONSTANCE. You were the one who encouraged him with your war stories. You were the one who admired his uniform, how handsome he looked when he...

Raymond J. Barry

HENRY. *[sharply]* That's enough.

CONSTANCE. Please, be kind, Henry. We must learn to be kind.

HENRY. I'm kind.

CONSTANCE. I know you're kind. I don't know why I said that.

HENRY. You said it because at times I'm unkind.

CONSTANCE. No, you're not unkind. I didn't mean to imply...

HENRY. But you didn't imply. You said it directly.

[pause]

CONSTANCE. That painting is so very beautiful.

HENRY. Yes, it is, isn't it?

CONSTANCE. I just love the colors... the controlled chaos of the painting.

HENRY. Yes. He should get back to painting.

CONSTANCE. Painting would be so good for him. *[pause]* Where did you say you went once you paid the forty dollar bill?

HENRY. The actual bill was thirty-three dollars. The tip came to forty.

CONSTANCE. Why such a large tip?

HENRY. Twenty percent isn't that large.

CONSTANCE. Seems like a great deal of money.

HENRY. I usually give two dollars for every ten charged.

CONSTANCE. What hotel did you say you went to after lunch?

HENRY. I didn't.

CONSTANCE. I'll stop asking.

[CONSTANCE walks into the kitchen. She putters about. Long silence with occasional clanking of dishes.]

HENRY. What are you doing in there?

CONSTANCE. Just working around the kitchen, cleaning, cooking, making things nice for myself.

HENRY. Cleaning? Or cooking?

CONSTANCE. Both cleaning and cooking.

HENRY. Well, you can't be doing both.

CONSTANCE. Sure I can. I know what I'm doing.

HENRY. Nobody doubts you know what you're doing.

CONSTANCE. *[puttering in the kitchen.]* Never mind.

HENRY. I know.

[pause]

CONSTANCE. *[from the kitchen]* Did anyone notice you?

HENRY. Yes.

CONSTANCE. *[from the kitchen]* Who?

HENRY. There was a guy near the elevators of the hotel. He saw us go up and later he saw us come down.

CONSTANCE. *[from the kitchen]* How much later?

HENRY. About an hour and a half.

[A glass breaks in the kitchen.]

HENRY. What was that?

Back Home

CONSTANCE. *[from the kitchen]* A glass. A glass broke.

HENRY. A glass broke?

CONSTANCE. *[from the kitchen]* Yes, a glass broke.

HENRY. How did the glass break?

CONSTANCE. *[from the kitchen]* It just broke, that's all.

HENRY. Be careful.

CONSTANCE. *[resumes washing dishes]* I'll be careful.

HENRY. That's what he should've been. Should've been careful.

CONSTANCE. *[from the kitchen]* What, dear? What did you say?

HENRY. What with those bombs all over the place, killing people, blowing their heads off, arms, their
legs...

[CONSTANCE enters living room.]

CONSTANCE. What was the room like in the hotel?

HENRY. Back to that again?

CONSTANCE. Just curious.

*[CONSTANCE vacuums loudly with a vacuum cleaner. This goes on for a while. The phone rings. CONSTANCE doesn't hear It. HENRY is reading the paper again. The vacuum cleaner drowns
out the ring of the phone. Finally HENRY hears the telephone. He shouts above the noise of the vacuum cleaner]*

HENRY. The phone's ringing. *[no response]* The phone's ringing! *[no response]* The phone's ringing!

CONSTANCE. *[vacuum cleaner off]* What, dear?

HENRY. The phone. The phone is ringing.

CONSTANCE. *[crosses to phone]* They hung up. Couldn't you have answered the phone?

HENRY. No. It's always for you anyway. Stop the damned noise with the vacuum cleaner. I can't hear myself think.

CONSTANCE. All right; just had to clean a little. *[pause]* Pete won the Purple Heart. He's says you won a medal for valor. That couldn't be true, could it? You weren't in the service.

HENRY. He's coming home. That's all that matters.

CONSTANCE. Yes, he's coming home. Did you tell him you won a medal for valor? I know what you did. You told me what you did. You told him you won a medal?

HENRY. He was a little boy then.

CONSTANCE. Well, that may be true, but you still told him a lie.

HENRY. He's hurt bad.

CONSTANCE. Did he say that?

HENRY. I can tell by the way he talked. You can tell, can't you?

CONSTANCE. The important thing is that he's coming home.

HENRY. Yup, getting out of that hell hole.

CONSTANCE. He seemed in good humor – even joked about the food.

Raymond J. Barry

HENRY. Yeah, he was in good humor.

CONSTANCE. We'll be ready for him. Won't we?

HENRY. I'm ready now.

CONSTANCE. We have to be strong.

HENRY. What strong? I'm strong.

CONSTANCE. We've got to be there for him.

HENRY. I have every intention of being there for him.

CONSTANCE. Just making sure that we're a team.

HENRY. I don't need this pep talk. I know what I'm in for.

CONSTANCE. "In for"? What do you mean by that? "In for!"

HENRY. *[reads the paper]* It's not going to be our usual routine. Stop nagging me.

CONSTANCE. No one is nagging.

HENRY. You're nagging.

CONSTANCE. If I am I'm sorry.

HENRY. Remember when he as a little boy, always playing basketball; always playing basketball. He was fast too, very fast. The things he could do with that ball, dribbling between his legs; total control - total control. He could shoot too. I'll say. He could shoot with the best of them. There wasn't a thing he couldn't do well on the court. Except maybe rebound. The boy never learned to rebound.

CONSTANCE. You and your basketball.

HENRY. Well, it's something to talk about, you know. Better than just sittin' here.

CONSTANCE. I'm worried for him. Aren't you worried?

HENRY. Of course, I'm worried. Who wouldn't be worried?

CONSTANCE. Let's have a nice party for him when he comes home.

Act One

-

Scene Two

[Living room of the same house. A young man, PETE, twenty-one, paralyzed from the waist down, dressed in full uniform complete with medals and confined to a wheelchair. Both CONSTANCE and HENRY stand before PETE at a loss for words. CONSTANCE gives him an embrace.]

CONSTANCE. It's nice to have you home, son.

HENRY. Yes, it's nice to have you home.

PETE. It's nice to be home.

HENRY. All the neighbors are excited about seeing you.

CONSTANCE. We're excited too.

Back Home

HENRY. Yes, we're excited.

CONSTANCE. It's just so nice to have you home.

PETE. Thanks, ma.

CONSTANCE. You want some pork chops with onions?

PETE. Maybe later.

HENRY. He's not hungry now.

CONSTANCE. I heard him.

PETE. *[at a loss for words]* Place feels good.

HENRY. You can have your old room back.

PETE. Thanks.

HENRY. It's nice to have you back, yeah.... nice.

CONSTANCE. Henry, would you take his bags to his room, dear?

HENRY. Yeah, right, let me get these out of your way.

[HENRY picks up the suitcases and exits. CONSTANCE and PETE are left alone.]

CONSTANCE. How are you really, Peter?

PETE. Fine. I'm just fine.

CONSTANCE. You can tell me everything.

PETE. This is kinda... new for me. I never had people do things for me like this. It's not comfortable.

CONSTANCE. Of course it isn't. You were always so independent.

PETE. How's dad taking this?

HENRY. *[entering]* Bags are in the room.

PETE. Thanks, dad.

HENRY. Would you like to say hello to the neighbors? They've all been asking for you.

PETE. I'd like to just stay home for a while, get used to things. You guys can go about your business and I'll get along fine.

HENRY. You're my business, Pete. I'm at your service. I'm retired, you know.

PETE. I knew that.

HENRY. Frankly, it was wrong to retire. I feel useless lately. Same old routine; read the paper in the morning, have coffee, go back to bed by eleven, catch up on my sleep. I never sleep at nighttime. Things always bothering me, keeping me awake. Don't know what to do with myself. Retirement isn't what it's cut out to be, believe me, son. I'm glad you're here though. I have plenty of time to take care of you.

PETE. I can take care of myself.

HENRY. Right.

CONSTANCE. *[awkward]* We still have your painting hanging. Isn't it beautiful?

PETE. Yeah, it's nice I guess.

CONSTANCE. Oh, you're too modest, son. You were so talented.

HENRY. You still like fishing, Pete?

Raymond J. Barry

PETE. Yeah... I don't know.

HENRY. Snappers are running. A little chum in the water and they'll start biting like crazy. How about tomorrow?

PETE. Yeah, maybe.

HENRY. We'll go tomorrow.

PETE. You seen Karen?

CONSTANCE. No, not much.

HENRY. I saw her about a month ago.

PETE. Where did you see her?

HENRY. In a restaurant.

CONSTANCE. What restaurant?

HENRY. Just a restaurant?

CONSTANCE. Not the Pangea.

HENRY. Could have been.

CONSTANCE. I see.

HENRY. What do you see?

CONSTANCE. Never mind.

PETE. What's going on?

CONSTANCE. Nothing.

PETE. Nothing?

HENRY. Missed the neighborhood over there, Pete?

PETE.. Yeah, saw a lot of stuff... didn't make much sense.

HENRY. Pathetic place. You gotta be stupid to live in a place like that; all that sand. Them rag-heads gotta be stupid. I hope we kill every last one of them dirty rag-heads. We ought to blow them back to the stone age. Sons-a-bitches.

PETE. It's more complicated than that. *[pause]* Did Karen say anything?

HENRY. She came over to my table.

PETE. What did she say?

HENRY. We didn't talk much.

PETE. What did she say?

HENRY. I told her you were hurt.

PETE. Did you tell her about my legs?

HENRY. I don't remember how I put it.

PETE. You don't remember?

HENRY. No, I don't remember.

CONSTANCE. You'll have to come clean with her sometime.

PETE. I know.

HENRY. I may have told her.

PETE. I guess she'll find out sooner or later.

CONSTANCE. Maybe she should have some warning.

HENRY. I may have told her.

PETE. Did you tell her or didn't you?

HENRY. I was dealing with more than one person.

Back Home

CONSTANCE. We needn't get into that.

HENRY. No, not her.

PETE. Who's her?

HENRY. Nothing.

PETE. I should call her now.

HENRY. Does it have to be now?

PETE. She probably knows I'm home.

CONSTANCE. She's got to be told.

HENRY. There's nothing to be ashamed of.

CONSTANCE. Yes, everything's normal in our happy home.

HENRY. You're our hero for goodness sake.

CONSTANCE. Our war hero.

HENRY. We're proud of you, son.

PETE. *[cross to phone]* I'll call her now. Her number is probably the same.

[PETE dials and listens to the ring. He hangs up the phone.]

CONSTANCE. Everything all right?

PETE. Yeah.

HENRY. Everything's not all right.

PETE. Yeah.

CONSTANCE. You don't have to say it.

HENRY. It's better to say it.

PETE. I don't mind saying it.

[MEL enters without knocking. He's sixty-seven, overweight and sportily dressed. The man has the look of being beaten by life with bags under his eyes and generally unhealthy in appearance. He likes to joke, smile and laugh, possibly to cover up what's really going on]

MEL. I'm here.

HENRY. Everyone knows you're here.

MEL. I just thought I'd say it.

HENRY. Well now that you've said it, you can go.

MEL. I'll go, friend, when I've said hello to the war hero. *[reaches for some peanuts on table]* You look good in your uniform, Pete.

PETE. Yeah,... thanks.

MEL. The medals.

PETE. Yeah.

MEL. Impressive, huh? Ribbons and medals all over him.

HENRY. Watch what you say, friend.

MEL. I'm watching.

HENRY. He just got home.

MEL. Welcome home.

PETE. Thanks.

MEL. Sorry you got hurt.

PETE. Yeah. Bomb went off... shrapnel... uh... left a scar.

Raymond J. Barry

MEL. Lucky you didn't lose your sight.

PETE. Yeah.

MEL. I am proud of you, kid. I got respect for what you done over there.

PETE. Yeah.

MEL. Just want you to know.

PETE. Yeah.

MEL. I got respect.

HENRY. You already said that.

MEL. I'm saying it again.

PETE. Thanks.

MEL. I fought, you know.

PETE. Yeah.

MEL. Vietnam.

PETE. Yeah.

MEL. Stupid war.

PETE. Yeah.

MEL. Gotta lotta respect.

PETE. Yeah.

MEL. Know exactly what you went through.

PETE. Yeah.

MEL. Still can't sleep some nights – stress.

PETE. Me too – post traumatic.

MEL. Yeah, lotta guys.

PETE. You still get it after all these years?

MEL. Yeah, still.

CONSTANCE. He'll be all right.

HENRY. He's our war hero.

CONSTANCE. We'll take care of him.

MEL. Gotta get away from your parents.

HENRY. What kind of stuff you saying?

MEL. You'll see.

PETE. What are you trying to say?

MEL. You'll see what.

HENRY. Why?

MEL. It's just the way it usually is when a guy comes home.

CONSTANCE. We'll take care of him.

MEL. It'll be too much for all of you.

HENRY. Why are you saying that?

MEL. You'll see.

CONSTANCE. You're frightening me.

MEL. I'll help.

HENRY. Help with what?

MEL. You'll see.

HENRY. He's not like you, friend. He's stronger than you.

Back Home

MEL. Nothing's happened yet?

HENRY. You know something we don't know?

MEL. About war, guys coming home from war. I'm proud I know you, Pete. The whole neighborhood is proud. You should hear them talking about you. A local boy, one of our own, a goddamn hero. *[MEL puts his arm around his shoulders.]* I've known you since you were a little boy and now you're saving the country. Boy, am I proud of you. If there's anything you need you just call out. There's not a person on the block who wouldn't help you. Need someone to push you around? We can do it. The neighborhood will work shifts pushing your chair. That's the least we can do after what you did for us.

CONSTANCE. Thanks to Pete we still have our freedom.

HENRY. The boy fought for our freedom. And paid the supreme price.

PETE. America was free before I went there.

MEL. You're kinda shy about being a hero, huh?

PETE. Yeah.

HENRY. He's a modest kid. Everybody makin' a fuss over him.

PETE. I'm a little tired of it. Maybe I should go to my room or something.

CONSTANCE. That'll be good for you, Pete.

PETE. Yeah,... I'll go to my room,... get some rest.

HENRY. He's a little tired. Maybe we can go fishing tomorrow.

PETE. Fishing? Sure,... fishing.

HENRY. That's it then. We're going fishing tomorrow.

MEL. I'll go fishing with you. I don't work tomorrow. I'll go fishing.

HENRY. What about you, Pete. You really want to go fishing?

PETE. Yeah, okay... fishing... yeah... I'll go.

HENRY. Good. We'll all go. It'll be good for you. Get outside and relax a little.

PETE. Yeah, relax a little.

[PETE wheels himself off stage.]

Act One
-
Scene Three

*[Next day, morning. Interior house. CONSTANCE is serving coffee. HENRY is winding up some fishing
tackle putting various hooks and plugs into the fishing basket.]*

HENRY. Pete!!! Wake up, Pete. It's time to go fishing.

CONSTANCE. Why can't he sleep a little later on his first day back home?

HENRY. It'll make him feel better to have some fun rather than sleeping all damned day. That's no way to live. It's a rule. You gotta have rules.

Raymond J. Barry

Get your ass outta bed and make a day of it is one of my rules. It should be his rule too.

CONSTANCE. But he's just gotten out of the hospital. He's just returned home.

HENRY. Don't you think I know he's just returned home?

CONSTANCE. Be kind, Henry. Be kind. *[knock on the door]* Someone's at the door.

[CONSTANCE answers the door. KAREN stands there. She's twenty-four and pretty, dressed simply in a skirt and blouse]

CONSTANCE. Why Karen. Hello, dear, hello. It's Karen everybody. It's Karen.

KAREN. I came to see Pete.

[PETE enters in his wheelchair. The shock of seeing him in a wheelchair is apparent. They're speechless for a moment]

KAREN. Hi.

PETE. Hi.

KAREN. I came to see you.

PETE. Yeah... great.

KAREN. I heard you were home.

PETE. Yeah,... I'm back.

HENRY. Pete's goin' fishing with his ole man. I got everything ready - new hooks and plugs, reels and poles.

CONSTANCE. It won't work, Henry. They've got things to talk about. Leave them be now.

KAREN. Maybe we could go to the park and... or... rather just talk; have a little time to ourselves.

HENRY. We're all set to go fishing. Why can't you wait till we get back?

CONSTANCE. You can go fishing by yourself, Henry.

HENRY. You can spend time together when we get back.

CONSTANCE. Or why don't you take me? I wouldn't mind spending some time with my husband for a change.

HENRY. All right. All right. You can come along.

CONSTANCE. Really? You wouldn't mind my coming with you? I'll have to get dressed. Give me a minute and I'll be ready.

HENRY. All right. Hurry up. *[pause]* This ought to be good.

PETE. You'll do some fishing together.

HENRY. Yep, I guess.

KAREN. It's a beautiful day for fishing.

HENRY. Why don't you all come too?

KAREN. I'm not much of a fisherman.

PETE. We haven't seen each other.

HENRY. No harm in trying. *[pause]* President is making a speech today about the war.

PETE. I won't be listening.

Back Home

HENRY. Right. Just thought I'd mention it in case you got time.

KAREN. It's really a nice day for fishing.

HENRY. Yep, I wonder what's taking her so long.

KAREN. You know how women are. Everything has to be perfect.

HENRY. I hear her coming. We can get outta here now. Leave you two alone.

[CONSTANCE appears in her improvised fishing garb.]

CONSTANCE. This is better. Going fishing with my husband. Lucky me, going fishing

with my husband. Come on, dear, take me fishing. This may be the start of a whole new thing for us. We'll become a fishing couple.

HENRY. Let's get outta here. We gotta pick up Mel.

CONSTANCE. Is he coming? I forgot he was coming. Oh, I wish he weren't coming.

HENRY. Well, he is, so learn to like it.

[They leave. Silence, PETE and KAREN alone]

KAREN. I missed you.

PETE. Yeah, what's left of me, minus a few extremities.

KAREN. Your soul isn't gone, Pete.

PETE. Soul... yeah, soul.

KAREN. I still love you.

PETE. Yeah, thanks. I guess...

KAREN. You're as beautiful as ever as far as I'm concerned.

PETE. Maybe you shouldn't have come.

KAREN. Why do you say that?

PETE. You and me – seems ridiculous.

KAREN. How could you say that?

PETE. We can't even have kids now.

KAREN. We could adopt.

PETE. Who would give a cripple a kid to raise?

KAREN. I've waited for you.

PETE. You shouldn't have.

KAREN. You can't just end it.

[KAREN tries to kiss him]

PETE. Stop.

KAREN. You're throwing in the towel then?

PETE. Maybe I don't love you anymore. I don't know.

KAREN. I don't believe that. What else are you giving up aside from me? Your life? The goodness you could bring to the world? What do you plan to live for now? Is there anything to struggle for without love in your life; without children, without a woman you care for? What's left without those?

PETE. When I was over there all I thought about was you. It was the only thing that made sense to me at the time. The daily horrors I

Raymond J. Barry

witnessed; people getting killed when we first went in, their kids getting blown up. Entire houses blasted with families inside, kids losing their arms, their legs. There wasn't any resistance from them. Hardly any return fire. We were invincible, all the modern weaponry. They didn't stand a chance. Most of the soldiers on our side were feeling a kind of macho euphoria that comes with overpowering the so-called enemy. But then guys started getting killed – bombs mostly, IED's mostly. Guys don't really know why they're fighting over there. I still don't know what I was doing there. I just don't know.

KAREN. You still love me, don't you?

PETE. I'm numb. I'm not the same. I probably won't paint anymore. I could never paint after seeing all that I saw. Just doesn't make sense to make art. It's the new me I'm dealing with; the new me who has to figure out all over again how to live. I don't know who this new person is. He's someone I'm still getting used to. I'm not sure I still like him.

KAREN. I like him, Pete. *[pause]* You have to believe in yourself again.

PETE. Myself? I don't believe in the whole setup.

[KAREN and PETE look at each other; neither knows what to say.]

KAREN. Oh, my God, it's past ten o'clock. I've got to get going.

PETE. You've got to go already?

KAREN. I've got to leave. I have an appointment.

PETE. How come you didn't mention it before?

KAREN. Why should I mention it?

PETE. Seems you would have mentioned it before.

KAREN. Why should I inform you of my private business?

PETE. I thought you were my girl, that's all.

KAREN. That has nothing to do with my private business.

PETE. My business is your business, honey. Your business is my business. Isn't that the way it is?

KAREN. If that's the way you want it.

PETE. That's the way it should be if we're going to get married.

KAREN. Oh, now we're going to get married? A year ago it was I who wanted to get married, but you wanted to go to war. Now suddenly you're all hot to get married.

PETE. You don't want to get married?

KAREN. Don't you realize things are different now?

PETE. What kind of different?

KAREN. Just different. *[pause]* It's nothing.

PETE. I know things are different but we can work it out.

KAREN. Goodbye for now. I'll call.

PETE. You're really going? You have to go?

KAREN. Yes, I'll call.

PETE. Yeah? Okay. Mom is having a dinner tomorrow night. You're invited. I'll see you then.

Back Home

KAREN. Goodbye, Pete.
PETE. Right. You'll be there. Right?
[KAREN is gone]

Act One

-

Scene Four

[Same day, early afternoon. HENRY, CONSTANCE and MEL are fishing from a row boat. All three hold their fishing poles extended over the water. They've been fishing for well over a few hours with nary a bite. There's an extended period of silence.]

HENRY. Yeah. *[fishing pole bends.]* Whoa! I got a nibble. Look, I got a nibble. Holy smoke, I got a strike. This son-of-a-bitch is big.
MEL. Get him in! Get him in!
CONSTANCE. Oh, my goodness, it's a real fish.
HENRY. Get him up. Get the damned net, Mel. Let's get this baby in.
MEL. *[reaches for the net.]* All right. Hold your horses.
CONSTANCE. Pull him in, Henry. Pull him in.
HENRY. I'm pulling.
[fishing pole bends under the strain of a live fish.]
MEL. I see him. He's a freakin' monster.
HENRY. Jeez, he's freakin' big.
CONSTANCE. Bring him in, Henry.
MEL. Goddamn, he's going under the boat. Hold on to that pole.
[HENRY can't maneuver the fishing pole. Finally the fish breaks the line. The pole straightens out.]
HENRY. Nuts, he got away!
MEL. The line broke.
HENRY. That's sixty pound test.
MEL. With sixty pound test, it should've held.
HENRY. That must've been a bluefish. They strike hard this time of the summer.
MEL. Bluefish in bay water? No way. You get snapper on bay water but no blues. Blues are ocean fish.
HENRY. I should've had him.
MEL. Nobody could bring that big baby in with that flimsy pole.
HENRY. No, I shoulda had him. If I coulda moved around more, I woulda had him. Mel was in my way.
MEL. I wasn't in your way. The pole is too light. That coulda been a big snapper or even an eel.
HENRY. It couldn't be an eel. Eels are bottom fish. We're fishin' on top.
MEL. But eels come up top sometimes. I seen eels come up on top. You

Raymond J. Barry

don't know what you're talkin' about.

HENRY. I shoulda had him.

CONSTANCE. Don't feel bad, Henry. There's more fish where that came from.

HENRY. I haven't hooked onto a fish that big for years. I'm outta practice.

MEL. You gotta practice fishing for big fish, just like anything else.

HENRY. How can you practice fishing? You just fish, that's all.

CONSTANCE. Maybe we should be getting back.

HENRY. Snapper will start to really bite when the tide comes up.

MEL. I've caught snapper at low tide.

HENRY. Snapper bite best when the tide's rising.

MEL. They bite best at low tide when the current is still.

HENRY. You don't know nothing about snapper.

MEL. I don't huh?

HENRY. No, you don't.

CONSTANCE. You men, always quibbling.

HENRY. *[to CONSTANCE]* That's enough outta you. Pay attention to your fishing. Just pay attention. You've already tangled your line three times. It takes me an hour to untangle it.

CONSTANCE. Be kind, Henry.

HENRY. *[to CONSTANCE]* Hold on to your pole. You'll get a bite and your pole will be dragged into the water.

CONSTANCE. I'm holding the pole.

HENRY. Well, keep on holding it tight. Don't let it go.

CONSTANCE. *[pole bends]* Oh, something's pulling on my line.

HENRY. You gotta bite. Pull up and hook him. You gotta bite, baby! *[CONSTANCE pulls the struggling fish up.]* That's it, pull up. Good. Get her in. That's it. Pull her in. *[pulls the fish in.]* There, you got him.

CONSTANCE. Oh, my, I haven't caught a fish since I went fishing with my daddy when I was a little girl.

HENRY. That's my girl all right. It's a sea bass. Must be five pounds of fish there. Good work. Good work, honey.

CONSTANCE. I like this fishing business. It's fun fishing, exciting! I'm going to come out and do it more often.

HENRY. I wouldn't mind the company. I'm getting tired of Mel.

CONSTANCE. If we did this together you wouldn't be running around with other women.

MEL. What's she talking about?

HENRY. Nothing. That only happened once and I told her all about it.

MEL. Told her all about what?

HENRY. Will you stop asking questions?

MEL. I'm a friend of the family. You can tell me anything.

HENRY. Just stay out of it.

Back Home

MEL. All right. Don't be such a grouch.

CONSTANCE. It's actually a thrill to catch a fish.

HENRY. It's a thrill to watch you catch a fish too.

CONSTANCE. Really, honey? You got a thrill out of watching me catch one?

HENRY. Oh, yes, you looked good wrestling with that fish, sexy too.

CONSTANCE. You thought I was sexy doing it?

MEL. That's enough, you two.

HENRY. Shuttup, Mel. *[to CONSTANCE]* You still look pretty good to me.

CONSTANCE. Why Henry, you haven't said that to me in the longest time.

HENRY. Well, you haven't caught a fish in the longest time.

[They embrace and kiss. MEL looks disgusted.]

MEL. You two should be getting back to your son. He shouldn't be left alone until he gets used to things.

CONSTANCE. You're right. I'm worried about him. I will never forgive you, Henry, for encouraging him to go to war.

HENRY. Any father would want his son to be a man.

CONSTANCE. He was a man before he went to war.

HENRY. I know. I know. Let's change the subject.

CONSTANCE. I don't want to change the subject. My son has come back from that miserable war a total mess...

[simultaneous]

CONSTANCE.	**HENRY.**
... a cripple, dependent upon people to get around. His life is ruined by that ugly war and you influenced him to go. I'll never, ever forgive you for that, Henry.	It wasn't my damn fault. He was a full grown man when he went and signed up. I didn't make him do it. I'm not to blame. He joined of his own volition.

CONSTANCE. You influenced him with your lies.

HENRY. He signed up on his own.

CONSTANCE. You influenced him.

HENRY. You better stop saying that, ya bitch, or I'll throw your damned fish back in the drink.

CONSTANCE. You and your war stories!

HENRY. *[throws the fish into the water.]* There, your damn fish is gone. Serves you right.

MEL. What'd you do that for, you jerk?

CONSTANCE. You threw my fish back into the water, you vengeful creature.

HENRY. We can't eat the fish anyway with all the arsenic in the water.

Raymond J. Barry

MEL. All that stuff about fish and arsenic and mercury in the water is a lotta bull. Come on, let's get outta here. We're not having any fun anymore with all this bull goin on. You say I talk too much. What a joke. You really know how to ruin a fishing party, Henry, with all your talk about arsenic and poison in the fish and stuff. Come on, let's go.

HENRY. Let's go home. Pull your lines up and let's row outta here.

CONSTANCE. You don't expect me to row, do you? You row. I'm not rowing.

MEL. Pull your lines in. I'll row.

CONSTANCE. Yes, somebody row. You row, Mel.

HENRY. Yeah, you row, Mel. Row us home.

MEL. *[He rows the boat.]* I'm rowing.

Act One

-

Scene Five

[Next day. Dinner time. Seated at the table are PETE and KAREN, CONSTANCE, HENRY and MEL. Everyone is slightly tipsy, eating and drinking, having a rousing time of it. The men are talking vociferously]

HENRY. Mel says it was an eel what broke my line, and we're fishin' on top! Everyone knows eels are a bottom fish! He don't know nothing. We're fishin' on top and he thinks an eel broke my line. Ha. Ha. Ha.
MEL. He don't know nothing.
HENRY. Eels are scavengers. They swim on the bottom, you dummy.
MEL. You can get eels on the top or bottom.
CONSTANCE. All right, you two, enough about fishing. There are other things to talk about. We have a war hero in our midst, after all - real war hero, my brave son, Pete.
MEL. Hear, hear. Here's to Pete. *[Everyone toasts.]*
CONSTANCE. Yes, here's to my beloved son, my Pete, who's put his life on the line for our sake while we've enjoyed the security of our beloved United States of America.
PETE.. Thank you, everyone. Thanks... *[much applause and cheers]* That's enough now. That's enough.
[applause and cheering die down]
CONSTANCE. Let's eat everybody. Enjoy yourselves and eat what the good Lord has provided for us.
[Everyone begins eating.]
HENRY. Pass the salt, please.
CONSTANCE. Surely, dear. One salt coming up. *[passes the salt.]*
MEL. Meat's good.
HENRY. Meat's very good. Enjoying your meat, Pete?
PETE. Yeah, meat's good.
MEL. Good food.
KAREN. Yes, very good, delicious.
MEL. You're a good cook, Constance.
CONSTANCE. Do you think so? That's so nice of you to say.
MEL. I mean it. Good-tasting food.
HENRY. He'd think anything was good.
MEL. It's good, good meat.
HENRY. You'd eat anything, whether it was cooked or not.
MEL. I like to eat.
HENRY. Mel here likes to eat, especially meat.
MEL. How bout you, Pete. Ya like to eat?

Raymond J. Barry

PETE. Yeah.

HENRY. He's eating isn't he?

MEL. Just trying to make conversation with my buddy here. He's the guest of honor tonight.

HENRY. That's right, my son, my war hero. Here's to Pete.

[They all toast, except for KAREN.]

MEL. To Pete.

CONSTANCE. To my son. *[toasting]* What's the matter, Karen. You're not drinking?

KAREN. Nothing. I'm fine. *[raises her glass]* Here's to Pete.

PETE. *[quietly]* Thanks, everybody.

MEL. I know what you're goin' through, Pete. Nobody can know unless they been through it themselves.

CONSTANCE. Don't be bragging, Melvin.

MEL. I been through it. Me and Pete know about war.

HENRY. Just quiet down why don't you?

MEL. All right, but I know about war.

HENRY. Big authority on everything.

MEL. What big authority? You're the one who thinks eels are bottom fish.

HENRY. They're scavengers, bottom fish. Ha, eels on top.

[simultaneous]

HENRY.	**MEL.**
You don't know nothing. They're bottom fish.	You can catch eels on top.

[simultaneous]

HENRY.	**CONSTANCE.**
Big authority on everything.	Have you been working on your...

CONSTANCE. ... your degree, Karen?

KAREN. I have only twenty credits to go for my teaching degree.

[simultaneous]

MEL.	**CONSTANCE.**
I've caught eels on top.	Isn't that wonderful, Henry?

HENRY. What's wonderful?

CONSTANCE. Karen has only twenty credits to go for her teaching degree.

KAREN. It's very expensive.

CONSTANCE. It's worth it.

HENRY. Pete went to college.

CONSTANCE. Yes, he did. Seems like only yesterday he graduated.

HENRY. Time goes by fast, real fast.

MEL. What did you study, Pete?

PETE. Anthropology.

MEL. What's that?

HENRY. It's college.

MEL. It's not college. It's a subject you get in college.

HENRY. What do you know about college?

MEL. I know plenty.

HENRY. You never went to college.

MEL. So what? I know about it.

CONSTANCE. Eat up. Eat up, boys. Stop bickering.

KAREN. They talk like children.

CONSTANCE. Boys will be boys.

MEL. Food's good.

[much eating and drinking]

CONSTANCE. When's the wedding date, you two lovebirds?

KAREN. We'll see what happens.

HENRY. Got anything to say about that, Pete?

PETE. Oh, we're getting married all right, but we're not rushing.

[simultaneous]

HENRY.	**CONSTANCE.**
Pete's brave enough for	Mel, have some more steak.
Marriage. He's not chicken-	**MEL.**
hearted, not after the way he	More steak, good. Thanks.
handled himself in the war.	Thanks, more steak.

[Mel piles a large piece of steak onto his plate]

HENRY. They've killed over four thousand men over there; damned bombs going off in broad daylight.

CONSTANCE. Terrible, just terrible, all the killing.

HENRY. Sometimes killing is necessary.

CONSTANCE. Oh, come now, dear. Killing? Necessary? You talk as if you've killed yourself.

HENRY. I've done some duck hunting in my day.

MEL. Duck hunting? Listen to him. He's done some 'duck hunting' he says. He compares 'duck hunting' to war.

KAREN. Please, let's stop talking about war. I can't stand talking about war.

CONSTANCE. Why, dear, what's the matter? Are you all right?

KAREN. My nerves. I can't stand this talk about killing.

MEL. Hey, Constance, this steak is delicious. *[to HENRY]* You don't know diddle. Listening to you talk about the war is like a comedy.

Raymond J. Barry

HENRY. I'm an American and I'm proud of what we're doing over there.

KAREN. Being proud isn't going to bring Pete's legs back.

HENRY. What kind of thing is that to say?

MEL. It's the truth, isn't it? Stupid dumb war, killing young kids, just like they did in Vietnam.

HENRY. What's the truth?

CONSTANCE. Don't, Henry.

KAREN. As long as only a few American lives are lost, that's okay – just as long as we continue the massacre in the name of peace, democracy and liberty for the rich.

CONSTANCE. Pete was fighting a war against terrorism, Karen.

HENRY. She shouldn't be talking like that.

PETE. Karen's right.

HENRY. What?

PETE. She's right to talk about it, and it's right what she's saying.

HENRY. It's right to avoid the subject too.

KAREN. No, it's not right to avoid the subject. The horrors that we're perpetrating over there are our responsibility!! Our responsibility!!!

CONSTANCE. Karen, don't talk that way. You sound like a Communist. We can talk about the war rationally. This is an open-minded family.

KAREN. Really? What aspect of war would you like to discuss, Constance?

CONSTANCE. Anything, darling. We're an open family.

KAREN. How about discussing how Pete is going to make a living, now that the government has used him as cannon fodder?

PETE. I'll work. I don't want anyone to support me.

HENRY. There, that solves it. Anyone want more meat?

MEL. No man wants his wife workin' for him.

KAREN. Pete doesn't have a wife.

CONSTANCE. But he will have a wife soon. Isn't that true, dear?

KAREN. We have to work a few things out.

PETE. We're still getting married.

HENRY. That settles that. Pass the peas.

MEL. Hungry tonight, friend?

HENRY. Real hungry. Pass the potatoes.

CONSTANCE. Save some for our guests.

HENRY. There's plenty. I mashed the potatoes myself with my secret formula.

CONSTANCE. The mashed potatoes are delicious, Henry.

HENRY. Little butter mixed in there and some warmed up heavy cream. Then a spot of pepper and salt. They're good, ain't they?

CONSTANCE. Oh, yes, very good, dear.

MEL. Nothing like good old American mashed potatoes, eh Pete?

PETE. Yeah, right.

Back Home

HENRY. Now that you're home you appreciate what a great country this is, huh, Pete? The cooking and stuff...

PETE. Right.

CONSTANCE. More potatoes, Mel? *[CONSTANCE passes the potatoes.]*

MEL. Don't mind if I do.

HENRY. He'll make a pig out of himself if you let him.

MEL. That's enough outta you. You can't catch bluefish in bay water either. Ha. Ha. They're ocean fish.

[simultaneous]

HENRY.	**CONSTANCE.**
Yeah, yeah, I've caught blues in bay water.	Pass the asparagus please, Pete.

[simultaneous]

MEL.	**PETE.**
You catch snapper in bay water, not blues.	Right. Here... asparagus.

[PETE passes the asparagus.]

MEL. I'll have some too.

[CONSTANCE passes MEL the asparagus.]

CONSTANCE. And a little taste of scotch for me. *[helps herself]*

PETE. I want to live normal. I'm gonna work.

MEL. *[eating voraciously]* Sure you'll work, Pete. Where?

PETE. I'll find something.

MEL. They treat vets like shit out there.

HENRY. That was Vietnam.

CONSTANCE. Pete is a war hero.

MEL. Being a hero won't help. Sleepless nights and bad dreams are all that's left when you get back. And a few lies from the government in the end

[simultaneous]

KAREN.	**CONSTANCE.**
Please, stop this talk.	Melvin's been drinking. Eat up and stop antagonizing.

[simultaneous]

HENRY.	**MEL.**
Eat your damned meat and quiet down.	Antagonizin' about what?

CONSTANCE. There are other things to talk about, more pleasant things.

Raymond J. Barry

If you want unpleasant subjects turn on the television.

[simultaneous]

KAREN.	MEL.
There's plenty of murder on television. We don't need more at dinner.	I'm not watching television now.
	PETE.
	Television lies anyway.

MEL. Pete knows what he's talking about. Television lies.

[simultaneous]

HENRY. *[to MEL]*	PETE.
That's enough out of you. I watch television all the time and there's no lies.	They don't say it the way it is. All they do is lie. Nothing but lies.

HENRY. What's Pete talking about?

MEL. Talking about television.

KAREN. Oh, you two, stop your stupidity. You know what he's saying. You know. Everyone knows.

MEL. Of course, everyone knows. Television lies. It's all run by the same people.

HENRY. Television is American. It was invented by America.

PETE. So what? America lies like television lies.

MEL. You tell him, Pete. Any desert?

CONSTANCE. Pumpkin pie.

HENRY. What's Pete talking about?

CONSTANCE. And ice cream.

MEL. I like ice cream.

HENRY. Me too.

MEL. Did you have any ice cream over there?

PETE. They'd give it to us at mess.

MEL. Bet it hit the spot.

HENRY. Ice-cream always tastes good.

PETE. Not when you've seen a guy's belly blown open by a bomb on the same day.

KAREN. Please, I can't stand this! *[runs to the bathroom]*

HENRY. They give you ice-cream after that?

PETE. Not automatically.

CONSTANCE. Karen is upset. Karen is everything all right? You men have got to stop this talk at dinner.

HENRY. So sometimes they give you ice-cream?

PETE. Yeah, sometimes.

CONSTANCE. I'll get Karen, poor dear. *[rises and knocks on the bathroom* *door]* Karen. *[knocking]* Karen?

HENRY. Where's everybody going?

MEL. She went to get Karen.

CONSTANCE. Karen, open the door, dear. They won't carry on any more.

HENRY. She's all right.

CONSTANCE. *[KAREN opens the door.]* There you are, dear. Come back to the table. They'll stop. We women aren't as callous as you men.

[CONSTANCE and KAREN return to the table.]

HENRY. You all right, Karen?

KAREN. Yes, I'm sorry. This talk upsets me.

CONSTANCE. She's fine now. Stick to pleasant subjects. No more war.

HENRY. Mel's to blame. Tell him.

KAREN. I can't stand this talk, this horrible talk.

CONSTANCE. All right, everyone, stop! No more war talk, Mel. It's upsetting Karen.

HENRY. Let's have a toast to Pete. My guy is a hero, my war hero, my son. Proud. Proud. Proud.

EVERYONE*[except KAREN]* Hear! Hear! To Pete! To Pete!

[much applause and cheering that dies down]

HENRY. Pass the pumpkin pie.

[pie is passed]

MEL. Good. Gimme my piece.

HENRY. Gimme, gimme, gimme.

[CONSTANCE swigs her drink while everyone eats pie.]

MEL. I went to Vietnam back in the sixties; saw plenty of guys get killed. I don't complain. I served my country as good as I knew how. Won the Bronze Star for valor. Someone stole it.

CONSTANCE. The Bronze Star? I'm impressed. Aren't you impressed, dear?

HENRY. Yeah, I'm impressed.

MEL. I don't talk about it much. It was a rough experience for me, but thank God I got through it. *[referring to HENRY]* You served too, didn't you, pal?

HENRY. Ah... yeah... I don't want to talk about it.

PETE. Dad went. He won a medal, like you did.

CONSTANCE. *[slightly tipsy]* Your father didn't win any medal.

PETE. Sure he did. You won a medal, didn't you, dad?

HENRY. Well, I... I was... ah... kiddin', Pete. You were a little kid when I told you that, and... I was kidding you... about the medal.

MEL. How come you told the kid?

PETE. You didn't really win a medal?

HENRY. No, I didn't. I was kidding, that's all. You were a little kid then. Now let's drop it.

CONSTANCE. Melvin, would you pass the sweet potatoes. *[slurred speech]*

Raymond J. Barry

I love sweet potatoes with scotch.

MEL. Here, eat your heart out. *[MELVIN passes the sweet potatoes.]* Guys were getting out of that war left and right in those days, pretending they were crazy, running off to Canada. Buncha cowards.

CONSTANCE. Melvin, are you calling Henry a coward?

MEL. Henry didn't run off to Canada, did he?

CONSTANCE. He didn't choose to go.

MEL. I thought he went.

CONSTANCE. Sometimes Henry exaggerates to impress his children.

HENRY. Goddammit!! Shut your mouth, mother.

CONSTANCE. Don't you tell me to shut my mouth!! Who the hell do you think you are?

HENRY. Shuttup about that stuff, dammit!!

CONSTANCE. Don't you dare tell me to shuttup!! I don't have to listen to you. You won't tell me to shuttup.

PETE. You didn't join up, dad?

HENRY. No, you got to understand... I was pretending... when you was a little kid... for your sake... so you'd grow up to be a man.

PETE. Why didn't you go?

HENRY. It just wasn't for me at the time.

MEL. What do you mean, it wasn't for you? They had a draft then. You had to go whether you wanted to or not.

HENRY. I didn't go, that's all. I just didn't go.

MEL. How'd you get out of it?

CONSTANCE. He had his ways.

HENRY. Shuttup, wife! I got nothing to say on the subject.

CONSTANCE. I've got plenty to say on the subject.

MEL. Pretty suspicious is all I got to say.

CONSTANCE. I've got so much to say on the subject that you'll never tell me or anyone else to shuttup again.

HENRY. Will you quiet down, Constance?

MEL. Pretty suspicious.

[simultaneous]

HENRY.	**CONSTANCE.**
[to MEL] You want a smack in the mouth?	I've had enough of that 'shuttup' business.

[Both MEL and HENRY rise and confront each other.]

[simultaneous]

MEL.	**CONSTANCE.**
Who's gonna give me a smack in the mouth? You?	Quiet down, my ass. For forty-two years I've been told to shuttup!

Back Home

HENRY.
Yeah, I'll give you a smack in the mouth.

Well, now I'm not going to shuttup. I'm going to say my peace.

[KAREN intercedes. Simultaneous talk]

KAREN.
All right, you two, that's Enough. Haven't you had enough of fighting?

CONSTANCE.
Telling me to shuttup.

PETE.
Why didn't you join up, dad?

HENRY. It was a different time then. War was looked down upon. Today it's a volunteer army. You guys weren't drafted. You went in on your own. We were forced to fight. Makes a big difference when you're forced to fight.

PETE. So why didn't you join up, dad?

HENRY. Aw, come on, Pete. Don't give me the third degree.

CONSTANCE. Be honest, Henry, darling.

HENRY. Don't give me advice. Okay? Just don't, when you're drunk.

CONSTANCE. Drunk is it? I'll show you how drunk I am! Henry pretended he was a homosexual just to get out of the army! *[CONSTANCE pours herself another drink.]* This is the last time you'll tell me to shuttup.

[simultaneous]

HENRY.
Son-of-a-bitch. You'll be sorry for this. It's not the way she makes it sound. The war hadn't broken out yet. It was back in nineteen-sixty-two. The real shooting hadn't started. Vietnam was a police action and little else. I just wanted to make money and start my life, that's all. Hell, I was only twenty-one at the time.

CONSTANCE.
Anyone want some more pie? There's plenty left. How about you, Pete?

MEL.
This is getting good. Gimme some more scotch. *[helps himself]*

PETE.
You were a homosexual, dad? Is that what you told them?

PETE. Were you a homosexual, dad?

HENRY. See what you did, Constance?

CONSTANCE. You wanted to know, right, son?

PETE. Yeah. Were you really a homosexual?

HENRY. Don't be stupid.

PETE. You told them you were.

HENRY. I just told them that.

Raymond J. Barry

PETE. Where'd you get the idea?
HENRY. I don't know. Somewhere.

[simultaneous]

HENRY.	**MEL.**
I didn't pretend to be like a woman or nothing like that - by walking like a woman or nothing, or swishing around or nothing. I just marked off a box on a sheet of paper they gave me. They sent me to a psychiatrist.	I'd like to see that. Wow, you are too much. You musta been convincing; musta really been a homo, right? Musta had it in you. Otherwise you'd never pull a stunt like you did.

HENRY. Everybody was pulling something in those days.
MEL. Not me. I went in like a man.
HENRY. Mr. Perfect.
CONSTANCE. *[slightly tipsy]* Pete went in like a man too.
PETE. What is this 'man' shit?
HENRY. It's important to be a man.

[simultaneous]

MEL.	**CONSTANCE.**
Look, Pete and me are men! Not faggots like him. We gotta act like one then. Can't be calling...	There's too much drinking going on here. Could you at least take hold of the situation, Henry?

MEL. ...ourselves faggots on purpose. That ain't being a man. Henry's a homo, not a man.
HENRY. Watch it, buddy.
CONSTANCE. Have some more desert, everybody... more meat for everybody!!!
[PETE erratically wheels his chair in circles.]
PETE. More 'meat' anyone?!! Meat to fill the belly?!! Have some meat. Vomit meat! Vomit meat! Vomit! Vomit!

[simultaneous]

PETE.	**HENRY.**
Meat! Vomit! Vomit! Vomit! Vomit! Funny full-bodied, healthy All-American boy. Little to say. Dead mind then. Dead. What came from my mouth then? Media ignorance until my	It's all right, son. Shuttup, boy! You're home now. There's nothing to be afraid of. Shuttup! You're talking like your nuts! Don't be afraid, Pete. It's all right. Don't be afraid of us.

Back Home

ass was handed to me. The absence of what? Sitting patiently, waiting for what? Dead, dead, dead, dead. Bomb, bomb, bomb, bomb lurking, bomb lurking! Bomb lurking!

You're my war hero, my big boy. You're my gallant hero. Come on now, Pete. Let's rest. Rest will do you some good. Yes, if only to rest. Lie down and rest. You can rest, son. Go lie down and sleep in your bedroom.

MEL. What bomb, Pete? There's no bomb.

KAREN. Pete, what do you want? You want to rest? Do you? You want to rest?

CONSTANCE. You're my baby boy, son.

PETE. No, mom, I'm a man! Machine gun! *[wheeling his chair in circles]* Who's talking here? Who's talking? I'm a man! I'm really a man! The ghost of what was. Wedges embedded too far, too far, too far. Shreds... embedded. But no more, no more. I'm a man, really a man!!! Wheelchair! Machine gun? Machine gun! *[spins around in his wheelchair]*

[simultaneous]

PETE.	**MEL.**
War hero - legs chopped off; driving automobiles from the hair-dresser to the shopping mall to the tanning salon and back to the ranch home; television reports; democracy. Killing, killing, killing. War mongers; Washington, wealth, wealth; big lie... Wrrrrrr. Wrrrrr. Wrrrrrr.	I come back from Nam like Pete, completely shell-shocked. **HENRY.** You never saw action. You made that thing up about the 'Bronze Star'. **MEL.** I saw action! I saw action! **HENRY.** How many gooks did you kill?

[PETE talking to himself, spins his wheelchair in circles and then exits the room. KAREN follows him, also exiting into his bedroom.]

MEL. Plenty, draft dodger, plenty.

HENRY. 'Bronze Star' my ass.

MEL. You don't know what I did. You told them you was a homo.

HENRY. Come on, do something about it.

[HENRY and MEL break into a clumsy wrestle to the floor with both men afraid of any real physical violence. It's more of a hugging session than a real fight. CONSTANCE doesn't bother to separate them, so harmless is their struggle. She stands and observes them making fools of themselves at her feet. After a beat PETE yells from offstage]

PETE. *[off stage]* What am I now? Who am I now? Am I a man, ma? Or

Raymond J. Barry

an insect? A bug devoured by some other bug? Crawling like a worm, half-eaten with my tail missing? What species am I? Am I a man, ma, a real man? What species am I? What species am I? Am I a man? A real man?

Act Two

-

Scene One

[Same evening, nighttime, very late. PETE is in the living room, sitting in his wheelchair, smoking a cigarette. He sits very still in silence, wearing a bathrobe. It is five o'clock in the morning. HENRY creeps into the room, dressed in pajamas.]

HENRY. Who's in there?
PETE. It's me.
HENRY. Pete, is that you?
PETE. Yeah, it's me.
HENRY. What are you doing up so late?
PETE. Nothing. I couldn't sleep.
HENRY. I couldn't either.
PETE. Haven't slept all night.
HENRY. Neither have I. *[pause]* Rough when you can't sleep.
PETE. Yeah.
HENRY. Mother's sound asleep.
PETE. That's good.
HENRY. I got too many thoughts going around in my head.
PETE. Yeah.
HENRY. Why couldn't you sleep?
PETE. Broke out in the sweats.
HENRY. You were sweating?
PETE. Yeah, sweating.
HENRY. You sick?
PETE. No, just stress.
HENRY. Stress? Why were you sweating?
PETE. Dreams, bad dreams.
HENRY. I can't remember my dreams.
PETE. You're better off.
HENRY. Dreams don't bother me.
PETE. They bother me.
HENRY. You mean the war?
PETE. Yeah, war.
HENRY. How do you get rid of those dreams?
PETE. I can't.

Back Home

HENRY. Sure you can. They gotta go away sometime.

PETE. I don't think so.

HENRY. You mean to tell me they'll never go away?

PETE. That's what I hear.

HENRY. Who told you?

PETE. The psychiatrist.

HENRY. What psychiatrist?

PETE. They sent me to a psychiatrist.

HENRY. Who?

PETE. The marines. The marine psychiatrist.

HENRY. What'd they send you to him for?

PETE. How do you know it was a "him?"

HENRY. Marines. You don't have women in the marines.

PETE. Oh, right.

HENRY. What's wrong, Pete?

PETE. I don't know – something.

HENRY. What something?

PETE. I'm not the same anymore.

HENRY. You're the same to me. You'll always be my son.

PETE. No, I mean I can't sleep.

HENRY. You sleep sometime, don't you?

PETE. No, never. I close my eyes and rest but I don't really sleep.

HENRY. What about dreams? You gotta sleep to dream.

PETE. It's always the same dream. As soon as I dream it, I wake up. It's always me with a gun, killing thousands of people by mowing them down – lines of them, just mowing them down, one row of men after another, men, women and children, young children, and babies, just killing them and not being able to stop, once I pull the trigger.

HENRY. You never did that.

PETE. I've been part of something that did.

HENRY. We didn't go in there and mow down women and children.

PETE. How do you know?

HENRY. I just know, that's all. We're Americans.

PETE. You're wrong. We do. I was part of it.

HENRY. You're not responsible.

PETE. Thanks for letting me off the hook.

HENRY. You gotta let yourself off the hook. You oughta start paintin' pictures again.

PETE. Don't have it in me.

[pause]

HENRY. I keep thinking about what happened.

PETE. What happened?

HENRY. At dinner.

PETE. Oh,... yeah.

Raymond J. Barry

HENRY. I don't feel right about it.

PETE. Yeah.

HENRY. I was young when I did that stuff with the draft board.

PETE. Yeah.

HENRY. I didn't know what I was doing.

PETE. Yeah.

HENRY. I thought I could get out of something.

PETE. Yeah.

HENRY. I was never gun-ho about the military.

PETE. Yeah.

HENRY. There are so few things a man can do that proves his character.

PETE. Yeah... character.

HENRY. What I think of myself is important to me; the things I did, what I avoided. What I faced. The choices I made along the way make a difference to me now. They mark what kind of man I was. You don't realize it when you're living out each decade, but when it's all done things become clear. They've become clear for me. I'm ashamed of what I did. I shoulda' joined up.

PETE. You might have been killed.

HENRY. That's what your mother said.

PETE. A lotta guys got killed in that war.

HENRY. I know.

PETE. A lotta guys got screwed up afterwards.

HENRY. I know. Look at Mel.

PETE. That could have happened to you. Instead you've lived a good life.

HENRY. I was a decent father.

PETE. Yeah.

HENRY. You always had enough. There was always a roof over your head and food on the table. I even coached you in basketball and helped you with your homework when you were little.

PETE. You did more than help. You wrote out the answers for me.

HENRY. Yep, funny about fathers and sons. Maybe because I never did anything special myself I wanted you to do something special. Remember how I used to push you in basketball?

PETE. Yeah.

HENRY. I pushed you too hard. I shouldn't have. It had to do with my own manhood, son. Not yours.

PETE. I always looked up to you then.

HENRY. What about now?

PETE. I was surprised by what I found out tonight.

HENRY. Sure. I know. I'm sorry.

PETE. Don't be sorry.

HENRY. It's getting late. I should go to bed. It's quiet at night around

Back Home

here.

PETE. Yeah. *[pause]* When I was a kid you told me stories about how you fought in Vietnam.

HENRY. There were no stories.

PETE. You told me stories.

HENRY. No, you're imagining things.

PETE. I still remember the stories.

HENRY. What stories?

PETE. War stories.

HENRY. That was Mel, not me.

PETE. Crawling on your belly through dismembered bodies, under barbed wire to retrieve ammunition for your machine gun unit. Remember those stories? You must have made them up. How you crawled on your belly through blown up bodies and guts all over the ground and grabbed the ammo for your unit? And how your commanding officer said he was going to recommend you for a medal? You told me that story when I was a kid. By the time I was eighteen I wanted to become a soldier like my father. I wanted to be like you.

HENRY. You had choices. You went to college.

PETE. I wanted to be you, a war hero.

HENRY. But that's not what I was.

PETE. You pretended to be. You fooled me..

HENRY. Pete, please, I'm sorry. I didn't know.

[pause]

PETE. I killed an unarmed man.

HENRY. You killed someone?

PETE. Yeah, I'm sorry about it.

HENRY. You were in a situation where killing was necessary.

PETE. This wasn't necessary.

HENRY. It was war.

PETE. I'm not a killer.

HENRY. Nobody ever said you were a killer.

PETE. I was afraid.

HENRY. Afraid of what?

PETE. Afraid of everything. Afraid of getting killed.

HENRY. You were in a war zone. Anybody would be afraid.

PETE. Some guys weren't afraid; the lifers, the professionals. They like killing. I didn't like it. I was afraid.

HENRY. You weren't afraid. You're a goddamned hero.

PETE. No, I was afraid, scared to death. In the beginning I doubted I could kill. It's not in my nature to kill. A real soldier can't think about what he's doing. He just does it and moves on, that's all, cut and dry. But I thought too much. I was guilty even before I fired my weapon. I knew the time would come when I had to prove myself, become a real

Raymond J. Barry

soldier like my dad. That day came finally during Fallujah. Remember Fallujah?

HENRY. We won that one.

PETE. Yeah, if that's what you want to call it. I fired my weapon that day blindly in the general direction of the enemy. I fired and fired. I was hundreds of yards away from any real action. There wasn't any real danger, but I was scared, really scared, avoiding any real confrontation during the entire battle, firing my weapon from behind the thickest wall I could find without looking or caring what I was aiming at - just protecting myself from getting hit. Some guys took chances. They were tough and brave and fought the way you read about in the newspapers. I wasn't one of those. I was scared and out to save my ass. Fact is, I didn't care who won the battle. It was their country and we were shooting the hell out of the place. Finally, our commanding officer told us to advance. I moved out with the rest of my unit, scared shit, still trying to protect myself, avoiding getting hit, always letting the others go in first, building to building, street to street. I was afraid I might have to shoot someone and pissed off at myself that I was afraid. Something in me was frozen. I couldn't shoot anybody and I didn't want to be shot. At one point my unit was searching an empty building that hadn't been bombed. Out of the corner of my eye I saw a figure dart across one of the rooms. It was an Iraqi. He seemed unarmed but I couldn't be certain. Sometimes they have bombs strapped to their bodies beneath their robes. I was so scared I couldn't think straight, daring myself to kill him, just to prove to myself that I was a real marine like the others in the unit. It was important to pretend to be tough like the others. I lowered my weapon at his head. A helpless look came over his face. His eyes pleaded with me to allow him to live, but I had to kill a living, breathing man to prove I was a real soldier like my father was. I fired my weapon into his head; blood all over the place, on my uniform, on the floor, on the wall. I stood there numb. It had been so simple. The Arab was dead. It was over. Other guys saw me kill. They started making jokes about it, calling him "rag-head" and stuff like that. Some of the marines shot him after he was dead. I laughed too just to be one of them, to be a real soldier. I wasn't scared anymore at least for that night. The next morning I looked at the Arab's body again, just to check out what I'd done. He was covered with flies by then; he smelled. Death was everywhere. The fear came back. I was frozen within the hour. It hasn't left me since. Only now I've killed, just for the sake of killing. I'm a killer. Nothing can change what I did.

HENRY. Have you mentioned any of this to your mother?

PETE. No.

HENRY. She wouldn't understand. *[pause]* You should marry that girl and live a normal life.

PETE. I can't make love anymore.

HENRY. Uh huh. *[pause]* I hear the birds. Sun's coming up. You should go into your bedroom, pretend you slept.

PETE. Pretend I slept?

HENRY. Yeah, so your mother doesn't worry.

PETE. Right... mom. I'll go back to bed.

HENRY. You wanna go fishing tomorrow?

PETE. Go fishing again? Is that all you do? Go fishing?

HENRY. It'd be a way for us to spend time together, be friends again like it was in the old days.

PETE. We'll talk about it in the morning.

HENRY. Okay then. Goodnight, Pete. Don't let the bedbugs bite.

PETE. Oh... yeah. Right.

[PETE wheels himself out of the room.]

Act Two
-
Scene Two

[Next day. KAREN is swinging PETE on a swing in the park. She's pushing him gently, taking care not
to have him fall. It's a nice day. The sun is shining; birds are singing and a soft breeze is blowing.]

PETE. You can push me harder.

KAREN. Okay, I'll push harder.

PETE. That's better. Whoa! That's almost too hard.

KAREN. You can take it. Your arms are strong. Just hold on tight.

[KAREN gives PETE one swoop into the air, safe enough not to throw him off.]

PETE. That's high enough.

KAREN. All right. You asked for it though.

PETE. This is just about right.

KAREN. Remember when we were kids swinging on ropes over the water on Hendrickson's Pit?

PETE. Yeah, I remember.

KAREN. We had a great time when we were kids.

PETE. Fishing every day.

KAREN. I used to watch you catch big carp with all different kinds of colors.

PETE. We had our own names for all of them.

KAREN. 'Pearly reds' were my favorites.

PETE. Yeah, white and orange. And then there were 'turners,'

Raymond J. Barry

remember?

KAREN. Oh, yes, the ones that were black and red.

PETE. Yeah, and the yellow and black ones. Some of those mothers were two and a half feet long.

KAREN. I know. Do you remember that one time when that huge goldie started swimming around the base of the cattails? He was three feet long and about four inches thick at his head. He was beautiful.

PETE. Yeah, I remember. Remember how the swans used to come up and hiss at us; they used to chase us away from the shore as if it was their territory.

KAREN. Yeah, those swans. They didn't want us messing with their babies.

PETE. And remember that big turtle I almost caught? We was standing on the bank of the little pond next to the Langdon house, and I see the head of this turtle. There's a sick fish floating on the water barely able to breathe. Suddenly the fish disappears and a half a minute later it comes up to the surface again, missing his head. The turtle bit his head off. It was amazing.

KAREN. My favorite thing were the caves you dug.

PETE. Yeah, the caves with candles in them for light. I used to take you in there. That's where I first kissed you.

KAREN. It's a wonder they didn't cave in on us. There were no supports or anything.

PETE. One did cave in on me. You grabbed my leg and pulled me out.

KAREN. I know. I remember. You went in again and came out with your sailor hat. That's how you were then, not afraid of anything.

PETE. You saved my life.

KAREN. Did I?

PETE. Sure. I still remember the weight of that dirt on me. I never could have gotten out by myself.

KAREN. Your leg was sticking out. Anyone would have done the same.

PETE. But you saved my life.

KAREN. I guess I did, Pete.

PETE. You're my love, my only love. The only love I ever had.

KAREN. Why do you say that?

PETE. Just felt like saying it. *[silence, PETE swinging gently]* Nice out here.

KAREN. Yes, very nice.

PETE. I prefer being out here rather than inside with them.

KAREN. There's something I want to tell you, Pete, but I don't know how.

PETE. What?

KAREN. I was determined to be myself when you came home. I'm usually hiding my life from people. Your family wouldn't understand. I usually give them some impression that I'm like I was when I was a little girl. And I am really. I mean... I will always be close to you.

PETE. What's going on?

KAREN. I'm afraid to tell you all of a sudden.

PETE. You? Afraid to tell me?

KAREN. Yes, I'm afraid. I've known you for so long.

PETE. Just blurt it out. I won't care what it is.

KAREN. I'm seeing someone else.

PETE. Someone else?

KAREN. Yeah, I'm seeing someone, a wonderful person, an artist. You used to paint, Pete, but you stopped for some reason. I wish you hadn't. It was so much a part of you at one time and now you seem empty without your work. His name is Rance and he paints all the time. I love his work. I've been seeing him all year and I think I love him.

PETE. I don't know what to do with that. Shit.

KAREN. I know. It's not something I planned. I never wanted to hurt you.

PETE. How'd that happen? I mean... we've known each other all of our lives. We wanted to get married when we were kids.

KAREN. I didn't choose this.

PETE. Bull, you gotta choose to be with another guy.

KAREN. No, it just happened.

PETE. How did it just happen? You made it happen.

KAREN. I just fell in love.

PETE. Jesus.

KAREN. I'm so sorry.

PETE. Yeah, I'm more than sorry. I'm pissed.

KAREN. I didn't plan this.

PETE. You mean you been sleeping with this guy?

KAREN. Yes.

PETE. Shit.

KAREN. Stop saying that.

PETE. What do you want me to say?

KAREN. I want you to be more understanding.

PETE. If you mean you want me to like it, I don't. You ought to straighten yourself out.

KAREN. And do what?

PETE. Learn about loyalty for a change.

KAREN. I'm not what you're implying.

PETE. Get me back into my chair. But don't touch me when you're doin' it.

KAREN. Don't say things like that to me.

[KAREN helps him into the wheelchair.]

Raymond J. Barry

PETE. I'll say what I want to say.

KAREN. We were always close. I've been hiding who I really am since you got home. I can't do it anymore.

PETE.. Just don't try any shit on me.

KAREN. What on earth are you talking about?

PETE. I don't like you touching me.

KAREN. You mean when I helped you into your wheelchair?

PETE. I just don't like it.

KAREN. You asked me to help you.

PETE. I didn't ask you. You just did it.

KAREN. No, that's not true. You asked me.

PETE. Just keep your damned hands off of me.

KAREN. Nobody is touching you.

PETE. Well just keep it that way, you whore.

KAREN. What did you say? What did you call me? How can you call me that? What about you? Who would be attracted to you anyway? You don't can't even walk.

PETE. What? What did you say?

KAREN. You can't even walk.

PETE. [flails in his chair, helplessly] You bitch. I'll break you.

KAREN. You aren't going to do anything. You're a cripple.

PETE. And you're a whore, sucking dicks.

KAREN. You keep it up and you'll be sorry.

PETE. I'll be sorry for nothing – fucking whore.

[KAREN grabs his wheelchair, tips it and shakes PETE onto the ground. Then she turns the heavy wheelchair upside down and throws dirt on it, kicking it in a rage.]

PETE. Lemme up! Lemme up!

KAREN. Get yourself up![violently kicks the upside down wheelchair.] I'll never forgive you, Pete. I'll never forgive you for what you said.

PETE. Lemme up, you whore.

KAREN. If you yell loud enough, maybe someone will hear you. If not you can spend the night here. I'll never forgive you, Pete, for what you called me.

PETE. Don't leave me here. For God's sake don't leave me on the ground like this.

KAREN. Why? You're a big man. You can take care of yourself.

[KAREN exits, leaving PETE with his arm dangling from the seat of the swing. He evaluates the situation
in silence, then calls out for help to no avail. The heavy wheelchair is overturned.]

PETE. Help! Help! Oh, what the fuck, you bitch whore! I'll show you! I'll get you, you bitch whore! [pause] I'm tired. Can't get anywhere. Help! Help me. Don't leave me here, you whore. Don't... leave... me. Don't

Back Home

leave...

[KAREN re-enters. Silence. PETE struggles to lift the heavy wheelchair.]

PETE. Go. I can take care of myself.

KAREN. If that were true you'd be on your way home.

[KAREN pulls the wheelchair upright.]

PETE. I can get home by myself.

KAREN. Let me help you.

PETE. Don't touch me. I can get home by myself.

KAREN. Don't be stupid. Let me help you.

[KAREN attempts to help PETE who skirts away on the ground, using the strength of his arms.]

KAREN. Stop making this so difficult.

PETE. What difficult? I can do it by myself.

KAREN. So do it. I'm just staying here to make sure you're all right.

PETE. I'm good by myself.

KAREN. It's dangerous in the park. It's getting late. Come on, let's go.

[PETE grovels in the dirt, pulls himself towards the wheelchair. He grabs the handles on the chair and yanks himself up but falls back to the ground in a heap. KAREN walks to him, reaches down to be of some help.]

PETE. Get away from me!

KAREN. Come on, let's go home.

PETE. I am going home. Just stay away from me.

KAREN. I'm sorry for what I said.

PETE. You go ahead.

KAREN. Not without you.

PETE. Don't wait for me.

KAREN. I'm not leaving you here.

PETE. Leave me alone.

KAREN. I won't.

PETE. Go home.

KAREN. Not without you. Get into your chair.

PETE. In my own time.

[PETE tries again to lift himself up, but falls. KAREN moves towards him, lifts him onto the chair but PETE throws himself down into the dirt.]

PETE. You will not help me!

KAREN. We can't stay here all night, Pete.

PETE. Go! Go! I keep telling you to go.

KAREN. I'm not leaving you.

PETE. I can do it myself.

[Again PETE attempts slowly but surely to raise his torso to the height of the chair and turns himself
around in a sitting position, but just before he successfully accomplishes this he falls in a heap

Raymond J. Barry

to the ground. No one speaks for a long while.]
PETE. All right. Help me.
[KAREN lifts PETE gently onto the chair. Not a word is spoken between them during the entire ordeal. PETE is finally sitting upright, stoically facing forward. KAREN pushes PETE out of the park.]

Act Two

\-

Scene Three

[Same day, early evening. Interior living room. HENRY and CONSTANCE are facing off with each other. The television is on with no sound, showing news of the war. Neither is watching it.]

CONSTANCE. What about the house? I should get the house.
HENRY. Why should you get the house?
CONSTANCE. I should get something. Why not the house?
HENRY. It's my house. I paid for it.
CONSTANCE. It's in my name too.
HENRY. That's because I put it in your name.
CONSTANCE. You put it in my name because I'm your wife. A wife has rights.
HENRY. So does a husband of thirty years.
CONSTANCE. So does a wife of thirty years.
[silence]
HENRY. That's settled then. I get the house.
CONSTANCE. Over my dead body.
[silence]
HENRY. Maybe we should stay together.
CONSTANCE. I'll think about it.
HENRY. Too late to get out.
CONSTANCE. It's not too late for me.
HENRY. Pete wouldn't like it. Splitting up would bring him down hard.
CONSTANCE. After you ruined him.
HENRY. I didn't ruin him.
CONSTANCE. You know better. You ruined his life.
HENRY. What about you? You did a nice job on him.
CONSTANCE. Pete and I are close.
HENRY. Close you call it.
CONSTANCE. What would you call it?
HENRY. I would call it mamma's boy.
[silence]
CONSTANCE. We should separate.

Back Home

HENRY. We probably won't.

CONSTANCE. Were just living together. There's no love. Just a man and woman living together, like strangers.

HENRY. In my house.

CONSTANCE. It's my house too.

HENRY. I told you. I paid for it.

CONSTANCE. Doesn't matter. My name is on the deed. *[pause]* You want to separate?

HENRY. Maybe.

CONSTANCE. You'd live alone.

HENRY. You would too.

CONSTANCE. I'm willing if you're willing.

HENRY. Yeah.

CONSTANCE. What do you mean, "yeah?"

HENRY. Just... nothing.

CONSTANCE. Nothing?

HENRY. Yeah, just nothing.

CONSTANCE. Why nothing? You must mean something.

HENRY. I don't know.

CONSTANCE. What don't you know?

HENRY. I just don't know.

CONSTANCE. I don't know either.

HENRY. Pete.

CONSTANCE. What about Pete?

HENRY. He was my last hope.

CONSTANCE. Last hope for what?

HENRY. For putting myself on the planet.

CONSTANCE. You're on the planet.

HENRY. I'm nobody. My kid coulda been somebody.

CONSTANCE. What do you mean by somebody? He's somebody. He's your son.

HENRY. There was an outside possibility that he could have done something.

CONSTANCE. We all do something – except you. You do nothing.

HENRY. He was my one opportunity to make my mark.

CONSTANCE. What kind of mark?

HENRY. Just a mark – just to do something great.

CONSTANCE. That's what you were using your son for?

HENRY. I wasn't using him. He coulda done something.

CONSTANCE. No matter which way you look at it, he needs our help after you sent him to that war.

HENRY. You keep saying that.

CONSTANCE. Sure I say it.

HENRY. You better not say it.

Raymond J. Barry

CONSTANCE. You sent him to war. You sent him to war.

[silence]

HENRY. How do you separate?

CONSTANCE. With lawyers.

HENRY. That costs money.

CONSTANCE. Sure it costs money.

HENRY. We don't have the money to pay fancy lawyers.

CONSTANCE. I get the house no matter what happens. And Pete's painting. That painting is mine too.

HENRY. To hell with the painting. You don't get the house. I get the house.

CONSTANCE. Pete needs a place to stay. He needs his mother.

HENRY. I'll take care of him in the house he grew up in.

CONSTANCE. Sure, you could talk about the medals you won in Vietnam.

HENRY. I didn't go to Vietnam.

CONSTANCE. I know that. What do you think I said it for?

HENRY. You said it because you wanted to bring it up again.

CONSTANCE. That's right, again and again.

HENRY. This is no good.

[silence]

CONSTANCE. I'll call my lawyer.

HENRY. What about Pete?

CONSTANCE. He should be with me. In this house. *[pause]* Will you still be seeing Jeanine?

HENRY. Once in a while.

CONSTANCE. You'll pay for your behavior.

HENRY. I already have. Nobody gets out of this thing alive. We all pay for just being here. The price is high for just being here. That's why I promised myself to be happy. I refuse to be down about anything, even my own son getting hurt in that goddamned war. I'm happy and I'm happy to be happy.

CONSTANCE. You pay for every slip-up.

HENRY. Hey, life is good, real good. You don't have to get nasty.

CONSTANCE. Nasty? I'm not nasty. Who are you calling nasty?

HENRY. You're the only one here, honey.

CONSTANCE. We just do not get along.

HENRY. You're always on me, interfering with my natural happiness.

CONSTANCE. I'm upset about Pete.

HENRY. Why me then?

CONSTANCE. You fed lies into his head; the medals.

HENRY. A medal is a symbol of having a pair of balls. I didn't have any medals, so I made them up, but I got a pair of balls. Doesn't mean my point wasn't right. Go out and grow yourself a pair of balls, boy. That's all I meant, nothing else. The marines was the way to grow a pair of balls, that's all.

CONSTANCE. Right, a pair of balls. It all narrows down to a pair of balls.

HENRY. You're picking on me again, interfering with my natural happiness. How about trying to be in a good mood for a change? That's what I do. I'm always in a good mood cause that's how I want to be.

CONSTANCE. What about Pete?

HENRY. I love the kid. What else do you want?

CONSTANCE. I'll call my lawyer. There may be a fight for the house.

HENRY. There will be. What else do I have? I need a roof over my head.

CONSTANCE. So do I.

HENRY. You can't have the house.

CONSTANCE. I'll fight for it.

HENRY. So will I.

CONSTANCE. Do you want that fight?

HENRY. Not necessarily.

CONSTANCE. Let's avoid it.

HENRY. How?

CONSTANCE. By finding a way.

HENRY. What way? What way?

CONSTANCE. Just finding some way.

HENRY. It'll always be the same.

CONSTANCE. Doesn't have to be.

HENRY. Pete just about breaks me.

[front door opens. PETE enters in wheelchair. HENRY and CONSTANCE regain their composure.]

HENRY. Well, there you are. Your mother was worried. You were gone for a long time.

PETE. Yeah, a long time.

CONSTANCE. Did you and Karen enjoy yourselves?

PETE. Yeah.

CONSTANCE. Is that all? Just, "Yeah?"

PETE. Is that all about what?

CONSTANCE. About your afternoon with Karen.

PETE. What about it?

CONSTANCE. Was it special?

PETE. Yeah, it was special.

CONSTANCE. How special?

PETE. Very special.

CONSTANCE. Have an appetite?

PETE. No.

CONSTANCE. I know you've been bonding after not seeing each other for such a long time? You have been bonding, haven't you?

PETE. We talked, swung on the swing, argued a little.

CONSTANCE. Hear that, Henry? They argued a little.

Raymond J. Barry

HENRY. Leave him alone.

CONSTANCE. We were worried about you.

PETE. Nothing to worry about.

CONSTANCE. Doesn't sound right to me. You and Karen arguing. What could have been that important – to argue with your own fiancée?

HENRY. Man and woman fighting, like Abraham and Sarah fighting in the Bible.

PETE. Screw the Bible.

CONSTANCE. How dare you say such a thing in our Christian home. How dare you say such a thing.

PETE. Your Christian home is what I grew up in.

CONSTANCE. That's correct, son, and you would fare well to re-acquaint yourself with the values you've learned within these four walls - American values of respect for family members.

PETE. I can speak for myself.

HENRY. Leave him alone, mother. They're all right, the both of them. They're a couple of kids, that's all, a man and a woman who fight and make up, that's all. Pete got hurt in the war, won a Purple Heart. His girlfriend doesn't like to see him wounded; puts her on edge. They argue about something unimportant. They're as nuts as they've always been. The woman walks away pissed about what happened to her man. It's normal; fighting cause they love each other.

PETE. Bullshit. Karen's a whore.

HENRY. What? What did you say?

PETE. Ask her. She's sleeping with another guy.

HENRY. What the hell are you saying?

CONSTANCE. You'll have to start going to church, son. It's not Christian what you're saying. Don't call your fiancée names, son. She's your wife to be. It's not Christian. We're Christian. We're Christian people. It's a sin to talk like that. What are you doing to Karen? She's always played by the rules. Now this is how you pay her back?

PETE. She's screwing another guy.

HENRY. What? You fought proudly for your country and that's how she pays you back. Hell, you've been together since you were little kids.

PETE. She's a whore.

CONSTANCE. Please, Pete, keep the conversation Christian. Remember - Christian values in this home. We're a Christian family.

PETE. I don't believe in God!

CONSTANCE. Blasphemy!!

[pause]

HENRY. Someday you'll look back on this time as a growing period, son. Everybody goes through their twenties and thirties, and when you turn forty, you give up all the things that are bad for you.

CONSTANCE. Oh, yes, like you and your whore-tramp!

Back Home

HENRY. That's it! What you need is to meet my friend, Jeanine.

CONSTANCE. Henry, you wouldn't dare.

HENRY. It's for him, mother, not for me. Pete needs a good woman, just to get him back to normal. Yep, the boy should meet my friend, Jeanine. She'll fix him up in a jiffy. Jeanine can turn any young kid into a man.

Act Two

-

Scene Four

[Same day, later that night. MEL and CONSTANCE waiting in the living room for the men to return]

MEL. How long before they get back?

CONSTANCE. Long time. Most of the night.

MEL. Out on the town, huh?

CONSTANCE. That's right. Out on the town.

MEL. Raping and looting.

CONSTANCE. Making a damned fool of himself.

MEL. Leaving you alone at home.

CONSTANCE. You get the picture.

MEL. At least you have me to protect you.

CONSTANCE. I don't need protection.

MEL. What do you need?

CONSTANCE. Company.

MEL. Company?

CONSTANCE. Yes, you are company, aren't you, Mel? You're my company tonight, while my husband is out on the town.

[Both characters freeze. KAREN appears with a letter in her hand on the other side of the stage. She reads the letter]

KAREN. Dear, Pete: I want to tell you that I love with all my heart both your soul and your impeccable character that remains unblemished by the hardship you've been through. It's not easy for me to say goodbye, having such feeling for you. We've been so close from the time we were children. Part of me wants so very much to continue our relationship. Another part insists upon saying what must be said. There is no other choice. Just know, when you read this letter, that I love you and wish always to be your friend. I care so very much for you.

[KAREN freezes. CONSTANCE and MEL continue.]

MEL. Wish he invited me to go with him.

CONSTANCE. And why would you wish that, Mel?

MEL. Oh, I would've enjoyed tagging along to make sure the old man

Raymond J. Barry

stays out of trouble.

CONSTANCE. No telling what he'll get himself into.

MEL. That's right. No telling.

CONSTANCE. Leaving me at home worried half to death.

MEL. Yep, not fair when you think about it.

CONSTANCE. Not fair at all.

MEL. Then again the world isn't fair, is it?

CONSTANCE. No, the world isn't particularly fair.

MEL. The world has a tendency to be unfair.

CONSTANCE. Yes, that's correct. It is an unfair world when it comes right down to it.

MEL. It's all one can do to keep one's head above the muck.

CONSTANCE. Yes, that's a good way of putting it – "above the muck."

MEL. I feel sorry for you, Constance, to have to put up with what you have to put up with.

CONSTANCE. I do the best I can.

MEL. Yes, you do, don't you? Everything you have to deal with, your husband out on the town, running around doing whatever he pleases.

CONSTANCE. Thank goodness you came by. Otherwise I'd be all alone.

MEL. Yes, you would, wouldn't you? All alone.

CONSTANCE. But I'm not all alone, am I? I'm with you. You came to visit.

MEL. To keep you company.

CONSTANCE. Such a good neighbor.

MEL. I try to be a good neighbor.

CONSTANCE. Well, you are a good neighbor, a very good neighbor.

MEL. It does my heart good to hear that.

[MEL reaches for CONSTANCE'S hand. KAREN continues reading her letter.]

KAREN. I'll not be marrying you, Pete. You've changed, not just physically but mentally as well. When you came home, I realized how different you are, Pete. A terrible cynicism has stolen that spark of joy that used there before you were wounded. That cynicism has destroyed our happiness together, Pete. I've hoped and prayed for the man I once knew to come back to me, but in my heart I realize that isn't going to happen. Your pain through this ordeal has won out by robbing you of hope. Pessimism has taken the place of that hope, regardless of what I say or do to make things right again. You've always been wiser than I. Please, dear Pete, recognize what is good in your life and find that joy again. Otherwise there's no reason to live.

[KAREN stops reading. CONSTANCE and MEL continue the scene.]

CONSTANCE. You're holding my hand

MEL. I'm just trying to be a good neighbor.

CONSTANCE. I don't mind. I'm all alone and there's no one here to comfort me.

Back Home

MEL. Except me, and, under the circumstances, I feel the urge to hold your hand.

CONSTANCE. Mel, did you ever think about getting married?

MEL. I don't know. I thought about it sometimes.

CONSTANCE. Of course you thought about it? Why wouldn't you have thought about it? You deserve to be loved, don't you?

MEL. Sure, I suppose so. I haven't thought of it that way.

CONSTANCE. Let's discuss it now.

MEL. Why do we have to discuss it?

CONSTANCE. So we can clarify the situation.

[CONSTANCE and MEL hold. KAREN continues reading her letter.]

KAREN. Marriage would be wrong for us, not only because of our obvious inability to have children, but also because I just cannot live in state of gloom for the rest of my life. I deserve more. I'm a good person. I'm a direct person, as you are. You told me in the park that day that you didn't love me anymore. I pray that's true, because I don't want to hurt you. You're such a fine person. You've already been destroyed by the wanton violence of war that you glorified so. I allowed you to go to war. I failed you, Pete. You left the best part of yourself back there and I can't wait for it to return. This can't continue. I will not be dragged down by your despair. The military was your dream, but it failed you, Pete. Its cause was not as honorable as you so earnestly believed, and I doubt you'll ever recover from the disappointment of that. You left the best part of yourself back there. But I must think of myself, Pete. This time I must think of myself. Please, remember that I'll always wish you the very best.

As ever your friend, Karen

[KAREN exits. CONSTANCE and MEL in the living room.]

CONSTANCE. I've forgotten all my troubles.

MEL. So have I. I've forgotten all about them.

CONSTANCE. Have you a few troubles as well?

MEL. Well, sure. I mean, I was in Vietnam, you know. I haven't had a whole night's sleep for thirty years.

CONSTANCE. I could help you sleep.

MEL. We're both in the same boat.

CONSTANCE. Yes, we are. Both in the same boat. Might as well row ourselves out of this backwater. Make love to me Mel.

[CONSTANCE and MEL embrace.]

Raymond J. Barry

Act Three

-

Scene One

[Same night, late. HENRY tiptoes into the house, pushing PETE'S wheelchair, careful to make as little noise as possible, so as not to wake up CONSTANCE. HENRY is drunk; collapses onto an easy-chair. No one speaks for a moment, leaving the room heavy with uncertainty. Finally HENRY gets up from the chair, turns the music on softly and gyrates his hips in a drunken imitation of what transpired at the strip bar from whence they came. HENRY dances as if JEANINE were in the room, which she is not. PETE watches]

HENRY. Yeah, give it to us, girl. Give it to a man, a red-blooded American male who loves pussy and his country. At-a-girl, Jeanine. You make me feel young again. *[making sexual undulations with his hips]* If I was twenty years younger I'd be over there killing Arabs, defending freedom for my country. Give us a good look at that sweet ass, honey. We want all you got, baby. See, Pete, maybe you want a personal lap dance in private. You'd do that, wouldn't you, Jeanine? Pete would appreciate a good woman to sit on his lap. *[HENRY is completely into his dance by now, exhibiting his memory of what transpired at the strip bar]* Give it to us, honey. Yeah, oh my, yes! I think I got a leak in my britches, Awwww!!! *[HENRY stops dancing. He's quite drunk, looks toward PETE]* Whatsamatter? Cat got your tongue? Did you like what you saw tonight. I just know you did. That's why I took you there. I knew you'd go for some good pussy once you were in the middle of it. I got good instincts, good instincts. I know how to heal you, Pete. You wait. With the right kind a influence I can make a real man outta you. You can bet on it. Just stick around me. *[dancing]* Whoopie! Whoopie! Whoopie!

PETE. Quiet down, father. You'll wake mom.

HENRY. *[slurred speech]* Father? You call me father? How come so formal? You don't have to be so formal. I'm your dad, remember? That's what you call me – your dad.

PETE. Yeah, dad.

HENRY. See that? I love it when you call me "dad." I want you to call me "dad" all the time. *[HENRY fetches a bottle]* You want another shot!

PETE. No. You better quiet down.

HENRY. *[drunkenly]* Not just, "No"... "No, dad." Dad. Dad! That's music to my ears. That's what you call me. "No, dad."

PETE. Right, dad.

HENRY. That's it. Now, really, you can tell me? You enjoy yourself tonight?

Back Home

PETE. Yeah,... great.

[HENRY tries to serve him his drink; PETE refuses.]

HENRY. That was some fine pussy back there, wasn't it? If you don't spend time with pussy, you can't learn about pussy. You haven't had the right influence. That's why your girlfriend is giving you a hard time. You wait and see. By the time I'm finished with you, you'll get enough pussy to last a lifetime.

PETE. Ah... I don't have to go to strip joints.

HENRY. *[drunken, slurred speech]* Oh, come on. Give it a chance. You seen a strip joint before. Ain't you seen a strip joint before, Pete?

PETE. Yeah, I saw one before.

HENRY. *[drunkenly]* Sure. Any soldier's been to a strip joint before. That's what soldiers do. They go to strip joints. If you can't appreciate a beautiful black woman dancing up there, then you're blood's not pumping through your veins. Jeanine is the lady I was talking to you about. She's my friend, real smart, graduated from Radcliff and working on her masters degree now. You was enjoying yourself, weren't you, Pete?

PETE. Yeah, sure.

HENRY. Did you like the lap-dance she gave you. You like the lap-dance?

PETE. Yeah, sure... the lap dance.

HENRY. *[loudly drunk]* Why do you think I invited the lady over to the table? So you could have a good time, that's why. Don't you get it? Real men spend time with women. She's a beautiful woman. So you spent time with her. *[HENRY gyrates his hips sexually]* She sat right down on you.

PETE. Mom might wake up.

HENRY. *[drunk]* Who's mom?

PETE. Mom's my mother.

HENRY. *[drunkenly]* Your mother? I don't want to be in some strange woman's house.

PETE. It's okay, she's your wife, dad. Talk softer. You're smashed drunk. Just keep it down. You'll wake her up.

HENRY. All right. All right. *[softly but still loud]* Dance for Pete again. *[HENRY'S mind is back at the bar]* Go on up to them and show 'em what you got. Make a man out of him. *[dancing himself wildly]*

PETE. What about mom? She might wake up.

HENRY. I told you. She won't wake up.

PETE. She could wake up with all the noise you're making.

HENRY. *[softer voice]* Then quiet down. You'll ruin all the fun.

PETE. What fun?

HENRY. You're having fun.

PETE. This isn't my idea of fun.

Raymond J. Barry

HENRY. Oh, I know you're having fun.

PETE. This isn't fun, dad. You're wasted drunk.

HENRY. Yeah, I'm drunk, and looking at Jeanine's ass is fun.

PETE. Jeanine's not even here, dad, and you got a foul mouth.

[HENRY dances around the room wildly, barely able to stand]

HENRY. Just dance, will you, honey? For my son. Make a man out of him. You gotta work for your money. Start moving your ass for Pete over there. You're wasting time. Jeanine give you a lap-dance, Pete. Relax; she's a friend of mine. I've known her for years.*[still dancing]* Okay, Jeanine, do your thing.

[HENRY falls down, tries to pick himself up]

PETE. Why don't we just go to bed?

HENRY. *[tipsy]* We ain't goin' to bed yet, you understand? The night's young. I ain't goin' to bed till I get my money's worth.

PETE. You got your money's worth.

HENRY. *[slurred speech, dancing]* Jeanine ain't made you happy yet. I paid her to turn you into a man, and I want her to give you a private lap dance. Dance for Pete, Jeanine. You can straighten him out.

PETE. I don't want a lap dance, dad. Jeanine's not here.

HENRY. What do you mean you don't want a lap dance?

PETE. We should go to bed.

[Henry dancing with imaginary partner]

HENRY. No, this is how you do it, honey. Follow me. *[HENRY gyrates his hips and dances in front of PETE, waving his crotch in his son's face. PETE is uncomfortable, looking up to the ceiling. HENRY encourages him to look at him]* That's it. You see, honey, this is how you do it. Get that pussy right into his face. Show him what a woman is all about. Just like this.

[HENRY dances his crotch into PETE'S face.]

PETE. Dad, please.

HENRY. *[gyrating his hips into PETE'S face]* Whatsamatter? She's tempting you. You're resisting her but she's tempting you and soon you'll weaken. You've got to weaken. *[dancing like a woman]* Any man would weaken. Look how sexy she is! And smart too. She graduated from Radcliff. Working on her masters. We been friends for years.

PETE. Mother will wake up. Keep it down. I'm going to bed.

HENRY. Don't go to bed! We're having a party. You'll learn from this. Here's how you do it. *[HENRY imitates JEANINE'S dance.]* Oh, yeah, honey. I like that. That-a-girl! Now you're doing it. Give it to me the way I like it. Turn the kid on too! Don't just dance for me.

PETE. I'm getting out of here.

HENRY. *[lunges for PETE'S wheelchair]* Goddammit! Get your ass back here!

[Suddenly CONSTANCE appears in the doorway, horrified at the

drunken sight of HENRY.]
CONSTANCE. Henry!!!
[MEL appears from the bedroom, half-naked. He carries his clothing in his hand while running across the living room and out the door, leaving everyone aghast.]
CONSTANCE. Out of my house, you drunken bastard! Out of my house!!! Out of this house!!! You drunk! Out! Out, I say!!! *[CONSTANCE changes her tone to ice.]* Get out of this house, Henry. I'll be leaving in the morning. You will sleep in the car tonight. If you need me for anything from now on, I can be reached at Melvin's address by letter only, preferably from your lawyer.
[CONSTANCE exits back into the bedroom. Long silence. Lights gradually out.]

Act Three

-

Scene Two

[Next day, early evening. Interior living room. HENRY collapsed on the couch. PETE in his wheelchair, reading KAREN'S letter. No one speaks. After a prolonged silence]

HENRY. Letter from Karen, eh? *[looks to Pete, no response]* From the look on your face, I've a good idea what it says. *[looks to Pete, no response]* It's going to be you and me, son, from now on – just you and me. *[looks to Pete, no response]* Remember when you were a young boy, Pete? When you were a young teenager? You were such a beautiful kid then. Young, strong, a little thin, but you had a pair of broad shoulders with muscles in your back. You had triceps too, already developed from years of basketball, football and doing thousands of pushups every week. A little man you were, and what an athlete. No one could cut and spin like you on the basketball court. You could shoot the ball like a professional too. You certainly had a pro's competitive spirit. Everything you did, you wanted to be the best. I admired that in you. Once, when you were playing football, you started the season brilliant – two or three touchdowns a game during the first half of the season. You looked great when you ran with the ball. I was proud of you. You seemed invincible. At least I thought you were invincible. You were my heart and soul then. You'll always be my heart and soul, boy. *[looks to Pete, no response]* Anyway, as the football season progressed, another running back began to show promise. Remember that kid, that fast kid? Conners was his name. That's what they called him – Conners. The kid had speed - burning speed. One game he scored four touchdowns. Remember that game, Pete? *[looks to Pete, no response]*

Raymond J. Barry

After that they didn't give you the ball much. You scored fewer and fewer touchdowns. And you lost your confidence a little. I could see what was happening. Your enthusiasm for the game was leaving you. Conners began to shine more and more. I saw you getting depressed, couldn't wait till the season was over, couldn't wait; began to hate the coach, began to hate the kid. Never said anything to either of them. There wasn't anything to say really. That other kid was better than you and that was all there was to it. What could I say? My heart went out to you though. I felt so bad. I saw your disappointment. You were used to being the star. You were special and used to doing great things on the field. I hated that coach because he wouldn't let you carry the ball. I could've killed the son-of-a-bitch for making you feel bad about yourself, but at the same time I knew it would teach you how cruel life can be, how unfair it can be and how the Lord makes us all different. Some of us are strong, some weak. Others are fast runners. Others are smart, others dumb. We just have to accept what God has given us and do our best, that's all.

[PETE drops KAREN'S letter onto the floor. He refers to painting on the wall]

PETE. That painting.

HENRY. What?

PETE. Something... not right about it.

HENRY. The painting? Your mother loved that painting.

[PETE wheels himself into the bedroom, leaves his father alone.]

Yep, you contributed a lot to that team, even though you weren't as good a runner as that fast kid, Conners. You hear me? *[no response from Pete in bedroom]* You're quiet today. I can understand that with your mother gone. Today you're dealing with a similar situation. Not only is everyone faster but you don't even have the legs to walk down the street. The coach isn't giving you the ball anymore like he used to and you feel left out. I see it in your face like you looked when you were a little kid, that disappointment in your eyes. You're like you were when you were a boy whose position had been stolen from you. Your legs are gone. Your mobility has been stripped. You look at yourself as a second-stringer, warming the bench, a substitute who can't carry the ball anymore. No more touchdowns for you. But there's room for linemen, Pete. Linemen never carry the ball either. A team can't win without linemen. The world can't function without them. You understand? *[looks to Pete, no response]* You can't just give up, Pete. You got to live. You gotta do something with your life, boy. *[looks to Pete, no response]* You don't hate me, do you, Pete? *[looks to Pete, no response]* Ain't there anything I can do to make things right? *[looks to Pete, no response]* I was so proud when you went in, son. I bragged about you to anyone who'd listen. It was as if you were doing what I'd

failed to do. You were facing the music. A real man faces the music, son; faces what life has to offer and doesn't run away from it like I did. I wanted to take short cuts so I could be a big shot. That never happened, and in the meantime I'm left with myself to look at in the mirror. I've avoided anything that might have meant sacrificing myself for something worthwhile, and I'm paying the price for it now. When I was young I was the center of the universe. I'm not the center of the universe. Nobody is. There are those who try, big shot politicians. You see them on television, making their promises. They seize power in some underhanded manner and choke the lifeblood out of the rest of us. They think of themselves as the so-called 'elite few' and the rest of us as the bewildered herd who don't understand enough to make choices. I would've been one of them if I had the talent. I didn't have the talent. Without the talent I'm a nobody, just one of the herd. *[pause]* Just you and me now, Pete. Your mother's gone for good. Yup, she's gone for good. Gotta learn to be alone now. Just you and me.
[PETE enters from the bedroom with a pistol pointed at HENRY. A shot rings out immediately.]
PETE. No, dad, it's just me now. *[HENRY'S face reflects the horror of being shot. He remains seated, as if in a trance and dies. Lights out abruptly]*

End of Play

Raymond J. Barry

Park Encounter

Characters

Erica: a corporate career woman in her fifties married to Paul. She has no children.

Edward: a corporate executive with a background in economics. He has been involved in loaning money to undeveloped countries and is about to quit his job.

Paul: husband of Erica who has worked with Edward, taking advantage of undeveloped countries.

Park Encounter is currently a work in progress.

CAST:
ERICA... Tacey Adams
EDWARD ....Raymond J. Barry
PAUL .... Bernard White

Raymond J. Barry

Tacey Adams, **Park Encounter**, 2009

Park Encounter

Park Encounter

[EDWARD *approaches ERICA on a bench, reads a book, Leo Tolstoy's short stories. EDWARD stands for a while with his own book. ERICA reads for some time without saying a word. Finally EDWARD speaks].*

EDWARD. I knew I'd see you again.
ERICA. I beg your pardon?
EDWARD. I knew you'd show up one of these days.
ERICA. I think you're mistaking me for someone else.
EDWARD. No, you are she.
ERICA. Who?
EDWARD. Just you.
ERICA. I have no idea...
EDWARD. Oh, you do; you do.
ERICA. No, I do not have the vaguest.
EDWARD. Come, come.
ERICA. No, really, I don't think I'm the right person.
EDWARD. Really?
ERICA. No, really, no.
EDWARD. I could have sworn.
ERICA. No, really, no.
> *[long silence; ERICA reads. EDWARD lingers.]*
EDWARD. Nice day.
ERICA. What? Oh, I'm sorry. I didn't hear you. I was reading my book.
EDWARD. I love the park on a nice day like this.
ERICA. Yes.
EDWARD. It certainly is a very nice day. *[pause]* What are you reading?
ERICA. I'm reading Tolstoy.
EDWARD. I've read Tolstoy.
ERICA. I'm enjoying his short stories.
EDWARD. I have a book too. Do you mind if I read here on this bench?
ERICA. Ah . . . no, I suppose I don't mind.
EDWARD. Such a pleasant bench beneath the fluttering birds and blue, blue skies in the presence of scurrying squirrels; a public bench shared by anyone who chooses to sit upon it.
ERICA. Do as you please then.
EDWARD. Thank you. It's just so lovely out here, isn't it?
ERICA. Lovely, yes.
EDWARD. My name is Edward.
ERICA. That's nice, Edward.
EDWARD. Aren't you going to tell me what your name is?
ERICA. *[reading]* No.
EDWARD. I understand completely. Can't be giving out one's name at the drop of a hat.
ERICA. I'm reading, so I'm really not hearing you.

Raymond J. Barry

128

EDWARD. Of course. I'll read too. *[EDWARD prepares to read, looks at her book]* Must be a good story.
ERICA. Oh, yes, I'm reading his short stories. I love it.
EDWARD. That's so nice.
ERICA. What's nice?
EDWARD. To love, to love something.
ERICA. I love reading.
EDWARD. I love everything about life, including the struggle it brings. I just love the struggle, don't you?
ERICA. The struggle?
EDWARD. Yes, don't you enjoy the battle of life?
ERICA. I don't look at my life as a battle.
EDWARD. You don't?
ERICA. People choose to make their lives difficult.
EDWARD. We do? What an interesting thought, that people actually have a choice. Do you really believe that?
ERICA. Believe what? Believe what?
EDWARD. That people choose or choose not to struggle.
ERICA. Yes.
EDWARD. That's all you have to say about the subject? Just, "Yes?"
ERICA. Yes.
EDWARD. What do you mean by "yes?"
ERICA. Just, "yes", I agree.
EDWARD. Yes, you do, don't you?
ERICA. I agree with my original statement that one does not have to struggle. There can be ease in one's life.
EDWARD. And there is great ease in your life. I can tell.
ERICA. How can you tell? I'm a perfect stranger.
EDWARD. I could have sworn I met you before. Regardless, we're getting to know each other quite fast I would say.
ERICA. I'd like to be left alone of you don't mind.
EDWARD. Of course, I don't mind.
ERICA. Thank you. Have a nice day.
EDWARD. And you the same.
     [heads turn out to fourth wall]
EDWARD. We're bombing again, aren't we?
ERICA. Always.
EDWARD. I thought so. I thought I heard bombs in the distance.
ERICA. Always bombs falling on those people.
EDWARD. What people?
ERICA. The enemy.
EDWARD. Oh, yes, the enemy. I don't have enemies.
ERICA. They're out there somewhere. Everyone has enemies.
EDWARD. I've read about them, those enemy people. Names are used to describe them as enemies, certain names; gunman, insurgents, terrorists and enemy itself. Ha, all of the above. Anyone can be called names. Anyone can become the enemy.
ERICA. It's up to us not to become the enemy.

Park Encounter

EDWARD. Yes, I agree. It's up to us. Wouldn't want to be called a name, an enemy name. I'm glad I'm not the enemy.

ERICA. We're all glad of that.

EDWARD. Wouldn't want to be them.

ERICA. You don't have to worry.

EDWARD. Really? I do worry. Everyone's bombing people, shooting people. A lot of shooting too everywhere. Shooting has become entertainment. Sometimes I dream of someone shooting someone. I'm not sure who, but it doesn't seem to matter. Don't you have dreams of people shooting people?

ERICA. I dream nice things.

EDWARD. Oh, but don't you have dreams of hurting people…

ERICA. Last night I dreamed…

EDWARD. … shooting people…

ERICA. …of a woman's severed head…

EDWARD. …bombing them?

ERICA. A woman's severed head…

EDWARD. It's part of all of us by now.

ERICA. … held a conversation with me.

EDWARD. All the shooting and bombing out there.

ERICA. The subject of our dialogue I don't remember…

EDWARD. Can't help but to dream about it, can you?

ERICA. … but the woman's severed head was pretty and attractive.

EDWARD. You dream of shooting and bombing, just like I dream of shooting and bombing. I know you do. You hear that bombing all day long. You can't help but to dream about it.

ERICA. Bombing protects my freedom.

EDWARD. But there's no freedom here. Our thoughts imprison us.

ERICA. I am a happy person.

EDWARD. You can be happy with the bombing still going on?

ERICA. The wars have nothing to do with my happiness.

EDWARD. Oh, they do. You aren't aware of their effect.

ERICA. I live with the sound of bombs; nothing significant about that. I just live with it and do my best.

EDWARD. You settle for that? Nothing but war surrounding us and you only do your best?

ERICA. What would you have me do? I can't do anything.

EDWARD. A sad state of affairs, not able to do anything.

ERICA. I didn't say I'm not able to do anything. I said I can't do anything about the wars. Please, listen to what I'm saying. Please, listen.

EDWARD. Sorry. You seem upset.

ERICA. Well, you have upset me. I am upset. You persist and persist so relentlessly.

EDWARD. I'm sorry for upsetting you. You're such a nice and decent person. We're all upset nowadays; constant sound of war in the distance, constant paranoia about the authorities checking up on us to see what we're up to. No wonder we're upset. Let me hug you so you'll feel better. I want you to feel better. Come here and let me hug you. You'll feel so much better if we hug. Come here. I'm warm and snuggly. Come here. Let's hug.

ERICA. Well, I . . . just this one time.

EDWARD. Attagirl. *[They hug]* There now. How does that feel?

ERICA. Much better.

EDWARD. Doesn't that feel good, a nice hug to console our hearts and souls.

ERICA. Yes, I feel much better. You can let me go now. I've had enough hugging.

EDWARD. Just a minute more, a little minute more.

ERICA. No, enough of this, no more hugging.

EDWARD. It's all right. You're enjoying our hug, aren't you? Aren't you feeling better being hugged?

ERICA. Please, let me go now. We've hugged enough.

[ERICA playfully struggles away from EDWARD]

EDWARD. It's okay. Hugging is good. People should hug more, especially when they're upset.

ERICA. Oh, you, you are up to something. You wouldn't let me go. That wasn't nice.

EDWARD. Nice?

ERICA. Yes, nice. You aren't very nice. Holding me against my will.

EDWARD. I suppose I needed to be hugged as well.

ERICA. Well, it wasn't very nice.

EDWARD. The wars have compromised my judgment.

ERICA. You held me against my will.

EDWARD. We all need contact with one another.

ERICA. I'll call an authorities if you come near me again.

EDWARD. All of us need to be hugged.

ERICA. I'm not noticing the wars enough to be bothered by them.

EDWARD. You are bothered. A simple hug and you're upset.

ERICA. You're a stranger to me. I'm not in the habit of hugging strangers.

EDWARD. You are upset.

ERICA. Yes, you've upset me even more. Please, don't go quite yet. I don't want to be alone. I'm upset.

EDWARD. I'm safe, harmless.

ERICA. I'm not questioning that. I'm not used to being hugged.

EDWARD. It's what we do. People hug.

ERICA. I don't hug as a general rule.

EDWARD. It is part of our culture to invade the space of others. Listen to that bombing. We invade the enemy's space.

ERICA. Oh, please, enough of your political rhetoric. Now you behave, or I'll call the authorities.

EDWARD. All right. I'll go. I'll go. *[EDWARD walks off stage, leaving ERICA alone. She sits, then stands, looking for EDWARD]*

ERICA. I know you are there.

EDWARD. How did you know I was there?

Park Encounter

ERICA. I have ways.
EDWARD. I wanted to apologize.
ERICA. That's decent of you.
EDWARD. I've been thinking about my behavior and I wanted to apologize for overstepping my boundaries.
ERICA. Accepted and good day.
EDWARD. Good day to you. May I sit.
ERICA. If you insist. Just don't talk.
EDWARD. No, no. I'll read. We'll both read.
ERICA. Very well then.
        [they read]
EDWARD. I've fallen in love with you.
ERICA. Really?
EDWARD. You are the cutest thing.
ERICA. Really?
EDWARD. Something so humane about you. You don't fit the mold. You haven't become ruthless yet. You're a kind person, a gentle and kind person. I feel your kindness.
ERICA. Thank you for those words but you really shouldn't.
EDWARD. I can't help it. I've fallen in love with you.
ERICA. That's foolish. Just drop it.
EDWARD. I'll do anything for you.
ERICA. Quiet down, little boy.
EDWARD. Do you have sex with your husband?
ERICA. Only once.
EDWARD. Was it good sex.
ERICA. Don't fantasize.
EDWARD. I was curious.
ERICA. We shouldn't be talking like this. The thoughts you have are mine as well. But we can't do anything about it.
EDWARD. Who are your enemies?
ERICA. I won't tell you, but I have them. We all have them.
EDWARD. That's just it. We don't know who our enemies are.
ERICA. We know. I know.
EDWARD. Who are they? The enemy?
ERICA. Men who hug me on park benches.
EDWARD. I get the point.
ERICA. It's not that I don't like you. It's that I wish you weren't here.
EDWARD. But I am, so we might as well negotiate. That's what civilized countries do. They negotiate.
ERICA. I'm not a country. I'm a person.
EDWARD. Yes, and a very interesting person at that. *[pause]* My mother died yesterday.
ERICA. Oh, I'm sorry.
EDWARD. No need to be sorry. She was very old.
ERICA. Well, I'm sorry anyway.
EDWARD. My daughter's husband is having an affair.
ERICA. Oh, I see.

Raymond J. Barry

EDWARD. He's cheating on her.

ERICA. That's upsetting.

EDWARD. Yes, don't you feel sorry for me?

ERICA. Sorry for your daughter is more like it.

EDWARD. But what about me?

ERICA. I'm sorry for you as well, I suppose.

EDWARD. But you're not sure.

ERICA. Naturally I'm more sympathetic with your daughter.

EDWARD. More so with my daughter than with me?

ERICA. Yes, that is correct.

EDWARD. I see. Just checking it out.

ERICA. Your daughter is the one whose suffering.

EDWARD. Yes.

ERICA. I'm reading now.

EDWARD. Right. *[pause]* I'm suffering too. Not much, but a little.

ERICA. I'm reading.

EDWARD. Right. I want my daughter to do well. And, as I said, my mother died. *[pause]* My father died too, back in nineteen-seventy-two.

ERICA. I'm sorry.

EDWARD. Don't be sorry. That's life.

ERICA. Yes, that is life.

EDWARD. I'm quitting my job this morning. I'm not doing that anymore.

ERICA. Very funny.

EDWARD. Don't laugh.

ERICA. I can laugh if I wish.

EDWARD. I know you can but don't.

ERICA. Really?!!!

EDWARD. I mean it.

ERICA. You mean what?

EDWARD. Everything I say, I mean. My conscience bothers me about what I do for a living. I'm ashamed of what I do for a living. It makes me tense at times along the forehead and down my temples, *[EDWARD touches his forehead and temples.]* a constriction that comes and goes on its own, a pulsation of blood vessels in my head. The source of it is my job which I hate. When a person hates what he does, he'll do anything to escape, anything to get my mind off it. I talk to strangers, for example, perfect strangers, but it can't be any kind of talk. It has to be talk that matters, real talk, the truth, or why bother to talk at all? Any lie makes my blood vessels constrict even more, as a punishment for lying. So I must not lie, you see. I must stop lying. Otherwise my life is a failure.

ERICA. Everyone's life is a failure to some degree.

EDWARD. Is your life a failure?

ERICA. Everyone's life is a failure to some degree.

EDWARD. There is something curiously correct about what you're saying. "Everyone's life is a failure to some degree." I like that

ERICA. I'm reading.

EDWARD. Don't read. Pay attention to me.

Park Encounter

ERICA. No.
EDWARD. All right.
ERICA. You're babbling!
EDWARD. Oh, yes, am I taking your attention away from your book?
ERICA. Yes, that seems to be the case. Now why don't you be silent...

[simultaneous]

ERICA.	EDWARD.
... and read your book and I'll read my book and between the two of us we can enjoy our independence.	That'll be fine, just fine if that's the way you want it. Fine, just fine. Fine. No more talking. Mum's the word from now on.

[silence]

ERICA. You're quite public about things. Can't you be more private? Just read and enjoy and stop trying to impress me.
EDWARD. Impress you? I'm not trying to impress you. Why on Earth would I try to impress you? We're strangers.
ERICA. You seem to need a great deal of attention.
EDWARD. Hardly. I happened to have shared a bench with you, that's all, on a day when I could have chosen another bench, and there you were. And it seemed such a natural thing to ask what you were reading, nothing more, nothing less. It was all purely innocent, you see, to simply open my mouth and say a few words, and then I began to read myself, and low and behold, I was completely taken aback by my reading material that describes the devilishness of our government and its tie-in with corporate interests. Are you following me?
ERICA. Another political pundit.
EDWARD. No, no, I'm not a political pundit. I barely vote. And I never talk politics. Don't have any interest.
ERICA. Neither do I.
EDWARD. Just live my life with blinders on.
ERICA. But you must have some reason for talking so much.
EDWARD. No, no reason. I'm ordinarily a quiet guy.
ERICA. You talk as much as anyone I know.
EDWARD. No, I don't. I don't talk; not much at all.
ERICA. You've done nothing but talk since you sat down on my bench.
EDWARD. I get it. You'd rather I didn't talk.
ERICA. I prefer a nice quiet afternoon of reading, that's all, a quiet afternoon with no one interrupting me. Now, please, you sit on your end of the bench and I'll sit on my end of the bench and let's ignore each other.
EDWARD. Fine. *[heads turn towards bombing in distance]* Those bombs again.
ERICA. They're always there. Ignore them.
EDWARD. Yes, I'll ignore them. Those bombs have changed me, you know; they've changed everyone, those bombs falling on our enemy. What if they're innocent people just tired of being pushed around? You

Raymond J. Barry

know, I'm closer to strangers than I ever was before, and that's
because of the bombing. I hate the bombing. I think of children hit by
those bombs. I care now about all people. I feel the urge to talk to
strangers with those bombs constantly falling on a population I don't
even know. They're not my enemy. You're one of those strangers I talk
to, lady. Can't a guy just open up and have a conversation? Do we all
have to be so isolated from one another? We can learn from each other.
We can exchange ideas and share, instead of being so goddamned
greedy all the time. We can learn to be generous with each other. We
can afford one friendship, one chance at being human. *[pause]* Oh,
listen, I'm so sorry. I've burned myself out lately. I just can't do it
anymore.

ERICA. Oh, you poor baby, feeling so sorry for yourself.

EDWARD. Don't patronize me.

ERICA. I'm not patronizing you.

EDWARD. You are! You're patronizing me. I won't have that. Now be my
friend. Show me how kind you are.

ERICA. I am kind! I am very kind!

EDWARD. I sense that, yes.

ERICA. We all have a touch of kindness! Kindness is what makes us
civilized! Kindness is what makes us human! Without kindness the
world would be in a sorry state.

EDWARD. Yes, kindness, one must project kindness.

ERICA. Well, we've settled that, haven't we?

EDWARD. Seems settled. You are kind and I am kind.

ERICA. Yes, we're both kind. That's been agreed upon. We've chosen to
be kind, as opposed to being unkind.

EDWARD. We have chosen to be kind. Do you believe you can choose to
be kind? Do you believe in free will?

ERICA. Free will? Why, yes, of course, I do. I do believe in free will; that
is, if you mean the ability to choose one's own destiny. Yes, of course, I
do. I do believe in free will. I make choices for myself. I certainly believe
in free will. I choose for myself. I certainly make choices for myself. We
all have to make choices for ourselves if we want to provide the best
opportunity for survival, and that requires the ability to choose for
oneself. That requires free will.

EDWARD. What choices have you made today?

ERICA. Choices? I've probably made numerous choices but I don't keep
track of them.

EDWARD. Oh, come on. You can remember your choices for the day.

ERICA. I suppose I can, if I make the effort. I do have an excellent
memory.

EDWARD. What did you choose then?

ERICA. Well, to be perfectly honest, I had a spat this morning . . .

EDWARD. A spat?

ERICA. Yes a spat . . . with someone whose identity I prefer not to
reveal, and decided not to go to work. That was a choice, mind you.
Instead I chose to go to the park and read my book. I was exercising

my free will by making a personal choice to read my book in the park to forget the unpleasant memory that lingered from earlier in the day.

EDWARD. So you had a spat with someone?

ERICA. We needn't get into that. It's much too personal.

EDWARD. Sorry, didn't mean to get personal.

ERICA. It's all right. I also chose to remain on this bench when you began chattering away like you did.

EDWARD. I'm enjoying your company. I like people.

ERICA. That's wonderful that you know that about yourself, that you like people.

EDWARD. I do like people. I hate to see people suffer.

ERICA. Just turn your head to avoid it, and you won't see people suffer.

EDWARD. That's why I'm leaving my job. I can't turn my head anymore.

ERICA. That's your choice, isn't it?

EDWARD. Yes, my choice not to turn my head. Nothing at all wrong with that, is there?

[ERICA listens to the sounds of the park]

ERICA. Listen. Do you hear something in the distance?

EDWARD. Hear what? Hear what? The traffic?

ERICA. No, silly, not the traffic. Children, children's voices in the distance. Do you hear the children's voices?

EDWARD. I do hear children's voices. It's a nice sound, children's voices, a very nice sound.

ERICA. Such innocence in their voices.

EDWARD. Children are innocent, aren't they?

ERICA. Listen to them playing, having fun.

EDWARD. They are having fun, lots of fun.

ERICA. Children's games.

EDWARD. Games and play.

ERICA. We adults have lost something.

EDWARD. And what is it we have lost?

ERICA. Our proclivity towards games and play.

EDWARD. Our proclivity towards games and play.

ERICA. The games have changed.

EDWARD. I know what you are driving at. The games have changed.

ERICA. Yes, grown up games; torn limbs and explosions. Listen to the children.

EDWARD. Such joy in their voices.

ERICA. Do you hear joy in my voice?

EDWARD. Why, I don't know how to answer that. Joy? In your voice?

ERICA. Yes, joy. Do you hear the sound of joy in my voice – like the children.

EDWARD. Well, not exactly like the children's voices, but there is a lilt of sorts.

ERICA. A lilt? A lilt in my voice?

EDWARD. Yes, I hear an inkling of happiness, a sort of upward inflection, not exactly like the children but somewhat in the family of joy.

Raymond J. Barry

ERICA. I'm glad there is some child left in me after a difficult morning. Yes, I have some joy left – after my spat . . . with that person . . . this morning.

EDWARD. Don't linger on that, whatever it was.

ERICA. It's too personal.

EDWARD. I'm not prying. Listen to the children.

ERICA. Yes, listen to them, the lilt of joy in their voices. I do love children. Most people are expendable, but not children, no not the children. It's the grownups who are expendable.

EDWARD. You keep saying that.

ERICA. Yes, I do and I mean every word. Oh, how I mean it. It's the way of the world. People come and go. We don't remember who just left. They've been replaced.

EDWARD. You mean me, don't you?

ERICA. You? Why you are a passing stranger soon to be forgotten.

EDWARD. I accept that, and desire nothing more.

ERICA. You're easily pleased.

EDWARD. A bit too easily pleased; compromise after compromise.

ERICA. You seem troubled.

EDWARD. Troubled? Who? Me? Troubled? Ridiculous. I'm in rare form today, rare form. I'm not troubled. Look, I'm dancing with joy. *[He does a little ballet]* Listen to my voice. Do I sound troubled?

ERICA. Well, I wouldn't have mentioned it if there wasn't a suggestion somewhere, somehow.

EDWARD. I don't mean to project anything too personal. That is, with my voice. I mean. . . . my voice doesn't project unhappiness, does it? I mean the authorities wouldn't pick up on anything . . . that is, if I smile and maintain a brightness in my speech.

ERICA. You do have a tendency to wonder into rather "gray areas," shall we say; all that chatter about the enemy, the bombing, your job, which, by the way should make anyone grateful; that is, the opportunity to maintain sustenance at a time when things are so very unsure. It's survival of the fittest out there, you know. Quitting your job, might not be the best thing at this time in history. It may not be the right thing. It's better to be on the inside rather than out; that is, if you want to survive.

EDWARD. Survive, survive.

ERICA. Well, survival is important, isn't it?

EDWARD. To a point.

ERICA. What point?

EDWARD. Dignity.

ERICA. Oh, yes, dignity, pride. We've all had moments of pride.

EDWARD. Nothing wrong with pride.

ERICA. Pride is expendable.

EDWARD. No, pride keeps us human. Pride is as significant as kindness. Without pride, we are willing to give our souls to the highest bidder.

[they turn their heads]

ERICA. I hear bombing.

Park Encounter

EDWARD. Yes, bombing, again bombing on a nice day like today. A nice day like today provides everything to live for, sunshine, fresh air, good company.

ERICA. *[looks up from her book]* Yes, lovely day.

EDWARD. I was in a completely different mood when I left my office today. I just didn't feel like beginning the day. Have you ever felt like that? I just didn't feel like it. Have you ever felt like that?

ERICA. Yes, of course, I have felt like that.

EDWARD. Then the sun came out and the breeze began to blow and I snapped out of it pretty fast. Then, later, I began to read my book, and in it there was a passage about the fall of Rome, and it made me nervous.

ERICA. Nothing to be nervous about. The fall of the Roman Empire happened a long time ago.

EDWARD. The fall of the Roman Empire is similar to our own fall, isn't it?

ERICA. Oh, please.

EDWARD. Well, think about it with all the corruption in our government.

ERICA. For someone who professes not to be a political pundit, you certainly talk a great deal about politics.

EDWARD. I don't mean to. I just find it interesting, that's all. *[pause]* Are you an honest person?

ERICA. Of course, I'm honest. What a bizarre question.

EDWARD. I've noticed a lack of honesty in our culture and I thought you might be dishonest yourself.

ERICA. Our country is very honest. Your assessment is flat-out wrong.

EDWARD. No, I see people cheating each other all the time. Hasn't that happened to you recently?

ERICA. Cheating?

EDWARD. Yes, cheating. Think hard now. Hasn't someone tried to cheat you recently? I bet they have.

ERICA. No, no one has tried to cheat me.

EDWARD. I don't believe you. People try to cheat you all the time, I bet.

ERICA. Only once.

EDWARD. There, you see?

ERICA. But that was an aberration.

EDWARD. How so?

ERICA. Well, I rented a summer house and put a security down on it and they refused to return the security, claiming I'd ruined some sheets and dirtied the floors. They made the whole thing up. I hadn't dirtied anything.

EDWARD. So they tried to keep the security.

ERICA. Yes, but that's not a reflection of everyone.

EDWARD. It is though. People are constantly trying to steal and cheat. We do the same to other countries, but corruption begins at home. We are a people who have lost our way, morally speaking. Are you aware of that?

ERICA. You're being a little harsh, aren't you?

Raymond J. Barry

EDWARD. Are you honest, an honest person?

ERICA. Of course, I'm honest.

EDWARD. Good. I feel safer then.

ERICA. No need to worry about me.

EDWARD. Oh, I'm not worried.

ERICA. Good.

EDWARD. I knew you were a generous person right away.

ERICA. You did? You knew?

EDWARD. Oh, yes, I knew right away.

ERICA. How did you know that?

EDWARD. From the way you shared your bench.

ERICA. That's normal. Nothing unusual about that.

EDWARD. I think it's unusual.

ERICA. There's nothing unusual about sharing a bench.

EDWARD. Oh, I don't know about that.

ERICA. You know, I don't mean to hurt your feelings, but you have a tendency to talk too much.

EDWARD. Someone has to do the talking.

ERICA. Do you really think so. I prefer to keep to myself and not talk. I have my reading.

EDWARD. You can both read and talk.

ERICA. Hardly.

EDWARD. You're doing both, aren't you?

ERICA. Yes, but I would have gotten much farther if I'd just read and you'd never have come along.

EDWARD. You're sitting on a public bench. You could have read at home. The general public passes here and the general public will occasionally open a conversation with you. "Hello, how are you? Lovely day we're having. Nice day for reading. Such a lovely day, isn't it?" I am the general public. I liked you and spoke to you. You responded. I even asked permission to sit next to you on this bench. How about that? *[pause]* I wish you liked me.

ERICA. *[looks up from her book]* I like you. Of course, I like you.

EDWARD. You behave as if you don't like me.

ERICA. Well, of course I like you. It's just that you're a stranger to me.

EDWARD. It's more difficult for a woman, isn't it?

ERICA. More difficult for what?

EDWARD. To express warmth to strangers.

ERICA. Yes. A woman has to be careful nowadays.

EDWARD. We've all become suspicious of each other; and with good reason I might add.

ERICA. Have we?

EDWARD. Are you really asking me?

ERICA. Yes, I'm truly interested.

EDWARD. Something mean-spirited about us as a people, trying to beat each other all the time, trying to win all the time.

ERICA. Win what?

EDWARD. Precisely; "Win what?" is the question.

Park Encounter

ERICA. There's nothing wrong with winning.

EDWARD. No? You're sure about that?

ERICA. Why would anyone want to lose?

EDWARD. Maybe losing isn't the alternative to winning.

ERICA. What would be the alternative?

EDWARD. How about sharing?

ERICA. Sharing what?

EDWARD. It's a foreign concept, isn't it?

ERICA. Now you're losing me. Please allow me to read my book in peace.

EDWARD. Of course, and I'll read mine. We'll share our reading experience together. Get it? "Share our reading experience?"

ERICA. Oh, yes, that is very funny. *[laughter]* Oh, my, I do enjoy reading in the park. I love it.

[silence; ERICA reads]

EDWARD. Oh, love. Ah, love.

[ERICA looks up and then returns to her book; silence.]

EDWARD. We only love a few times in our lives.

ERICA. *[reading]* Yes... ah... yes.

EDWARD. For me it's only happened four or five times. The first love, of course, when I was a teenager; Emily was her name. Boy, I still remember the first time we kissed each other goodnight. I ran all the way home, leaping up into the air and running. I was in a euphoric state, leaping into the sky, running all the way up to the moon and back again. My God, I was completely transformed by that simple kiss, sent to heaven in one instant, in love all at once. My God, I was in love. Were you in love when you were a teenager? *[ERICA continues reading]* Excuse me. Were you in love when you were a teenager?

ERICA. Oh... ah... certainly not. Please, I would like to read uninterrupted.

EDWARD. Of course, by all means. Don't mind me. I'm just reminiscing. *[silence for a while]* The second time I was in love was also during my teenage years. My goodness, I was completely overwhelmed by that little girl. Her name was Ellen. Oh, she was sweet, such a sweet little girl, but she was Jewish and her father didn't want me in the picture. Her father wanted his daughter to date only nice Jewish boys which I wasn't, but my God, I loved her. It was a pure love too, a clean and pure love that I've never experienced since. Somehow love became tainted after that, mostly by sex, which is a powerful force and an important ingredient of love, but as soon as sex became part of the experience, something innocent was lost. Love was mixed with possessiveness then. Have you ever been possessive? *[ERICA doesn't respond]* Excuse me, I'm sorry to disturb you. Have you ever been possessive?

ERICA. I beg your pardon?

EDWARD. Have you ever been possessive?

ERICA. Please, would you mind? I'm trying to read.

EDWARD. Oh, sure, right. Sorry.

[silence; ERICA reads; bombs bursting in the distance]

Raymond J. Barry

EDWARD. The third time I was in love was also with a Jewish girl, but this time sex was involved, real sex, which made the relationship stormy; we fought all the time. Of course, we loved each other, but, my goodness, with all that fighting we didn't stand a chance. The fourth time I was in love, I actually married the woman. She was the most beautiful of all of them. This was a German woman. Oh, my God, she was beautiful, so gorgeous, but that made things even more complicated. Everyone noticed her beauty, just everyone. Men were so attracted to her and she was just so insecure. Of course, I was jealous and possessive, didn't have the confidence necessary to remain calm when men were attracted to her. Somehow I took it as a personal threat. Ridiculous. Have you ever been jealous?

[ERICA doesn't respond.]

EDWARD. Excuse me, have you ever been jealous? Miss?

[ERICA doesn't respond. EDWARD touches her.]

ERICA. Don't touch me!!

EDWARD. Sorry. I was just asking if you'd ever been jealous?

ERICA. None of your business. Don't touch me.

EDWARD. I know. I heard you. I won't. We got divorced eventually, and after that I fell in love with a terribly insecure black woman, who thought I was looking to leave her at the drop of a hat.

ERICA. *[looks up from her book]* Look, mister, I'm not interested in your love life.

EDWARD. I can understand that.

ERICA. You should share your conversation with someone else. I'm not interested.

EDWARD. I was talking to myself.

ERICA. Yes, you were, because I wasn't listening.

EDWARD. You heard a little of what I said, didn't you?

ERICA. No, not a word.

EDWARD. But I was speaking very loudly.

ERICA. I agree, and I wasn't listening.

EDWARD. I'd be willing to bet you overheard some of it.

ERICA. Not a word. I was reading my book.

EDWARD. Just a few phrases here and there?

ERICA. *[putting her book down]* What do you want from me? Can't you see how oppressive you are? Do you have to impose yourself upon me? I didn't ask for your company. Now, please, be a gentleman and leave me alone.

EDWARD. All right. All right.

[ERICA reads; silence for a while. ERICA looks up and then checks to see if EDWARD is still there. He is staring at her.]

EDWARD. You're looking at me.

ERICA. Yes, I'm looking at you.

EDWARD. Don't mind me. I'm just an old man.

ERICA. What a thing to say.

EDWARD. It's the truth.

ERICA. Yes.

Park Encounter

EDWARD. What do you mean, "yes?"

ERICA. Yes, just yes.

EDWARD. You say "yes" quite often, don't you?

ERICA. I'm somewhat agreeable.

EDWARD. You are. That's the trouble with people nowadays. We don't know what's really going on, but we agree with everything.

ERICA. I don't agree with everything. We're strangers, buddy. We have no obligation to each other. I don't care about you and you don't care about me. It's every man for himself in this world, "survival of the fittest" and up to each individual to provide for his own happiness. You've obviously failed in that regard.

EDWARD. I really like you. *[no response]* You have a fine spirit about you. *[no response]* It's you who should be thanked.

ERICA. For what? Thanked for what exactly?

EDWARD. Thanked for being such a nice person.

ERICA. I'm not really nice. Don't think you can take advantage of me.

EDWARD. You seem nice. You seem like the kind of person who could be a good friend.

ERICA. I've had friends. They passed by the wayside.

EDWARD. Why?

ERICA. This is much too personal.

EDWARD. Sorry.

ERICA. You're getting into my personal life and I won't have it.

EDWARD. Would you enjoy going for a walk?

ERICA. Most certainly not.

EDWARD. Just thought I'd ask.

ERICA. Out of the question.

EDWARD. Trying to be nice. Just thought I'd ask.

ERICA. I'm waiting for someone.

EDWARD. You think I'm the enemy?

ERICA. One never knows.

EDWARD. You'll contact the authorities about me?

ERICA. No, I wouldn't do that.

EDWARD. People are doing that nowadays.

ERICA. I haven't told on anyone. Well, maybe one person, but in her case it was obvious.

EDWARD. Who was she?

ERICA. Just a friend.

EDWARD. Your friend?

ERICA. She turned out to be an enemy.

EDWARD. Then you did the right thing.

ERICA. Oh, yes.

EDWARD. Wonder what she did?

ERICA. Always talking about kindness and generosity. She was up to no good.

EDWARD. Then you did the right thing.

ERICA. Yes, I did the right thing.

EDWARD. You got rid of your friend, as you should have, I suppose.

Raymond J. Barry

ERICA. Yes, she's out of my life. She complained about things.

EDWARD. I complain about things.

ERICA. I know you do. I've been aware of that.

EDWARD. Good thing we're friends.

ERICA. There are no friends. Just people on our side or enemies on the other side, the ones who should be bombed, destroyed. That's the way the world has evolved over time. We have to be honest with ourselves and refuse to sentimentalize. Some people are important. Others are not. Some people are expendable. Others are not.

EDWARD. I mean no harm.

ERICA. I'm sure you mean no harm, but I would like some privacy. I would like to relax and read my book. *[rises from the bench]* It was very nice talking to you.

EDWARD. Are you leaving?

ERICA. No, you're leaving. You must go now. You ask too many questions.

[simultaneous]

EDWARD.	**ERICA.**
I'll stop asking questions.	You must stop asking questions.

EDWARD. What shall we say to each other?

ERICA. Anything.

[simultaneous]

EDWARD.	**ERICA.**
Anything?	Yes, anything that's not personal.

EDWARD. Everything is personal.

[simultaneous]

EDWARD.	**ERICA.**
Sure it is.	Everything is not personal.

ERICA. We can talk about lots of things that aren't personal. The beautiful park, for example. The birds, the trees, nature and reading. I love reading on this bench. I met my husband Paul right here on this bench.

EDWARD. On this bench?

ERICA. Yes, this bench became precious to us. He stood right there and asked me my name. I was reading at the time and didn't want to be bothered, but he was so tall and impressive looking. I couldn't resist responding.

EDWARD. You've been married for years?

ERICA. That's what I said.

EDWARD. Oh, I see.

Park Encounter

ERICA. I don't talk to strange men as a rule, but Paul was special. He was different than most men. As soon as we began speaking we felt something. At least I did. We've been coming to this bench ever since. We love it so, our bench. We never argue here; at home - but not here. The stress of daily living leaves us when we sit on our bench and the triviality of life is forgotten providing a feeling of love between Paul and me. *[emphatically]* Now you really should go. I want you to go. This is my territory, you see. This is a sacred place for me and my husband. This is where we met before we took our wedding vows. Paul and I will not be imposed upon by a common beggar who can't take care of his own needs! You, sir, are the worst kind of predator. Now be a nice man and find another place to nest before Paul arrives.

EDWARD. But I've fallen in love with you, Erica. Don't you ever long to connect with people? To reach out and hug everyone who crosses your path, just to tell them not to be afraid, that there's nothing to fear, nothing to run away from, and that I am a kind person, who has nothing but goodness on my mind, nothing but goodness and kindness, and gosh wouldn't it be just so nice if we were friends, good, close friends who will do everything in our power to benefit the other. Isn't it possible to just reach out and give me a hug?

ERICA. *[standing]* Oh, Paul is coming. I see Paul in the distance. Oh, Paul! Paul! Paul! Over here! Over here!

EDWARD. *[hides behind a bush, stage left]* I must go. It's Paul.

ERICA. No, I think it'll be okay. I want you to meet Paul.

EDWARD. I can't. I'm not confident. I'm in transition. I'm not at my best.

ERICA. Don't be silly. You look fine. You are fine. Paul! Over here! That's funny. He's turning the other way. It's not Paul after all. It looked so much like Paul, with the same broad shoulders and manly gait.

EDWARD. Paul has a manly gait?

ERICA. Oh, yes, very manly his gait.

EDWARD. I see. You must be very attracted to him.

ERICA. Yes, I am.

EDWARD. I see. I wish you liked me.

ERICA. I like you.

EDWARD. You really do?

ERICA. I hardly know you.

EDWARD. That doesn't matter. We can like each other.

ERICA. We all need to be liked.

EDWARD. Why are people so mean to each other then?

ERICA. There are certain people who can't be trusted. It ruins it for everyone.

EDWARD. You mean the enemy?

ERICA. Yes, that's it, the enemy.

EDWARD. What if there were no enemy? What if the so-called enemy were just a fabrication made up by men for their own personal gain?

ERICA. I'm sorry, I just think you are bizarre.

EDWARD. Are you attracted to me?

Raymond J. Barry

ERICA. You are bizarre. I have a husband!!

EDWARD. Aren't I likeable?

ERICA. No, I don't like you.

EDWARD. Oh, you do.

ERICA. Do you think I like everyone who accosts me on a park bench and interrupts me from my Tolstoy?

[heads turn in direction of bombing]

EDWARD. The bombing is closer than before. Is the enemy fighting back? Weren't they supposed to be helpless? Aren't they helpless?

ERICA. They're just closer, that's all.

EDWARD. Yes, the enemy has never fought back. There's nothing to worry about. Bomb after bomb; limb after limb; child after child.

ERICA. I'm happy. I'm very happy. I'm a very happy person. I'd like to spend this time relaxing. It's my day off from work.

EDWARD. Your day off from work, meaning you work six days a week for some company?

ERICA. Yes, I work.

EDWARD. You spend most of your time working, don't you?

ERICA. Yes, most of my time, just like the rest of the world.

EDWARD. Some have escaped that oppressive pattern.

ERICA. I suppose you don't work.

EDWARD. I don't. I'm quitting my job. I own my own soul.

ERICA. Well, aren't we awfully judgmental.

EDWARD. Trust me, I'm on your side.

ERICA. That's comforting.

EDWARD. The working woman.

ERICA. Yes.

EDWARD. Hard at work.

ERICA. Yes.

EDWARD. Very little time for folks like me.

ERICA. I'm not in the habit of bothering with strangers.

EDWARD. You work for a corporation, don't you?

ERICA. That's none of your business.

EDWARD. Which one is it?

ERICA. I'm not telling.

EDWARD. Typical. Corporate people always withhold information. You're a secretive bunch.

ERICA. I'm not part of any group.

EDWARD. That's it. Keep it to yourself. Protect the cabal.

ERICA. What cabal?

EDWARD. The cabal you work for. You're not fooling anyone. You're part of the giant conspiracy that's vying for global power, jockeying for control of all the natural resources out there, oil in particular, so you can manipulate the rest of the world.

ERICA. You're crazy.

EDWARD. That's the normal reaction, the easy reaction, but it won't work this time. I know too much.

ERICA. I like my life, Eddie. I'm proud of myself. I've worked very hard

Park Encounter

to shape my life into something I respect. I like money, both the challenge of earning it and the self-satisfaction that comes with shaping a life-style that appeals to me, the comfort of a soft bed at night and money in my pocket that will provide a meal in a restaurant any time I want it. I enjoy stylish clothing and feminine shoes that make me look attractive. All of that takes money which I and my husband earn by working hard. There's no need for me to feel guilty about my enjoyment of earning money either. It is a rare pleasure for me to have something that brings self-esteem. There is little out there in the world that brings joy to me, so very little. Do you like my shoes?

EDWARD. Oh, yes, I like them. I like them very much.

ERICA. They're expensive. I like them too.

EDWARD. Pretty legs.

ERICA. Thank you. I take care of myself by belonging to an expensive gymnasium.

EDWARD. You treat yourself very well.

ERICA. And why not? Nothing wrong with treating myself well, is there? *[no response]* You seem judgmental with your holier-than-thou attitude. What puts you on such a high pedestal? Who, aside from yourself, put you there? What is it about you that makes you better than I? Have you done anything that merits attention. Anything I don't know of?

EDWARD. I won the Binai Brith Award for good citizenship in my senior year of high school.

ERICA. Really? Then why do you feel so superior to me? Is it because you hate corporations and think it is immoral to earn large sums of money? What permission have you given yourself to stand above us all? I'm a worthy person too.

EDWARD. You are a worthy person.

ERICA. You condescend to me. Do you know that? You condescend as if you have a right but you don't have a right. You seem to think that you know the right path, that the way of business is for some reason not moral simply because of the profit it brings to those who engage. What's wrong with profit? Why have you decided that wealth is an evil thing? What gave you that idea? *[no response]* Do you like my outfit?

EDWARD. Oh, yes, I do. It is very pretty, very nice.

ERICA. It is expensive, very expensive.

EDWARD. I bet, from the looks of it.

ERICA. I enjoy looking good.

EDWARD. I understand. I enjoy looking good too.

ERICA. You don't look good.

EDWARD. I don't?

ERICA. No, you don't look good, something out of place about you; something doesn't add up.

EDWARD. It has taken a while for me to learn how to present myself.

ERICA. Yes, I can see that. You don't quite pull it off.

EDWARD. I don't?

ERICA. Something is missing – balance mostly, a lack of balance. You're

Raymond J. Barry

desperate, too desperate. Learn to accept things the way they are. Learn to go with the flow. You'll be better off. You're trying too hard. Don't try so much. It's not appealing.

EDWARD. It isn't?

ERICA. Not really. A woman doesn't like to see a man so desperate. It is not manly. You're not manly when you talk the way you do. Who cares about those things you seem so concerned about. Just make some money, buy a house and hide in it away from the troubles of the world. Nothing is going to change anyway. You can jabber away about all sorts of things, but nothing will be different. You'll be delivering the same speech twenty years from now and everything will be the same. There'll still only be the winners and the losers in the end. And you'll be on the wrong side. You'll be one of the losers. You're already a loser, quitting your job like that. What an immature thing to do just to "own your own soul." Such rhetoric really. Where did you pick up such foolish ideas and be foolish enough to believe you could actually cut off your income. Immature, so terribly immature.

EDWARD. You're making me feel bad about myself.

ERICA. You're trying much too hard. Relax. Let things unfold on their own without so much effort.

EDWARD. I like you. I really like your spirit. I think you're great, absolutely great, and attractive too. I don't want to be a pest. It's just . . . well, I've had a job for years working for a large company, and so, you see, I'm in the middle of everything I was accusing you of before, and, I simply need to talk, that's all. Just want to talk. I'm an economist. What do you do?

ERICA. I don't want to tell you what I do for a living, Eddie.

EDWARD. Fair enough. You don't have to tell me. Fair enough. I'm about to quit my job. But I haven't the courage. I've gotten used to the money, but I should quit. They pay me well, but the work . . . As I say I'm an economist, but often I lie about economic forecasts. I'm not an economist really. I dabble. I make projections, that's all, but I just can't do it anymore, persuading undeveloped countries to borrow huge sums of money, which puts them in debt forever and then we've got them. I'm talking about greed primarily, taking advantage of the world's weak. I don't know. I feel guilty about my part in the whole thing. It's confusing. It's such a dirty business, Panama, Ecuador, Chile, Nicaragua. I shouldn't be talking about this to strangers. I shouldn't. I'm trapped. Thank you for listening.

ERICA. Do you like my jewelry?

EDWARD. Oh, yes, I like it. It looks good.

ERICA. My jewelry cost money. It is expensive but I can afford it with my so-called corporate salary. The corporation I work for provides a life-style that I'm in agreement with. I'm proud of myself to be a part of it, proud that I can afford expensive jewelry and clothing. I'm on the winning side. You're on the losing side with all of your foolish rhetoric. If you don't learn to go with the flow, you're going to find yourself in trouble, deep trouble.

Park Encounter

EDWARD. What kind of trouble?

ERICA. You'll see. You're not part of the team, buster. You're nothing more than a mangy beggar on the outside, trying to expose everyone on the inside, as if we were bad people because we make money. So what if we make money? So what if we have a powerful influence? The corporate sector is what makes the world go round, and I'm part of it and proud of that. What's wrong with winning?

EDWARD. Tolstoy wrote about the relationship between the rich and the poor.

ERICA. I'll fix you. I'm going to call the police.

[simultaneous]

ERICA.	EDWARD.
I'm trying to have a calm day. Now, please, allow me to read my book and stop interrupting me.	I'll stop! I'll be good. Please don't call the police. It would create too much of a fuss. See? I'm reading again.

[silence; ERICA reads; EDWARD reading out loud from his book]

EDWARD. "Ecuadorian rainforests are precious, as are the forests of North America, the Savannas of Africa, or the icecaps of the Arctic. Every one of these represents a battle line, forcing us to search the depths of our individual and collective souls."

ERICA. Ho – hum.

EDWARD. You don't care, do you?

ERICA. No, I don't care.

EDWARD. All you care about is your Tolstoy and your Paul.

ERICA. That's my choice.

EDWARD. Where is Paul anyway? When's he getting his big ass here?

ERICA. Never mind Paul. He'll be here.

EDWARD. I have things to talk about.

ERICA. Oh, don't I know it.

EDWARD. Yes, I have plenty to talk about with Paul.

[heads turn upward to sound of helicopter]

EDWARD. Police helicopters overhead.

ERICA. Don't talk to me, please.

EDWARD. If the police didn't exist, would we behave the same?

ERICA. They probably know you're not wanted here.

EDWARD. I'm wanted here.

ERICA. Not by me you aren't.

EDWARD. Do you really mean that, miss? I don't know your name. Please tell me your name?

ERICA. My name is Erica.

EDWARD. Erica. *[looks above]* Them and their helicopters, Erica, spying on our every move.

ERICA. Police don't bother me.

EDWARD. They disgust me.

ERICA. Police protect us.

Raymond J. Barry

EDWARD. Little boy scouts with their guns and clubs and handcuffs.
ERICA. Police insure my safety.
EDWARD. I don't need police to tell me what to do. *[helicopter sound diminishes in distance]* Good, they're flying away to bother someone else. Listen. *[listens to the birds]* The music of birds is a far more beautiful sound than helicopters that grate the nerves and make us feel we're being watched. I don't like being watched. We can make choices without them interfering. I won't be interfered with. I will do what I please. I refuse to give in to them. Watch this. *[EDWARD shouts to the sky]* I refuse to give in to you, Mr. Policeman!! *[EDWARD spots something above.]* Another plane passing by. I wonder what this son-of-a-gun wants.
ERICA. Just passing by.
EDWARD. Probably carrying bombs.
ERICA. Yes, destroying the enemy.
[heads turn towards bombing in the distance; EDWARD stands, crosses downstage toward sound of the bombing]
EDWARD. Bomb after bomb, destroying the enemy. Don't you trust me, Erica?
ERICA. Don't have to trust you. We'll never see each other again.
[ERICA gets up]
EDWARD. Wait a damned minute!
ERICA. Don't talk to me that way! Who do you think you are?
EDWARD. I'm Edward. That's all, just Edward.
ERICA. Well, Ed, it's been nice knowing you.
[ERICA attempts to go]
EDWARD. No, please, don't go quite yet. Let's make a time to meet one another, just one more time. Please? You're a nice person, a special person. Maybe it's possible to form a friendship, some kind of friendship. I'm getting old and people don't talk to me much anymore and I'm sort of, well . . . lonely. There I've admitted it.

[simultaneous]

EDWARD.	**ERICA.**
Would you meet me one more time, I'm nice. I'm a nice person. I really am a nice person. I can tell you're a nice person too. I'm lonely and out of touch with people in my life, and I just like you, that's all, and I want to be your friend.	Look, Ed... if that's really your name, I appreciate your interest, but, you see, I have a life and a husband. We've been married for years, so I can't be traipsing off with any stranger who starts talking to me. Leave me alone. Just leave me alone.

[Slow turn of their heads toward sound of bombs exploding in the distance. Heads turn slowly back. EDWARD takes a small step towards ERICA. She moves away from him]
EDWARD. Are you afraid of me?

Park Encounter

ERICA. You wouldn't hurt me, would you?
EDWARD. I long for something personal between us.
ERICA. What do you mean by personal?
EDWARD. Where we know secrets.
ERICA. I have no secrets.
EDWARD. You have absolutely no secrets?
ERICA. No, none.
EDWARD. I long for something more, more substance in our conversation, more substance. You don't say anything. All you do is talk. Oh, God, my head, the tension in my head!
ERICA. *[exits]* You're frightening me.
EDWARD. No, you mustn't go. I won't allow it. You must stay.
ERICA. You can't make me stay. I'm leaving.
EDWARD. No, you're not. *[grabs ERICA'S arm]*
ERICA. Don't touch me!
    [ERICA screams]
EDWARD. Take it easy, lady! You don't have to scream! I'm not raising my voice, am I? I'm not flailing my arms and kicking my legs, am I?

[simultaneous]

EDWARD.	**ERICA.**
I'm clean-shaven and well-groomed. My hair is combed. Why would I be accused of raving? I simply care. Somebody has to care, so I'll be the one. It's so easy not to care, so easy to ignore what they are doing, so easy to give up.	You're raving!! Officer! Officer! Officer!......... Police! Is there a policeman in the area? Over here!...... Officer!

ERICA. Officer! Officer!

[simultaneous]

EDWARD.	**ERICA.**
What are you doing? Don't call a cop! I'm not hurting you! Stop it. You're making a huge mistake! All right, all right, I'll shut up. I'll be a good boy. See, I'm reading my book.	Officer! Over here. *[pause]* This man is bothering me. *[pause]* He won't leave my bench! *[pause]* Officer! *[pause]* Please, help, help!

ERICA. I want you to leave my bench.
EDWARD. It's not your bench. It's a public bench.
ERICA. You are harassing me.
EDWARD. No, I'm not. It's my word against yours.
ERICA. You think you can steal my bench from me, but you're wrong.

Raymond J. Barry

No one is going to steal my bench from me. I have rights too. The rudeness of your behavior, the outright rudeness. *[She looks inside her purse.]* Just wait till I show you what I have here. If I can find it. I know I have it somewhere.

[simultaneous]

ERICA.	EDWARD.
Here in my purse. You'd better leave immediately if you know what's good for you. You'd better. Just wait. It's in here somewhere. All right, I've	I won't hurt you. If you only knew how harmless I really am. I couldn't hurt a flea. I just need help with things, some little bit of help with things.

ERICA. Got it right here. Here it is right here.

[ERICA brandishes a tiny penknife, a small one, but nonetheless a knife.]

ERICA. Here, now what do you have to say to me? Not so communicative now, are you? Nothing coming out of your mouth now, is it? Well, well, speak. Say something. Cat got your tongue? My, aren't you the quiet one.

EDWARD. I'm not afraid of dying.

ERICA. This is my bench. You get off this bench and leave this place. Leave me alone.

EDWARD. No.

ERICA. I'll stab you.

EDWARD. No, you won't.

ERICA. I might.

EDWARD. I don't think so.

ERICA. Why?

EDWARD. I don't pose any threat to you. We're both harmless to each other.

ERICA. You're not harmless. You annoy me.

EDWARD. That doesn't merit a death penalty.

ERICA. I just want to be left alone.

[bombs in the distance; heads turn out to audience]

EDWARD. They're bombing again.

[heads turn back to each other]

ERICA. I'll stab you.

EDWARD. Please do.

ERICA. I will stab you.

EDWARD. I want you to.

ERICA. No, you don't.

EDWARD. Yes, I do. Stab me.

ERICA. I will.

EDWARD. You probably won't but I want you to.

ERICA. I'll do it.

EDWARD. Have you ever felt love for a perfect stranger?

Park Encounter

ERICA. Yes... no.
EDWARD. You said "yes" first.
ERICA. I meant "no." It was a mistake.

[simultaneous]

EDWARD.	ERICA.
I feel love for you, a perfect stranger, threatening me with a knife and so vulnerable, so sensitive, at your wits' end.	Yes... no... you'd best stop talking to me and leave before something terrible happens. Something could happen. Something terrible could happen.

EDWARD. Like what? What would happen? You have the knife. You have the power. You're safe from me. I can't do anything to you. You'll stab me.
ERICA. No, I will... do something.
EDWARD. Come here, closer to me.

[simultaneous]

EDWARD.	ERICA.
I'm at my wits end too; nowhere to turn, nowhere to go. I can't even go	No, be careful. You're harassing me. I have every justification to attack.

EDWARD. . . . home. People are looking for me. You'd be doing me a favor by stabbing me with your little penknife. Why don't you do it?
ERICA. My husband is coming.
EDWARD. You knew I would come.
ERICA. I didn't know.
EDWARD. You knew I would.
ERICA. I resisted you from the beginning.
EDWARD. You resisted and I persisted.
ERICA. Get away.
EDWARD. You don't sound very convincing.
ERICA. I don't?
EDWARD. No, you don't.
    [EDWARD grabs ERICA and kisses her; she breaks away from him. Silence; she sits on the bench, facing the audience]
ERICA. How dare you. How dare you force me to be intimate. You forced me. What I just did was not usual for me. I'm not used to kissing strangers. Usually I'm rational. My behavior is usually well thought out. I plan things ahead. I've always planned things ahead. This wasn't planned. My book! My book! My book! Where is my Tolstoy. I must read.
EDWARD. Yes, read. Go ahead, read.
ERICA. Yes, I shall.

Raymond J. Barry

EDWARD. Concentrate on your Tolstoy.

ERICA. How dare you treat me like a common tramp. What puts you on such a high pedestal? Why are you the custodian of the planet? Who placed you in that position? Your "holier-than-thou" attitude implies that you're better than I. Exactly what is it that makes you better? Have you done something special I'm not aware of, something that merits special attention? Anything special about you that I don't know of?

EDWARD. No, nothing special.

ERICA. Then why do you feel so superior to me? Why do you treat me like a whore? Is it because I work for a corporation? Do you think I'm immoral because I earn large sums of money? You have no job, no income. You'll be begging on the streets soon. Just give it some time. You'll be begging on the streets. I see them every day, those beggars. They quit their jobs too once, and now they have nothing. They judged the system too and now they have nothing. Those beggars in the street resisted the flow of things when they shouldn't have, so the system took care of the problem by getting rid of them, by depositing them onto the street in the gutter. That's where you're going to end up if you quit that good job of yours - in the gutter. I'll never end up in the gutter. I'm too proud to end up in the gutter, too proud to be kissing strangers. If my husband should find out. *[looks off into distance]* Oh, there he is. Thank God. Paul! Oh, Paul.

[simultaneous]

ERICA.	**EDWARD.**
[referring to EDWARD] Stay where you are! He's already seen you. He can't help but to see you talking to me. *[back to PAUL]* Over here, Paul. Over here. Paul! We're over here! Yes, come Paul, darling. Come here, darling.	Is he coming? Is that he? My God, I know that man. I've done business with that man. I do know him. We've had dealings with each other, yes. I do know him.

ERICA. You know him. You know my Paul? Oh, Paul is really coming. Brace up. Make yourself presentable, and, above all, stop slouching. Sit up. You're slouching. Oh, yes, it's him. It's my husband. Hello, Paul!! Paul, darling, over here!! He's coming. Please, straighten yourself up. You look haggard. Smile a bit. Try to alter the mood here. Smile and, please, sit up straight. For God's sake take that expression off your face.

EDWARD. I'm looking my best. I'm smiling.

ERICA. Let's pretend we're reading.

> *[PAUL enters surreptitiously, elegantly dressed in a business suit, cautiously sits down between them on the bench. From his furtive manner one could deduce that someone might be*

Park Encounter

following him.]
ERICA. You took long enough.
PAUL. Had errands.
ERICA. Errands?
PAUL. Yes, numerous errands.
ERICA. I see. *[pause]* Have you no reading material?
PAUL. That's one errand I forgot.
ERICA. I see, absentminded.
   [silence, ERICA reads. EDWARD reads. PAUL sits.]
PAUL. Lovely day.
EDWARD. *[looking up from his book]* I was just commenting about that.
PAUL. I beg your pardon?
EDWARD. The day. I was just commenting about the day. Lovely.
PAUL. Yes, lovely.
ERICA. Edward, this is my husband.
EDWARD. Hello, Paul.
PAUL. You know my name?
EDWARD. The oil man.
ERICA. Oh, yes, Edward says you know each other.
EDWARD. Oh, yes, Paul, the oil man, destroyer of natural wildlife, barbarian killer of indigenous people and all that is beautiful on our planet.
PAUL. For Erica's sake, I'll let that one slide. Up to your old tricks again, eh, Eddie?
EDWARD. No tricks... and, please, don't call me Eddie.
ERICA. He likes to be called Edward. It's more elegant, less rural.
EDWARD. *[referring to ERICA]* Your wife is charming. You've done very well for yourself, Paul, very well indeed.
PAUL. Thank you. Erica and I have a good life, a civilized life.
EDWARD. Yes, oil.
PAUL. Oil, yes. Thank God for oil, good old oil. Made us rich.
EDWARD. I'm rich too. I have a million.
PAUL. Oh, I have quite a bit more than a million.
EDWARD. I've got to make more money.
PAUL. Sure, a million isn't enough. You've got to make two, three million.
EDWARD. Or a billion. That would cover it.
PAUL. Yes, that would make ends meet. Ha, ha, ha!
   [PAUL AND EDWARD howl with laughter.]
ERICA. *[uncomfortable pause]* My husband is a very important man.
EDWARD. *[uncomfortable pause]* Your wife is reading Tolstoy.
PAUL. You actually know what my wife is reading?
EDWARD. It came up in our conversation, Tolstoy; she's reading his short story, 'The Death of Ivan Illyich.' Have you read Tolstoy?
PAUL. No time for books.
EDWARD. Right busy, busy, busy. How's business? Still milking them for all they're worth? Sly, clever Paul.
PAUL. Come, come now, Edward, you've had a hand in it. You know

Raymond J. Barry

very well how things work.

ERICA. Edward has been up to something not quite on the up and up.

PAUL. You've heard bits and pieces, have you?

ERICA. Edward said a few things.

EDWARD. Various issues, Ecuadorian rainforests, illegal drilling.

PAUL. Get off your soapbox, Edward.

EDWARD. I'm just getting started; the dam in Ecuador flooded the land of indigenous tribes.

PAUL. You received a pay hike.

EDWARD. Blood money. . .

[simultaneous]

EDWARD.	**PAUL.**
. . . we destroyed people's land, their livelihood. The majority of people didn't benefit. Most of the people have	The country benefited. Hydro-electric power provides electricity for the surrounding area.

EDWARD. . . . no electricity. Only the rich owned factories that used electricity. Only the rich own the dam.

PAUL. We're comfortable. That's the main thing.

EDWARD. You're comfortable. I'm not. I'm getting out.

ERICA. Oh, yes, he's quitting his job, darling.

PAUL. We're not discussing business here, are we, Eddie?

EDWARD. It would take two of us to talk. Everything seems driven by money.

ERICA. Paul and I do good things with our money. Paul and I are generous givers. It's good for the soul to be generous.

EDWARD. A generous couple.

PAUL. After the wars came the bombing and with the bombing our soldiers lost arms and legs, not as many arms and legs as the enemy lost, but enough for Erica and me to donate our money. My wife and I are very good people. Hearing those bombs every day has made us conscious of our fallen heroes, debilitated wrecks of men really. We have a heart, my wife and I, constantly donating our money.

EDWARD. The wars have brought out the best in you and your wife.

ERICA. We don't have to fight in the wars. We are safe and sound. And so we give our money to our heroes with no arms and legs.

EDWARD. All your money?

PAUL. No, not all, only some of it.

EDWARD. How much?

PAUL. That's personal if you don't mind.

EDWARD. Oh, come on, you can tell me.

ERICA. A great deal of money.

EDWARD. A great deal of money for our fallen heroes.

PAUL. For our fallen heroes, yes. We are good people. Erica and I are very good people.

EDWARD. How much for a loss of limb?

PAUL. We don't itemize arms and legs that way.

Park Encounter

EDWARD. Well, then how do you know what is done with the money?

PAUL. We know. We know. There are ways.

ERICA. We are good people.

EDWARD. Do you save the money that's left over from the money you give?

ERICA. Yes, we save the rest for a rainy day.

EDWARD. That's smart, very smart.

ERICA. Oh, we're smart people, my husband and I.

EDWARD. I sense that, yes. *[Bombing goes off in the distance. Heads turn.]* Those damned, noisy wars. What did you do with your money before the wars began?

ERICA. I don't remember that far back.

PAUL. The wars have always been there, Eddie.

ERICA. I've grown used to the bombing. The sound offers a rhythm for the day, music of sorts.

EDWARD. Of course, we don't hear the screaming.

ERICA. No, we're too far away to hear the screaming. Although the bombing is getting nearer these days, isn't it, darling?

PAUL. Yes, it is getting nearer, much nearer lately.

ERICA. Makes me wonder what's going on.

EDWARD. We're probably losing.

PAUL. Losing? We're not losing. Impossible to lose. Oh, heavens, no. How could we be losing? We've spent so much money.

EDWARD. We'll have to spend more money.

PAUL. No, Eddie, we are not losing. We could never lose. But enough of this shameful talk of losing. This is rest time. We're in the park. Enjoy the scenery, my friend. Oh, this is nice; fresh air, a cool breeze. Look at the squirrels, and the birds flying above. Yes, this is a lovely spot. Tell me, Eddie, what are you really doing here with my wife?

EDWARD. At first I didn't know she was your wife, but she was reading Tolstoy, and who else's wife would be reading Tolstoy?

PAUL. Ha, reading Tolstoy. That's a good one, Tolstoy.

EDWARD. Yes, it is, a good one. Tolstoy.

    [EDWARD AND PAUL uproarious laughter]

PAUL. Oh, boy.

ERICA. Oh boy is right. Well, this is nice. You two know each other.

PAUL. Yes . . . *[another sputter of laughter]*. . . oh, boy, oh, boy . . . ah . . . . geez where is this life of mine taking me? I try to do the right thing, but what do I know? How could I come to the park to meet my wife and not know that Edward would be here with her? How could I not know that? I'm still naïve. What have I done to deserve this?

ERICA. You haven't done a thing, darling.

PAUL. He doesn't fool me. He's not here by chance.

EDWARD. Not if Tolstoy has anything to do with it.

PAUL. Tolstoy has everything to do with it, or at least the woman reading him. She has nothing to do with our business, you know. She is my wife.

EDWARD. Yes, I know.

Raymond J. Barry

ERICA. I've already made that clear.

PAUL. So you did.

EDWARD. You've both got that fact firmly established.

PAUL. Good, that was my intention, nothing more, nothing less.

EDWARD. I'll read my book and leave you two alone.

>*[pause; EDWARD reads.]*

PAUL. So, my dear, how long have you and Eddie been at it?

ERICA. "At it"? I don't like the way that sounds, darling.

PAUL. I know him, Erica; his charming flow of words, his alleged concern for mankind. I know him very well.

>*[bombs explode in the distance]*

EDWARD. Ha. Ha. Ha. Ha. *[chuckles at something he's reading]* Ha. Ha. Ha. Ha.

PAUL. Something funny?

ERICA. Don't bother with him.

PAUL. He could be laughing at me.

ERICA. Don't encourage him.

PAUL. I'll try to ignore him.

EDWARD. Ha. Ha. Ha. Ha.

PAUL. He's guffawing now.

ERICA. Just let him be.

PAUL. Were you talking to him before?

ERICA. A little. Nothing to speak of.

PAUL. Mustn't carry on with strangers.

ERICA. We spoke briefly.

>*[EDWARD'S laughter subsides.]*

EDWARD. Not as briefly as she makes out.

ERICA. We didn't speak much.

EDWARD. I consider it to be a rather lengthy . . .

>*[simultaneous]*

EDWARD.	**ERICA.**
. . . and informative conversation about all sorts of things.	It was inevitable that one of us would speak. He just walked up to

ERICA. . . . my bench and sat.

EDWARD. I wanted to rest.

ERICA. We were sitting side by side.

PAUL. Was it a friendly chat?

ERICA. On his side, yes. I was withholding.

EDWARD. She spoke as much as I.

ERICA. Liar!!!

>*[silence; ERICA and EDWARD face off; PAUL simmers; more*
>*silence; bombs in the distance; heads slowly turn]*

ERICA. Those bombs are getting closer, darling.

PAUL. Don't worry about the bombs. We're safe, my dearest. We have each other.

Park Encounter

ERICA. Are you sure?

PAUL. Of course I'm sure. When haven't I been sure?

ERICA. You're always sure, aren't you, darling?

PAUL. One has to be sure.

ERICA. I'm sure I'm safe. That's the important thing.

PAUL. We're both safe.

EDWARD. What about me? Aren't I safe too?

[simultaneous]

PAUL.	ERICA.
You'll never be safe!	You'll never be safe!

EDWARD. I don't feel safe.

ERICA. You aren't safe.

PAUL. No, you aren't safe. You have made enemies, Eddie, boy.

EDWARD. We've all made enemies.

PAUL. But you've not only made enemies with me. You've made enemies within the group.

EDWARD. Oh, yes, the group.

ERICA. What group?

PAUL. Edward knows what group. I don't have to tell him. They're looking for you, Eddie boy.

EDWARD. I've done nothing wrong.

PAUL. There has been talk.

EDWARD. What talk?

PAUL. Reference to a certain party who might divulge important, private information.

ERICA. He was talking about his work.

PAUL. Yes, our work.

EDWARD. I'm leaving the group.

PAUL. You'll be lonely, Eddie, boy.

EDWARD. I can't lie anymore. I have a conscience.

PAUL. Forget conscience. Just enjoy the profits. Wasn't it fun to be one of the group? Didn't you like the way people treated you, how they listened to what you had to say, how they served you? Gave you anything you wished, wine, women, money.

ERICA. He's a fool. He has so little money. It'll be gone before he knows it.

PAUL. Once you're in, it is impossible to leave without repercussions.

EDWARD. Repercussions? What repercussions?

PAUL. Come, come now, Edward, you little worm. Don't be naïve.

EDWARD. I'm not used to being hunted.

ERICA. Perhaps I should call the authorities.

EDWARD. I should leave the area.

PAUL. Stay, Edward, change your mind.

ERICA. We have a future and we will help you.

PAUL. Enjoy what you have established for yourself.

ERICA. I was confused once.

Raymond J. Barry

PAUL. You must never quit, Ed.

ERICA. And then Paul straightened me out.

PAUL. Retire, yes, but quit, no. Bow out peacefully when you get tired, but don't quit. You know too much. You've seen too much. There's too much at stake.

ERICA. Don't give up, Ed.

EDWARD. I'm not giving up. I'm just beginning.

PAUL. Beginning what?

EDWARD. You'll see.

PAUL. What are you up to?

EDWARD. You'll see.

PAUL. What is on your mind, Ed. Tell me.

EDWARD. Fresh air, trees, water, fish, birds, and, above all, peace of mind. Thank God I have no children.

[silence; Paul simmering]

PAUL. You knew I was coming.

ERICA. Yes, I knew.

PAUL. And still you couldn't wait.

EDWARD. Wait for what?

PAUL. Wait for me, your husband.

ERICA. I was waiting while we spoke.

EDWARD. People speak to each other while they wait.

ERICA. I spoke to Edward while I waited. I shouldn't have spoken while I waited but I did speak while I waited.

EDWARD. It's normal for people to speak to each other while they wait.

ERICA. It is normal, darling.

[silence; ERICA and EDWARD read; Paul simmers]

PAUL. I am her husband.

EDWARD. Yes, we've been through that already.

PAUL. So, you can understand my concern.

EDWARD. Of course, I do understand. I was a stranger to her at the time of our conversation.

PAUL. That is my point.

EDWARD. Of course, a point well taken.

ERICA. I had no idea that you knew each other at the time, darling.

EDWARD. Yes, your wife and I have a few things in common.

[silence; EDWARD reads; PAUL simmers]

PAUL. What did I tell you about talking to strangers?

ERICA. I know. You were right.

PAUL. I wish you would listen to me.

EDWARD. No harm was done.

PAUL. I arrived in the nick of time.

EDWARD. We were getting along. Weren't we Erica?

PAUL. He knows your name? You gave him your name?

ERICA. Of course. It's normal to give one's name.

PAUL. Not normal.

EDWARD. What's in a name?

PAUL. The beginning of friendship.

Park Encounter

EDWARD. Exactly. Is it not allowed?

PAUL. Not with strangers.

ERICA. All people are strangers until they become friends.

EDWARD. I see, so I'm to be ignored.

PAUL. We haven't ignored you.

EDWARD. Somehow I feel cut off from you, as if I don't matter, as if I could die right here on the spot and you wouldn't even notice.

ERICA. What a morbid sense of humor you have.

EDWARD. I'm not joking.

ERICA. Neither am I joking. You are very morbid.

EDWARD. I am not morbid and you'd better stop saying that if you know what's good for you.

ERICA. What was that?

EDWARD. I'm not being morbid. I love life with all of its nooks and crannies.

PAUL. What was that you said about, "If she knows what's good for her."

EDWARD. Just a figure of speech.

[simultaneous]

ERICA.	**PAUL.**
Don't threaten me!	Don't threaten her!

EDWARD. No one is threatening you.

[simultaneous]

PAUL.	**ERICA.**
You threatened my wife!	You threatened me!

EDWARD. I wouldn't do that.

[simultaneous]

PAUL.	**ERICA.**
You just did!	You just did!

EDWARD. Look, I'm nice. I'm a nice person. I have respect for people, even the ones who have given their lives over to oppressive forces that are evil.

PAUL AND ERICA. What oppressive forces?

EDWARD. You work for a corporation, don't you? *[pause]* Look, I would like to be your friend.

[ERICA goes back to her reading. PAUL simmers.]

PAUL. Couldn't wait for me. Couldn't show your husband the common courtesy.

ERICA. Stop carrying on.

PAUL. Couldn't restrain yourself. Had to open a conversation with him, had to communicate with a strange man. Couldn't wait for your husband.

Raymond J. Barry

EDWARD. *[looks up from his book]* You're carrying this on a little far, aren't you, Paul?

PAUL. We've been through this before. Infidelity of sorts.

EDWARD. For merely speaking with a person?

PAUL. Not just a person. You're a colleague of mine, and not just speaking; revealing personal details, I suspect, details I would rather keep private; the most intimate . . . the most personal information about our life, our money, my career, the implications of my work.

ERICA. It's all right, darling. Nothing was revealed. *[to EDWARD]* I'm in a prison.

EDWARD. I can see that.

ERICA. *[to EDWARD]* It's repressive, restricting. I cannot breathe without repercussions.

EDWARD. I can see that.

PAUL. What are you saying?

ERICA. I cannot breathe with you around.

PAUL. You would say that in front of him, a perfect stranger?

EDWARD. I can be trusted. Your husband runs the roost, I see.

PAUL. Nobody runs the roost, Eddie.

EDWARD. There's always a stronger party in marriage and in war.

PAUL. We're both strong.

ERICA. Yes, both very strong.

PAUL. Very strong. Our relationship is based upon mutual strength.

ERICA. Yes, mutually strong.

PAUL. We have each other's interest at heart.

ERICA. That's so.

PAUL. Our relationship is stronger than strong; it's powerful.

ERICA. Much strength, power and money.

PAUL. Deep and trusting.

ERICA. Speaking of trust, Edward has been communicating about some dealings he's had with impoverished countries in the world.

[simultaneous]

ERICA.	PAUL.
And let's see, he's afraid of losing his money. He's only got a million. And he's going to quit his job. Something about not being able to do it anymore.	What? You mean to tell me that he just came up to you and began talking about all the most intimate, the most personal information about his life, his career, his work?

ERICA. Then he roughly grabbed me by the shoulders and pressed his body against mine and stuck his wet tongue stuck down my throat and kissed me . . . and I told him what you mean to me, darling.

PAUL. *[shocked]* What? You kissed my wife?

EDWARD. You didn't have to tell him everything.

ERICA. Of course I did.

EDWARD. You could have lied . . . a little.

Park Encounter

ERICA. That's not our way, is it, Paul?

PAUL. I swear to God I don't know what our way is anymore. You've been kissing.

ERICA. Truth is our way and always has been.

PAUL. The truth is that you've been kissing.

ERICA. And forgiveness is our way too, darling.

PAUL. The kissing hurts; it truly hurts.

ERICA. I don't know what came over me. Mischief, attraction, general naughty behavior.

[simultaneous]

ERICA.	**PAUL.**
He forced me.	It hurts. The kissing hurts.

EDWARD. I'm sorry. She started it.

ERICA. You would blame it on me.

PAUL. It doesn't matter who started it.

[simultaneous]

PAUL.	**EDWARD.**
It hurts terribly.	It matters to me.

EDWARD. . . . who started the kissing.

ERICA. *[to EDWARD]* You forced me to kiss you.

[simultaneous]

ERICA.	**PAUL.**
Your lips were all over mine, wet lips.	You forced my wife to kiss you with

PAUL. . . . those wet lips of yours? But she was my wife.

[simultaneous]

PAUL.	**EDWARD.**
Mine. Her lips were mine.	I didn't know you were her hubby, Paul.

EDWARD. Otherwise I would have kept my wet lips to myself.

PAUL. Why would you kiss him, Erica? We have plenty of money. We have millions. Why would you kiss him? I have more influence than he. It wasn't always like that. I had to work for success in the beginning of my career.

[simultaneous]

PAUL.	**ERICA.**
And this is what I get. I was so naïve. Remember, Erica, when I first began? How difficult it was?	It just happened. Edward was going out of his mind just a moment ago He seemed to be

Raymond J. Barry

And now this... this... kissing business is what I get in return.

cracking, seemed troubled by something, his life or something.

PAUL. You hurt your husband, Erica.

ERICA. We kissed only once. He forced me.

PAUL. You allowed it. You could have kicked him in the balls.

ERICA. I would have kicked him in the balls, but he forced me. Real love is never a smooth ride, my darling. Whom one picks for a mate is a large factor in life. A good person? A bad person? And to what qualities are we attracted? Goodness? Generosity? Kindness? Gentleness? Marriage requires a sane existence for it to last. Love is an elusive emotion . . .

PAUL. You could have kicked him in the balls.

EDWARD. You can't just kick . . .

[simultaneous]

| **EDWARD.** | **ERICA.** |
| a man in the balls. | Don't be upset, darling. |

PAUL. Oh? How can I not be upset? My wife and my colleague, plotting against me . . .

[simultaneous]

| **PAUL.** | **ERICA.** |
| . . . with their wet lips and tongues. | What gives you that idea, darling? |

PAUL. Look at him. Look at the guilt on his face.

EDWARD. Nonsense . . .

[simultaneous]

| **PAUL.** | **EDWARD.** |
| Guilt is written all over his face. | I have nothing to be guilty about. |

PAUL. Really? Nothing? Why are you here? Surely there is a reason you are here.

EDWARD. There is such a thing as happenstance . . .

ERICA. He was a nuisance, kept harassing me into a confrontation.

EDWARD. Such a thing as just wandering by . . .

ERICA. I asked him to leave several times.

EDWARD. . . . and stumbling upon a public bench to sit.

ERICA. He refused. Suddenly his wet lips were on mine.

PAUL. *[to EDWARD]* You seduced my wife with your wet lips?

EDWARD. I was reading on a public bench.

PAUL. Her public bench.

Park Encounter

ERICA. Yes, my public bench.

EDWARD. No one owns a public bench.

ERICA. But I was here first.

EDWARD. Your wife flirted with me.

PAUL. Making things up about my wife.

ERICA. I wouldn't flirt with such a man.

PAUL. He is repulsive, isn't he?

EDWARD. I'm not repulsive. I'm very good-looking.

PAUL. Ha, listen to him talk about himself.

EDWARD. Well, you put me in a position of defending myself. The bench was mine for the sitting. Your wife was there. She spoke. I spoke. It was as simple as that. Two passing ships in the night.

PAUL. Two passing ships and one shipwreck of a marriage.

ERICA. No, Paul, two passing ships still afloat. Our marriage is still afloat. He roughly grabbed me by the shoulders and kissed me and stuck his tongue deep down my throat.

PAUL. You were overpowered? He assaulted you?

EDWARD. No, I was overpowered by threat of a knife. Show him the knife.

ERICA. There was no knife.

PAUL. Overpowering my wife!

EDWARD. There was a knife. I did my best to preserve my honor.

PAUL. You stole my wife's honor.

EDWARD. Never.

ERICA. Two men fighting over me.

PAUL. I am fighting, as I must fight, for my wife's honor.

EDWARD. I refuse to fight over nothing.

PAUL. *[standing in wife's defense]* You call my wife nothing?

EDWARD. *[standing]* Your wife is nothing to me.

[silence; EDWARD and PAUL face off, frozen nose to nose, and slowly retreat]

ERICA. The sky is so blue today; clouds so puffy and white. It is a Godsend, this universe of ours. The air is fresh, the sun, the trees, the leaves on the trees. It's quite beautiful, this park, and particularly this spot in the park. We all suffer so. It's necessary to find a retreat somewhere, some getaway where one is able to gather one's thoughts, away from the bombing, away from one's enemies, in order to find peace of mind, in order to find calm in the eye of the storm of everyday living. *[ERICA listens]* But I do hear something.

EDWARD. The sound of a motor.

ERICA. An automobile coming.

EDWARD. And one pigeon cooing.

ERICA. Yes, one pigeon cooing. The pigeons have arrived. Yes, a hearty breed, the pigeons. *[heads turn; bell ringing]* Oh, there are more birds. Look, look at the birds, darling.

PAUL. Never mind the birds. I'm hurt, terribly hurt; his wet tongue, wet lips on yours.

EDWARD. They are beautiful those birds.

Raymond J. Barry

ERICA. Something about their sound, how they make that sound, that little squeaky sound.

PAUL. I never trusted him with his puffy, puckered lips.

EDWARD. Yes, something about the peeping sound of birds.

ERICA. Something about how they rub their little beaks together and make that squeaky, little sound. Birds are truly a wondrous miracle, a wondrous miracle.

EDWARD. Yes, nothing like birds. How about you, Paul? Don't you love the chirping birds?

PAUL. Never mind birds. I haven't time for birds. I'm hurt, terribly, terribly hurt.

ERICA. Yes, nothing like birds. Edward loves birds, don't you, Edward?

EDWARD. I do love birds. I too find birds to be a wondrous miracle, a wondrous miracle.

[ears perked at sound of bell ringing]

ERICA. Oh, there is the sound in the distance of a bell ringing. Such an optimistic sound, the sound of ringing bells.

EDWARD. Yes, most optimistic, the sound of ringing bells.

ERICA. Such a lush sound, the ringing of bells, reminds me of when I was a little girl, going to church, praying for goodness in the world. Something having to do with the future in a bell ringing, signifying the time of day, the hour, the half hour, future hours.

EDWARD. Yes, future hours, years and decades to come. If only bombs were bells.

PAUL. We must have war, Ed.

ERICA. Bombing the enemy facilitates change for the better, for the improvement of mankind. War makes the world a better place. That's what we're all fighting for, isn't it, to make the world a better place for our offspring, so they too can fight the enemy?

EDWARD. I've never seen this enemy. Who is this enemy?

PAUL. We make it up as we go along. You know that. You are my enemy, Eddie. You kissed my wife.

ERICA. It doesn't mean we don't like you, Edward.

PAUL. Any enemy must be destroyed. That's why war is necessary, Eddie. You of all people know that. As unpleasant as that may sound, wars have been part of men's lives since time began. Why should things change now? Our survival is at stake, Eddie. We must wage war, to support our way of life. Our general comfort involves change, Eddie. Whenever there is change, someone gets hurt. It is unavoidable. It is normal. The strong always survive. The weak don't. And the strong are more comfortable. Comfort is insured by war with the uncomfortable. Business is constantly developing new means of comfort for the betterment of all mankind, Ed. Someone is bound to get hurt whenever there is a transition that improves the quality of life. Just as long as it's not us, big boy. Yup, just as long as it's not us. The weak have always had to be moved aside, haven't they? I never heard you complain about that. We don't live in tents anymore, big boy. We live in massive, comfortable buildings with beautiful views and air conditioning that cools when it's too hot. The natives had to go or we had to go. I'm still here and so are you, so guess who won that battle. Today the enemy is out there resisting our good intentions again, so naturally we bomb them. What else can we do? We'll eliminate them too for the general good of our people; not their people – our people. It's between them and us. Your betrayal won't be tolerated, Eddie boy. You'll see. You'll be eliminated like the rest of those self-righteous fools, who think they can stop progress. You can't stop progress, Eddie, and you won't walk away with my wife either. I'll nip that one in the bud right now. It's a shame a man of your education should make the choices you've made. Poor judgment, Eddie. You know how to play that game. You have been part of what happens behind the scenes, part of the system all your life, but you're outside the inner circle now. You dared to bite the hand that fed you, Eddie boy. I know the right people who will support my decision to throw you to the wolves. You're in great danger, Eddie boy. So foolish. You know where the power lies and what we are capable of doing when a fool hampers progress. God is on my side. God approves, Ed. God approves of what the group does for the world.

EDWARD. I don't believe in your God.

PAUL. Of course you don't. Otherwise you would go with the flow. Otherwise you would stop badgering my wife.

EDWARD. We only talked.

PAUL. You call that innocent communication?

EDWARD. I do call it innocent communication.

ERICA. I should have kicked him in the balls.

PAUL. You have done enough damage. I'll take care of it.

ERICA. You'll protect me, won't you, darling?

PAUL. Yes, you're safe. I know how to handle this. It's every man for himself in this world, Eddie. You are on your own now. Kissing my wife.

ERICA. He says he has a million but I don't believe it.

PAUL. It has taken me decades to find the right woman, Eddie. You should have known better than to tamper with something so precious; kissing my wife, my wife who nourishes me at night when I have finished with business.

EDWARD. I meant nothing by it. She was attractive to me. I didn't mean anything by it.

ERICA. Treating me like a common whore like that. He treated me like a whore, darling.

PAUL. And you're not a whore, are you?

ERICA. No, I'm not. I have pretty legs, but I'm not a whore.

PAUL. You do have pretty legs, doesn't she Ed? Doesn't Erica have pretty legs?

EDWARD. Yes, yes, she has pretty legs. I mentioned that before.

PAUL. You mentioned that my Erica has pretty legs? Why would you do that, Ed? Don't you realize how much she means to me? I can't live without my Erica. *[turns to Erica]* I'm sorry, Erica, I was late coming here. I allowed Edward to observe your legs. It does hurt. I suppose you observed my wife's buttocks as well.

EDWARD. I did observe your wife's buttocks, but I was thinking of more important things than your wife's buttocks.

PAUL. What could be more important than my wife's buttocks?

ERICA. Yes, what could be more important than my buttocks?

EDWARD. Lots of things; the constant bombing, exploitation of people; imbalance of wealth, overwhelming power in the hands of the government, lack of power for the people.

PAUL. And these, you say, are more important than my wife's buttocks/

ERICA. Hit him with something, Paul.

PAUL. Do you realize what you are suggesting, Eddie?

ERICA. Hit him with a rock, or a stick.

PAUL. Quiet down, my darling. My wife is as important to me as my mother was when she was alive.

EDWARD. My mother died yesterday.

PAUL. I'm talking about my mummy, not your mummy! It's my mummy who is at stake here when you mess around with Erica, my one and only Erica, and my dearest mummy, as well as our wealth and all of the advantages that come with being part of the group!

ERICA. I still think you should hit him with something, darling. You heard what he said about my buttocks.

PAUL. Never mind your buttocks. If you had kicked him in the balls to begin with, none of this would have happened.

ERICA. I'll make it up to you, darling.

PAUL. The question is how, and when.

EDWARD. I should leave now. The authorities . . .

PAUL. Oh, no you don't. You owe me, Ed. You owe me and I want payment for what you have done to us.

ERICA. You do owe us, Edward. I'm not comfortable now that you've been feeding all of those ideas into my mind that have ruined my confidence. I'm not as confident as I was. Are you confident, dear. Are you confident?

PAUL. No, not completely confident now that I think about it. I'm usually sure of myself, but not as confident as I was with Eddie challenging everything that matters, my wife, my mummy, the workings of the group that keep us on top.

EDWARD. I said nothing about your mummy.

PAUL. What? What did you say about mummy?

ERICA. What did you say about my Paul's mummy?

EDWARD. I said nothing. I . . . I must go now. I said nothing about anyone's mummy. I was talking only about the insanity of war, the insanity of selfish government, the insanity of exploiting people by stripping them of their dignity, stripping them of ideals that encourage human dignity. Trying to live in an insane world that pretends the insanity in which we live is not really insane at all when in fact that world is more insane than I am insane but my insanity is more noticeable than the insanity of the world with people's faces so red and

Park Encounter

their voices so loud and their expressions so tortured that they can never undo the insane impression they leave on other countries who are surely frightened of our unpredictable insanity that could become unhinged at a moment's notice if things don't go our way. Dropping bombs on people who are insane enough to imagine they wouldn't drop the same bombs on another insane group of insane people if they had a sane chance to drop bombs for the sake of sanity, for the sake of the insane world's insanity in order to make the insane world sane when there isn't a possibility of finding an ounce of sanity in the rubble that will remain after those insane bombs are dropped first once and then again and again, until they are all insanely dead and the world will become sane again but there will be no sane people left to live in it but at least the world will be sane without people to live in it, without insane people to live in it. I must go.

ERICA. Something in me wants to hit Edward over the head with a rock.

PAUL. You're mean today, Erica.

ERICA. I wasn't mean before I met Eddie.

PAUL. We have to be mean to win.

ERICA. Hit him with a brick, Paul.

PAUL. There is no brick. Do you see a brick?

ERICA. There's always a brick lying around somewhere.

EDWARD. Don't hurt me with a brick. I must go.

PAUL. You hurt me, Eddie, so it is logical that I would hurt you with a brick. That's how war gets started, big boy.

ERICA. Find a brick, love, and bring it to me. I'll do the hitting. Or a stick. A stick will do. A brick or a stick.

EDWARD. Don't resort to violence. Let's negotiate. That's what civilized countries do. They negotiate. We don't need any more violence with bricks and sticks, bombs and business.

ERICA. Did you find anything, darling?

PAUL. *[wandering around, looking for a weapon]* No, dearest, not yet. I could punish him with my shoe. My shoe might work.

EDWARD. Don't hit me with a shoe. I'm harmless.

ERICA. Harmless Edward? You've done nothing but protest since you arrived. Hurry, dear, find a rock or a club. We'll fix him.

EDWARD. I must go.

ERICA. Hit him, Paul.

PAUL. With what?

[simultaneous]

ERICA.	**EDWARD.**
Anything. I don't care. Throw the bench on him.	That's what we've been taught, to hurt each other.

ERICA. Hit him, Paul. He's babbling. All day babbling, babbling, babbling about rain forests.

[simultaneous]

Raymond J. Barry

EDWARD.
We're full of hate for each other. Well, I won't have it. Do you hear me? I won't have it. I don't feel that way towards you. I am kind and gentle.

ERICA.
The forests of North America, arctic ice caps. Get a rock. Hit him with a rock.
There's a rock over there.

ERICA. Hit him with that rock.

EDWARD. Oh, come on, we can be friends. I'm good. I'm a good person. We all feel the same thing.

PAUL. I feel what you feel? Hardly.

ERICA. Two men sharing their feelings. Hit him with something, darling. Make him bleed. Bash his face in, the little prick.

PAUL. It's not necessary, darling.

[simultaneous]

ERICA.
Sure it is. He's the enemy. Kill him.

PAUL.
You should watch who you're kissing honey.

EDWARD. She almost stabbed me with her penknife.

PAUL. My wife is not to be messed with.

ERICA. I tried to read my book, but he kept talking and talking. I could barely escape.

EDWARD. You never tried to escape.

ERICA. I tried but you held me captive with your wet lips. Hit him. I can't stand him.

EDWARD. It's my park too and my bench. I'm staying put.

[PAUL has been moving in back of EDWARD. He finds a large rock]

ERICA. Hit him, Paul!

PAUL. Give me your little penknife, you kissable little bitch.

ERICA. Here it is, darling. Don't hurt me. What are you going to do with it?

PAUL. Now I'll take care of him. Take that!

[PAUL stabs EDWARD in the chest, who is totally dumbfounded. EDWARD rises, then falls back onto the bench with a horrified expression on his face. The knife hasn't penetrated more than half an inch, since it's a little pocket knife.]

EDWARD. I'm stabbed. You have stabbed me with Erica's little penknife. It hurts.

PAUL. I'm glad it hurts. Kissing my wife.

ERICA. You shouldn't have done that, Paul.

PAUL. I shouldn't have? Why shouldn't have I?

ERICA. It's going to cause us trouble.

PAUL. They're looking for him anyway.

EDWARD. Your wife . . . Oh, it hurts. She took part in our relationship willingly.

Park Encounter

[EDWARD is weaving around in circles.]
ERICA. This will give you plenty to talk about in the future with helpless women sitting on park benches.
[EDWARD weaves around in circles and finally lands himself on the park bench.]
ERICA. He's bleeding. What if he faints?
PAUL. Nothing if he faints. He just faints, that's all, and we walk out of the park and wish him luck.
EDWARD. Please . . . I'm weak . . . don't leave me here.
ERICA. *[holds up the knife]* It was only a little penknife.
EDWARD. But it hurts. I'm hurt. Get somebody. *[EDWARD falls to the ground.]* Oh, my goodness, something is wrong.
ERICA. He's faking it. Sit up, Edward. You're slouching, looking all crumpled.
EDWARD. I can be crumpled in my condition.
ERICA. Sit up. You look a mess.
EDWARD. I'm losing blood.
ERICA. *[to EDWARD]* You can get home, can't you, buddy?
EDWARD. I'm Edward, not buddy.
PAUL. Let's get out of here.
ERICA. No, we're going to stay here and watch him squirm.
PAUL. What if he dies?
EDWARD. Ouch! This stab wound hurts. *[gets up from the bench, weaving around in circles]* I must go now.
ERICA. He won't die. It was only a little penknife.
EDWARD. Oh, god, I'm losing a lot of blood. I could die. I can feel it running down my pant leg. I'm feeling weak. . . just lie here until somebody helps me.
ERICA. He's exaggerating. He's faking it. He's been faking it ever since he started up with me. He's a fake.
PAUL. You cheated on me.
EDWARD. I'm losing blood, . . . feeling weak.
ERICA. He's a fake.
EDWARD. My mind . . . , the utter hollow space, nothing left. . . Oh, my God.
ERICA. I'll call the authorities. *[ERICA takes out her cell phone; makes a call]*
PAUL. Yes, call them.
ERICA. I will. I'm calling them. It's ringing.

[simultaneous]

EDWARD.

Oh, I'm dizzy. I'm feeling faint, drifting, out of breath, losing blood and have nothing smart to say. Want to write it all down and deliver it to my best friend, but there are no best friends. They've

ERICA.

Hello, yes, I'm Erica Swinton, wife of Paul Swinton, the oil man, and I'm at the park in front of bench number thirty-five near the large oak tree and there's a man named Edward

Raymond J. Barry

all been betrayed. You, Erica, have deceived me into believing we might have something special. But we don't have something special. I've failed. here, who has been threatening to quit his job for one thing, and for another he has been badgering both me and my husband, and, well, he...

ERICA. . . . seems a little out of control. He casts aspersions upon the police. Before he was talking about a constriction in his brow and he's been communicating on a very personal level both to me and my husband, breaking the rules . . . His name? . . . His name is Edward. What's your last name Edward?

EDWARD. Ahh, I'm bleeding . . . weak.

ERICA. He's not cooperating. Yes. Yes. Fine. He'll be here; bench number thirty-five.

[ERICA hangs up the phone]

EDWARD. Help me, I'm not feeling well.

ERICA. He's a phony prick.

EDWARD. I am not.

PAUL. You're really mean today, honey. Let's keep the spirits up. I'll tell a joke. You want to hear a joke?

ERICA. Your jokes never make me laugh.

PAUL. This one will, one joke, a joke between us. Here goes. There was a fellow who thought of himself as being important.

ERICA. Ho, ho, ho!

PAUL. That's not the end of the joke.

ERICA. Hit him with a rock, and let's get out of here.

PAUL. He's a nice guy.

ERICA. I'll do it. [ERICA hits him with a rock; hearing something] Listen, I hear a chainsaw in the distance. Hear the chainsaw? Someone is cutting wood.

PAUL. Wood, darling? What kind of wood?

ERICA. Let me look. *[she rises from the bench to look]* No, it's not a chainsaw. It's a grass cutter. A man is cutting the grass. He's edging the grass around the church with the bells.

PAUL. Edging the grass, is he?

ERICA. Yes, dear, he's edging the grass.

PAUL. There's that damned bell again.

[simultaneous]

EDWARD.	ERICA.
More bells ringing. Yes, more bells, lots of bells today.	That suggests a future, doesn't it? Making the lawn look nice?

ERICA. It's so important to have a future.

EDWARD. You've hit upon it.

ERICA. Hit upon what?

Park Encounter

EDWARD. The future. That's what is missing, the future.

ERICA. You think the future is missing?

PAUL. Hogwash. I see an automobile driving over a grave and I think of the future, what's lying ahead. Where is the automobile driving to? That question implies a future.

ERICA. You're right, darling, an automobile driving over a grave. We do have a future.

[simultaneous]

PAUL.	**ERICA.**
A car door is slamming. Who slammed that car door? Who walked out of that car? That's definitely the future.	And I hear a hooting owl and a pigeon and another automobile engine and a dog barking. They hint of the future too.

ERICA. And another car door slamming. Who could be walking out of that car? Who could be arriving in the future? Someone. Someone. We have a future, as long as we protect ourselves from the enemy.

PAUL. Yes, and realize who the enemy is.

ERICA. You mean him?

PAUL. You know who I mean.

ERICA. Yes, I know who you mean. Let's get out of here before the authorities come.

PAUL. The authorities won't care about him. He's wounded, no use to anyone. *[staring intently at EDWARD]* Don't worry. We're safe.

ERICA. Are you sure, darling?

PAUL. Of course I'm sure. When haven't I been sure?

ERICA. You're always sure, aren't you, darling?

PAUL. One has to be sure.

ERICA. I'm safe. That's the important thing.

PAUL. We're both safe.

> *[ERICA and PAUL exit, leaving EDWARD dead on the ground. Bombs in the distance that can be heard by the audience]*

End of Play

Raymond J. Barry

Mother'Son

Characters

Mother: a possessive single woman who controls her son by supporting him and feeding him. Her husband is dead.

Son: a middle-aged man who spends his time eating and living with his mother. He is separated from his wife and refuses to get a job.

Wife: married to SON and in competition with the MOTHER for control of the SON.

History

The World Premiere of **Mother'Son** was performed at the **Omaha Magic Theatre** in Omaha, Nebraska, in September, 1993. Artistic Directors were Joanne Schmidman and Megan Terry. **Mother'Son** was named the **Outstanding Play of 1993** by the Omaha World Herald.

CAST:

MOTHER .... Judy Jean Berns
SON..Raymond J. Barry
WIFE .... Kim O'Kelley

DIRECTOR ....Bill Bushnell

Mother'Son was performed at the **Met Theatre**, Los Angeles, California, 1994, produced by Holly Hunter.

CAST:

MOTHER .... Judy Jean Berns
SON..Raymond J. Barry
WIFE .... Kim O'Kelley

DIRECTOR ....David Saint
ASST. .... Tom Draper
SET .... Yael Pardess
LIGHTING...Rand Ryan

Raymond J. Barry

Mother'Son was performed at the **Edinburgh Festival** in Edinburgh, Scotland, June 1994, **Pleasance Theatre**, produced by John Goodman and David Arrow.

CAST

MOTHER	Judy Jean Berns
SON	Raymond J. Barry
WIFE	Kim O'Kelley
DIRECTOR	David Saint
DESIGN	Markus Maurette

Mother'Son was performed at **Smokebrush Center For the Arts**, Colorado Springs, Colorado, 1993.

CAST:

MOTHER	Judy Jean Berns
SON	Raymond J. Barry
WIFE	Kim O'Kelley
DESIGN	Markus Maurette
DIRECTOR	David Saint
ASSISTANT DIRECTOR	Tom Draper

Mother'Son was performed at the **Open Fist Theatre Company** in Los Angeles, California, July-August 2001. Martha Demson, Artistic Director.

CAST:

MOTHER	Laura James
SON	Jon Stafford
WIFE	Terri Smith
DIRECTOR	Russell Milton
STAGE MANAGER	Hillary Holt
COSTUME DESIGNER	Van Ramsey

Raymond J. Barry, Judy Jean Berns, **Mother'Son**
Met Theatre, Los Angeles, 1994

Raymond J. Barry, Judy Jean Berns, **Mother'Son**
Edinburgh Festival, Scotland, June 1994

Raymond J. Barry

Raymond J. Barry and Holly Hunter, producer, **Mother'Son**, 1994

John Goodman, Producer   David Arrow, Producer
Back When Back Then,
Theatre for the New City, New York City, Magic Theatre, San Francisco

Mother'Son

Mother'Son

[The stage is white and rectangular with walls covered with walls covered with yellowed newsprint. Newspapers cover the seams of five doors, making them invisible to the eye. One door is on the center of the upper wall while the other four doors are on both side walls, two on each side. They are closed at the outset of the play. A white stool stands downstage right center. There is a blackout. Son enters from stage right masking and sits on the stool in the dark. The Son can be somewhere between the ages of 38 to 48. He is fat and unkempt with oversized black shiny shoes, black socks, oversized green khaki work pants, a plaid shirt and a dark jacket buttoned with only one button at the top, stomach protruding below. His belly could possibly be a pillow. It is not necessary that his fatness be realistic. A spot comes up on him.]

SON. I could almost touch them with my finger tips, every belief, every ethic, all the shoulds and should nots, the clunking, the dunking, the thumping, the biting, the tearing, the ripping of old, long gone wishes of what must happen and what should happen but did not, could not, will not. Things didn't work out that way, never could to begin with, standards too high or too low. That's how it went, a familiar terrain, a bit bumpy, large boulders in the way, but pretty scenery, grazing cows, pigs, chickens, farm unification, all unified, brought together in my head, a skull not cracked but weakening, breaking but not cracked, leaking but not cracked, solid full with impressions heavy, some "unidentifiable" that settles down into the pit of me, the inward center, apart from the rest, and I'm used to it. Back to my own track, back to that. I thought of my mom. Hi, mom. [Refers to Mother's spirit in audience.] Ma, when I take a hatchet to your head and blood spills onto the floor as it did when daddy punched you in the face, we'll play some dancing music, ma, or maybe Prokofiev or Bartok, composers both, whom you generously introduced to me when I was young and uneducated. Oh, how it made a difference, ma, knowing all those things you wanted me to know. Any bit of esoteric gave me such an edge in this world.

But this is not a tenable situation, ma, in the middle of the onslaught, the attack, the waterfall Niagara beating me over the head, whacking me with its whopping wap, waps as I pretend to be a big bopper in the midst, surrounded, no place to hide, no place, joining them in the end, while I integrate a foreign value system into my own with time out for lunch, coffee breaks. Don't try too hard. There's a

Raymond J. Barry

certain wisdom in that, and I'm used to it. Back to my own track, back
to that. I thought of my mom. Hi, mom. [refers to mother's spirit in the
room] Clear choice, ma, clear choice. If I could make one, one clear
choice that makes sense. I should work on an occupation maybe, but I
don't have any real talent, like a pro baseball player or a doctor or
something like that, so maybe I should get involved in some kind of a
cause, like anti-nuclear war. No, that's not something I can get excited
about. But it's time to do something, ma, anything, or I shall die of
inactivity. Stagnant, non-doing creature am I, a beast in hibernation
with these unforgiving bloodshot eyes of mine, looking, looking at the
most mundane ordinary, all too familiar in slow motion - addictive,
kaleidoscopic river of nonsensical images, complete with stick-figured
creatures, dressed to suit every occasion, bow tie, whatever, every
article, every gesture, all clothing, socks and shoes to match, all
matching, and that is the confusion, ma, the matching of us all, one to
the other - identical appearance, disappearance of me into them, them
into those others, those "other others" into those "other, other, others,"
and these bloodshot eyes of mine observing it all. A hibernating ox-ape
am I with a hair chin and crusted layers of sweat, cracking when I roll
across my bed mattress, as long and as wide as a floor or a tundra, and
I'm used to it. Back to my own track. Back to that. I thought of my ma.
Hi, ma.

Ma, what vacuum are you filling? What empty hole in the dark
pit of your stomach remains empty? I know of emptiness too. All of my
choices make no sense. You seem to make sense to yourself, ma. Tip me
off. Explain to me what it is that I am missing. What is your wisdom,
ma? I see no pattern here, no reason within my yawning, howling head,
and I am used to it. Back to my own track, back to that. I thought of my
ma. Hi, ma.

I wait for something to big to happen, ma, bigger than a whale
of all beings. So big. Bigger than anything else that is big, a bigness that
bulges beyond the boundaries of being bound and released to the
winds, flying out to the big beyond, a booming big bulge that bustles
forth and brushes the backs of the big boys in business. I run. I run in
rambling circles, circumnavigating the outer perimeter of the perameter,
farther out from the center than ever before, farther and farther out,
where the original point will have to wait until the next lucky life. I'm
willing to wait, ma; worry perhaps while I wait, and while away my time
with happenstance beginnings together with endings, not the big end,
but endings, every moment an ending, a little one and I'm used to it.
Back to my own track. Back to that. I thought of my ma. Hi, ma.

Ma, shall I sit, stand or lie here? Shall I answer the telephone or
ignore its bleating ring? Shall I eat? Shall I starve? Shall I read? Shall I
think? Shall I do nothing? The choices are decided by my guilt and the

wish to control the child in me who wants very much to dance nude on the sidewalk, uttering a gleeful scream at the height of each soaring leap, dancing, leaping with spins and tap steps in between. The leaping is the most fun of all, ma.

[Son is downstage right. Mother enters upstage left door pushing a table on wheels. She crosses downstage left. The table has on it a head of romaine lettuce, two large carrots, radishes, two cucumbers, some parsley, two large tomatoes, along with a small cutting board, a small knife, a large knife, a vegetable scraper, a large bowl, a small bowl, a small bottle of salad oil, vinegar and paper towels in a roll. The age difference between mother and son need not be realistic but her hair should be gray. She can be anywhere between forty-eight to eighty years old, dressed in a dress and an apron - the universal mother.]

MOTHER. It's so nice having my son home again. It's been a long time since mother and son have been together, hasn't it? I've missed you, son. I'm glad you're back. You had me worried for a while when you were living with that bitch. You weren't yourself as I know you. You seemed so unhappy. I'm glad you made the move finally to come live with your mother. Are you hungry? Do you want anything to eat? [she prepares a salad for Son]

SON. No, mother. I'm not hungry.

MOTHER. You should eat something. It would be good for you.

SON. I'm hungry but I can't eat.

MOTHER. You're hungry. I'm glad you finally said that. I'm going to cook you something whether you eat it or not.

SON. I'm hungry for something but it isn't food.

MOTHER. [holds up lettuce] Maybe you'd like a delicious salad with crispy lettuce leaves, nice and crisp and washed to keep the germs off them and break them up into little bite-sized pieces.

SON. [crosses to table stage left] Where did you get crispy lettuce, ma?

MOTHER. Crispy lettuce grown in our own back yard, son.

SON. Crispy lettuce grown in our own back yard, ma, crispy lettuce that you planted in the beginning of the summer?

MOTHER. That's right, son, broken up into bite-sized pieces, little bite-sized pieces.

SON. [sits on stool downstage right] Ma, I don't want a goddamned salad.

MOTHER. You don't? You'll change your mind, son. People change their minds. That's what's so wonderful about people. They change their minds. I'll also add a nice sliced green cucumber, a big juicy one, fresh from the garden, chopped up into little bite-sized pieces.

SON. [to audience] I could eat a building or a whole city, ma.

MOTHER. [To audience. Picks up a carrot.] A big orange carrot next...

SON. [to audience] An entire universe...

MOTHER. [to audience] fresh from the garden...

Raymond J. Barry

[simultaneous]

SON.	MOTHER.
...if I wanted to satisfy this gnawing, aching, yearning within me.	also chopped up into little bite-sized pieces...

MOTHER. *[picks up a tomato]*...I could put tomatoes into it...
SON. *[to audience]* I could swallow mouthfuls of concrete.
MOTHER. *[to audience]*...big ones that taste so juicy fresh in the mouth.
SON. *[to audience]* I could eat steel girders...
MOTHER. *[to audience]*...sliced tomatoes...
SON. *[to audience]*...bolts and all.
MOTHER. *[to audience]*...no quartered...
SON. *[to audience]* I could chew up the sidewalks we walk on...
MOTHER. *[to audience]*...still mouth-sized if quartered.

[simultaneous]

SON.	MOTHER.
...the chairs we sit on, the glass in our windows, window frames and all.	I'll even put in some decorative touches, a few cut up radishes for color... as well as taste.

SON. *[to Mother]* I could chew, chew, chew the world, ma, one piece at a time...
MOTHER. *[picks up parsley]* Some parsley leaves for green.
SON. *[to audience]* until it is all gone...

[Voices should soften, simultaneous to audience:]

MOTHER.	SON.
[making salad stage left] I don't have peppers. What a pity. I don't have anything red or green the way peppers look. Nothing like peppers for color. Then I'll put together a lovely salad dressing just the way you like it, a touch of vinegar with that tangy taste you always loved. And last but not least, pepper and salt. I know how you love your salad seasoned with pepper and salt.	*[sitting stage right]* until it has disappeared, all of it, destroyed, swallowed, and digested. To wash it all down I'll drink up the lakes and rivers. Afterwards I'll throw it up again and leave it in a wet, mucous pile, concrete, glass, all of it, wetted with digestive juices from my stomach. *[faces her]* Maybe I'll piss on the pile of vomit for good measure.

MOTHER. *[turns to Son]* Mother has not forgotten what her boy likes. How does that sound, son?

SON. *[Pause. Sits stage right. Faces audience.]* Ma, is it you who carried me on your shoulder that Christmas long ago while Dad was raging like a wild bull, smashing the Christmas tree against the wall...

MOTHER. *[Upstage left at table. Faces audience.]* I tell you it was intolerable.

SON. *[to audience]*...back at the house at nine Glenwood?

MOTHER. *[to audience while making salad]* It was unspeakable,

SON. *[to audience]* Ma...

MOTHER. *[to audience while making salad]*...the torture,

SON. *[to audience]*...was it you who carried me on your shoulders?

MOTHER. *[to audience while making salad]*...in which I found I was stuck...

SON. *[to audience]* Ma...

MOTHER. *[to audience while making salad]*...like in a vice...

SON. *[to audience]*...was that really you?

MOTHER. *[to audience while making salad]*...between him and my own private needs,

SON. *[to audience]* What quick thinking, ma.

MOTHER. *[to audience while making salad]*...to achieve...

SON. *[to audience]* You saved my life,

MOTHER. *[to audience while making salad]*...to be recognized,

SON. *[to audience]*...our lives,

MOTHER. *[to audience while making salad]*...to be loved.

SON. *[to audience]*...didn't you?

MOTHER. *[to audience while making salad]* Yes, I wanted to be loved.

SON. *[to Mother]* Or did you?

MOTHER. *[to Son while making salad]* And I still want that.

SON. *[to Mother]* Since you were the cause of his rage...

MOTHER. *[to Son while making salad]* I want to be loved by my children.

SON. *[to Mother]*...at least in part?

MOTHER. *[to Son while making salad]* Do you hear me?

SON. You probably can't admit to it...

MOTHER. I need to be forgiven.

SON. *[to Mother]*...but it was you who behaved like such a bitch...

MOTHER. *[to Son]* My son!

SON. ...that he couldn't live with it anymore.

MOTHER. *[turns to making of salad]* I'm not listening anymore.

SON. *[stands and approaches Mother]* Now you are old...

MOTHER. I mean what I am saying.

SON. ...and you refuse to remember.

[simultaneous]

Raymond J. Barry

SON.	MOTHER.
But down deep inside... you must know. How could you not know?	*[She sings to drown him out.]* THE OBJECT OF MY AFFECTION HAS CHANGED MY COMPLEXION FROM WHITE TO ROSEY RED...

SON. You remember but you refuse!

MOTHER. *[turns to Son]* I refuse!

SON. *[directly to Mother stage left of table]* Tell me.

MOTHER. I refuse.

SON. You can't refuse.

MOTHER. I can.

SON. Not to me you can't.

MOTHER. I can.

SON. Mother, if you don't talk about this now I will never forgive you.

MOTHER. Then never forgive me. I won't.

SON. That's your last word on the subject?

MOTHER. Yes, that's the last word.

SON. All right then. *[Son exits downstage right.]*

MOTHER. There are some things that are private. My life is my own and none to know about. It is mine for me and only me.

[Son re-enters downstage right with a yellow flower, smelling its fragrance. He stands stage right.]

MOTHER. Aren't you formidable to inquire about it says in the Bible respect your parents are the only thing you have to obey me for if you don't you will be punished by my anger, slashes across your face, nail marks from my fingers in your arms from my squeezing too hard. I meant it to be an affectionate touch but my rage, you see, urged me to squeeze unnecessarily hard. *[Mother crosses to Son, sitting stage right. She embraces him.]* My child, my young child, why didn't you tell me what I was doing when I was doing it? I knew it was happening but I didn't realize, you see. I was so ill, so very ill at the time. If only I could change the past.

SON. *[Sits on stool stage right. To audience.]* The mother of the house was not ordinary. She refused to cook.

MOTHER. *[to Son]* Who gives a fuck? You have two hands. You cook.

SON. *[to audience]* She hated to cook.

MOTHER. *[To audience. Crosses back to table.]* The road of life I have wandered only to arrive at this deadly impasse with my son, my only son, who has such difficulty now in his middle-age life.

SON. *[to audience]* The mother of the house was too neurotic to cook.

MOTHER. *[to Son]* I wasn't made to cook. I was made to be a dancer.

SON. *[to audience]* She hated cooking.

Mother'Son

MOTHER. *[to Son]* Such difficult effort for so little in return; my love for you, my son, return my love. It is real.

SON. *[to audience]* Years went by and she refused to cook.

MOTHER. *[to Son]* Cook yourself.

SON. *[to audience]* The kids cooked and occasionally the father.

MOTHER. *[makes salad]* I loved your father.

SON. *[to audience]* The father who was Irish and rough...

MOTHER. *[makes salad]* At times he was a brute,

SON. *[to audience]*...and had a number of cooking jobs in his youth...

MOTHER. *[working at salad at table]*...a terrible brute to me... beating me when he was drunk...

SON. *[to audience]* So he knew how to cook.

MOTHER. *[working on salad at table]*...never coming home and never forgiving me for whatever it was that he thought I had done. He would fly off in jealous rages whenever I showed interest in anyone or anything whether it be a person or my pursuit of art or whatever.

SON. *[Sits stage right. To Mother.]* Ma, we have been silent too long. Not enough words have been spoken.

MOTHER. *[to Son at table]* Yes, I have felt it too, my son. I know your ache. I do. Forgive me, son.

[They cross to each other and embrace center stage.]

SON. *[embrace with Mother]* I long to go to church. I long for a God. I long for some force to worship.

MOTHER. *[embraced]* That's a good thing to wish for, son.

SON. *[embraced]* I long for a divinity that will protect me from stress.

MOTHER. *[embraced]* That's a good thing to want, my son. That's a good thing.

SON. *[embraced]* I am obsessed with this longing. I am blessed with it.

MOTHER. *[breaking slightly from the embrace]* What do you mean, son?

SON. Never mind.

MOTHER. What you need is a good wife.

SON. *[crosses stage right away from Mother]* You always go back to that.

MOTHER. *[downstage center]* Well, it's true, my son. You need to be cared for by your mother. That's what wives are for.

SON. *[crosses upstage right]* You never listen to me. You always go back to that wife business.

MOTHER. *[crosses back to table., continues making salad]* Well, it's true, son.

SON. *[crosses downstage right]* Did you just hear what I said about God?

MOTHER. Yes, son.

SON. Why do you ignore what I said?

MOTHER. You don't know what you want, son. You don't know what you want.

SON. Why do you insist upon that?

Raymond J. Barry

MOTHER. I'm not insisting, my boy, calm down. When you were little you used to play baseball when you became tense. Why don't you go outside now and play catch with the neighbor's children. It would be good for you.

SON. Not now, ma.

[Silence. Son exits downstage right. He returns with a small table and places it next to the wall downstage of the upstage right door. On the table is a small white vase into which he has placed his yellow flower. There is an extended silence during which he places his stool next to the table and sits.]

MOTHER. What are you thinking, son?

SON. Nothin', ma. I'm not thinking anything.

MOTHER. *[crosses to him upstage right]* Come on now, son. I know my boy. What's on that little mind of yours?

SON. I don't know, ma. I'm not thinking anything. Honest, ma.

MOTHER. You are cute when you fib to me. Don't you be a little fibber now. *[whacks him on the back of the head, crosses back to salad table]* You can tell your mother who loves you more than anything in the world.

SON. *[turns his head away]* I don't know, ma. I wasn't thinking anything. I just look that way.

MOTHER. Then look your mother in the eye why don't you?

SON. I'm not thinking anything. I swear, ma.

MOTHER. Come on, son. You can tell me. What is it you're thinking?

SON. All right, I was thinking something but it was not very important.

MOTHER. Come on, son. Tell me what it was. Let me decide how important it is.

SON. All right. I'll let you decide.

MOTHER. Well, what is it?

SON. I never did what my dreams wanted me to do, ma. Never. But that may change since I'm trying to move forward a little, just get my ass to move forward a little. Just an inch at a time will do, just an inch toward that place in which I could have been had the stars been in the right place at the right time but they weren't. *[crosses to her stage left with his stool]* They were elsewhere, somewhere else, and had there been better weather during the birth, the popping of my embryo out of your womb, *[He rises from his stool, crosses to downstage right and then haphazardly wanders back to his stool as he delivers the rest of the speech.]* with a few hairs on my bald head, mouth open, no teeth, wailing, wailing, crying out for some clarity about where I was. I didn't know, you see, ma, and who would with all the slime. I still don't know what is going on with all the slime, like the lights are out or some shade has been pulled down and my hat is over my head, covering my eyes making it awfully difficult for me to comprehend the signals I'm getting, considering the bombardment of them upon me, splattering my comprehension, confusing my grasp of concepts and issues, the big issues, the big concepts, the whole picture, so to speak, that had been splintered into a thousand particles like tiny pieces of glass, little slivers of what truly is the big picture of it all, that couldn't and still can't be comprehended.

MOTHER. *[at table, making salad]* You should stop living in the past, son.

SON. *[center stage right of table]* I'm not living in the past.

MOTHER. Yes, you are. You're living in the past. You definitely are.

SON. *[crosses to small table stage right, carries stool with him]* I didn't want to get involved in this conversation. You kept probing me until I gave in. It wasn't my idea to bring any of this up. You know that now, don't you? *[He sits on stool next to table.]*

MOTHER. Yes, I know what you're saying.

SON. You ask me what I was I thinking and then blame me for what I was thinking.

MOTHER. I wasn't blaming you for what you were thinking.

SON. You knew what I was thinking.

MOTHER. I didn't know what you were thinking.

SON. You wanted to talk about the subject. I didn't.

MOTHER. Please stop, son.

SON. I didn't want to talk. I even said so.

MOTHER. All right, already. You go on like a broken record.

SON. Well, I don't like being cornered into unpleasant conversations.

MOTHER. All right; will you stop this? I am growing tired of this, promptly tired of it.

SON. *[rises from the stool, crosses to her at the table]* You know, I'm glad you're getting tired of it, mother. I don't want you to ever do that again.

MOTHER. I won't.

SON. I don't like being used like that, mother.

MOTHER. I know.

SON. *[still next to her at the table]* I don't like being used for your own purposes. I'm tired of being manipulated. I'm tired of manipulative people, particularly women.

MOTHER. All right.

SON. *[crosses away from her to upstage right, sits on stool next to table]* I'm tired of it all.

MOTHER. I understand. Don't get so excited. I didn't mean to excite you so much. I really didn't mean to get you so excited. I really didn't.

SON. Well you did, you son of a bitch.

MOTHER. *[abruptly turns to him]* Don't you use the male form with regard to me. You'd better not. If you know what's good for you, you'd better not. *[chases him with a cucumber in her hand around the stage in a circle]*

SON. *[ends up downstage left]* Don't make me laugh, you bitch.

MOTHER. *[center stage right of table]* That's better.

Raymond J. Barry

SON. Oh you. *[Silence. Gradually they look at each other and crack a smile that turns into laughter.]*

MOTHER. We are funny aren't we?

SON. Yes, we are funny.

MOTHER. Somehow we continue through it all. We just keep going.

SON. Yes, you just keep going.

MOTHER. Not just me, you too.

SON. Yes, you too. You just keep going.

MOTHER. I wonder how we do it.

SON. Yes, I wonder how you do it.

MOTHER. Beats me.

SON. When you use an expression like that, "beats me," I know you're lying.

MOTHER. How can you say I'm lying? How do you dare say I'm lying? You don't know me if you think that. No, if you think I'm a liar you don't know me very well at all.

SON. I know you, mother.

MOTHER. You know what I'm willing to allow you to know, son.

SON. That's true of everyone.

MOTHER. I suppose.

SON. When you say, "beats me," I know you're lying.

MOTHER. Such a harmless expression. How can it be so significant to you?

SON. My instinct tells me things, that's all. My instinct is all I have, that's all.

MOTHER. I'm not a liar. I just leave things out.

[Pause. They smile at each other.]

SON. We do communicate easily, don't we? *[Son crosses from downstage right to downstage left and continues upstage making a circle around Mother who is making a salad at the table. He skips while he moves.]*

MOTHER. Yes we do. Indeed we do.

SON. We never argue. We just discuss.

MOTHER. Yes, that is correct.

SON. Somehow we find clarity.

MOTHER. Yes we do. Indeed we do.

SON. It's a miracle the way we do it.

MOTHER. Kind of, yes, it is a miracle.

SON. *[From upstage center he fakes a punch toward his mother. She doesn't see it.]* I give the credit to you. I couldn't do it myself.

MOTHER. I had a certain wisdom in bringing you up.

SON. I know what you mean.

MOTHER. I allowed you to do your own thinking.

SON. *[He circles her, skipping along the outer perimeter of the stage.]* I know.

Mother'Son

MOTHER. I know I made mistakes but I did encourage you to think for yourself.

SON. Yes, I'll give you that.

MOTHER. And we always talked. We always did talk.

SON. We do have a unique way of talking.

MOTHER. Yes, we do. Indeed we do. *[Pause. Mother methodically chops a carrot in a steady rhythm.]*

SON. Ma, can I invite a guest to dinner?

MOTHER. I don't think it would be just.

SON. What are you talking about?

MOTHER. Oh, life, life.

SON. What are you talking about?

MOTHER. Nothing, life, life.

SON. Stop saying that.

MOTHER. All right, all right.

SON. I don't know what's wrong.

MOTHER. Everything's wrong.

SON. Mother, everything's not wrong. You make it wrong. A simple thing, a guest.

MOTHER. I know exactly what's wrong.

SON. Wrong with what?

MOTHER. Nothing's wrong. I didn't say anything was wrong.

SON. You didn't? I think you did. I think you said something was wrong.

MOTHER. Well, I didn't mean it if I said it.

SON. You didn't mean it? I bet you did mean it and you forgot what the meaning was.

MOTHER. Maybe that's it. I forgot what the meaning was.

SON. Yes, that's it. You forgot what the meaning was. So what was the meaning you were forgetting...

MOTHER. Oh, life, life.

SON. Mother, stop saying that.

MOTHER. How can I? Son, I wanted to have dinner with you alone tonight. Why is that impossible? I think that is a simple request. I believe it is a simple request. I really do.

SON. You're holding onto your anger, mother.

MOTHER. I'm not holding onto my anger, goddamnit! I'm letting go. I'm free of it. Get rid of it. Get rid of me. Get rid of it all. I don't care. I don't count. You count but I don't count. I'm here to cooperate with you. I'm here to obey. Well, I'm totally tired of it. There's nothing wrong with me or my anger, nothing at all.

SON. May I have a glass of water?

MOTHER. Get your own goddammed water! I'm tired of waiting on you! And there's nothing wrong with my anger.

SON. You're raising your voice a shade too much.

Raymond J. Barry

MOTHER. [shouting even more] Well that's too goddammed bad.

SON. You don't have to react like that, mother.

MOTHER. Who are you to tell me how I am supposed to react? I have every right to feel what I am feeling.

SON. I don't want to argue, ma.

MOTHER. You don't want to argue, son?

SON. No, I do not.

[Mother picks up a cucumber and approaches Son with it. He stands next to his stool and backs away from her downstage right.]

MOTHER. Maybe you should argue.

SON. I won't do that, ma.

[With the cucumber, Mother crosses downstage right to Son. He crosses away from her to downstage left.]

MOTHER. [crosses downstage right to downstage center] Maybe you should fight for what you want, fight for your rights.

SON. I have no rights - only resentments.

MOTHER. But you don't feel good without a fight, son.

SON. Feeling good never mattered to me, ma.

MOTHER. It should, son. That's all we have.

SON. That's not all we have.

MOTHER. Then what else is there?

SON. Dignity and... death.

MOTHER. [crosses towards Son in pursuit to downstage left] What a cop out.

SON. [crosses away from her to upstage right] No, more of a comfort. I'm too weary to fight.

MOTHER. Then you're as good as dead.

SON. I don't think so.

MOTHER. [crosses to Son, menacing him with the cucumber, to upstage right] Fighting keeps one alive.

SON. [crosses away from her threatening cucumber to downstage right corner] I don't think I can fight. I don't like it.

MOTHER. [She pursues him with cucumber and corners him downstage right. She pokes him with cucumber.] Nobody likes it, son. You've got to fight. Besides there is a healthy way to fight. You can fight and then forget about it afterwards. You don't have to hold onto it. You can let it go.

SON. [protects himself from her pokes with cucumber] I don't like fighting, ma.

MOTHER. Then you're not sticking up for your rights, son.

SON. I have a right not to fight.

MOTHER. [continues poking him] But you want to fight, don't you? You want some satisfaction, some way to express your needs. How can you have that if you keep your mouth shut?

Mother'Son

SON. I can find some way, ma.

MOTHER. How, by killing someone?

SON. Yes, I would like to kill someone. I'd like to rap one of those suckers right in the mouth.

MOTHER. *[crosses stage left to table, makes salad]* You sound angry, son.

SON. You bet I'm angry. I'm wild with angry. I want to ram something down those little suckers' throats. I want to beat the crap out of those little, sweet-smelling pricks.

MOTHER. That's what you're really feeling, isn't it, son?

SON. Yes, those pricks.

MOTHER. You've really got a bad case of anger, son.

SON. Cocksuckers! Fucking cocksuckers!

MOTHER. Easy, son. Take it easy.

SON. I can't take it easy, ma. It's driving me crazy.

MOTHER. You should have taken it out on them when you had the chance.

SON. Fucking exploitative pricks.

MOTHER. You're the one to blame.

SON. Assholes! ! !

MOTHER. You're just cursing your own shortcomings.

SON. I'll kill them. I'll kill them.

MOTHER. You don't have the balls to do that. You're a coward. Anybody who doesn't fight for his rights is a coward.

SON. I'm brave. I do brave things.

MOTHER. You look brave but you're not brave.

SON. I'm brave. I do brave things.

MOTHER. *[making salad]* You don't do anything, son. You just endure.

SON. I do things.

MOTHER. *[downstage left at table]* You do safe things to make up for what you don't do, little compensative acts that amount to nothing because the real issues are never faced.

SON. I'll kill the bastards!

MOTHER. You won't kill anyone and you know it.

SON. *[slowly crosses to Mother stage left]* Yes, I will. I'll kill you if you keep it up, ma. I'll kill you.

MOTHER. *[makes salad, ignores him]* You wouldn't do that.

SON. *[stops upstage center]* I wouldn't?

MOTHER. No, you wouldn't.

SON. Maybe I would. You can't be totally sure, ma.

MOTHER. Stop fooling around, son. I'm trying to help you.

SON. *[menaces her again]* You made me angry.

MOTHER. You were angry already.

SON. *[threatening her]* But I didn't know it.

MOTHER. *[She holds her ground unafraid.]* So I allowed you to experience

Raymond J. Barry

something you shouldn't block out.

SON. *[attacking]* Then you've got to suffer the consequences.

MOTHER. *[turns to him]* Stop the nonsense.

SON. *[backs away from her]* I'm going to kill you, ma.

MOTHER. Stop it.

SON. It's not nonsense...

MOTHER. *[crosses back to table]* You know, I've been observing you for a few days and it strikes me that you are very isolated from your friends. *[Son stops, stands center stage right.]* Why don't you visit a few people just to reestablish contact? It couldn't hurt. Maybe they could offer a few suggestions about what you could do with yourself. It couldn't hurt. *[She continues making the salad.]*

SON. *[crosses to downstage right center, faces out to audience]* I am visiting people, ma. I'm visiting ghosts in my head. They visit me actually. They come upon me in the nighttime when I am alone. I welcome them.

[simultaneous, soft, to audience:]

SON.	MOTHER.
I know when they are coming.	It's not healthy.
{pause}	
I know when they are coming.	It's not healthy.
{pause}	
I know when they are coming.	It's not healthy.
{pause}	
I know when they are coming.	It's not healthy.
{pause}	
I feel them in the air above me.	It's not normal. You need
They are my friends.	distraction sometimes.
{pause]	
They are the memories of people.	It's not good to be self-
[pause]	involved. *[pause]*
They are the memories of people.	
[pause]	It's not good to be self-
They are the memories of people	involved.
who have had effect upon me at	
some past time. They visit me	*[pause]*
and we have dialogue. We talk to	It's not good to be self-
each other sometimes for hours.	involved. You should get
	outside of yourself more.

[soft, to audience.]

Spirits of people, ghosts, ghost	Maybe it's not important. I

Mother'Son

people, visitors in the night, my comrades,

don't know. I live alone. But I at least have friends I care about...

SON. People...
MOTHER. ...and...
SON. ...who...
MOTHER. ...who...
SON. ...have...
MOTHER. ...care...
SON. ...be-
MOTHER. ...about...
SON. -trayed...
MOTHER. ...me.
SON. ...Me.

[simultaneous]

SON.

People who have betrayed me and who are now reestablishing contact. The friends, half friends who meant something to me once.

MOTHER.

... and who care about me. It gives my life a well-roundedness which I need desperately. I need contact with others.

MOTHER. *[to Son]* My contact with you is very important.
SON. *[He skips to stage left and circles up around the perimeter of the stage.]* I discovered something long ago, mother.
MOTHER. Find a friend, son.
SON. That my friends were not really friends at all.
MOTHER. It'll be good for you.
SON. My approval meant something to them.

[simultaneous]

SON.

They sought it out by pretending to be my friends. They weren't. They all betrayed me when they felt strong. They turned on me.

MOTHER.

[making a salad]
It would make me happy to see you laughing with a person at a table in a cafe or somewhere nice where people congregate to share with each other their thoughts.

[Son grabs the stool from the stage left wall and places it center stage right. He sits on it.]

Raymond J. Barry

Son. She visits me. She comes down upon me at night and lays her soft body on my own.

Mother. You still think about her?

Son. Yes, I do.

Mother. If you don't straighten out your thinking about this you're going to end up a sad, bitter man.

Son. I think about her every day.

Mother. You have to be careful, son.

Son. I'm constantly thinking about her.

Mother. I understand your pain but I am afraid for you.

Son. Sometimes I could die without her.

Mother. Your father did this to you with his warped thinking about women.

Son. I wish she was never part of my life.

Mother. He had a double standard, that one.

Son. *[out to audience]* She makes love to me while I lay in a semiconscious state.

[Wife appears in the upstage window.]

Mother. He carried on in a way I wouldn't tell you about...

[simultaneous]

Son.	**Mother.**
[Stands, crosses stage right. To audience:] She whispers into my ear. She says, "I love you," over and over again and I nod in agreement, hoping the night will never end with her on top of me, with her on top of me. She visits me.	*[chops vegetables aggressively]* But when it came to me I was in a prison. I wasn't permitted. I was under lock and key not knowing which way to turn, never sure if he would come home drunk or if he would become violent. I grew to hate him. I loved him but I hated him with a passion.

[Wife leaves window.]

Son. Ma, that was your life.

Mother. But you are like him in many ways. You are a jealous man, son. You hold a grudge against her. You search for reasons to hate her. You hunt down her ghost day after day.

Son. But I love her.

Mother. Let her go, son. Let her go. Remember only what you can learn by. Otherwise you will grow old and weak before your time and you will die bitter. Soften your heart, son.

Son. Shut up, ma. You're beginning to bother me.

Mother. There I go again. I am consumed by hatred and a bitter wish that it all had happened in a different way.

SON. *[He circles the perimeter of the stage, skipping gently.]* Don't be so hard on yourself, ma.

MOTHER. No, it's true. That's how I feel.

SON. You're too hard on yourself.

MOTHER. You're young. You can't understand.

SON. You're just being too hard on yourself.

MOTHER. Things happened so unexpectedly. They rather surprised me. Just when I was going so good. I got messed up.

SON. I know, mom. It's okay.

MOTHER. I didn't expect life to be what it turned out to be. I just didn't.

SON. Yes, I know.

MOTHER. I could accept the madness I was living in when I was a girl but I didn't anticipate what happened later on. I'm still learning to live. You have a chance. Don't make the same mistakes I made, my son. I was rigid. I thought I knew it all. I was unaccepting and intolerant. Now I know better. People don't know what to expect. I didn't expect it, that's all. I just didn't expect it.

SON. *[stopping stage center right; no longer skipping]* Yes, mom.

MOTHER. If only someone had told me. If someone had warned me then things would have been very different. And now look at me.

SON. Yes.

MOTHER. Look how I am.

SON. Yes.

MOTHER. I am a decayed failure.

SON. Who says so?

MOTHER. "Who says so?" he says. That's very amusing how you verbalize that. "Who says so?" You probably said that at school, didn't you? You probably picked up that expression from the other kids in school and you are still saying it. "Who says so?" That's very amusing really, very amusing indeed.

SON. I don't know what to say.

MOTHER. You don't.

SON. No.

MOTHER. You can't possibly comprehend what I am saying. *[She continues to chop her carrot in a long, steady rhythm. Long silence. She suddenly bursts into a long burst of laughter and stops abruptly. Again a long silence. Son stands stage right of his stool.]*

SON. *[after prolonged silence]* Ma, would you talk to me?

MOTHER. *[PAUSE.]* You know I love you very much, don't you, son? You know that don't you?

SON. [PAUSE.]Thank you, mother, my mother.

MOTHER. *[PAUSE.]* You were such a cute baby but right from the beginning you were difficult. You were so big. It was a difficult birth. The

Raymond J. Barry

nurses tied a big yellow ribbon onto your crib for being the biggest baby in the hospital. *[She takes a small box of toys out of the drawer of her table and crosses to stool center stage right. She takes a small truck out of the box and winds it up. She places it on the floor and it goes slowly towards the Son's foot. It hits his foot. There is more silence.*

SON. Ma, sometimes, am I talking too loud? Am I talking too soft?

MOTHER. I hadn't thought of it.

SON. You hadn't? Sometimes I press my voice down to give it a stronger sound.

MOTHER. Yes.

SON. Particularly when I don't have confidence.

MOTHER. You seem confident now.

SON. But I'm not.

MOTHER. You're not?

SON. No. That's why I'm asking you how I'm coming across.

MOTHER. You're coming across well, very well.

SON. Do you think so?

MOTHER. Yes, I do. I really do.

SON. I'm not confident. I'm not sure how I'm coming across.

MOTHER. Don't worry. You cut a striking figure.

SON. But how does my voice sound?

MOTHER. Slightly desperate.

SON. Well, I identify with my desperateness so I allow it to reflect in my voice. But seriously, ma, am I coming across all right? Am I myself? Do I seem real? Do I seem earnest? I'm feeling desperate, ma. I'm so insecure. Do you really love me? Do you? Do you? Please, mother, tell me. Please, tell me, tell me.

MOTHER. Yes, I do love you. Relax. Take it easy.

SON. There's a tape inside my head that tells me I'm no good.

MOTHER. You have that too?

SON. You bet I do.

MOTHER. I hear that tape.

SON. We both do. It tells me I'm no good.

MOTHER. No, you're good.

SON. Good for nothing.

MOTHER. No, you're good for something.

SON. If I am I can't find it. There's a large hole in me. I can't seem to fill it. Even when I eat.

MOTHER. You'll get used to it, son. I have.

SON. I'm not myself. I want to sink my teeth into some food, soft and chewy, sinewy or beefy, pulpy or wet, spongy and springy, that when it goes down, fills the labyrinth within me up to my ears, the abyss that is called my being, the hole that is me, the whole hole of me that won't be filled but rather gets emptier every day, a hole more wide, more crevassed, deeper, emptier with each activity, with each business that fills the hours, the time abundant, the hole, the wide open, the broad expanse, the wideness that is me, the nothing of me, the emptiness of me.

MOTHER. That's quite a recipe.

SON. I look like a pear, puffed up like a cream puff, soft and pudgy, puffed and swollen, stretched and misshapen, flopped, slurped, slubbering, blubbering out into another form, filled fop fupper, blubbering, slubbering, slurping, flirping, flupping, sclupping into a fat slob who loses his chance to scluck in the fluck, fluck, fluck, fluck...

MOTHER. Shuttup! *[She puts toys back into the box and then back onto the shelf of her table, stage left.]*

SON. What? *[He crosses fearfully to the upstage right corner.]*

MOTHER. Shut up I said! You're thinking about too many things at one time. Deal with things one at a time! That's the only way to accomplish anything. Deal with things only one at a time, not everything at once. You think too much. You should do something!

SON. Do what?

MOTHER. You should do something, anything.

SON. *[crosses downstage right]* I don't want to do anything.

MOTHER. Sure you do, son. Sure you do.

SON. No, mother, really, I don't want to do anything.

MOTHER. You've got to do something eventually.

SON. I don't know what to do.

MOTHER. Sure you do, son. Think.

SON. I'm thinking but I'm not coming up with anything.

MOTHER. Try as hard as you can and I will too.

SON. I can't think of a thing.

MOTHER. Eat your salad first and then we'll talk about it.

SON. Do I have to, ma?

[Mother crosses stage right, grabs him by the arm and takes him to the table where he sits on his stool that she places for him. She puts a bib around his neck.]

MOTHER. Yes you do have to, son. You need energy. Now eat this. *[Mother places a bowl of salad on the stage right side of the table. Son goes to the table, sits.]*

MOTHER. Mother has not forgotten what her boy likes. Eat this and enjoy. It's lovely salad made to suit your tastes. That's how your mother cares for her son. She serves him salad. *[He spears a piece of tomato. Silence for a long period while he is eating. She stands left of the table and watches him.]*

SON. It's good.

MOTHER. Sure it's good, son. I knew you were hungry. I know what you like.

Raymond J. Barry

SON. It's very good, this salad.

MOTHER. Yes, son. You eat. It's good for you.

SON. I didn't think this salad would be so good.

MOTHER. What did you think, son?

SON. I thought it would be all cold and wet with no body, no substance.

MOTHER. Mother made you something light because her boy wasn't feeling like eating.

SON. I feel like it now, mom.

MOTHER. Yes, I see that, son.

SON. I would even like some more.

MOTHER. Then have some more.

SON. This tastes better than concrete buildings.

MOTHER. What?

SON. Oh nothing. I was just talking, ma.

MOTHER. Yes, I know you were just talking, son, but what did you say about concrete, about
eating concrete?

SON. Nothing, I was just joking, ma.

MOTHER. You are a funny one; you are a funny one.

SON. Yes, I know, I am funny.

MOTHER. The things that come out of your mouth.

SON. Yes, I am funny sometimes.

MOTHER. Eat as much as you like.

SON. Thank you, mummy.

MOTHER. You called me, mummy. Did you hear yourself? You called me mummy. You haven't called me mummy since you were a little boy.

SON. I'm a little boy now, mummy.

MOTHER. See? You did it again. You talk like a little boy.

SON. I'm a little boy, mommy, eating his salad like a good little boy should eat his salad.

MOTHER. Easy, son, you don't want to carry this behavior on too far.

SON. Sorry, mother. I lost my grip for a moment there but things are under control now.

MOTHER. Well, that's a relief. Boy, you're eccentric. You're really eccentric.

SON. Am I talking loud now, mother?

MOTHER. I can't tell.

SON. Well, listen.

MOTHER. I am listening, but I can't tell.

SON. Am I talking normal?

MOTHER. You appear to be.

SON. That's because I'm eating. If I wasn't eating my salad I'd be speaking much louder.

MOTHER. You're getting a little louder now.

Son. I am? Is my voice deep?

Mother. Sort of normal.

Son. Is there cabbage by any chance? I can eat cabbage without getting too fat. I'm fat from eating so much. I'm really feeling very fat. There is a little roll of flesh below my belly button. My belly is swelled up and hanging in folds. I try to hold it in but it hangs out. My chest and shoulders are still firm but this food I'm pouring into my big swelling belly is ruining my shape. This salad is good.

Mother. I know, son. You don't have to keep saying that every time you take a bite.

Son. It nourishes me.

Mother. I knew it would.

Son. It makes me feel big and strong.

Mother. That's what nourishment does, son. There are other kinds of nourishment, spiritual nourishment. That's why your mother wants you to go outside of this house and meet new friends.

[Wife appears in upstage center window.]

Wife. I hear you but your words are bouncing off me like bricks.

[Son gets up from his stool and crosses to downstage right corner.]

Son. Bricks can be loaves of bread if given in a love offering.

Mother. What are you talking about?

Son. Did you hear her voice?

Mother. Whose voice?

Wife. I am kissing you.

Son. Don't!

Mother. Who are you talking to?

Wife. You know you hunger for it.

Son. What do I hunger for?

Mother. If you're hungry eat your salad.

Wife. Don't be bashful.

Son. Come. Let me see you with my eyes!

Mother. Who are you talking to?

[Wife disappears from the window. Pause.]

Son. *[downstage right looking out to the audience]* We should do something.

Mother. Yes, I agree, we should do something. The question is what?

[pause]

Son. *[turns to Mother]* Why don't we sit?

Mother. What? Sit? You want to sit.

Son. Yes, let's just sit. That's doing something. Lots of people sit.

Mother. You mean just... sit?

Son. Yes, that's it. Just sit down.

Mother. What do we do when we are sitting for a while?

Son. Wait and see.

Raymond J. Barry

MOTHER. You get stranger every day.

SON. *[He crosses stage left and grabs both stools and places them downstage right. He keeps his bowl of salad.]* Everyone can't be the same. Now please, mother, come sit with me for a while and let us share our presences with each other.

MOTHER. All right, I'll sit with you for a while but only for a while.

[They both sit simultaneously staring out to the audience. There is no pause here in the dialogue.]

MOTHER. I'm busy, you know. I'm a very busy person. I can't be sitting doing nothing even if it is with my only son.

[They stare out to audience in an upright position. The dialogue continues without pause.]

SON. *[He lays his head on her lap. Again no pause in the dialogue.]* How does it feel?

MOTHER. *[Facing audience.]* We're sitting together, mother and son.

SON. Yes, we're sitting together, mother and son. How does it feel?

MOTHER. It feels fine. [*Son lays his head in her lap.*]

SON. Good. It feels fine to me too. [Pause.] What a day we're having.

MOTHER. It is a nice day.

SON. Perfect harmony.

MOTHER. Yes, harmony.

SON. Things should always be like this.

MOTHER. Did you enjoy your salad?

SON. It was good.

MOTHER. Good. I'm glad. *[She stares at her hand.]* This is how it should always be between us, just sitting together and enjoying each other's company.

SON. I knew you would enjoy sitting and doing nothing.

MOTHER. I don't really feel like I'm doing nothing.

SON. Well, it's true. You're sitting and doing nothing.

MOTHER. I've always encouraged you to do things. I never encouraged you to just do nothing.

SON. Nevertheless, that's what you're doing. You're doing absolutely nothing. You're sitting and doing nothing.

MOTHER. *[She forces his head off her lap.]* I don't like to think of it as doing nothing.

SON. We don't have to talk about it. After all, you are having a good time sitting and doing nothing.

MOTHER. Yes, it is a good time just sitting and doing nothing.

SON. One could even say that there is depth in this experience.

MOTHER. Yes, you are right. Anything between mother and son has depth automatically.

SON. *[looks at Mother's hand There is no pause in the dialogue.]* What is it, mother?

MOTHER. Nothing really. I keep noticing a tiny growth upon my hand, on the back of it. Not a growth - just a spreading or rather a swelling of the skin. It's nothing really, nothing more than a symptom of my age, my aging. We change. Can't be helped.

SON. Oh, well, yes. You're right, I suppose. It can't be helped.

MOTHER. *[She gets up, takes her stool back to stage left of the table.]* Now that you're starting all over again, son, I bet you're thinking about your future. What are you going to do? What kind of a job would you like? You're not getting any younger, you know. You're a middle aged man now. You have to begin to think about your future. *[crossing upstage and around to downstage right]* You can't just sit.

SON. On the contrary. That's exactly what I want to do, mother. *[eats salad]* I want to sit.

MOTHER. Sitting's all right for a couple of days but...

[simultaneous]

MOTHER.	SON.
...eventually you'll have to take action. You have to do something son. Maybe you should go to college. That would be nice. You could become a lawyer or something like that.	I want to sit. I want to sit for a long time, I think. Sitting has become my way of life. I like sitting. Sitting is meditative to me.

SON. I sit naturally, automatically, so it must be right for me, occupationally speaking.

[Mother crosses to Son's stool downstage center right. Simultaneous:]

MOTHER.	SON.
I would be very proud to have a son who is a lawyer. I would be very proud of that. You wouldn't have to decide right away, of course. Just being in school would expose you to so many things you could become interested in.	*[Son should slow this down.]* Other people sit. Why shouldn't I? I see them all the time, sitting around tables in men's clubs, sitting in bars, sitting in parks, sitting all the time, just sitting.

SON. Napping is also something I would enjoy doing.

MOTHER. You know, I heard the transit authority is hiring men.

[simultaneous]

MOTHER.	SON.
That's a wonderful occupation. I	I love the peace of a nap.

Raymond J. Barry

MOTHER	SON
understand they pay thirty thousand dollars per year for starters...	Napping comes naturally and I could become quite dedicated to it...

[Both actors stop suddenly... then start... then stop... then start... twice. Then they resume their speeches.]

[simultaneous]

MOTHER.	SON.
...and they train people themselves. If you don't want to go to school, they would take you, I'm sure.	There's nothing like a good long nap in the afternoon while the world outside is busying itself.

SON. There's something attractive about doing nothing, ma.

MOTHER. *[takes away salad]* You're such a big strapping boy. I'd be willing to bet lots of people would want to hire you to work for them. You're one of the lucky ones.

SON. I like not workin' when everyone else is workin', ma.

MOTHER. *[Kicks Son out of his seat. Takes his stool and places it next to the table.]* You're a pisser, son.

SON. *[crosses stage left, circles around to the downstage right exit]* I have an imp in me, ma. I love being contrary. Whatever other people do, I don't want to do.

MOTHER. You ought to cooperate with people more, son.

SON. I got my mind on something, ma.

MOTHER. We all have our minds on something, son.

SON. But I got my mind on something important, ma. I can't work right now. *[exits downstage right]*

MOTHER. You can work like everyone else, son.

SON. I got my own kind of work, ma.

MOTHER. Bullshit, son.

SON. I can't work right now.

MOTHER. *[at downstage right door]* You have to work, son. Everybody has to work. I'll tell you to your face. You're a lazy son of a bitch, not working. You ought to be ashamed of yourself.

SON. *[opens upstage right door]* Don't come off in my face like that, ma. *[slams door shut and goes quickly to upstage left exit by crossing in back of the set]*

MOTHER. *[goes to upstage right door]* I can't help it. I'm pissed that you don't work.

SON. *[crossing to stage left in back of the set]* I work but it's not the kind of work you're talking about.

MOTHER. You're bullshitting, son. You don't work.

SON. *[crossing to stage left while in back of the set]* I work but I don't do the kind of work you're talkin' about.

MOTHER. *[at upstage right door]* Our neighbors have mentioned that you don't work. They also told me you have little piggy eyes.

SON. *[enters from upstage left door]* I don't have little piggy eyes and I do work.

MOTHER. *[at upstage right door]* You do have little piggy eyes. I'm looking at them right now.

SON. *[They cross in step from stage left to stage right.]* You better not say that again, ma.

MOTHER. A fact is a fact.

SON. Just don't say the fact out loud.

MOTHER. *[crosses to him upstage left]* You see? You admit it's a fact. *[They stop stage left.]*

SON. I'm not admitting anything.

MOTHER. *[exits upstage left door]* You did and you know you don't work.

SON. I do my own kind of work. I got my mind on my work right now. I can't get my mind off my work. That's work. Worrying about work is my work. Worry is work. The kind of work you want me to do involves just showing up. You don't worry about your work. That ain't work.

MOTHER. *[Enters upstage left with a tin garbage can. Places it stage left of table.]* I worry. I worry.

SON. You're too simple to worry.

MOTHER. I worry. I worry too much.

SON. Nobody worries too much.

MOTHER. I worry too much. I'm worried about my health a lot and my girl friend.

SON. *[offstage left]* You don't know what I'm talkin' about.

MOTHER. I don't have to know what you're talking about, son. I know what I'm talking about. You're a lazy galoot. You don't work.

SON. *[crosses to stool downstage right and sits]* My work is inside me. My head is working all the time. I can't stop it. I don't have to try to work, ma. I'm working anyway. My head does the job. It's always in motion in spite of me.

MOTHER. You don't do anything.

SON. What do you call doing something?

MOTHER. You know, doing something, moving around, accomplishing something.

SON. My mind is always working, working, working.

MOTHER. So tell me what you're talking about.

SON. I can't stop working.

MOTHER. Work, right?

SON. I'm always working.

MOTHER. Doing something for money, right ?

Raymond J. Barry

SON. You may not see me working but I'm working, ma.

MOTHER. That's what we're talking about for chrissakes.

SON. You may not see it but I'm working.

MOTHER. You put your time in, get some money and split. That's all.

SON. My work is like the edge of a razor scraping the surface of my brain.

MOTHER. Nothing complicated.

[simultaneous]

MOTHER.	**SON.**
That's work, son. That's work. Not the bullshit you're talking about. What is this internal stuff? I don't get it. You either do something or you don't.	I'm not involved with the world, ma. I pretend to be involved with the world but I'm not involved with the world. It pisses me off. It really pisses me off.

[Son stands downstage right.]

MOTHER. Hang in there, son. Don't be such a wimp!

SON. I don't want to be a wimp.

MOTHER. You don't have to be a wimp, goddamnit! You don't have to be. Be a man! Be a goddammed man.

SON. I'm not a man. I'm a pussy. I'm evasive.

MOTHER. Stop avoiding. Just stop it. Put a stop to the whole goddammed thing.

SON. I can't.

MOTHER. If you say you can't, then you can't. Stop defeating yourself. Just stop it.

SON. I wish I could.

MOTHER. Stop wishing and do it. Just do it.

SON. I'm such a pussy. I'm bigger and tougher than everybody but I got no guts.

MOTHER. Then get guts, you pussy.

SON. I don't know if I can. I don't know how. I just don't know how.

MOTHER. Stop hiding from yourself.

SON. I can't.

[simultaneous]

MOTHER.	**SON.**
Yes, you can. Stop saying you can't. Stop saying that, goddamnit. You can. Be a man. Be a man. Be a man for once.	I can't. I know I can't, ma. No, I can't, ma. I really can't. No, I can't, ma. I can't. I'm paralyzed. I'm not a man. I'm not. I can't. I can't.

MOTHER. You're such a pussy! *[She exits upstage right. Son follows her to the exit, then he crosses upstage right, crosses downstage left, crosses downstage center to upstage center as he mumbles.]*

SON. I'm not a pussy. Big macho guy. Big macho guy with a lotta gals; big macho guy with a lotta beautiful gals under my arm, macho guy, big macho love with a lotta beautiful gals under my arms and feelin' their beautiful feminine asses with my big, macho hands; big, macho guy with plenty of ass to feel with my big, macho lover hands... *[He pantomimes squeezing a woman's ass, bumping, grinding and dry humping as he mumble's utterances about mauling her while making love. This speech should be improvised, semi-verbally with low, guttural tones and bits of phrases expressed with body movements that describe the frustration of his inadequacy which is compensated for by much chest pounding and exaggerated male gestures. Occasionally the speech should be sprinkled with words like "Cadillac", "blow job", "spiritual" and "TV" thrown in whenever it suits the actor. The result should be a sound and movement dance at the end of which he is reduced to his usual weakened state.]*

SON. *Big macho* love. Get a little blow job with big my macho hands driving her little head down, down onto my big macho dick and, "We'll get married after you do it to me, honey," your big macho man, driving around in my big macho Cadillac with my little gal - big macho guy. *[He pantomimes pushing a woman's head down upon his penis while he describes macho love, and when he is finished, he physicalizes the driving of the Cadillac, using the full perimeter of the stage.]*

SON. Big macho Cadillac with a lotta gals, big macho lover, making big macho phone calls in my big macho Cadillac - stocks and bonds and dividends and jumbo loans, jumbo loans and money, money, money, money on my macho portable, big macho telephone, getting a big macho blow job with my big macho hand, driving her little head down, down on my big macho dick and, "We'll get married after you do it to me, honey," while I watch my little macho TV on my macho Cadillac and spiritual, spiritual, spiritual! Big macho man with my big macho telephone, TV, Cadillac, blow job, macho, macho, macho, Cadillac, TV, telephone, blow job! I can't. I can't. I'm a pussy. I'm a pussy. *[Son calls helplessly for his mother downstage right.]*

Ma! Ma! Where are you, ma?

MOTHER. *[enters dressed in a coat with a handbag and carrying a role of blue toilet paper]* What is this?

SON. *[downstage left]* Toilet paper.

MOTHER. How many times do I have to tell you? Don't buy colored toilet paper. The dye is bad for you.

SON. *[crosses upstage right center]* I'm sorry. My instincts told me to buy white paper but I didn't.

Raymond J. Barry

MOTHER. Next time follow your instincts.

SON. *[crosses stage left of table]* I will. I'm sorry.

MOTHER. *[crosses away to table]* And stop saying you're sorry. You're always apologizing for yourself. I'm sick of it.

SON. I want to stop doing that.

MOTHER. I wish you would because I'm sick of it.

SON. *[crosses to her stage right center]* I'll try to correct that. Be patient with me, please.

MOTHER. You try my patience no end, believe me.

SON. *[crosses around table stage left]* I know. I'm sorry.

MOTHER. *[Crosses downstage right. Sits on taller stool. Takes out compact mirror.]* There you go again. Stop it.

SON. It slipped out.

MOTHER. *[puts on her lipstick]* Control yourself. You're saying it out of habit.

SON. *[crosses in front of table, stage left]* Habit, yes.

MOTHER. You've got a habit of apologizing for yourself.

SON. *[crosses stage left center to right of table]* I guess I do.

MOTHER. You've got to retrain yourself to think positively.

SON. *[crosses in back of table]* Yes, you're right. Think positively about myself.

MOTHER. You're totally boring otherwise. Don't you think you're boring?

SON. Yes, I do think that. It must be boring to be with someone who's constantly apologizing for himself. I'll try to stop.

MOTHER. Good. *[She puts her compact and lipstick into her handbag and starts to go.]* I'm going.

SON. *[crosses to her stage right center]* Where are you going?

MOTHER. I'm going out.

SON. Can I tag along?

MOTHER. No, you cannot tag along. How many times do I have to tell you? I don't want you tagging along everywhere I go. Don't you have any independence? You should have more independence. I don't respect dependent people. They repulse me. You repulse me when you become so dependent.

SON. I'm not a bad person.

MOTHER. I'm not saying you're a bad person, my dear, but something is amiss.

SON. I have bad habits.

MOTHER. Yes, that's it. You have very, very bad habits. Now, I'm going. *[She stands and crosses upstage center.]*

SON. *[crosses around table upstage left]* Wait!

MOTHER. What is it now?

SON. I don't want you to go for some reason. I don't want to be alone.

MOTHER. What?

SON. I know it's silly but I want you to stay with me.

MOTHER. What?

SON. I'm afraid.

MOTHER. Afraid of what?

SON. I don't know.

MOTHER. How can you not know?

SON. I'm not sure what I'm afraid of. Please, just stay here, ma. Just stay. I'm going to go crazy if you go. I'm going to go absolutely nuts. I'm going to eat everything in sight, absolutely everything, the chairs, the tables, everything - everything. Nothing is safe, absolutely nothing. Nothing, nothing, nothing - not even you. I'll eat you alive, ma, gobble you down, swallow you into the pit of my stomach and eat, eat, eat, eat! *[pause]*

MOTHER. Do you want to tell me what's really troubling you, son?

SON. Nothing.

MOTHER. You can tell me.

SON. Maybe I can but I don't want to tell you.

MOTHER. You're so secretive.

SON. Everyone keeps secrets, ma. There is always that little private part that wants to hide. Maybe it's shame. Maybe it's shame. *[He moves along the back and stage left wall, skipping and hopping as she speaks.]*

MOTHER. You've lost everything as far as I can see. You've lost just everything there is to lose; your wife, who wasn't the right girl for you anyway. You left your bicycle out in the rain and it rusted so you can't do your paper route anymore. You don't even do your yard work. Even your health looks bad. Your skin doesn't look right. Just look at all the broken blood vessels on your cheeks. Your behavior isn't in keeping with this family. Your father would be ashamed.

SON. *[Both are upstage center.]* Don't bring him up again, okay? I dealt enough with him when he was alive. I don't need to deal with him now.

MOTHER. Don't talk disrespectfully about your father, son.

SON. I'm not talking disrespectfully about him. Just give me breathing space will you? Just give me some breathing space. *[crosses to upstage along the back wall and downstage right toward the stool]* I'm fighting for my life, ma.

MOTHER. I know you are, son. You already failed once.

SON. Once? I've been failing all along.

MOTHER. *[upstage right behind the table]* I know you have. I didn't want to say it.

SON. I wish more people would say it. It might put a match under my ass.

MOTHER. You'll never do anything.

SON. I'll do something tonight. It's gotta be tonight. I'll be ready tonight.

MOTHER. What are you gonna do tonight?

Raymond J. Barry

SON. I promise you I won't be tight tonight.

MOTHER. What are you gonna do tonight?

SON. I haven't been going after my objectives. I've been thinking too much.

MOTHER. What are you gonna do tonight?

SON. I'm held back. I think too much.

MOTHER. Son, will you tell me what you're going to do tonight?

SON. I know exactly what to do tonight. I know exactly what to do. Tomorrow my confidence might go away. I can feel it now but the feeling is rare. I seldom feel this strong. It's great when it's here but I don't have it all the time.

MOTHER. *[to upstage left exit]* Well, whatever it is, I hope for your sake it's tonight.

SON. Yeah, me too.

[The upstage center door falls down like a draw bridge. His wife appears. The Mother and Son stand there speechless for a moment. Son then runs to downstage right exit.]

WIFE. Him. I want to speak to him.

[All move and then stop suddenly.]

MOTHER. You're looking for trouble coming here like this.

[All move and then stop suddenly.]

WIFE. I want to talk to him.

MOTHER. He doesn't want to talk.

SON. Mommy! *[talks like a child]*

MOTHER. It's all right, son.

SON. Mommy, it's her.

MOTHER. I know, son.

WIFE. *[crosses downstage right to Son]* I knew you'd be here. I knew it.

SON. *[crosses from downstage right to downstage left]* What is it? What do you want?

WIFE. Just wanted to see how the little boy was doing.

MOTHER. *[crosses center stage to Wife]* He's doing fine.

WIFE. Are you talking for him?

MOTHER. At the moment, yes.

WIFE. Mind if we spend a few minutes alone?

MOTHER. Yes, I do mind.

WIFE. Well, in that case we can relate without inhibiting each other, I presume?

MOTHER. You've never inhibited yourself before.

SON. What does she want, mummy?

MOTHER. Don't worry, son. Mother is here. Everything is under control.

WIFE. Under your control.

MOTHER. Yes, under my control, as it should be.

SON. What do you want?

Mother'Son

WIFE. Easy, little mama's boy - take it easy.

SON. What do you want from me?

WIFE. We'll get to that in due time.

MOTHER. We'd both like you to be brief.

WIFE. Oh don't worry about that. I'll be brief all right. I'll be brief.

SON. *[crosses from stage right to Mother center stage]* What does she want, mummy? What does she want? I want her away.

WIFE. You want me away, is it? What a quaint way of putting it. You're becoming more articulate as you grow older, remarkable development.

SON. *[center stage next to Mother]* She make fun.

MOTHER. Quiet down, son. Quiet. *[She crosses back to stage left.]*

WIFE. You've done a lot for the boy, mother. You've done a great deal. I see the improvement. Why, he'll be running for president before we know it.

MOTHER. He's not usually like this - only when you're near him.

WIFE. Oh, really?

MOTHER. Yes, really.

WIFE. My memory is vague, of course, but I distinctly remember an adult when I think of your son.

MOTHER. Yes, he is an adult but since he lived with you he lost his balls! *[Wife crosses to Son downstage left. Son runs to Mother center stage. Wife continues to chase him until he ends up downstage left where he began.]*

WIFE. Hear that, boy? What do you think of that? Hear the way she's talking about you?

MOTHER. Don't be so damned harsh with him.

SON. *[crosses to Mother center stage]* I hurting you with me.

WIFE. Like you're some kind of a sniveling idiot.

SON. I nervous.

MOTHER. You know how you affect him.

WIFE. You're letting her talk like that about you too.

SON. It's not clear to me how I should be.

MOTHER. You're doing it on purpose.

WIFE. You always were weak.

MOTHER. You leave that boy alone. Do you hear me?

SON. How should I be, mummy?

WIFE. *[downstage center]* Be any way you want. My, aren't we getting a bit stout?

SON. *[pause. Crosses downstage left]* Yeah, I've been eating.

WIFE. Little pudgy.

SON. Yeah, pretty bad.

MOTHER. He's healthy. That's all.

WIFE. *[crosses stage right]* I see that. And you make him healthy, I presume, by stuffing his mouth.

SON. *[crosses to Wife stage right and retreats from her to stage left]* I eat

Raymond J. Barry

by myself. Mummy doesn't make me.

WIFE. I need some bread.

MOTHER. Bread? What bread?

SON. I don't have much.

MOTHER. What? Bread? We have bread.

SON. I don't have much the last time I counted.

WIFE. Gimme what you got.

MOTHER. We have bread but you don't count bread.

SON. She means money, ma.

MOTHER. Oh, money. Right. I understand. Money.

SON. Yeah, money. I'll give you what I got.

MOTHER. *[downstage left to Son]* No, you won't. You won't give her nothing.

SON. Yes, I will. It doesn't matter, ma. Money doesn't matter to me.

MOTHER. Give me the money then. I'm the one who works her fingers to the bone. Give me the goddamned money.

WIFE. *[downstage right]* Tell her to leave the room.

[Son crosses upstage left.]

MOTHER. *[crosses stage right to Wife]* Asking for money... the nerve of this bitch. You just want me out of here so you can take advantage of him.

WIFE. I'll lay this out to you as simply as possible. I miss you.

MOTHER. You want to coerce him into giving you money.

WIFE. We had some good times together when she wasn't around.

MOTHER. Well, I'm not leaving this room.

WIFE. Things haven't been the same since.

MOTHER. I'm staying to protect my son.

WIFE. I want what we had back.

MOTHER. Your kind doesn't fool me.

WIFE. I also need money.

MOTHER. I know what you're here for.

SON. *[upstage left]* I'd like to deal with this like a man, mummy.

WIFE. I want you back and I need your help with the rent.

SON. *[crosses upstage center]* Men are supposed to pay the rent, mummy.

WIFE. Also, there's a large American Express bill.

SON. Men are supposed to pay all the bills, mummy.

WIFE. I need help with my American Express bill.

MOTHER. You have some nerve, you bitch.

SON. I'd like to meet this new challenge like a man, mummy.

MOTHER. *[crosses to Son who crosses downstage left]* You never pay the bills here, son.

SON. *[crosses downstage center]* That's another issue, mummy.

WIFE. I've come back for you, mama's boy.

MOTHER. I'm the one who makes ends meet.
WIFE. I want you again.

[simultaneous]

MOTHER.	**WIFE.**
You never lift your butt off your chair to help your mother out.	I have that American Express bill to pay. It's on my mind all the time.

SON. *[crosses to Mother downstage left]* Mummy, what shall I do, mummy?
MOTHER. Don't go with her, son.
SON. *[crosses upstage center]* I want to be a man, mummy.
MOTHER. Pay my bills why don't you?
WIFE. Pay my bills!
MOTHER. Pay my bills and take care of your mother like a good little boy should take care of his mother.
SON. *[crosses downstage center]* I want to be a big strong man who pays all the American Express bills, mummy.
WIFE. You're a sniveling, fat weakling.

[simultaneous]

MOTHER.	**WIFE.**
I'll make you a man, son. I'll make you a strong man.	Get away from your mother and take charge.

[downstage left]
MOTHER. I'll show you how to...

[simultaneous]

MOTHER.	**WIFE.**
...get up off your fat ass and go to work. Get out there and fight like a man.	Take me in your arms and run away with me.

SON. *[crosses upstage center]* I'm a big strong man, mummy.
MOTHER. That's what I've been telling you for months.

[simultaneous]

MOTHER.	**WIFE.**
Get out there and fight like a man.	Get away from your mother for God's sake.

SON. *[crosses to Mother downstage left]* Mummy, what shall I do?

Raymond J. Barry

MOTHER. Steel yourself, son, steel yourself. Earn your keep.

[simultaneous]

MOTHER.	**WIFE.**
You sniveling, fat slob. Make your mother proud of you.	You sniveling, fat slob. Make your woman proud of you.

SON. *[downstage center in front of table]* I confused, mummy.
WIFE. *[crosses downstage right above table]* Love me like you used to.
MOTHER. *[crosses to table]* Son, don't you see how she wants to use you?
SON. I not think straight.
WIFE. *[climbs onto table, grabs him]* Climb on top of me, mount me, show me that I am yours.
[Mother grabs Son in front of the table. Both women are holding Son.]
MOTHER. I gave you life, for God's sake.
SON. I awful inside.

[Both women converge on Son downstage center. Simultaneous, very soft, loud whisper:]

WIFE.	**MOTHER.**
I awful inside. I awful inside. What kind of talk is that? You're reverting back to your childhood. See what she's doing to you? I'm capable of turning you into a real man. You will love me with your body and support me. It's your last chance. Theodore. Come home with me and be mine. Let me mold you into something you can be proud of for once in your life. Take me with all your powers. Put your energies where they should be. Let's have a life together.	I brought you into the world and nurtured you when you were little. I breast fed you until you became a fat, little roly-poly baby. I fed you salads and cabbages and brought you into manhood. I protected you from evil women in the world who wanted to take you away from your mother. You will not leave me now. You WILL NOT. I will not allow it. This bitch will have you over my dead body. Over my dead body she will take you away from me... over my dead body. Don't listen to her. You're mine.

MOTHER. He wasn't the same after he left you.
WIFE. He didn't leave me. I threw him out.
[volume builds]

[simultaneous]

MOTHER.	**WIFE.**	**SON.**
You have ruined	He was slim when I	*[crosses down-*

Mother'Son

him. Look at him. He used to be slim. Now he's fat. He's lost his figure. He's eaten too much. He's become anxious and sedentary. You won't take him away from his mother. He wants what his mother has for him.

got rid of him. Now he's a fat slob. You kept on feeding him. I loved the way he was. You ruined him but I still love him.

stage right] Now wait a minute! I'm in control here. I'll say who's doing what and where and how. I'll decide who's going off with whom. I pick up the tab and control my own destiny. I do. I do. I do.

Son. *[crosses downstage left and interrupts their banter]* You just shut up, both of you! You just back off, both of you. I'm the man of this house. I'm masculine. I have the balls here. I have the deep voice that commands attention. I'm the one who runs things. I'm the boss here. I'm the one who pushes his weight around. I do. I do. I do. I do.

Wife. *[downstage right]* It's nice to see you come to your senses.

Son. *[downstage right in front of table]* I'm sorry I shouted. Maybe I got a little carried away.

Mother. No, son, you did fine.

Wife. You asserted yourself. It was nice to see.

Mother. *[crosses downstage left to Son]* I've never seen you behave like that, son. You were so... manly.

Son. Did I frighted you, mother?

Mother. I was a bit taken aback.

Son. *[crosses to Mother downstage left of table]* I'm sorry ma. I didn't mean to frighted you... I... just had to express this frustration I was experiencing while both of you were pulling at me, pulling at me, pecking away at me like two birds, pecking, pecking, pecking. I couldn't control myself any more. I shouted. I'm so sorry for raising my voice. I shouted. I am so sorry for that.

Wife. *[Downstage right, pulls her stocking up. Her thigh is exposed.]* You made me proud of you. I like seeing you assert yourself. I like that.

Son. *[confidentially]* Mother, would you leave the room for a moment?

Mother. What for, son?

Son. Don't ask questions. Just leave.

Mother. I'm your mother, son. I won't leave. I have a right to be here. If she's here why can't I be here?

Son. Get out, mother.

Mother. It's my house, son, I won't leave.

Raymond J. Barry

SON. You'll leave, mother. You'll leave because it is your son's wish for you to leave. You'll leave because I'm telling you to leave - now.

MOTHER. I'll leave son. But you are cruel to your mother. You are very cruel to your mother.

[She exits downstage right after which she sits upstage right offstage. Her shadow is cast on the upper hallway wall where it is visible to the audience. There is an interminably long silence during which time Wife and Son wait for each other to speak. He stands at the downstage left corner of the table. She sits on his stool downstage right.]

SON. You want some coffee?

WIFE. I've given up coffee.

SON. You've given up coffee?

WIFE. Yes, it's bad for my nerves.

SON. Coffee's bad for your nerves?

WIFE. I had been drinking twenty to thirty cups a day.

SON. Wow, twenty to thirty cups.

WIFE. That's a lot, isn't it?

SON. I'll say it's a lot.

WIFE. By three o'clock in the afternoon I was literally shaking. My hands were shaking and I would feel dizzy.

SON. I would think so.

WIFE. Finally I realized it was the coffee that was doing it so I switched to tea but the tea had the same amount of caffeine in it so I wasn't doing myself much good. I was drinking the same amount of tea.

SON. I didn't know tea had the same amount of caffeine in it as coffee.

WIFE. Oh, yes it does. Actually it has more.

SON. But you drink tea now.

WIFE. Not the caffeine type, herb-type tea, caffeine free.

[simultaneous]

WIFE.	**SON.**
There's a difference.	There's a difference?

WIFE. Herb tea doesn't have caffeine.

SON. I see.

WIFE. Eventually I eliminated caffeine from my diet altogether. I just stopped drinking caffeine-containing beverages.

SON. Caffeine-containing beverages?

WIFE. I don't even drink Coca-Cola.

SON. Does it contain caffeine?

WIFE. Yes it does, but I don't drink it.

SON. You don't drink Coca-Cola either?

WIFE. No I don't but I'm still nervous.

SON. That's odd, isn't it?

Mother'Son

WIFE. I don't get dizzy as much but I'm still nervous. My hands get clammy and wet sometimes.

[simultaneous]

WIFE.	**SON.**
I don't know what it's from.	I wonder what it's from.

WIFE. Sometimes I lose feeling in one of my fingers but I don't know what that's from either.
SON. Your finger gets numb?
WIFE. Possibly bad circulation. I've eliminated all the bad things from my diet...

[simultaneous]

WIFE.	**SON.**
...and still I have strange sensations.	That must be a strange sensation.

WIFE. I wish I could eliminate them all.
SON. One would hope so.

[simultaneous]

WIFE.	**SON.**
I don't think about it much. Actually it's not...	It must be strange walking around with a numb finger.

WIFE....the whole finger that's numb - just the tip of my finger. I just forget about it if I can.
SON. You just forget about it?
WIFE. Yes, I just forget about it.
SON. How do you manage that?
WIFE. Oh, I focus on other things.
SON. Like all the beverages that you've given up?
WIFE. Sometimes, yes, I focus on some of the beverages I've given up. I do get signals to drink them upon occasion. When that happens I wrestle with the thought until it goes away, which takes my mind away from my numb finger. Or else, if I'm not receiving "drink caffeine beverage" signals I focus upon whatever task is at hand at the moment. I can take my mind off my numb finger that way.
SON. Which finger is numb?
WIFE. Oh, it's not numb now. It's only numb sometimes. It's not numb now.
SON. Which finger gets numb when it gets numb?
WIFE. It's this one, my pointer mostly. Sometimes my middle finger, but

Raymond J. Barry

mostly this pointer here.

[She shows him. He puts his mouth on it and sucks it.]

WIFE. What are you doing?

SON. I'm sucking your finger a little bit.

WIFE. You silly. Why are you doing that?

SON. I'm hoping you will feel my suck. Do you?

WIFE. Oh, yes, I do.

SON. *[He releases her finger and returns to the stage left corner of the table.]* Good. Then it's not numb now.

WIFE. No, it's not numb now.

[Silence. Son crosses away from her downstage left. Wife places her hand upon her brow.]

SON. What's the matter?

WIFE. I have a constriction around my temples and along the sides of my head, an invisible activity of blood vessels that affects my circulation, a tightening as if a vice were gripping my skull. It affects my circulation.

[Silence. Both face the audience during the following scene.]

WIFE. *[sitting on stool downstage right]* You miss me?

SON. Yeah.

WIFE. How much?

SON. I dunno.

WIFE. Come on. How much?

SON. I guess a lot.

WIFE. You guess?

SON. Yeah.

WIFE. You're not sure?

SON. Less as time goes by.

WIFE. But you still think about me sometimes?

SON. Oh, yeah. You miss me?

WIFE. Yeah.

SON. Why did you come here?

Wife; I need money.

SON. How much?

WIFE. A lot.

SON. How much?

WIFE. Enough.

SON. Stop beating around the bush. How much do you need?

WIFE. Fifteen hundred dollars.

SON. You haven't changed.

WIFE. I've changed.

SON. Maybe. After all you came back.

WIFE. I knew you needed to see me.

SON. That's not it. You just wanted to work me for money.

WIFE. *[crosses to him center stage]* Don't make remarks like that. I don't deserve it. I've been doing pretty well for the past couple of years on my own.

MOTHER. *[Her shadow can still be seen on the upstage wall. From offstage:]* Everything all right, son?

WIFE. I've worked...

SON. Yes, mother.

WIFE. ...and I've never taken anything from anyone. I hate asking anyone for anything.

MOTHER. *[offstage]* Just holler if you need me, son.

WIFE. I don't like it.

SON. I will.

WIFE. I have my pride, you know.

MOTHER. *[offstage]* I'm right here, son.

WIFE. Why don't you get rid of her?

SON. Don't blame my mother. It was my decision to come here. It was my choice - not hers. Actually my whole life is my choice. She's got nothing to do with it.

WIFE. The hell with your mother. How 'bout the money?

SON. You got a pair of balls.

WIFE. Why?

SON. Askin' me for money. You got some pair of balls.

WIFE. You should be glad I'm askin' you. It shows I still care.

SON. What? By askin' me for money?

WIFE. Who else would I ask it from?

SON. Some rich guy who wants to screw you.

WIFE. There are plenty of people out there but I wanted to ask you.

SON. Doin' me a favor, huh?

WIFE. Come on. You know you're the only one I can really count on.

SON. *[crosses downstage center to her]* Maybe you can't count on me anymore. Maybe I don't want to be counted on.

WIFE. Then maybe I came to the wrong person.

SON. Maybe.

WIFE. You don't have any money anyway.

SON. Maybe.

WIFE. Do you?

SON. Maybe.

WIFE. I guess I came to the wrong person.

MOTHER. *[offstage]* Son, are you all right in there?

SON. Yes, mother, I'm fine.

MOTHER. *[offstage]* You call me if you need anything.

WIFE. *[crosses to upstage center]* Shut up, you bitch!

MOTHER. *[offstage]* What? What did you say?

SON. *[crosses to Wife center stage]* Hey, don't start up with her.

MOTHER. *[offstage]* What did she say to me?

Raymond J. Barry

Son. Nothin' ma. She was talkin' to me.

Mother. *[offstage]* She'd better be aware of whose house she's in.

Wife. *[upstage right]* Fuckin' hag.

Son. Hey, back off.

Wife. How can you put up with that?

Son. How'd I put up with you?

Wife. What's that supposed to mean?

Son. *[crosses downstage left]* You know what it means. She's nothin' compared to you. All you bitches are the same. You're all out of your fuckin' minds.

Wife. Don't start.

Son. Yeah, I know, don't start. Just take it but don't start giving it back. Is that it? Why are you here anyway? For years you wouldn't have anything to do with me and now you want to ask me for money?

[simultaneous]

Son.	**Wife.**
What happened when I needed something? What happened when you wouldn't even look at me when I passed you in the streets? What about then, huh? Where were you then? You'd better stop it. You'd better knock it off if you know what's good for you. Just stop it. Cut it out, you damned bully. Don't go on with this. Shut your face, you goddammed bully. You're becoming infantile.	You're living with your mother. You don't work. You never leave the house. You're fat and you won't get off your fat ass to do anything about it. You're just a sniveling little mama's just a little boy. Oh, you boy, want me to stop it. Poor little baby wants mommy to stop it, doesn't he? Poor little baby doesn't like it when mommy behaves this way. Mommy has to be nice to him at all times.

Wife. Infantile? Infantile?

[simultaneous]

Son.	**Wife.**
You're a bully, you damned bully. You're bullying me. Bully, bully, bully, bully, bully. You better knock it off. Bully! Bully! Bully! Bully! Bully! Bully! Bully! Bully!	Baby is using big new words, isn't he? His development is coming along nicely. Isn't it? His vocabulary is growing. My! My! My! My! My! My! My! My!

[Wife sticks her face into Son's face. She punches him on the shoulder.]

Wife. You better shut your damned mouth if you know what's good for

Mother'Son

you.

SON. *[wanders around stage holding his arm exaggerating the pain]* My arm hurts. Why did you do that? You really hurt me. You really pack a wallop. You know that? You really do. My arm hurts. *[He continues to wander around the stage in agony. She approaches him to help at which point he frightens her with a loud noise and laughs. They both laugh at his joke.]*

SON. Are you having sexual intercourse with anyone?

WIFE. Don't ask me that.

SON. Why?

WIFE. Because I don't want to tell you.

SON. But why?

WIFE. Why do you want to know?

SON. I thought you might want to share a secret with me.

WIFE. I'm not involved.

SON. Yes you are.

WIFE. No I'm not.

SON. You haven't slept with anyone since you kicked me out.

WIFE. No, not anyone. I haven't.

SON. Don't bullshit me.

WIFE. I haven't. It's not important.

SON. It's important to me.

WIFE. No, it's not important.

[Son walks to her and kisses her. Wife attempts to gather bags and leave. He picks her up with one arm and drags her toward the table as they speak.]

SON. I want to screw you.

WIFE. *[stage right of table]* We can't.

SON. Just one more time.

WIFE. No.

SON. You know you want to. *[knocks everything off the table, lays her on it and gets on top of her]*

WIFE. What about your mother?

SON. I love you.

WIFE. I love you too.

SON. Make love to me please.

WIFE. I knew I shouldn't have allowed us to be alone.

SON. Just one more time before we never see each other again.

WIFE. You're not hearing me. Stop it, goddamnit! Stop it!

SON. I'll make you feel good. Please, please.

WIFE. Don't be crazy!

[Suddenly they are passionately kissing, embracing, caressing like a pair of wild animals on the table. Mother enters upstage right wearing rubber gloves. She snaps one of them and they freeze in a prolonged silence.

Raymond J. Barry

Mother has altered herself into a sex-pot, wearing spike heels, a black slip, and a rose tucked behind her ear. She is dressed to compete with the Wife over her man.]

MOTHER. Son, why do you call me "mother" all the time?

SON. *[frozen on top of wife, alert]* We don't have to get into that now.

MOTHER. *[crosses downstage right]* No, we do have to get into that now. It's about time she knew what was up between us. I think it might clarify our situation. Don't you think? Don't you think it would clarify our situation? Then she might leave us alone.

SON. Relax.

MOTHER. Relax, you say. Relax? I am relaxed or hadn't you noticed? I'm asking you a simple question, that's all. Why do we have to carry on this charade indefinitely? Let her know. Let her know.

SON. Quiet.

WIFE. What is she talkin' about?

SON. Nothing.

WIFE. What do you mean, nothing?

SON. Nothing. That's all. Nothing.

MOTHER. Don't be a fibber. Don't be a little fibber.

[She places his stool stage right center. He is startled by the sound of it landing on the floor.]

MOTHER. Come over here. Get on over here, boy.

[He continues to face Wife who is on the table. He slowly and with great conflict backs toward stage right center to the stool. He stops uncertainly.]

MOTHER. Come on. Don't be bashful.

[He continues with great difficulty avoiding Wife's eyes as he backs toward Mother.]

MOTHER. Come on, boy. Hurry up.

[He finally arrives at the stool, looks at it with horror and turns his body toward it. He still hasn't looked at Mother.]

MOTHER. That's a good boy, come on. You know what to do.

[He hesitates and then with great trepidation he steps onto the stool with his hands down at his sides.]

MOTHER. That's a good mother's boy. Come on now. What's next?

[He struggles to obey Mother by unzipping his fly and unbuckling his belt. He pulls his pants down slowly. Then he pulls his white jockey underwear down as well. His bare bottom faces the audience. Mother's rubber glove is on her right hand. She places her right hand on his ass and gives it a squeeze.]

MOTHER. Such a nice fanny. Now, give me a kiss.

[He kisses her on the cheek but Mother shifts the kiss to a deep soul kiss with her tongue in his mouth. He breaks away from her, jumps off the box and runs to the stage right wall, attempting to rub the kiss from his mouth, spitting and vomiting.]

Mother'Son

SON. Get away from me! Get away from me! Get away from me!

MOTHER. *[crosses to him stage right and pins him to the wall by the ears]* Don't push me away like that. Don't you ever push me away like that. You'd better show some respect if you know what's good for you. *[crosses to him stage right]*

SON. I'm sorry.

MOTHER. *[stage right]* Being sorry isn't enough. You'd better show respect to me. You'd better show this young lady to the door and allow us some peace and quiet around this house. Yes, you'd better do that, and now, since that's what I want you to do so you'd better fucking well do it if you know what's good for you; if you fucking damn well know what's good for you.

SON. *[zipping up his pants]* I'm sorry I've offended you, but please don't carry on like this in front of her. Please don't do that. *[crosses to stage left]*

MOTHER. *[crosses to center stage, picks up the Wife's bags and throws them out the upstage exit]* To hell with this woman and out of my house, I say! Out, out of my house is what I say and what I want! And I want it now! I'm tired of this. Do you hear me? I'm tired of it, coming here for money. How dare you!

WIFE. *[stage left]* Shut up this bitch, will you?

SON. *[crosses to downstage right]* I can't. She'll go on like this for hours.

MOTHER. *[throws both stools to the upstage right back wall]* Out of my house, I say.

WIFE. I'm not leaving.

MOTHER. You are leaving.

WIFE. I am not.

MOTHER. You are. You have no place in his life anymore. You are history.

WIFE. He loves me.

MOTHER. I doubt that.

WIFE. Ask him.

MOTHER. All right, I will. Do you still love this bitch?

WIFE. Answer her.

SON. I... don't know. She affects me.

MOTHER. But do you love this bitch?

SON. I used to love her.

WIFE. *[crosses to Son downstage right]* You still do. Tell her.

SON. I love mummy now. *[He turns to the wall downstage right.]*

MOTHER. You may leave now. You may go. *[Wife hesitates.]* Get your ass out on the street and sell it. Just get the fuck out.

WIFE. Okay, I'll go.

MOTHER. That's right, bitch, go.

WIFE. I'm going.

Raymond J. Barry

MOTHER. Hurry, bitch.

WIFE. All right! All right! I'm going.

MOTHER. You'd better.

WIFE. I feel sorry for you.

MOTHER. You don't have to feel sorry for me.

WIFE. You're going to die.

MOTHER. So are you, bitch.

WIFE. *[Wife leaves upstage center. Offstage:]* You fucking bitch.

[There is an uncomfortable pause. No one moves. Mother looks at Son and Son avoids her gaze. He stares at the floor in silence.]

MOTHER. *[approaching him downstage right as she pulls down the straps of her slip]* We do communicate easily, don't we? We never argue. We just discuss. Somehow we find clarity. *[pause]* It's a miracle the way we do it. I give the credit to you. I couldn't do it myself. I had a certain wisdom in bringing you up. I allowed you to do your own thinking. I know I made mistakes but I did encourage you to think for yourself. And we always talked. We always did talk. Would you like something to eat? *[She touches his back as he turns to the downstage right wall.]*

SON. *[this interruption can happen at any one of the above lines whenever the actor wishes.]* SHUT UP! SHUT UP! SHUT UP! *[He turns away from the downstage right wall and faces her.]*

MOTHER. Son, you are cruel to me. You are cruel.

SON. I am not, mother. I am not. You must not say that. I am not cruel. What a terrible thing to say. I'm feeling bad things about myself. I get so vague when I stand accused like this. You are backing me against the wall like a trapped animal. That's what I am, a trapped animal, your trapped animal. You take that back. Please, I beg of you, take that back.

MOTHER. Take what back?

SON. I... I'm... not sure. You made me not trust you. I don't know why you made me not trust you. I don't trust you.

MOTHER. *[crosses stage left to table]* You trust me all right. Otherwise you wouldn't be here with me.

SON. *[drops to his knees]* I don't want to leave you forever. I don't, mummy. I don't want to leave you forever. I truly do not. You represent incorrectly. You represent incorrectly. You are not just with me. You are not just. You are not.

MOTHER. *[picks dishes and utensils up from the floor, places them on the table]* You talk strange, son.

SON. I am so hurting. I hurting, mummy.

MOTHER. "You hurting." What kind of talk is that?

SON. I hurting. I hurting. I hurting, mummy. Do something about it, please. Do something about it. Make me feel better.

MOTHER. Son, get hold of yourself. You are a grown man.

SON. I know I not a grown-up, mummy, not now. I know I not, mummy.

Mother'Son

MOTHER. *[crosses stage left to Son]* Stop calling me "mummy." That's not my name. I am not a "mummy." I simply am not an infant's mother. I am the mother of a big, strapping boy who happens to be a man, a grown man with independence and strength if he wants it. You better straighten yourself out if you know what's good for you.

SON. *[Mother pulls him to his feet. Crosses to table stage left.]* I know what's good for me and it isn't you. You aren't good for me. That's why I'm going to be a monster and eat you, my mother. I'm going to eat my mother. I'm going to eat my mother. I'm going to eat my mother.

[He does a short, playful spurt of hopping - then stops.]

MOTHER. *[picking up dishes and utensils, placing them on the table]* No, please don't eat me! *[laughing]* Oh, stop it, my boy. Please stop it. You're just too funny. You're one of the funniest people I've ever seen. You are truly an amusing man. Now please be real.

SON. *[picks up knife from table, stands downstage center]* Shut your goddamn trap. This is real, bitch. I'm going to eat you up alive. I am. I'm going to eat you up alive. *[They turn their heads to the audience while playing the scene as if they are talking to each other.]* Now let me see. Should I cook you first?

MOTHER. No!

SON. No, you say. I shouldn't cook you before I eat you, my mother?

MOTHER. No! *[simultaneously heads turn out to audience downstage left]*

SON. I don't know. You're a little tough, sinewy. If I cook you first you'll be more tender. Besides, if I cook you I won't have to bite into that ugly skin of yours. If I cook you, the skin will change, texture and color and all.

[simultaneous]

MOTHER.	**SON.**
Stop being ridiculous. Stop it. Don't frighten your mother. It's not fair to me. It's not fair to your mother. You're not being fair! Listen to me. You're not being fair!	I want to cook you first, but how can I get you into a pot? No, seriously...how can I get you into a pot? You're too big. I'll have to chop you up into little bite-sized pieces.

MOTHER. You're not being fair!

SON. *[aggressively]* Fair? What is fair, mother? What is fair? What are you talking about? Fair? I don't have to be fair. That's not what I'm about. I've lost all sense of fairness. You were never fair.

[Heads turn back to each other.]

MOTHER. That's not true.

[They circle the table downstage left.]

SON. Never.

Raymond J. Barry

MOTHER. I have always been fair.

SON. You always thought of yourself first.

MOTHER. I have always been fair.

SON. Always it was you who came first.

MOTHER. I have always thought of you first.

SON. No matter what was happening to me.

MOTHER. Honestly, son, I have.

SON. I was always some form of entertainment for you.

MOTHER. *[upstage left]* Now please, son, please stop this ridiculous behavior. I'm tired of this.

SON. *[stalking her]* You are tired of this?

MOTHER. Yes, I am. I want you to stop it. You are frightening me.

SON. You can't fit into the pot.

MOTHER. Oh, God, God, there you go again - always carrying on.

SON. I'll have to chop you up into little bite-sized pieces.

MOTHER. Don't talk that way to me. I am your mother.

[Wife appears in the upstage window]

WIFE. Would you like something to eat?

SON. I know you are my mother. That's why I want to eat you. "Mother" means "eat."

MOTHER. No, son. "Mother" does not mean "eat."

WIFE. You should eat something.

SON. "Eat" means "mother."

MOTHER. No. "Eat" does not mean "mother."

WIFE. I'll cook for you.

SON. Mother, eat. Mother, eat.

MOTHER. Mother, no eat. Mother, no eat.

[During the following pages of dialogue the Mother runs with Son hot in pursuit. Cross to downstage left corner. Wife in the upstage window.]

SON. Cooked mother. Cooked up mother!

[simultaneous, wife in the window,
speaking softly so as to allow dialogue to be heard.]

MOTHER.	WIFE.
Help!	Maybe you'd like a delicious
SON. Don't shout!	salad with crispy lettuce leaves,
MOTHER. Help!	nice and crispy and washed to
SON. Don't shout, mummy.	keep the germs off them and
MOTHER. Don't, son.	break them up into little bite-
SON. Mummy, don't shout.	sized pieces. I'll also add a nice
MOTHER. I won't shout.	sliced green cucumber, a big
SON. If you shout people will	juicy one, fresh from the garden,
hear you.	chopped up into little bite-sized
MOTHER. I won't shout.	pieces. A big orange carrot next,

Mother'Son

SON. They will hear you.
MOTHER. It's all right.
SON. You don't want people here in our home, do you?
[They turn out to audience.]
MOTHER. Don't panic, son. Don't. Mother loves you.
SON. Mother loves me?
MOTHER. Yes, mother loves you, son. She does.
SON. I know mother loves me. That's why I want to eat mother, so all that love can be inside my tummy. Love tummy. Love mummy.
[turn to each other]
MOTHER. Put that knife down! You're just making an asshole of yourself.
SON. I'm not making an asshole of myself. I'm making a stew of you.
MOTHER. Don't threaten me, junior. Just don't you threaten me. *[She exits downstage left. Son chases her off stage.]*
SON. *[simultaneously offstage]* I'm going to make a mother's stew of you and eat you! There, that's for dear old dad, and this is for the lumps you left in my mashed potatoes, you old bitch! You fucking old bitch! You fucking goddammed bitch!

fresh from the garden. I could Put tomatoes into it, big ones that taste so juicy fresh in the mouth. Sliced tomatoes, no quartered, still mouth-sized if quartered. I'll even put in some decorative touches, a few cut up radishes for color as well as taste. Some parsley leaves for green. I don't have peppers. What a pity. Nothing like peppers for color. Then I'll put together a lovely salad dressing just the way you like it, a touch of vinegar with that tangy taste you always loved. And last but not least, you will eat your mother's heart.
[Wife is in the window. Softly]
Cooked mother's heart. Dorsal and ventricle, aorta cut thoroughly clean through, valves halved, halved heart, cut in half, half of mother's heart.
Cooked heart.
Cooked mother's heart with cut aorta vessel.
Cooked mother's heart.

Cooked mother's heart.

Cooked mother's heart.

Cooked mother's heart.

[Mother screams as if she is being hacked to death. Then silence.]
WIFE. Cooked mother's heart. Cooked mother's heart. Cooked mother's heart.
[Red lights appear on Son and upstage entrance. He holds the knife in one hand and a sharpener in the other. He stands in the light for a moment and then walks downstage center in red light.]
SON. When I was a little boy I looked at everything with enormous delight. There were flowers, animals, hot sunshine in summer, people, beautiful people, pretty dresses, black patent leather shoes that I loved

Raymond J. Barry

to wear; oak trees, ducks in a pond and swans, fishes swimming, black, rich earth that was fertile and grew corn and ferns, bones of dinosaurs that were always a special treat for me to see every year at the Museum of Natural History. I also had a fondness for birds. I loved all birds, still do in fact. They were a wonder to me when I was a little boy as they are today even though I don't notice them as much. I was amazed by sky, big sky that went on forever up, up to the stars and beyond, beyond. And also the seasons, the change of seasons that came with regularity each year. Those seasons reminded me of chapters in a book, long chapters, that as soon as they unfolded reminded me of God's power. Then I began to learn things from others.

MOTHER. *[offstage]* You know I love you very much, don't you son?

SON. I shall eat my mother's heart. I shall feel her love within me forever and ever, mother to son unified in a marriage of flesh. We are the flesh family. We are the flesh family.

WIFE. *[offstage]* Love me like you used to.

SON. Memories, impressions of who I am in place of me.

MOTHER. You don't know what you want, son.

SON. Convincing characters substituting my former self, my softer self.

WIFE. *[offstage]* You miss me?

SON.....my true self,

MOTHER. *[offstage]* You sound angry son.

SON.....the me who I was and no longer am,

WIFE. *[offstage]* I want what we had back.

SON.....that wide-eyed kid who stared out into space and expected that things would be good and not bad...

[simultaneous, softly]

SON.	MOTHER.	WIFE.
[onstage]	*[offstage]*	*[offstage]*
with an expression on my face that children and animals possess, a gentle expectancy that some kind person would bring a new toy soon and that will be great fun, and I'll play with that new toy together with old toys and invent new games that will be	Pay my bills! Pay my bills and take care of your mother like a good little boy should take care of his mother. Get out there and fight like a man. Fight for what you want. Fight for your rights. I brought you into the world and nurtured *[enters upstage left]* you when you were	Pay my bills! How about the money? How about the money? How about the money? You're reverting *[enters upstage right]* back to your childhood. See See what she is doing to you? I'm capable of turning you into a real man. You will love

Mother'Son

fun, and when my mommy comes she'll bring me my bottle and I'll take a nap and dream of lollipops and horses and trucks with wheels and when I wake up I'll put on my new baby sneakers and walk around the house with my shovel and pull the cat's tail and life is good with my mommy and my daddy taking care of me and they are nice to me and they are nice to each other and the world is a big toy for me to play with a big handle on it too to swing around and bang against my sandbox and life is so much fun. It's so much fun. It's so much fun. It's so much fun. It's so much genuine fun. Fun! Fun!

[BLACKOUT.]

little. I breast fed you until you became a fat little roly-poly baby. I fed you salads and cabbages and brought you into manhood.
I protected you from evil women in the world who wanted to take you away from your mother.
I will drive you out of your mind.
I will drive you out of your mind.
I will drive you out of your mind.
I will drive you out of your mind.

me with your body and support me. It's your last chance, Theodore. Come home with me and be mine. Let me mold you into something you can be proud of for once in your life.
Take me with all your power.
Put your energy where it should be.
Let's have a life together.
Let's have a life together.

End of play

Raymond J. Barry

Mother'Son

Costume Plot

Son

    black dress shoes
    black socks
    green "dickie" pants
    white V-neck T-shirt
    white briefs - underwear
    fat pad
    light blue-green patterned dress shirt
    dark grey dress jacket/sportcoat
    tan belt

Mother

    blue-and-white-checkered cotton dress
    tan low-heeled shoes
    knee-high nylon socks; tan
    small multicolored waist apron
    offstage: tan raincoat, tan gloves

Wife

    black fitted jacket
    black button-down scarf
    white-and-brown patterned, light cotton dress [to knees]
    white nylon hose [to thighs]
    black high heels

Property List

MOTHER

gray metal stool (30")
small decorative white vase
restaurant type, woodblock kitchen table on wheels
plastic toy box: filled with Legos, small wind-up cars (2) inside
utensils: small cutting knife (2) for salad
           large butcher knife, 9" blade
           large metallic bowl
           wooden cutting board
           colander
           various bowls, different sizes
           pots
           one large pot (for vegetable throw away)

individual wooden salad bowl
forks (many)
square plastic container to hold silverware
vegetable peeler [2]
various plastic containers, Tupperware
paper towels (one roll)
Italian salad dressing
cans of food (2) - peas, string beans, etc.
plastic salt and pepper shakers (filled)
vegetables: two heads of romaine lettuce
                three carrots
                two cucumbers
                two large tomatoes
                five radishes
                parsley
cloth dish rag
waist apron
toilet paper (blue)
pocket purse (black)
lipstick
compact
rouge
rubber surgical gloves
band aids (on kitchen table in case of emergency)

Son
small white stool (18")
small wooden vase stand (30"
flower (real, with smell)
large band of ropes
stage blood
knife sharpener
metallic outdoor garbage can

Wife
purse
compact
assorted unpaid bills with envelopes
small cloth handbags filled with belongings, clothes, blankets, etc. (5)

Raymond J. Barry

Back When-Back Then

Dedicated to the memory of Fifi Oscard.

Characters

Father: a man in his sixties who channels his deceased wife by wearing her dresses.

Robert: his near-do-well son who confronts his father regarding their past.

History

Back When-Back Then has been performed in the following theatres:

ANDREW'S LANE THEATRE, DUBLIN, IRELAND, SEPTEMBER AND OCTOBER, 2000.

CAST:

ROBERT .... Tom Draper
FATHER .... Father-Raymond J. Barry

Artistic Director .... Pat Moylan
Administrator ....Laura Condon
Producer..Myra Donnelley
Design .... Markus Maurette

THEATRE FOR THE NEW CITY, NEW YORK CITY, NEW YORK, NOVEMBER, 1997.

CAST:

SON .... Tom Draper
FATHER ....Raymond J. Barry

Artistic Director/Producer......................... Crystal Field
Producers .... Myra Donnelley,
David Arrow, John Goodman
Director .... Martha Gehman
Design ....Markus Maurette

Raymond J. Barry

MAGIC THEATRE, SAN FRANCISCO, CALIFORNIA; JUNE, 1997.

CAST:

ROBERT .... Tom Draper
FATHER... Raymond J. Barry

Artistic Director... Maime Hunt
Producers .... David Arrow and John Goodman
Director .... Martha Gehman
Design .... Markus Maurette

ARCADE THEATRE, LOS ANGELES, CALIFORNIA, NOVEMBER, DECEMBER 1996.

CAST:

ROBERT .... Tom Draper, Jack Black
FATHER... Raymond J. Barry
VALOIS... Kim Gillingham

Artistic Directors......Michael Patrick King, Tracy Poust, Dan Bonnel
Director ....Michael Patrick King
Set/Lights....................................Michael Patrick King

SMOKEBRUSH CENTER FOR THE ARTS, COLORADO SPRINGS, COLORADO, MARCH/APRIL, 1996.

CAST:

ROBERT .... Jack Black
FATHER... Raymond J. Barry
VALOIS .... Kim Gillingham

Artistic Director.. Kat Walter
Director ....Gregory Wagrowski
Design .... Markus Maurette

STARK RAVING THEATRE, PORTLAND, OREGON, MARCH, 1997.

CAST:

ROBERT .... Tom Draper
FATHER ....Raymond J. Barry

Artistic Director .... David Demke
Producing Director...............................Myra Donnelley
Director .... Martha Gehman
Design .... Markus Maurette

CARMEL FESTIVAL, CARMEL, CALIFORNIA, JULY 1997

CAST:

ROBERT .... Tom Draper
FATHER ....Raymond J. Barry

Director .... Martha Gehman

Raymond J. Barry

Raymond J. Barry, Jack Black, Kim Gillingham, **Back When-Back Then**
Magic Theatre, San Francisco, 1997

Back When-Back When set by Markus Maurette
Andrew's Lane Theatre, Dublin, Ireland, September, October 2000

Back When-Back Then

Tom Draper, **Back When-Back Then**
Theatre for the New City, New York City, November 1997

Raymond J. Barry

Raymond J. Barry, Tom Draper, **Back When-Back Then**
Andrew's Lane Theatre, Dublin, Ireland, September 2000

Raymond J. Barry, Jack Black, **Back When-Back Then**
Magic Theatre, San Francisco, June 1997

Raymond J. Barry, Jack Black, Kim Gillingham,
Back When-Back Then
Magic Theatre, San Francisco, 1997

Raymond J. Barry

Raymond J. Barry, Tom Draper, **Back When-Back Then**
Theatre for the New City, New York City, November 1997

Myra Donnelley, producer, **Back When-Back Then, Foul Shots**,
Portland, Dublin (Ireland), New York City

Back When-Back Then

[FATHER sits stage right center in a chair facing audience, his figure more visible as the lights come slowly up. He is fifty-seven to sixty-two years old and wears a flower-print dress with bare shoulders and woman's slippers. He sits, facing the audience, in a dirty room cluttered with junk, with two hardback chairs next to a table CENTER STAGE. A bottle of scotch lies on the table with two empty glasses. The room is enclosed by high walls with an entrance upstage center. Downstage right, amidst piles of debris, there is an old ramshackle refrigerator that tips to one side, besides which lies a mattress on the floor. Upstage center stands a ladder that leads nowhere.]

FATHER. Get it done. Get it done. Clean the cat; wash her. I was only giving the cat a bath and that seemed innocent enough. Her fur had to be washed, after all. "How could I know," comes the obvious question but then again I was in the habit of ignoring the damage my hands could impose. For so many years they had taken action on their own.

The water was warmish, considerate temperature for the animal. I try to be considerate, although the greater part of me is selfish - a murderer's shortcoming. Flea-tick, toxic shampoo squirted onto her matted coat, a bath for a cat who hates baths, as all cats hate baths and certainly this one did. Scratched me too to emphasize her protest, her claw sticking my tender biceps like a drug addict's needle, puncturing its smooth surface to alter me from rational to raging with my hands repeatedly crashing down upon her spine as well as her stomach, the brutish Cain destroying his unsuspecting brother, Abel. Like Cain I seem to have forgotten the fragile nature of living flesh and find my hands beating upon it, beating upon it, beating upon it a bit too often.

Soot drained from her supple coat as my insults rebounded from the kitchen ceiling, words like "stupid" and "dumb" to keep the sweet beast in her place. Her body grew more limp by the second, indicating from her lack of resistance that she was accepting her bath, although she did whine in protest before she was inconsiderately tossed onto the tile floor where she finally lay to rest. Something so complete about the death of a spouse. Did I say "spouse"? A slip of the tongue; I meant cat, yes, the bathing of my cat.

[Robert enters downstage left. He is thirty three, wears a shiny, blue, double breasted suit with a white shirt and black shoes.]

ROBERT. You should try to control your temper.

FATHER. Go easy on me.

ROBERT. You never went easy. Why should I go easy?

Raymond J. Barry

FATHER. I don't want to fight.

ROBERT. I don't either.

FATHER. So let it go.

ROBERT. All right. *[Robert exits downstage left.]*

FATHER. But there are other considerations here, having to do with softness rather than hardness. My softer side rejects these Wurlitzer-like impulses to kick my loved ones in the shins whenever I dance in the shadow of self-doubt. I was never in agreement with the accepted notion of manhood so why not allow my softer side to speak, the side that ambles to a halt in the face of gruff growling and wild farting of male crowds, macho swearwords with much mooing and mawing, flexing and bulling, tobacco chewing, cigar-smoking animal-like behavior that never made much sense. I too have shoved myself into the weight of bodies to clear a space for my big ass, pointing my elbows a good distance to my left and to my right to steal the territory of others. Selfish me.

[Robert enters downstage left.]

ROBERT. There's so much to say.

FATHER. Say it.

ROBERT. I don't know where to begin.

FATHER. It begins with me. I'm your father.

ROBERT. Yes, my father.

FATHER. My temper.

ROBERT. Yes.

FATHER. My inability to control my temper.

ROBERT. You do have a temper.

FATHER. How I explode - without thought, not able to think.

ROBERT. You scream often.

FATHER. Yes, at the top of my lungs.

ROBERT. Yes, difficult to listen to - difficult to watch.

FATHER. I wish I could stop. I don't know where it comes from, the source of it, a place that's deep.

ROBERT. No one else can speak when you're like that.

FATHER. Yes, no one. I've done terrible things.

ROBERT. Everyone has.

FATHER. No, not everyone. I have.

ROBERT. You're not that bad.

FATHER. No, I'm bad. I've done terrible things.

ROBERT. What things?

FATHER. Things you don't know about, bad stuff. My anger got the best of me.

ROBERT. What bad stuff?

FATHER. Stuff you don't remember anymore. You were a little boy. You don't remember.

ROBERT. What stuff?

Back When-Back Then

FATHER. Stuff. I don't know what came over me.

ROBERT. Is that what the dress is all about?

FATHER. Don't mention that.

ROBERT. All right. *[Robert crosses downstage left.]*

FATHER. Don't mention that.

[Robert stops dead in his tracks and then walks toward the downstage exit.]

Don't mention that.

[Robert stops, then exits downstage left.]

I prowl through the streets in the deep of night, grim faced at the edge, seeking approval of local street vagabonds, my mind shattered like broken panes. Fling-dress and high-heeled, be rejected, be rejected. Who cares about the myriad of insults that follow me? Shaking strangers' hands always curbed my appetite for being who I really am. I'm not implicated in the usual scandals but it is not my game to avoid scandal either. *[Father rises from his chair and crosses upstage right.]* Who's to say what looks right on a man? Nylons demonstrate the clean sheen of my legs' smooth surface while spangled dresses heighten the stake driven through my heart.

[Robert enters downstage left and crosses to the table. Father returns to the table. Father and Robert face each other, separated by the table.]

ROBERT. When mom died something permanent was suddenly taken away.

FATHER. I know it sounds like a lie with everything that happened...

ROBERT. I searched for a replacement but I was so young.

FATHER. But I miss her too.

[Robert and Father turn their heads to the audience. They cross DOWN STAGE toward the audience.]

ROBERT. I began planting tiger lilies in our yard...

FATHER. I was addicted to her.

ROBERT. ...and shrubbery...

FATHER. Even the battles we had...

ROBERT. ...and trees.

FATHER. ...became a necessity to me.

ROBERT. Their roots...

[They split apart, ROBERT going STAGE LEFT and FATHER going STAGE RIGHT, facing the audience.]

FATHER. All the shouting...

ROBERT. ...would grow deep...

FATHER. ...and abuse...

ROBERT. ...into the soil...

FATHER. ...mixed with long silences...

ROBERT. ...and they would be there...

FATHER. ...when we refused...

Raymond J. Barry

ROBERT....forever.

FATHER....to talk to each other...

ROBERT. They blossomed..

FATHER....made me feel...

ROBERT....every Spring...

FATHER....alive.

ROBERT....reconfirming that life doesn't just disappear.

[They cross downstage, again towards each other, facing audience.]

FATHER. A man needs a contest and mine was my wife.

[simultaneous]

ROBERT.	FATHER.
I planted thousands of tiger lilies, tiger lilies, a blinding orange, a wildflower with tremendous endurance. I have the same endurance. I vowed to be everything mother wanted me to be.	I had to win that contest with your mother or I couldn't call myself a man. Measure of my manhood - her acceptance or rejection of me - more than anyone I met at work or in the bars.

[Father and Robert sit simultaneously; Father STAGE RIGHT and Robert STAGE LEFT of the table.]

ROBERT. Remember those orange tiger lilies I planted all over the yard?

FATHER. They bloomed only a short part of the summer. The rest of the year the dead stems just stuck up all over the yard.

ROBERT. Mother had run away. I wanted to plant flowers. I needed to plant something permanent, something that grew. Her absence took the wind out of me. I had to establish roots for myself.

FATHER. You don't live here anymore but I do and I have to put up with the damned daffodils.

ROBERT. They're pretty, aren't they?

FATHER. Yeah, they are pretty - when they bloom. There wasn't any grass left when you got done.

ROBERT. There wasn't grass before, unless you call "crab grass" grass.

FATHER. What ya mean crab grass? That was grass.

ROBERT. No, it wasn't. It was crab grass.

FATHER. You wouldn't know crab grass if you saw it.

ROBERT. I know crab grass and that was crab grass.

FATHER. No, that was real garden grass and you turned it over to plant your damned daffodils.

ROBERT. They were tiger lilies.

FATHER. No, no, they were daffodils. I know a daffodil when I see one.

ROBERT. You don't know shit.

FATHER. I don't, huh? I know you killed all the grass for your damned

Back When-Back Then

daffodils.

ROBERT. Tiger lilies! Tiger lilies! Tiger lilies! You never mowed the lawn anyway. It was always a foot and a half high with all the junk layin' around! At least the flowers made the place look like someone cared!

[Robert sits. Pause optional.]

FATHER. Remember Cleo, Cleopatra?

ROBERT. The cat?

FATHER. Yes.

ROBERT. My cat?

FATHER. Your cat.

ROBERT. What about her?

FATHER. Nothing.

ROBERT. You're not saying anything. You begin to say something and then you stop.

FATHER. It's not easy to talk. I'm not used to it. I don't like talking.

ROBERT. You don't have to. Don't talk.

FATHER. I want to but it's not easy.

ROBERT. So we don't have to.

FATHER. I loved that cat too, you know. I had her a good dozen years before you were born and I always looked after her, changed her kitty litter, fed her, wire brushed her, washed her, took her to the vet. Yeah, I got used to her. She was my cat before she was yours.

ROBERT. I was a little kid when we had her. I barely remember her.

FATHER. You loved that cat. You used to sleep with her at night.

ROBERT. I know. I did. I remember.

FATHER. Cats are nice to sleep with.

ROBERT. Yeah.

FATHER. You used to sleep with her.

ROBERT. Yeah.

FATHER. *[ambles back to his chair next to the center stage table]* I gave her a bath every once in a while to take care of her coat. I liked her coat to be shiny and smooth and brushed. I used to brush her with the wire brush. She was a sweet cat.

ROBERT. Yeah, she was sweet.

FATHER. When I scratched her stomach she would get this dreamy-eyed look as if she was experiencing complete pleasure. She would just space out. She was your cat and you loved her.

ROBERT. It was a long time ago.

FATHER. I remember it as if it were today.

ROBERT. I don't know quite what we're talking about here.

FATHER. *[sits]* We're talking that's all. Getting things out. I'm talking about your cat.

ROBERT. She was your cat, too.

FATHER. Yeah, but she was mostly yours. I may have done all the work

Raymond J. Barry

for her, emptied her kitty litter and all, but you were more connected to her.

ROBERT. I'm not sure what the point is here. She was part of the family, that's all. We all owned her - even mom.

FATHER. I killed her.

ROBERT. What?

FATHER. I killed the cat.

ROBERT. What are you talking about?

FATHER. That's what I did. I didn't mean to but I did it.

ROBERT. It's all right. That was a long time ago.

FATHER. You didn't know where the animal went, you were so little. You didn't understand death.

ROBERT. Why are we talking about this? I don't care what you did.

FATHER. I lost my temper. She scratched me when I was giving her a bath. My mind snapped. Thank god my cat was not my son.

ROBERT. What?

ROBERT. Pretty soon now I'm going to walk right out that door.

FATHER. That's your prerogative.

ROBERT. I may never come back.

FATHER. We all have to do what we have to do.

[pause]

ROBERT. Well, I guess I'll go.

FATHER. No don't go.

ROBERT. Why? We're not getting anywhere.

FATHER. Where do we have to get?

ROBERT. Nowhere in particular.

FATHER. Everywhere you go you have to bring yourself along. You can't run away. Might as well stay right here.

ROBERT. Seems best to leave.

FATHER. I'll follow you out there. You'll hear my whispers.

ROBERT. When I was out there I felt you near me.

FATHER. See? I told you so. I'll be there. You can't run away from me so easily.

ROBERT. So I came back...

FATHER. Sure you came back. We all come back.

ROBERT. ...to find out what happened back then.

FATHER. Back then?

ROBERT. Yes, back then.

FATHER. Back when?

ROBERT. The time when you and mother...

FATHER. Don't say it!

ROBERT. But you asked.

FATHER. JUST DON'T SAY IT!

ROBERT. All right. But it has to be mentioned sometime.

Back When-Back Then

FATHER. No, it can be forgotten.

ROBERT. I can't forget so easily. Neither can you.

FATHER. But we can try.

ROBERT. I'll try.

FATHER. Yes, do.

[Robert tries to forget.]

ROBERT. I'm trying.

FATHER. Yes.

[Robert tries to forget again.]

ROBERT. I've forgotten.

FATHER. Good.

ROBERT. Have you?

FATHER. I've rearranged my thoughts a little, yes.

ROBERT. So have I. I haven't really forgotten but my thoughts have been rearranged.

FATHER. Yes, rearranged, indeed.

ROBERT. Some have been shuffled a few steps ahead to replace the ones that were there.

FATHER. Same with me.

ROBERT. But there's a pressure in the back of my mind.

FATHER. Same with me.

ROBERT. You want me to stay?

FATHER. Yes, I want you to stay. Why don't you stay?

ROBERT. Why do you want me to stay?

FATHER. I miss you already.

ROBERT. You do?

FATHER. Not that I can't live without you. I certainly can.

ROBERT. But you want me to stay?

FATHER. Yes, don't go. Stay.

ROBERT. How long should I stay?

FATHER. Stay long. It's okay.

ROBERT. Like how long?

FATHER. Stay forever.

ROBERT. Forever?

FATHER. Yeah, forever.

ROBERT. I couldn't stay forever.

FATHER. Then stay for five minutes.

ROBERT. Only for five minutes?

FATHER. Yeah, only for five.

ROBERT. That's not very long, not a very long time.

FATHER. Seems long to me.

ROBERT. See? I knew you wanted me to go.

FATHER. No. I don't want you to go. You can stay.

ROBERT. Only for five minutes?

Raymond J. Barry

FATHER. Stay ten. I don't care.

ROBERT. Why would I stay?

FATHER. Communicate a little.

ROBERT. I've had enough communication.

FATHER. Had your fill, huh?

ROBERT. Yeah.

FATHER. Well, then I suppose it is time for you to go.

ROBERT. I guess so.

FATHER. So long.

[pause]

ROBERT. I want to give you a hug.

FATHER. A hug? What hug?

ROBERT. You know. A big hug before I leave.

FATHER. Naw, I don't go for that kind of stuff much, hugging.

ROBERT. It's all right. We can hug.

FATHER. Naw, it's not masculine.

ROBERT. Not masculine, you say?

FATHER. No, it's not very manly, hugging, not between men. Men don't do much hugging.

ROBERT. They should.

FATHER. I don't think so.

ROBERT. Well do it anyway.

FATHER. It doesn't feel right to me.

ROBERT. It'll break down barriers between us.

FATHER. Break down barriers?

ROBERT. Sometimes it's necessary to break down the hardness between men.

FATHER. What hardness?

ROBERT. You're all blocked up.

[Father rises from his chair, crosses stage right.]

FATHER. I'm a normal guy, that's all. I'm not hard.

ROBERT. I imagine you're afraid to give me a hug.

FATHER. I'm not afraid of anything.

ROBERT. No, you're afraid.

FATHER. I just don't like this hugging stuff, that's all.

ROBERT. You don't have to like it. Just do it. It's an expression of love and tenderness, that's all, just a simple expression.

FATHER. Well, I don't like it.

ROBERT. *[approaches Father downstage right]* Come on, try it. Come on, at least let me hug you.

FATHER. Go easy on me for Chrissakes.

ROBERT. You don't have to hug me back.

FATHER. *[escapes to downstage left]* Can't you see I don't like this?

[After a struggle, Robert hugs Father, whose arms dangle from his sides.

Back When-Back Then

Robert throws Father's arms around him and both men awkwardly stand hugging until Father breaks away and crosses to stage left.]

ROBERT. I love you, dad.

FATHER. Yeah, I know.

ROBERT. How do you know?

FATHER. You hugged me and you told me.

ROBERT. Do you love me?

FATHER. Sure I do.

ROBERT. Why don't you say so?

FATHER. I never behaved like this with anybody.

ROBERT. Not even with mom?

FATHER. That was different. She was a woman and she happened to be my wife.

ROBERT. You probably still didn't hug her.

FATHER. Sure I did. I hugged her all the time.

ROBERT. Did you tell her you loved her?

FATHER. Sure. I told her once in a while.

ROBERT. Once in a while?

FATHER. Yeah, once in a while. That's enough.

ROBERT. How often was once in a while?

FATHER. Often as I thought was necessary.

ROBERT. Not often enough.

FATHER. Now don't be so quick to pass judgment on me.

ROBERT. I was there.

FATHER. You didn't know what our marriage was all about. Hell, you were never married.

ROBERT. I witnessed most of it.

FATHER. You witnessed through a child's eyes.

ROBERT. Children know what they're looking at.

FATHER. What about what I'm looking at?

ROBERT. Of anyone they know more what they're looking at.

FATHER. A man who doesn't understand what it is to be a man.

ROBERT. What does that mean to you?

FATHER. Hugging doesn't have a thing to do with it.

ROBERT. I think it does.

FATHER. That's the generation gap for you.

ROBERT. Hugging has everything to do with being a man.

FATHER. All that soft stuff.

ROBERT. Opening your heart is part of being a man.

FATHER. Opening your heart - hogwash. Go out there and get a job. Open your heart to that

ROBERT. That's only part of it.

FATHER. That may be but it's a big part of it. Once you learn how to work then you can start opening your heart.

Raymond J. Barry

ROBERT. I wish I never said it!

FATHER. It's all right you said it.

ROBERT. I want to sit on your lap, daddy.

FATHER. You're too damned heavy. Look at your big ass. You're thirty two years old for goodness sake.

ROBERT. I want to sit, daddy. I want to sit.

FATHER. Then sit but not on my lap.

ROBERT. I'm grown up now.

FATHER. You're not repressed enough to be grownup.

ROBERT. I'm free! Wowee!

FATHER. Learn to inhibit yourself.

ROBERT. I'm going to talk more. Wowee!

FATHER. Inhibit yourself. Stop waving your arms. You're behaving like a child.

ROBERT. I'm going to kick my legs. Wowee!

FATHER. Don't kick your damned legs. For god's sake, don't do that.

ROBERT. I'm going to scream.

FATHER. You'd better not.

[ROBERT screams.]

FATHER. Shuttup! Shuttup!

[Robert slams his chair upstage left and sits with his back to the audience. Father sits stage right of the table and stares at the bottle of scotch. Pause.]

One day when you were a baby I gave you a bath, a bath like any other bath, wet like any other bath as if I was bathing the cat - wet - with soap and bubbles and splashing water and washcloths and boats and floating alphabet letters, the accoutrements that came with all of your baths.

[Robert does not face his Father.]

ROBERT. Wow!

FATHER. That's all you've got to say?

ROBERT. Definitely.

FATHER. Just wow?

ROBERT. Yes. That's all I can think of.

FATHER. Not a suitable reaction. You cried. Babies cry and the noise of it crinched my brain. "Damned kid, damned kid," words released on my breath - never managed to shout them so shamed I was, and you, a shitting, pissing infant child, sprouting like a petaled plant with each day's sun nurturing your vitality and screamed and screamed and screamed.

ROBERT. I didn't mean to scream.

FATHER. Oh course you didn't. I know that. You never meant it. I know what it means not to mean it. I never meant half my life either. I never meant it but I did it.

Back When-Back Then

ROBERT. Wow!

FATHER. I am a brute.

ROBERT. Indeed. Wow!

FATHER. My hands are big.

ROBERT. You do have big hands.

FATHER. Impatience pressed at them when I was giving you that bath. Whatever limb I was grabbing had to cooperate or I would break it off for resisting. My hands yanked your hair as I whispered insults into your tiny ears, destroying the fabric of our trust, washing you as if you were the cat, the parent devouring the child.

ROBERT. Wow!

FATHER. Could you be more specific?

ROBERT. How's this? My heart is broken in many sections.

FATHER. I grabbed so hard and whispered so intensely into your tiny ears that you screamed and screamed and screamed in that hard porcelain sink, that same brittle, uncompromising bed where your fragile cat had only one year before been put to rest, too old for my abuse.

ROBERT. What more can I say?

FATHER. There must be something. Surely there must be something.

ROBERT. "Wow" seems to cover it. I've always said, "Wow." From the time I was little I said, "Wow." I find myself still saying it. "Wow" this and "Wow" that or "Wowee." That's a good one. "Wowee, you beat me unconscious," or "Wowee, you broke mother's nose," or "Wowee, look at all that blood," and maybe you'd like to give a repeat performance of that and I could experience it as an adult, get whacked a little in the head as an adult so as to recreate the anguish of the child in me who has forgotten what resulted from your many blows when I was too young to fend for myself, too young even to record that event in my memory. "Wowee" and "Wow" seem to express the extremity of that bonding event between father and son. *[Pause. Robert sits stage left. At the same moment he sits, Father rises from his chair and slowly moves stage right.]* You know, I'm funny. I'm a funny guy. I have a sense of humor.

FATHER. Yes.

ROBERT. I could make you laugh.

FATHER. You're making me laugh now.

ROBERT. Really? You don't seem to be laughing.

FATHER. I'm laughing inside.

ROBERT. Right. Did I say something funny?

FATHER. No, but you are funny.

ROBERT. Did you know that before I told you?

FATHER. I think I did, yes.

ROBERT. I guess I shouldn't have mentioned it.

Raymond J. Barry

FATHER. No, it's good you mentioned it.

ROBERT. You knew I was funny.

FATHER. But I didn't know you knew.

ROBERT. I knew. I wanted to make you laugh.

FATHER. You can still do that.

ROBERT. Don't feel funny anymore.

FATHER. Oh, go on. You're funny. Have a go of it. Make me laugh.

ROBERT. I'll tell a joke. I'm actually funny.

FATHER. But you don't have balls, son.

ROBERT. I do have balls.

FATHER. You never had balls before.

ROBERT. People change.

FATHER. Really?

ROBERT. I have balls. I'm funny.

[Robert and Father abruptly turn their heads to the fourth wall as if they hear something.]

ROBERT. Someone is slamming a door.

FATHER. I hear it too. Don't allow it to distract you from our conversation, son.

ROBERT. I'll try to stay with our line of thinking, father.

FATHER. That's it, son. *[They turn their voices UPSTAGE.]* What's that? Do you hear that?

ROBERT. Yes.

FATHER. Sounds like voices. I swear to god it's voices. Sounds like your mother.

ROBERT. I hear her too.

FATHER. She visits me often just to remind me.

ROBERT. Remind you of what? *[They turn their heads out to fourth wall simultaneously and rise from their seats. FATHER crosses to STAGE RIGHT. ROBERT crosses to STAGE LEFT.]*

FATHER. There, you hear that? She's here. Can't you hear it, son?

ROBERT. Yes, I hear it.

FATHER. See? See what she's doing? She's here, the bitch. She won't leave me alone. This is what I have to put up with.

ROBERT. Calm down. She couldn't mean any harm. Mom loved us. She wouldn't want to hurt us in any way. Come on, dad, relax. I'll tell you a joke.

FATHER. All right.

[Robert pantomimes a chicken with his arms folded up like wings at the sides of his body. He makes clucking chicken sounds.]

ROBERT. There was a chicken man and he had a cat. The cat was a cantankerous old cat who meowed and meowed. *[ROBERT makes spitting sounds of a cat.]* Finally the man decided to give the cat a bath so he poured a nice warm sink of water and put the cat into it. The baby

Back When-Back Then

went down the drain.

[Pause. Robert clucks like a chicken.]

FATHER. That is funny. That is a pretty funny joke all right.

ROBERT. See, I am pretty funny.

FATHER. Yes, you are. Quite funny. Good sense of humor, son, very good sense of humor.

ROBERT. It's important to make people laugh. Most folks appreciate a good belly laugh.

FATHER. I certainly do.

ROBERT. If you can make them laugh they trust you more.

FATHER. Makes sense, all right.

ROBERT. Do you trust me more after I made you laugh?

FATHER. You know, I haven't thought about it but I have an idea that I do. It softened the energy here. That's for sure.

ROBERT. Yes, there's more relaxation in the atmosphere, isn't there?

FATHER. Yes.

ROBERT. There's a glimmer in your eyes.

FATHER. You have the same glimmer but that should be expected of you. You're young.

ROBERT. I have things to look forward to.

[They sharply turn their heads out to the audience as if they hear something. There is a silence as they listen after which they turn back to each other and continue their conversation.]

[simultaneous]

FATHER.	**ROBERT.**
Yes, you do, don't you? When you're young you'd better take advantage of it so you can prepare yourself for being old. I worked hard when I was young.	That's the great thing about being young. That's why I'm working so hard now while I have the energy to do great things. Then when I'm old I can rest on my laurels.

FATHER....but somehow I tripped over my own feet. Now I still have to plug along - no time for rest, no time at all for rest.

ROBERT. I'll take care of you if something goes wrong.

FATHER. No, I'm too proud for that.

[They sharply turn their heads out to the audience as if they hear a sound.]

[simultaneous]

FATHER.	**ROBERT.**
I couldn't accept your help. I'll have to go it on my own.	Don't look at it that way, dad. I'd be happy to help you.

Raymond J. Barry

[They sharply turn their heads back to each other.]

ROBERT. You helped me when I needed it.

FATHER. Yes, I helped you but you're expected to do that when you're a father.

ROBERT. I'll help my son when I have one.

[They slowly turn their heads out to the audience as if they hear something.]

[simultaneous]

FATHER.	ROBERT.
Yes, you'll help your son. That's what a good boy should do for his children. That's what is expected of you.	I'm going to be the best father in the whole wide world. I'm going to work very hard for my children.

FATHER. That's what you should do, son. That's what I did for you.

[They simultaneously dance up and downstage like joyful children.]

ROBERT. Life is just play for me.

FATHER. That's what's so great about being young, son. You can do so much playing.

ROBERT. I want to play all the time.

FATHER. Old people have such worries all the time, mostly about money, worrying about money all the time.

ROBERT. I love to play.

FATHER. We lose our ability to play. It's a shame.

[Robert sits stage left of the table.]

ROBERT. I've had such fun except when you were drinking too much and fought with mother. That wasn't fun.

[Both men freeze. Father stands stage right.]

FATHER. What are you driving at, son?

ROBERT. Nothing, father. I'm not driving at anything. I'm just talking, that's all. I'm just pointing out what's been fun and what hasn't been fun, that's all.

FATHER. Are you accusing me?

ROBERT. No, I'm not accusing you.

FATHER. Well, you'd better not. I did my best, you know. I did my level best. It took a lot of guts to bring you up. It took a lot of strength and guts and "stick-to-itiveness."

ROBERT. "Stick-to-itiveness," yes.

FATHER. I could have run away from my responsibility but I didn't.

ROBERT. Yes, dad.

FATHER. I stayed put and did my job.

ROBERT. Yes, dad.

FATHER. I could have run away and you never would have seen me again.

ROBERT. Yes, dad.

FATHER. I did my best, you know, what with your mother and all. I did my level best, kept my head in there. I did.

ROBERT. I know you did, dad, and I'm proud to be your son too.

FATHER. You don't behave like you're proud.

ROBERT. I try to respect you, father.

FATHER. No, you don't behave like it.

ROBERT. I listen to what you have to say all the time.

FATHER. It's when you remember things that you get into trouble with me.

ROBERT. I can't help remembering, father. Things just pop up in my head and they have to be said.

FATHER. They don't have to be said. Just ignore them.

ROBERT. You once told me never to ignore the truth.

[Father crosses to the back of Robert who sits stage left of table.]

FATHER. Well, I meant what I said but you go too far with it. You dredge up bad stuff, boy. You dredge up the kind of stuff you can't do anything about anymore. What can I do about all that stuff you dredge up? It's done and it's past. Let it go, son. Let it go.

ROBERT. But I still remember, father.

FATHER. So remember but don't talk to me about it.

ROBERT. If we talk about it, it might bring us a little closer.

[Father bends down to Robert, stage left of table. Robert cowers.]

FATHER. What? We're pretty close now aren't we?

ROBERT. Yes, dad.

FATHER. We have a very close father and son relationship now, don't we?

ROBERT. It's just that...

FATHER. It's just that. It's just that. It's just that. Why do you persist? Why are you challenging me about this?

[Father leans closer to son's head. Robert cowers.]

FATHER. Remember when you were lighting fires, son, how fascinated you were with the glow from each new match, hypnotized by each new flame? You burned up the pit, remember that, son? It was hot that summer and all the dry twigs caught fire. You did it, didn't you, son? All the bull rushes and woods and cattails went up in a flash. Fire engines came from the surrounding five towns just to put out your fire. Remember that, son? A hundred acres at least. Almost burned the houses down in the surrounding area. Firemen watered down those houses with their hoses. You started that fire, didn't you, son? It was so big and furious. I couldn't believe you would start such a big fire. Most of your fires were smaller.

[pause]

Raymond J. Barry

ROBERT. Look, dad, there's someone I'd like you to meet.

FATHER. Meet? What meet?

ROBERT. A woman. Someone I'd like you to meet later if it's all right to bring her over.

FATHER. You want me to meet her? What for?

ROBERT. I don't know; just to meet her, that's all.

FATHER. What is she a woman?

ROBERT. Yes, she's a woman, someone I care about, I guess.

FATHER. What do you want me to meet her for?

ROBERT. Because you're my father.

FATHER. I'm your father? I know I'm your father. What's that got to do with meeting a woman?

ROBERT. I just thought it would be a good thing to do.

FATHER. I don't want a woman in my place. This is my place and I don't want a woman here. It's too dirty and I'm not gonna clean it up for a woman.

ROBERT. You don't have to clean it up.

FATHER. What? Leave it dirty?

ROBERT. You could clean it up a little maybe.

FATHER. Why do I have to meet her?

ROBERT. I care about her.

FATHER. So? That's all right.

ROBERT. So maybe I want your approval.

FATHER. I approve. It's okay.

ROBERT. Don't you want to meet her?

FATHER. Naw, I'll meet her someday if you stay with her long enough.

ROBERT. Just like that, huh?

FATHER. What are you doin' with this woman anyway? Do you sleep with her?

ROBERT. Sometimes.

FATHER. You better watch out for that, boy. You'll have to make a living if you get married.

ROBERT. I'm not afraid of that.

FATHER. You're not afraid of that, huh? You can't prove it by me. No, sir, you can't prove it by me.

ROBERT. I'd do what's expected of me. I'm trying to get myself together. I've been seeing a therapist.

FATHER. A therapist?

ROBERT. She wanted me to deal with some things between us.

FATHER. She did, huh? Just what exactly is a therapist, anyway?

ROBERT. You know, a psychiatrist.

FATHER. Jesus Christ.

ROBERT. What's wrong?

FATHER. Now you're seeing a psychiatrist. What is she, a woman?

Back When-Back Then

ROBERT. Yes, she's a woman.

FATHER. Jesus Christ. What does she tell you?

ROBERT. She doesn't tell me anything.

FATHER. Then what do you go to her for?

ROBERT. I go to her so I can function better.

FATHER. Jesus Christ.

ROBERT. There are some things about myself that are self destructive.

FATHER. Self destructive. What?

ROBERT. I'm tripping over my own feet.

FATHER. Just get a goddamned job and stop the bullshit. A therapist. Ha.

ROBERT. You wouldn't understand.

FATHER. I don't need to understand. Do you pay this lady?

ROBERT. Yes, I pay her.

FATHER. How much?

ROBERT. Sixty.

FATHER. What sixty?

ROBERT. Sixty an hour.

FATHER. Jesus Christ.

ROBERT. It's cheap.

FATHER. And she doesn't tell you anything?

ROBERT. I do most of the talking.

FATHER. Jesus Christ.

ROBERT. That's how it's supposed to be. I talk and she listens.

FATHER. What's the difference between talkin' to her or talkin' to me?

ROBERT. Maybe no difference.

FATHER. You know what I'm gonna say now, don't you?

ROBERT. I know, yeah.

FATHER. Why don't you give me the sixty?

ROBERT. Very funny.

FATHER. What the hell are you doing with yourself? How do you pay for this shit?

ROBERT. Odd jobs.

FATHER. And with the few measly bucks you make you want to pay a woman psychiatrist sixty bills an hour?

ROBERT. Yes. It's important to me.

FATHER. Get a real job and your problems will be over.

ROBERT. You never got a real job, you dumb bastard.

FATHER. What? What did you say?

ROBERT. You never got a real job.

FATHER. No, you called me dumb, didn't you?

ROBERT. I didn't mean it. It just came out.

FATHER. You called me dumb. Now get this straight. You're talkin' to your father and I may not be everything you would like me to be but I

Raymond J. Barry

am what I am and that's the best I can do.

ROBERT. I'm sorry. I didn't mean it.

FATHER. Don't forget I had a struggle bringing you kids up. I didn't want the life I had but I did it anyway and you know why? Because I had kids, that's why.

ROBERT. I'm sorry.

FATHER. You put kids in the world you don't give up on them. You got to see it through even though your marriage is killing you and your kids don't like you and you got no money.

ROBERT. All right. I didn't mean it.

FATHER. You still got to see it through. You must feed those kids and put a roof over their heads no matter what and that ain't dumb, get it? It ain't dumb. I didn't sacrifice my whole life just to be called dumb.

ROBERT. All right. Stop.

FATHER. You've got some arrogance callin' me dumb. Just because you finished two-and-a-half stinking years of college you can call me dumb, huh? Let me tell you, you got a lot to learn.

ROBERT. You've got a lot to learn too.

FATHER. I'm smart enough to finish what I started. You're living proof of that.

ROBERT. I'm sorry.

FATHER. You never finished anything in your life.

ROBERT. I finished things.

FATHER. Always quitting jobs, dropping out of school.

ROBERT. All right. Stop.

FATHER. That's dumb. That's what I call really dumb.

ROBERT. Let's drop it.

FATHER. You're the dumb one. I can do more things with one hand than you could ever dream of doing.

ROBERT. I know.

FATHER. Short order cook, dishwasher, laying sheet rock, diggin' ditches, bricklayer, any kind of cement work, longshoreman at a time when you worked with a hook. Machines do all the work today.

ROBERT. They weren't real jobs.

FATHER. I could even drive a "semi" if I had to and I did it all for you kids, you dumb arrogant kids who don't know shit.

ROBERT. A job isn't real until you love it. Then it's real.

FATHER. I'll tell you what's real, boy. You and your sisters had to eat, that's what's real.

ROBERT. Look how you live in this filth hole.

FATHER. You and your sisters were my reason for everything I did from getting up in the morning with my head splitting so bad that I couldn't even see straight.

ROBERT. You should have been a fisherman.

Back When-Back Then

FATHER. To get to the damned job no matter how much I hated it - for you, boy, so you could fill your belly and become the sniveling, whining pussy that you've become.

ROBERT. A job isn't real until you love it.

FATHER. Everyone has to eat and that's fundamental. That's the nut of it. Get a goddam job for chrissakes. Be a goddam man.

ROBERT. I am a man. What about you in that goddam dress?

FATHER. *[pause]* Don't mention that. Don't mention that. Don't mention that. *[Pause. Father crosses stage right.]*

ROBERT. Look, dad, I'm sorry I hurt your feelings.

FATHER. You can't touch me, boy. What do you think I am, a pussy? You ought to know better than to call me dumb. I ain't dumb.

ROBERT. I know you're not.

FATHER. I might be rough but I ain't dumb.

ROBERT. I don't think you're dumb, dad.

FATHER. Yes, you do. You said so.

ROBERT. I didn't mean anything by it.

FATHER. You didn't? Then why did you say it?

ROBERT. It just slipped out.

FATHER. It must have been there to begin with for it to slip out later.

ROBERT. Don't you ever say things by mistake?

FATHER. No, I always know what I'm saying.

ROBERT. I'm glad we talked.

FATHER. You call this talkin'?

ROBERT. It's good to talk about things that are difficult.

FATHER. I call it yellin' at each other.

ROBERT. It's better to get the emotion out, dad.

FATHER. Get what out?

ROBERT. Just release it and get it out.

FATHER. I got nothin' to get out.

ROBERT. You do. We all do.

FATHER. I worked all my life.

ROBERT. You should have been a fisherman, dad. You loved fishing. You went fishing whenever you had the chance. Remember? You loved to surf cast. That was the only thing you did consistently with your spare time. It was the one thing you did with me. I looked forward to those fishing trips. You loved to take me with you. At least I think you did except when I tangled the line. Then you used to yell at me and I would get very quiet all day and you would feel bad. You hated to hurt my feelings, didn't you? You were a good guy basically but you had such a rotten job in those days. You never did what you wanted to do. You wanted to be a fisherman. That was obvious. The only magazine you ever read was *Field and Stream*. Fishing provided the only communication we ever had. We never even caught a fish.

Raymond J. Barry

FATHER. Oh, go on.

ROBERT. No, I remember. Now that I look back on it, I don't think that was the reason we went fishing. We didn't expect to catch anything. We went for the adventure of it.

FATHER. We caught a few.

ROBERT. We never caught anything. You used to dress in those waders and go out up to your chest in the waves and cast a plug miles out to sea. You looked great when you cast. It was great exercise. You really knew what you were doing.

FATHER. We must've caught something. We went all the time.

ROBERT. We never caught anything. That was the story of your life in a way; always tryin' but never catching anything.

FATHER. I caught a few.

ROBERT. It didn't matter to you. You just wanted to be near the water. You looked beautiful during the summers, always tanned and strong, in great athletic shape. If you had committed to being a full-time fisherman you would have caught more fish. But without a total commitment you were an amateur. You were a short-order cook then. That wasn't the real you. The real you lay at the bottom of the ocean where the fish were. The tides and the surf and the winds were what excited you the most.

FATHER. You kids always had a roof over your heads...

ROBERT. You were a natural fisherman...

FATHER. ...and food on the table.

ROBERT. ...but you were afraid to do it for a living.

FATHER. Don't forget that.

ROBERT. That's where your spirit was.

FATHER. I always held up my responsibility...

ROBERT. but you were hiding from yourself...

FATHER. ...to my kids.

ROBERT. ...all the time,

FATHER. That's me too.

ROBERT. ...either by drinking...

FATHER. Don't forget that.

ROBERT. ...or by pretending to be something you never were.

FATHER. Even when I was out in the bars...

[simultaneous]

FATHER.	**ROBERT.**
You were always doing what You thought other people wanted you to do. That's why you were so unhappy	... I knew I had kids home who had to eat. I always brought food home to the table.

Back When-Back Then

[They abruptly and simultaneously turn out to the audience as if they hear something. They stare out through the fourth wall.]

FATHER. Don't talk.

ROBERT. What? *[pause]*

FATHER. Don't talk.

ROBERT. Why? *[pause]*

FATHER. Do you hear something?

ROBERT. I hear the wind. *[pause]*

FATHER. Listen closely.

ROBERT. It's the wind.

[Pause. Father and Robert rise from their chairs.]

FATHER. It's more than the wind. Your mother's in this room.

ROBERT. I can't hear her.

FATHER. You can't?

ROBERT. No, for sure, I can't.

FATHER. Even if you strain to hear?

ROBERT. Even if I strain I can't hear.

FATHER. Nothing at all?

ROBERT. That's right nothing.

FATHER. You must hear something. There definitely are sounds in here.

ROBERT. Of course there are sounds in here. There are always sounds in here. There are always some sounds.

FATHER. And you can hear those?

ROBERT. Yes, I can.

FATHER. What about other sounds, some presence in here?

[Again they hear something and cross upstage. Their attention is toward the ceiling.]

ROBERT. What's that? Do you hear something?

FATHER. It's her.

ROBERT. Do you hear what I hear?

FATHER. It's my partner in war.

ROBERT. I feel her next to me.

FATHER. Yes, sir. She's here all right, somewhere in this room. She's here.

ROBERT. I feel mother hugging me.

FATHER. Her scent has wafted into my nostrils for years, from her dress. Her garment is a conduit that allows your mother and me to bond.

ROBERT. I want to bond with mother too.

FATHER. Hold my hand, son. Come on, don't be afraid. Hold my hand.

[Robert crosses upstage right and grabs Father's hand. Robert drops to his knees.]

There, son, that doesn't hurt, does it? Father and son - holding hands. Your mother wouldn't mind that, you know. I've held your hand before when you were a little boy. We took walks then - to get ice cream mostly.

Raymond J. Barry

[With Robert on his knees, they stroll hand in hand from the table to downstage center. They walk in a circle around the stage.] You liked vanilla - never chocolate. I always ended up eating half of yours after I finished mine. Ice cream was our big event of the day. You liked me to hold your hand when you were a cute kid with your short pants and sandals. I'm glad you're holding my hand, son. No one has done that for a long time. Every day I stare at my hands, son, as though they aren't part of me. I can't control them, you know. If they wish to beat then they'll beat regardless of what I want. They do the beating and the rest of me is dragged by them. No one can stop them. My fists go into action by themselves. I don't instruct them to fly out as they do.

ROBERT. I hit a woman once, dad.

[Father and Robert stop walking, upstage right.]

FATHER. What? You did?

ROBERT. Yes. She recognized something in me that could be baited.

FATHER. Shit. I did that to you.

ROBERT. No, I did it to myself.

FATHER. I'm your model for chrissakes. I taught you how to behave.

ROBERT. You didn't do it to me.

FATHER. You got your male image from me.

ROBERT. You didn't do it, father. It was me. She wanted to be hit.

FATHER. Don't you ever say that, son.

ROBERT. It's true.

FATHER. No woman wants to be hit.

ROBERT. She wanted to be hit.

FATHER. Don't justify yourself that way.

ROBERT. She kept goading me and goading me until I couldn't hold it in anymore.

FATHER. You're ruined with that type of thinking.

ROBERT. She knew what she was doing.

FATHER. You're ruined.

ROBERT. Don't feel bad, dad.

[Father and Robert, holding hands, walk in a circle again. Robert is still on his knees.]

FATHER. Don't you ever hit a woman. Control yourself and do what you have to do with words. Never strike a woman or even put your hands on a woman. They'll never forgive you for it and you'll never forgive yourself. Walk away from it, son. Walk away from it.

ROBERT. That happened only once.

FATHER. If you don't come to grips with the horror of that kind of behavior, son, you'll end up alone. You've got to recognize the beast in you, boy, and spear it in the heart. Otherwise you'll go on talking like that for the remainder of your life, claiming the woman wanted to be hit. Shame on you, boy. Shame on you. No woman wants to be hit.

Back When-Back Then

ROBERT. What about mother? Did she want to be hit?

[They stop walking. Robert squeezes his father's hand so tight that he can't leave his grip.]

FATHER. Shut up.

ROBERT. No, seriously. Did she want to be hit?

FATHER. Don't bring that up again, boy.

ROBERT. Answer me.

FATHER. I warn you.

ROBERT. Don't threaten me, dad.

FATHER. That's enough.

ROBERT. Did she want to be hit?

FATHER. You've become the worst part of myself.

ROBERT. I didn't hit the girl as hard as you hit mom.

FATHER. Stop it.

ROBERT. Oh, there was blood...

FATHER. Put an end to this right now.

ROBERT.....but not as much blood as came out of mom.

FATHER. Stop it.

ROBERT. Mom was covered with blood, remember?

FATHER. Goddamnit.

ROBERT. All over her nightgown was red blood.

FATHER. Shut your evil mouth.

ROBERT. The girl I hit only had a little cut over her eye. It was nothing more than a black eye.

FATHER. Please stop, son.

ROBERT. But ma was covered with blood. You really bashed her.

FATHER. You don't have to keep bringing it up.

ROBERT. I didn't like hitting that woman.

FATHER. Of course you didn't. It's a shameful way to behave.

ROBERT. You pushed me to say it.

FATHER. Maybe I did but don't fear me, please.

[simultaneous]

ROBERT.	**FATHER.**
It has to be spoken about if either of us is going to be healed.	I never felt quite right every time I lost control with your mother.

[abrupt stop]

ROBERT.	**FATHER.**
We have to talk about all of the events that have been swept under the rug. No more disguises, dad.	I'd never quite get over it and then it would happen again and I'd spend the rest of my time justifying it.

[abrupt stop]

Raymond J. Barry

ROBERT.
No more pretending for us. It's
time to bring it out into the
open. It'll bring us closer
together. That's how it was for
me - jumping on your shoulders
in the middle of the night and
pulling you off her every time
you came home drunk.

FATHER.
I think I hurt myself more than I
hurt her. Don't you take after
your father, son. Don't you take
after your father. You can't
forget that, can you? You keep
returning to the same old theme.

ROBERT. You would have killed her.
FATHER. No I wouldn't have. I knew when to stop.
ROBERT. You knew when to stop? But why did you begin in the first
place?
FATHER. Your mother was no picnic.
ROBERT. I know that but that's no excuse.
FATHER. I know it's no excuse.
ROBERT. It sounded like an excuse.
FATHER. You must think I'm capable of murder, boy.
ROBERT. You behaved like a murderer. You murdered our spirits.

[simultaneous]

ROBERT.
I'll never forget waiting in bed
until you came home not
knowing what kind of mood
you'd be in. I never slept until
your car pulled in and then
waiting for you to come into the
house. I knew you'd be
smashing furniture, breaking
lamps, kicking holes in the
walls and singing that grim
song about mom being a whore
and a slut.

FATHER.
I know... You don't have to keep
bringing it up. I know. I know.
That's enough now. That's
enough. I didn't know how it
was affecting you, that's all. I
didn't know. I was drunk and
didn't know better. That was a
long time ago. You don't have to
keep bringing it up.

FATHER. What about what she did to me? That's violence too.
ROBERT. No, violence is when a man strikes out at his wife.
FATHER. No, violence is when a wife cuts a man's balls off, son. That's
violence, the slow, insidious violence that kills a man, destroys any good
he might feel about himself. Once the violence became part of our daily
diet there was no way to give it up. The punches were foreplay before we
made the sky explode with the pure passion of raw sex. We were both
addicted to violence.

Back When-Back Then

ROBERT. She didn't encourage your brutality.

FATHER. Oh, but she did, son. Oh, she did. She constantly played at my insecurities until slowly I became the man she wanted me to be. Her own father had deserted her and I was paying the price for it.

ROBERT: Why do you wear that dress, dad?

FATHER. You ask too many goddam questions about what doesn't concern you.

ROBERT. It does concern me. You're my father. Anything you do concerns me.

FATHER. Why should it?

ROBERT. Because I love you.

FATHER. Ha, love. What do you know about love?

ROBERT. I know what I feel. I'm not comfortable with you dressed like that.

FATHER. These are my clothes, not yours. I'm the one who should be comfortable.

ROBERT. It's odd.

FATHER. You dress well.

ROBERT. Thank you.

FATHER. You have a nice color scheme there.

ROBERT. Thank you.

FATHER. Must have taken some planning to put that outfit together.

ROBERT. Actually I didn't think about it much.

FATHER. But you do a hell of a lot of thinking about what I wear.

ROBERT. My outfit doesn't offend anyone. *[sits stage left of table]*

FATHER. You're so cocksure of yourself, aren't you? All that macho stuff, pushin' your weight around, shovin' yourself around as if you're a big man. I don't have to shove my weight around. I know I'm a man. I don't have to prove it. In the meantime I'll wear what I want to wear.

ROBERT. I don't push my weight around.

FATHER. Most men are frightened to death of the woman inside them, frightened to death of it like they're gonna be labeled "queer" or something.

ROBERT. Right.

FATHER. Are you afraid of that?

ROBERT. I don't know.

FATHER. Bullshit, you know. You're afraid. That's why you have to dress like everyone else. Look at those dumpy clothes, blue, shiny. You got no style. You look like shit.

ROBERT. I look all right.

FATHER. Bullshit. You don't even care what you look like but you got all these opinions about what I wear.

ROBERT. Any son would wonder why his father wears a dress.

FATHER. Out of respect for your dead mother if you must know. I've put

Raymond J. Barry

myself into solitary confinement for my crimes and this is my prison uniform while I serve a life sentence. I know I'm no good.

ROBERT. Don't say that.

FATHER. I'm everything you said I was, all of it.

ROBERT. You're a lot of things.

FATHER. See these hands, son.

ROBERT. But your whole life is based upon mother.

FATHER. Look at my hands.

ROBERT. You drink because of her.

FATHER. The calluses are from work.

ROBERT. You beat people up.

FATHER. The wrinkles are from age.

ROBERT. You spend time with whores.

FATHER. I should give my hands a face lift.

ROBERT. And now that she's gone...

FATHER. My skin has aged.

ROBERT. ...you wear dresses because of her.

FATHER. Seems looser.

ROBERT. It's time you begin to live for yourself.

FATHER. I wouldn't know where to begin. *[pause. FATHER looks at his hands.]* I dream at night that I've severed my hands from my wrists. I want no part of my hands. They're the brutes - not me. *[FATHER dances a little STAGE LEFT.]* So.

ROBERT. So.

FATHER. So what's going on?

ROBERT. Nothing much.

FATHER. "Nothing much," you say. There must be feelings, certain feelings.

ROBERT. Yes, there are.

FATHER. There are. I know.

ROBERT. Yes.

FATHER. Certain feelings of contempt for your old man.

ROBERT. No, I don't think so.

FATHER. Oh, come now. There must be.

ROBERT. My feelings are complicated. You know I love you very much, don't you, dad?

FATHER. I don't quite know what to say.

ROBERT. You must know that, don't you?

FATHER. It touches me when you say that. I mean... it means a great deal to me when you say that.

ROBERT. I mean it.

FATHER. Well, thank you for saying that, son. I... ah... don't quite know what to say.

ROBERT. Don't say anything, dad. Just accept it.

Back When-Back Then

FATHER. I do. Believe me, I do. It touches me. There could have been so much more in my life. I could have done so much more if I had given myself the chance. I kept tripping over myself. I could have been a better father.

ROBERT. You did the best you knew how.

FATHER. No - choices son. I could have made better choices. The love between your mother and me crumbled, bit by bit, piece by piece and we didn't even know it. We were both so unconscious, you see. I would have liked something to come home to also, you know, something aside from a house of screaming kids and no love, no nothin'. I have a soft side as well. A man has feelings, you know. A man needs to be held, you know. It must have been tough for you too.

ROBERT. I got through it all right.

FATHER. Yes, you did, didn't you? You're a hell of a lot farther along than I was when I was your age with your schooling. You have two-and-a-half years of college behind you, don't you?

ROBERT. Yes, two-and-a-half, right.

FATHER. You should have finished but what the heck. Why did you say you left school?

ROBERT. I ran out of money.

FATHER. Oh, yes, right.

ROBERT. I was paying for the whole thing myself.

FATHER. Right.

ROBERT. You never helped me.

FATHER. Stop your damned whining.

ROBERT. I'm not whining. You asked me.

FATHER. You brought it up.

ROBERT. No, you brought it up.

FATHER. No, you brought it up.

ROBERT. I did not and who cares anyway?

FATHER. You blame me for your failure.

ROBERT. Who cares about college?

FATHER. I care.

ROBERT. I work - part time.

FATHER. Look at yourself. What do you do, for chrissakes?

ROBERT. I work at the docks.

FATHER. If you're satisfied then I'm satisfied.

ROBERT. I unload fruit.

FATHER. You don't even work full time, for chrissakes.

ROBERT. Nothing wrong with that.

FATHER. You don't even work full time.

ROBERT. What do you care?

FATHER. Just watch out, boy.

ROBERT. I pay my way.

Raymond J. Barry

FATHER. I worked all my life doin' shit work with my hands, not my brain, and I'm tellin' you it ain't a life. It's a prison term. You oughta find a way to go back to college and get your education.

ROBERT. Like you did, huh?

FATHER. All right, look at me. No don't look away. Really look at me. You think I like who I am? I don't. And you know why? Because I'm a dumb ox, that's why. I'm a beast of burden, bred and trained to load and unload trucks or load pipe or sweep floors or whatever else some rich asshole doesn't want to do himself. So take a good look at your old man, boy, because this is how you're going to end up if you don't wake up. You have to make your life work, boy. You have to make it work 'cause if you don't, everything will come down on you all at once. Don't be like your father, boy.

ROBERT. All right. All right.

FATHER. You say it's all right but it isn't all right. You've wasted too much of your life already.

ROBERT. I haven't wasted my life, dad. It all counts. Nothing is wasted. It's all a learning process.

FATHER. Is that what your psychiatrist told you for sixty bucks an hour?

ROBERT. I wish I never said it.

FATHER. It's all right you said it.

ROBERT. I want to sit on your lap, daddy.

FATHER. You're too damned heavy. Look at your big ass. You're thirty-three years old for goodness sake.

ROBERT. I want to sit, daddy. I want to sit.

FATHER. Then sit, but not on my lap.

ROBERT. I'm grown up now.

FATHER. You're not repressed enough to be grown up.

ROBERT. I'm free.

FATHER. Learn to inhibit yourself.

ROBERT. I'm going to talk more.

FATHER. Inhibit yourself. Stop waving your arms. You're behaving like a child.

ROBERT. I'm going to kick my legs.

FATHER. Don't kick your damned legs. For God's sake don't do that. You're not making sense, boy.

ROBERT. Yes, raving, babbling. What a terrific thrill it is to pay rent for a roof over my head. Imperative! A job. Make money. Make money. Make money, money, money!

FATHER. That's what I've been tellin' ya for years, boy.

ROBERT. Well, in that case we're on the same wave length, more stuck together if you will, more stuck together. I'm going to scream.

FATHER. You'd better not.

ROBERT. AAAAAAGH! AAAAAAAGH *[ROBERT screams.]*

Back When-Back Then

FATHER. Shuttup! Shuttup!

[Robert runs up to the top of the ladder. Father looks at him in wonderment.]

FATHER. What are you standing there for?

ROBERT. Nothing. *[pause]*

FATHER. Well you're standing there waiting for something, aren't you?

ROBERT. Not really.

FATHER. You seem to be. You must be used to it.

ROBERT. Used to what?

FATHER. Used to waiting for something to happen.

ROBERT. I guess so. I guess we're all waiting for something to happen.

FATHER. *[crosses to ladder UP STAGE RIGHT]* I'm not. I know nothing's going to happen 'cause that's the way life is. Nothing ever happens unless you make it happen. That's what you got to learn, boy. You got to learn to stop waiting and make something happen. You got to learn to take initiative.

ROBERT. Here we go again.

FATHER. All right. All right. I'll stop. I know I'm a bit of nag. *[near ladder UPSTAGE RIGHT.]* I've spent so much of my life waiting for others to tell me what to do that it pains me to see my own son develop the same goddam habit, that's all. I care about you. *[FATHER goes down on his knees.]* Don't you see that, son? I genuinely care about you. Please forgive me for being a nag.

ROBERT. I forgive you, father.

FATHER. All right then. You want a drink or something? *[Father rises, crosses to the table and pours himself a drink.]*

ROBERT. No thanks.

FATHER. I'm going to have one.

ROBERT. Right.

FATHER. I need to relax.

ROBERT. Right.

FATHER. Nothing wrong with relaxing.

ROBERT. Right.

FATHER. Don't worry. I'm not going to overdo it.

ROBERT. I know.

FATHER. Them days are gone forever.

ROBERT. Yeah.

FATHER. You ever drink?

ROBERT. A little.

FATHER. You ever overdo it?

ROBERT. Oh, yeah, once or twice.

FATHER. You know how rotten that feels then. I mean, the next morning.

ROBERT. Yeah.

FATHER. I've had many a next morning. I'm used to it. Wasted a lot of

Raymond J. Barry

time drinking, a lot of time.

ROBERT. Yeah.

FATHER. Got nothin' to show for it either. I don't know. I don't know. *[Robert doesn't respond.]* I wish I did know. I wish I did. *[Father takes his first sip of scotch.]* Nothing like the warmth of scotch, nothing like it. *[Robert doesn't respond.]* God, life is bleak - just bleak. Waiting, waiting for something interesting to happen. Been waiting all my life for something interesting to happen. The other kids? Where are they now?

ROBERT. Upstate I think. The youngest gave up drinking.

FATHER. That's good.

ROBERT. The oldest got cancer, almost died.

FATHER. What kind?

ROBERT. The kind that eats you alive.

FATHER. But she lived?

ROBERT. Yes, barely.

FATHER. That's good.

ROBERT. Her husband is sick too - bad heart.

FATHER. Lost contact with both of them. Time went by and the visits became phone calls until the night I ripped the phone out of the wall and then finally an occasional note I never returned. Even they stopped. Something natural about it, I suppose. Kids become adults, lose touch, develop their own interests, their own obsessions. It's only natural. Can't blame myself. When they were little I couldn't wait for them to grow up, but now I miss the sound of children in my house.

FATHER AND ROBERT. "When the kids grow up!" *[FATHER stops.]*

FATHER. I would say to myself as if my troubles would be over but that's not how it's worked out. Surprisingly I've been lonely, son. Made it that way, I suppose. My existence is no better than when I was struggling to keep everyone fed. Now there's nothing to fight, nothing to demand of myself. A darkness surrounds me and I just wait. There's nothing but waiting. For what, I haven't figured out. When you were born I thought I'd have some reason to go through all of it but after a year it was the same; just more responsibility, that's all, just one more mouth to feed, that's all. Your existence made it more difficult to escape it all. Couldn't run away from my responsibility. God knows I thought about it, but I couldn't run away. You hear me, boy?

ROBERT. Yeah.

FATHER. I didn't run away. That's one thing I can say for myself. You can give me credit for that.

ROBERT. Yeah.

FATHER. That's all you got to say?

ROBERT. I guess so.

FATHER. Just "yeah"?

ROBERT. I didn't run away either.

Back When-Back Then

FATHER. You didn't run away? Why would you run away? Where would you run to anyway? You had no place to run. You know that.

ROBERT. *[climbs down ladder, crosses to table]* I could have found a place.

FATHER. You have to have guts to run away when you're a kid.

ROBERT. I stayed to protect mom. That took guts.

FATHER. You stayed to protect mom from what?

ROBERT. Why do you really wear that dress, dad?

FATHER. I don't want to talk about it.

ROBERT. Why don't you want to talk about it?

FATHER. I don't want it used against me.

ROBERT. I wouldn't use anything against you.

FATHER. You can't know that.

ROBERT. I'm not a vindictive person.

FATHER. You might try to get even with me.

ROBERT. I've got secrets too. I'd like to tell you one secret.

FATHER. Please don't.

ROBERT. I'm going to.

FATHER. I wish you wouldn't.

ROBERT. I was a shy boy, extremely shy.

FATHER. I wish you wouldn't tell me this.

ROBERT. One time when I came down the stairs I smelled fish. The whole house smelled of fish.

FATHER. I remember. I remember.

ROBERT. I didn't know if I was smelling things or what...

FATHER. I was something all right.

ROBERT. ...but the place definitely stunk.

FATHER. I can't believe the shit I used to pull.

ROBERT. You were sprawled out on the couch and you know what was all over you?

FATHER. No, what?

ROBERT. Maybe I shouldn't tell you.

FATHER. No, tell me. We're finally talking, right?

ROBERT. Yeah, we're finally talking.

FATHER. So tell me. What was all over me?

ROBERT. Naw, maybe I shouldn't.

FATHER. No, go on. Here have another drink. *[FATHER attempts to pour more scotch into Robert's glass. The bottle is half full.]*

ROBERT. Condoms.

FATHER. What?

ROBERT. Condoms.

FATHER. What do you mean, condoms?

ROBERT. You know, scumbags.

FATHER. Watch your language.

Raymond J. Barry

ROBERT. You were covered with condoms, all over your legs and belly. There was an empty box of condoms and your cock was hanging out.

FATHER. No it wasn't.

ROBERT. Yes, it was. I saw.

FATHER. Are you sure?

ROBERT. Yes, I'm sure.

FATHER. You must be imagining things.

ROBERT. No, I'm not imagining things. I saw it with my own eyes.

FATHER. You were a little kid then. You didn't know what you saw.

ROBERT. I knew. And then I walked into the kitchen. There was a big tuna fish on that green Formica table in the kitchen. Remember that table, dad?

FATHER. Yes, I remember, the green Formica table in the kitchen, right?

ROBERT. Yeah, in the kitchen. Anyway, there was a huge tuna fish on it...

FATHER. Oh, yeah.

ROBERT....with the tail hanging over one end...

FATHER. I remember now.

ROBERT....and the head on the other end...

FATHER. Boy, what a memory you got, boy.

ROBERT....and it stunk to high heaven.

FATHER. What a memory.

ROBERT. The smell was so thick I had to hold my nose.

FATHER. Nothin' gets by you. I bought that fish from a fisherman in a Freeport bar. He sold it to me for a couple of bucks and a few drinks. I remember now. I brought it home to eat.

ROBERT. To eat?

FATHER. Yeah, to eat. I shoulda' put it into the refrigerator.

ROBERT. You were drunk.

FATHER. Yeah, I know. Ha. Ha. Ha.

ROBERT. You weren't thinking straight.

FATHER. What a wild man I was.

ROBERT. That fish really smelled... and you on the couch passed out with those condoms all over your belly. What were the condoms for, dad? You didn't sleep with mom. Why would you have condoms?

FATHER. What's past is done.

ROBERT. You were messing around, weren't you? Here, have another drink, dad. It'll help you talk about it a little. That's what we're doing, isn't it? We're talking.

FATHER. Yeah, we're talking but I don't remember any condoms. You're just makin' that up. I remember the tuna fish but I don't remember any condoms.

ROBERT. They were scattered all over your belly as if you had tried to put one on in your drunken stupor.

Back When-Back Then

FATHER. You don't know what you're talkin' about, boy. I was just drunk, that's all.

ROBERT. You must have been lonely. You never slept with mom.

FATHER. Don't ask questions.

ROBERT. What did you do for sex?

FATHER. That stuff is none of your business.

ROBERT. That stuff is alien to your Catholic upbringing, isn't it?

FATHER. Alien? What is "alien"? What does that mean? Speak English.

ROBERT. You always called mom a whore but you were the one who did the whoring.

FATHER. Shuttup.

ROBERT. Why should I? We're talking, aren't we?

FATHER. I don't know what you're doin' with this shit.

ROBERT. Dad, don't you see? All the accusations you used to direct at mom about her running around with men?

FATHER. She hadn't slept with me for years.

ROBERT. You were the one running around, weren't you, dad?

FATHER. Why shouldn't I have messed around?

ROBERT. All I saw related to the issue of sex was a box of opened condoms on your belly.

FATHER. Drop it.

ROBERT. That's what I understood a marriage was.

FATHER. It's none of your business.

ROBERT. It's my business when it comes to the woman I care about. Then it becomes an issue, a big issue.

FATHER. Your lady friends are your own affair - not mine.

ROBERT. Except for one thing, dad. I'm not capable of having a relationship.

[simultaneous]

ROBERT.	FATHER.
I can't allow myself to feel love towards anyone. Love to me is brutality and cruelty.	Stop feeling sorry for yourself. You talk like a woman. Wake up. 'Cause nobody's gonna do it for

FATHER. ...you. Be a man for a change.

ROBERT. Oh, yeah, that "be a man" business. How did you get the syphilis, dad?

FATHER. Syphilis? I never had the syphilis. The Board of Health sent that notice to the wrong house, son.

ROBERT. Did you get syphilis from another woman?

FATHER. I didn't get the syphilis. I was exposed to syphilis.

ROBERT. From a man?

FATHER. Not from a man! What do you take me for, boy? Some kind of a

Raymond J. Barry

homo?

ROBERT. From a man?

FATHER. I didn't get the syphilis from a man. I got it from a woman!

ROBERT. What woman, daddy?

[Pause.]

FATHER. Just a whore at a bar. A whore at a bar. And I exposed your mother to syphilis at the Bricklayers' Convention,

[simultaneous]

ROBERT.	**FATHER.**
... the Bricklayers' Convention in Florida.	The Bricklayer's Convention in Florida.

FATHER. We slept together, your mother and I,...

[simultaneous]

ROBERT.	**FATHER.**
... at the Bricklayer's convention.	At the Bricklayer's convention?

FATHER. Other men were at the Bricklayer's Convention with their wives...

ROBERT. She wasn't your wife really!

FATHER. ...and they were getting it.

ROBERT. You simply lived together!

FATHER. Why shouldn't have I gotten it?

ROBERT. You had a silent agreement...

FATHER. She was my wife...

ROBERT. ...to ignore each other!

FATHER. I needed her bad that night.

ROBERT. You had a truce!

FATHER. So I forced her...

ROBERT. You violated her!

FATHER. ...and I exposed her to syphilis.

ROBERT. By raping her!

FATHER. I didn't realize I had it.

ROBERT. Never, never again!

FATHER. We all have needs, you know.

[simultaneous]

ROBERT.	**FATHER.**
She was so furious, so insulted that her needs would have been put aside. You begged her to go	And those needs, if they are not fulfilled, leave us, empty or even at times slightly desperate if they

to the Bricklayer's Convention.   are not fulfilled.

FATHER. Your mother was a dyke! A dyke! She was with a woman and pretended all those years, gave the impression that I was the guilty one, gave you kids that impression that I was the one who was nuts.

ROBERT. You were nuts, Dad. How could she tell you? You would have smashed her in the face.

FATHER. You sided with her.

ROBERT. That's right. I sided with her. I was proud of her. She had guts enough to accept who she was and get on with it. Damned right I sided with her. I didn't care what she was. She was my mother and she was involved with a woman. So what? She had respect for me and you never did.

[simultaneous]

FATHER.	**ROBERT.**
I was made to believe I wasn't good enough. Not good enough? I'll show her! I'll prove I'm good with my hard fists to her cheekbone - fighting myself really.	You never even looked at me but she did. She took care of me the best she knew how even though she could barely take care of herself. Who else was I supposed to side with?

FATHER. She was a homosexual woman.

ROBERT. I didn't care about that then and I don't care about it now. She was a great woman as far as I'm concerned. She managed to survive in a hellish, murderous environment and she had a right to be who she was. She had one relationship that gave her support and love, something every human being needs. She happened to have gotten it from a woman. So what? I've watched you beat people, fight, punch mother, smash lamps – all kinds of craziness and yet she's the guilty one here. What kind of hypocrisy is that? What am I to understand? I have a short fuse too and I hate that in myself but where do you think I picked it up? I learned rage from my own father. If it wasn't for her I'd be like you, hating queers, blacks, Yellows, Jews and anyone else who might be different but I'm not like you. I'm like her. I'm softer than you. I like all people and the oppressed I like a little bit more. Look at yourself. You're wearing a dress, for chrissakes, a dress! And yet you point fingers at her. Mommy loves you, daddy.

FATHER. What? That's not what she said, son. She said the opposite. You're changing the words. Listen to him, mother.

ROBERT. She said she loves you, daddy.

FATHER. *[to dead MOTHER beyond the fourth wall]* He's changing the words.

Raymond J. Barry

ROBERT. I'm a big boy now.

FATHER. *[to MOTHER beyond the fourth wall]* He's changing the words. What about that, mother? Making his own interpretation.

ROBERT. My mind wanders.

FATHER. You've got to focus on the truth, boy. Can't make things up.

ROBERT. I was taking a short cut.

FATHER. Yes, a short cut at our expense, distorting the facts.

ROBERT. I wasn't trying to hurt anything, papa

FATHER. But that wasn't what your mother said, boy.

ROBERT. Let me be.

FATHER. Don't change the words, boy. We have to trust the words.

ROBERT. Words never meant much.

FATHER. Oh, no, they did. They were like darts aiming at our vital parts.

ROBERT. So what would you like to do now, daddy? Wowee! Maybe kiss me or hug me? No, you don't like hugging, right? I remember. You don't like hugging. Wowee! So what means of expression do you like? Kill me? Hit me? Smash me? Hurt me? Maim me? Wound me? Yelling or cursing? Wowee! Or backslapping like two Brahmin bulls, farting in a china shop? What can we do but talk, daddy and try our best to understand?

FATHER. You said you loved your papa, son.

ROBERT. That's not what I said! You're changing the words.

FATHER. Stop badgering me, son.

ROBERT. I'll badger if I want. I want to scare you.

FATHER. You're not vicious enough to scare me. I'm the vicious one around here, son. You'll have to take a back seat to your father.

ROBERT. I won't. I won't. I'm vicious too. Watch! Grrrrr. Grrrrrrrrr.

[ROBERT pretends he's a mad dog down on all fours. FATHER keeps his distance from him, STAGE RIGHT.]

FATHER. Look at yourself. Aren't you silly? Anyone can growl. Even I could do that. Yes, anyone can growl.

ROBERT. Grrrrrrrrr. Grrrrrrrrrrrr.

FATHER. You're having the time of your life, aren't you, son?

ROBERT. Grrrrrrrrrr... I'm a dangerous beast. Grrrrrrrrrrrr...

FATHER. You're so indulgent, Robert.

[ROBERT chases his father around the table on all fours.]

FATHER. Boy, why don't you get back up on your feet? Give me some breathing space.

[ROBERT is still behaving like a vicious beast. It has become a bit too serious for him.]

ROBERT. Nobody takes me seriously around here. Grrrrrrrrrrrrrrgh!

[FATHER attempts to pet ROBERT upon the head.]

FATHER. You're a pesky little feller. Yup, that's what you are, a little pesty.

Back When-Back Then

ROBERT. Now I'm really mad. Grrrrrrrrrgh! GRRRRRRRGH!

[ROBERT bites FATHER'S leg

FATHER. Hey, stop biting my leg, you dangerous beast.

ROBERT. I'm the vicious one. Grrrrrrrr. Grrrrrrr. GHRUFF! GHRUFF! *[barking]*
GRUFF! GRUFF! *[barking]*

FATHER. You bit me, you little mongrel! You bit me!

ROBERT. Hold my hand, please, father.

FATHER. Not right now, Robert. I'm busy.

ROBERT. You can hold my hand.

FATHER. No, I won't hold your hand.

ROBERT. Grrrrrrrrrrgh! [He barks.] Ghruff Gruff!

FATHER. Don't be a pest, son.

ROBERT. I hate you, daddy.

FATHER. So? My life is about finished anyway.

[ROBERT growls and barks menacingly. He chases FATHER around the table.]

ROBERT. GHRRRRRRRRGH! I'll show you. I'm as dangerous as you are.

[ROBERT bites FATHER'S leg.]

FATHER. What are you doing? Stop biting my leg, you dangerous beast! Oh, Jesus! Sweet Jesus!

ROBERT. I'll show you! I'll show you how vicious I am!

[ROBERT dances and barks wildly around the room.]

ROBERT. Changing my words. Changing my words.

FATHER. No one is changing your words, son.

ROBERT. Changing my words. Changing them.

FATHER. I've stuck to your words religiously, son. Now quiet down.

ROBERT. I have to pee, daddy.

FATHER. Control yourself, boy. Be a man.

ROBERT. I'm a big boy now. Bigger than you ever imagined. I'm Mr. Bossy Pants. I'm going to tell you what to do instead. *[He barks.]* Growlll. GHRUFF! Fire in my brain.

[simultaneous]

ROBERT.	**FATHER.**
Fire, fire, fire.	Robert, stop it at once. Inhibit
RUFF! RUFF! Make fires!	yourself. Stop waving your arms.
RUFF! RUFF! Make fires!	You're behaving like a child.
RUFF! RUFF! Make fires!	

FATHER. Don't be rebellious, son.

ROBERT. Rebellious? Like this, father? Light fires! Light fires! Out there like this? RUFF! RUFF! Wowee! I'm going to scream.

FATHER. You better not.

Raymond J. Barry

[ROBERT screams.]
FATHER. Shuttup. Shuttup.
[FATHER and ROBERT turn out to the audience. The following chorale is done directly to the audience by both actors. Each actor is required to maintain his through-line during the overlapping of monologues.]
FATHER. I destroyed it,
ROBERT. Things permanent die.
FATHER.....our marriage,
ROBERT.....heart beat...
FATHER.....our family,
ROBERT.....dead fish...
FATHER.....beat it to death...
ROBERT.....burnt hut...
FATHER.....smashed it.
ROBERT.....dead mother. *[They walk toward audience.]*
FATHER. Drinking became an excuse to behave like a monster.
ROBERT. I search...
FATHER. I was "stewed"...
ROBERT.....for *other* possibilities.
FATHER.....as if it didn't matter.
ROBERT. Avoid men...
FATHER. Fist smashing on her cheekbone.
ROBERT.....who crack jaws...
FATHER.....break her nose,

[simultaneous]

ROBERT.	**FATHER.**
...for a pastime, escape to a world of daffodils. Tiger lilies birch trees, nourishing elements permanent, offsetting the death of a smashed mother abused. Oh, those birch trees, tiger lilies, growing hope for me to trust, wailing, wailing, wailing...	....her face, reduce her to the lower depths that my physical strength could impose. Heavy muscled arms bashing her teeth - her bloody mouth. Nightgown, pillows sprayed with blood. Crying wife, children in the background wailing, wailing, wailing...

FATHER.....like a chorus at the sight. Greek tragedy, Irish Catholic weekend, crashing new lamp through plaster wall and the songs I made up and sang every night...
[Father sings. Robert plugs his ears as he actively moves back and forth from upstage to downstage.]
FATHER AND ROBERT. "She's a bum. She ain't no goddamn good and she's a bum. Cunt! Whore! Bitch! Cunt! Whore! Bitch!"

Back When-Back Then

[Actors suddenly freeze. Pause. The following chorale begins softly and builds. At some point they can take it out to the audience.]

FATHER. When your mother refused to sleep with me I didn't know what was wrong.

ROBERT. I planted pink lilac...

FATHER. She wasn't attracted to me.

ROBERT. beautiful lilac...

FATHER. I worked with my hands.

ROBERT. ...that bloomed every Spring.

FATHER. I was ashamed of my hands...

ROBERT. A big bush of lilac...

FATHER. ...filthy dirty from work

ROBERT. ...outside the kitchen window.

FATHER. I didn't like who I was...

ROBERT. It bloomed next to the glass...

FATHER. ...wasn't proud of what I did for a living.

ROBERT. ...where you could see it...

FATHER. She made me feel that way...

ROBERT. ...when you ate breakfast...

FATHER. ...with her education...

ROBERT. ...in the morning.

FATHER. ...about art and everything.

ROBERT. The flowers' perfection...

FATHER. I didn't appreciate...

ROBERT. ...reminded me...

FATHER. ...who I was...

ROBERT. ...there was goodness...

FATHER. ...next to her.

ROBERT. ...to live for...

FATHER. Dirty fingernails.

ROBERT. ...and permanence...

[Actors continue to face audience while overlapping their monologues.]

FATHER. Stinky armpits.

ROBERT. ...with deep roots...

FATHER. I was an animal...

ROBERT. ...that held the earth together.

FATHER. ...and I knew it.

ROBERT. I needed to witness...

FATHER. Even my own wife...

[They turn heads toward each other.]

ROBERT. ...the permanence...

*[Actors face audience while overlapping their monologues.
Simultaneous:]*

Raymond J. Barry

ROBERT.	FATHER.
...of blooming flowers in the absence of my mother. Blooming flowers strengthened me in the absence of my mother. I'm still not quite sure why she left. It amazed me. I remember her proud and erect like those lilacs. I thought of her when I saw them reach up to the sky.	...couldn't stand my body odor. I couldn't stand myself. I washed every time I found the chance but I had to work all day. Can't take a bath there. Whenever I came home from work the first thing I did was to take a bath. She still would have nothing...

FATHER.....to do with me, hated the sight of me. My son picked upon her energy too. He behaved like she did.

ROBERT & FATHER. He wouldn't speak to me much, refused to touch me. I didn't feel good about myself.

[FATHER crosses to STAGE LEFT. ROBERT crosses to STAGE RIGHT.]

ROBERT. That joke I told you before?

FATHER. Yes?

ROBERT. It wasn't that funny.

FATHER. It was funny.

ROBERT. No, it wasn't that funny.

FATHER. I laughed.

ROBERT. You faked it. I knew.

FATHER. All right you caught me.

ROBERT. You mean you really faked it?

FATHER. Yes.

ROBERT. Oh. I didn't realize.

FATHER. But you suggested I faked it.

ROBERT. I was just testing you.

FATHER. Oh. I see. And I failed the test.

ROBERT. You merely told the truth.

FATHER. But I wouldn't have if I knew it mattered to you.

ROBERT. You would lie?

FATHER. I don't mind lying when it comes to little things.

ROBERT. Little things?

FATHER. I'm capable of maintaining that level of honesty.

ROBERT. Yes, you seem to be. You do enjoy my company, don't you?

FATHER. Yes, I do. It's nice you're here.

ROBERT. I'm a funny guy.

FATHER. Yes, I can see that.

ROBERT. I can get a rise out of people. Wowee! I have to laugh.

FATHER. You are funny, a funny person. Might as well take things light. You're a man now and I'm a man. Neither one of us asked to be here but we're here so let's make the best of it. Okay?

ROBERT. Okay.

FATHER. Okay. Let's drink to that. *[FATHER pours a drink for both of them. Robert takes a glass of scotch.]*

ROBERT. I'll only have one.

FATHER. Good. Let's drink to our friendship.

[Lights black out around them. They do a slow motion pantomime of a raucous drinking bout with much back slapping and cavorting. Legs kick high and arms are extended with much belly laughter between the two of them. Slowly the slow motion, friendly drinking behavior turns nasty as the father hits the son a little too hard. Pretty soon the slow motion party transforms into a slow motion beating of the father towards his son. The spot light stays on the father while the son crawls OFF STAGE. FATHER speaks beyond the fourth wall to MOTHER.]

FATHER. Glad you came, mother. Wow. Wowee. I've been in mourning with you gone and with you went the war we waged. I still miss that war, mother. I still miss our mutual wish to destroy each other. Our battle confirmed that I was alive. I found you, one fine night, tongues in mouths, clothing all over the place, a woman stranger lying in what was once my bed. You had broken the rules, had to pay the price. What if the kids had seen you fornicating, tongues to bare asses and the kids walk in? What then? What then in my house? What death sentence would be adequate? Your woman friend ran out half naked into the night and I focused on you, mother, gave you the whipping you deserved. I'll never forget the look in your eyes that night, a combination of fear with acceptance, like the eyes of a fish dangling on a hook. We had run out of time, mother. You never quite recovered from that whipping, my love. Months later, after you died, I piled your dresses in a heap in the middle of this very floor. I don't know why , but I found my hands picking up one of your dresses and suddenly I put it on - secretly as if I was wearing your skin with your familiar smell in its fabric. As soon as I wore it I could hear your voice faintly calling to me but when I took the dress off it stopped. Ever since that night, wearing your dresses has become my way to continue a dialogue with you. Whenever I need to be close to you I wear it. The garment is a conduit that allows us to bond. Wow. Wowee.

[Lights come fully up. Robert sits silently downstage left, facing the audience. He is dressed in a dress. Father crosses to downstage right of the table. He speaks to Mother, who he imagines is in the room. He uses a falsetto voice whenever Mother speaks from his mouth.]

FATHER. Look at him, mother, why don't you, just sitting there staring at his thumbs.

[Pause. Father looks out to Mother above audience.]

FATHER. Where did we go wrong do you suppose? I gave him what I

Raymond J. Barry

could. I always got up in the morning and went to work. He should have modeled himself after me. *[pause]* Look at him. He hasn't moved. All he does is sit. If we were outside I'd hit him with a stone. This morning I wished he would work but now I just wish he would move. Hey, son, what's on your mind? *[ROBERT doesn't respond.]* I wish he would speak. Robert. Hey, Robert. Cat got your tongue? You haven't spoken to me in the longest while, son. *[no response]* Run out of words, Robert? He's digesting his food. *[No response.]* Sure, he's digesting his food. We're all digesting our food. *[No response. Father looks out to Mother.]* Tell him I love him, mother. See how that hits him. What? No, you tell him. For once do as I say, dear. What? Oh, me? Oh, all right. *[to Robert]* Your mother says I love you, son. *[pause]* He's not saying anything back. You tell him, mother. *[listening to mother]* Don't tell him that for God's sake, you embarrass me. *[Father answers himself as if he's speaking to Mother.]* I agree. It was a nice thing to say, but now is another time. Feelings shift. I am really embarrassed, mother. *[listening to Mother]* Never mind. Don't make up words. You make up words and I never said them. *[Father answers himself as if he's listening to Mother.]* No, no, I never said them. *[Father answers himself as if he's talking to Mother.]* You said them and he heard them. *[listening to Mother]* You're stubborn, mother. That's what I love about you the most - your stubbornness. *[Father answers Mother.]* I love that, that you love me. I just love that. *[listening]* The stubbornness part? *[Father answers Mother.]* Oh, I love that too, but not as much. *[listening]* Oh, I get it. Just the "loved you" part. *[Father answers Mother.]* Yes, mother.

ROBERT. Mom loves you, dad!

FATHER. Goddamnit, son, that's not what she said.

ROBERT. Yes. Underneath words...said.

FATHER. Don't be changing the words on us, boy. There can be nothing gained by changing our words.

ROBERT. She said...

FATHER. That's not what she said, son.

ROBERT. I heard sadness...love.

FATHER. Sadness isn't love, son.

ROBERT. Both afraid... Both afraid.

FATHER. Right now I don't mind being afraid.

ROBERT. *[ROBERT rises from his chair and meets FATHER in front of the table, CENTER STAGE. ROBERT speaks to FATHER while FATHER speaks to the dead MOTHER beyond the fourth wall.]* Mend it! Mend it! For my sake, dad!

FATHER. I hate to ask you this in front of him, mother...

ROBERT. Furious! Furious!

FATHER. ...but... we all have needs, you know...

ROBERT. Needs put aside...

FATHER. ...and those needs...

ROBERT. Bricklayers' convention...

FATHER. ...that is, if they are not fulfilled...

ROBERT. Bricklayers' convention...

FATHER. ...leave us, you know...

ROBERT. All those bricklayers...

FATHER. ...er... empty...

ROBERT. But she gave in! She gave in!

FATHER. ...or even at times slightly desperate if they are not... fulfilled. *[Father suddenly turns to Robert as if Robert is Mother.]* And if there is to be a rejuvenation, if you will, of our relationship, is it possible that, er... we could at some point manage to rub... er... that is, combine our... that is... our bodies could be brought together in such a way as to make... er... love? You know what I'm trying to say, don't you, dear?

ROBERT. She didn't hear, dad.

FATHER. Well, tell her yourself.

ROBERT. Not straight in my mind.

FATHER. You know, son, we both could be part of her life. I wouldn't mind that, you know. It wouldn't bother me. *[No response.]* Interested?

ROBERT. No.

FATHER. Well, then, what are you interested in?

ROBERT. Wrestling.

FATHER. Wrestling? But we both have dresses on.

ROBERT. It didn't make any difference before.

FATHER. It was your mother's.

ROBERT. She didn't mind. She's dead.

FATHER. She may be dead but she's watching us right now.

ROBERT. Let her watch.

FATHER. All right then but take it easy on me, boy.

[The two men begin their wrestling match, slightly bent over, dressed in the mother's dresses. They lock arms, head to head, FATHER obviously stronger than the son. FATHER grabs ROBERT'S leg and the younger man is turned upside down by the larger, heavier man. In a short time ROBERT is pinned to the floor. He fights furiously and escapes. The older man tires and ROBERT overthrows his father.]

ROBERT. I won fair and square. I'm the wrestling champ now.

[FATHER gathers himself to his feet. ROBERT develops an exaggerated swagger that used to be his father's. FATHER rises.

FATHER. You should be spanked with the hairbrush the way I did in the old days.

ROBERT. Fuck you and your hairbrush.

FATHER. You know what this is all leading to. You know.

ROBERT. What is it leading to, daddy? A whipping with a hairbrush on my bare ass? Those days are gone forever.

Raymond J. Barry

FATHER. We'll see about that. You been asking for this and I'm gonna give it to you.

ROBERT. Go on. I dare you, you old fuck! Lay a hand on me and you'll be sorry!

FATHER. You been asking for this.

ROBERT. Come on, you bad daddy. Catch me if you can.

FATHER. I'll catch you and when I do, you'll have a pink ass, believe you me.

ROBERT. Fuck you, you old fool. *[runs out the door]*

FATHER. Fucking coward. Fucking coward. Fucking cowardly little punk bastard of a son of mine. Good for nothing kid who never did anything worthwhile in his life.

[ROBERT pounds on the door from outside.]

ROBERT. Hey, daddy, let me in.

FATHER. Let him hang out there for a while, dear. We're busy. I'm out of breath. I've lost my breath.

ROBERT. Hey, open up the door, will ya?

FATHER. I'll just leave him out there, dear. Mind if I turn the lights down a little bit lower?

[FATHER signals for the lights to go down. ROBERT pounds on the door.]

ROBERT. Let me in, will you? There's a crowd gathering out front.

FATHER. Get away from the door then. I don't want people outside my house. Can't you see I'm busy?

ROBERT. Open the door, please. Have a heart. People are laughing at me with this dress on.

FATHER. Go home, boy! If only I had it all to do over again, my darling. When I was young I had a chance. I felt good about myself then, fishing, always fishing with my best friend, Joel. Joel was a great fisherman and he was my best friend, taught me how to fish for goldfish in a big freshwater lake called Hendrickson's Pit near where we grew up. Joel taught me how to mix Wonder Bread and water and a spoonful of vanilla.

[ROBERT pounds on the door.]

ROBERT. That's my mother, you bastard!

FATHER. He'll quiet down eventually, darling. He knows his old man means business. Do you smell something, dear? I smell smoke. Yes, it's smoke. He's at it again, little firebug. Little firebug's burning the house down with me in it. The whole place is going up in smoke with me in it. What was I saying, dear? Oh, yeah... vanilla and Wonder Bread without the crust and how to use a bent pin on a line of thread tied to a bamboo pole and how to chum for fish by putting a big glob of Wonder Bread and vanilla into a nylon stocking.

[ROBERT pounds on the door. FATHER sits on a pile of tires as if he is floating on water.]

Back When-Back Then

ROBERT. Let me in!

FATHER. Go home, boy! Anyway, dear, Joel and I would put our lines right next to the nylon stocking chum bag and we could catch as many as a hundred and seventeen goldfish in a day. That was our record and they were all pretty –all gold and black or white or white and red, just beautiful... and... and... just beautiful. And some of those goldfish were that big, that big. *[FATHER measures with his hands.]* I must have had a marvelous childhood. Did a lot of fishing. I'm on your side, dear. You know that, don't you? I'm on your side. Where are you, sweetness? Come here. I'm here. Where are you? I feel you coming toward me. Ah, here... That's it. Here, put your hands on me. My god, they're cold. They seem very knowledgeable, your hands, very knowledgeable. Don't be so timid, darling. Take over, my darling. Glad you came, my darling. Glad you came, my darling. Glad you came, my dear.

[Smoke is filling the room going up in flames. FATHER calls to his dead wife.]

[BLACKOUT.]

End of Play

Raymond J. Barry

Foul Shots

Characters

Father: a man learning to read from his son.

Son: an educated man who teaches his father how to read but resents past events in his father's history.

History

Foul Shots was performed as a work-in-progress at the **Triangle Theatre** in Portland, Oregon, September-October 2004.

CAST:

FATHER ....Raymond J. Barry
SON...Russell Milton

Director .... John Ferraro
Stage Manager...................................Carol Ann Smith
Costume Designer..................................... Van Ramsey

Foul Shots was performed as a work-in-progress (under the title *And then I did this, and then I did that*) at the **Odyssey Theatre** in Los Angeles, California, January-February 2005. Ron Sossi, Artistic Director.

CAST:

FATHER ....Raymond J. Barry
SON...Russell Milton

Director .... John Ferraro
Lighting Designer...John Fejes
Costume Designer..................................... Van Ramsey
Production Stage Manager .... Leah Roobini

Raymond J. Barry

Foul Shots was performed as a work-in-progress at the **Electric Lodge** in Los Angeles, California, March 2005.

CAST:

FATHER.. Raymond J. Barry
SON .... Joseph Culp

Director .... Michael Arabian

The World Premiere of **Foul Shots** was performed at the **Theater For The New City** in New York City, in September-October, 2005. Artistic Director, Chrystal Field.

CAST:

FATHER.. Raymond J. Barry
SON .... Joseph Culp

Director .... Michael Arabian
Set Designer ....Markus Maurette

Raymond J. Barry, Joseph Culp, **Foul Shots,**
Theatre for the New City, New York City, September, October 2005

Foul Shots

Foul Shots

[TWO MEN ON A WHITE STAGE: FATHER sits on a wooden stool, STAGE RIGHT of a CENTER STAGE wooden table. Both characters can be played either by a white Caucasian or African American men. A solid wooden chair is STAGE LEFT of the table. This is the SON'S chair. SON stands UPSTAGE CENTER dressed in a formal, tweed jacket and shiny, black shoes. He speaks with a somewhat affected English accent, compared to the FATHER, who uses an uneducated, working class dialect. FATHER wears a blue work-shirt, brown janitor pants and scuffed, brown shoes. Surrounding them UPSTAGE at a sharp right angle are two stark white walls that will be written upon with different colored chalk to illustrate the SON'S lesson. FATHER reads with difficulty from a non-descript, hardcover book. He's having difficulty.]

FATHER. Th... e e e... r r r... e e e... th... e e e... re... th... rrr... e e e... t... h... r r r r... eee... th... r r r... e e e e...

SON AND FATHER. Th... th... th... there.

FATHER. *[stops reading]* 'There'. I'm discouraged, son.

SON. Don't be discouraged, father. Come on now, you can do it. You can do it.

FATHER. No, I don't think so, especially at my age.

SON. Age has nothing to do with it, father.

FATHER. I'm an old man.

SON. You're as old as you think you are.

FATHER. That's easy for you to say, son. You have your whole life ahead of you.

SON. As you do. You can still enrich yourself.

FATHER. You think so?

SON. I do, dad.

FATHER. *[shoves hands in SON'S face]* Look at the dirt on my hands.

SON. They're not dirty.

FATHER. No, they are dirty.

SON. I don't see any dirt.

FATHER. You don't have to see it. I know it's there, that dirt.

SON. You're imagining things.

FATHER. Imagining things? No, my hands have always been dirty, ever since you were little.

SON. I never noticed.

FATHER. Dirty from work, dirty under the finger nails, dirty in the pores of my skin. You never had to grovel in the dirt the way I did when I was raising you.

Raymond J. Barry

Son. Everyone grovels one way or another.

Father. You never had to grovel like your father, boy.

Son. What's that got to do with your lesson?

Father. Too much wax in my ears, too much dirt in the pores of my skin to learn. Besides, I'm too old. I don't believe in myself anymore. I never had much school.

Son. We can change that. When you do learn how to read, books will become your tools.

Father. I've never had much to work with.

Son. You're marvelously gregarious.

Father. *[FATHER rises from his chair, crosses stage right of table.]* Watch it.

Son. Why do you say that?

Father. Don't insult me.

Son. I'm not insulting you, father. I was saying something nice.

Father. You were?

Son. Of course, I was. You communicate well. You have 'people skills'.

Father. I do?

Son. Of course you do.

Father. I'm not looking for a handout.

Son. Nobody is giving you a handout.

Father. I tried to teach myself how to read once, but I couldn't figure it out.

Son. You'd have to learn phonetics and then there is the issue of grammar.

Father. Yeah, it's tough.

Son. You'll catch on. Here, try it again.

[SON opens the book to correct page.]

Father. I can't.

Son. Sure you can. Just sound out the vowels.

Father. What are the vowels again?

Son. Aaaaa, eeeee, iiiiiii, ohhhhh, oooooo.

Father. Aaaaaaa, eeeee, iiiiiii, ohhhhh, ooooo?

Son. That's right. Pick them out first.

Father. *[cross to stool stage right of table]* What do I do with them?

Son. Sound out the vowels.

Father. Th... eeeereeee.

Son. That's it. You're doing it. "There..."

Father. A a a... reeee...

Son. "There are!..." That's right. That's great.

[FATHER stops, rises from his seat, crosses to stage right, then circles the stage.]

Father. I... don't think I can go on.

[FATHER finds his way UPSTAGE.]

Foul Shots

SON. You must go on.

FATHER. *[stage left]* What's the use?

SON. You give up so easily.

FATHER. I can't concentrate, my son.

SON. But you simply must concentrate.

[FATHER pacing upstage and downstage left]

FATHER. I'm tired. Let's rest.

SON. No, we must continue. Begin with basics. Before one learns to read, one must make a choice to read. You seem doubtful. You must eradicate that doubt before any reading can be accomplished, before anything can be accomplished for that matter. You have 'free will', you know.

FATHER. *[stops pacing stage left]* I do?

SON. Of course you do. You're not the product of your environment entirely. You made choices along the way that enabled you to survive.

FATHER. I did?

SON. Oh, yes, you did, dad.

FATHER. Like my choice to marry your mother?

SON. Yes. That's not exactly the choice I had in mind, but, yes, that was a choice, I suppose.

FATHER. It didn't feel like a choice when I did it.

SON. *[cross stage left]* It sounds to me like an act of passion.

FATHER. Watch it!

SON. Watch what?

FATHER. Watch what you say about your mother.

SON. I didn't say anything about mother.

FATHER. Yeah, well, you watch it anyway.

SON. Oh, come on. I'm here to help you.

FATHER. Oh,... yeah, help me... to read, right.

[FATHER crosses downstage right, sits on stool.]

SON. You can use me, you know, in a positive way. I'm educated and you're not.

FATHER. I know as much as you do about livin'.

SON. I wouldn't argue with you there.

FATHER. Maybe even more.

SON. Nonetheless, I am educated. That counts for something.

FATHER. I'm beyond bein' educated.

SON. Beyond?

FATHER. Yeah, I can't do it.

SON. No, you can be taught. How's this for example? *[crosses to upstage wall]* A noun is the name of a person, a place or a thing.

[SON writes "A noun is the name of a person, place or thing" on upstage wall.]

FATHER. A noun is a... I don't get it. I've had a tough time of it lately.

Raymond J. Barry

Son. Never mind that, dad. Now then, what is a noun?

Father. A name of a person...

Son. No, not "name of". When we get into names we're dealing with something special.

Father. But you said "name of" first.

Son. You imagined I did but I most certainly did not say any such thing.

Father. Oh, I thought you did.

Son. No, I did not.

Father. Oh...

Son. Now then, what is a noun?

Father. It... It's... not name of...

Son. That's right.

Father. It's a person, a place or...

Son. You shouldn't be hesitating at this point. You should know the answer.

Father. I'm sorry. I forgot.

Son. You mustn't forget so readily.

Father. So readily?

Son. Yes, so easily. You mustn't forget so easily. Please try to remember, father.

Father. I shall ... er... I will... ah...

Son. And stop stammering. You must learn to answer with authority. Stop stammering. One would think you have no confidence in your answer.

Father. Yes, I'm... I'll be stronger...

Son. One would have the impression you don't feel right about yourself.

Father. Sometimes I don't, son. I mean I don't feel exactly right about myself.

Son. Well, we're going to make a special effort to change that. Now then, a noun is a person, a place or a thing. *[SON refers to definition on upstage wall.]* Repeat that if you will.

Father. A noun is a... a... a word describing a person... a place or... a thing.

Son. Not exactly; not 'a word describing'. It's important to be precise about this. 'A word describing' is not part of the definition.

Father. Yes, "'A word describing' is not part of the definition."

Son. Precisely, precisely. Now finish the entire statement.

Father. A noun is ah... not "name of" and not "a word describing." A noun is a... ah... a person, ah... ah... a place or... ah... ah... I'm sorry. I can't remember the last one.

Son. You certainly can if you try. It requires effort.

Father. I'm trying very much, son. It just isn't coming.

Son. You're so lazy!!! A lazy good for nothing!!! *[FATHER rises from his stool, crosses downstage left]* No, that's not what you are. You're nothing

Foul Shots

of the sort. Please, forgive me, father. I try to be kind but there's so much resistance in you, so much resistance.

FATHER. *[downstage left]* Why are you the boss here?

SON. *[upstage right]* I'm trying to offer you something, father.

FATHER. No, you're trying to make yourself important by bossing me around.

SON. I'm teaching you. I'm improving your situation by making you literate. I'm a teacher. I have a gift.

FATHER. Everybody got some kinda gift.

SON. But my gifts are greater than yours.

FATHER. My mind jams up. So what? I don't know what happens to me. I am all frozen inside. So what? Whenever I have to remember the details I can't do it.

SON. You can do it. You're a perfectly intelligent being. I can tell by your eyes you can do it. You've got blocks, that's all. You're blocked.

FATHER. I know.

SON. Don't be afraid.

FATHER. I can't help it.

SON. I'll help you, father. That's what I'm here for.

FATHER. I know. It's just so hard for me.

[FATHER sits on stool, stage right of table]

SON. Just be patient with yourself. Don't push yourself too hard. We can spend as much time as you wish.

FATHER. I know.

[SON crosses to upstage wall and points to word, 'THING' written on it.]

SON. You know what a thing is, don't you?

FATHER. Ah... ah... a thing?

SON. Yes, a thing.

FATHER. A thing? Yes, a thing... ah... What a thing is? Yeah, I do know what a thing is.

SON. Name one.

FATHER. *[stage right]* Name one thing?

SON. Yes, one thing.

FATHER. Ah... One thing?

SON. One thing.

FATHER. Ah, yes, one thing... Me!

SON. You? But you couldn't possibly be a 'thing. You are a person to be sure. Things aren't people and people aren't things. They are two separate realms. You have a soul, and 'things' don't have souls. Our soul is the very thing that separates us from 'things'.

FATHER. But you said persons and things are both nouns so they are the same.

SON. Yes, father, persons and things are both nouns, but they are not the same. One has consciousness. The other does not. You are

Raymond J. Barry

conscious so you are a person and not a thing.

FATHER. What is 'conscious'?

SON. Well, a fair enough question. It is a certain awareness we experience, to be awake to some degree.

FATHER. Do persons become 'things' when they fall asleep?

SON. Certainly not. Then they are dreaming.

FATHER. Oh, I see, 'things' don't dream?

SON. Certainly not.

FATHER. How do you know 'things' don't dream?

SON. It is obvious 'things' don't dream.

FATHER. It's not obvious to me 'things' don't dream.

SON. But they are 'things', and therefore they don't dream, and 'things' are nouns. All 'things' are nouns, all 'things' in this room are nouns and they can't dream.

FATHER. I do dream!!

SON. *[cross stage left of table]* Yes, you do dream. You are not a thing. All objects in this room, all 'things', as we see them, are inanimate and they do not dream: the chair, the table, our pencils, our pens, the paper upon which we write our ideas, all books, your shoes, your socks, your pants, my shirt and your shirt as well; the room itself... *[cross downstage left]* all remain inanimate objects that cannot think, dream nor deduce conclusions from various premises upon which they are based. In short, these objects have no souls, and, for that matter, haven't even a brain and furthermore have no consciousness, which is that specific characteristic that allows us persons to make decisions, otherwise known as...

FATHER. Decisions? Ah... Choosing, choice.

SON. Yes, choice or choosing, or better known as 'free will'.

FATHER. Oh, yeah, 'free will'.

SON. You have 'free will' because you are alive and conscious and have a soul, be it black or white, depending upon the sins you have committed, but we needn't get into that now. Your sins have no significance here.

FATHER. Why do you talk that way?

SON. I picked it up in London.

FATHER. You picked it up in London?

SON. Yes, in London... Good then. Can you name me some more 'things'?

FATHER. Ah... ah... some more things? Yes, some more things. Yes, I can name some more things.

SON. Would you name some more things?

FATHER. Yes, some more things. Ah... ah... floor... wall... ceiling... light... chalk, chalk-board.

SON. Yes, that is correct. You see? You got the right answer. How do you feel about that?

Foul Shots

FATHER. *[celebrates, downstage left]* I got the right answer!!!

[FATHER sits, stage right]

SON. Yes, you're answer was right, a new beginning for you. There will be other right answers as well and soon you'll be feeling like a new man. Now then, let me ask you this. *[crosses to stage left wall]* Is love a noun? *[Writes 'LOVE' on stage left wall]*

FATHER. Is... ah... love... a noun?

SON. Yes, is love a thing?

FATHER. Ah... Is... love... a thing? Oh, well... ah... love irritates me...... and hurts me. It tortures...

[simultaneous]

FATHER.	**SON.**
... me when I sleep at night. It drives a stake through my heart. Love runs into my finger tips and makes my palms sweaty.	Now, now, now! Listen to me! I did not ask you what love does. I asked you if it is a thing. Tell me if it is a thing, something, some definite thing that it can be...

SON. *[cross to SON, stage right]*... called. Forget all these participial phrases, forget about all that. You haven't covered enough material for that. Answer me! Is love a thing?

FATHER. Love?

SON. What is love? Is it a person? *[refers to word, 'person' on wall]*

FATHER. No.

SON. *[refers to word, 'thing' on wall]* Is it a thing?

FATHER. Love is a feeling I had once towards your mother, more punishing than death itself, a feeling I'll never forget that drives me crazy to the point where, when I was in love I couldn't eat, couldn't sleep, couldn't behave the way I was used to, forcing me into a state of frustration that wouldn't go away, and now that I'm thinking of it I'm becoming frustrated all over again, that, combined with my usual frustration is slowly driving me up the wall in frustration...

[simultaneous]

FATHER.	**SON.**
... forcing me again to take my frustration out on you, my son. Love rushes into my temples and freezes my brain.	We will have order here! Order here in this classroom! We will have order here! Order! All right, that's enough!

SON. Let us move on. *[crosses to stage right wall]*

FATHER. Thank God.

Raymond J. Barry

SON. You're complicating the issue. God is a separate issue, a bigger issue.

FATHER. *[sits on stool, right of table]* I was just wondering if 'love' is a noun.

SON. As you should. As you should. Not the time to probe it, however, a subject for the shelf if you please and let us trust that blind faith will take care of it.

FATHER. Things are dead then?

SON. Not exactly dead as they have never been alive to begin with.

FATHER. I see. And if you break a 'thing' open there is nothing?

SON. Yes, nothing, absolutely nothing.

FATHER. *[refers to his shoe]* And if I rip apart an old shoe there'd be no pain involved, whereas if the same were done to me there'd be great injury; my soul would be affected.

SON. Oh, yes, indeed.

FATHER. As well as my 'conscious'?

SON. My god, you're bright!

FATHER. It's better to be a 'thing' then.

SON. Oh, no, no, no! By saying that you welcome defeat. After all, you aren't an old shoe. You can be educated. You are being educated at this very moment. Come now, let us move instead to the subject of 'place'.

[SON writes 'PLACE' on stage left blackboard wall. FATHER sits on stool, stage right of table]

FATHER. Place?

SON. Yes, place.

FATHER. What place?

SON. Any place.

FATHER. Like here, for example?

SON. Here would be fine.

FATHER. And somewhere else too?

SON. And somewhere else too.

FATHER. Any place?

SON. Yes, any place. Words that describe any place are also nouns.

FATHER. Like where?

SON. Anywhere.

FATHER. Even London.

SON. Careful now. You're getting into the area of proper nouns.

FATHER. Then how should I describe London?

SON. Just call it a city, a big city.

FATHER. It is a big city.

SON. Yes, it is.

FATHER. I saw a picture of it once.

SON. I've lived there.

FATHER. What was it like?

SON. Brownish gray. But the parks were green.

FATHER. Oh. What were you doing in London?

SON. I taught there, daddy.

FATHER. Do you feel qualified to teach?

SON. Of course I feel qualified to teach, daddy! I was born to teach, daddy! I taught everything I knew at the time, daddy! I don't limit myself to specific subjects! The entire array of knowledge is always at my finger tips! I just let my words fly like seeds falling to fertile earth! I nurture those seedlings into full-grown, healthy trees, until a forest of magnificent ideas is born, whose trunks are cut down eventually by greed, avarice and ignorance!

FATHER. Did you have a good time in London?

SON. A good time? Is that all you think about? A good time? My dear father, I of all people never have 'a good time'. *[crosses upstage of table to stage right]* I'm too serious to have 'a good time'. Remember that. And I don't expect you to have 'a good time' either. 'A good time' is not our purpose here. I am suffering the anguish that comes with caring a great deal about what you learn. You of all people must suffer also and forget about 'a good time'. No one is having 'a good time'. Life is generally sad. People are sad. I am sad. *[twists FATHER'S ear]* Aren't you sad, papa?

FATHER. Oh... ah... sad? Yes, I'm sad.

SON. *[upstage of table]* Excellent! You have the beginning stages of true consciousness. All great men are sad, Camus, Beckett, James Joyce, the whole lot of them, all sad. It's the price one must pay in order to be conscious.

FATHER. What does it mean to be conscious?

SON. Not yet! Not yet! You must wait until the right time comes. Meanwhile I suggest you accept sadness. Embrace that emotion. Nurture that condition, fertilize it if you will. Do not try to escape sadness. Otherwise it will come back to haunt you more so than before.

FATHER. What about happiness, son?

SON. Forget the notion of happiness for it will betray you in the end. Are you not paying attention to me, father? Don't you believe what I have to say?

FATHER. *[on stool]* Oh, yes, I do believe it.

SON. Good. Let us return to that familiar sensation of sadness. I'm a teacher. I have complete understanding of these matters. *[crosses upstage to back wall]*

FATHER. I am so dumb.

SON. I said sad, not dumb! Sad, sad and not dumb. Have you no intellect whatsoever, daddy? God, you exhaust me. Can't you make the distinction between sad and dumb?

FATHER. Yes, master.

SON. Watch it! You're swimming delicate waters there. I am benevolent.

Raymond J. Barry

You know that, don't you, father? I am a benevolent son.

FATHER. All I know is that I am learning a lot.

SON. But it's important for you to believe that I am benevolent.

FATHER. Oh, yes, I do believe that.

SON. Good. All right then, back to basic knowledge. Allow us to move onward into new areas... of enlightenment. *[SON gives open book to FATHER, sitting on stool]* Read this.

FATHER. I can't. The script blurs my eyes.

SON. Unblur them then and read.

FATHER. I can't see the words.

SON. You must make an attempt, father.

FATHER. But I can't see the words.

SON. Do it!

FATHER. I'll try. *[He prepares himself and then reads]* "So ma.. . ny... al... ter... na... tives."

SON. Pull it together! You're stammering again!

FATHER. "So many al... ter... na... tives from what... at

SON. My god, firm up a bit. You're stammering!

[FATHER stands]

FATHER. Enough!!!

SON. Sorry?

FATHER. Your constant interruptions make it impossible.

SON. Without me you'd be nothing.

FATHER. Don't talk to you me like that, goddammit!

SON. It's my place in the world to instruct, father.

FATHER. Not when I'm finally getting it.

SON. You were faltering! You were faltering!

FATHER. I was doing the best I could.

SON. Continue then.

FATHER. All right. *[SON moves his stool far to STAGE RIGHT. He sits]* "So many de... par... tur... es from what one mig g g... h... tt

SON. Might.

FATHER. 'Might'. Yes... might nor... mally sa... vo... oo ...r

SON. Savor.

FATHER. ...savor... as... the tra...a... th."

[FATHER stands, places book on table]

SON. Troooth.

FATHER. Trooth. Yes, trooth. Truth... savor as the truth. There, how's that?

SON. *[sits, stage left]* Lot of hesitancy. Sort of bumbled through it if you ask me.

FATHER. What do you want? A speed-read?

[FATHER paces stage right – upstage and downstage]

SON. My goodness, you are difficult, dad. My goodness, I've never come

Foul Shots

across this kind of resistance quite before.

FATHER. You're the one whose breakin' balls.

SON. Never mind the vulgarity. We don't need vulgarity in my class room.

FATHER. You're killing my joy for knowledge, boy.

SON. Joy for knowledge? Poppycock.

FATHER. You seem to enjoy my struggle.

SON. I'm giving you my very best.

FATHER. There's no need to talk to me like that.

SON. No need is it?

FATHER. Yeah, there's no need to look down on me.

SON. Am I not to be given any credit whatsoever?

FATHER. You've discouraged me, boy. Anyone who survives as long as I have has to be smart.

SON. You reduce everything to food on the table, a roof over your head.

FATHER. Why make it complicated?

SON. There's such a thing as a higher level.

FATHER. *[pacing upstage to downstage]* That's up to me. If I don't need a higher level, there's no reason to get excited about it.

SON. Pure knowledge has value all by itself.

FATHER. Hogwash. Knowledge of what? I know what I need to know. You expect sadness. Sounds stupid to me.

SON. I'm a great thinker.

FATHER. Oh, yeah? What do you think? That life is sad? That's dumb. Real dumb.

SON. You're not sensitive enough to understand.

FATHER. I gotta be a pussy to understand how to live?

SON. It's important to be informed.

FATHER. Survival is informed!

SON. But that's so primitive, like a cave man. You're nothing more than an animal.

FATHER. I know it's hard for you to believe, but you got to watch what you say to me. I ain't a 'thing'. I got feelings, you know.

SON. Come now. Have you no backbone?

[simultaneous]

FATHER.	**SON.**
You've bullied me into failure. My failure is your failure. If only you had a softer touch. You've taken the heart out of me, boy.	I've been nothing less than nurturing. Your failure is yours and not mine. There, there, father, don't baby yourself. You exaggerate.

FATHER. I don't want to do this anymore. Find another victim to mess

Raymond J. Barry

up.

SON. Sit down. Sit down and concentrate.

FATHER. No, I won't sit down! *[crosses to SON stage left. They move in a circle around the table.]*

SON. *[cross to downstage left corner]* Don't approach me, father.

FATHER. I'm not gonna hurt you.

SON. Then sit!! Sit down!!!

FATHER. Must I sit down, oh master?

SON. Stop behaving ridiculously.

[FATHER crosses to stool stage right, places it next to table, sits.]

FATHER. I would like to be your friend, son.

SON. We will be unified but on my terms, not yours.

FATHER. Why always on your terms?

SON. The past, remember the past.

FATHER. That was a mistake, a terrible mistake.

SON. A mistake!? A mistake!?

FATHER. Can't I be forgiven ever, by anybody?

SON. You're only hope is education.

FATHER. I want to be understood, son.

SON. I understand you.

FATHER. Do you? Do you really?

SON. Of course I do.

FATHER. Why of course? We're so different.

SON. You're not that different from me. We're both human.

FATHER. But I'm dumb. All my life I wanted to be smart, son, not just smart but very smart, like you. When I was young I worked very hard at my school work but I never could quite get it. All I could do was memorize, one definition after another, but I never knew what to do with them once I learned them. I was always behind, could never understand what was going on. I'd look up at the blackboard and things would get muddled in my head. Everyone else knew what was going on but me. I was lost, so lost. When you were born I didn't want you to go through the same thing. I pushed you, maybe a little too hard. I want your forgiveness, son.

SON. *[downstage left]* That's fine. Just confine your feelings to words and not actions.

FATHER. I am a man of action. I'm hard-working. I've always been hard-working.

SON. *[crosses stage left of table]* Mother would question that.

FATHER. I provided for her! I always provided for her!

SON. Calm down. Just calm down.

FATHER. Don't tell me to calm down, goddamnit! Don't insult me! You're not better than me, boy! You're my teacher and nothing else, just my teacher!

Foul Shots

[simultaneous]

SON.

You will sit down! You will not approach me in a threatening manner! You're just sensitive right now. I don't want to injure you in any way, dad.

FATHER.

I'm not threatening. I don't know. I've been injured enough.

SON. I'd like to show you that I can be kind.
FATHER. You seem kind, son, the kindest person I know.
SON. You must learn to control your feelings.
FATHER. I'm a bundle of nerves.
SON. You've got to get a handle on yourself.
[FATHER picks up book, presents it to SON]
FATHER. Teach me, son.
SON. Become more socialized.
FATHER. That's my last request, my last one.
SON. It's time for a change. I'll give you all the help I can.
FATHER. It's generous of you, son.
SON. The most important thing is the mind.
FATHER. I haven't used my mind for years.
SON. It is easier than you think...
FATHER. If only it could be so easy.
SON. ...if you change your attitude.
FATHER. I want so very much to die an educated man.

[simultaneous]

SON.

That's the stuff, dad. For god's sake, dad, Stand alert. Stand alive.

FATHER.

Yes, I'm doing it. I'm standing tall and powerful.

[FATHER and SON, simultaneously, stage left; SON crosses to stage right]

[simultaneous]

SON.

Get a hold of yourself. Do something constructive with yourself. Reach in and pull the best out of yourself. Stand up! Stand up! Stand strong! Stand powerful! Reach in and pull the best out of yourself, the very best

FATHER.

Yes, yes, I'm yanking from within what has been lost for years, my best self, alert, intelligent. I am a powerful person who can take can take charge of my full potential. I am intelligent! I'm even smart.

Raymond J. Barry

of yourself. Pull... pull... pull!   I... I... I...

[DECEASED MOTHER enters]

MOTHER. Come now, boys, don't fight. Don't fight.

FATHER. Is that you, you old bitch?

MOTHER. Yes, it's me. You've got to stop getting at each other so much, constantly at each other.

FATHER. He's the one, not me.

MOTHER. There you go again, posing as the innocent one.

FATHER. I'm almost innocent.

MOTHER. Oh, now then, dear, we both know better.

FATHER. Oh, mother, you always sided with him, always with him.

MOTHER. Who else would I side with?

FATHER. Your husband, that's who you'd side with.

MOTHER. You're no husband of mine.

FATHER. I was your husband once.

MOTHER. Once, but no more. I ended that, didn't I?

FATHER. Yes, you ended it. I've missed you, you know. I've missed you.

MOTHER. You should have thought of that when it counted.

FATHER. I had no way of knowing.

MOTHER. You had me in the palm of your hand. There was no need for your abuse.

FATHER. I'd be different today, honey.

MOTHER. And don't call me honey.

FATHER. Oh, sorry, how 'bout ex-wife?

MOTHER. That's more like it.

FATHER. I never forgot you, dear.

MOTHER. We couldn't forget, could we?

FATHER. You were the best thing in my life.

MOTHER. That's sweet of you to say but it is too late.

SON. Don't make friends.

MOTHER. We want to make friends.

SON. No, don't make friends.

MOTHER. We must mend bridges. Or else there will be endless bickering.

SON. The bickering is more comfortable than mending bridges.

MOTHER What an odd thing to say.

SON. Pretending that the past is healed is worse than living with it.

MOTHER. Your father and I are trying our best.

FATHER. I'm trying my best.

MOTHER. Your father is trying his best and I am trying my best. We're discussing things. We're trying our best.

SON. The big lie.

MOTHER. Don't be so harsh, son. Isn't he harsh, dear?

Foul Shots

FATHER. I can't talk to him. Maybe you can talk to him.

MOTHER. We always knew how to talk to him before.

SON. Talk is cheap.

MOTHER. "Cheap" you call it. Did you hear what he said, dear?

FATHER. It's an noun. He taught me that 'talk' is a noun. Talk is 'noun' and I'm a 'noun' too. At least that's what he told me.

MOTHER. A noun? Why are we drifting to nouns?

FATHER. Everything is adjectives, verbs and nouns to him. He don't talk about what we're talking about. Thinks he's smart. Says life is sad.

MOTHER. Is that what you think, son? Life is sad? Is that what you think?

FATHER. 'Life' is a noun to him. It's not really life. It's some kind of noun, telling a 'thing'. You know, some 'thing' which is a noun. He taught me that, mother.

MOTHER. Stop interrupting, father.

FATHER. 'Father' is a noun too.

MOTHER. Stop with this academic drivel.

FATHER. That's how he talks to me. I never can get to anything real with him. Always with this gobbledygook.

MOTHER. I've always been able to talk with him. Talk with me, my boy. Say something nice about our family.

SON. Our family doesn't exist anymore.

MOTHER. We're here now, aren't we?

FATHER. Here and 'conscious'.

SON. You're not conscious. How can you call yourself conscious?

FATHER. I'll call myself anything I damn well want to call myself and you're not gonna stop me.

MOTHER. Don't argue, boys, my boys.

FATHER. He can't stand it that I'm conscious. He's the only one who can be conscious. I can't be conscious. Only he can be conscious.

SON. You don't even know what the word means.

MOTHER. Don't insult your father, son.

SON. He insults himself with his ignorance.

FATHER. He thinks he's accomplished something with his life just because he can read. What a joke.

MOTHER. He sent himself through college. That's something.

FATHER. What? You and me had nothing to do with it, huh?

MOTHER. We helped a little, I suppose.

FATHER. More than a little. He wouldn't even want to go to college if it wasn't for you. You're the one who persuaded him to go to college with all your high-falutin' talk about art and stuff.

MOTHER. Well, it did mean something, didn't it? In the long run of things it did mean something.

FATHER. He thinks he's better than everybody. When you died he got out

Raymond J. Barry

of control with that education stuff. Can't even talk to him anymore about nothing.

SON. You're the one who can't talk.

FATHER. I can talk. I can talk. Been talking all my life.

SON. You don't say anything, just words.

FATHER. You should talk. You're the one with just words.

SON. At least I know what I'm talking about.

FATHER. Yeah, but I don't know what you're talkin' about.

MOTHER Open your ears, dear. You always were a little thick.

FATHER. Now don't start on me, mother.

MOTHER. No, you don't start on me. You don't have the same power over me now, father.

SON. Stupid! Stupid!

MOTHER. I am not stupid! I will not be called stupid!!

FATHER. Anyone who would light a match near a gas heater to check a leak has to be stupid.

MOTHER. You will not call me stupid!

FATHER. Any woman who overrides her husband's authority has got to be stupid.

MOTHER. Your authority means nothing to me when I can't breathe.

FATHER. You can breathe. Unless you're too stupid to know how to breathe.

MOTHER. Don't call me stupid.

FATHER. You don't work. That's stupid. A law degree and you don't work.

MOTHER. I was too busy with the children.

FATHER. I'm the busy one, layin' brick all day. I'm the provider, the one who's haulin' ass.

MOTHER. Oh, yes, and I don't do anything, not anything for the family. If it weren't for me he'd be uneducated like their father.

FATHER. I'm the one who fed him.

MOTHER. I fed him too in my own way.

FATHER. You spoiled him. That's what you did.

MOTHER. I taught him about art, culture. I civilized him.

FATHER. Look at your son. Look at what you did to him.

MOTHER. I'm proud of my son. I've had enough. I've had enough.

[DECEASED MOTHER disappears. Abrupt silence. FATHER and SON, suddenly break into an attenuated laugh that subsides abruptly to another silence. Both men cross to their respective chairs]

SON. My God, I'm exhausted. You suck every bit of energy from me, do you realize that? Your density is a major obstacle for me; you torture me with your thickness, your dullness. Surely, nobody can be as dull as you appear to be. You're playing at it a bit, are you not?

FATHER. I'm trying my best. You ask complicated questions.

[FATHER sits on stool, stage right of table]

Foul Shots

SON. Ah, yes, the futility of it all! To imagine that you could possibly comprehend the subtleties of what I have to teach. I'm surely an optimist, a dreamer, to believe so very much in you.

FATHER. Aren't we friends, son?

SON. I have no friends! How can you possibly be my friend!! You are my father and my pupil. I don't take friendship lightly, daddy.

FATHER. I don't got no friends either.

SON. There, you see? What did I tell you? You and I are friendless!!! Ah, yes, life is sad, sad, sad!!! But then I am a teacher. I serve mankind so all is not lost. But in your case there is so little by way of hope. You're hopeless.

FATHER. Don't talk to me like that! I'll learn to read. There's hope, some hope.

SON. And upon what, may I ask, do you base that assumption?

FATHER. I must believe that. Otherwise there is no point.

SON. *[crosses to FATHER, stage right]* No! No! No! There is a point to all of this. The point is the pure, unadulterated beauty of learning!!! Learning is in itself beautiful!!! The vast capacity of your mind is like a canvass upon which an artist paints a masterpiece. I am the artist and your mind is a blank canvass. I am molding that mind into a lovely, thinking machine with which, from certain premises, you may draw certain conclusions that clarify your consciousness.

FATHER. What then is consciousness?

SON. Not yet! Not yet! You mustn't take such gigantic leaps. There is a process you must abide by first.

FATHER. Ah, yes, the process. I forgot.

SON.*[gives FATHER book]* You're always forgetting process. Your mind isn't disciplined.

FATHER. My mind has always been my worst shortcoming.

SON. *[sits stage left of table]* But we're going to turn that around, aren't we? You're going to educate yourself, daddy. If I can do it, then you can do it. I've picked myself up from the bootstraps, risen from the bowels of deprivation and transformed myself into a man of letters.

FATHER. You seem to be fighting yourself, boy.

SON. What fighting? I read with ease. I have information at my finger tips.

FATHER. You don't seem to have much fun.

SON. Fun? *[crosses to stage left wall, writes the word, 'FUN']* Fun? Fun? Fun is a vulgar noun. Fun is the name of a thing. Fun is for the masses. I have no time for fun.

FATHER. I like to have fun.

SON. You're typical bourgeois. Indulgent, all of them, looking for a quick fix to spruce up their dull lives.

FATHER. My life isn't dull. I have fun.

Raymond J. Barry

SON. Ah, yes, fun, fun, fun. And what, pray tell, is fun for you, daddy?

FATHER. I like to fish.

SON. Ah, yes, fishing; the proverbial fisherman with a fishing pole in his hands, fishing for meaning in his life.

FATHER. No, I fish for fish.

SON. Did you catch any fish, daddy?

FATHER. Sometimes. *[pause]* What are we talking about here?

SON. Big fish, daddy?

FATHER. Sometimes they were big. *[pause]* What are we talking about here?

SON. Smelly fish, daddy?

FATHER. Fish always smell a little bit. What do you ask that for?

SON. My father, the smelly fisherman, the drop-line specialist, foraging for meaning in his life.

FATHER. I'm not foraging for nothing, boy. Go easy on me, son. Go easy on me. Fishing never hurt nobody.

SON. It did when it became more important than us.

FATHER. What us?

SON. You know, you and me, us.

FATHER. What are we talkin' about here. *[pause]* Tell me about London.

SON. The parks are green.

FATHER. The parks?

SON. Yes, the parks in London are green. There is little sun, you see, and adequate rain, so the parks are green. The grass and trees are green with leaves. Something lush about it all. *[crosses upstage]*

FATHER. What else?

[SON crosses back toward FATHER]

SON. What are you driving at?

FATHER. I'm not driving at nothin'.

SON. Yes, you are. You're suggesting something.

FATHER. No, honest, I'm not suggesting nothin'. I'm just curious.

SON. You? You're curious? Curiosity is typical of great artists and inventors and intellectuals like myself. I am curious but surely you of all people cannot be curious.

FATHER. I'm curious about London. How did you feel while you were in London?

SON. I was extremely calm at the time, so calm it was unnecessary to speak. In fact I barely spoke.

FATHER. You talk too much now.

SON. How dare you!

FATHER. I take it back.

SON. How dare you criticize my well-intentioned verbiage.

FATHER. You seem to make a lot of noise.

SON. How dare you!

Foul Shots

FATHER. Your mouth is always opened, making noise.

SON. It wasn't like that in London. In London, as I say, I was very calm, very quiet.

FATHER. Were you lonely?

SON. *[cross to stage left wall]* Enough! Enough! Back to 'things'. Back to education.

FATHER. Oh, yes, persons, places and things.

[FATHER rises from his chair, crosses stage left, paces upstage and downstage]

SON. *[paces upstage right]* Yes, exactly that. The platform upon which everything stands, the parts of speech, the labeling effect, the categorization of all parts of life, starting with the noun, *[referring to the word 'NOUN' written on stage right wall]* the simple noun, the common noun. And ultimately moving forward to *[cross to stage right wall]* adjectives. *[writes 'ADJECTIVES' on wall]* Repeat after me. An adjective is a word...

FATHER. An adjective is a word...

SON. ...that describes how many...

[SON writes definition of an adjective on stage right wall]

FATHER. ...that describes how many...

SON. ...what kind and modifies a noun or a pronoun.

FATHER. ...what kind... What's the use? I can't learn this stuff. I should go back to working with my hands. *[sits on chair, stage left]*

SON. No, you should not! Working with your hands will get you nowhere in your life. You can work with your brain as I do. Now repeat the definition of an adjective to me.

FATHER. If I have to.

SON. Yes, you must. It's necessary.

FATHER. Oh, all right. An adjective... What was it again?

SON. Listen! Listen! Listen! An adjective is a word that describes how many, what kind and modifies a noun or a pronoun.

FATHER. What is a pronoun?

SON. Stop with your evasive techniques!!! You are evasive, evasive, evasive!!! Remember, blind faith is what will get you somewhere in your life, not insignificant facts that change over the course of time. Simply do the work and your reward will follow.

FATHER. All right. I'll try. An adjective is a word that tells... I don't remember.

SON. It is a word that describes how many, what kind...

FATHER. How many what? What kind of what?

SON. Don't ask questions, nincompoop! Just say it!

FATHER. But I don't know what I'm saying.

SON. You don't need to know. It will fall into place in its own time. Be patient. Now, sir, be a good fellow and recite the words I give you. An

Raymond J. Barry

adjective is a word that describes how many, what kind..

FATHER. An adjective is a word that describes how many, what kind...

SON. ...and modifies a noun or a pronoun.

FATHER. ...and modifies a noun or a pronoun, which I don't understand what it is.

SON. You are insubordinate! You'd better learn to abide by the laws of this classroom, sir, or you'll be a sorry one!

FATHER. I failed.

SON. No, you have not failed but you are trying my patience.

FATHER. I have failed. I can't remember what an adjective is.

SON. Listen to me. How many! What kind!

FATHER. How many what? What kind of what?

SON. No, no, no, no! Simply say the words. My god, you exhaust me.

FATHER. An adjective is how many and what?

SON. Listen to me, you nincompoop!!! An adjective is a word that describes how many, what kind and modifies a noun or a pronoun!!!

FATHER. You fascist!!!

SON. What did you say?

FATHER. You fascist!!!!

SON. Fascist? Fascist? Where on earth did you learn that word?

FATHER. The word dribbles out of you like molasses.

SON. Again, insubordination!

FATHER. I failed.

SON. At the risk of being called a "fascist" I will say you have not failed and you will not fail. You have too much will-power to fail!!!

FATHER. I have no will-power. I'm a failure.

SON. You must stop saying that, you cowardly pupil you!!! Now, brown house. What kind of house? Answer?

FATHER. Brown.

SON. Yes, – brown. Brown is the adjective. Get it? A few houses. How many houses?

FATHER. A few.

SON. *[stage right]* Yes! You see? 'brown' and 'a few', both are adjectives and both should be regarded as such. *[crosses to stage right wall]* Now use your sterling imagination to describe some more examples.

[FATHER runs downstage right to SON threatening him with stool poised to hit him]

FATHER. Dumb me; stupid me. What kind of me? Dumb and stupid me. What are the adjectives. Why dumb and stupid, of course. Don't be afraid, son. No one is going to hurt you. I'm not as cruel as you. Just allow me to read a little bit. I'll show you what I can do.

SON. Book's on the table.

FATHER. Yes, I'm going to struggle through that book just to improve myself. I'll begin here and now. *[He crosses to table, puts down stool, sits*

in it, picks a page and reads] Wh... en we we... re. W... w... w... w... Lot of
'w' sounds. F... f... fir... st m... m... m... a... rried in London.
SON. *[downstage right]* London? Is that what you said? London?
FATHER. *[shows him the word in book]* Yes, that's what it says here.
London.
SON. Just checking.
FATHER. *[crosses up-center stage]* Please, if I'm gonna flow with this,
don't interrupt me.
SON. I'm sorry, but you stumble so.
FATHER. Well, stop it.
SON. You will not order me.
FATHER. You will not order me. You will coax me but you will not order
me. You will find ways of building my confidence, but you will not order
me.
SON. *[crosses upstage right]* I make the rules in my classroom!
FATHER. *[cross to SON]* That's not a good way of educating, by ordering.
We must have instruction without punishment.

[simultaneous]

FATHER.	**SON.**
Otherwise I'll shut down altogether and my mind will never learn the knowledge you want to teach. There is my freedom to consider here. Otherwise I can't learn. I won't learn.	No, we must have punishment! Order! Insubordinate! You are insubordinate! Order in the classroom!

SON. You refuse to accept my terms?
FATHER. *[stage right]* Yes, I refuse.
SON. Illiterate! You are an illiterate, a failure of a man!!
FATHER. I'm a man. I'm a real man.
SON. A real man would know how to read.
FATHER. But I am a real man.
SON. You can't even read.
FATHER. Reading has nothing to do with my manhood.
SON. No, reading has everything to do with your manhood.
FATHER. What I do determines my manhood, not what I read.
SON. And you do nothing, absolutely nothing! Not a book has been read!
In your entire life not a book has been read! Might as well put you
behind a machine, like a monkey, and have done with it! Show you how
to press buttons, like a monkey, and leave it at that!
FATHER. I've loved my wife and children. I've taken care of them.
SON. That isn't manhood.

Raymond J. Barry

FATHER. My babies I have taken care of, supported and raised.

SON. Woman's work.

FATHER. You were too goddamn selfish for family!

SON. Watch it! Watch it! Watch it! Watch it! Shut your fucking mouth about family, fucking family. What of my accomplishments? What of my degrees?

[simultaneous]

SON.	**FATHER.**
What of my abilities, my ambition to succeed, my power in a world full of neer-do-wells?	Your degrees mean nothing, considering the way you treat your father!

FATHER. You, sir, are selfish!!!!

SON. *[down center stage]* And you, sir, are illiterate. Which is worse? I'll show you what you are, you stupid, cross-eyed feather-head!

FATHER. *[down center stage]* You fascist, dictating Nazi. Don't you call me a stupid cross-eyed featherhead!

[simultaneous]

FATHER.	**SON.**
Don't you tell me, because I'll walk all over you, you rotten, no good! You fascist, you! I'll show you. I'll walk all over your face! Don't you tell me,	You muscle-headed, sinew-brained beef-caked ball of protoplasm! You jerk! You jerk-headed, junk-skulled moron! You muscle-headed, sinew-brained,

[sudden silence, then back to argument]

FATHER. *[cont'd]*	**SON.** *[cont'd]*
... because I'll walk all over you, you Rotten, no good! You fascist, you! I'll show you! I'll walk all over your face. Don't you tell me, because I'll walk all over you, you rotten no-good!	beef-caked ball of protoplasm! You jerk! You jerk-headed, junk-skulled moron! You muscle-headed, sinew-brained, beef-caked ball of protoplasm! You jerk! You stupid, cross-eyed featherhead!

[A sudden pause. FATHER crosses to stage left without losing eye contact. Argument begins again abruptly and simultaneously]

FATHER. *[cont'd]*	**SON.** *[cont'd]*
Don't you tell me, because I'll walk all over you, you rotten, no	You muscle-headed, sinew-brained beef-caked ball of

Foul Shots

good! You fascist, you! I'll show you. I'll walk all over your face! Don't you tell me. protoplasm! You jerk! You jerk-headed, junk-skulled moron! You muscle-headed, sinew-brained.

[FATHER crosses downstage left]

SON. I'm terribly, terribly sorry for my part in this. *[no response]* I stated those insults out of a wish to injure you. *[no response]* Please say something, daddy. I feel terrible lately, too much of groveling, tasteless, uninspired, uneducated humanity. I'm responsible for them all. Anyone who walks into my classroom is automatically my responsibility. It's just too much work. Please forgive me. *[no response]* I wish you would talk to me, daddy. It makes no sense to remain angry. After all, we need each other, don't we? You need me to learn, and I need you to teach. Teaching is important to me. Without it, my knowledge is meaningless.

FATHER. You hurt my feelings.

SON. I know I did, and I'm terribly, terribly sorry for that.

FATHER. You called me a stupid, cross-eyed feather-head.

SON. That was a terrible thing to say, daddy. You mustn't take it seriously. It just popped out of my mouth in the heat of passion.

FATHER. You meant it.

SON. I was speaking from a place of anger. 'Feather' and 'head' don't even go together.

FATHER. Feather-head.

SON. Feather isn't an adjective, father. Feather doesn't tell 'what kind'. 'Feather' is the name of a 'thing'.

FATHER. Now I've forgotten what I learned.

SON. Your knowledge will come back to you when the proper time comes.

FATHER. No, it won't come back.

SON. I did this to you.

FATHER. You hurt me.

SON. Please, I feel terrible about it.

FATHER. It was almost true what you said.

SON. It's not true.

FATHER. That's what hurts.

SON. You're not a feather-head at all.

FATHER. There was some exaggeration, but it was almost true.

SON. And you're certainly not a cross-eyed idiot.

FATHER. That's the part that's almost true. I'm not only a feather-head but I'm a cross-eyed idiot too.

SON. What of other things I said? What of those? I called you 'brilliant' numerous times.

FATHER. I wish you had more confidence in me.

Raymond J. Barry

SON. But how can I possibly be confident in you? You plainly fail to see the beauty of learning.

FATHER. I would like you to be my friend, son.

SON. We've already been through that.

FATHER. I like you, son. I know you mean the best for me, but you destroy while you pretend to build. You're not building really. You're merely exercising power, flexing your muscles to push your weight around. You like crushing people. You've crushed me. Well, I won't be crushed anymore. I've had enough of being crushed. I'm my own boss. You're not my boss. I'll do what I want, do as I see fit. You think you know more than I do, but there are some things I know. *[crossing upstage right. SON sits in chair, stage left]* I know all sorts of things that ordinary people don't know. I know about tensile strength, for example, how far I can push myself in any given situation. Who needs to read for that? I'm tough, tougher than most - if not all. I know all kinds of things, having to do with games and fishing. I love fishing. I've fished for sunfish and carp, big carp, with all different kinds of colors, and slimy eels, blowfish, flounder, fluke and mackerel; I've even bagged me a rock-fish and blues and weakfish. *[cross to SON, stage left]* And I baited the hook myself with blood worms and crickets and dried dough balls and killies and spearing; the fluke go for the spearing. And I've jacked too, speared 'em with a jacking spear, eight-pronged spear with a twelve foot handle, and crabs and clams. *[moving to downstage right]* I'm educated. I know how to tread for clams with my bare feet, caught bushels of them with my bare feet; even hunted for duck when I was a boy, hid in a blind and waited for them with stools, fake wooden ducks, bobbing up and down in the cold, so cold; couldn't keep my hands warm, blew on them to keep them warm, a hunters' trick, and gardening too. I'm educated. I'm an educated man. *[facing SON who is sitting on stool, stage left of table]* I know how to mow a lawn, I tell you, and how to make a compos heap out of dead things, like weeds and dung and anything that don't serve any purpose for ordinary persons. But I know how to make a compos heap out of them so I'm educated. I can solder pipe for your toilet, sweat pipe, no-hub pipe or threaded pipe, any kind of pipe. It don't make no difference. So don't tell me I'm no dummy. It took a long time for me to accumulate so much knowledge, a long time, so don't tell me; don't tell me nothing! *[cross behind SON, behind stage left chair, menaces SON with hand]* Touch my hand, son.

SON. *[crosses to stage right]* What?

[FATHER chases SON, downstage right corner]

FATHER. Touch my hand.

SON. Don't come any closer.

FATHER. Why? I'm your father, son. I'm gentle.

SON. You have a certain menace about you.

Foul Shots

FATHER. Don't be fooled by how I look. Touch my hand.

[SON leans away from FATHER, downstage right]

SON. Please, take your hand away from me. Don't come any closer. You will not touch me ever again!

FATHER. Still afraid of a little touch?

SON. This is not my usual method.

FATHER. It's my method, son. Now touch your father's hand, boy.

SON. You're my father, and, besides, you're a man.

FATHER. So are you a man.

SON. Men don't hold hands.

FATHER. They don't? Even when they're father and son? What the hell happened to you in London, son?

SON. *[cross to stage left]* Sunny London.

FATHER. I thought you said it was brownish gray.

SON. I don't remember everything. I'm on medication, you know.

FATHER. *[cross down center stage]* You are? On medication?

SON. Yes, anti-depressant.

FATHER. How come?

SON. I'm depressed.

FATHER. Oh. What is that?

SON. Hard to explain.

FATHER. Never mind then. You take some kind of pill?

SON. Yes, a pill. It balances out my chemistry so I feel better.

FATHER. What do you have to feel?

SON. I don't know – just better.

FATHER [crosses center stage left] Let's get a beer then. That'll make you feel better.

SON. You don't understand. I'm clinically depressed.

FATHER. What the hell is that?

SON. *[downstage right corner]* It's a term that describes a state of mind that is unable to function.

FATHER. *[center stage left]* When I feel bad I just move on.

SON. You can do that. I can't.

FATHER. You can do it too. You just move on.

SON. You don't care about anything so you can do that.

FATHER. I care about my own ass.

SON. Right.

FATHER.

What do you care about?

SON. I care about everything but my own ass.

FATHER. Maybe you should start thinking about your own ass.

SON. Somehow I don't think about my own ass.

FATHER. What do those pills do?

SON. They make me feel better. They take away the darkness.

Raymond J. Barry

FATHER. What darkness?!!

SON. The part of me that wants to let go of everything.

FATHER. Let go of everything? *[cross downstage left]* Shit, I did that years ago.

SON. No, I mean really let go of everything.

FATHER. You mean everything?

SON. Yes, everything.

FATHER. What do you mean, 'everything?' You mean 'everything'?

SON. Yes, like die.

FATHER. Oh, yeah, die. *[crosses to SON]* Shit, I wouldn't mind dying.

SON. I wouldn't mind dying either. But I'm afraid to die.

FATHER. I ain't afraid.

SON. I care. You don't. *[upstage left of table]* Tell me you love me.

FATHER. *[cross downstage left corner]* Shit... Men... don't... talk that way. I don't... say... that stuff to nobody. I'll tell you one thing though. You oughta get off them pills.

SON. No, I need them to get through each day.

FATHER. You need a pill to get through each day? You ought to be ashamed of yourself.

SON. Fuck it! Tell me you love me, you prick! *[cross to FATHER, stage left]*

FATHER. Aw, shit! Will you stop it!... *[cross to upstage right]* Why do you have that phony accent?

SON. I picked it up in London.

FATHER. Why do you keep talking that way?

SON. It sounds better.

FATHER. Better than what?

SON. Better than how I used to talk.

FATHER. I don't understand a word you're saying.

SON. You understand me.

FATHER. You should talk more natural.

SON. This is natural.

FATHER. Natural to who?

SON. Natural to me.

FATHER. You sound like someone I knew once.

SON. Who?

FATHER. Your mother!

SON. Oh, maybe I should talk about Pat?

FATHER. What do you mean, Pat?

SON. You remember Pat.

FATHER. He didn't talk like that.

SON. What do you mean, 'he'?

FATHER. Did I say, "he"?

SON. Yes, you said 'he'.

Foul Shots

FATHER. I didn't mean 'he'. I meant 'she'. I... didn't mean... 'he'. I meant 'she'... Come on, let's move away from this stuff.

[FATHER crosses downstage left and then upstage left]

SON. What 'stuff'?

FATHER. Just this 'stuff' where we have to say stuff like this to each other.

SON. I don't mind talking about this 'stuff'.

FATHER. You should mind.

SON. Oh, why is that?

FATHER. You mean to tell me you want to talk like this to each other?

SON. Yes, I do. I want to talk about this stuff to each other.

FATHER. Aw, Jees, you gotta be kidding.

SON. Why would I be kidding?

FATHER. You can't just say stuff like this to each other. It ain't right.

SON. You love me, don't you, father?

[FATHER crosses to upstage right. SON follows]

FATHER. Aww shit! Will you, stop it? I can't stand this stuff.

SON. What stuff?

FATHER. *[crosses downstage right]* Just this stuff. It disgusts me, all this talk. Who taught you how to talk like this?

SON. You did.

FATHER. What do you mean me? I didn't teach you this stuff.

SON. Sure you did. I heard you say, "I love you," many times.

FATHER. Bull, I never said anything of the kind.

SON. *[crosses to FATHER, downstage left]* Yes, you did, to your lover on the phone every day around four o'clock after I came home from school and mother was at work!!! Remember, dad, on the phone, talking to your girl friend? Pat was her name! I think it was Pat! You used to say, "I love you, Pat," then! You were pretty free-wheeling with expressing your feelings to her, daddy! How about
me? How do you feel about me?

FATHER. You're a pain in the ass. *[cross upstage right]* That's how I feel about you, dragging me through all these goddamn lies. All of it is lies.

SON. I'm not lying, father.

FATHER. You sound like a lot of hot air if you ask me. You haven't even lived for goodness sake. You ain't even married.

SON. No, I'm married.

FATHER. What? You're married?

SON. I never told you.

FATHER. You never told me?

SON. But I'm married.

FATHER. *[cross to table, sit, facing audience]* Why wouldn't you tell me?

SON. I just never got around to it.

FATHER. You should've told me.

Raymond J. Barry

SON. It was a little sudden. I never should've done it.

FATHER. You kept such an important thing from your father?

SON. We broke up.

FATHER. You're already broken up?

[SON sits on table, facing audience]

SON. We didn't get along.

FATHER. Can you beat that? Married and divorced, all in the same breath.

SON. It wasn't right for us.

FATHER. *[sits on table, facing audience]* You can just take it or leave it when you get married nowadays, huh?

SON. Yeah, take it if it works and leave it if it doesn't. I was sure I'd leave her some day.

FATHER. When you know something for sure, it'll happen.

SON. I know a lot of things for sure and they don't happen.

FATHER. They will if you're sure of them.

SON. I'm not sure of anything.

FATHER. Oh, yes, you are, son. All that talk about life being sad. You seem pretty sure of yourself when you say that stuff.

SON. It's true. I see sadness all around me.

FATHER. You see what you want to see.

SON. Sadness is there, right in front of your eyes.

FATHER. With all your knowledge you're still tripping over yourself.

SON. I read every day.

FATHER. Books. What about people? What about your wife?

SON. People are a waste of time. My work is what counts.

FATHER. Your work is cold, son. It doesn't breathe. It can't hold you at night. Take it from me. I been sleeping alone for years.

SON. You got what you deserved.

FATHER. We all make mistakes. Your mother was too goddamned good for me, that's all. She knew what fork to eat at dinner.... and how to move a spoon away from her when she ate a bowl of soup. I didn't know nothin' about forks and spoons. You just ate the food where I come from, that's all, just ate the food and left the table. Your mother was just too goddamned classy for me. I didn't know nothin' about class. My armpits smelled when I came home from work. I was a animal, a suspicious animal. Why did you break up?

SON. Who knows?

FATHER. Don't give me that. You know. You know.

SON. I left, that's all.

FATHER. Why?

SON. I don't know why. We didn't get along. She said I made her feel stupid.

FATHER. You make me feel stupid too.

Foul Shots

Son. That's different. You are stupid. Besides, you're my student.

Father. You make all of your students feel stupid?

Son. Students are stupid until I teach them how to be smart.

Father. I was smart before you started to teach me.

Son. You couldn't even read.

Father. What's that got to do with smartness?

Son. Smart people can read.

Father. I get by just fine without reading. That shows how smart I am.

Son. You're as dumb as they come.

Father. You do to me what you did to your wife.

Son. That was different. I loved my wife.

Father. I loved your mom too, very much.

Son. Well she's dead!!!

Father. All right, enough of this. *[gets up from table, crosses to stage left wall]* Back to my lesson. Tell me what a... a.. a adjective is.

Son. *[writes a word on fourth wall]* 'Cheap.'

Father. What do you mean, "cheap?"

Son. The 'cheap' father couldn't spend his money freely.

Father. What?

Son. 'Cheap' is the adjective, modifying the noun, 'father', which is you.

Father. What do you mean, me? I'm not cheap.

Son. *[down center stage]* Yes, you are cheap!! You're cheap with your money and you're cheap with your feelings!!! You're cheap with every part of yourself. Your cheapness has robbed you of any chance of having a decent life. *[cross upstage right]*

Father. *[stage left]* You're a real smart ass, aren't you?

Son. *[center stage]* I did go to college.

Father. *[down stage]* I paid for it.

Son. *[up center stage]* No, you, didn't. I was on scholarship.

Father. I paid for most of it.

Son. You sent me twenty five dollars right before I graduated.

Father. I sent you more than that.

[simultaneous]

Father.	**Son.**
I couldn't afford your damned college.	You didn't take any interest. You were too busy

Son. *[up center stage]*... having sex with Pat.

Father. I don't remember any goddamned Pat.

Son. *[upstage of table]* Oh, you do. You do. You remember Pat, for goodness sake! You remember Pat! You talked on the phone and sometimes she would come over. You'd slip her in the side door while I was upstairs; slip her into your bedroom and whip off a piece for an

Raymond J. Barry

hour. You'd always manage to get Pat out of the house before mother came home from work. You remember Pat, all right.

FATHER. *[downstage of table]* Let's get a beer, son. Tell me some reading.

[FATHER picks up book from table. SON smashes it from his hand.]

SON. What would you like to read, father? How about some legal documents, your divorce from mom for example?

FATHER. What you doing, boy?

SON. *[upstage of table]* Don't you get it? I don't know who I am, you weak fuck excuse for a man!!! You never showed me what's a man supposed to feel, what's he supposed to do! How was I supposed to act? I don't know because you never knew!! I limp through my life like you limp through yours and neither of us can stand up on our own two legs! I want to be perfect but I'm not perfect. I'm imperfect. That's what I learned from you, my father, how imperfect I am. My pills. Where are my pills? *[He searches through his pockets, downstage right, violently throws his jacket on the floor]*

SON. Goddamnit! I cannot find my pills.

[downstage right; silence while SON rummages through his jacket, looking for pills.]

FATHER. Ah,... I would like to be your friend, son. Look how smart you are. You're a great teacher. I don't understand a word that comes out of your mouth you're so smart. Come on, boy, let's have a good time. Life is so short. There's no point in fighting. Let's have a good time.

SON. You can't decide to have a good time and then just do it.

FATHER. Sure you can, son. Sure you can. All you do is have a good time, that's all. Just decide to and then do it, by deciding to do it, that's all. There must be some reason why we stay in this room together. It can't be all bad between us. It can't be all bad, can it? We must be having a good time some way. Otherwise we wouldn't be staying in this room together like this. It wouldn't be possible for us to stay in this room together like this, would it?

SON. You can't just decide to have a good time. That's not how it works. I'm not having a good time. I'm questioning things.

FATHER. Don't question so goddamn much. Just enjoy what we have together. Come on over to the table, son. Come on, sit at the table with me, boy.

[SON comes to the table]

FATHER. Now sit down, son.

SON. I don't want to sit down, father.

FATHER. Sure you do, son. Sure you do.

SON. No, I don't.

FATHER. Every son wants to rest his ass once in a while with his old man.

SON. It's not just resting my ass. It has more to do with artificially having a good time.

FATHER. What's artificial about it? Just have a good time, that's all. Just make a decision that this time with your old man is gonna be the cat's meow, and that's all there is to it. There is such a thing as making it happen, you know. People do make it happen. You got bad habits, boy. You allow yourself to be taken over by bad feelings when you don't have to allow it. You can rule the roost, boy, when it comes to having a good time. You don't have to let yourself go down the tubes so easy.

SON. I don't know what 'a good time' is.

FATHER. That's a shame, son. Everybody got to have some kind of a good time. Otherwise they'll shrivel up and die. Gotta find a way to relax. Gotta have fun. Come on, boy, let's have some fun.

SON. What fun? There is no fun.

FATHER. What an old stick in the mud you are. You're older than me for Chrissakes.

SON. Then how can we have fun?

FATHER. Just by talking about it there's something beginning to happen, isn't there? You're beginning to have fun, ain't you? This is fun, talking about fun, isn't it? See? You're beginning to smile. I can see you smile.

SON. All right; all right, you old whippersnapper, you.

FATHER. What did you call me? Did you call me an old whippersnapper?

SON. I suppose I did – an old whippersnapper of a father. That's what you are, dad. An old whippersnapper of a father who can just decide to have fun when he wants to.

FATHER. And you're having fun now, aren't you? You're having some real fun now, aren't you?

SON. I suppose I am, you old whippersnapper. I suppose I am, you old buttercup.

FATHER. Don't get out of hand now. Keep it light, but keep it manly.

SON. Isn't 'buttercup' manly enough for you, father?

FATHER. Manly? A buttercup manly? It don't sound so much like a real man as far as I'm concerned.

SON. What about male buttercups?

FATHER. That's a joke, right? You're joking me, right?

SON. They have to reproduce, don't they? Buttercups must have the male and the female. Therefore it is appropriate to call my father 'buttercup'.

FATHER. All right. Since we've decided to go ahead and have a good time, we might as well just have a good time and call each other 'buttercup'. I don't mind being called buttercup really. It don't bother me. It's all in fun anyway. All in fun while we're having a good time in the same room with each other. That's why we stay in the same room together – because we're having such a good time, callin' each other 'buttercup'.

SON. You're the buttercup – not me.

Raymond J. Barry

FATHER. Anybody can be the buttercup – not just your old man. You could be the buttercup too.

SON. Nope, I'm not the buttercup. I'm having too much of a good time to be the buttercup.

FATHER. You can have a good time and be the buttercup. That's what having a good time is – calling each other 'buttercup' and 'whippersnapper'. That's what having a good time is.

SON. You know, I am having a good time.

FATHER. So am I. So am I.

SON. You changed my mood entirely.

FATHER. I suppose I did a little, but it was you who changed the mood yourself.

SON. Me?

FATHER. Yep – little ole you gave yourself a good time and nobody else. You decided and took the bull by the horns and low and behold look what happened. You're feeling good.

SON. Yeah.

FATHER. You seem mopey again, son. Whatsamatter?

SON. Nothing.

FATHER. Come on, aren't you havin' a good time?

SON. Yeah.

FATHER. Good. You don't seem to be havin' a good time.

SON. I'm mulling things over, analyzing things.

FATHER. That's the trouble with you, son. "Mullin' things over. Analyzing things." What for? You don't have to mull things over, analyze things. That's ridiculous. Just live your goddamned life, boy. Have a good time. Enjoy! Enjoy!

SON. I am enjoying myself.

FATHER. Are you really, son? I'm happy to hear that. I'm so very happy to hear that. Down deep inside I want a happy son.

SON. Yes, father, and that's what you have too. One, big happy son, all your own

FATHER. Yup, that's right, boy.

SON. Only thing is, you can't even tell your own son how you feel about him. You're cheap, stingy.

FATHER. Go easy on me, son. Everyone got problems. Don't make such a big goddam deal about problems. You can choose a good life if you make it good, not sad, but goddamn good, and stop blaming me for your problems.

SON. Easy for you to say.

FATHER. No, it's not easy for me to say. *[upstage right]* My father made mistakes too. Who gives a damn? I made it livable, that's all. I insisted on making it goddamn livable! What do you expect, everything to be easy? That's not how it works, boy. You gotta make some effort in this world.

SON. I educated myself.

FATHER. Big fucking deal.

SON. I am my work. That's all I think about, my work.

FATHER. A job ain't nothin' but a way to put food on the table. That's all it is. In the end your family, your kids, your mother, your father. That's all that counts. You gotta take care of those. Who gives a damn what a 'noun' is if you can't hug it in the end. Death is too close to ignore the people you care about. Otherwise you'll die of loneliness.

SON. You just don't get it, do you?

[FATHER goes down to his knees]

FATHER. You want me to go down on my knees and confess my sins, but I'm not going to after all I done for you. *[slow cross on knees to SON, downstage right]* You forget, kid, I changed your dirty, shitty diapers when you were a baby. I worried about you. I worried a lot about you. I was concerned for you. Still am. Nobody worried about you more than me. I couldn't sleep some nights. Tossing and turning, thinking about my son. No, really, I worried.

SON. You did worry, did you? *[crosses from downstage right to downstage left]*

FATHER. Oh, yeah, I did. I worried all the time.

SON. Funny, I never knew.

FATHER. How could you know? I never told you.

SON. You never told me much of anything.

FATHER. Oh, go on, I used to talk about things.

SON. Funny, I don't remember talking much.

FATHER. We used to small-talk a lot.

SON. You were always so tired from working.

FATHER. Layin' brick.

SON. What a waste of a life.

FATHER. Oh, now then, son, don't be going overboard.

SON. You would actually spend your entire life laying brick?

FATHER. I'm proud of it.

SON. Are you proud of me?

FATHER. You bet. I am.

SON. How proud?

FATHER. This proud. *[extends his arms]*

SON. About the size of a big fish.

FATHER. Well, I suppose, if you want to talk about it that way.

SON. Tell me you love me.

FATHER. *[cross upstage left]* Aw, Jeez! Will you stop it. Men don't talk like that!!!!

SON. Men can say they love their sons!!!

FATHER. I 'm not one of them guys who talks like that!!!!

Raymond J. Barry

SON. Sure you are. I heard you talking like that to Pat!!!

FATHER. [stage right] Pat is all you talk about!!!! Fuck Pat!!!! Fuck Pat!!! Fuck Pat!!!

SON. I'm ready to give up on you.

[SON gathers his books from table. FATHER runs to him, blocks his way. SON moves to stage left]

FATHER. No, no no, don't give up on me, son. Please, please help. I got nothing without you. I'm flexible.

SON. What's come over you, dad? Don't you realize what you're doing to our trust? How can I teach such a rebellious student? Have you no idea how ignorant you are? Why you are outright stupid. You can't think. You can't read. The only thing you can do is listen and you aren't willing even to do that. What has come over you for goodness sake?

FATHER. I guess I'm just dumb.

SON. [cross to stage right wall] No, you're not dumb. You have shown yourself to be an academic. In this short span of time you have grasped the more subtle elements of grammar, and without that comprehension God knows what a hopeless case you would be. [cross to upstage wall] But encouragingly you are blessed with an active brain, sir, and that fact has been demonstrated over and over again by your immediate grasp of the subjects we have wrestled with. [cross to stage left wall] Don't give up now, dad, when you are on the brink of discovery. You should think more positively. Use adverbs that are happy.

FATHER. [stage right] Such as what?

SON. Like, for example, 'gleefully'. That's a happy word, 'gleefully'.

[SON dances around the stage in a gleeful manner]

FATHER. I've seldom used the word.

SON. Well, you can start now.

FATHER. How would I use a word like 'gleefully?'

SON. The student learns 'gleefully'.

FATHER. I don't learn gleefully. I learn with great resistance.

SON. That is irrelevant! Again you are mixing form with content which will lead you astray every time. You must stick with the subject at hand.

FATHER. Gleefully!

SON. Gleefully, I walked away from the mother of my children and never returned. [writes 'GLEEFULLY' on wall] Notice the 'ly' word 'gleefully'. It's the adverb, modifying the verb 'walked', telling how I walked; that is, gleefully.

FATHER. Is that what you did, son? Did you walk away from your kids and never come back? Did you desert your kids, son? Is that what you did? Did you desert your kids?

SON. Come now, father, give me an example of an adverb, an 'ly' word.

FATHER. What happened to you in London, son?

[SON turns to stage left wall, long pause]

Foul Shots

Son. Children... some children somewhere.

Father. Children somewhere?

Son. Never mind... two... boys... Never mind.

Father. Don't give me that 'never mind' business. What children?

Son. Two little boys... with wavy hair.

Father. What? Wavy hair?

Son. Enough of that, father. Back to your lesson.

Father. Wavy hair runs in the family, son.

Son. Never mind, father. Back to our lesson. Let's get back to our lesson.

Father. We can talk, son. I would understand.

Son. I can't talk. I can only teach. Teaching is all I know.

Father. There's got to be more in you than plain teaching.

Son. No, I'm a plain teacher and nothing more.

Father. You could be a husband as well someday, son, or even a father.

Son. No, never a father.

Father. But you must be a father someday if you were to live out a natural life.

Son. No, I'm not a real father.

Father. What of those two boys you mentioned? Are they yours?

Son. Enough of that, daddy; enough! Let's discuss other things.

[FATHER sits on 'teacher's chair,' stage left of table. SON slowly paces around the stage]

Father. Such a sensitive lad. And so secretive as well. What happened in London, son.

Son. Not really a man... I became the baby sitter for our children, taking the boys to school, dropping them off,... depressed, going back to bed, sleeping.... sleeping until four in the afternoon, waking up just before she came home from work and then pretending I'd done something constructive with the day. She knew. She always knew I'd been sleeping while she was struggling to make a living for the both of us. She made the money. I spent the money... on frivolous things, a forty-inch television to occupy the empty hours. She always knew... She lost respect for me. But I couldn't help myself. I was clinically depressed. I went to another woman, just to give myself some resemblance of dignity... If someone would love me... think I was attractive, then that would equalize how I felt inside.

Father. Not a bad life if you ask me. Beats laying brick.

Son. You really mean that, don't you?

Father. Of course, I mean it. Anyone would like to spend the day in bed. That's a good day for anyone.

Son. You really are stupid, aren't you?

[SON, stage right, begins pacing around the room. FATHER stage left approaches table]

Raymond J. Barry

FATHER. You had wavy hair once.

SON. Yes.

FATHER. When you were little.

SON. Yes.

FATHER. You were cute.

SON. Yes.

FATHER. Then you got bigger.

SON. Yes.

FATHER. Taller.

SON. Yes.

FATHER. You developed muscles.

SON. Yes.

FATHER. I'll never forget when you took your shirt off one day and I saw these muscles on your chest and back. I couldn't believe what I was seeing.

SON. Yes.

FATHER. You had become a man, someone I had to contend with all of a sudden.

SON. Yes.

FATHER. Then you were off to college and I never saw much of you after that.

SON. Yes.

FATHER. There were a few visits here and there but that's about it. You seemed.. What did you call it before?... 'depressed' at one point.

SON. Shattered nerves.

FATHER. Yes, shattered nerves is what it looked like too.

SON. Yes.

FATHER. You were pretty quiet during those days.

SON. Yes.

FATHER. It was shortly after you came back from London, I think.

SON. Yes, back from London.

FATHER. There was some kind of woman, wasn't there at that time?

SON. I'm alone. I'll always be alone.

FATHER. That's a shame, son. I stayed with your mom to the bitter end. She left me.

SON. That's precisely why I'm alone!

FATHER. What about those wavy-haired boys?

SON. Stop it, father!

FATHER. Wavy-haired lads.

SON. Please, don't bring that up again.

FATHER. It's a sore point with you, is it?

SON. Nothing I wish to talk about.

FATHER. I like to push things for a change just to keep a balance.

SON. Yes, you do.

Foul Shots

FATHER. You've pushed enough. Now it's time for me to do a little pushing.

SON. Enough of pushing.

FATHER. I agree. But without the pushing things stay the same between us.

SON. Nothing wrong with that.

FATHER. But I haven't learned to read yet.

SON. I'm weakening on that front.

FATHER. Don't weaken, boy. Keep your nose to the grindstone.

SON. Easy for you to say.

FATHER. Hard work will get you there. Don't give up on me now, boy. Don't give up on me.

SON. Your mind is like a sieve. I'm impatient, father, always impatient.

FATHER. You were impatient with those wavy-haired boys as well.

SON. Yes, I admit it.

FATHER. Couldn't stick with them when the going got tough.

SON. Enough, daddy.

FATHER. *[presents book to SON]* Teach me, boy.

SON. I've run out of knowledge.

FATHER. What? You've run out of knowledge?

SON. Yes, I've run out of purpose.

FATHER. Well, which is it – purpose or knowledge?

SON. I've run out of...

FATHER. Say it, son. Does it have anything to do with those wavy-haired boys?

SON. Father, I wish...

FATHER. What, son? You can tell me. You certainly can tell me. Speak, son.

SON. We've never spoken.

FATHER. But we can speak now if we make the effort.

SON. *[pacing]* No.

FATHER. Tell me the most difficult thing you could possibly say.

SON. *[upstage right]* Daddy, I would like to cut your throat with a very sharp razor.

FATHER. What?

SON. *[approaches table]* Daddy, I would like to cut your throat with a very sharp razor.

FATHER. *[stage left of table]* Oh, well, I guess that's it then, is it?

SON. I guess so.

FATHER. You got no respect for me whatsoever then, huh?

SON. Respect for what?

FATHER. I was insecure during those days. Didn't know what I was doing. Everything you did I wanted you to be the best at, the very best. You had to do things perfect, not just do them like everyone else, but do

Raymond J. Barry

them perfect. I wanted you to be a great man, son. Not an asshole like me. I guess I hounded you too much. I might've been too rough with you. I don't know. I hit you too many times, I suppose, but goddamnit, you weren't gonna be like me. You just weren't gonna live that kind of life. I know. I know. I pushed you until you couldn't breathe. I hounded your ass when maybe I shouldn't have. Made you stay up all night to do your work, memorize your words when you were little. And the sports! Now that's something I coulda' been good at, if I had the confidence. I never had the confidence. You had the confidence. You could shoot a basketball I tell you, and run – boy you could run, could run with a football when you were little. After a while I thought it was me running. You'd make a touchdown and I thought it was me doin' it. You had the confidence I never had. You managed to do what I could never do. Didn't have the

ability. Didn't have the balls really. You had the courage in the beginning, until something happened to you. Changed at some point. Things were different between us after you gave up sports. I just was so disappointed in you when you quit everything. Look at you. You're too weak for sports really; didn't eat right. That's the one thing I couldn't force you to do. Never could force you to eat. You always threw up whenever I shoved the food down your mouth. That's the one thing I couldn't force you to do, the one thing I couldn't make you do. You wouldn't even drink your goddamned milk.

Son. You were a son-of-a-bitch to put it mildly. Remember how I used to miss my foul shots?

Father. You made your foul shots, son.

Son. No, I didn't.

Father. You made your foul shots.

Son. One after the other.

Father. You didn't miss them.

Son. Kept missing them.

Father. You made your foul shots.

Son. Until it became ridiculous.

Father. Don't say you missed them, son.

Son. The rest of my game was good.

Father. You made your foul shots!

Son. But always kept missing my foul shots.

Father. Don't you ever say you missed your foul shots...

Son. Couldn't help it.

Father. ...when you made your foul shots!

Son. You used to get so angry.

[simultaneous]

Son.   **Father.**

Foul Shots

Kept missing, missing, missing my foul shots until the game became all about your reaction to missing my foul shots. I kept missing, missing something. You wanted me to be the best? But I'm not the best. I never was the best. I didn't have it in me. You were never the best. How come you want me to be best when you never made it.? You never did anything. You drove me crazy with your constant requirements for perfection but you never did a thing yourself. You can't even read! How can I teach you? You're too dumb. It's like teaching a horse, some kind of beast that can't think. All you can do is pull wagons. Why? That's how you used to talk to me. Can't make your foul shots! Can't make...

Aw, hell, son, I don't care what you do so long it makes you happy. You can forget about those stupid foul shots. I just wanted you to be the best, son, just the best. Nothing wrong with that. Don't say that, boy. Never say that. You've got to be the best or why even bother with your life? I made you. I didn't have to make "it."

I did things. Teach me, son. You can teach me.

Don't talk to me like that, son.

Don't talk to me like that.

All right, you're overstepping your boundaries now.

SON. ...your foul shots! Can't make your foul shots. You're not making any adjustment in your foul shots.

[simultaneous]

SON.
Remember when you used to say that

FATHER.
You're making all this up.

SON. ...to me, father? You're not making any adjustment in your foul shots!

[simultaneous]

SON.
Not making any adjustment in your... foul shots! Bend your legs! Bend your legs! Remember, dad? All the instructions you gave me? Remember? Remember what you put me through, you

FATHER.
It's not true. It just isn't true. You're makin' this up. You're overteppin' your boundaries now, son. It just isn't true.

Raymond J. Barry

dumb bastard.

FATHER. Don't call me that, son.

SON. God knows what you were trying to accomplish, you dumb bastard.

FATHER. Please, don't call me that, son.

SON. That is, aside from completely destroying my confidence, you dumb ox.

FATHER. Teach me how to read, son.

SON. I'll teach you nothing.

FATHER. Teach me how to read.

SON. You can't grasp anything just like I couldn't make my foul shots.

FATHER. Stop feeling sorry for yourself, son.

SON. Who are you to say stop feeling sorry for yourself? I'm a grown man.

FATHER. Then behave like a goddamned grown man.

SON. Hey, I'm the teacher, not you!

FATHER. If you're the goddamned teacher then teach. Otherwise, shut your yap about your foul shots. The world is in ruins and your talkin' foul shots. Nothing pleased me then. I couldn't help myself.

SON. Yes, well, I can't help myself either.

[SON crosses from stage right of table to chair where FATHER is sitting, grabs him by the back of the neck. The two men wrestle to the floor where a battle ensues. FATHER separates himself from the fray and crawls away from SON.]

SON. *[on his knees]* You are my student and your performance under my tutelage is a direct reflection of my reputation. You'd better perform well or I will have a reason. You will learn to read and fast and not only will you learn to read you will learn to read here and now. You're too dumb to read but I will teach you anyway. How am I doing so far, dad?

FATHER. With regard to what?

SON. Am I a good teacher?

FATHER. I don't know much more than I did before.

SON. I've taught you things now, dad. I've taught you things.

FATHER. Name one thing I've learned.

SON. *[twists FATHER'S ear]* You know, grammar, prepositional phrases.

FATHER. Nope, can't say that I know those.

SON. Oh, come on now, dad. I've taught you something. Gosh, you're stupid. You've got to shape up now. Get with it. I'm not wasting my time on you, am I? Am I wasting my time?

FATHER. I don't know nothin' after all the money I spent on your education.

SON. I'll pay you back.

FATHER. You don't have any money.

Foul Shots

SON. How do you know how much money I have?

FATHER. Anybody who misses his foul shots when he's a kid can't make any money when he's grown up.

SON. That's it. I'm charging you for this lesson!

FATHER. Your approach is all wrong. We should go out and have a beer, just relax a little and talk about old times, talk about us, talk about life. That would warm us up a little so the relationship would be easier and we'd like each other better and there'd be more trust between us. *[FATHER lets go of SON'S arm]*

SON. Fuck trust. Just listen to your lesson.

FATHER. I don't like your lesson.

SON. You don't like my lesson like you don't like my foul shots.

FATHER. Fuck your lesson and your foul shots.

SON. *[twists FATHER'S ear]* Fuck you, dad.

FATHER. Is that how you talk to your own father?

SON. Maybe yes. Maybe no.

FATHER. Better straighten up, boy. Come on, let's get a beer.

SON. What about our work?

FATHER. Fuck work. Always working, working. Don't you ever get tired of it? That's not what life is all about. You can't just work yourself to death all the time. That ain't no fun.

SON. *[release ear, cross stage left]* You sound so ignorant.

FATHER. *[stands, stage right of table]* I am ignorant and stupid to boot.

SON. You're not applying yourself, that's all.

FATHER. Not applying myself, my ass.

SON. You've got to take it personally. That's what you used to tell me about my foul shots.

FATHER. I don't remember any goddamn foul shots. You're not a little boy anymore. You're my teacher.

SON. I have nothing to teach but my hatred, my anger. I can't dissolve my anger. This is what you created, dad, your son, the one you groomed for greatness, the one who missed his foul shots, the one who became frozen. The one who can't tolerate imperfection, the one who can't do anything but teach.

[SON gathers his books and crosses to door. FATHER crosses to stage left wall]

FATHER. I lo... ovve you. *[inarticulate attempt. FATHER feels himself along the BACKSTAGE wall, similar to an ape, learning to speak for the first time]* I lo... ove you. I lo... ve you. I lo... ove you. I lo... ove you, son.

[FATHER cross to SON, upstage right]

SON. Then why do you insist upon approaching me? You mustn't approach me like you are. I won't stand for it.

[simultaneous]

Raymond J. Barry

FATHER.
I have rights too, you know. Space is for everyone. That's democracy. I'm in such need. If you only knew. Please, make an exception in my case. I'm so afraid. I just want closeness, to be close to you. Men can be close.

SON.
Your space is your space and my space is my space. There is no democracy in a classroom. You must back off. We're all in need. There's nothing I can do about that. No, men mustn't be close, not too close.

[FATHER grabs SON, embrace]
FATHER. My father never held me like this.
SON. Nor did mine.
FATHER. I wanted him to hold me like this, but I couldn't ask him.
SON. Nor could I.
[While in an embrace FATHER walks SON downstage towards audience. Their walk continues to down center stage]
FATHER. What did you call it before? The noun thing, 'love', which is a thing, that eventually developed into our father and son thing... whatever is left between us, , when it comes to the big issues of 'what kind' and 'how many', tellin' to what degree and how much and why and what, what, what you mean to me will never be said again quite this way, since we don't talk, and what did you call it before?... a noun... 'heart', which is a thing,... my heart... and... what? A verb? That is an action - 'aches', my heart... aches. My heart... aches. My god-awful heart aches.
[Lights dim.; men in embrace]

End of Play

Pornographic Panorama

Playwright's notes

During the eighties, I worked as a laborer, renovating lofts in Manhattan, laying pipe in basements of Manhattan loft buildings. In this setting I wrote 'Pornographic Panorama', a play that describes different characters I encountered at the job when I was penniless, fortyish and very much in limbo. Working-class men surrounded me on the job and were the source of many of the play's character ideas, particularly with regard to 'Mulligan,' although heightened as my imagination saw fit to describe the decayed spirits of a man with no ethical standards. At the time I lived in the Lower East Side of Manhattan where life was cheap, indulgences were abundant and values were reversed from those of the middle-class suburb where I had been raised. Human beings in this play relate to each other as if they are replaceable. Similarly, in some countries, such as Rwanda and Yugoslavia "ethnic cleansing" has been part of their past. Although the play appears not to be political, it is a microcosm of how groups often are willing to dehumanize individuals to serve an expedient purpose.

Characters

Ralph: an English Professor, forty five.
Bartender: a man who serves food and drink, fifty years of age.
Mulligan: a big bully, a plumber by trade, forty five.
Cicero: a sexy laborer, thirty eight.
Beau: a carpenter, forty eight.
Molly: a woman in her thirties searching for something better.
Mrs. Mulligan: a wife of Mulligan, forty five.

Raymond J. Barry

History

The World Premiere of **Pornographic Panorama** was performed at Stark Raving Theatre in Portland, Oregon, May 15, 1999.

Rick Mullins was awarded Portland's Drammy Award for Best Actor, 1999, for his performance in the role of Mulligan.

CAST:

RALPH .... Steve Boss
BARTENDER... Jim Whilhite
MULLIGAN.. Rick Mullins
CICERO .... David Seitz
BEAU.. Jim Hartley
MOLLY.. Adrienne Flagg
MRS. MULLIGAN..................................... Nancy Wilson

ARTISTIC DIRECTOR........................... Myra Donnelley
DIRECTED BY .... David Demke
SET DESIGN..................................... Jeffrey D. Woods
LIGHTING DESIGN .... Angela Meyer
SOUND DESIGN .... Mel Fletcher
COSTUME DESIGN................................. Uta Krepulat
PROPS MISTRESS .... Torrey Cornwell
STAGE MANAGER .... Jennifer L. Hartman

Pornographic Panorama poster, Stark Raving Theatre, Portland, 1999

Raymond J. Barry

Pornographic Panorama

Act One

-

Scene One

[Interior of a bar, New York City. Seated on a barstool is Ralph, an English professor. He is slender of build and short, wears glasses, and combs his hair with a part. There is something boyish and at the same time intelligent about him, a combination that would not be unattractive to women. He is forty, but could look younger. The bartender is big, full bellied, and bald; about fifty to early sixties.]

RALPH. Gimme a drink.

BARTENDER. What do you want?

RALPH. Make it a beer. I'll stay away from the hard stuff.

BARTENDER. What kind do you want?

RALPH. I'll make it a Coors. That kind doesn't use preservatives. Does it?

BARTENDER. We don't have Coors.

RALPH. You don't have Coors?

BARTENDER. That's right.

RALPH. Why not?

BARTENDER. How should I know why not?

RALPH. How do I know what you know? Lighten up, will you?

BARTENDER. What do I know?

RALPH. How do I know what you know? What's the matter with you, yellin' like that at me?

BARTENDER. I'm not yellin'. What are you, hung over or something?

RALPH. No, I'm not hung over.

BARTENDER. You guys are all alike...

RALPH. Whattaya been drinking?

BARTENDER. ...wasting time drinking, hanging out...

RALPH. You gotta drink to look the way you do. You been drinking.

BARTENDER. ...never doing anything worthwhile.

RALPH. You're ugly. Look at those broken blood vessels all over you, all over your nose and cheeks.

BARTENDER. You're all alike.

RALPH. You smell of alcohol. That's why you're so sensitive about the subject.

BARTENDER. All right, I don't want to get into a discussion with you about this.

RALPH. You're already in a discussion with me about this.

BARTENDER. I am?

RALPH. 'Course you are and you brought the issue up.

BARTENDER. I did?

RALPH. 'Course you did.

BARTENDER. Well, now I'm taking myself out of it.

RALPH. All right, take yourself out of it.

BARTENDER. I am.

RALPH. All right.

BARTENDER. What do you mean, "All right"?

RALPH. Just what I said. All right.

[Long pause. Ralph sips his beer. Bartender moves away and begins drying glasses.] What do you think about a woman who doesn't work?

BARTENDER. She's smart.

RALPH. Yeah, I know what you mean. She must be pretty smart, right? I do all the goddam work and she doesn't work. That's pretty good, right?

BARTENDER. Yeah, she's smart.

RALPH. I mean, I wouldn't mind if I was makin' a lot of money, but I'm not. I supported her for five years, and now I need some help, but she won't work. Says she has a problem with it.

BARTENDER. We all have problems with it. After all, who wants to work?

RALPH. I don't mind working.

BARTENDER. You don't?

RALPH. Well, think about it. You work, right?

BARTENDER. Right.

RALPH. Well, what if you didn't? What would you do with yourself? Play with your peter? I mean, what would you really do with yourself? You'd be sitting around on your ass complaining about how tough life is. That's what you would be doing, and believe me, life would not be any better for it. You'd be bored.

BARTENDER. So why don't you tell her to work?

RALPH. She won't. She says she will, but in the meantime she won't. I know she won't. She's got some kind of a block about the whole thing. You can't change a person.

BARTENDER. That's right. You can't change a person.

RALPH. I used to think you could change a person, but you can't. People don't change. I don't change that much and the things that are important to me today will probably be important to me ten years from now. I don't know. Does your wife work?

BARTENDER. Yeah, she works. When the kids began to grow up she began working and she's been working ever since. She's pretty good in that way.

RALPH. Well, I don't know. People don't change and I'm not gonna fool myself about it. I don't feel right about the whole thing. I guess I should just leave her.

Raymond J. Barry

BARTENDER. What are you asking me for? I got nothing to do with your business.

RALPH. I don't mean to bring it to your doorstep.

BARTENDER. You know how many guys come in here with their troubles all day and all night long?

RALPH. Sorry.

BARTENDER. I get the same thing day in and day out.

RALPH. Take it easy. I won't mention it anymore.

BARTENDER. What am I, your doctor or something?

RALPH. I didn't mean to aggravate you.

BARTENDER. What the hell are you doin' for me for chrissakes?

RALPH. What are you talking about for chrissakes?

BARTENDER. I'm not interested in this bullshit.

RALPH. Calm down.

[Pause. The bar is quiet as the two men call a truce. A group of workmen come in; roughneck types, used to hard physical labor. Their clothes are dirty from a day's work and they each have a grubby, unshaven look. Their rowdiness breaks the silence of the bar. They appear to be in a good mood as they approach the bar and order.

Mulligan is the biggest of the four men. He looks as if he weighs two hundred and fifty pounds with big hands and dressed in overalls. Cicero is smaller and dark. He maintains a quiet intensity with a brooding look that could possibly ignite. He wears tight jeans, work boots, and a T-shirt. Beau is genuinely a nice man and for that reason easily browbeaten by Mulligan. He's got a softer physical presence than the others.]

BEAU. Gimme a beer.

CICERO. Make it two.

MULLIGAN. Gimme a shot of Martell.

BEAU. Oh boy! Nice to sit down.

CICERO. Yeah, nice. I killed myself today.

MULLIGAN. What do you mean you "killed" yourself?

CICERO. I did.

MULLIGAN. That'll be the day when you kill yourself.

CICERO. I busted my chops.

MULLIGAN. Okay. I believe you.

CICERO. I was working with a jackhammer all goddam day. That thing is tough. My hands are killing me, and the goddam thing was broken so I kept having to put the bit back in.

MULLIGAN. Okay. You killed yourself.

CICERO. Busting through fucking cement is hard enough without having to do it with a broken jack.

BEAU. It was better than using your dick, wasn't it?

[They all laugh an uproarious, unabashed laughter, enjoying themselves thoroughly.]

Pornographic Panorama

MULLIGAN. Or your cunt! *[More laughter. By now Ralph and bartender are picking up on the conversation and enjoying the ridiculous humor.]* Gimme another shot of Martell. *[Bartender gives him the shot.]* How much is it?

BARTENDER. For you, three bucks.

MULLIGAN. What am I drinking, gold?

BARTENDER. Don't order it if you can't afford it. You know how much it costs?

MULLIGAN. I work all goddam day long and I gotta pay an arm and a leg for a decent drink.

BEAU. Might as well gimme another beer.

CICERO. Yeah, gimme one too.

BARTENDER. Lemme see, that should be a buck and a quarter for the beers and three for the cognac for a grand total of five fifty.

MULLIGAN. Take it outta here. *[Mulligan throws a ten dollar bill on the bar.]*

BEAU. Cheers!

MULLIGAN & CICERO. Cheers!

BEAU. *[referring to Ralph]* Buy that man a drink.

RALPH. Thank you, sir.

BEAU. You're quite welcome. Always willing to buy a drink for an Irishman.

RALPH. I'm not Irish.

BEAU. That's all right. What are you drinking?

RALPH. Just a beer.

BEAU. You can have more than that if you want.

RALPH. I don't want more than that.

BEAU. You're smart; have what you like.

RALPH. Give me a Beck's.

BARTENDER. One Beck's.

BEAU. Take it outta this. *[Beau throws a bill on the bar.]*

RALPH. Did you gentlemen have a hard day's work?

MULLIGAN. *[referring to Ralph]* He didn't, but we did.

RALPH. Work is what keeps the spirit high, the children eating, and the world spinning, so they say.

BEAU. If it wasn't for the working man this country wouldn't be what it is today.

RALPH. I know that. However, the term "working man" overlooks another working force in this country, namely the working woman.

BARTENDER. Oh, no, here we go again.

BEAU. No, he's right!

RALPH. Thank you.

BEAU. Women work today. They gotta, when Martell is three bucks a glass. It's too tight today for the woman not to work.

RALPH. I agree with you thoroughly.

BEAU. They gotta work. A man can't do it all by himself.

Raymond J. Barry

RALPH. I was just talking a while ago with our bartender about the same subject.

MULLIGAN. What do you do?

RALPH. I am a teacher.

MULLIGAN. You are a teacher of what?

RALPH. I am a teacher of English literature.

BEAU. English literature? Let me ask you something? What is literature? No, seriously.

RALPH. Well, it simply is a word that describes all of the written material of a given country. There are studies in French literature, Italian literature, and so on.

MULLIGAN. Do you call that work?

BEAU. Of course, that's work.

MULLIGAN. No, let him answer.

RALPH. Yes, it's work.

MULLIGAN. Let me ask you something else. Is it boring? Don't you get tired of all those books and stuff? I remember when I was in school I hated most of it because it was boring. I just couldn't take it. But if you gave me a good hard job to do with my hands, I got off on it.

RALPH. Do you feel the same today?

MULLIGAN. I feel different than I did when I was a kid. Always the same thing day in and day out. It's hard for a man to do that routine every day, year after year, without a change. A pound of flesh for each dollar I make.

RALPH. What exactly do you men do?

MULLIGAN. *[referring to Beau]* He's a carpenter. Stand up when I introduce you. *[Beau stands up and Mulligan slaps him on the top of his head, which sits him down.]* And this fellow here, his name is Cicero. He's a laborer. You might've guessed from what we were talking about before. And I'm a plumber. My name is Mulligan. What's your name?

RALPH. My name is Ralph. Pleased to meet you. *[Ralph gets up and approaches the working men. Beau shakes his hand first, then Mulligan. He then approaches Cicero and offers his hand.]* I don't believe I shook your hand.

CICERO. I don't believe you did either.

RALPH. Well, my name is Ralph. *[Ralph extends his hand, but is rejected.]*

CICERO. That's nice, Ralph.

BEAU. Don't mind him. We're all working the same job around the corner.

RALPH. What kind of a job?

BEAU. Building reconstruction, renovation, completely new plumbing, rewiring, new beams, and so on.

RALPH. Sounds like tough work.

[Mulligan laughs in obvious derision of Ralph's comment. Beau pinches

Pornographic Panorama

him lightly on the shoulder to shut him up. He does so.]

MULLIGAN. How much money do you make on your job?

RALPH. I beg your pardon?

MULLIGAN. I said, how much money do you make on your job?

RALPH. It's none of your business.

MULLIGAN. You think you make more money than me?

RALPH. Now wait a minute.

MULLIGAN. You heard me. Answer the question.

RALPH. Yes, I heard you.

MULLIGAN. You know, I don't like the way you talk. *[He reaches for a beer bottle which has not been finished quite yet. Beau and Cicero restrain him. He is furious. Finally they drag him to the other side of the bar and Cicero stands beside him in an effort to quell his anger.]*

RALPH. Well, I really am sorry for this. I didn't want the fellow to get so upset. I was trying to be friendly.

BEAU. I'm sorry, too.

RALPH. He certainly is oversensitive, isn't he? A man could get himself killed just for being a school teacher. Ha. Kind of absurd.

BEAU. Here, let me buy you a drink.

RALPH. No, really, I should be going.

BEAU. I'll tell you what. Before you go, maybe if I can get him to drink a shot with you as a sort of truce.

RALPH. I don't want to aggravate your friend any more than is necessary.

BEAU. It might be better than to leave with him so upset.

RALPH. Well, I don't know if it really matters that much if he is upset.

BEAU. *[yelling across the bar to Mulligan]* What do ya say? You want a shot and shake hands? *[no response.]*

RALPH. I'll probably never see him again, and even if I did I'm not sure if I actually said anything that offensive anyway.

[Beau goes over to Mulligan, puts his hand on Mulligan's shoulder.]

BEAU. Come on, ease up a bit. The guy's all right. He didn't mean any harm. He doesn't understand about us, that's all. So now he understands. Come on over and have a shot with him on me. Come on, shake his hand.

MULLIGAN. I don't want to shake his hand.

CICERO. We know you don't, but at least have a shot.

BEAU. Come on. *[He nudges him to come over.]*

CICERO. It's free.

BEAU. Get over there. It ain't gonna hurt you. *[By taking him by the arm they are able to get Mulligan to Ralph.]* Bartender, let's have a setup over here. What do we got here? Who wants what here? Mulligan gets a Martell. What do you want, Cicero? Give me a Martell too. What do you want, Cicero? Why don't you have a Martell too, Ralph? Just one. Give my friend, Cicero, one.

Raymond J. Barry

RALPH. No, I don't think I should.

BEAU. It's okay. I'm only talking about one. Whatcha have, two beers? You're not gonna get drunk on that. I guarantee.

RALPH. Not with beer.

BEAU. Come on, have one. Bartender, give Ralph one too. That makes one, two, three, four so far. Why don't you have one for yourself?

BARTENDER. No, I better not. [He pours the cognac.] Let's see, that's one, two, three, four Martells. Four times three…

RALPH. No, wait.

BARTENDER. …twelve dollars even. Grand total. [He starts taking money from the individuals.]

RALPH. Let me pay for this.

BEAU. No, I'll pay this.

MULLIGAN. I got it.

BARTENDER. Come on, gentlemen, don't quibble.

RALPH. Take this. [He forces a twenty on the bartender, which he finally takes.]

BARTENDER. Okay. I owe you eight dollars change.

RALPH. Keep two for yourself.

BARTENDER. Thank you, sir.

RALPH. You're welcome.

MULLIGAN. Thanks for the drink.

BEAU. Yeah, thank you.

RALPH. I would like to make a toast to all the people in the world who work with their hands.

[Everyone drinks.]

MULLIGAN. I make a toast to all the English teachers in the world.

[Everyone finishes their drinks.]

Bartender, give us another setup.

[Beau grabs both of their hands and puts them together.]

Hey, okay, all right.

[Molly enters the bar, alone. She pretends not to notice anybody. She sits at a table. The bartender gives her a menu.]

BARTENDER. Do you know what you want, Miss?

MOLLY. I'd like a little white wine if you please. Also a small salad.

BARTENDER. Bar wine?

MOLLY. Yes, I think so. Bar wine will be fine.

RALPH. Hello, Molly.

MOLLY. Hello, Ralph.

RALPH. Do you mind if I join you?

MOLLY. No, I don't mind at all. I haven't seen you in quite a while.

[Ralph joins Molly at her table.]

RALPH. I've been working pretty hard.

[Cicero laughs as the three workers watch the scene.]

Pornographic Panorama

How've you been doing?

[Bartender brings her wine to the table.]

MOLLY. Oh, I've been taking care of myself.

RALPH. I bet you have.

MOLLY. I'm looking for work.

MULLIGAN. This guy bothers me for some reason.

CICERO. He's a harmless faggot.

MOLLY. I've been out of work.

RALPH. If I hear of anything I'll leave word at the bar.

CICERO. Don't let him get to you.

MULLIGAN. Yeah, he's a faggot.

MOLLY. Keep your ears open.

RALPH. I will.

MULLIGAN. Is he talking about us?

BEAU. Take it easy. He's not talking about us.

MULLIGAN. I swear he's talking about us.

MOLLY. Do you know them?

RALPH. Briefly. One of them, the sullen, big one over there tried to brain me with a bottle before because it came out in the conversation that I read books for a living.

MOLLY. Are you serious?

RALPH. We all shook hands on the matter, so it's safe. You don't have to worry.

MOLLY. What an asshole.

MULLIGAN. I wonder what that bitch sees in him.

BEAU. Mulligan, why don't you cool it? If you try to be friendly with him you might be able to get an introduction to her. You understand? Put a smile on your stupid-looking face.

CICERO. Yeah, look more friendly. You notice how the guy doesn't even give us the time of day after she come in?

MULLIGAN. Yeah, I notice.

CICERO. I'm gonna walk over there.

BEAU. I dare you.

CICERO. I wouldn't mind fucking her.

BEAU. She's fair game.

MOLLY. Listen, I have an eerie feeling that maybe we shouldn't be sitting together.

BEAU. She came in here alone. Go on over.

CICERO. Give me a minute.

MULLIGAN. Chicken shit.

BEAU. Go on.

[Bartender brings salad to Molly's table.]

MOLLY. You sure do strike up strange friendships with weirdo people.

RALPH. I was here first and they struck up a conversation with me.

Raymond J. Barry

MOLLY. And, of course, you being who you are, dove in right away.

RALPH. You might say that.

CICERO. I'm going over an' say hello.

BEAU. Ya wanna drink first so you don't have to order from the table?

CICERO. Yeah.

BEAU. Bartender, give my friends another round.

MULLIGAN. Thanks, Beau. Are you really going over there?

BEAU. He's spontaneous. That's the best way to do it — like not know what's gonna happen.

MULLIGAN. What are you gonna say?

CICERO. I don't even know.

MULLIGAN. He don't even know.

BEAU. He's got balls, man.

MULLIGAN. What a crazy guy.

BEAU. No, he ain't crazy. Maybe you want to go over there, Mulligan?

MULLIGAN. Not me.

MOLLY. What happened since the last time I saw you?

MULLIGAN. I wouldn't know what to say.

MOLLY. You never got in touch.

BEAU. Then Cicero is elected.

MOLLY. You're really something, you know?

BEAU. When are you gonna do it?

MOLLY. You make me think there is something really nice going on between us and all of a sudden I don't see you anymore.

CICERO. I don't know. When I feel like it.

MOLLY. There's something about that I don't like.

CICERO. When I feel like it.

RALPH. I was somewhat busy.

MOLLY. Bullshit. You just didn't want to get involved.

RALPH. That may be true.

MOLLY. So why didn't you say that?

RALPH. Look, if I don't want to be involved I just don't want to be involved and that's all there is to it. I have a right to feel that way.

MULLIGAN. I think she's pissed off at him.

MOLLY. You sure as hell talked a lot different when I first met you, when you were trying to get a good piece of ass.

RALPH. Keep your voice down.

BEAU. Go over now, it's perfect. Did you hear what she said?

CICERO. Yeah, I'm going. *[He crosses to table.]* Hi, folks.

RALPH. Hello, Cicero.

MULLIGAN. Boy, he's got some pair of balls.

RALPH. This is Molly, a friend of mine.

BEAU. Yeah, he does, doesn't he?

RALPH. Molly, this is Cicero.

BEAU. That's okay.

RALPH. He is a carpenter and works with that couple over there.

BEAU. Because you'll get a chance to show your balls later.

RALPH. Molly's an old friend.

BEAU. Trust me.

CICERO. How long have you known each other?

MOLLY. Well, I...

RALPH. We've known each other for about ten years.

CICERO. And you never got married?

RALPH. No, never got married. *[pause]* Can I offer you a drink, Cicero?

CICERO. I have one. *[He stares at Molly.]* Where do you live?

MOLLY. In Manhattan.

CICERO. Just in Manhattan?

MOLLY. Yes, just in Manhattan.

CICERO. That's pretty general.

RALPH. She's not in the habit of handing out her address, Cicero. You can understand that.

CICERO. Yes, I can understand that, I guess. Still, I'm your friend now because we shook hands before, and on the basis of that she should trust me.

MOLLY. Well, I don't.

CICERO. Why not? I'm a nice guy.

MOLLY. How nice?

CICERO. Try me and see. You don't mind do you, Ralph? *[Cicero takes Molly's hand and pulls her from the chair to the jukebox. He throws in a coin, picks exactly the right number, and begins to dance with her very close. The song is something slow and sexy, perhaps by Stevie Wonder. They dance awkwardly at first because she resists, but Cicero knows what he is doing, and eventually they dance well. Ralph sits down, not knowing what to do. Beau comes over to the table, leaving Mulligan behind.]*

BEAU. They dance pretty good.

RALPH. You think so?

BEAU. Yes, don't you?

RALPH. Yes, I guess so.

BEAU. Hey, Mulligan, don't they dance good?

MULLIGAN. Yeah. *[He imitates her dancing.]*

BEAU. See, he thinks they dance good too.

RALPH. That's great.

BEAU. You don't seem so enthusiastic.

RALPH. I guess I'm not.

BEAU. What's the problem?

RALPH. No problem.

BEAU. Don't sound like it.

Raymond J. Barry

RALPH. Well, if you must know, it was rude of Cicero to come over here and interrupt our conversation like that.

BEAU. Maybe it was a bit rude, but then again he knew you had no intention of introducing us to your friend. You made that perfectly clear.

RALPH. Look, Beau, I don't want an argument with you. I don't know exactly why you have something against me, but I suspect it is because I am different from you. I can't help that. I'm me and you are you. People are different. That's the way the world is and nobody, especially me, can help that. If I could in any way make you feel more comfortable about me, believe me I would be more than happy to accommodate you. But I can't. I dress differently because I have different work. It may not be work to you, but it is work to me, goddammit. I am an assistant professor at a college and some day, if I publish enough, I may be a full professor. I don't understand what is with you working men that gives you such an odd way of looking at the world. You shouldn't be threatened by my type. I mean no harm first of all, and secondly I can't do what you do. I had to find another way.

BEAU. But your way is easier.

RALPH. How can you say that my way is easier?

BEAU. It is. Sittin' in a chair all the time reading books, writing. You can't tell me it ain't easier.

RALPH. What makes you so damn sure? You can't make sweeping generalizations like that.

[During this conversation, Cicero and Molly have become more sensual with each other as they dance behind Beau and Ralph. The music has stopped and they are returning to their seats.]

BEAU. I can't? Why not?

RALPH. Because... *[Beau is distracted by the return of Cicero and Molly.]* Well, hello. You two seem to be having a good time. I didn't know you wanted to dance with Molly. I would have invited you myself. Here, finish your salad.

MOLLY. Have it yourself.

RALPH. No, thank you. How about you two? Anyone want to finish the salad?

BEAU. Hey, Mulligan, you want some salad?

MULLIGAN. *[who has been drinking steadily]* Yeah. I'll take a smidgen of a bite.

CICERO. "A smidgen of a bite." What kind of talk is that? You studying to be a professor of English literature?

BEAU. Lay off that "professor of English literature" business. You don't want to hurt Ralph's feelings, do you?

RALPH. Oh, stop it, please.

MOLLY. Ralph, calm down. They don't mean anything. Right?

BEAU. Right.

Pornographic Panorama

CICERO. Right.

MOLLY. You mean it?

BEAU. Sure, I mean it.

MOLLY. What about your friend here?

BEAU. He means it too.

MOLLY. He better.

CICERO. I mean it. *[Cicero puts his hand on her thigh.]*

MOLLY. Don't get too familiar. *[Molly takes his hand off.]*

RALPH. Well, Molly, maybe we better be going.

BEAU. What's the rush?

[By this time Mulligan is really bobbing and weaving.]

MULLIGAN. Yeah. Why go now?

CICERO. You're not going with the creep, are you?

RALPH. I beg your pardon?

CICERO. You've already begged my pardon tonight, haven't you?

MOLLY. Now, listen, I'm not somebody's piece of meat. You all understand? I go with anyone I want, you all get that? Nobody, but nobody, tells me who I am going to go or come with. Get it? There's not one son of a bitch here who is man enough to control my mind in that way. Bartender, gimme a check.

[Bartender brings the check to Molly. She takes money out of her purse and gives to the bartender, along with the check. He retreats back to the cash register and gives her change. She leaves a tip and puts the rest into her bag.]

Now, gentlemen, I have a terrific idea. Why don't we all go up to my apartment and have a party?

RALPH. You must be absolutely insane.

MOLLY. Insane? Why would I be absolutely insane?

RALPH. Molly, don't you... ?

MOLLY. Look, I'm making a simple invitation to you all. There's nothing insane about that, is there? I'm not insane. I'm friendly... *[to Cicero]...* and I'm willing to do something about that part of myself. Ralph, you jealous all of a sudden? What the hell, it's Friday night and early, so why not? Let's have a party and if you guys want to leave for someplace else in an hour, it's okay by me. Ralph, I want you to come too. Come on over for a drink. It'll be okay. These guys are all right.

[BLACKOUT.]

Act One
-
Scene Two

Raymond J. Barry

[Interior, the apartment. Lights come up and we are already in the middle of the conversation. The four men and Molly are arranged about the apartment casually. There is a sofa. It is white. Molly and Ralph are sitting on it. The sofa has a pale, almost white, floral print. It is upstage left at an angle. There is also a rocking chair, which Mulligan has chosen to sit in. He rocks back and forth from time to time as the mood suits. He is the drunkest. The rocking chair is facing the audience stage right. Mulligan therefore can be seen gazing out into the fourth wall and relating to the other people on stage at the same time. Cicero can move around from stage left to stage right depending on the director's judgment. Of all the men, he is most driven by the sexual desire to have Molly. She knows this. Beau is downstage left staring upstage right. We see the back of his head. Of course, the positions of all actors change as the scene progresses.]

RALPH. So anyway, I worked for my doctorate for the next eight years.
BEAU. Boy, that's pretty good.
CICERO. Yeah, that's pretty good.
RALPH. You think so?
CICERO. Sure. [to Beau] This guy has been talking for a half an hour about himself.
MOLLY. Maybe you're jealous.
CICERO. Maybe I am.
MOLLY. Maybe you'll do something about it.
CICERO. Maybe I will.
BEAU. I wish I was smart.
CICERO. You seem pretty smart to me.
MOLLY. Don't put yourself down, Beau. You're a nice fellow. Anybody want another drink?
MULLIGAN. Let's cut the bullshit and get down to business. I'll have another one of those — whattaya call them?
MOLLY. Courvoisier.
MULLIGAN. Yeah, Courvoisier.
MOLLY. It's almost the same stuff you were drinking at the bar.
MULLIGAN. It's strong stuff.
MOLLY. But it's a little better quality.
MULLIGAN. It's a little better?
MOLLY. Yes, it is.
RALPH. I'm glad we came!
MOLLY. Anybody else want some?
RALPH. Yes, me. I'm having a good time.
CICERO. You should be having a good time. You talked about yourself ever since we got here.
RALPH. Only because I was asked.
CICERO. Who asked you?

Pornographic Panorama

BEAU. Come, you two, knock it off, will you? *[to Ralph]* It's unusual for a guy to educate himself.

MOLLY. It is unusual.

BEAU. There must have been some special influence from the family to get you started with the books. I know my family influenced me.

RALPH. Oh, yes, I had a lot of varied influences. My father drank.

MULLIGAN. My father used to get loaded too. One time he brought home a tuna fish about three feet long. He was so drunk he started swinging it around like it was a baseball bat or something. He hit walls with it and the fish's guts kept on splattering all over the living room where we used to sleep on the couch. When I walked into the kitchen in the morning, a big tuna fish was hanging over both ends of the table, a tuna fish with big eyes staring right at me.

MOLLY. That's a scream.

MULLIGAN. He probably brought it home, thinking it would be good food for the family or something. I don't know. Funny.

[Mulligan gets up from the rocking chair and exits to the bedroom. No one notices.]

MOLLY. That is really funny, Mulligan.

CICERO. *[referring to Mulligan]* Now I know where you got your brains from.

RALPH. Both sides of my family were very different. On my mother's side there was culture and a lot of it. In her family practically everyone was an artist and they were educated, whereas my father's side was more primitive.

CICERO. What is this? Your life story? *[to Ralph]* You talked about yourself ever since we got here.

MOLLY. Dance with me, Mr...

RALPH. Beau is his name.

MOLLY. Oh, yes, Beau. Yes, Mr. Beau, hold me close and dance with me. *[Molly forces herself into his arms.]* Hold me with your arms, your big, strong arms, and dance with me.

BEAU. There's no music.

MOLLY. I'll sing. I'll make the music for both of us. I'll fill the rafters with song, so to speak. *[Molly sings, making up the lyrics and forcing Beau to dance with her.]*

> DANCE WITH ME, MY LOVER,
> COME DANCE WITH ME.
> I NEED THE KIND OF MAN
> I SEE BEFORE MY EYES.
> RIGHT NOW.
> DANCE WITH ME, MY DEAR.
> COME DANCE WITH ME
> UNTIL THE TIME OF DAY

Raymond J. Barry

HAS TURNED INTO AN ETERNITY.
DANCE WITH ME, MY DARLING.
COME DANCE WITH ME.
AND LET YOUR EYES SPARKLE
LIKE WINE IN MINE.
I'M NOT SURE IF ALL WE'VE
GAINED CAN EVER FOLLOW UP
THE RIVER OF LOVE THAT
FLOWS FOREVER.

BEAU. I don't dance too good.

CICERO. She's got your number, Beau.

BEAU. I like the way you sing.

MOLLY. Thank you. *[Molly forces Beau to spin wildly.]*

CICERO. She knows how cute you are.

BEAU. You make it up as you go along?

MOLLY. Yes, impromptu.

BEAU. I wish I could do that.

MOLLY. Oh, but you can.

BEAU. It's pretty good.

MOLLY. You talk spontaneously, don't you?

BEAU. Yeah, I guess so.

MOLLY. Then add song to it.

BEAU. Oh, I get it. I get it. Just sing along with the words.

MOLLY. Yes, that's the ticket. *[She pirouettes out of his arms into Cicero's arms.]*

CICERO. Easy there, lady. You don't want to get too wild.

MOLLY. Really? Why not?

CICERO. Because you might fall and hurt yourself.

BEAU. Molly, come into the bedroom for a minute. Okay?

MOLLY. Into the bedroom? Why would I go into the bedroom?

BEAU. I want to talk to you about something.

RALPH. Don't go into the bedroom, Molly.

MOLLY. Don't worry, I won't.

CICERO. Shut up, you little prick.

RALPH. Don't talk to me that way.

CICERO. What are you, kidding? After all the mouth of yours we've been hearing tonight? Don't make me laugh.

[Mulligan re-enters from the bedroom with one of Molly's dresses on over his underpants and work boots.]

MULLIGAN. I hope you don't mind.

CICERO. Why, you're lovely, Mulligan...

MULLIGAN. I thought I'd make myself more comfortable.

CICERO. ...a real piece of ass.

RALPH. Mulligan, you're too funny.

MULLIGAN. You think I'm funny?

RALPH. You're really funny.

MULLIGAN. Why, because I'm makin' myself more comfortable?

RALPH. Yeah, because you're fooling around.

MULLIGAN. I'm glad you think so. I always wanted to be funny.

RALPH. I can't get over you!

MULLIGAN. How do my legs look? Pretty good or what? I mean, do I look terrific? *[Mulligan struts across the room.]*

CICERO. I wouldn't mind a little piece myself.

MULLIGAN. If you're good to me I'll give you a little bit.

CICERO. If I want to be good to you, Mulligan, I'll be good to you. It's got nothing to do with your pussy.

MULLIGAN. Nothing to do with my pussy? Why, I'll hit you with my pocketbook if you're not careful. No pussy for you.

RALPH. This guy's a riot.

MOLLY. He's a real showman, isn't he?

RALPH. Yeah.

MULLIGAN. Come on, Cicero, you put something on.

CICERO. Like hell I will.

[simultaneous]

MULLIGAN.	**MOLLY.**
What the hell is this. Everyone says let's have a party and I'm the only one who parties. Are you guys game or what?	Come on, what's going on? You guys wanted to party and Mulligan is the only one willing to have a little fun.

CICERO. You ain't gonna find me making an ass out of myself.

RALPH. Mulligan, you're too much.

BEAU. I want to talk to you for a minute.

MOLLY. You want to talk to me about what?

BEAU. Come into the bedroom and I'll tell you.

MOLLY. Well, I don't know.

BEAU. Come on, it's not gonna kill you.

MOLLY. Okay, but make it fast.

MULLIGAN. What's he doing?

CICERO. Who knows?

[Beau and Molly exit into the bedroom.]

RALPH. What the hell is going on in there?

CICERO. Leave them alone.

RALPH. I'm going in there.

MULLIGAN. Leave them alone.

CICERO. They must be having fun.

MULLIGAN. Yeah, they know what they're doing.

RALPH. I'm going in there.

Raymond J. Barry

CICERO. They're adults.

RALPH. I don't trust him in there with her.

CICERO. They know what they're doing.

RALPH. What the hell is going on?

CICERO. What are you gonna do next summer, Ralph?

RALPH. What do I know what I'm gonna do?

MULLIGAN. Anybody want a drink?

RALPH. What does it look like I'm gonna do?

CICERO. Yeah, give me a drink.

[a moan from the bedroom.]

RALPH. I hear a noise from the bedroom.

CICERO. One of those cognacs.

RALPH. What the hell is that?

MULLIGAN. One of those Courvoisiers?

[Another moan from the bedroom.]

RALPH. Jesus Christ, I gotta go in there.

CICERO. Yeah, one of those Courvoisiers.

MULLIGAN. You got it.

RALPH. I care for her.

CICERO. She's all right.

RALPH. I'm worried.

CICERO. Don't worry.

MULLIGAN. What are you worried about?

RALPH. Her.

CICERO. She's probably having fun.

RALPH. I'm tired of this bullshit. I'm going in there. *[Ralph enters the bedroom. Cicero tries to stop him, but he's too late. Cicero and Mulligan are left in the main room. They wait.]*

MULLIGAN. What's going on?

CICERO. I don't know.

MULLIGAN. It's quiet in there.

CICERO. I know.

MULLIGAN. Should we go in?

CICERO. Wait a while.

MULLIGAN. You think we should wait?

CICERO. Yeah, maybe we should wait.

[They sit for a while. It is quiet. Ralph finally comes out. He looks stunned. He sits on a chair, speechless. Mulligan and Cicero look at each other, not knowing what has happened.]

MULLIGAN. What happened, Ralph?

[No answer.]

CICERO. Ralph, can you tell us what happened?

[No answer.]

MULLIGAN. Ralph, you look as if you feel really bad.

Pornographic Panorama

CICERO. Something must have happened.

MULLIGAN. Can you talk to us, Ralph? *[Long pause. Another moan from the bedroom.]* I'm going into the bedroom.

CICERO. He looks bad.

MULLIGAN. Yeah.

CICERO. What's going on with you, Ralph?

RALPH. Her...

MULLIGAN. You wait here with him. I'm going in there and I want you to stay with Ralph here.

CICERO. Okay. He doesn't look so good. *[Ralph looks increasingly more shaken. Mulligan slowly crosses to the bedroom and walks in. Ralph and Cicero are left alone in the living room.]* What happened, Ralph? What's going on in there? You can talk to me, buddy. You can trust me. I ain't gonna hurt you. I'm not like those other two. I got feelings. You can really trust me. Honest. I think I know what you're going through. I can tell by your face. You're paralyzed, aren't you? I know. And you can't move and you can't talk? I've been like that. Sometimes because of a woman, too. Sometimes I would even cry. Can you imagine, Ralph? Me, crying?

RALPH. Her... She...

CICERO. You spoke, Ralph. Are you feeling all right?

RALPH. Her...

CICERO. What happened in there?

RALPH. What I saw...

CICERO. What did you see? *[At that moment, Mulligan re-enters the room. He too looks as if something is off. He is quiet and distant. He sits, not saying a word.]* Mulligan, what's going on? *[Mulligan does not answer.]* Come on, talk to me. What happened? *[Mulligan doesn't answer. Cicero approaches him.]* For Chrissakes, you look like you lost your mother or something. What the hell happened? I'm going in there.

RALPH. No...

CICERO. What's with you guys? Why can't you talk? What is it? What's going on? I came here for a party, not to be weirded out by you guys. *[Cicero runs into the bedroom.]*

RALPH. Can you talk, Mulligan?

MULLIGAN. *[after a long time]* Yeah.

RALPH. What do you think?

MULLIGAN. I don't know.

RALPH. What should we do?

MULLIGAN. I don't know. Stop asking me all these questions.

RALPH. Well, we've got to do something.

MULLIGAN. I guess.

RALPH. You guess? What is that supposed to mean?

MULLIGAN. I guess we got to do something.

Raymond J. Barry

RALPH. You bet we do. *[long pause]* Should I get Cicero? He's been in there a long time.

MULLIGAN. I guess so.

RALPH. Hey, Cicero. Come out here, will you?

[Cicero comes out and leans against the wall at the door to the bedroom.]

CICERO. Jesus Christ!

RALPH. Take it easy. Sit down.

CICERO. I can't sit down.

[Long pause. Another moan from the bedroom.]

RALPH. You can sit down.

CICERO. I can't sit down.

RALPH. Now sit. We have to put our heads together. We've got to do something. *[Molly comes out of the bedroom door, perfectly intact.]* Molly, are you all right?

MOLLY. No, I'm not all right.

RALPH. Can I do something for you?

MOLLY. No, you can't do a thing for me and neither can anyone else in this room.

MULLIGAN. Take it easy, Molly.

MOLLY. Don't tell me to take it easy, you old fag.

MULLIGAN. I told you not to talk to me that way. Not now or any other time.

MOLLY. Listen, you drag queen, I'll talk to you any way I please.

[Mulligan gets up from the chair and moves toward her in his dress.]

[simultaneously]

MULLIGAN.	**MOLLY.**
Who the hell do you think you're talking to? I'll rip your head off if you say another word.	Nobody's gonna tell me how to talk. Not you or anybody else. Understand? So shut your damned mouth.

[Ralph holds Mulligan away from her.]

RALPH. Stop it, both of you! This is craziness! Get away from her now! Get away!

[simultaneously]

MULLIGAN.	**MOLLY.**
Don't tell me, Ralph. That was my best friend in there and she's responsible. She alone is responsible. And I'm gonna get her for it. I am. I'll pay her back if it's the last thing I do. You	I'll do the same thing to you as I did to him. So stay away from me, mister. I'm responsible for him. Right? I'm responsible? Why am I responsible for him? He's the one responsible for his

Pornographic Panorama

understand?   own goddam self.

MOLLY. You hear that, Ralph? He's threatening me.
RALPH. Sit down, Molly.
MOLLY. You heard it. He's threatening me.
CICERO. Yeah, sit down. Mulligan, come on.
[Ralph takes Mulligan by the arm and steers him to the sofa.]
RALPH. Molly, what happened? Can't you tell us? Relax and tell us.
MOLLY. I don't know.
RALPH. You can tell us.
MOLLY. No, I can't.
RALPH. I told you not to go in there with him.
MOLLY. You told me?
RALPH. I did tell you, didn't I?
MOLLY. What am I supposed to do, everything you say? All you animals are the same.
MULLIGAN. I ain't no animal.
MOLLY. Who says so?
MULLIGAN. I say so.
RALPH. Now stop it, you two. Stop it.
MOLLY. He better stay away from me or I'll take care of him too.
RALPH. Don't talk that way, Molly.
[Mulligan gets up, runs over to Molly, and punches her in the face.]
MULLIGAN. There now, maybe you'll shut your face. Maybe you'll shut your face now.
[Ralph goes to her. Molly is unconscious.]
RALPH. Get away from her. Molly, are you all right?
[Molly gradually regains consciousness. She stumbles into the kitchen.]
You shouldn't have done that.
MULLIGAN. I don't give a damn!
CICERO. You shouldn't have hit her.
MULLIGAN. Don't tell me I shouldn't have hit her.
CICERO. What'd you do that for? *[Cicero grabs the shoulder strap on Mulligan's dress and it rips.]*
RALPH. We were all having a good time until you began to ruin it for all of us. If you don't like the party, well, you should just leave.
MULLIGAN. Fuck you, schoolteacher. *[Mulligan attempts to fix dress. Another moan from the bedroom.]*
CICERO. What are we gonna do about him?
[Molly returns from the kitchen.]
MOLLY. I want you all to get the fuck out of here!
CICERO. We can't just go.
MULLIGAN. *[trying to fix the strap on his dress]* This dress is ruined.
MOLLY. You get out of here, all of you!

Raymond J. Barry

MULLIGAN. You ripped my fucking dress, you prick.

CICERO. Just wait till I tell the guys on the job about you.

MULLIGAN. Tell them what?

CICERO. I swear to God, you're just like a goddam woman, ain't you?

MULLIGAN. We was havin' a party.

CICERO. Some party.

MULLIGAN. You mean I can't go out with you?

CICERO. You're behavin' like a fag.

MULLIGAN. You mean every time I go out with you you're gonna bring it back to the job?

CICERO. Be a man. Get outta that fucking thing.

MULLIGAN. What are you, a big man who's scared to loosen up a little?

CICERO. I ain't scared.

MOLLY. I want you guys to get the fuck out of here.

RALPH. Calm down, Molly.

MULLIGAN. What do ya mean, you're not scared?

MOLLY. He's scared.

MULLIGAN. You're frightened to death that you might find out something about yourself that you don't like.

MOLLY. You're both scared. That's why you punched me.

MULLIGAN. That's why you can't play around with the rest of us.

MOLLY. You was punchin' the faggot in yourself.

RALPH. Shut up, Molly.

MULLIGAN. That's why you're so scared.

CICERO. You're behavin' like a fag.

MULLIGAN. Here, put on a fucking dress like me and loosen up a little. *[Mulligan picks out a dress from the clothes closet.]* Go on. Put it on. It'll be good for you. *[He throws the dress at Cicero's feet.]* Go on. Pick it up. *[Cicero doesn't move. No one moves. There is a long silence.]*

CICERO. You know, Mulligan, you're taking your life in your hands. *[Cicero crosses to a bottle of brandy, pours himself a drink.]*

MULLIGAN. Who says so?

[Cicero looks at him. Everyone is still.]

CICERO. I guess I'm supposed to say "I do". But somehow I don't feel like gettin' into this. Besides, I know your wife.

MULLIGAN. What's that got to do with it?

MOLLY. You're married?

RALPH. Molly, please.

MULLIGAN. No, really, what's she got to do with it?

CICERO. Nothin'. I just know you got a wife and kids. I wouldn't want to get into this kind of talk with a guy who's married like you are.

MULLIGAN. You're married too.

MOLLY. All these guys are married, and them trying to fuck me like I was a hunk of meat.

CICERO. So what's this dress shit?

MULLIGAN. Just pick it up and put it on like a man. What are you, afraid of it?

CICERO. I just don't want to do it, that's all.

MULLIGAN. What do ya think, you get to do everything ya want?

CICERO. Yeah, so what?

MULLIGAN. Is that a man, Cicero, or a spoiled little kid?

RALPH. Maybe we should lighten the party up a little, Mulligan.

MOLLY. He's scared.

MULLIGAN. That's what spoiled little kids do — anything they want.

RALPH. Let's get back into the spirit of things.

MULLIGAN. That's what you're doin' now, Cicero.

RALPH. We're gonna have a party, all right?

MULLIGAN. You're sulking like a little brat.

RALPH. Isn't that right, Cicero? We're gonna have a party.

MULLIGAN. Big man.

CICERO. Fucking bullshit.

MULLIGAN. Now why do you say something like that?

CICERO. Get off my ass.

RALPH. Leave him alone, Mulligan.

MULLIGAN. Why are ya so afraid, Cicero?

RALPH. Can't you see he doesn't want to play?

MULLIGAN. He wants to play all right.

MOLLY. Yeah, Cicero, join in.

CICERO. You're all nuts.

MULLIGAN. You're a little chicken shit. *[He goes toward Cicero, picks up the dress at his feet, and taunts him with it. Cicero backs away as he approaches him. They circle the room with Cicero moving backwards and Mulligan approaching him.]*

CICERO. You're all a bunch of faggots.

MULLIGAN. What do you mean by that, Cicero?

CICERO. Back off. I'm gettin out of here. *[Cicero approaches the door, but Mulligan blocks him.]*

MULLIGAN. Oh, no you don't, boy.

RALPH. Come on, boys, let's play.

MULLIGAN. Remember, I'm bigger'n you are.

RALPH. Don't fight, fellas.

MULLIGAN. I work harder and I'm stronger and I'm as much of a man as you even though I got a dress on.

MOLLY. I'll tell you what, Cicero, if you put my dress on I'll go into the bedroom with you.

RALPH. Don't say that, Molly.

MULLIGAN. How 'bout dat, Cicero.

MOLLY. How would you like that, Cicero?

Raymond J. Barry

MULLIGAN. There, Cicero, you'd get to fuck her.

CICERO. Shut the fuck up, Mulligan.

MOLLY. Don't listen to him.

MULLIGAN. If you fuck her you'd be a big man.

MOLLY. You want me, don't you, Cicero?

MULLIGAN. Wouldn't that appeal to you?

MOLLY. I know you want me, Cicero.

CICERO. I didn't come here for this.

MOLLY. Don't give me that. You came here for my pussy and you know it.

CICERO. You think you're somethin'.

MULLIGAN. Stop the bullshit. Here's some nylons for ya. *[Mulligan throws the nylons at Cicero.]*

MOLLY. Cicero, put those nylons on at once!

CICERO. Fuck you. *[But Cicero begins to put them on.]* You promised me you'd come into the bedroom. Don't double-cross me.

MOLLY. Look what it does for your legs, Cicero. You look truly beautiful.

CICERO. Don't rub it in.

MOLLY. Just think what you'll get afterwards. Just think.

RALPH. Let's all be civil to one another.

MOLLY. Shut up, Ralph.

RALPH. Don't speak to me like that. I'm a person too.

MOLLY. Oh, Cicero, you look gorgeous.

MULLIGAN. You see that, Cicero? You don't feel any different, do you? Hey, Molly, ya got any makeup around?

MOLLY. Don't, Mulligan. Cicero needs our encouragement. That's it, Cicero.

MULLIGAN. And when you get the dress on I want you to fuck me.

[Cicero slips on the dress.]

MOLLY. No, I'm his present.

MULLIGAN. We'll see. How's your manhood doing, Cicero?

RALPH. You are evil, aren't you?

MULLIGAN. Is that an official schoolteacher opinion?

RALPH. Don't mock my profession any longer, you hear me?

MOLLY. Don't worry about it.

RALPH. You ape.

MULLIGAN. Who are you calling an ape?

MOLLY. Don't start again. Please, let's get into the spirit of this.

MULLIGAN. It's great being a woman, isn't it?

CICERO. *[smiles]* Beats being on the job.

MULLIGAN. That's the boy, Cicero. Now you're catching on.

[Ralph is checking through his pants pockets and jacket.]

RALPH. I knew it. I lost my wallet.

MOLLY. What? You lost it?

RALPH. Goddammit!

MOLLY. That's terrible.

RALPH. Who took my wallet?

MOLLY. That's absolutely awful.

RALPH. My credit cards, my money.

MULLIGAN. Well, don't look at us.

RALPH. I must have had three or four hundred bucks in the damn thing.

MULLIGAN. It didn't get taken by us.

RALPH. All right, you guys, which one of you took my wallet?

MULLIGAN. I didn't.

CICERO. I didn't.

RALPH. Well, it must have gone somewhere.

CICERO. Yeah, it must have gone somewhere.

RALPH. Come on, which one of you took it?

MULLIGAN. Molly or Beau must have.

MOLLY. Don't give me that.

RALPH. Well, somebody must have taken it.

MOLLY. I didn't take it and neither did Beau.

RALPH. It didn't disappear by itself.

CICERO. Can never tell how it disappeared.

MOLLY. This is my house and nobody steals in my house.

RALPH. That's bad. I had a lot of money in it, and my credit cards.

MULLIGAN. What's the difference, schoolteacher? You didn't work for the money.

RALPH. You people aren't helping me find my wallet.

MOLLY. Maybe it dropped somewhere. *[Molly gets down on her hands and knees to search.]*

MULLIGAN. Look at that, huh? Look at that nice butt. Nice view, huh, Cicero?

CICERO. Yeah, nice. What are we doing here anyway? I got a wife and kids home. I should be home.

MULLIGAN. Ain't Molly gonna give you a present first before ya go?

RALPH. Hey, you two Neanderthals. What are you bullshitting about? Come help find my wallet.

CICERO. Crawl over to that end, Mulligan.

MULLIGAN. I'm crawling over, but don't peek under my goddam dress and try looking at my underwear. *[uproarious laughter from both of them]*

CICERO. Your balls are showin'. I peeked before and they're showin'.

MULLIGAN. I can see the crack of your ass up your dress. *[out of control laughter]*

CICERO. You're bullshitting me.

MULLIGAN. No, I'm not. Just like you can see my balls, I can see the crack of your ass if I get my head down low enough. *[They again have a grand time laughing.]*

Raymond J. Barry

CICERO. You're bullshitting me.

MULLIGAN. No, I'm not. I can get my head way down here close to the ground and get my eye in place to see right up your dress and see the crack of your ass. *[laughing, mocking themselves]*

CICERO. Shit, that's embarrassing.

MULLIGAN. You shouldn't be embarrassed. I'm your buddy. We're asshole buddies, remember?

CICERO. Yeah. *[Ralph and Molly have crawled into the bedroom area in their search for the wallet.]* Hey, they crawled into the bedroom. She's in there with the schoolteacher. Son of a bitch. She's in there with the schoolteacher.

MULLIGAN. It's okay. You'll get sloppy seconds or maybe thirds. Who knows if Beau got to her before. If you're so hungry for a woman you can have me. *[laughter]*

CICERO. You're a fucking pig.

MULLIGAN. I'm not so bad.

CICERO. You ain't my cup a' tea.

MULLIGAN. How do you know? You ain't never had a taste. *[Now Mulligan is serious.]*

CICERO. A taste of what?

MOLLY. *[offstage from the bedroom]* Stop it, Ralph. Stop it.

MULLIGAN. A taste of my pussy.

CICERO. What the fuck are you talkin' about?

MULLIGAN. You know what I'm talkin' about.

CICERO. You're a crazy motherfucker the way you talk about my ass and everything.

RALPH. *[offstage from bedroom]* Just roll over a little bit.

MOLLY. *[offstage from bedroom]* Ralph, let's get back to the wallet business.

CICERO. You ever pull this bullshit on the job and I'll kick your butt.

MULLIGAN. You been flirting with me all this time.

MOLLY. *[offstage from bedroom]* No, Ralph, not now, baby.

RALPH. *[offstage from bedroom]* You see? You called me baby.

MULLIGAN. Even on the job I see how you look at me.

CICERO. Fuck this. You're being an asshole. *[Cicero tries to exit. Mulligan blocks his way.]*

MULLIGAN. I knew you looked at me as an asshole.

CICERO. What the fuck are you talking about?

MULLIGAN. I've never been nothin' but a goddam hole to you all this time. Even on the job.

CICERO. I'm getting the fuck out of here. *[Cicero tries to exit again, but Mulligan blocks him.]* You talk weird.

MULLIGAN. You ain't goin' nowhere.

CICERO. You're weird, Mulligan.

MOLLY. *[offstage from bedroom]* Stay away from me, Ralph.

CICERO. You know how weird you are?

MULLIGAN. I like you telling me that when you're dressed in that outfit.

MOLLY. *[offstage from bedroom]* You got no right to do this, Ralph.

CICERO. You're a fucking fag.

MULLIGAN. How 'bout I "put the wood" to you?

CICERO. I'll kick your balls in if you so much as come close to me.

MULLIGAN. What kind of way is that to talk?

CICERO. Just don't give me any shit.

MULLIGAN. Do I sense a weakness in you? Is your manpower being questioned or what? I see weakness in your face, Cicero. You're afraid and I'm not. What is that all about?

MOLLY. *[offstage from bedroom]* You come at me again and I'll kick you right in the balls.

MULLIGAN. Men aren't afraid, are they? If you were really a man you wouldn't be afraid now, would you? There's something soft in you.

RALPH. *[offstage from bedroom]* Come on now, please allow me.

MULLIGAN. I see you takin' those coffee breaks every time you could, when your buns was freezin' in cold weather and your hands was hurtin' from your skin crackin'.

MOLLY. *[offstage from bedroom]* You men. You pathetic male egos.

MULLIGAN. I watched you, Cicero, and I says to myself, "He ain't got no balls," and you know somethin'? I was right 'cause I can see the fear in your eyes right now. I'm gonna fuck you tonight, chicken boy.

CICERO. You better back off, Mulligan. Hey, you two in there, you hear this?

MOLLY. *[offstage from bedroom]* Hey, Mulligan, you hear what's goin' on here?

MULLIGAN. Yeah, Molly. Can't do much for you, honey. I'm busy.

RALPH. *[offstage from bedroom]* Leave them outta this.

CICERO. Throw me my pants. I'm getting outta this fucking thing.

MULLIGAN. You look better in your pretty dress. You want to hug me?

CICERO. No. Stop this shit.

MULLIGAN. I know you want a hug. Come on, let me hug you. *[Mulligan approaches Cicero.]*

CICERO. You get away from me, you son of a bitch.

MULLIGAN. Come on, Cicero, get loose.

CICERO. I don't want to. Leave me the fuck alone.

MULLIGAN. Be with me, buddy.

CICERO. I got kids.

MULLIGAN. They aren't your excuse for anything. You got to stand on your own two feet, Cicero. You can't hide behind them. They aren't proof of anything.

CICERO. I got a wife.

Raymond J. Barry

MULLIGAN. Your wife and kids ain't you. A man wouldn't hide behind his wife and kids.

MOLLY. *[offstage from bedroom]* Oh, shit, you cocksucker. Ralph, stop it now.

RALPH. *[offstage from bedroom]* You were willing to do it with Cicero.

MOLLY. *[offstage from bedroom]* I only wanted him to put on the dress.

MULLIGAN. I like you in a dress when it lifts up a little like now. *[Mulligan grabs Cicero's dress, lifting it up as high as possible.]*

CICERO. Knock that shit off. *[Cicero tries to reach his pants.]*

MULLIGAN. I like those woman's legs of yours. But seriously, don't you want to be buddies? You know, I watch your back and you watch mine. Two guys who protect each other at all times when something is needed by the other one when there is something that I can get for you that you can't get by yourself because you're too weak to pull it off by yourself and I back you up because we've got a special feeling for each other, as of this occasion when I'm telling you to lift up your dress and let me stick my dick into your ass. Have you ever done that before? I bet you have.

CICERO. No.

MULLIGAN. You have.

CICERO. No.

MULLIGAN. I can tell you have.

CICERO. How?

MULLIGAN. I have a way of knowing.

MOLLY. *[offstage from bedroom]* Ralph, be gentle. Please be gentle.

CICERO. What way?

MULLIGAN. Some understanding that men have between each other. I have that understanding. I know what you've done. I know what you haven't done. You've fucked in that "special" way. You've been a man's man.

CICERO. No, I haven't.

MULLIGAN. But you know what I'm talking about, don't you?

CICERO. I think I do.

MULLIGAN. You understand what I gotta do to you to make you feel right?

CICERO. I don't know.

MULLIGAN. You want to be a man, don't you? You want to be without all that nervousness in your head that you got.

CICERO. I... Yeah.

MULLIGAN. Then bend over.

MOLLY. *[offstage from bedroom]* Oh shit, Ralph.

CICERO. Leave me alone.

MULLIGAN. C'mon, Cicero, let's have a party. Just you and me.

CICERO. This is weird.

MULLIGAN. It's only weird if you make it weird. It's not weird. It's life. We got life ahead of us. You like me, don't ya?

CICERO. Not right now. I feel weird.

MULLIGAN. But you liked me in the past, didn't you?

CICERO. You never came on like this before.

MULLIGAN. So what? You like me. I know you like me.

CICERO. I like everyone I work with. This is weird. I feel weird.

MULLIGAN. I feel weird too. *[Mulligan gets closer.]* There's nothing wrong with being weird. Things are weird, that's all. Things have a tendency to get weird. That's life. That's the way life is. If you're a man you got to face life. No question about it. That's what being a man is.

CICERO. Maybe we oughta go. I wanna go.

MULLIGAN. Let's get something straight. You ain't goin' nowhere until the night's over, and this night is not over. We got plenty of living ahead of us.

CICERO. This place gives me the creeps.

MULLIGAN. You're not scared, are you?

CICERO. Sort of. I just don't feel right.

MULLIGAN. You're too much of a man to be scared. Just relax. *[Mulligan begins rubbing Cicero's back gently.]* There, take it easy, buddy. You don't mind me calling you "buddy," do you?

CICERO. My name's Cicero. You know, just plain Cicero.

MULLIGAN. Sorry, I didn't mean to insult you.

CICERO. You didn't insult me. It's just my name.

MULLIGAN. Are you scared now? *[Mulligan continues to rub Cicero's back.]*

CICERO. That's not the word. I'm just not used to this.

MULLIGAN. Life is full of surprises. Relax your shoulders. That's it. Just drop them. Don't that feel good?

CICERO. Yeah. I guess so. I feel kinda scared. I ain't never let a guy rub my shoulders before.

MULLIGAN. It's okay to be scared. We're all scared. Every one of us big strong men is scared. It don't matter.

CICERO. I ain't never heard a guy talk like you, Mulligan.

MULLIGAN. Trouble is we got to keep it in all the time. It's about time we fought for ourselves more.

CICERO. You got a way with words, I gotta admit.

MULLIGAN. It's about time we let our fears come out, let them be said.

CICERO. You know how to get your way, all right.

MULLIGAN. I just let myself say what I want, that's all. I just allow myself.

CICERO. I don't hear them in the other room anymore.

MULLIGAN. They're probably having a good time.

CICERO. You think he's fucking her?

MULLIGAN. Yeah, I do.

CICERO. I don't hear anything.

MULLIGAN. Why don't you lay down and let me give you a massage.

Raymond J. Barry

CICERO. Maybe you should stop this shit for a while. I don't like how I feel.

MULLIGAN. Why stop?

CICERO. Because I don't feel right.

MULLIGAN. Did you feel right before tonight?

CICERO. I don't feel normal.

MULLIGAN. What's so great about feeling normal?

CICERO. I always felt normal.

MULLIGAN. Who wants to feel normal?

CICERO. What do you mean?

MULLIGAN. Normal is dull.

CICERO. I never felt dull, but I felt normal.

MULLIGAN. That's not so great, normal. Normal is just the way everyone else is.

CICERO. Right now I don't feel normal doin' this.

MULLIGAN. So? Don't feel normal then. You're not normal. You're unusual.

CICERO. I don't like the sound of that.

MULLIGAN. You don't have to feel normal.

CICERO. I think I want to be normal. *[Mulligan grabs Cicero around the neck and drags him back down to the floor.]* What are you doin'? Huh? Shit. Let me go, will you? C'mon. Shit. Let me go. *[Mulligan forces Cicero's dress up over his underpants, attempting penetration. Lights go down for a few seconds to indicate that time has passed. Lights come up. Ralph is standing there, staring at them long enough to see what's going on. Mulligan suddenly jumps up.]*

MULLIGAN. Get outta here!

RALPH. Oh, excuse me.

MULLIGAN. Oh, yeah... yeah... schoolteacher... poppin his head in where he doesn't belong.

RALPH. Excuse me. I was looking for my wallet and...

[Cicero moves off to the corner. His underpants are down to his knees. He lifts them up.]

MULLIGAN. Jesus... Look... Look... I don't know, Ralphy... You... just come in like that... You scared me...

CICERO. Shit.

MULLIGAN. We were just... ah... foolin' around.

RALPH. Yeah, fooling around?

MULLIGAN. Yeah, we was wrestling... ah... you know... ah... wrestling, foolin' around.

RALPH. Wrestling? Two grown men, wrestling?

MULLIGAN. Yeah,... ah... Cicero... ah... challenged me to... ah... wrestling match. We were wrestling each other... for fun.

RALPH. Honestly, Mulligan, do you expect me to believe that?

MULLIGAN. You... don't believe me?

RALPH. No, not really.

MULLIGAN. Well, what would you call it?

RALPH. I would call it hanky panky.

MULLIGAN. You mean hanky panky as in hanky panky?

RALPH. Yes, hanky panky as in hanky panky.

MULLIGAN. Are you gonna send me up to the principal's office, schoolteacher?

RALPH. Just what is it you've got against me, Mulligan?

MULLIGAN. I don't like schoolteachers just like I don't like prison guards.

RALPH. Just what did school teachers ever do to you, aside from preventing you from burning the school down for recreation?

MULLIGAN. All you "do gooders" make me sick, like you know something I don't, like you got a right to make the rules and I don't.

RALPH. *[To Cicero.]* You haven't seen my wallet by any chance?

MULLIGAN. Believe me, if I see your wallet, you'll be the first to know.

RALPH. I paid for my drinks. I hope I didn't leave it in the bar.

CICERO. I'm getting out of here.

BEAU. *[from the bedroom]* Geaooorgh!

CICERO. I gotta go to work tomorrow.

MULLIGAN. Don't panic, Cicero.

CICERO. I'm not panicking. I just want to get back to my kids, that's all.

MULLIGAN. Your kids can wait. We ain't through partying yet.

CICERO. Oh, no, Mulligan; that's where you're wrong; the party is over for me.

MULLIGAN. Molly made a promise to you.

CICERO. She can keep her promise. Lemme outta here.

RALPH. The man wants to leave, Mulligan.

BEAU. *[from the bedroom]* Goorghuff! georguff! Geeorgff!

MULLIGAN. Stick around. I'm not finished with you yet.

CICERO. You're finished with me. You can bet on that. I'm sorry I got mixed up in this shit.

RALPH. I know what Cicero is saying.

CICERO. It's just too much for me.

RALPH. It's not right.

MULLIGAN. Look, you guys, nobody has to know.

RALPH. I could lose my job if somebody found out what I been up to tonight.

MULLIGAN. I'll keep my mouth shut. You can count on it.

CICERO. I'm scared.

MULLIGAN. Everyone's scared. What does being scared got to do with anything?

CICERO. Take your shit out on them cause I'm leaving.

[Mulligan pushes Cicero away from the door.]

Raymond J. Barry

MULLIGAN. We got business.

CICERO. We got no business.

RALPH. If it means anything to you, Cicero, I wish you would stay.

MULLIGAN. Scared don't mean shit after you're in deep enough.

RALPH. You're clever, Mulligan.

MULLIGAN. You get your licks in too, Ralphy boy.

RALPH. It means a lot to me to have another man here, Cicero, while Mulligan is purging his masculinity.

MULLIGAN. You do all right for yourself too, don't you, Ralphy boy? You get a lot of pussy for a schoolteacher.

RALPH. Cicero, please stay.

MULLIGAN. Look at Ralphy boy squirm with his bullshit, guiding young kids who ain't involved with the puke shit yet because they're too fucking young and still in school and they still think there's somethin' to give a shit about with their sweet, big bright eyes and all that hope in their minds.

RALPH. I happen to love children.

MULLIGAN. Not enough for you to change yourself for them, teacher boy. *[to Cicero]* The party's not over yet, Cicero. Molly promised you something for wearing her dress. *[to Ralph]* I build buildings, while you destroy kids' minds, you cheap fuck. *[to Cicero]* We can still party, Cicero, have a good time. *[to Ralph]* You still got pussy hairs in your teeth, Ralphy boy.

RALPH. You've lost all sense of decency, Mulligan.

MULLIGAN. When I was a kid with hopes and dreams in my head they were stomped by pricks like you.

RALPH. Just what do you have against my profession?

MULLIGAN. Teachers made me cry when I was trying to get my arithmetic right.

RALPH. I've got nothing to do with your arithmetic. You're plainly not a nice person.

CICERO. Ahhhhgh!

RALPH. What's wrong, Cicero?

CICERO. Nothin'. I'm gettin' out of this thing while I still got a pair of balls left.

MULLIGAN. WhatSamatter, Cicero, don't you like your little crinoline dress?

[Mulligan approaches Cicero.]

CICERO. No! Stay... away from me. I... ah... gotta... gettin' outta here... gotta go home to my kids and wife. Aaaaaaaagh!

RALPH. I for one would like you to stay, Cicero, at least until I find my wallet.

CICERO. I'm gettin'... outta this thing. Oooough! *[Cicero begins to remove his dress.]*

Pornographic Panorama

RALPH. What did you do to him, Mulligan?

MULLIGAN. Wrestling. Maybe he bumped his head or something.

RALPH. Cicero, can I help you in any way?

MULLIGAN. Leave him alone, schoolteacher.

RALPH. I'm just trying to help him.

MULLIGAN. He doesn't need any help, right Cicero?

CICERO. Help? Do I need any help? *[flying around the room erratically]* Aaaagh!

RALPH. Jesus, what did you do to him, Mulligan?

MULLIGAN. I already told you I didn't do nothing to him.

RALPH. You must have done something. Look at him. Here, Cicero, let me help you.

[Ralph attempts to help Cicero on with his shoe.]

MULLIGAN. I told you, schoolteacher, leave him alone.

RALPH. I'm not here to take orders from you.

MULLIGAN. You're not, huh? We'll see about that.

[Mulligan approaches the couch where Ralph is helping Cicero put on his shoe. Suddenly, Cicero runs to the opposite side of the room.]

CICERO. No! No! Keep him from me, bad daddy, bad daddy! Keep him away! Keep him away! Bad daddy! Bad daddy! *[He speaks like a little boy.]* I want bad daddy away! Away! Not good! Not good! Not good! Bad daddy! Away! Go! Go! Away!

RALPH. Stay away from him. He's afraid of you.

MULLIGAN. Now why would he be afraid of me? I never did nothing to him. We were wrestling, that's all. Just wrestling. He musta' bumped his head or something.

RALPH. You're lying. I can tell you're lying.

MULLIGAN. You can, eh, schoolteacher. Schoolteacher can always tell when his good little boys and girls are lying. Why don't you get a job where you have to deal with grownups?

RALPH. You've done something to him. Cicero, are you all right. It's me, Ralph.

CICERO. I not good, anymore. I not good. Bad daddy! Bad daddy! Not good!

RALPH. You animal, Mulligan

MULLIGAN. He's all right. He's just faking it.

CICERO. Away... Bad daddy... be away.

RALPH. It's me, Cicero. Here, I'm your friend. You don't have to worry. Just let me get this dress off. *[Ralph helps him off with his dress.]* Where's his pants?

MULLIGAN. I got 'em.

[Mulligan steals Cicero's pants from the floor and holds them behind his back.]

RALPH. Give him his damned pants!

Raymond J. Barry

[Cicero, wearing only his underwear and suddenly in a rage chases Mulligan.]

MULLIGAN. I'm keepin' your pants and you're stayin'. You're my bitch now.

[Mulligan dances around the room with Cicero's pants.]

CICERO. Bad daddy, give me pants, pants, pants!

[Cicero chases Mulligan with intent to kill. Molly staggers into the room with Beau on her shoulder. She throws him down on the couch but he falls to the floor. Beau has blood on his mouth and is barely conscious.]

MULLIGAN. Gotcha pants, Cicero, and you're my bitch.

RALPH. Mulligan, give Cicero his pants at once or there will be consequences.

MOLLY. *[Beau attempts unsuccessfully to rise and then falls in a heap.]* Beau, wake up. Wake up.

MULLIGAN. What kinda consequences, schoolteacher? Am I gonna get expelled?

RALPH. You will be punished!

MULLIGAN. Oh, punished like with a steel rod bashed over my knuckles or a strap whipped on my bare ass like in the old days?

RALPH. You will be left back and forced to repeat a grade.

MOLLY. Come on, Beau. Get your ass up.

[Molly attempts to prop Beau up on the couch.]

CICERO. Beau's pants then; Beau's pants.

[Cicero loosens Beau's belt and pulls Beau's pants down.]

MOLLY. Get away from him, Cicero. Leave the poor bastard's pants on him.

[Cicero takes Beau's pants off.]

CICERO. These pants; pants, pants.

[While the dialogue continues Cicero takes Beau's pants off and puts them on.]

RALPH. Mulligan, stay in your corner.

MULLIGAN. Go to hell, schoolteacher.

RALPH. Open your book to page one hundred and seventeen, chapter eleven.

MULLIGAN. Ralphy boy is losing it, Molly. You'd better call a doctor.

MOLLY. I want to be alone with Beau. All of you to get the fuck out of here.

RALPH. Not before the facts are brought to light. Mulligan has abused Cicero and he should be sent to the principal's office immediately.

CICERO. *[articulate again]* Don't bad daddy. Bad daddy. Wife and kids. Wife and kids.

[Cicero has Beau's pants on and is buckling his belt in absence of a shirt.]

RALPH. The perpetrator of the crime is, as usual Mr. Mulligan, one of the most depraved students in our entire school system. Now I ask you, should we allow one bad apple to ruin the entire barrel? We're good people. Are we not? Does this individual have the power to influence the good intentions of all of us? Now I ask you.

MOLLY. Ralph is educated. He's read books.

MULLIGAN. That's right, English literature.

RALPH. That is correct, sir, English literature. That is my work and I am very proud of it.

MULLIGAN. You'd be proud of your dick if you had one.

RALPH. I beg your pardon.

MOLLY. Don't listen to him, Ralph.

MULLIGAN. Just cause you fucked him don't mean he's worth protectin'.

MOLLY. Shut your fuckin' mouth!

RALPH. I shouldn't have come here.

MULLIGAN. You're having a good time, aren't you, teacher boy?

RALPH. I don't like what you and your friends are about.

MOLLY. Now, now, boys, beneath all of your bluster, each one of you needs love.

MULLIGAN. I don't need nothin'.

MOLLY. Cicero, don't you need some affection of some kind?

MULLIGAN. He doesn't know what he needs.

MOLLY. What if a woman showed that she cared for him? *[Molly does a flirtatious turn with her body.]*

RALPH. You don't do much for him, Molly.

MOLLY. Let's pretend I do. Let's all of us just pretend, and each person can express his attraction in whatever way he wishes. I pick Ralph. He's the man for me. *[Molly throws her arms around him.]*

RALPH. What if I don't want you?

MOLLY. Then go after someone you like.

RALPH. But what do I do with you hanging all over me?

MOLLY. Discard me at your will.

RALPH. All right. *[Ralph throws Molly off him.]*

MOLLY. All right, that's fine. Now I react accordingly. "Why, you cad! How dare you throw me away like a piece of trash? " See what I mean? We can simply play it out to its logical end and then everyone switches partners like this. *[Molly attempts to dance with Cicero.]* Well, hello there.

RALPH. He's not in a dancing mood.

MOLLY. Oh, go on, you're a wonderful dancer, Cicero. *[Cicero doesn't respond.]* Find a partner everyone! *[To Cicero.]* I love you. I love you. I love you. *[Molly grabs Cicero's legs and buries her head into his knees.]*

RALPH. All right, Molly, I'll play for a while. *[Aims his attentions towards Beau.]* How ya doing, Beau?

MOLLY. Aren't you paying attention to me, Ralph?

BEAU. Oeerghuff!

CICERO. *[To Molly.]* Leave me alone', lady.

Raymond J. Barry

RALPH. No, Molly. I'm focusing my attention on Beau.

MOLLY. But he's a guy.

RALPH. It's only a game, Molly. *[to Beau.]* Would you hold my hand, Beau?

BEAU. Ooeerguff! Ooooeeeguff!

RALPH. You can, it's all right, Beau. It's just a game.

BEAU. Oooogruff! Oooogreeoff!

MULLIGAN. How about you, Molly? Would you give me some? *[Mulligan goes down on his knees.]* "I love you madly!"

RALPH. *[To Ralph.]* You're not afraid of this, Beau, are you?

MOLLY. *[To Mulligan.]* I'm busy, Mulligan.

MULLIGAN. *[To Molly.]* You must be kidding.

MOLLY. I love you, Cicero. Please, love me back.

RALPH. *[Turns suddenly away from Beau to Cicero.]* Please, hold my hand, someone. I'm afraid.

[Molly runs to Beau who again has fallen onto the floor.]

[simultaneous]

MULLIGAN.	**MOLLY.**
[To everyone.]	*[On couch with Beau.]*
I want to be naked in front of all of ya'.	Would you love me, Beau? I mean like a little? Would you please, Beau?

BEAU. Oooeeerguff! Oooooeeerguff!

MULLIGAN. First off with my shoes. *[Mulligan takes his shoes off. Molly grabs Beau.]*

[simultaneous]

MOLLY.	**RALPH.**
Beau's repulsive, but I'm in love with him.	*[to Cicero]* I've noticed you from a distance and I've been...

RALPH. ... dying to say something to you, anything that would break the ice.

MULLIGAN. Just let me fuck you just once, Molly.

CICERO. I'm not really into this, man.

MULLIGAN. *[to Cicero]* Ha, that's a laugh.

CICERO. *[To Mulligan.]* Shut the fuck up, why don't you.

RALPH. Don't pay any attention to him

CICERO. Prick.

MOLLY. Beau, speak to me. Beau!

BEAU. Ooooreeeuff! Oooooeerruff!

RALPH. Where are you from?

CICERO. Louisiana.

RALPH. You don't have an accent.

MULLIGAN. All right, everybody. Switch partners. *[Ralph walks up to Mulligan but Mulligan is focused on Molly.]*

[simultaneous]

RALPH.	**MULLIGAN.**
You know, I swear I've seen you somewhere before.	Now I'll fuck the bitch.

[Molly mounting Beau on the couch, begins to have sex with him.]

[simultaneous]

MOLLY.	**RALPH.**
Beau, give it to me, honey; that's it, baby. Let me get that big man's cock stuck into my cute little pussy.	Shame on you, Mulligan, shame on you. What do you think your punishment should be?

BEAU. Ourcugh! Oeeorguff! Orrgeuff!

MOLLY. That's it, honey, stick it in and pull it out.

MULLIGAN. This whole place is gettin' on my nerves.

MOLLY. Yeah, honey. Yeah.

MULLIGAN. I feel like killin' somebody.

[Mulligan dances around the room with Cicero's pants like an ape.]

RALPH. You're already staying after school and being left back a grade.

MULLIGAN. Ha. Ha. Ha. Hey, Molly, when you're finished give me some.

MOLLY. I only do it to gentlemen, Mulligan.

MULLIGAN. Pretend I'm your girlfriend.

MOLLY. You're a prick so you don't get any.

MULLIGAN. I'll give you my panties after we're finished. Or better yet I'm wearing your dress. You can pretend you're fucking yourself.

MOLLY. I don't fuck nobody wearing my dresses.

[simultaneous]

MULLIGAN.	**RALPH.**
Shit, Beau's half dead and his tongue's cut out. What the fuck do you see in him?	That's enough, everybody. You're all misbehaving. You'll all have to stay I in school after the bell if you don't shape up immediately. And I mean immediately. Mulligan, stop dancing
MOLLY. He's quiet for one. That's more than I can say about a loud mouth bastard like you.	

Raymond J. Barry

RALPH. ...and pay attention. Molly, Cicero, gather round and listen to your grammar lesson.

MULLIGAN. Fuck you, schoolteacher.

MOLLY. Beau has a nice, fat cock, a magnificent cock even though he's half dead.

BEAU. Geuggrff. Geoggruff. Gooorgh.

CICERO. Stay away from me, Mulligan.

MULLIGAN. I'm dancin'. You can't blame a guy for dancin'.

CICERO. Just dance your ass away from me.

[Cicero puts on his shirt.]

MULLIGAN. We're the labor pool of America!

CICERO. Yeah, hard working fags like you.

RALPH. Order in my classroom!

MULLIGAN. We're what this country is built on!

RALPH. Order, I say, in my classroom!

CICERO. You're the labor pool all right.

[simultaneously]

CICERO.	**RALPH.**
You'll end up in the joint. You won't last in normal life. Just stay the fuck away from me.	Order! Order in my classroom! I will have order here! Order here. Order!

MULLIGAN. Shut the fuck up, schoolteach. Your ass is sucking wind.

RALPH. I'll have you expelled.

MULLIGAN. Not if I quit school

RALPH. If you quit you won't have a future.

MULLIGAN. All right, everybody, switch partners again! *[Nobody moves.]* ALL RIGHT, EVERYBODY SWITCH PARTNERS AGAIN! *[Nobody moves.]* Whatsa matter here? Why doesn't anybody want to switch partners when I call it? What's goin' on here?

CICERO. Nobody wants to be with you. That's why.

MULLIGAN. Tough shit. They gotta be with me. What the fuck is the matter with you guys? I'm a good lay. What am I, chopped liver or something?

CICERO. You're a prick.

MULLIGAN. A prick that you like.

MOLLY. Come on, Mulligan, play the game. Be a sport.

MULLIGAN. Nobody's gettin' laid.

CICERO. That's not always the point of everything.

MULLIGAN. What, in this kind of game?

RALPH. Sex isn't everything.

MULLIGAN. It is everything.

RALPH. There are lots of ways of showing one's affection.

MULLIGAN. Let's get down to brass tacks. Who's gonna gimme some? *[silence]* All right, then. I'll take what I want without goin' through this game shit.

RALPH. Order in my classroom! Order, I say!

MULLIGAN. Bullshit. Gimme some head, school teacher.

[Mulligan corners Ralph, grabs him and lowers him onto his knees, forcing him to perform fellatio.]

MULLIGAN. *[Mulligan pulls his hard-on out, most likely back to audience.]* Now Ralphy boy, this'll shut your mouth.

RALPH. How dare you. I am a teacher... a hgaraaph! *[Mulligan's penis muffles his voice.]*

MULLIGAN. Attaboy, schoolteacher, suck!

[simultaneously]

MULLIGAN.	**RALPH.**
Hey, Molly, ya finished with Beau yet? I'm ready for you, honey, any time you say. I'm ready for you. Come on, Ralphy boy, suck on it before I get expelled from school.	Gurgle! Gaarph! Gooki! **BEAU.** Gooeeerph! Gooorph! **RALPH.** Gaaphruff! Gapruffruf! **BEAU.** Geeoorhph! Gooorerhruff!

RALPH. Gurgle! Gaarph! Gooki!

MULLIGAN. He talks like Beau with a cock in his mouth.

BEAU. Gooeeerghuff! Geeoorghuph! Goooreeephuf!

MOLLY. We should have them in a chorus. Ha. Ha.

MULLIGAN. Yeah, a cock chorus. Ha. Ha. Ha.

CICERO. I'm leavin'.

MULLIGAN. *[Manages to grab Cicero by the neck while Ralph performs fellatio on him.]* Hey, wait a minute. You can't go yet. The whole party is just beginning to bust out. This is when the action starts.

CICERO. I don't need this kind of action.

MOLLY. *[Still humping enthusiastically on top of Beau whose leg is loosely hanging above the back of the couch.]* Come on, Cicero, you're next just like I promised.

CICERO. You don't have to keep your promise.

MOLLY. I want to keep my promise.

RALPH. Hold still, Mulligan. *[Ralph is still performing fellatio on Mulligan.]*

MULLIGAN. Come on, Cicero, you worked hard all day. Relax.

[Ralph stops performing fellatio.]

RALPH. I suppose Cicero is disgusted with all of us.

MULLIGAN. What him? We're asshole buddies. Nothin' could disgust him.

RALPH. I'm disgusted with myself. *[Ralph rises to his feet.]*

Raymond J. Barry

MULLIGAN. Don't stop now for chrissakes. I'm almost coming.

RALPH. I feel empty.

MULLIGAN. Empty?

RALPH. Everything is empty.

MULLIGAN. What are you talking about?

RALPH. All of it.

MULLIGAN. Feeling down, Ralphy Boy?

RALPH. Just empty. Out of gas.

MULLIGAN. Well, come alive, Ralph! Come alive! Find a reason, Ralph! Look at the mess my life is in. Do I let it get to me? No, I won't allow my joy for life to get sidetracked.

RALPH. No, I feel immoral.

MULLIGAN. Immoral? You? You're a fucking schoolteacher for chrissakes. What's wrong with immoral? Come on, you guys, don't give me that immoral shit.

MOLLY. Assssssssshhhh!

MULLIGAN. Molly's coming and you want to go?

RALPH. I just feel so dirty.

MULLIGAN. Come on, Ralph.

RALPH. I'm just shocked at myself.

MULLIGAN. You should try some honest work, Ralph.

RALPH. No, teaching young people is the future of us all. They are truly beautiful in their innocence.

MULLIGAN. Don't take it to heart, Ralphy boy.

BEAU. Geeooorghuf. Geeoorguff!

[Mulligan blocks the entrance. Molly dismounts Beau.]

MOLLY. The party's young.

MULLIGAN. You got a lot of spirit, lady.

RALPH. I have no spirit.

MOLLY. Yes, I do have spirit, Mulligan.

MULLIGAN. Yeah, you got spirit, all right.

RALPH. I'm losing all enthusiasm for everything.

MOLLY. Come on, Ralph, don't kill the spirit of the party.

MULLIGAN. After all, what's more important than spirit?

RALPH. My heart isn't in it anymore. All this... play acting.

MOLLY. My pussy smells like halibut. *[Molly laughs uproariously.]*

RALPH. I'm losing heart for things.

MULLIGAN. Come on, Ralph. It's just a party game like *Spin the Bottle* when we were kids.

RALPH. I just want to mope around.

MOLLY. Yeah, come on, Ralph, don't poop out.

RALPH. No, I can't anymore.

MOLLY. Come on, Ralph, pick up your head and smile.

RALPH. It wouldn't do anything for me.

Pornographic Panorama

MULLIGAN. Yeah, come on, Ralph, you're not the only one here.

RALPH. I don't have any spirit all of a sudden.

MULLIGAN. You're bringin' us all down.

RALPH. I'm depressed.

CICERO. He's "depressed," he says.

MULLIGAN. What's "depressed"?

CICERO. It's when you don't smile at nothing.

MULLIGAN. Like Beau?

MOLLY. No, Beau's practically dead.

CICERO. It's when you don't feel like goin' to work in the morning.

MULLIGAN. I always go to work.

RALPH. You no doubt have the constitution of an ox, Mulligan.

MULLIGAN. I never miss a day.

RALPH. You can go on forever without thinking about it.

MULLIGAN. Even when I'm hung over I go to work.

RALPH. That's what gets me into trouble, thinking about things.

MULLIGAN. Whattaya mean?

MOLLY. I understand, Ralph. I understand.

RALPH. I'm losing my grip on the world.

MULLIGAN. You, of all people, need to party.

RALPH. I'm out of touch with the flow of things.

MULLIGAN. You gotta forget about things.

RALPH. I wish I was Beau.

MULLIGAN. Why Beau? Beau's dead.

RALPH. He can't be all dead.

MULLIGAN. He's as good as dead.

MOLLY. Watch how you talk. He's my lover.

MULLIGAN. No wonder he's dead.

RALPH. I don't feel like going on anymore.

MULLIGAN. You gotta go on.

RALPH. It doesn't matter anymore.

MOLLY. The guy's real down.

MULLIGAN. You gotta put bread on the table.

CICERO. He sounds real down.

MOLLY. Lift your head up, Ralph.

MULLIGAN. Yeah, Ralph, lift your head up in the air.

CICERO. Come on, Ralph, get that goddam head up.

MULLIGAN. If you got a pair of balls, then lift your fuckin' head.

RALPH. Who cares about my head or my balls?

MULLIGAN. The ladies do.

MOLLY. You have a nice head, Ralph.

MULLIGAN. See? They care about your fucking head.

MOLLY. Yeah, Ralph, you got a nice one — nice balls, too.

MULLIGAN. Yeah, Ralph, see?

Raymond J. Barry

RALPH. I wish I were Beau. I'm gonna kill myself.

MOLLY. No, don't do that, not in my house.

MULLIGAN. Yeah, do it.

MOLLY. Stop encouraging him, Mulligan.

MULLIGAN. I want to see him do it.

MOLLY. He may mean it.

MULLIGAN. He does mean it.

CICERO. Mulligan, you should think about what you're saying.

MULLIGAN. I can tell by how he says it.

RALPH. Hold my hand, someone.

MULLIGAN. Go on, Ralph, do it.

MOLLY. You always like it when somebody's having a hard time.

MULLIGAN. Hey, what the fuck are you talking about?

MOLLY. Listen to what the guy is sayin', for chrissakes.

MULLIGAN. He ain't sayin' nothin'.

RALPH. Nothing really matters.

MULLIGAN. If he wants to kill himself, let him. That's his business.

MOLLY. Ralph, there has to be something good about your life.

RALPH. It doesn't matter anymore.

MOLLY. Surely something matters.

RALPH. No, nothing I can think of.

MOLLY. Something's got to matter.

RALPH. Somebody, please, hold my hand.

MULLIGAN. I'll hold it. *[Mulligan approaches Ralph and holds out his hand to him.]* Here, take my hand.

RALPH. Such a large, square hand... *[Ralph takes Mulligan's hand in his own.]*

MULLIGAN. From layin' cement all my life.

RALPH. ...and calloused and hard.

MULLIGAN. I've laid enough cement to cover the world.

RALPH. You're a simple person, Mulligan.

MULLIGAN. Makes my hands square.

RALPH. That's the difference between us.

MULLIGAN. I just do what I want.

RALPH. It's that simple for you?

MULLIGAN. Yes, it's that simple.

RALPH. That's it, huh?

MULLIGAN. I just do what I like.

MOLLY. Ralph, there has to be something good about your life.

CICERO. You're an animal, Mulligan.

MOLLY. Stop antagonizing him!

MULLIGAN. Not now I'm not. Not when I'm holdin' his hand I'm not. I don't have to do that. I could just say "fuck it" to the guy and that would be it. I don't have to be like this to him.

Pornographic Panorama

CICERO. No matter which way you cut it, you're a prick.

MULLIGAN. Fuck you.

MOLLY. Pay attention to Ralph, both of you.

RALPH. You don't have to pay attention to me, really.

MOLLY. We don't want you to kill yourself, Ralph.

RALPH. I'm not worth this kind of attention.

MOLLY. Yes, you are, Ralph. We like you, Ralph. Look, even Mulligan likes you. He's holding your hand. That means he likes you. He's nurturing you. It's called nurturing.

RALPH. I know what it's called.

MULLIGAN. You're a schoolteacher. That's like bein' nothing. You got hands like a girl. You might as well kill yourself.

RALPH. I want to cash it in.

CICERO. You're a cruel son of a bitch, Mulligan.

MULLIGAN. Why don't you slit your throat?

RALPH. Yes, good.

MOLLY. Don't talk that way, really. It makes me nervous.

RALPH. I'm sorry to be causing so much of a stir.

CICERO. Just cheer up.

MOLLY. Why don't you try on one of my dresses? That would cheer you up.

RALPH. No, I don't want to.

MULLIGAN. You could knock your brains out on the fuckin' wall.

RALPH. It wouldn't do any good. I'd still feel the same way.

MULLIGAN. Just try it. *[Mulligan lets go of Ralph's hand, crosses to a wall.]*

MOLLY. Mulligan, stop it.

RALPH. There must be a way.

MULLIGAN. Knocking your brains out is one alternative.

RALPH. I'll jump out the window.

[simultaneous]

CICERO.	MOLLY.
Don't jump out the window.	Don't jump out the window.
You'll kill yourself.	You'll kill yourself.

RALPH. I'm going to kill myself.

MULLIGAN. Go on! Jump!

[Ralph gets up from his chair and walks to the window. He lifts his leg up and dangles it outside. He hesitates.]

RALPH. I'm a little scared.

MULLIGAN. By the time you hit the cement it'll be over.

RALPH. It'll probably hurt.

MULLIGAN. No, it won't hurt. You'll fly through the air, that's all. It won't hurt.

Raymond J. Barry

RALPH. You think so?

MULLIGAN. Yeah, it won't hurt.

RALPH. I'm still scared.

MOLLY. Maybe you don't want to do it.

CICERO. You have reservations?

RALPH. Yeah, I'm not sure it's the right thing.

MOLLY. Is there another way, Ralph?

CICERO. Do you have any pills?

MOLLY. Just for a headache.

MULLIGAN. He'll have a headache if he jumps out the window. Give him one for when he hits the pavement. Give him two.

MOLLY. Do you want a pill for a headache, Ralph?

RALPH. Maybe.

MULLIGAN. Whattaya mean, maybe?

RALPH. I don't know what I mean.

MULLIGAN. Then jump.

RALPH. I don't know anything anymore.

MULLIGAN. Get it over with.

RALPH. All right.

MOLLY. You're absolutely sure?

RALPH. How can I be sure?

MOLLY. Close to being sure?

RALPH. Sort of sure.

MOLLY. Think before you leap.

RALPH. I'm thinking. I'm frightened.

MULLIGAN. Go on! Jump!

RALPH. I'm tired of all this bullshit. *[Ralph jumps. No one goes to the window. There is a long pause.]*

MOLLY. He jumped.

[pause]

CICERO. I know why he did it.

MULLIGAN. I don't. I don't understand why a guy would do that. There's always another angle to get you through it.

CICERO. He didn't like life.

MULLIGAN. Nobody likes life but you don't have to do that.

MOLLY. Everyone has their own way. We're just better off than he is, that's all.

CICERO. Not really.

MULLIGAN. I know I am. I'm alive.

CICERO. That's nothing.

MULLIGAN. Whattaya mean, "That's nothing"?

CICERO. Ralph is gonna be fine, Mulligan. We're the ones who have to worry. We're the ones who have to find new reasons for every day.

MULLIGAN. I don't give a fuck.

Pornographic Panorama

CICERO. You, Mulligan, are the most honest one in this room. You don't give a damn, do you? You move from one person to the next, using them up to suit your needs and throw them away when you're finished. Take what you can and throw away the rest, and you don't blink an eyelash — no guilt, no reservation, just nothing. You don't pretend. We're all playthings to you, plain as day. None of the usual sentimental stuff gets in your way.

MOLLY. I'm not like that.

CICERO. You are, Molly, but you don't realize it. You're afraid of being alone. You had to have company no matter what the price. It didn't matter what took place in this room as long as you were distracted from yourself. You'll put up with anything to reduce the panic inside.

MOLLY. This talk bothers me.

MULLIGAN. Don't take his bullshit serious, Molly.

MOLLY. Ralph went out the window and nobody's doing anything about it.

MULLIGAN. He knew what he was doin'.

CICERO. Yes, he did know. He was afraid though. He was afraid of leaving us.

MULLIGAN. He flew out that window like a big striped-assed bird.

CICERO. He didn't want to be alone, even in death. That fear stayed with him until the end.

MULLIGAN. He was afraid of hurting himself.

CICERO. That was only part of his fear.

MULLIGAN. He even said so.

CICERO. It's difficult to leave the safety of the crowd.

MOLLY. I don't like this talk.

MULLIGAN. I don't like this shit either.

MOLLY. That's tough what you don't like. You're not nice, Mulligan.

MULLIGAN. I don't try to be nice, cause "nice" don't mean shit in this world. "Nice" is bullshit. Everybody's "nice". Everybody pretends he's "nice" but nobody's really "nice". You either lie about being "nice" or you get honest and be who your really are, a mean sonofabitch out for yourself and pull no bones about it. That's the way I am because I was taught to be that way by teachers and parents and relatives who pretended to be "nice" when they wanted only one thing, that we needn't get into cause it ain't "nice". The world changed me just like it change Ralphy boy right before our very eyes. Ralphy ain't "nice" either. In fact he wasn't "nice" when he walked in here tonight although he pretended to be "nice". He'd been programmed by that nice "teacher" shit for years, while pretending all the time to be a model citizen for all the "nice" boys and girls, but underneath all that crap he was like the rest of us, figuring out an angle so you can make it to the next year, when another angle will come along to get you through the year after that. The angles

Raymond J. Barry

and double crosses come and go year after year, day after day, and when you're a respectable schoolteacher you may go a life time without gettin' caught. But Ralphy boy got in over your head this time. He ran out of angles and double crosses to the point where he didn't want to do it no more. The whole world is phony so don't blame me for not playing the "nice" game you have to play to live in it. I intend to keep finding "angles" and "double crosses" until, just like Ralphy, I've had enough, and then I'll be the one to jump out the window.

[There is a loud pounding on the door which results in much scampering around in the apartment. We see Molly picking up articles of clothing that have been strewn upon the floor.]

MOLLY. Who is it?

[pause while the banging continues]

Who is it?

[pause while the banging continues]

Who is it?

MRS. MULLIGAN. *[From the other side of the door.]* Is my husband in there?

MULLIGAN. Oh, shit. It's my wife. *[general flurry to gather themselves]*

MOLLY. Wait now everyone. We can all be rational, can't we? There are a number of factors that have to be considered here.

MULLIGAN. Shuttup, I can't think straight.

MOLLY. Since when have you ever thought straight, Mulligan. Now, as I was saying, I definitely am of a mind to accommodate her in every way possible.

MULLIGAN. Not a peep outta you, Molly, if you know what's good for you. Help me, will you, Cicero? You're a good talker. Shut Molly up, and get rid of my wife. *[Cicero glowers at Mulligan with vengeance in his heart.]*

CICERO. I don't know what to say to her.

MULLIGAN. Say anything, goddammit. Say anything. *[Mulligan, dressed in Molly's dress, exits into the bedroom. Finally, after much pounding, Molly goes to the door and opens it. There in the hall stands a very plain looking woman dressed like a housewife. She is a sturdy, physically strong, heavy-set woman around forty five with glasses and her long hair tied in a bun. Mrs. Mulligan forcefully walks in and looks past Molly.]*

MOLLY. Come in.

MRS. MULLIGAN. Thank you. *[She walks further into the apartment.]* I'm sorry to bother you. My husband didn't come home so I was worried and I decided to go out to his usual hangout and, well, to make a long story short, someone, the bartender in the downstairs bar, told me he might be here.

MOLLY. What bartender?

[simultaneous]

MRS. MULLIGAN.	MOLLY.
The bartender at the bar, an acquaintance of mine at the bar down where my husband drinks. He doesn't drink. I mean, he's not a drinker but he had a drink there...	Come in and sit and have something like maybe a drink or some food. There's some food in the refrigerator. Why don't you have something...

MRS. MULLIGAN. ...when he was finished with work and he didn't come home so I was worried and I thought I'd come here and... today's payday. Mulligan is his name. The bartender downstairs told me he might be in this apartment.

MOLLY. These are some friends of mine... a... This is Beau. He's had too much to drink, and a...Cicero, Cicero. Yes, Cicero. That's Cicero. He's a construction worker.

CICERO. Hello.

[Everyone stands in awkward silence.]

MRS. MULLIGAN. Well, I guess he's not here. I suppose I'll go. I'm really worried about him. Today was payday.

MOLLY. I can imagine.

[simultaneously]

MRS. MULLIGAN.	MOLLY.
Well, I'm sorry to interrupt your party. You were having a nice time and I'm sorry, but I just had to come looking for him.	Yes, it's terrible not knowing where your husband is. I haven't known where mine is for over five years now. I've given up.

[Mrs. Mulligan turns to exit.]

CICERO. He's in the bedroom.

MOLLY. Shut the fuck up.

MRS. MULLIGAN. What?

MOLLY. Oh, my God, what'd ya tell her for?

CICERO. He's in the bedroom.

MRS. MULLIGAN. What?

CICERO. I work with him on the job.

MOLLY. You dumb bastard! What is on your mind, Cicero? What'd you tell her for?

MRS. MULLIGAN. What?

[simultaneously]

CICERO.	MOLLY.
You heard me. Why are you saying, "What! What! What!"	He's kidding. He's not telling the truth. There's no one in there. We've

Raymond J. Barry

You heard me. He's in the bedroom. That's what. He's in the bedroom. Go in the goddam bedroom.

been having a party so everyone's a little bit drunk. He's just bullshitting.

[After a long, indecisive pause, Mrs. Mulligan walks into the bedroom. She disappears for a moment.]

MOLLY. Why did you tell?

CICERO. Part of the party spirit, that's all. No more than that.

MOLLY. You prick. You got yourself in trouble.

CICERO. If I'm in trouble then you're in trouble.

MOLLY. You told, not me.

CICERO. Yeah, but you're in trouble too.

MOLLY. Stop it. This is serious now.

[Mrs. Mulligan re-enters the living room. She stands there looking at them for a long time. No one can look her in the eye.]

MOLLY. What ya' looking at?

[silence]

MOLLY. What ya' thinking?

[silence]

MOLLY. That's not your husband, is it?

[silence]

MOLLY. The guy's someone else, that's all. He came in here and had a few drinks, that's all.

[long silence]

MOLLY. Why aren't you talking? What'sa matter with you? Say something.

[long silence]

MOLLY. I hardly know the guy. He came over with these guys for a party. I don't know him. He's none of my business.

[long silence]

CICERO. Mulligan and Beau had a fight.

[Mulligan walks in dressed in his dress.]

MULLIGAN. What the fuck are you talking about?

CICERO. Mulligan hurt him.

MULLIGAN. You fucking weirdo. What the fuck are you talkin' about? *[He approaches Cicero, but the lighter, faster Cicero escapes. Mulligan attacks again, but again Cicero is faster physically. Mulligan winds up flying onto the floor after slipping onto his ass.]*

MOLLY. Come on now. Stop this.

CICERO. Mulligan and Beau were a couple of faggots together. They was fucking each other up the asshole during lunch breaks on the job. They had a faggot lover's spat and Beau lost.

MULLIGAN. *[getting up]* You son of a bitch.

Pornographic Panorama

[*Molly goes to Mulligan and contains him.*]

MOLLY. Cicero, stop it! The guy doesn't need this. [*Mrs. Mulligan remains silent. She stands for a long time watching them all.*] She's in shock. The whole thing's a shock to her. Is there anything I can do for you? Would you like to sit down?

[*no response*]

MOLLY. What's up, lady? Can I get you a glass of water or something? [*Molly goes to the sink and comes back with a glass of water.*] What's goin' on? Here's some water. Drink it down. [*Mrs. Mulligan doesn't take the water.*] How come you don't say nothin'? Maybe you'd like a real drink? I'll get you a real drink. [*Molly fetches a bottle of brandy and pours her a glass.*] Here's some brandy. It'll warm your stomach. [*Mrs. Mulligan doesn't take the drink.*]

CICERO. Beau's still here, Mulligan. He's waiting for you. He wants you to do him up the ass.

MULLIGAN. I'm gonna cut you in your face, motherfucker.

CICERO. You see, Mrs. Mulligan? Your husband is full of violence. He did that to Beau with a pair of scissors. They're faggots together on the job. Ain't that something? They both got wives, but they're faggots together when they're away from home. That's the "bitch" in Mulligan. I've seen that part of him myself.

MULLIGAN. I'll kill you.

[*Mulligan breaks loose and starts throwing bottles and glasses at Cicero.*]

CICERO. Most people wouldn't believe it until he begins to lose it, but when he does, it gets dangerous. Mulligan is a mean, vicious faggot capable of committing murder.

MULLIGAN. I'll fucking kill you. [*Glasses bounce off Cicero as he ducks away, trying to avoid being hit.*] I'll fucking kill you! [*Molly tries to restrain Mulligan who by now has peaked into total rage, a pit bull out of control.*]

CICERO. Look at Beau. Mulligan did that to him because Beau wouldn't leave his family and go off with him. Look at him. It's all that faggot shit. It's pathetic.

MRS. MULLIGAN. Who is this man? ! ! !

[*pause.*]

MULLIGAN. This is Cicero, honey. We work together on the job.

MRS. MULLIGAN. Have you spent your paycheck yet?

MULLIGAN. No... I... er... I was just having a few beers, hon.

CICERO. This is too good to be true.

MRS. MULLIGAN. A few beers? Isn't that quaint? What on earth do you have on?

MULLIGAN. Just foolin' around.

MOLLY. You're weird, Cicero.

CICERO. I'm weird, huh. It's not me who cuts people's tongues out with sharp scissors.

Raymond J. Barry

[Mrs. Mulligan points at Mulligan in a rage.]

MRS. MULLIGAN. Get that fruity thing off. What on earth is going on with you? Kids at home, waiting to be fed and me running all over town to find you and you foolin' around in a dress no less. Where are your clothes?

MULLIGAN. Ah... back there... in the back.

MRS. MULLIGAN. Whose dress is that anyway and why are you wearing it? You look like a cheap tart. Come on, tell me. Whose dress is that?

MULLIGAN. *[He points to Molly.]* Hers.

MRS. MULLIGAN. And who's she?

MULLIGAN. Her name is Molly.

MRS. MULLIGAN. Sounds like a common trollop.

MOLLY. Easy, lady.

MRS. MULLIGAN. Why are your clothes in the bedroom?

MULLIGAN. Honey, could we put a hold on the questions until we get outta here?

MRS. MULLIGAN. Just answer me. Why were you in the bedroom? Molly's bedroom, I presume.

MULLIGAN. I... ah... was just foolin' around so I went in the bedroom and put on the dress.

MRS. MULLIGAN. I suppose Molly was in there with you at the time.

MULLIGAN. No, nobody was in there with me.

MRS. MULLIGAN. Molly wasn't in the bedroom?

MULLIGAN. No, she was in the living room.

MRS. MULLIGAN. Why would she be in the living room when you were in her bedroom?

CICERO. A guy was in there with him.

MULLIGAN. Shut your damned mouth.

MRS. MULLIGAN. *[referring to Beau.]* What's the matter with him?

MULLIGAN. Ah... er... nothing.

MRS. MULLIGAN. What do you mean nothing. He's bleeding from the mouth.

MOLLY. He had too much to drink.

MULLIGAN. Yeah, that's right; he had too much to drink.

MRS. MULLIGAN. He's not moving.

MULLIGAN. He moves. I've seen him move.

MOLLY. Yeah, he moves. He's moving.

CICERO. I don't see him moving.

MULLIGAN. Who cares what you see.

CICERO. You don't have to care. It's Beau we're talking about and he's not moving. I don't even see him breathing.

MRS. MULLIGAN. What've you done with him?

MULLIGAN. I haven't done anything with him.

MRS. MULLIGAN. Don't give me that. You've done something with him.

MULLIGAN. There are two other people in the room.

MRS. MULLIGAN. Yeah, I know, but you're the guilty one. I can see it in your eyes. Get out of that fruity dress. Why are you wearing that dress anyway?

MULLIGAN. Nothin'. Just foolin' around. I'll take it off.

MOLLY. Go get your pants, little boy, and don't forget your lunch box.

CICERO. Ha. Ha. Big tough Mulligan's mother is here to take him home.

MULLIGAN. Lay off. Cicero had a dress on just a few minutes ago.

CICERO. So? What does that mean? It was your idea.

MULLIGAN. You asked to put it on.

CICERO. No, I didn't.

MULLIGAN. Yeah, he was beggin' to put a dress on. Beggin'. Just like he begged me to put my dick up his ass.

CICERO. Mrs. Mulligan, you got a big problem with your husband.

MRS. MULLIGAN. I know. I know.

MULLIGAN. I'll deal with you later.

CICERO. You're not dealing with me anytime. Get your dress off, sweets.

MOLLY. Shuttup, Cicero.

MRS. MULLIGAN. I'm going in there with you.

[Mrs. Mulligan follows him into Molly's bedroom. Their voices can be heard while we watch the reaction of Cicero and Molly in the living room.]

MRS. MULLIGAN. *[From the bedroom.]* Why are you hanging out with such riff raff? Why didn't you come home? You got your pay check?

MULLIGAN. *[From the bedroom.]* Yeah, I got it. I got it.

MRS. MULLIGAN. *[From the bedroom.]* Well, where is it?

MULLIGAN. *[From the bedroom.]* It's in my wallet.

[Mr. and Mrs. Mulligan re-enter the living room. Mulligan carries his clothes in his hand.]

MRS. MULLIGAN. Let me see it.

MULLIGAN. You don't have to see it.

MRS. MULLIGAN. I'd like to see it just to make sure you have it.

MULLIGAN. Honey, you can trust me. I have the check.

MRS. MULLIGAN. I don't know why it's such an issue to show it to me.

MULLIGAN. I cashed it. All I got is cash.

MRS. MULLIGAN. How much cash?

MULLIGAN. Don't worry about it. I have most of my money.

MRS. MULLIGAN. How much is most of your money?

MULLIGAN. A lot.

MRS. MULLIGAN. A lot of cash?

MULLIGAN. Ah... No, a lot of striped-assed birds.

MRS. MULLIGAN. Don't be funny.

MULLIGAN. I'm not being funny.

MOLLY. Isn't this something? The big construction worker, builder of buildings, getting picked up from school by his wife.

Raymond J. Barry

CICERO. Don't forget your lunch box, Mulligan.

MRS. MULLIGAN. Don't you have sense enough to come home with your paycheck?

MULLIGAN. Yeah, my paycheck.

MRS. MULLIGAN. Let me see your wallet.

MULLIGAN. What for?

MRS. MULLIGAN. So I can count your money.

MULLIGAN. I don't need you to count my money, honey.

MRS. MULLIGAN. What do I care about your need?

MULLIGAN. That's the trouble with you. You don't care about anybody but yourself.

CICERO. Who do you care about, Mulligan?

MULLIGAN. None of your business.

CICERO. For a minute there I thought you sounded generous.

MULLIGAN. Generous this. *[Mulligan grabs his joint.]*

CICERO. Now we're back to normal.

MRS. MULLIGAN. Don't be vulgar.

MULLIGAN. He's used to it.

MRS. MULLIGAN. Just never mind. Don't be vulgar.

MOLLY. Listen to his mommy telling him.

CICERO. And he's listening.

MOLLY. Attentively.

MRS. MULLIGAN. Put your pants on, little boy.

CICERO. Get your pants on, little boy.

MRS. MULLIGAN. And make it snappy.

CICERO. And make it snappy, little boy.

MULLIGAN. Knock it off, Cicero.

CICERO. Not the big lover boy now, are you?

MULLIGAN. Knock it off.

CICERO. Don't give me that shit, Mulligan. We all know who did what to who and why tonight.

MULLIGAN. I'll get my pants on, honey.

MRS. MULLIGAN. Don't "honey" me.

RALPH. Does your husband wear dresses very often?

MRS. MULLIGAN. My husband never wears dresses.

[Mulligan puts his pants on.]

MOLLY. I never expected that Mulligan would have such a nice wife.

MULLIGAN. Why wouldn't you expect that?

MOLLY. I just never would expect it.

MRS. MULLIGAN. Thank you for saying that.

MOLLY. Oh, it's quite all right, really. Must be nice to have a family. Any kids?

MRS. MULLIGAN. Thirteen.

MOLLY. Jesus Christ! Thirteen kids and him running around in dresses.

CICERO. That's what I call a full life.

MRS. MULLIGAN. Full! You call that full? No paycheck; children at home hungry. Oh, lord, oh, lord. Hand to mouth; hand to mouth. Nothing ever gets easier.

CICERO. He must be some model for the children.

MOLLY. Yeah, it must be great to have a dose of Mulligan every day when you get up in the morning.

[Mulligan has taken the top of the dress partially off and struggles to put one pant leg on beneath his dress.]

MRS. MULLIGAN. Hurry up! Hurry up!

MOLLY. Hurry up, Mulligan. Your wifey is waiting for you.

CICERO. Yeah, mommy calls.

MULLIGAN. I'll get to you on Monday, Cicero.

MRS. MULLIGAN. Oh, your bark is bigger than your bite.

MULLIGAN. What'd you say?

MRS. MULLIGAN. I said your bark is always bigger than your bite.

MULLIGAN. Hell it is. *[Mulligan tumbles onto the ground, entangled in the swathes of clothing that trip him up.]* If I can just get this leg in here I'll be all right.

CICERO. Get your pants on Mulligan. Ha. Ha.

MOLLY. Well, it's awfully nice to meet you.

MRS. MULLIGAN. Hurry up. Get your pants on.

[A wallet falls out of the pants.]

MOLLY. That's Ralph's wallet. *[Mulligan tries to hide the wallet.]* You have Ralph's wallet.

MULLIGAN. What are you talking about? It's my wallet.

[Mulligan has his pants on by now and has put the wallet into his back pocket.]

MRS. MULLIGAN. Come on. Come on. Get your leg into those things. *[Mulligan is now hopping around on one leg.]* Running around town, looking for you night after night. I swear to God what you put me through. It's cruel. You're cruel. Do you realize that?

MULLIGAN. Yeah, I'm sorry.

CICERO. You're cruel, Mulligan.

MULLIGAN. That's enough outta you.

MRS. MULLIGAN. You come to these places, but you can't come home when you finish work? Why don't you want to see your wife and children?

MULLIGAN. I do... I don't know...

MRS. MULLIGAN. You don't know? What don't you know?

CICERO. He doesn't care about anything.

MRS. MULLIGAN. What did you say?

CICERO. I said he doesn't care about anything.

MULLIGAN. What do you know?

Raymond J. Barry

CICERO. I know.

MRS. MULLIGAN. Who is he?

MULLIGAN. We work together.

MRS. MULLIGAN. You care. Don't you care?

[Mulligan flinches as if he's going to be hit.]

MULLIGAN. Yeah, I care. I care... about the kids.

MRS. MULLIGAN. You care about me too, don't you?

MULLIGAN. Yes, I care about you.

MRS. MULLIGAN. How much do you care?

MULLIGAN. A lot.

MRS. MULLIGAN. How much?

MULLIGAN. A lot.

CICERO. He doesn't care about anything.

MRS. MULLIGAN. Why does he keep saying that?

MULLIGAN. Knock it off, Cicero.

CICERO. It's true; he doesn't care.

MULLIGAN. Stop sayin' that.

MRS. MULLIGAN. What's he to you?

MULLIGAN. Nothin'. I work with him.

CICERO. He doesn't care about his job. He goofs off.

MULLIGAN. You don't have to get into that.

CICERO. I feel the need.

MRS. MULLIGAN. Why does he say you don't care?

CICERO. He doesn't.

MULLIGAN. I care.

CICERO. You don't care about nothing, your job, your friends or your family.

MULLIGAN. I care about my job. I'm a union man.

CICERO. Your union doesn't care either. It protects you from being fired when you sleep on the top floor of the job.

MULLIGAN. I don't sleep. I work. I work hard.

CICERO. You sleep on the top floor under the sink. I see you. But you can't get fired, cause of the union.

MULLIGAN. The union protects me.

CICERO. Right, the glorious union.

MULLIGAN. You got a hard-on for the union?

CICERO. You can't get fired so you don't give a shit about nothin'.

MULLIGAN. Give it up, will ya? You done it too. You slept on the top floor too.

CICERO. I know, and we can't be fired.

MOLLY. Big working men.

MULLIGAN. What're ya tryin' to prove, Cicero? You goof off too. Everybody goofs off. That's the game ya play. What's the difference anyway? The boss makes the big money and we get shit.

Pornographic Panorama

MRS. MULLIGAN. No wonder you can stay out all night after night. You're sleepin' during the day.

MULLIGAN. I'm not sleepin'. I'm workin'.

MOLLY. America's work force.

CICERO. You don't get satisfaction from your work.

MULLIGAN. What are you talkin' about? Do you mind tellin' me what you're talkin' about?

CICERO. What we do all day we don't care about.

MULLIGAN. Yeah? So what?

CICERO. So we leave the job feeling like shit, knowing the work we're doing is below what we're capable of doing and we don't feel right about ourselves because we've learned how not to care which is catching and bleeds into our marriage and our friendships so that we start not caring about those things too, and when we don't care about anything there's no way to feel good about yourself so you try to numb yourself with anything that comes your way. Your job doesn't do it for you and neither does your marriage and your kids and pretty soon you don't go home anymore after work because you don't care about your home just like you don't care about your job, and "not caring" has become a bad habit that takes over your whole existence but it's all right because your union protects you and you can't be fired. It gets to the point where we don't even care what hole you stick it into, dogs, cats, sheep, horses, a man, a woman, our wives, even our kids, as long as it's warm and wet and a hole of some kind, as long as you get your rocks off. Any screw is a good screw, just like any job is a good job so long as it pays money. Everything has been reduced to gissom and money. Well, I care, Mulligan; I care just a little bit and I've got to hold onto that for dear life. If I don't I'm a dead man.

MRS. MULLIGAN. You should've gone to college.

CICERO. I did go to college... for a while.

MULLIGAN. He was too dumb to stay there.

MOLLY. Spare us, Mulligan. How long did you stay in school, Cicero?

CICERO. Nothin'. Not for long.

MULLIGAN. He was too dumb.

MRS. MULLIGAN. Oh, shuttup, you big oaf. What college did you go to, Cicero?

CICERO. Just a college... I don't want to talk about it.

MULLIGAN. He got some sense and became a union man where you get paid.

CICERO. Yeah, A union man who doesn't give a shit about nothin'.

MOLLY. You give a shit, Cicero.

MRS. MULLIGAN. Yes, I can tell by the manner in which you speak that you take pride in your life.

CICERO. I'm here, aren't I?

Raymond J. Barry

Mrs. Mulligan. We're all here. What's that got to do with one's pride?

Mulligan. Let's go, honey. We've hung out enough.

Molly. Don't be in a hurry.

Cicero. Yeah, we're enjoying this.

Mulligan. Let's go.

Mrs. Mulligan. I'd like to sit here just for a minute and drink my brandy. *[Mrs. Mulligan takes the glass of brandy that was poured for her before.]* I'm tired of being pushed.

Mulligan. I'm tired of stayin' here.

Mrs. Mulligan. Always being pushed, day and night, scrubbin' floors, cleaning, babies' diapers.

Mulligan. How do you think it is for me?

Mrs. Mulligan. Never mind you. You're out with the boys.

Mulligan. My one pleasure of the week.

Mrs. Mulligan. Wearing dresses.

Mulligan. Don't make a big deal about that.

Mrs. Mulligan. If I don't make a big deal about it, then who will?

Mulligan. I was just playin'. What's wrong with playin'?

Cicero. I could name a few things.

Mulligan. Nobody's askin' you.

Cicero. I don't have to wait to be asked.

Mulligan. That's a matter of opinion.

Cicero. My opinion is the only one that matters.

Mulligan. Come on, honey, let's go.

Mrs. Mulligan. Oh, you can hang out but I have to leave. Is that it?

Mulligan. Yeah, that's it. Come on, I'm leavin'.

[Mulligan strides out the door.]

Mrs. Mulligan. Let him go.

Molly. I agree. Let him go.

Cicero. He'll be back.

Mrs. Mulligan. What makes you think so?

Cicero. He's not going to leave you with us.

Mrs. Mulligan. I'm an adult.

Cicero. Yeah, I know, but he wouldn't want us to compare notes.

Mrs. Mulligan. Perhaps you're right.

[Mulligan re-enters.]

Mulligan. You coming?

Mrs. Mulligan. Yes, I'm coming - when I'm good and ready.

Cicero. She wants to get to know us, Mulligan.

Mulligan. She does, huh?

Cicero. Yeah.

Mulligan. Let's go.

Mrs. Mulligan. I'm not leaving quite yet.

Mulligan. I wish you wouldn't carry on in front of them.

MRS. MULLIGAN. Oh, yes, we have to keep up with appearances.

MULLIGAN. I don't give a shit about appearances.

CICERO. Then why don't you wear a dress on the job?

MULLIGAN. Right.

[Silence.]

MOLLY. I like this party.

MULLIGAN. You like any party.

MOLLY. Maybe I do. You want to make something of it?

[Silence.]

MRS. MULLIGAN. That man doesn't seem to be breathing.

MULLIGAN. He's breathing.

MRS. MULLIGAN. No, I don't think so. His chest isn't moving up and down.

MULLIGAN. He's breathing through his asshole.

MRS. MULLIGAN. I've heard enough of that talk.

MOLLY. Yeah, Mulligan, give your old lady a break.

MULLIGAN. I'm givin' her a break. The guy's breathin'. Poke him with a stick or something.

MOLLY. You do the poking. I don't want nothing to do with him anymore.

CICERO. Ha. Ha. Ha. Ha. Ha.

MOLLY. What's so funny?

CICERO. You don't want anything to do with him.

MOLLY. What's so funny about that?

MULLIGAN. Ha. Ha. Ha. That is funny.

CICERO. Isn't it funny?

MULLIGAN. Yeah.

MOLLY. I still don't get why it's so funny.

MULLIGAN. You don't have to get it.

CICERO. You didn't mind him before.

[Both Mulligan and Cicero laugh. They stop suddenly. Pause.]

MRS. MULLIGAN. I'm not understanding this.

MOLLY. Would you like another brandy?

MRS. MULLIGAN. Oh, yes, I would like another.

MULLIGAN. No, she wouldn't.

MOLLY. You've got nothing to do with it.

MRS. MULLIGAN. You've got nothing to do with my thirst for brandy.

MOLLY. Here's your brandy.

MRS. MULLIGAN. Thank you.

[Mrs. Mulligan drinks with her eye on Mulligan. Silence.]

MOLLY. You know, come to think of it, it looks to me like Beau isn't breathing.

MULLIGAN. Poke him with a stick or something.

MRS. MULLIGAN. Don't be disrespectful of the dead.

MULLIGAN. He's not dead.

Raymond J. Barry

CICERO. He's practically dead.

MULLIGAN. Well, if he's practically dead he may be dead pretty soon.

CICERO AND MOLLY. That's true.

[Silence. Mrs. Mulligan drinks her brandy.]

MRS. MULLIGAN. How'd you say his mouth got cut?

MULLIGAN. I didn't say.

MOLLY. You said.

MULLIGAN. What'd I say?

MOLLY. You said he took a nose dive.

MULLIGAN. A nose dive?

MOLLY. Yeah, you said he fell right on his face.

MULLIGAN. Naw, I didn't.

MOLLY. You did.

CICERO. I heard it.

MRS. MULLIGAN. So did I.

[Silence.]

MULLIGAN. Poke him with a stick or something to see if he moves.

CICERO. He was moving before.

CICERO AND MULLIGAN. Ha. Ha. Ha. Ha. Ha.

MOLLY. Why are you laughing?

MULLIGAN AND CICERO. Nothing.

[Silence.]

MOLLY. He sure is still.

CICERO. Sure is. The party might be over for him.

MULLIGAN. Sure might be.

[Silence.]

MOLLY. I'll blow in his ear.

CICERO. Yeah, blow in his ear.

MULLIGAN. Maybe I should blow up his ear.

CICERO. You stay away from him.

MULLIGAN. Why?

CICERO. Respect for the dead.

MULLIGAN. He's dead?

CICERO. He looks dead.

MOLLY. I'm blowing and he looks to me dead.

MULLIGAN. He looks dead to me too.

[Silence. Molly blows into Beau's ear.]

MOLLY. Somebody help me drag him over here.

MULLIGAN. What're ya draggin' him over there for?

CICERO. Good question.

MULLIGAN. What're ya draggin' him over there for?

MRS. MULLIGAN. Never mind that; help the woman out for a change.

MULLIGAN. I'm helpin'. I'm helpin'.

MRS. MULLIGAN. All right then.

Pornographic Panorama

CICERO. If you're gonna help, then I'm gonna help.

MRS. MULLIGAN. That's it, you two strong men. We ladies need a helping hand once in a while. Which reminds me. How much do you have left of your paycheck?

CICERO. Tell her how much, Mulligan.

MULLIGAN. Not at a time like this, honey, when I'm in the process of draggin' a dead body from one place to another. Where are we draggin' him anyway?

MOLLY. Over here, next to the window where the air is fresher. It might be easier for him to breathe here; that is, if he's still alive.

MULLIGAN. I'm beginning to think there's little chance of that.

MRS. MULLIGAN. I knew he wasn't breathing from the first moment I walked in here.

MOLLY. Grab a leg, gentlemen, and let's get him over to the window.

MULLIGAN. You mean the one Ralph jumped out of?

MOLLY. That's the one.

MRS. MULLIGAN. Ralph? Who's Ralph?

MULLIGAN. Just a fellow, honey. He got sick of it all and jumped out.

MRS. MULLIGAN. I've thought of doing something like that for years now.

MOLLY. We all have. We just don't mention it much.

CICERO. That's right. I never mention it.

MULLIGAN. I don't think about it. I just keep going.

CICERO. You're like a horse, Mulligan.

MRS. MULLIGAN. That's right. He is like a horse. I've lived with him all my life and he's like a horse, whereas I'm more like a sheep.

MOLLY. Nothing wrong with a sheep. You get warm wool from a sheep and leg of lamb.

MULLIGAN. Good meat from a sheep.

MOLLY. I love leg of lamb. Pull him over here men.

MULLIGAN AND CICERO. We're pulling.

[They pull the body to the window.]

MRS. MULLIGAN. A sheep always follows. I'm a follower – not a leader. I follow my husband's lead all the time.

MOLLY. That can get you into trouble. You men grab an end now and lift him up.

MRS. MULLIGAN. Oh, it has gotten me into trouble, a lot of serious trouble. You heard my description before of my life.

MOLLY. Sounded like mine when I was married. Okay now, Cicero, get his big behind up to this sill.

CICERO. What are we doing? Throwing him out the window?

MULLIGAN. What do you think we're doing?

CICERO. Yeah, but like I was just obeying orders without knowing for sure what I was doing.

MULLIGAN. Well, you know now so start lifting.

Raymond J. Barry

CICERO. He's heavy.

MOLLY. Careful men. Don't hurt yourselves.

MRS. MULLIGAN. I've never been to one of your parties before.

MULLIGAN. We don't throw people out the window at all my parties.

CICERO. But it's a pretty much "anything goes" type of thing with your husband.

MRS. MULLIGAN. Oh, I know. I know. I've lived with him long enough to know. I see him when he comes home at night. He's a...

MULLIGAN. Hoist up, Cicero. Get his ass up.

MRS. MULLIGAN. ...bizarre man to live with. Comes home dressed in costumes, constantly playing dress up for no particular reason really. At first he'd dress up like Santa Claus to entertain the kids and that was a lot of fun for us. Then Halloween became an occasion for him to carry on. Then he began dressing as Bat Man with the cape and hooded mask; once he even came home with Robin. God knows who that man was. Can you imagine? To wake up with Bat Man and Robin staring down at me, both men drunk as can be. I was frightened to death at first, until I realized it was only him. A week later he came home dressed like the devil with a pitch fork and a little pointed tail. He even developed a laugh like the devil. Frightened the kids half to death.

MOLLY. I would imagine. The devil walking around in your own house. Come on, boys, lift.

MRS. MULLIGAN. Not very pleasant. That's for sure. Another time he came home dressed...

MOLLY. Now give it the old heave ho!

[They throw Beau out the window.]

MRS. MULLIGAN. ...as Tarzan and I had to play the part of Jane for the rest of the evening just to please the man. Finally he passed out dead drunk. One year he had a yen for cowboys. The Lone Ranger was his favorite with the mask and silver guns. He even rented a horse to ride up to the house with. That's when we lived in the suburbs before we lost our home. The costumes became more and more bizarre as time went by from grandmother outfits with a gray wig to football player outfits with real shoulder pads to farmer outfits and superman capes and tights.

MULLIGAN. He won't feel a thing. He's practically dead already.

CICERO. Two guys out the window in one night.

MULLIGAN. It's a party. You've been to a party before.

CICERO. Yes, I've been to a party before.

MRS. MULLIGAN. Last year he came home dressed in a policeman's uniform and arrested me with real handcuffs. He raped me repeatedly that night, and, you know, things got out of hand with the handcuffs. He had to call a locksmith to get them off me the next day. I was afraid of him then. Do you have any more brandy? *[Molly pours her more* *brandy.]* Funny what happens to a couple when the trust goes. You can never repair that. I never enjoyed my husband's dress up games after the handcuff evening. There was something about being controlled... left a permanent mark. I tried to forget about it but the suffocation has stayed with me until now, the threat of being handcuffed and thrown down on the bed to be mauled and raped by my husband who is supposed to love me. Do you have the bottle of brandy? That's right, give me the whole bottle. I suppose I'm drinking a bit too much.

MOLLY. She's finishing off the rest of the brandy.

MULLIGAN. You ought to watch out for that stuff, honey.

MRS. MULLIGAN. And why should I watch out do you suppose?

MULLIGAN. That stuff has a kick to it.

MRS. MULLIGAN. Oh, a kick, eh? You can party but I'm not allowed. Is that it?

MULLIGAN. I just want you to have a healthy respect for the stuff, that's all.

MRS. MULLIGAN. *[As she pours herself another shot.]* I listen to you but I don't listen. The trust is gone and somehow no matter how hard I may try I can't bring myself to give him the benefit of a doubt. Yes, the trust is gone.

MULLIGAN. We trust each other, honey.

MRS. MULLIGAN. You know better than that.

MULLIGAN. We trust each other.

MRS. MULLIGAN. For years you been pushin' me around from one end of the block to the other. Do this, sweep up, take care of the kids, mend my underwear, take out the garbage, make the bed, wash the floor, wash the walls, change the baby's diapers, change the sheets, wash the sheets, take the kids to school, cook the breakfast, cook the dinner. "My noodles are too well done. My noodles aren't well done enough. Pack my lunch. Make my sandwiches, make a desert, buy the right desert. Bye bye, honey. Spread your legs. No, don't spread your legs. You don't have what it takes," or "I wish you had what it takes," or "What would it take to make you change? I wish you would change. I wish you weren't you. You're not good enough for me. You're not good enough, not good enough, not good enough. *[Silence.]* Those are my prayers every day. Obviously I don't love him anymore.

MULLIGAN. What're you talking about, honey? You gotta love me.

MRS. MULLIGAN. Mr. Cicero is right. You don't care about anything.

MULLIGAN. Sure I care, honey. You gotta love me.

MRS. MULLIGAN. No, it's not like it used to be.

CICERO. In fact nobody cares about anything in this room.

MULLIGAN. Honey, you don't really mean that, do you?

MRS. MULLIGAN. Of course I mean it. Why wouldn't I mean it?

CICERO. We're all filling time for each other.

Raymond J. Barry

MULLIGAN. You love me and I love you.

MRS. MULLIGAN. Sounds so nice when you say it.

CICERO. You ought to divorce him.

MOLLY. What a brazen thing to say.

CICERO. No, seriously, she ought to cut the guy loose.

MULLIGAN. You got a big mouth.

MRS. MULLIGAN. That's the way it is. I don't love you anymore, and I'm leaving you and taking the kids. [*Mrs. Mulligan serves herself another drink.*] Where's that fellow you had here just a moment ago? The one bleeding from the mouth.

MOLLY. He's gone.

MRS. MULLIGAN. Gone? Where did he go?

MOLLY. He left just a few minutes ago.

MRS. MULLIGAN. I didn't see him go.

MULLIGAN. You been drinking.

MRS. MULLIGAN. I may have been drinking but I didn't see him go.

MULLIGAN. You don't have to see everything.

MRS. MULLIGAN. I don't have to see everything but I didn't see him go.

MULLIGAN. You sound like a broken record.

MOLLY. Don't talk to your wife so disrespectfully.

MRS. MULLIGAN. See? That's what I mean about the trust being gone. I don't have to live with him though. We'll go our separate ways.

MULLIGAN. You're talkin' too much. Let's go home, honey. Stop foolin' around.

MRS. MULLIGAN. Yes, I know. "Just fooling around." I've heard it all before, "Just foolin' around." Well, I've had enough of this to last me forever. I hate my husband's guts. It's over for us. Oh, my, I've had a bit to drink, haven't I? [*Mrs. Mulligan attempts to stand up.*] Oh, well, I'll sleep it off during the night. I'll be fine in the morning, just fine. Goodbye, husband; good evening to all of you. I've lingered in this marriage long enough. Time to get some rest. Oh my, the world is a dizzy place tonight, a dizzy place. The party is over for me. You have your paycheck? Oh, yes, I already asked you that. [*Mrs. Mulligan exits.*] [*Silence. All eyes are on Mulligan.*]

MULLIGAN. She'll come back.

[*Pause.*]

MULLIGAN. What the hell. She'll come back.

MOLLY. No, she won't.

MULLIGAN. Yeah, she'll come back.

MOLLY. No, she won't.

MULLIGAN. Why do you say that?

MOLLY. I heard the sound of her voice.

MULLIGAN. Yeah? So what?

MOLLY. I know the sound. of a woman who has given up. Something both weak and strong about that sound.

MULLIGAN. But she'll come back, won't she?

MOLLY. You don't seem to get it, Mulligan. She just left you for good.

MULLIGAN. But she couldn't have. We've been together for fourteen years.

MOLLY. She snapped. When a woman snaps, it's over.

MULLIGAN. Oh, shit. What am I supposed to do?

MOLLY. Change your ways with the next one.

MULLIGAN. I don't want a next one. I want this one.

MOLLY. You can't have everything you want.

MULLIGAN. Yes I can. I can have her. She's mine. She's my wife.

MOLLY. She's not yours anymore.

MULLIGAN. I gotta get her back.

CICERO. You didn't give a shit before.

MULLIGAN. I give a shit.

CICERO. You don't give a shit where you stick your dick.

MULLIGAN. We don't have to get into that.

CICERO. Your wife finally got smart.

MULLIGAN. She ain't leavin' me.

CICERO. She already left and you got nothin'.

MULLIGAN. I got something.

CICERO. Oh, yeah? What do you got?

MULLIGAN. I don't know but I got somethin'.

CICERO. You're left holdin' your dick.

MULLIGAN. No, I got somethin'. I got somethin'.

MOLLY. You'll probably learn something from this, Mulligan.

MULLIGAN. I got nothin' to learn.

CICERO. Famous last words from a man with no pride.

MULLIGAN. I got pride. I'm proud. Who are you to talk about me that way?

CICERO. I'm the guy who just watched your wife leave you, buddy.

MULLIGAN. Please, don't, Cicero.

MOLLY. Did you hear him? He said, "please".

CICERO. Yeah, he said, "please".

MOLLY. I haven't heard him say, "please" all night.

MULLIGAN. I'm sorry you're so down on me, Cicero.

CICERO. No, you're not.

MULLIGAN. I always covered your ass when you wanted to take a nap on the job, didn't I?

CICERO. Yeah, sure, Mulligan, you covered my ass all right, but I'm not interested in having my ass covered anymore. I want something better. I've become like you, and I don't like who that is. I feel replaceable. I could have been a rubber doll tonight and it wouldn't have made any difference. We were all rubber dolls, yellin' at each other, getting' drunk, screwing. One rubber doll was as good as the next. It's the same at job.

Raymond J. Barry

We're all replaceable. It's all about the money and nothin' else. It's time for me to fight for something better so I can like myself again so my kids can like me as well. See you, Molly.

[Cicero exits. Silence. Mulligan and Molly stand alone with Beau on the floor.]

MULLIGAN. What's buggin' him?

MOLLY. I don't know. Something.

MULLIGAN. Right, something.

[Silence.]

MOLLY. Let's stop pretending, Mulligan. You know what he's saying.

MULLIGAN. Yes, I know what... wait... I don't know what he's saying. He's unhappy about one thing or another.

MOLLY. Okay, we can play this game if you want.

MULLIGAN. What game?

MOLLY. You know what game.

MULLIGAN. Game?

MOLLY. You want to play dumb with me go right ahead. But you're not fooling anyone.

MULLIGAN. I'm not, aren't I?

MOLLY. No, not really. You're just playing dumb.

MULLIGAN. I don't mean to play dumb.

MOLLY. No, you mean it but it's not working.

MULLIGAN. Sorry.

MOLLY. You can't get away with it anymore.

MULLIGAN. I see that.

MOLLY. You can be yourself.

MULLIGAN. I don't really know who that is.

MOLLY. He's somewhere inside of you.

MULLIGAN. I lost touch with that part of myself a long time ago.

MOLLY. You seem to be doing fine now.

MULLIGAN. Yeah, I don't know.

MOLLY. You don't have to know maybe.

MULLIGAN. People laugh at me.

MOLLY. I don't laugh at you.

MULLIGAN. I feel bad that she's leaving me.

MOLLY. You could go after her.

MULLIGAN. I don't think it would make much difference.

MOLLY. That might be true.

MULLIGAN. Yeah, she's going this time.

[Pause.]

MOLLY. You can stay on the couch if you want.

MULLIGAN. No, I gotta go. *[Mulligan prepares to leave.]* You know, I hear you, and I... ah well... I want to cry out to you that what you're saying is a lie, but if I did that you wouldn't... anyway... *[Mulligan weeps.]* Oh, shit. I don't know how to get myself out of this with my skin so thick. *[Pause.]* Look, I don't know who I am, and there's a part of me that doesn't care one way or the other. Why should I care? The more I care, the more there is this outpour of... like a big engine driving me. I'm afraid... I'm afraid, and the plain fact is at some point I got carried away with myself... and I don't want to carry on with that... Part of me is soft inside for my wife... and the kids and... them walking out on me. This is just the beginning of the price I'm gonna pay. Without them I don't have a diving board to jump off. It's all a free fall now and I'm not sure where I'm going to land. "Till death do us part, right?" "Till death do us part?" Aw shit, I can't take this with the kids and everything. This is killing me. Those are my kids too, and I'd do anything for them, anything. They're my reason for working. I love my kids. What's wrong?

MOLLY. I know you have to go but I wish you wouldn't. I wish you would stay on the couch or just talk to me for a while.

CICERO. I just can't. I got my kids, my wife.

MOLLY. I know that but just for a little more time before you go? You can't just leave me like this, can you? You really can't just leave me by myself. I don't know what I'll do really but I can't be left alone, not after tonight. I just have to have someone stay with me tonight. Please... stay... Please.

MULLIGAN. I have to go, Molly.

[Mulligan leaves. Molly is speaking to herself.]

MOLLY. Don't go. I need someone, anyone to communicate, someone to touch. Cicero? Beau? Mulligan? Ralph? Oh, yes, Ralph. Surely, you're here. Please, someone anyone, please, stay here. Come, talk to me. Talk to me. Touch me. I need someone to talk to. No, please, wait... Don't leave me here alone... not now. Would you please, hold me. I beg of you, hold me. Don't let me be alone. *[Molly finally turns toward the bedroom.]* Please... I can't be alone... not tonight or any other night. *[She walks to the window and lifts her leg over the sill. She sits for a while and calmly ponders her next move while the lights dim.]*

End of Play

Raymond J. Barry

A Piece of Cake

Characters

Albert: roommate of Mervin and spy for the government, late thirties.
Mervin: roommate of Albert and people-pleasing spy for the government, late thirties to early forties.
Buford: Ruth's husband, late thirties to early forties.
Ruth: Buford's unfaithful wife, thirty-five or so.
Herman: Government provider of cake supply in his fifties.

History

The World Premiere of **A Piece of Cake** was performed at **The Stark Raving Theatre** in Portland, Oregon; Artistic Director, Jim Wilhelm, July-August 2000.

CAST:

ALBERT .... Tom Beckett
MERVIN.. Danial Flint
RUTH ....Megan Harris
BUFORD...Jared Roylance
HERMAN .... Don Baham

DIRECTOR .... Jim Wilhelm
LIGHTING..Jeff Woods

Raymond J. Barry

A Piece of Cake

Act One

-

Scene One

[Mervin and Albert are in their home, a modest, neat room furnished with an off-green, disheveled couch, an old wooden table and two hard-backed wooden chairs. In the upper stage left corner stands a dresser. A closet is upstage right. There are no pictures on the walls, and the room contains nothing personal. A stage right exit leads to the outside and a stage left exit leads to the bedroom. When referring to the environment outside, the actors can relate to imaginary windows in the fourth wall.]

[Albert is a tall man in his late thirties, dressed in baggy green janitor pants, work boots, and a plain blue shirt. Mervin is slightly older, late thirties or early forties, dressed in a dark brown, baggy jacket and dark pants also too big for him.]

ALBERT. It's so barren out there.

MERVIN. Yes, very empty.

ALBERT. Gives me the creeps.

MERVIN. There is something unsettling about it.

ALBERT. I long for crowds of people, hoards of them milling about.

MERVIN. Wishful thinking.

ALBERT. I want to rub elbows with people. I want to smell them. Human odor tells me I am alive and connected to the world.

MERVIN. You sound lonely.

ALBERT. Yes, I am lonely. I want very much to see sweating bodies. I long to touch those bodies. I long to rub them with my own.

MERVIN. Sensual.

ALBERT. Yes, I am a sensualist. It's so empty out there. It sends chills up my spine. I'm cold. I'll die of solitary confinement.

MERVIN. I'm here.

ALBERT. Yes, but that's something else. I'm talking about something beyond us. I'm talking about social interaction. I long for a populated, active world that stimulates me. I long for a society that is vital. Look out there. There is nothing. Only sky. Where is mankind? There must be more than this.

MERVIN. At least the sun is shining.

ALBERT. Yes, it is, isn't it?

MERVIN. It's warm.

ALBERT. Yes, warm sun. Sun is healthy.

MERVIN. Yes, it is healthy. Without it plants can't grow.

ALBERT. Without it humans can't live.

MERVIN. Warm, warm sun.

ALBERT. But where are the people? Where is activity? Where is mankind? There must be more than this. There must be.

MERVIN. Yes, there must be, but what if there isn't?

ALBERT. What do you mean?

MERVIN. What if there isn't?

ALBERT. Are you trying something? You're trying something.

MERVIN. I'm not trying anything.

ALBERT. You're trying something.

MERVIN. No, I'm just posing a question.

ALBERT. It's a nasty question if you ask me.

MERVIN. I'm not trying to be nasty.

ALBERT. But you're trying something.

MERVIN. I'm not trying anything.

ALBERT. You wouldn't admit it if you were.

MERVIN. How can you say that? How can you say such a thing after the length of time you have known me?

ALBERT. I can say it.

MERVIN. You're not thinking about what you are saying.

ALBERT. That I admit.

MERVIN. Well, at long last you admit it.

ALBERT. Yes, I admit it. I do admit it.

MERVIN. Thank you for that. Thank you for admitting it.

ALBERT. You're welcome. You're very welcome. *[pause.]*If only there was a future for us all. That would make all the difference.

MERVIN. Yes, a future would make a difference.

ALBERT. A sense of things moving forward.

MERVIN. Yes, forward momentum.

ALBERT. People would have something to look forward to, have some hope, some optimism.

MERVIN. Yes, some sense of goodness in the world.

ALBERT. But, alas, that is not the case.

MERVIN. No, it is not.

ALBERT. Look at the sun.

MERVIN. Yes, the sun.

ALBERT. Hot sun.

MERVIN. Yes, hot, so hot.

ALBERT. Scorching the earth, transforming it into a desert.

MERVIN. Yes, a desert; hot like a desert.

ALBERT. The people — where are the people?

MERVIN. They're nowhere to be seen.

Raymond J. Barry

ALBERT. They're hiding from the sun in their homes.

MERVIN. Yes, like us.

ALBERT. Hiding from other people in the world. Hiding from social contact, from interaction, separate. I'm tired of it. You hear me?

MERVIN. I hear you.

ALBERT. I'm tired of being separate.

MERVIN. I'm a bit tired of it too.

ALBERT. I want to run outside into the hot sun and risk contact with other people.

MERVIN. You mustn't stay in the sun.

ALBERT. I want to crash through the doors of those ranch homes and insist upon social interaction.

MERVIN. Me too.

ALBERT. I want to argue with them and take a stand.

MERVIN. Me too.

ALBERT. I want to heighten my consciousness...

MERVIN. Yes.

ALBERT. ...by probing other minds.

MERVIN. That would be most exciting.

ALBERT. We think alike, don't we?

MERVIN. Yes, we do.

ALBERT. We seldom oppose one another. That's what I miss the most. Opposition.

MERVIN. I suppose you're right about most things.

ALBERT. Never mind that. Are you with me on this? Are we going to storm the community? Are we going out into the sun?

MERVIN. I think we are this time. I think we are.

ALBERT. I want to wear a suit. I want to look my best.

MERVIN. I think I'll stay just the way I am.

ALBERT. All right, but I'm going to change into my best outfit. I want to look presentable for the people. Just to show that my intentions are honorable.

MERVIN. So our neighbors don't think we are a couple of freaks.

ALBERT. Yes, that's exactly the reason. I don't want to alienate anyone with antisocial behavior. I want to look nice.

MERVIN. Do I look nice?

ALBERT. Oh, yes, you look perfectly fine. You won't do much of the talking anyway, so you can dress any way you like.

MERVIN. All right.

ALBERT. But I'm going to wear my suit. I want to be as charming as possible for this mission. It means a lot to me.

MERVIN. I'll stay the way I am.

ALBERT. I don't want to be insecure in any way. Looking presentable is very important.

A Piece of Cake

MERVIN. I hope I look nice.

ALBERT. This will only take a minute.

MERVIN. Take your time.

ALBERT. Just a quick change, starting with the removal of the old... *[He takes off his clothes.]*

MERVIN. I'm patient.

ALBERT....and replacing that with the new. *[Albert takes a black suit out of his closet.]*

MERVIN. I like your suit.

ALBERT. Do you? I do too. It's very smart, isn't it? It was given to me years ago by a friend. I wear it on special occasions, like this one. *[As Albert talks, he puts on his suit.]*

MERVIN. It's really nice.

ALBERT. I know.

MERVIN. I suddenly feel like a slob.

ALBERT. Don't be silly. You look perfectly fine.

MERVIN. I hope I look nice.

ALBERT. I love the way you look.

MERVIN. You're not just saying that?

ALBERT. No, I'm not just saying that. I sincerely mean what I'm saying. I have to look better because I'll do most of the talking.

MERVIN. That's probably true.

ALBERT. Besides, you're a good looking fellow, much better looking than I.

MERVIN. That's true.

ALBERT. You have that to your advantage.

MERVIN. I hadn't thought of that.

ALBERT. It takes me to remind you of your strengths. Well, are you ready?

MERVIN. Ready as I'll ever be.

ALBERT. Then let's go.

MERVIN. We're off.

[They exit.]

Act One

-

Scene Two

[Albert and Mervin have been wandering through the suburban community for hours. They are tired when they come upon a well-kept white house that is neat and pretty. The scene takes place inside the living room of that house with the front wall divider separating inside from outside. The audience can look into that living room through the fourth wall, which is the downstage side of the house; Albert and Mervin

Raymond J. Barry

approach the white picket fence of the house.]

ALBERT. This must be the place.

MERVIN. I hope so. I'm getting tired of this.

ALBERT. Be patient. There must be someone around here who wants human contact.

MERVIN. I suppose you're right.

ALBERT. They can't all be as antisocial as the others we visited.

MERVIN. I suppose. I'm still getting tired.

ALBERT. Chin up. I have a hunch this is going to be it.

MERVIN. Why don't you knock on the door or something?

ALBERT. All right. Let's go through this white picket fence and get started. Those last people were absolutely rude. It can't go on like that forever.

MERVIN. Should I knock on the door?

ALBERT. Yes, most definitely, but you let me do the talking.

[Mervin knocks on the door. Inside Ruth appears from the kitchen, an attractive woman about thirty-five, old enough to have had a long term marriage. There is a sexuality about her.. She approaches the door and looks through the peephole.]

RUTH. Who is it?

ALBERT. Just a couple of friendly neighbors.

RUTH. Yes?

ALBERT. We thought we'd drop by and interact with you a bit.

RUTH. I don't understand.

ALBERT. *[to Mervin]* This bitch is probably as difficult as the rest. *[to Ruth]* There's nothing to be afraid of, madam. We were tired of spending all our time by ourselves so we decided to visit.

RUTH. I can't let you in.

ALBERT. We want to socialize a bit, make small talk about contemporary issues, no more than that.

RUTH. I'm sorry.

ALBERT. We might even borrow a cup of sugar.

RUTH. This doesn't seem right.

ALBERT. I realize how out of the ordinary it is, but my friend and I thought we would take a chance.

RUTH. I can't allow two strange men to enter my home.

ALBERT. Without risk there is nothing gained.

RUTH. It's too much of a risk. We haven't had visitors here for years and we don't intend to begin now.

ALBERT. That's not very friendly.

RUTH. I fully realize that, but you're being awfully presumptuous coming here like this.

ALBERT. We're nice people, I assure you.

A Piece of Cake

MERVIN. Come on.

RUTH. I have nothing to say to you.

ALBERT. We mean no harm.

MERVIN. Let's go.

ALBERT. We simply want to break the ice, that's all.

MERVIN. She's just like all the rest.

ALBERT. No, I won't give up so easily.

MERVIN. She doesn't want to socialize. *[Pause, during which the men linger outside Ruth's door, wondering what to do.]* This is certainly one gigantic pain in the ass.

ALBERT. Now don't get testy.

MERVIN. But she won't let us in.

ALBERT. Things will turn out.

MERVIN. She doesn't want to socialize.

ALBERT. Maybe there's another entrance.

MERVIN. Are you crazy?

ALBERT. I'll go around to the side and find an open window.

MERVIN. We're going to find ourselves in serious trouble if you pull something like that.

ALBERT. We're not hurting anyone, are we? We just want social contact, that's all. A little social interaction won't hurt a fly. That's what's so lacking in our lives today.

RUTH. If you don't go away...

ALBERT. We're so damned isolated from one another that it's inhuman.

RUTH. ...I'll call the authorities.

MERVIN. She's calling the authorities!

ALBERT. Keep her busy. I'm going around back.

MERVIN. What should I say?

ALBERT. Anything as long as she's preoccupied.

MERVIN. I don't know what to say.

ALBERT. Think of something.

MERVIN. The neighbors might come.

ALBERT. Don't be silly. You know better than that. I'm going around back. *[He leaves.]*

MERVIN. All right. *[Pause; to Ruth on the other side of door.]* I guess you think we're a couple of burglars or even worse than that, what with all the serial murderers and mass murderers around nowadays, but I assure you that we're just a couple of lonely guys who have been isolated too long and have decided to take tangible steps toward solving that problem. It's probably the same with you, isn't it?

RUTH. You'll have to go now. Please.

MERVIN. Don't be afraid. You're separating yourself from the world just as we did. We mean absolutely no harm. It's time someone took initiative and broke through the barriers that have destroyed the social

Raymond J. Barry

fiber of our community.

RUTH. I don't want anyone in my home, do you hear?

MERVIN. People don't care about each other enough. Everyone is off by themselves without the normal support system that people need. My friend and I wish to communicate with others.

RUTH. I want to be alone. Please respect my wishes.

MERVIN. We just happened to pass by and noticed your lovely house. It's an attractive dwelling. You have excellent taste indeed.

RUTH. Thank you. I accept that as a compliment.

MERVIN. It is a compliment. A sincere compliment. You have a beautiful home. You must be very optimistic to have built such a lovely place. It reflects a positive attitude toward life.

RUTH. Thank you.

MERVIN. Your voice sounds kind. I like that. Kind people have always been a favorite of mine. Ever since I was a little boy, trying to figure out what life was all about, somehow I always gravitated towards kindness.

RUTH. You sound kind, too.

MERVIN. Oh, I am kind. I'm the kindest person. I've never injured anyone in my whole life, if that's at all possible. At least I think I haven't. I've tried my best not to be mean to anyone and I truly believe I have succeeded. *[In the dull light we see the silhouette of Albert climbing through the back window quietly. Ruth doesn't see him. His torso dangles into the living room while the lights come up gradually.]*

RUTH. You don't sound like a person who would want to hurt anybody.

[Albert has entered the room.]

ALBERT. He isn't.

RUTH. How dare you! How dare you! How on earth did you get in here?

ALBERT. Don't get excited please. I climbed through the window. I took that liberty. I don't mean any harm. My friend and I simply want to socialize, that's all.

RUTH. What exactly do you mean by... socialize?

ALBERT. You know, what people used to do in the old days. We used to talk to each other, argue about issues, drop over to each other's homes, tell each other stories — in short, share common experiences, thoughts, with one another. Allow me to introduce my friend. You'll like him. He's a harmless sort of fellow.

RUTH. I feel I have no choice.

ALBERT. No, you do have a choice. This is your home and we are guests in your home. Your home is your castle and we don't mean to intrude. *[Albert goes to the door, unlocks it, opens it and allows Mervin to enter.]*

MERVIN. Hi.

ALBERT. Mervin. This is... What is your name?

RUTH. Ruth. Ruth Pumpernickel.

MERVIN. That's a bread, isn't it, some sort of bread?

A Piece of Cake

RUTH. Yes, it's the name of a bread.

MERVIN. *[laughs uproariously]* The name of a bread. That's funny.

ALBERT. Please don't be rude, Mervin.

MERVIN. All right.

ALBERT. We're not here to be rude.

MERVIN. I'm sorry.

ALBERT. No, apologize to Ruth.

MERVIN. I'm sorry, Ruth.

ALBERT. May we call you by your first name?

RUTH. Yes, of course.

[pause]

ALBERT. Well, Ruth, nice home you've got here.

RUTH. Thank you.

ALBERT. May we sit for a while?

RUTH. I have no choice.

ALBERT. No, that is not true. This is your home and we are guests. We do not mean to intrude upon you. We just want to socialize. We've been lonely — very lonely.

RUTH. That's apparent.

ALBERT. Yes, it is apparent. It seems to be the human condition nowadays. May we sit?

RUTH. Yes, I suppose.

MERVIN. Thank you, Ma'am.

RUTH. You're welcome.

ALBERT. Well, what should we interact on?

RUTH. I don't have the vaguest.

ALBERT. Really? There must be something pressing against your brain. Come on, Ruth, out with it. There are so many poignant issues today. There must be something upon which we can have an exchange, some pertinent subject that merits our attention.

RUTH. I don't think so.

ALBERT. Gosh, the world is strange today, isn't it? Everyone is so obedient and cooperative. What a world we live in. No dialogue at all taking place between people, no argument over contemporary issued. No one cares anymore. What a disgrace! And we're not doing anything about it. No one speaks up. What do you think about that?

RUTH. Nothing.

ALBERT. Typical, typical. That's the way today. Nobody has anything to say.

RUTH. I certainly don't.

ALBERT. What about you, Mervin? What have you to say?

MERVIN. It's terrible.

ALBERT. Yes, it is, isn't it? But Mervin here is no help since he always agrees with me. He never argues. A nice man really, this fellow, Mervin,

Raymond J. Barry

but "nice" isn't enough. There has to be opinion. There has to be some difference of opinion so that a consensus can be arrived at. That has to happen from the grass roots, from the suburban housewife, say, who holds the collective consciousness within her bosom. Yes, the housewife must be heard. Her opinions must be heard.

MERVIN. I love the way you talk.

ALBERT. Thank you, Mervin. Hopefully it will encourage others to do the same. I love your home, Ruth. You have excellent taste.

RUTH. Thank you.

MERVIN. Could I have something cold to drink? We've been walking all day in the sun.

RUTH. Yes, of course.

ALBERT. We hate to trouble you.

RUTH. No trouble.

ALBERT. You know how it is when it gets hot. That sun is murder.

RUTH. I'll get you something. *[Ruth exits to the kitchen.]*

MERVIN. Don't you think we should go in there with her?

ALBERT. Relax. Ruth isn't our enemy. She's our neighbor. We have to establish trust with her or our mission will be meaningless.

MERVIN. But we forced our way into her home.

ALBERT. I'm not going to treat her like a house prisoner. She wouldn't interact socially if we did that to her. Ruth will come our way.

RUTH. *[re-enters]* Here's some juice. I trust that will suffice.

MERVIN. Thanks a lot.

ALBERT. Mervin was just saying that we forced ourselves into your home, Ruth. What is your opinion about that?

RUTH. You did.

ALBERT. Yes, but it seemed to be the expedient way to socialize. I hope you understand. That was our motive - nothing more than that.

RUTH. I see. Of course, you understand I'm frightened to death by your methods.

ALBERT. That is unfortunate. Is there anything we can do to make you feel more comfortable?

RUTH. None other than taking a quick exit.

ALBERT. That I cannot agree to as I am starved for titillating conversation, Ruth. *[pause]* So, what is your opinion about our society today?

RUTH. I have no opinion.

ALBERT. You have no opinion? None at all? Surely you must have an opinion.

MERVIN. She has no point of view.

ALBERT. Yes, she has no point of view. But some opinion must be had. Some statement must be made. Don't you think so, Ruth?

RUTH. No, I have no opinion.

A Piece of Cake

ALBERT. You can't continue hiding what you think, madam. People simply must venture from their homes to speak out. Mervin and I did exactly that.

MERVIN. We took a risk.

ALBERT. Yes, we took the risk to make contact and affect people, to probe their minds, to stimulate conversation about important issues of the day.

MERVIN. We're trying to be good neighbors.

ALBERT. We are attempting to light a fire under your ass, woman. You can't hide forever.

MERVIN. We're community minded.

ALBERT. Yes, we have social conscience.

MERVIN. We like you.

ALBERT. We are high-leveled men who care about the world in which we live.

MERVIN. You're a nice person.

ALBERT. We care about our fellow humans...

MERVIN. We like what you're about...

ALBERT. ...and we want you to care since you are our neighbor.

MERVIN. ...even though you are non-communicative.

RUTH. Isn't everyone today?

ALBERT. Yes, that's what he's saying. We're all hiding in our homes. Television is our only contact with the outside world.

RUTH. Did the both of you break into my home to complain to me about my television?

MERVIN. Please, please, don't belittle this mission of ours, Ruth.

RUTH. You've got some nerve coming in here like this.

ALBERT. There is a great deal at stake and we all know it.

RUTH. You bet there's a great deal at stake. What do you expect...

MERVIN. We are not frivolous people.

RUTH. ...that I'll serve tea and confess all of my sins

ALBERT. We have embarked upon a serious mission at great risk.

RUTH. I'm outraged by this intrusion.

MERVIN. We are well aware of the threat of the authorities.

RUTH. Communication with a couple of fools doesn't interest me. You're both repulsive. I wish you would leave now.

[Buford walks in, a corporate, good-looking man in his late thirties to early forties, surprised at the presence of Albert and Mervin. He immediately takes off his suit coat and hangs it in his closet. There is an air of familiarity about him, indicating that he is the man of the house.]

BUFORD. Hello.

ALBERT. Hello.

MERVIN. Hello.

RUTH. Thank God you're here. These men broke in. I can't get them out.

Raymond J. Barry

I've been frightened to death. *[Ruth runs to Buford's protective embrace.]*

ALBERT. We can explain everything. We were simply trying to discuss current issues with your wife. I... er... we don't mean any harm. You see... we aaa... we came out of our house and went visiting. We ended up here. Isn't that right, Mervin?

MERVIN. Right.

BUFORD. I see. Won't you sit down?

[BLACKOUT.]

Act One
-
Scene Three

[Lights come up. All four characters sit around a dinner table laughing uproariously. BUFORD is telling a joke. RUTH is joining in the telling of it. ALBERT and MERVIN are laughing huge belly laughs. There is prodigious eating of food and drinking of wine.]

BUFORD. So I am in the file room and she comes in and sits right down on it.

RUTH. He's such a joker. *[laughing]* Oh, I can't get a hold of myself. It's too, too funny.

BUFORD. Sometimes that office just fractures me with its contradictions. *[laughing]* It is too funny, too, too funny for words.

MERVIN. It is... *[laughing]*... too, too funny. Yes it is.

ALBERT. Go on, Buford, tell us some more. *[laughter]*

BUFORD. So the next day they deliver a message that all races must be segregated while working. You know, separate offices for each one, blacks in one office, whites in another and so on... and I say to the man who's passing down the order, we'll do better than that. We'll put everyone in a separate building. *[laughter]* Oh God, it's funny, just funny as hell.

[The loud laughter trickles to a halt, after which there is an uncomfortable silence.]

ALBERT. Hasn't it been awfully hot lately?

BUFORD. Yes, the world is baking before our very eyes.

ALBERT. The foliage on the trees was burned off from the last bomb blast.

BUFORD. Yes, terrible thing really.

ALBERT. Yes, I miss the greenery.

BUFORD. I saw a bit of greenery last month.

ALBERT. We all miss the greenery.

BUFORD. A refreshing sight, greenery.

A Piece of Cake

ALBERT. The youngsters who grew up without greenery are different somehow.

BUFORD. Greenery brings out the poetry in me.

ALBERT. They seem so unenlightened, no creativity.

MERVIN. I saw a flower once.

BUFORD. A flower?

RUTH. Where?

MERVIN. It was a chrysanthemum, I believe, or at least a related species, a mutation of some kind from that family. It was beautiful. I tried to hide it by piling rocks around its roots, but it did no good. The next day its stem had been crushed by one of those wandering bands of children. I saw them running away as I approached.

ALBERT. The ignorance we have to deal with today. It's just too amazing. Say, Ruth, this veal is absolutely wonderful.

BUFORD. Thanks. It's my own recipe.

ALBERT. Don't you love it, Mervin?

MERVIN. Yes, I love it.

ALBERT. Say Buford, how do folks in your office feel about the bomb?

BUFORD. Oh... why, they think it's an absolute blast. *[laughter]* And it is, I might add. No, seriously speaking, it's a terrible threat to mankind. It really is, but what can one do but carry on. Carry on is what I say and carry on is what I intend to do. Everything is so eerie today as if some strange force is controlling us. We're being watched. And all those diseases breaking out everywhere. Look what happened to the homosexual population. Totally eliminated by one unknown disease. I'd be willing to bet that was no accident.

ALBERT. Got rid of the cocksuckers.

[Everyone laughs but Buford.]

BUFORD. But if it's they first, who could be next?

MERVIN. How do you know what you're saying is true?

BUFORD. They appropriated nothing for a cure for the virus, did they?

MERVIN. They started the epidemic? You don't know that for sure.

ALBERT. But it's an interesting idea, isn't it?

BUFORD. That's how the whole thing started.

MERVIN. You just heard it but you don't know for sure.

ALBERT. It could be true.

BUFORD. Homosexual people were singled out.

ALBERT. Such experiments have taken place. That much we know.

RUTH. Watch what you say.

ALBERT. We're interested in the big issues.

MERVIN. Do you have a disease, Ruth?

RUTH. It's time for you and your "buddy" to change the subject.

ALBERT. That's enough, Mervin.

BUFORD. It's good you came over.

Raymond J. Barry

ALBERT. Mervin and I knew we were doing something important when we left the house today.

BUFORD. Ruth and I haven't spoken to a soul in the neighborhood for years.

MERVIN. Months have gone by without us seeing or speaking to anyone.

RUTH. Makes one think. Something is awry these days.

BUFORD. Ruth, would you fetch some cake for our guests?

RUTH. Would you be interested in some cake?

MERVIN. Some cake?

BUFORD. Perhaps cake will settle your meal.

ALBERT. Some... cake?

RUTH. Yes, some cake.

BUFORD. What do you say, gentlemen?

RUTH. We have... cake.

BUFORD. A piece of cake to settle your dinner?

ALBERT. Where did you get... cake?

RUTH. Buford managed it.

BUFORD. Never mind where it came from.

RUTH. He has connections.

MERVIN. Cake connections?

BUFORD. We have cake, that's all.

MERVIN. Yes, I'd like some cake. Albert would too.

ALBERT. I'll speak for myself, thank you, Mervin.

RUTH. Well, you do want some cake, don't you?

ALBERT. Yes, I'll have some cake.

[Ruth exits to the kitchen. The three men sit uncomfortably in silence. Finally, Buford breaks the ice.]

BUFORD. The little wife. I love her.

MERVIN. I'm getting to like her myself.

ALBERT. She's got something going for herself.

MERVIN. Now I know why she looks so good. She's eating the right food.

[Again there is an uncomfortable silence.]

ALBERT. What other complaints do you have?

BUFORD. Complaints?

ALBERT. Yes, things you notice.

BUFORD. It's an odd way to put it. Complaints?

MERVIN. We certainly don't mean it to be odd.

BUFORD. "We"?

ALBERT. Yes, Mervin and myself don't mean it that way.

BUFORD. What way?

ALBERT. Oh, I don't know.

BUFORD. It sounded strange. I'm not complaining.

ALBERT. More wine?

BUFORD. No, thank you.

A Piece of Cake

MERVIN. I'll have some.

ALBERT. You've had enough, Mervin.

BUFORD. I have a good life.

MERVIN. But I want some more wine.

ALBERT. Dammit, Mervin, you've had enough.

BUFORD. What do you expect me to do, be honest with you? How do I know who's listening?

MERVIN. But I only had a few glasses.

ALBERT. That's enough now. We've got work to do.

MERVIN. Okay. Okay.

[A bomb blasts in the far distance. There is a long silence.]

BUFORD. What kind of work?

MERVIN. Oh, you know, visiting people, talking.

BUFORD. I see.

RUTH. *[Re-enters with the cake]* Here we are. Plenty for everyone.

BUFORD. Thank you, sweetheart.

MERVIN. Good-looking cake.

ALBERT. Chocolate.

MERVIN. I haven't had cake since I can remember.

RUTH. Buford gets it.

BUFORD. That's enough, dear, don't be talking about our trade secrets.

RUTH. It's around, that's all.

BUFORD. We have cake. That's all there is to it. Just cake.

MERVIN. Good cake.

BUFORD. Mervin was just explaining what kind of work they do, honey.

RUTH. Oh, really? I'd be interested in that.

MERVIN. I forgot what I was going to say.

ALBERT. Whatta dope.

MERVIN. Well, everybody was talking at once. I lost my train of thought.

ALBERT. Ha, "train of thought" he calls it!

MERVIN. I was thinking about the cake. Where did you get the cake?

BUFORD. Mervin, you're enjoying the cake, aren't you?

MERVIN. There's some kind of illegal business going on in this household.

BUFORD. What does it matter where it came from?

MERVIN. I can smell something illegal, some special privileges with this cake.

BUFORD. We're sharing the cake with you, aren't we?

MERVIN. Albert, maybe we can take the cake with us. Ask them.

[uncomfortable pause]

BUFORD. May I ask a serious question?

ALBERT. Yes, of course.

RUTH. I know what you're going to ask.

BUFORD. I bet you do. Sirs, I would like to ask for whom do you work?

Raymond J. Barry

[Albert and Mervin stand up abruptly, horrified at this question.] There, there, gentlemen. There's no need to be alarmed. I'm, after all, asking a simple question that should offer no particular reason for this kind of reaction. What's it all about? Why are you so upset all of a sudden?

RUTH. I mistrusted them right from the beginning.

BUFORD. Why?

RUTH. Why? Look how they gained access to our home.

BUFORD. Contain yourself, dear.

RUTH. The big one over there climbed through the living room window, for goodness sake.

BUFORD. Lower your voice, dear.

RUTH. You call that normal "encounter" with another human being? I don't.

BUFORD. We can discuss this rationally, can't we?

RUTH. We can if we both are in a rational mood, but I happen to be outraged by this whole thing, completely outraged, completely and totally outraged. These men are as phony as can be.

BUFORD. Is this true? I feel it's true. Is it true?

MERVIN. We are lonely, that's all, and had the need for human contact.

BUFORD. Who do you work for?

MERVIN. "Work for"?

ALBERT. We aren't working for anyone.

BUFORD. Then why are you asking questions?

MERVIN. Albert and I were starved for conversation.

BUFORD. I'm beginning not to believe that.

ALBERT. It's true. We were lonely.

MERVIN. Could I have some little thing to drink? I mean aside from wine. Something stronger.

BUFORD. Yes, of course. Get him something, won't you, dear?

RUTH. I want to listen!

BUFORD. Yes, of course.

RUTH. Stop sending me on all these errands!

BUFORD. Yes, of course.

ALBERT. Chauvinist. Absolute chauvinist.

BUFORD. I think that's quite enough out of you, quite enough.

RUTH. As you say, darling.

MERVIN. Where's my drink? I can't say a thing without my drink.

[Buford goes to the bar and pours him a drink.]

ALBERT. Stop making such a fuss.

MERVIN. You must get my drink for me. You must.

ALBERT. Mervin can give an explanation.

BUFORD. I do wish one of you would. *[He hands Mervin a stronger drink.]*

ALBERT. You tell the story, Mervin.

BUFORD. I wish one of you would damn well start or I'll throw both of you

A Piece of Cake

the hell out.

ALBERT. He's getting impatient.

MERVIN. Okay, I'll begin. You see, we are both sharing the same house and because of that we have spent...

ALBERT....a lot of time together.

MERVIN. Are you explaining or am I?

ALBERT. We can both tell it.

MERVIN. You have some nerve, Albert.

ALBERT. It's our shared experience.

MERVIN. *[He gathers himself to begin again.]*And because we spend a lot of time together...

ALBERT. We naturally communicate to each other more than...

MERVIN. That's hardly the point.

ALBERT. It depends upon the slant you take.

MERVIN. Communication is only part of my explanation. I don't know what your explanation is, but it's only part of my explanation. You know what my explanation is now, don't you?

ALBERT. Don't tell that!

MERVIN. Why not? I'm not ashamed.

ALBERT. I know that. Nobody is suggesting that you would be ashamed.

MERVIN. I'm tired of hiding.

RUTH. Hiding from what?

BUFORD. Don't interrupt him. He'll come out with it in his own time.

RUTH. Hiding from what?

BUFORD. Do you hear me? Don't interrupt him.

RUTH. Don't tell me what to do.

MERVIN. Stop interrupting me, please.

BUFORD. Please, someone say something.

MERVIN. I will.

ALBERT. Our volunteer will begin. Begin, Mervin. Speak. Shed some light on the subject. Everybody stop talking. Let him take his time now.

RUTH. Begin.

MERVIN. Life has been unbearable.

ALBERT. It has been sad, but it seemed at first normal.

MERVIN. First a few friends began to die off.

ALBERT. We thought nothing of it.

MERVIN. People do die.

ALBERT. They simply go.

MERVIN. Never to return again.

ALBERT. It seemed normal.

MERVIN. Jose Lope de Vega died first.

ALBERT. Yes, I think you're right, Mervin.

MERVIN. He was the very first.

ALBERT. We thought nothing of it aside from the sadness of it all. He

Raymond J. Barry

died of pneumonia; a little strange perhaps in the middle of summer.

MERVIN. We let it pass.

ALBERT. There was no reason why we should have believed anything strange was going on.

MERVIN. Life went on as usual.

ALBERT. Until we began to notice other people were disappearing.

MERVIN. All of our friends were killed.

ALBERT. Dead forever and gone from the face of the earth.

MERVIN. And only for one reason, their sexual preference.

RUTH. They're a couple of queers!

ALBERT. That's enough, Mervin!

BUFORD. Yes, I knew something was odd about them. I knew it.

MERVIN. Would anybody like some more cake?

BUFORD. No, Mervin, no more cake!!!

[A tense standoff. The last remark has put a cloud over the room.]

ALBERT. You've put your foot into it, Mervin.

MERVIN. I'm sorry.

BUFORD. Rotten queers.

RUTH. These filthy queers have some nerve coming in here like this.

ALBERT. We've been so lonely. We've been hiding, you see, and terribly lonely.

BUFORD. Despicable low life.

MERVIN. Don't call us that.

ALBERT. Don't report us, please. Don't. It doesn't make sense. There are so few of us left. We can't make a difference to anyone.

RUTH. Disgusting.

MERVIN. Please don't be so harsh with us.

RUTH. What about the virus? How do you know we haven't caught it from you?

ALBERT. We only have the usual diseases that everyone has.

RUTH. You sat down with us and shared our cake.

ALBERT. We haven't been infected with the virus.

MERVIN. No. We don't have it. They missed us.

BUFORD. You can't be sure.

RUTH. You sat down with us and shared our cake. Now we could be infected.

ALBERT. We don't deserve this treatment. We're not that different from you. We eat, sleep, try to live in this crazy world.

RUTH. Break into the house, intrude upon people.

ALBERT. Only to make contact. Human contact.

MERVIN. Albert, maybe we can take the cake with us. Maybe they won't mind. Ask them.

BUFORD. You were on your way out, I believe.

ALBERT. All right, Mervin. I'll ask. Buford and Ruth, can we take the remains of the cake home with us? It would mean a lot to Mervin, and seeing as how you seem to have access to more cake, perhaps you could allow us to have this one.

RUTH. This is the only cake we have.

MERVIN. Somehow I don't believe you. There's more cake around here somewhere.

BUFORD. You can't take the cake out of the house. Someone will see you.

ALBERT. We'll take the risk if you'll give it to us.

RUTH. Get out of this house and leave the cake here.

MERVIN. Selfish bitch.

RUTH. Out of here, I say.

MERVIN. You want us to leave?

BUFORD. You'd better leave, without the cake.

RUTH. Out now!

ALBERT. We'll go, but we'll be seeing a lot of each other.

BUFORD. You'd better leave.

MERVIN. Goodbye and thanks so much for the cake.

ALBERT. We want to go anyway.

MERVIN. I don't want to go.

RUTH. Don't think of staying now. You're on your way out.

BUFORD. Get out of here before someone sees you.

MERVIN. We don't like to be pushed out. Your wife is pushing us out.

BUFORD. You were leaving.

MERVIN. Yes, we must go; out into the sun.

ALBERT. Yes, out into the hot sun. Come on, Mervin, we've overstayed our welcome.

[They exit. lights out.]

Act One

-

Scene Four

[lights up; Buford and Ruth's apartment.]

RUTH. I want that window gated. Anyone who would do such a thing has to be off the beam.

BUFORD. Couldn't we just hug for a bit on the bed?

RUTH. You know we don't share the same bed together. It's dangerous. *[pause]* But why us? What could their interest be in us?

BUFORD. They came by chance. We were nice to them, that's all.

RUTH. You were nice to them.

BUFORD. You gave them cake. *[pause]* Couldn't we just caress?

RUTH. No, we cannot. If they were found in our house we could be implicated.

Raymond J. Barry

BUFORD. We won't catch anything. I don't have a rash. *[He approaches her.]* They weren't discovered in our house, were they?

RUTH. What about me? I'm contagious too.

BUFORD. I'll be careful. I'm not broken out. It's been so long. *[He approaches her.]*

RUTH. They must never again be part of our lives. *[He approaches her. She holds him at bay.]* Stop being silly. You know it would be dangerous.

BUFORD. But I'm safe today. I'm not broken out.

RUTH. There's got to be some way to deal with them.

BUFORD. Darling, you're allowing this thing to run away with you. *[He approaches her. She crosses to the other side of the room.]*

RUTH. Despicable characters, sex perverts. They should have their privates removed. *[He continues to make advances.]* Please! Stop approaching me! We can't do it.

BUFORD. I can't stand not having it for so long. It's inhuman. Do me with your mouth. We can't get anything from that.

RUTH. Don't push. Don't be pushy. You're too damned pushy. *[She dodges his advances.]* We should tell someone about them.

BUFORD. No, Ruth. That's the wrong thing to do. People mustn't tell on each other.

RUTH. What do you suggest? That we go to their house and become bosom buddies?

BUFORD. We can't go around turning people in.

RUTH. They are bound to find out anyway.

BUFORD. It would be wrong.

RUTH. I don't trust them.

BUFORD. Make love to me with your mouth.

RUTH. Can't you suggest anything?

BUFORD. No. Come to bed.

RUTH. No, just sit. *[He approaches her.]* I said sit. *[He sits.]*

BUFORD. Please take care of me. I'm so lonely. Why are you so interested in them?

RUTH. One of them climbed through our window.

BUFORD. Is that really so important?

RUTH. To me it is. You allow this sort of thing to happen once and it'll happen again.

BUFORD. You sound so concerned.

RUTH. I am concerned. People can't be climbing through our window every time the sun gets to them.

BUFORD. It won't happen again. They know us now. They'll knock on our door. Now come to me.

RUTH. I want to tell someone. *[She goes to him, gets down on her knees.]*

BUFORD. Forget it and take care of me for now.

[Ruth unbuttons his fly, the lights go down.]

A Piece of Cake

Act One

-

Scene Five

[Lights up; Ruth and Buford's apartment. There is a portly gentleman visiting who has brought with him boxes and boxes of bakery goods; cakes, cookies, etc. He is preferably an overweight black man, but the part could be played by a heavy white person as well.]

HERMAN. The goods are all fresh. You folks will have a ball. I'm sure of that. Sweets for everyone.

BUFORD. You're a clever one.

RUTH. A good friend.

HERMAN. I enjoy doing business with folks I like.

RUTH. You're very kind.

BUFORD. Would you like something sweet while you're here?

HERMAN. Oh, no, thank you. I have to watch my waistline.

RUTH. You have discipline, don't you?

HERMAN. Well, you might say so, but generally speaking I'm an eater.

BUFORD. A regular jolly fat man is what you seem to be.

HERMAN. Ha. I suppose so.

[Pause.]

RUTH. We have some information for you.

BUFORD. Ruth...

RUTH. Our home was invaded by two homosexual males.

BUFORD. They were diseased, at least according to what they told us.

HERMAN. Everyone is diseased today. That's common.

RUTH. They may be infected with the virus.

HERMAN. Probably they are. Why did they come here?

RUTH. They came here by chance.

HERMAN. Do they know you?

RUTH. Of course not!

BUFORD. They picked our house out by some whim.

RUTH. They said they wanted to discuss issues.

HERMAN. What issues?

BUFORD. Current events.

HERMAN. What scum.

RUTH. What troubles me is that they escaped. How could they have been overlooked?

HERMAN. A few escaped, but we're slowly closing in on them.

RUTH. Despicable little queers.

HERMAN. Why did you wait so long to tell me?

Raymond J. Barry

RUTH. We're telling you now.

HERMAN. You could have called me immediately.

BUFORD. We were... unsure what to do.

RUTH. Buford told me not to tell you. He explained to me that we have to be loyal and not to inform on anyone.

HERMAN. Did you say that, Buford?

BUFORD. Well, not exactly... I...

RUTH. You did say that, Buford.

BUFORD. All right. I said it.

HERMAN. You should have told me immediately. There's going to be trouble.

BUFORD. What kind of trouble?

HERMAN. I'll have to confer with my colleagues, but there may be a consequences.

BUFORD. We gave you the information.

RUTH. I did. You didn't.

BUFORD. You disloyal little bitch.

RUTH. You got yourself into this. You should have known better.

HERMAN. I think I'll have a pastry after all. *[He reaches into a box full of pastries and begins eating.]* You know, Buford, for all I know you could be a homosexual yourself.

BUFORD. Don't give me that.

HERMAN. What kind of a lover is he, Ruth?

RUTH. Well... uh...

HERMAN. You can tell me.

RUTH. Well, you know how it is...

HERMAN. Yes, I know how it is.

RUTH. No one has sex anymore.

BUFORD. Who do you think you are to ask my wife a question like that?

HERMAN. Does Buford engage in oral sex?

BUFORD. What kind of an animal are you?

HERMAN. Just doing my job. What about it, Ruth? Does Buford engage in oral sex?

RUTH. Yes... He wants oral sex... from me.

HERMAN. Then he could be a homosexual himself, couldn't he?

BUFORD. But we're diseased!

HERMAN. It's just a possibility, that's all.

BUFORD. We can't indulge in usual sex. We're infected; we would kill each other.

HERMAN. This pastry is good, very good.

BUFORD. What have you done, Ruth? You've turned this all around. I'm not the guilty one here. They are. I shouldn't stand accused here. They should.

RUTH. A person has to do what a person has to do nowadays.

A Piece of Cake

BUFORD. But look at what you've done. You have turned against me, for God's sake. After all we've been through.

RUTH. It's a question of priorities.

BUFORD. You're so cold, so very cold.

HERMAN. You should have known better, Buford.

BUFORD. It was a confusing situation when I arrived home from work.

HERMAN. I should have been informed sooner.

BUFORD. They were already here with my wife, and I didn't know what to make of it.

HERMAN. You're saying Ruth encountered them first?

RUTH. Yes, but it was a tricky situation. You see, one of them jumped through my window and the situation seemed a bit dangerous. I was left in a very uncertain frame of mind.

HERMAN. You were uncertain?

RUTH. Very uncertain... Not uncertain about my loyalty, mind you, but uncertain nonetheless.

HERMAN. Uncertain nonetheless?

RUTH. Yes.

[Herman reaches for another pastry.]

HERMAN. These pastries are certainly delicious. I'm certain of that, truly certain of that.

RUTH. Truly certain of the pastry?

HERMAN. Yes, truly certain.

BUFORD. So you see, Inspector...

HERMAN. Why do you call me Inspector? I'm not an inspector.

BUFORD. I'm trying to be respectful.

HERMAN. I'm not an inspector. That requires a special kind of training. I simply provide cakes, bakery goods for you. Nothing more. I'm not an inspector. I don't do any inspecting. I provide bakery goods.

BUFORD. The point I was trying to make was that the situation was confusing at best.

HERMAN. A real friendship was beginning to evolve, was it?

BUFORD. Not a friendship.

HERMAN. This is wonderful pastry.

BUFORD. More of a curiosity.

HERMAN. I love the taste of this pastry.

BUFORD. I'm loyal.

HERMAN. You just delayed a bit.

BUFORD. Just a bit... out of confusion. You can be sure of that. I would have reacted sooner if only I was sure who they were. There was no way of knowing.

HERMAN. You can't tell an effeminate male when you see one?

BUFORD. Not always. These weren't effeminate. They seemed a bit strange, but they weren't effeminate. They seemed like men.

Raymond J. Barry

HERMAN. Do you know, Buford, that you are somewhat effeminate?

BUFORD. I... am?

HERMAN. I love this pastry. I'll have another. *[He reaches for another.]*

BUFORD. I... wasn't aware of that.

HERMAN. Well, one seldom is. Your manner, however, is quite effeminate.

BUFORD. I always felt like a man.

HERMAN. Look at yourself now, for example. How you snivel and carry on in your defense.

BUFORD. I'm a man though.

HERMAN. You can hardly call that a man's behavior.

BUFORD. Sexually I'm a man. I desire my wife.

HERMAN. This pastry is good.

BUFORD. We can't have intercourse, that's all. We're both diseased.

HERMAN. If you keep this subversive behavior up you'll pay the price.

BUFORD. If you do that to me it would be unjustified. I'm a man I tell you. I'm a complete man!

HERMAN. Any children?

BUFORD. You pig! *[Buford grabs him by the throat.]*

[simultaneous]

RUTH.	**BUFORD.**
No, Buford, don't! You're only making things worse! My God, Buford, you're making things worse. Stop it! Stop it!	Look at you accusing me! You fat blob of pig meat! I'm a complete man. I tell you. I'm a man, not a queer! I'll kill you! I'll kill you!

[Herman rolls around the floor with Buford on top of him, grappling as they knock into furniture and boxes of baked goods flying in every direction. Buford rises to his feet.]

BUFORD. You fat pig! Who's the real man now, huh? You pig. Get up. Get up!

HERMAN. You knocked the pastry out of my mouth. *[Herman starts to laugh. Buford is slowly won over and begins to laugh too. Herman rises to his feet.]*

HERMAN. I need my pastry, you know. You have quite a temper there, Buford; a real man's temper. Have to be careful about what I say to you. You're compensating for something. That's what men do, you know. The more woman in a man, the more he has to make up for it and the most obvious way is to resort to physical violence.

BUFORD. I'm not usually a violent man.

HERMAN. Well, apparently this discussion touched a nerve.

RUTH. You completely lost control, Buford.

BUFORD. Look, I apologize. You both have been digging at me and I couldn't hold it in any longer. I'm loyal as much as anyone.

HERMAN. We'll see what comes of this.

RUTH. Just remember I was the one who told you.

BUFORD. The more I defend myself, the more guilty I become.

HERMAN. I'll be in touch with both of you. In the meantime, keep the cake.

[Herman exits. Ruth and Buford are alone. Buford paces while Ruth sits. Silence for a long time.]

BUFORD. You violated a trust between us.

RUTH. Don't blame me.

BUFORD. No telling what will come of this now.

RUTH. It's out of our hands.

BUFORD. He doesn't believe me.

RUTH. Just continue as if nothing happened.

BUFORD. But something did happen, something very dangerous happened.

RUTH. He believes you. He just questions the delay.

BUFORD. You put me in a bad position with him.

RUTH. I had to protect myself. I'm sorry, but your position on this matter is dangerous.

BUFORD. Your own skin comes first.

RUTH. That's not fair to me.

BUFORD. Is that how it is?

RUTH. I care for you, but I'm not going down the tubes with anyone.

BUFORD. That's fine, but two can play at this game. You overstepped boundaries this time.

RUTH. What do you mean by that?

BUFORD. We'll see what happens. *[He changes his clothes.]*

RUTH. Where are you going?

BUFORD. I'm going to take care of business.

RUTH. What business?

BUFORD. You'll find out.

RUTH. No, really. What business?

BUFORD. You're not my confidant anymore.

RUTH. Don't be foolish. Talk to me. Where are you going?

BUFORD. I'm going to straighten a few things out with those two men.

RUTH. Don't try to find them.

BUFORD. You started this.

RUTH. There'll be trouble.

BUFORD. Now I'm going to finish it.

RUTH. You don't want to be implicated.

BUFORD. I'm already implicated, thanks to you. *[He leaves.]*

Raymond J. Barry

Act Two

-

Scene One

[Mervin and Albert in their own home. There is a far away explosion.]

ALBERT. There's bombing again.
MERVIN. It gets on my nerves. *[Mervin paces. Albert sits at the table.]*
ALBERT. Why don't you relax? Just sit down and relax.
MERVIN. I'm nervous.
ALBERT. You're always nervous.
MERVIN. No, I'm not. That's not true and you know it.
ALBERT. You always seem to be fidgeting.
MERVIN. What do you mean, "fidgeting"?
ALBERT. You should see yourself sometimes. That's why Ruth and Buford became suspicious.
MERVIN. I'm not always fidgeting.
ALBERT. You were so nervous the whole time and constantly eating cake.
MERVIN. Sometimes I'm very calm.
ALBERT. They suspected we were hiding something.
MERVIN. I did my best, for goodness sake.
ALBERT. Your best wasn't good enough. You seemed desperate.
MERVIN. I am desperate.
ALBERT. Well, relax.
MERVIN. I want to be normal.
ALBERT. We're on the right side.
MERVIN. I don't feel normal.
ALBERT. We've been very clever.
MERVIN. We're so out of touch.
ALBERT. Everyone is out of touch.
MERVIN. But it's driving me crazy.
ALBERT. Take it easy.
MERVIN. I can't take it easy.
ALBERT. We had contact with Ruth and Buford, didn't we? At least we had contact. We did what we were told.
MERVIN. You had to break into their house.
ALBERT. It turned out all right, didn't it?
MERVIN. Up to a point.
ALBERT. You got some good cake.
MERVIN. I can't stand it.
ALBERT. What do you propose?
MERVIN. I don't know. I just don't know.
ALBERT. At least we're not infected.
MERVIN. How do we know that? We can't tell that for sure. They could

A Piece of Cake

contaminate our water. There are any number of ways they could get rid of us.

ALBERT. Stop the paranoia.

MERVIN. It would be very easy to single us out and eliminate us.

ALBERT. We're on the right side.

MERVIN. One day spots on our skin appear and we know they have no use for us anymore. It's just a matter of time.

ALBERT. They still have use for us.

MERVIN. When they are finished with us, goodness knows what they'll do.

ALBERT. What happens will happen.

MERVIN. You mean we shouldn't try to affect anything?

ALBERT. We never do anyway. Might as well just sit.

MERVIN. Just sit around.

ALBERT. Yes, that's the best thing.

MERVIN. All right. *[They sit for forty counts.]* This isn't doing much for me.

ALBERT. Me neither.

MERVIN. Should we show some affection for each other? Some emotional expression that represents some depth of feeling for each other.

ALBERT. I suppose it'll be all right.

[They embrace and kiss.]

MERVIN. That was nice.

ALBERT. Yes.

[Pause. Count of ten.]

MERVIN. I'm so lonely. Thank goodness you're here.

ALBERT. Yes, thank goodness.

MERVIN. I have some memory of when things were different, long ago.

ALBERT. I know. Me too.

MERVIN. My chest hurts again. Every day it hurts. Something is wrong.

ALBERT. I love you.

MERVIN. What did you say?

ALBERT. I said, "I love you."

MERVIN. That's sweet.

ALBERT. I mean it.

MERVIN. I love you too. You're my only friend.

ALBERT. Yes, we're friends. Close friends.

[Mervin reaches out his hand toward Albert. They hold hands for a while. Then they let go.]

MERVIN. Another day.

ALBERT. Perhaps.

MERVIN. We'll wait through it.

ALBERT. I suppose.

MERVIN. We're waiting now. For what, I don't know.

Raymond J. Barry

ALBERT. For something good to come of it.

MERVIN. What good?

ALBERT. Some good thing will come of it. I held your hand, didn't I?

MERVIN. Yes, you held my hand.

ALBERT. We kissed.

MERVIN. That was good...

ALBERT. You said you loved me. I said I loved you.

MERVIN. ...very good.

ALBERT. And worth waiting for.

MERVIN. Yes, worth waiting for, indeed. *[Pause]* I'll wait some more. Maybe some more good things will happen.

ALBERT. They will.

[pause]

MERVIN. I'm so lonely.

ALBERT. Everyone's lonely.

MERVIN. Thank goodness you're here.

ALBERT. Yes, thank goodness. Let me make you some soup.

[Mervin does not respond. He wraps himself in a blanket. Albert leaves the room towards the kitchen. There is a knock upon the door. Mervin lifts his head and listens carefully; another knock. He struggles to get up, while keeping himself wrapped in the blanket. He stumbles forward toward the door, pauses for a moment and calls.]

MERVIN. There's someone at the door.

ALBERT. *[from the kitchen]* Well, let them in.

MERVIN. I'm afraid.

ALBERT. *[enters from the kitchen]* Let them in!

MERVIN. I'm afraid.

ALBERT. Sit down. I'll do it.

MERVIN. Maybe we shouldn't open it.

ALBERT. By now they've heard our voices. We have to open it. *[Albert goes to the door.]* Who is it?

[Mervin sits in his seat.]

BUFORD. *[from outside]* Your friendly neighbor.

ALBERT. Our friendly neighbor?

MERVIN. It's him.

ALBERT. Are you sure?

MERVIN. Of course I'm sure. Don't you recognize his voice?

ALBERT. I have to open it.

MERVIN. Leave him outside.

ALBERT. It's probably a friendly visit.

MERVIN. Don't answer the door.

ALBERT. I have to.

MERVIN. No, please, don't. *[Mervin rises and tries to stop him, only to fall in a pile on the floor.]*

A Piece of Cake

ALBERT. Don't be ridiculous. *[Albert opens the door.]* Come in. *[Buford enters.]*

BUFORD. Thank you. I'm sorry to intrude upon you like this.

ALBERT. I'm glad you did.

MERVIN. I'm not.

BUFORD. It took hours to find you.

MERVIN. We don't want to attract attention to ourselves.

BUFORD. Going from physical description is a tedious process, but they have it computerized. They wanted to know why I wanted to visit. They didn't like it.

MERVIN. We can't hide like animals!

ALBERT. Stop shouting.

MERVIN. We have done nothing wrong!

ALBERT. It hurts my ears, Mervin. I can't take your whining.

BUFORD. They finally narrowed it down to three sets of males who live within walking distance.

MERVIN. I'm not feeling well.

BUFORD. Has he been drinking the water?

ALBERT. No, I don't know what's wrong.

BUFORD. I'm glad I found you.

ALBERT. Really? I am too.

BUFORD. I want to be friendly.

MERVIN. Careful.

ALBERT. Don't start.

BUFORD. I know my wife behaved badly toward you. Her behavior disturbed me. How inhospitable it was. I want to make it up to you.

MERVIN. Don't trust him.

ALBERT. Quiet! Don't be rude.

BUFORD. I'm under suspicion too. My own wife turned me in.

ALBERT. She did?

MERVIN. Don't trust him.

ALBERT. Quiet!

BUFORD. Yes, she did. She violated our trust after all this time.

ALBERT. What did she turn you in for?

BUFORD. I understand Mervin's paranoia about me.

ALBERT. Nonsense, he's not feeling well.

MERVIN. I have a disease. Very catching.

ALBERT. Don't make up things. He's exaggerating for attention.

BUFORD. He has a right to be suspicious of me.

MERVIN. Yes, I do, don't I?

ALBERT. Don't listen. What did she turn you in for?

BUFORD. Nothing.

MERVIN. Don't trust him.

ALBERT. Come on, Buford, tell us. You know it's something. It's got to be

Raymond J. Barry

something.

BUFORD. It's too... personal.

MERVIN. How corny.

ALBERT. That's enough out of you!

BUFORD. Don't be too hard on him.

ALBERT. You're being obnoxious.

BUFORD. He doesn't like me for a good reason.

MERVIN. That's the smartest thing you've said so far.

ALBERT. Enough, I say. Tell me, Buford.

BUFORD. No... I can't.

ALBERT. You can tell me.

BUFORD. It's embarrassing.

ALBERT. Only a few things can embarrass me.

MERVIN. I have a contagious disease.

BUFORD. You do look ill.

ALBERT. He's pretending.

MERVIN. He doesn't know. I am definitely sick.

ALBERT. Don't listen to him.

MERVIN. It could be contagious.

ALBERT. He's being obnoxious on purpose.

BUFORD. He's not feeling well.

MERVIN. You bet I don't feel well, and you're going to get it. I breathed on you.

ALBERT. Go into the other room, will you!

MERVIN. I will not be ordered around! I simply will not allow you to order me around!

ALBERT. Then stop! There is pressure on us all here. You are not the only one involved. This nice man is relating something personal and I will not allow you to inhibit him. Please forgive him; he's not himself.

BUFORD. My wife is the same. She embarrasses me on purpose.

ALBERT. Yes, that's what Mervin does.

MERVIN. It doesn't matter what either of you say. I'm deathly ill.

BUFORD. Mervin will trust me more as time goes on.

ALBERT. I'm sure he will.

BUFORD. Let me ask you, are... or rather... do I look like a real man to you?

MERVIN. A real man?

ALBERT. I'd say so, yes.

MERVIN. You got a dick, don't you? Ha, ha, ha, ha, ha.

[Mervin and Albert laugh at this.]

BUFORD. No, seriously, am I in any way, say, like a woman?

MERVIN. Oh, you mean like us?

ALBERT. You mean like the way we are with each other, like sexually?

BUFORD. No, I know who I am sexually, but I'm just curious how I present myself to other people. I mean am I in any way effeminate?

ALBERT. Well, that's a difficult question to answer.

MERVIN. You seem like a normal guy to me.

ALBERT. What about us, Buford, do we seem effeminate?

BUFORD. Come to think of it, no, neither of you have any noticeable effeminate characteristics.

ALBERT. We're men's men, so to speak.

MERVIN. I have a chill.

BUFORD. I never would have suspected anything if Mervin hadn't mentioned it.

ALBERT. Good old Mervin, spilled the beans.

MERVIN. I can't stop shaking.

ALBERT. Stop complaining, Mervin.

MERVIN. Look, Albert, look at my hand. It could be contagious.

ALBERT. Did your wife accuse you of being one of us?

MERVIN. This rash says it all.

BUFORD. Yes.

MERVIN. I have something. Look at this rash on my hand.

ALBERT. But a rash could be anything.

MERVIN. Oh, God, I'm going to die. I'm going to die.

ALBERT. Sometimes I wish you would.

MERVIN. Don't be talking like that. I'm sick. I have that rash that's been going around. *[He falls on the floor.]*

ALBERT. Ignore him.

MERVIN. Now I'm on the floor and I can't get onto the chair. And you're too preoccupied to do anything about it.

ALBERT. He's a fool.

BUFORD. I forgive him; really.

ALBERT. Tell me, Buford, your wife turned you in because you're one of us? Why would she do that? You have always been loyal, haven't you?

BUFORD. Yes, within reason.

ALBERT. Within reason?

BUFORD. People like us are in danger.

MERVIN. We've got him now.

ALBERT. Quiet.

MERVIN. But we've got him now.

ALBERT. Let him talk.

BUFORD. I've said enough.

ALBERT. Don't pay attention to Mervin. Speak your mind.

BUFORD. No, it's unimportant.

MERVIN. Go on, speak your mind.

BUFORD. No, it's okay.

ALBERT. Shut up, Mervin.

MERVIN. But he was saying things.

Raymond J. Barry

ALBERT. Will you shut your mouth!

BUFORD. Let's change the subject.

MERVIN. Let's not and say we did.

BUFORD. Who are you people anyway?

MERVIN. That's right. Who are we? You don't really know, do you? Nobody knows who we are but us. Right, Albert?

ALBERT. Quiet, Mervin.

MERVIN. What about you, Buford? You hate us, don't you, Buford?

BUFORD. I don't really hate you.

MERVIN. You've been told how disgusting we are so you hate us.

BUFORD. I wish you hadn't come into my life, but I like both of you.

MERVIN. Who do you like more, us or Ruth?

BUFORD. Ruth is my wife so you shouldn't be compared. On the other hand, things aren't so good between Ruth and me lately so I would say, for the moment, I like you better. For the moment, that is.

MERVIN. Even though we're a couple of queers.

BUFORD. Yes.

MERVIN. He's saying things.

ALBERT. Shut up, Mervin!

MERVIN. This is so clever what we are doing.

BUFORD. What's so clever? I'm being honest.

MERVIN. We know it. You'd say the truth to a couple of queers, but you wouldn't say the truth to your own wife. Interesting, isn't it?

ALBERT. That's enough, Mervin.

MERVIN. Stop telling me when it's enough!

ALBERT. Well, you'll say something you shouldn't if you're not careful.

BUFORD. Like what?

ALBERT. Oh, nothing.

MERVIN. We have to be careful about things or we'll get ourselves in trouble.

BUFORD. What kind of trouble?

MERVIN. What?

BUFORD. What do you mean by trouble?

MERVIN. I'm hard of hearing.

BUFORD. What kind of trouble?

MERVIN. I can't hear you.

BUFORD. Is he playing a joke on me?

MERVIN. We are playing a joke on you.

BUFORD. Well, stop it, will you?

MERVIN. A bad joke.

BUFORD. Things are too serious for jokes.

ALBERT. What things?

BUFORD. They are onto all of us.

MERVIN. Oh, yes. Watch out!

A Piece of Cake

ALBERT. Don't mind Mervin. He's been under a lot of pressure.

MERVIN. Kiss me, Albert.

ALBERT. Stop that shit, Mervin.

MERVIN. No, really. Kiss me, Albert.

ALBERT. Get away from me or I'll kick your ass.

BUFORD. You don't have to restrain yourselves in front of me. I know what you are, both of you. There's even a part of me that envies you.

ALBERT. You envy us? Why?

BUFORD. Because you have someone to trust.

MERVIN. You have Ruth.

BUFORD. No, I don't.

MERVIN. She's pretty.

BUFORD. I don't trust her.

ALBERT. You sound bitter, Buford.

BUFORD. She betrayed me.

ALBERT. Really bitter.

BUFORD. I don't mean to be.

ALBERT. Sounds to me like you don't know who you can trust nowadays.

MERVIN. Buford can't trust us.

ALBERT. You can't trust us, for example.

MERVIN. We're just a couple of queers.

ALBERT. Can you trust us, Buford?

BUFORD. You have caused me a lot of trouble.

MERVIN. I suppose we have.

ALBERT. Stop picking on Buford, Mervin. He's become our friend.

BUFORD. I was angry when I came here.

MERVIN. But now we're getting along pretty well, aren't we? We all have similar problems.

BUFORD. But I haven't done anything.

MERVIN. Neither have we. We're in the same boat. Might as well join us.

BUFORD. What are you encouraging us to do?

MERVIN. Oh, nothing, just hide with the rest of us.

BUFORD. I can't hide.

ALBERT. That's right, Buford.

BUFORD. There's no place to go.

MERVIN. There's no place we can't find you.

BUFORD. Did you say, "We"?

ALBERT. Mervin...

MERVIN. Oh, my, I've spilled the beans.

BUFORD. I'm getting out of here.

ALBERT. And where would you run, Buford?

MERVIN. There's no place to run.

BUFORD. But you're a couple of queers.

MERVIN. Might as well admit it.

Raymond J. Barry

ALBERT. There's no place to run.

BUFORD. You... are in the same situation I'm in.

MERVIN. Oh, really?

ALBERT. That's quite enough, really, Mervin.

MERVIN. Yes, Albert. We're very clever.

ALBERT. Stop calling yourself clever.

MERVIN. But we are. We're very clever.

BUFORD. I'm leaving. *[Buford attempts to leave. Albert and Mervin block his way.]*

[simultaneous]

MERVIN.	**ALBERT.**
No, don't go! Isn't it a bore to not trust the sun. Remember all the good things, the beautiful rain and sex, real sex, intimate sex between couples before infection? That's how it has to be again, Buford.	No, don't go! Remember when it was fun to get a suntan? Remember when sex was available? The people are frustrated, Buford. Couples don't even trust each other. People have to be controlled.

BUFORD. Yes, I remember.

MERVIN. People, before they were infected,

ALBERT. People have to be controlled...

MERVIN. ...were outspoken,

ALBERT. ...by elimination if necessary.

MERVIN. ...too outspoken.

ALBERT. Gays were influential.

MERVIN. As were writers, painters and performers.

ALBERT. Artists and gays could influence thinking then.

[simultaneous]

MERVIN.	**ALBERT.**
We had talent and political power. We had to be eliminated.	We had talent and political power. We had to be eliminated.

BUFORD. Disgusting queers.

MERVIN. Upon what do you base that?

BUFORD. You said so.

MERVIN. Oh, I said so. What if I was lying?

ALBERT. You've said enough.

MERVIN. No, Albert, I'll say what I damn well please. You've got nothing to do with it.

ALBERT. If I kick your ass I'll have something to do with it.

MERVIN. Don't get physical with me. Give me a big kiss instead.

A Piece of Cake

ALBERT. Stop that shit.

BUFORD. I want to leave.

[Mervin blocks the exit.]

MERVIN. No, don't leave. You mustn't leave.

ALBERT. We have you now. You can't leave.

BUFORD. What do you mean, you have me? I'm going.

[Mervin grabs him and throws him halfway across the room.]

MERVIN. I didn't mean to do that. I meant only for you to think before you act. You can't run from us. For God's sake, you don't even know who we are, do you?

BUFORD. You disgust me.

MERVIN. Buford, you don't even know what you're disgusted by. Kiss me, Buford.

BUFORD. Get away from me!

MERVIN. Kiss me.

BUFORD. I'm married.

MERVIN. You hate her.

BUFORD. I love her.

MERVIN. You don't know what you love. If there wasn't a mirror in your bathroom you wouldn't even know you existed. You don't even know who we are.

BUFORD. Who are you?

MERVIN. We are clever.

BUFORD. Who are you... both of you?

MERVIN. But, Buford, do you love me is the question.

ALBERT. Stop playing with his brain.

BUFORD. I want to go home to Ruth.

MERVIN. She betrayed you. You can never go back to her.

ALBERT. That's right, Buford, you're one of us.

MERVIN. We'll break you down unless you agree.

ALBERT. Yes, we'll break you down. Then where will you be?

[BLACKOUT.]

Act Two

-

Scene Two

[Ruth has arrived at Herman's unit, which has a noticeable sumptuousness about it that contrasts radically with the units of both couples. There is a soft, luxurious couch in one corner and a comfortable easy chair on opposite side of the living room. Lush, beautiful abstract paintings hang on the wall, painted loosely with rich, subtle colors.

Raymond J. Barry

Everything in the room suggests good taste and supply. There is a door in back that leads to the cake-room.]

HERMAN. Please, do sit down and make yourself comfortable.
RUTH. Thank you.
HERMAN. My time is your time.
RUTH. I'm so nervous, never having been in this position before.
HERMAN. No harm will come to you.
RUTH. It's difficult for me to ask anything from a man of your influence.
HERMAN. Now, now, we're all human beings, after all.
[Uncomfortable pause.]
RUTH. I just had to come. You were so difficult to find. At first the center wouldn't allow me to visit you.
HERMAN. They called and I gave permission.
[Bomb blasts in the distance.]
RUTH. They did change their minds rather suddenly.
HERMAN. Your interests are my interests.
RUTH. Sometimes words come from my mouth that Buford, my husband, disapproves of...
HERMAN. I'm listening.
RUTH. ...and believe me, he's always correct in his position; that is... with regard to... ah... certain issues... ah.
HERMAN. What issues?
RUTH. Oh, just issues that come up during the course of our day.
HERMAN. What kinds of issues?
RUTH. Just normal, everyday issues that he might bring home from work, for example.
HERMAN. Issues that bother him with regard to work?
RUTH. Oh, no, he was never bothered.
HERMAN. He was never bothered?
RUTH. Oh, of course, everyone is bothered occasionally.
HERMAN. Am I bothered?
RUTH. I suppose you are bothered from time to time.
HERMAN. When am I bothered would you think?
RUTH. Random situations with your wife maybe, or with a friend.
HERMAN. What if I told you that I have no wife, and I have no friends either.
RUTH. Really? Well, I wouldn't have guessed that.
HERMAN. My wife betrayed me.
RUTH. Really? How sad.
HERMAN. Is your marriage a happy one?
RUTH. Oh, yes, we have a perfect marriage.
HERMAN. It didn't appear to be perfect late this afternoon.
RUTH. I was merely revealing the truth.

A Piece of Cake

HERMAN. You did the right thing.

RUTH. I didn't realize the repercussions that would follow.

HERMAN. You did place your husband in a... "precarious" position.

RUTH. He's so distracted by what's happened.

HERMAN. He's been suspect for some time now.

RUTH. For what reason, "suspect"?

HERMAN. Certain attitudes he's projected from time to time that have... shall we say... come to my attention.

RUTH. I was never aware of any attitudes.

HERMAN. Perhaps you have the same attitudes and therefore his are not as noticeable as they otherwise might be.

RUTH. I have no attitudes.

HERMAN. Surely none that I detect.

RUTH. Those men broke into our unit.

HERMAN. Scum. Nothing but scum.

RUTH. They're the source of all of our troubles.

HERMAN. Buford delayed in contacting me.

RUTH. He was afraid of the consequences.

HERMAN. Well, my dear, look at the consequences that came from withholding information.

RUTH. There must be leniency for Buford.

HERMAN. Would you like some cake?

RUTH. Cake? Oh my goodness. I didn't come for cake.

HERMAN. But some... cake would settle your nerves.

RUTH. I never expected this.

HERMAN. Please, have some... cake.

RUTH. Well, if you insist I suppose I could have a small piece of cake.

HERMAN. Come over here and look into the cake room.

RUTH. *[She looks into the back.]* Oh, my goodness! Nothing but cake. Cake after cake after cake.

HERMAN. You see? I'm a man of substance.

RUTH. And to think, this all came from your job.

HERMAN. It isn't a job, really, not for me, the pleasure of winnowing out the sledge in our system, those who fail to contribute anything of worth.

RUTH. Like Albert and Mervin, the two homosexuals?

HERMAN. Your husband is much more of a threat than those scum.

RUTH. Buford is innocent.

HERMAN. I'll get some cake.

[Herman goes into the back room. Ruth stays outside.]

RUTH. I never expected this.

HERMAN. Good things always come to the deserving. *[Shouting from the back.]* What kind of cake would you enjoy the most.

RUTH. *[Calling to him.]* I'll be happy with anything. Don't go through a lot of trouble.

Raymond J. Barry

HERMAN. *[Calling from the back.]* I'm looking at the selections back here; strawberry short cake, vanilla icing, chocolate fudge. I'm taking a few mouthfuls myself. Oh, my goodness, I just put my finger into the crust of the lemon meringue.

RUTH. *[Calling to him.]* Eat a whole piece if you like. I'm patient.

HERMAN. *[Calling from the back.]* I'm making a little piggy of myself.

RUTH. *[Calling to him.]* I'm patient, although I have to admit I'm getting a touch eager for my piece.

HERMAN. *[Calling from the back.]* What kind do you want?

RUTH. *[Calling to him inside.]* I don't know for sure. I didn't expect cake so I'm completely surprised by this.

HERMAN. *[He enters with a big chocolate cake.]* How does this one strike you?

RUTH. Oh, my goodness, I really didn't expect this.

HERMAN. Here is your reward for your honesty, my sweet.

RUTH. Honesty is the best policy.

HERMAN. Plenty of cake in the house, pounds and pounds of cake.

RUTH. You must have such influence to have so much cake.

HERMAN. Yes, I have nothing to worry about with all this cake lying around.

RUTH. You seem so sure of yourself.

HERMAN. You could call it confidence... cake confidence.

RUTH. Yes... cake confidence.

HERMAN. Imagine everyone with a full supply of cake.

RUTH. Do you think that would be possible?

HERMAN. Of course it's possible once we winnow out the undesirables, and, believe me, my dear, that is slowly happening, the result of which will be more cake for all.

RUTH. Panacea at last, after all the sacrifice we've made.

[A bomb blasts in the distance. Herman cuts a piece of cake for Ruth.]

RUTH. Those bombs.

HERMAN. Your nerves seem shattered. Here's a nice big piece of cake for you to chew on.

[Herman serves Ruth a piece and leaves the rest on the table.]

RUTH. Oh, thank you much. Thank you. Thank you. My goodness, such a large piece of cake.

HERMAN. There's more where that came from.

RUTH. Oh, I don't want to over extend my welcome.

HERMAN. Don't worry about that. I enjoy your company. Eat up. Eat up.

RUTH. Aren't you having any?

HERMAN. Yes, of course, but I enjoy watching you eat cake. The second that sugar rush hits you will be as exciting for me as it will be for you, and then will come the let down afterwards. It's always the same, with some variables, depending upon the individual.

A Piece of Cake

[Ruth eats the cake.]

RUTH. This beautiful cake is so very tasty, luscious cake, sweet toothy taste of cake on my big, hungry, wet tongue.

HERMAN. Is that how you usually speak or did the excitement of the cake get the better of you?

RUTH. Oh, my goodness, I'm in such high spirits now. I'll say anything that pops into my mind.

HERMAN. You have a little chocolate frosting on your lip.

RUTH. Oh, my.

[Ruth wipes the frosting from her lip.]

HERMAN. You are a sensualist.

RUTH. I am, aren't I?

HERMAN. Your taste buds are operating at full force.

RUTH. I suppose they can't help themselves.

HERMAN. In many ways I can't help myself.

RUTH. How do you mean?

HERMAN. I enjoy watching you eat... cake.

RUTH. I'm going to make this last as long as I can. It's simply delicious.

[Silence. Ruth eats awkwardly, aware that Herman is staring at her.]

HERMAN. I like you, Ruth.

RUTH. That's very kind of you.

HERMAN. You have a winning way about you.

RUTH. I've been told that by my husband.

HERMAN. Well, now you're hearing it from me.

RUTH. That's very kind of you.

HERMAN. I'd like to know you better.

RUTH. Oh, my goodness, you're a man of such... influence.

HERMAN. And how would you know of my... influence?

RUTH. Well, your endless supply of... cake, for example.

HERMAN. Yes, that tells something.

RUTH. I notice how men relate to you as if you're important.

HERMAN. Perhaps we could be friends.

RUTH. Friends?

HERMAN. Would you like another piece of cake?

RUTH. You're spoiling me.

HERMAN. An attractive woman like you should be spoiled.

RUTH. You make me blush. I'm making a pig of myself.

HERMAN. Hardly. You've been deprived for a long time now.

RUTH. I could eat cake forever.

HERMAN. You are pretty, you know, a very attractive woman. How's your... cake doing? Want some more?

RUTH. Some more... cake?

HERMAN. Yes, would you like some more?

RUTH. Well, I didn't really expect... cake when I came.

Raymond J. Barry

HERMAN. Nevertheless, it's being offered to you.

RUTH. Cake soothes my nerves.

HERMAN. Yes, it will relax you.

RUTH. You are kind.

HERMAN. I sense we're going to be very close friends.

RUTH. It must be marvelous, having cake.

HERMAN. How easily we converse.

RUTH. Yes, there is a certain ease between us.

HERMAN. Perhaps some good will come of this.

RUTH. But my husband...

HERMAN. Please don't bring him up again.

RUTH. But my original intention was to...

HERMAN. I must insist!

RUTH. ...point out his innocence.

HERMAN. You persist with this banter about your husband while I'm sharing my cake with you. *[Herman gathers himself.]* I'm sorry. I haven't shared my cake with a woman for such a long time.

RUTH. A man with so much cake and no women?

HERMAN. Once the cake supply ends the women leave me.

RUTH. You're attractive to women only for your cake?

HERMAN. *[He lies down next to her.]* It seems that way, only for my cake, my endless supply of cake.

RUTH. Must make one suspicious of mankind in general.

HERMAN. Oh, yes, until I met you.

RUTH. You seem to enjoy my company.

HERMAN. You're the first woman I've met who appreciates me for who I am.

RUTH. Your cake is still very much a part of you.

HERMAN. I suppose. I can't get away from that.

RUTH. Buford will come home soon. I must finish my cake and go back.

HERMAN. I can't help myself. I'm attracted to you. There I've said it.

RUTH. But a man of your... influence.

HERMAN. It is shocking, isn't it?

RUTH. Desirous of someone so insignificant?

HERMAN. You little buttercup.

RUTH. Oh, I'm not a buttercup.

HERMAN. Oh, surely you're my little buttercup.

RUTH. My husband seldom mentions my attractiveness.

HERMAN. But surely you have lovers.

RUTH. I'm infected with the virus.

HERMAN. We're in good fortune then. I'm immune to that nasty little bug, part of the fringe benefits that come with my position.

RUTH. You're immune?

HERMAN. Yes.

A Piece of Cake

RUTH. What that must be to a person.

HERMAN. It's a powerful position to be in during this stage of our development.

RUTH. This cake is so delicious.

HERMAN. I find you delicious. Am I attractive to you in any way?

RUTH. I am attracted to your... influence.

HERMAN. And, of course, you like my... cake.

RUTH. Oh, yes. Very much.

HERMAN. You know by now what's on my mind, don't you?

RUTH. I have my suspicions.

HERMAN. Is it possible that I might have my way?

RUTH. I'd have to think about that.

HERMAN. I admire your loyalty to your husband.

RUTH. I do have feelings for the man but my current cake supply is low.

HERMAN. What fortunate destiny that you have come into my sorry life.

RUTH. Why sorry with your endless supply of frosted cake?

HERMAN. Oh, that's nothing compared to my despair.

RUTH. Despair? A man of such... influence?

HERMAN. Day in and day out, people only out for themselves, scouring the countryside for some mischief or another. I have to keep a watchful eye.

RUTH. Your position sounds like an important one.

HERMAN. There must be someone with whom to share the spoils so to speak.

RUTH. Share the cake.

HERMAN. Yes, share the cake. You have a way with words, don't you, you little buttercup?

RUTH. I really didn't expect cake when I came.

HERMAN. You've brought me pleasure. I therefore offer you pleasure.

RUTH. Pleasure for pleasure.

[Buford goes down on his knees.]

HERMAN. Yes, my dear, pleasure for pleasure. Shall we?

RUTH. Shall we what?

HERMAN. Surely you know.

RUTH. You have to say it.

HERMAN. I'm shy.

RUTH. You? Shy?

HERMAN. Yes, I'm so tongue-tied I can't say it.

RUTH. I have you wrapped around my little pinky.

HERMAN. You do.

RUTH. A man of such... influence, with so much... cake.

HERMAN. Yes, all of that and yet so lost.

RUTH. Just the two of us in your unit, a man of such... influence.

HERMAN. Your nervous condition is what concerns me most.

Raymond J. Barry

RUTH. You are so kind, really kind.

HERMAN. I've been known to care about my fellow man.

[Bombs blast in the distance.]

RUTH. Oh, my God!

HERMAN. Did you say "God"?

RUTH. I didn't mean it... I... I'm so brittle lately, so easily frightened. I can't control my nerves. *[Herman places his beefy arm around her shoulder.]*

HERMAN. You make my blood boil, my little buttercup.

RUTH. You're so blunt.

HERMAN. Take your clothes off. I want your cake-filled body.

[Herman attempts to kiss Ruth.]

RUTH. I didn't come here for this.

HERMAN. You think you didn't but really you did. Eat cake. Eat cake. Eat your cake.

[Herman attempts again to kiss Ruth.]

RUTH. I want very much to eat my cake.

HERMAN. You've eaten cake before. Now finish this piece.

[Herman at last kisses her.]

RUTH. Yes, I'm eating my cake.

[Herman and Ruth kiss passionately. Ruth is carried by Herman into the privacy of the cake storage room. Bomb blasts in the distance. Lights dim.]

Act Two

-

Scene Three

[Lights up. Albert and Mervin enter Herman's unit as if they are familiar with it. Mervin holds the end of a rope that leads outside the entrance.]

HERMAN. *[From the cake room.]* Oh, my goodness. This is better than cake. Oh, oh, oh, how marvelous and at my weight. Oh, my goodness! Oh, stop. It tickles. No, no; it tickles. Oh, my goodness.

MERVIN. Herman's getting laid.

ALBERT. We shouldn't eavesdrop.

MERVIN. Since when are you so moral?

MERVIN. I can be moral.

ALBERT. You've never been known to be moral.

[Erotic sounds come from the back]

ALBERT. Maybe we should leave.

MERVIN. And go where?

ALBERT. Back to our unit. Where else?

MERVIN. I don't trust that place.

ALBERT. Nonetheless, it's the only home we have.

A Piece of Cake

MERVIN. I'm going to make myself at home right here. *[He sits.]*

HERMAN. *[From the cake storage room.]* Oh, my God! Oh, my God!

MERVIN. He's even referring to God.

ALBERT. People do that when they forget themselves.

MERVIN. I said "God" once.

ALBERT. You're saying "God" now.

MERVIN. It's only a point of reference from the past.

ALBERT. Nevertheless, you said "God".

MERVIN. What of it, huh? You want to make something of it?

[Mervin puts up his dukes. He looks ridiculous.]

HERMAN. *[From the cake storage room.]* Oh, heavens!

ALBERT. Don't get aggressive, Mervin.

MERVIN. Don't get aggressive, my ass. You want to make something of it?

ALBERT. Let's go now.

MERVIN. You want to?

ALBERT. Yes, we can't get much done here.

[Ruth's pleasurable moan comes from inside.]

ALBERT. The old geezer is immune. He can have his pick of any of them.

MERVIN. I wish I liked women.

ALBERT. I'm almost a woman.

MERVIN. I know, but I wish I liked real women.

ALBERT. Probably no more interesting than what I can offer.

MERVIN. Maybe. Everyone's infected. We're infected.

ALBERT. I know that. Don't you think I know that?

MERVIN. Don't let them hear you.

ALBERT. All right, but you bring up the most sensitive issues that I would rather forget.

MERVIN. Sorry.

[Bombs go off in the distance.]

MERVIN. Those bombs.

ALBERT. Necessary until they're all wiped out.

MERVIN. We'll survive, won't we?

ALBERT. We're here, away from those skirmishes.

MERVIN. Bands of roving urchins with little more than mischief in their minds.

ALBERT. Just keep up our daily work and everything will be fine.

[Ruth's pleasurable moan from inside.]

MERVIN. Somebody's really getting it good from that fat pig.

ALBERT. Quiet, he'll hear you.

MERVIN. I wish I could get some.

ALBERT. You're not immune.

MERVIN. You don't have to keep rubbing it in. *[Another groan from the back room.]*

Raymond J. Barry

He's really giving it to her.

ALBERT. Fat pig has control over everything.

MERVIN. We're lucky to be working for him.

ALBERT. What luck? We're good at what we do, very good I might add.

[Pause.]

MERVIN. Why are we waiting here?

ALBERT. Where else would we go?

MERVIN. Home to our unit.

ALBERT. And do what?

MERVIN. Talk.

ALBERT. We can talk here.

MERVIN. Maybe they'll come out soon.

ALBERT. All flushed and satisfied.

MERVIN. While we sit here holding our dicks.

ALBERT. Maybe Herman would be willing to make us immune.

MERVIN. Are you kidding? He's just using us and then we'll go the same route as the rest of the queers.

ALBERT. At least he's "queer friendly".

MERVIN. What gives you that idea?

ALBERT. He hires us.

MERVIN. In case you don't remember, he's responsible for the deaths of thousands of our brethren.

ALBERT. How do you know?

MERVIN. I don't, but my instinct tells me it's true. Of course it's true.

ALBERT. At least we got some cake out of the deal.

MERVIN. Hopefully there's more where that came from.

[Herman comes out, half dressed.]

HERMAN. Oh, you two here? Oh, my goodness, I didn't expect you to be here. Oh, my goodness, that little session was almost as good as cake.

MERVIN. Nothing is good as cake.

HERMAN. Just a figure of speech.

ALBERT. How'd you manage with that big belly of yours.

HERMAN. Doggy style.

ALBERT. I see.

HERMAN. Yep, anything can be accomplished if one is willing to wait for a solution.

MERVIN. I'm willing to wait.

ALBERT. You have to wait with those looks.

[Ruth comes in. Albert and Mervin can't believe their eyes.]

RUTH. Oh, what are you two doing here? Herman, what are they doing here?

ALBERT. We suspect you had a good time, doggy style.

MERVIN. Don't be vulgar, Albert.

ALBERT. How quickly you've forgotten your husband, Ruth.

A Piece of Cake

RUTH. I'm rerouting for the sake of security.

MERVIN. For the sake of saving your ass.

ALBERT. We didn't expect her to be here.

HERMAN. She's my guest. You're all my guests.

ALBERT. Remember us, Ruth?

MERVIN. She's not saying anything.

ALBERT. What is there to say?

MERVIN. They've bonded, which leaves us out in the cold.

HERMAN. Nonsense. You still work for me.

RUTH. They are your employees?

HERMAN. Oh, come now, Ruth. Don't be naïve.

RUTH. I had no idea.

HERMAN. Your naiveté' is part of your charm, my little buttercup.

ALBERT. Is she truly on board, or is she just saving her ass?

HERMAN. You're all saving your asses, all of you.

MERVIN. Aren't you saving your ass as well?

HERMAN. My ass has been saved, considering my influence.

MERVIN. You and your influence.

ALBERT. Quiet, Mervin.

MERVIN. I can express myself.

ALBERT. Just button your lip.

HERMAN. That's enough, Mervin.

ALBERT. Don't mind Mervin, sir. We're trying too hard, fighting for our lives so we don't end up like Buford or the rest of our kind.

MERVIN. We're defensive.

ALBERT. Yes, that's it. We're defensive.

MERVIN. We're not operating on all cylinders.

ALBERT. You have no idea what it feels like to be different.

HERMAN. Stop whining, the two of you.

MERVIN. We're obedient.

HERMAN. Of course, you are. Otherwise you'll meet the same fate as your colleagues.

MERVIN AND ALBERT. No! Not us! We'll be good! We'll be good!

RUTH. The big one broke into my unit.

ALBERT. Herman put us up to that.

HERMAN. Don't start babbling.

MERVIN. She's one of us.

HERMAN. Nonetheless, our business is private.

MERVIN. But you've bonded.

HERMAN. Who knows how long that will last.

RUTH. Darling, what are you saying?

ALBERT. She's made a lifetime commitment.

MERVIN. The same commitment she made to her husband.

HERMAN. State your business, gentlemen, and then take your exit.

Raymond J. Barry

ALBERT. You're talking a different tune in front of her.

MERVIN. He's two-faced as they come, but we knew that all along, didn't we?

ALBERT. Don't say it to his face for goodness sake.

MERVIN. Where else would I say it, to his ass?

HERMAN. Come, come, gentlemen, the point! Get to the point.

ALBERT. Pull in the beast, Mervin.

[Mervin gives a tug on the rope he's been holding at the other end of which is tied around Buford's neck. He's pulled in with his head lowered.]

MERVIN. We've broken Buford's spirit like a crushed cake.

ALBERT. Mervin, let me say it.

MERVIN. Don't hesitate then. Speak!

ALBERT. We have done the deed, crushed him as requested.

MERVIN. Rooted out his misdemeanors and buried him with guilt.

ALBERT. I've never heard you so eloquent, Mervin.

MERVIN. You haven't?

ALBERT. No, you're so eloquent.

MERVIN. I'll continue then. We were extremely clever tonight, again proving our worth to you, sir. "Buford" I believe is his name, sir, spilled the beans so to speak, poor devil, didn't have a spark of self-esteem left after what we put him through; just tore him apart and left him groveling on the ground, begging to be forgiven. Chances are he might not even survive the night after we literally pelted him with allusions to his effeminacy, which could possibly be the case, given his girlish wiggle when he walks.

RUTH. He doesn't wiggle.

MERVIN. He wiggles.

RUTH. No, he definitely doesn't wiggle.

ALBERT. He was asking for trouble.

MERVIN. Thought he could bully us...

ALBERT. But we showed him, didn't we, Mervin?

MERVIN. We burrowed into his soul.

ALBERT. Until he couldn't tell which end was up.

MERVIN. Now he's broken.

ALBERT. But still dangerous.

MERVIN. You must be careful of him.

ALBERT. He's unpredictable.

MERVIN. I wish you would allow me to tell it, Albert. I have a way with words.

ALBERT. A way with words, my ass.

MERVIN. He started galloping like a horse...

ALBERT. Running like a horse...

MERVIN. ...just a few minutes ago.

ALBERT. ...right down the boulevard.

A Piece of Cake

RUTH. Herman, what have these men done to my husband?

HERMAN. The result of trained interrogation.

MERVIN. We convinced him that he was one of us.

ALBERT. He couldn't take it.

MERVIN. He confessed when we were clever enough to press the right buttons.

ALBERT. I pressed the right buttons.

MERVIN. You don't have the imagination to press the right buttons.

ALBERT. You're always taking the credit.

HERMAN. Stop bickering! ! You, "men," for want of a better word, make him communicate; I don't have any use for a man who is mute. Wound him, cripple his strengths, but leave him functional for goodness sake.

MERVIN. I'll get him to talk.

ALBERT. I should be the one and not you.

MERVIN. For once allow me to show my skills.

HERMAN. Let him try.

MERVIN. Thank you, master.

HERMAN. Stop the nonsense and get to work.

MERVIN. [Mervin approaches Buford.] Buford, we are two of a kind, you know, both helpless in the face of our uncertain futures. We are merely two little fishes swimming in a huge sea of man-eating sharks, or rather fish-eating men who are hungry for our cute little tails as we wiggle from rock to rock.

ALBERT. My goodness, he's the most insipid fellow.

MERVIN. You love me, Albert. Don't deny it.

ALBERT. He talks too much.

HERMAN. Let him continue.

ALBERT. All right, but when I can't stand it any longer I'm going to join in. We work well in tandem.

MERVIN. Oh, no, not Albert. I.. I...I am the one. I deserve the accolades for my cleverness. Buford speak, speak for me. Speak for me! I'm the one who deserves the credit. I'm the one who speaks of little fishes being nipped by fish-eating sharks in man-infested seas!! Buford I've always been a loser. I've never won at anything, and from the time I was a small boy I have always been related to as a low life on the basis of the way I am, which I really can't help since I was born this way, and that can't be changed. When I find myself in a position of power I turn into the very fish-eating shark that has been nibbling on my tail all of my life, lying and cheating and bullying the weak fishes in the sea in the same way that I have been abused all of my little life. I've carried this whole thing too far, Buford. [Bombs explode in the distance. Everyone except Buford is startled.] At first I just went along with Albert, but then when I realized how clever I was with my uncanny talent for confusing you into saying just about anything, my power ran away with me, and I daresay I

Raymond J. Barry

became cruel. But it is not my nature to be cruel, Buford. You may think I'm saying this just to coerce you to speak, but you must believe that I realize how terribly ugly I have been. Try to believe me, Buford. I am so sorry for causing your pain. I myself have been laughed at, spat upon, beaten almost to death because of my way, and somehow I have become as inhuman as my tormentors. Please, please, forgive me, my friend. Please, speak to me, my friend, speak to me, or I will carry the guilt of having done harm to you to my grave.

[Mervin is holding onto Buford's legs by now.]

ALBERT. I'm speechless.

HERMAN. Apparently Buford is speechless as well. He hasn't responded in the least.

ALBERT. Still you have to give Mervin credit for coming up with that stuff in a pinch. I didn't know he had it in him.

RUTH. He seemed sincere.

HERMAN. You don't know the man.

ALBERT. You're a good liar.

MERVIN. I was just doing my job.

ALBERT. Lying.

MERVIN. Not lying.

ALBERT. You lied to Buford and you even convinced yourself you were telling the truth.

MERVIN. "Surviving" is the operative word here.

ALBERT. You do have a way with words..

MERVIN. I try my best with whatever is asked of me.

HERMAN. That's why you're so valuable, Mervin.

MERVIN. Thank you, master.

ALBERT. What about me? Aren't I valuable?

MERVIN. Don't be jealous, Albert. You know what is at stake here.

ALBERT. That's fine for you to say when you're getting all of the attention.

MERVIN. What about you? You always get the attention.

HERMAN. Gentlemen. Gentlemen.

BUFORD. C... C... C... C... ake.

HERMAN. He's responding.

ALBERT. Look at that. He responds to cake.

MERVIN. Everyone responds to cake.

RUTH. You may have some cake, Buford. Would that make you happy?

[Ruth fetches some leftover cake and places it into his hand.]

BUFORD. C... C... C... ake.

ALBERT. He's broken.

MERVIN. Don't gloat.

ALBERT. You're the one gloating with that speech you gave.

MERVIN. Just trying to make sense of it all.

A Piece of Cake

ALBERT. There are so many jokes I could have told in the same length of time.

MERVIN. I would like to hear a joke.

ALBERT. You never laugh at my jokes.

MERVIN. I'll laugh.

HERMAN. Maybe Buford would like to tell a joke.

ALBERT. No one ever wants to hear my jokes.

MERVIN. I'd like to hear your joke after Buford tells a joke.

RUTH. Come on, Buford, darling, tell us a joke. Speak to us, dear.

HERMAN. He'd better start talking soon or you two will pay the consequences.

ALBERT. For simply doing our best?

MERVIN. We are expendable then?

HERMAN. Just get him talking.

MERVIN. Tell us a joke, Buford.

ALBERT. Tell us a joke. Come on Buford.

[Buford attempts to talk.]

BUFORD. T... T... Th... ere.

ALBERT. He spoke. Quiet everyone.

BUFORD. There... w... was... a... m... an who...

RUTH. Who, Buford? Please, darling, continue.

BUFORD. There... w... as a man who... broke...

ALBERT. What "broke," Buford. What "broke"?

MERVIN. It's a joke, Albert. Let him tell it in his own way.

HERMAN. Quiet, idiots, let him speak.

MERVIN. He's more expressive when he's encouraged.

HERMAN. I said quiet!

RUTH. Fascist.

HERMAN. Buttercup, please, don't call me that.

BUFORD. I... I... I.

ALBERT. He's responding in his typical effeminate manner.

BUFORD. T... T... T... unit... behind... my unit... my wife... my wife... breathe.

Broke... spirit... together...

MERVIN. Ha. Ha. Ha. Ha. Ha. That's the funniest joke. "Broke his spirit". Don't you get it?

BUFORD. Spirit together... go together... suffocate... breathe... fall behind.

[simultaneous.]

BUFORD.	**MERVIN.**
Make... l... l... love and if possible and... breath together... love ... air... together... would my wife... come with me once... m... m...	Ha. Ha. Ha. He made a funny joke. Albert why aren't you laughing? Ruth? Herman, encourage him, laugh. He

Raymond J. Barry

more t... t... time... back... root
of experience... origin of...
experience... not to overlook...
other possibilities...
suffocate.

made an offering. He's telling a
joke. It's Buford's joke. I'm
laughing, Buford. I'm your
friend. I get the humor of your
joke, you old jokester, you.

RUTH. Buford, It's me, darling. You spoke and we all heard you. Mervin even laughed. Buford, make an effort to recognize who I am. Darling, I'm nothing but an appendage to all this, a victim of circumstances.

HERMAN. Nonsense, you're very much implicated.

RUTH. But I'm with you now.

HERMAN. You are mercenary, aren't you?

RUTH. I'm loyal to you.

HERMAN. That's no doubt what you said to your husband.

RUTH. I left my husband for you.

HERMAN. What do you see in a fat, black man?

RUTH. Your influence; your cake. I'll show you that you're alive.

HERMAN. You've already shown me.

RUTH. Then why are you not trusting me?

BUFORD. To fly... over walls.

HERMAN. I'm jealous of your husband's influence. He must be taken care of.

BUFORD. Flying... over walls.

RUTH. But how?

BUFORD. Reaching summit... away from earth.

HERMAN. He's guilty.

RUTH. Of what?

HERMAN. He's guilty of collusion.

RUTH. Too general.

HERMAN. Don't challenge me! Collusion. Do you understand?

RUTH. Yes. Yes, collusion.

BUFORD. Rise in rebellion...

MERVIN. Buford is a broken man.

ALBERT. Don't be so hard on him.

BUFORD. Might take us to the moon...

HERMAN. He's too good-looking. We must get rid of him so you'll be mine.

RUTH. But I am yours.

HERMAN. Not completely mine.

BUFORD. Suffocate. Might take us to the moon.

HERMAN. Have some cake to soothe your nerves.

RUTH. I don't want cake.

HERMAN. You see? You don't even want cake.

MERVIN. Doesn't want cake?

A Piece of Cake

ALBERT. Surely she wants cake.

RUTH. And what does cake prove?

HERMAN. It proves you're not thinking straight when it comes to your husband.

RUTH. Nonsense, I'm stuffed with cake.

HERMAN. No one can be stuffed with cake.

RUTH. Well, I'm stuffed with cake.

BUFORD. New land... my life...

HERMAN. You're distracted by your love for your husband.

RUTH. You must leave my husband out of our business. He's no threat to you.

BUFORD. I'm... not... gone... Ruth.

HERMAN. I'm jealous. The thought of him putting his hands on you simply kills me. It simply kills me.

RUTH. I didn't come out of a vacuum. I do have a past.

HERMAN. I'm so fat. You couldn't love me. I'm so terribly fat.

RUTH. Maybe you could thin down a little, darling. Eat less cake.

HERMAN. Eat less? Yes, then you might fall for me.

RUTH. I've fallen for you already, dear.

HERMAN. Impossible. It's my influence you're attracted to and my supply of cake.

RUTH. I truly am loyal, completely loyal to you.

HERMAN. Your husband must be taken care of. Albert, fetch the needle.

MERVIN. Can't I be the one?

HERMAN. No, let Albert fetch the needle.

MERVIN. I've done more to break Buford's spirit than he.

ALBERT. You made that long, faggy speech, that's all.

MERVIN. Yes, but it was from the heart.

ALBERT. Herman asked me to fetch the needle and I'm going to do just that.

[Albert exits into the back.]

RUTH. You know I'm loyal, don't you?

HERMAN. We're going to give you a little test.

RUTH. I've had enough of tests.

HERMAN. We've all had enough of tests, but, nonetheless, they still go on, test after test. Right, Mervin?

MERVIN. Right. After all the tests you've given me I'm still hanging around.

HERMAN. Yes, you are, aren't you, in spite of a few close calls. We'll have to make our tests more difficult.

MERVIN. Oh, no, don't do that. Let me hang around longer. I can serve you as I have been doing.

[Albert returns with a hypodermic needle.]

ALBERT. The tool is ready, sir.

Raymond J. Barry

HERMAN. Fifty milligrams.

ALBERT. That's correct, sir.

RUTH. Do I have to be around for this?

HERMAN. Ruth, would you do the honors?

RUTH. My goodness. Me? Do the honors?

HERMAN. That's right. Just to show your loyalty.

RUTH. But I can't. He's my husband. I couldn't.

HERMAN. Oh, come now, you can do it for our sake.

BUFORD. R... R... Run... ning.

RUTH. He's still talking.

BUFORD. ...and, and, and try... ing... across.

RUTH. I can't do this.

HERMAN. Have some cake first. That will give you the strength. Come on, Ruth, let's get this over with.

RUTH. I'd prefer to go back to my unit.

HERMAN. You have to administer the inoculation.

RUTH. No, I can't do that.

HERMAN. Yes, you can.

RUTH. But I'd rather not.

ALBERT. Don't be emotional about it.

HERMAN. You must. It's an important detail.

RUTH. Can't you take care of it, honey?

ALBERT. Just do it as if it's your job.

RUTH. But I can't.

[simultaneous]

HERMAN.	**ALBERT.**
Ruth, you've got to detach yourself from him.	Do it, Ruth. Do it. Then you'll be free.

RUTH. He's my husband. I love him.

HERMAN. You love me too just a little.

RUTH. No, I love him.

HERMAN. Your cake rations will be cut short.

RUTH. Somehow that matters to me.

HERMAN. You've been softened by my supply of cake.

RUTH. No one is safe.

HERMAN. You're safe. I have influence.

RUTH. I'm drawn to you even in front of my husband.

HERMAN. This is the best way to detach yourself from him.

MERVIN. Otherwise we'll always suspect you.

RUTH. I can't... I hate needles.

HERMAN. The inoculation will give us a new beginning.

ALBERT. Your husband will always be an issue.

HERMAN. Do it for our sake, buttercup.

A Piece of Cake

ALBERT. You'd better do it.

RUTH. Can't you just infect his water.

ALBERT. No! You must finish him yourself.

HERMAN. It's the only way I can trust you.

MERVIN. Give yourself to Herman.

ALBERT. He's fat but give yourself to him anyway.

MERVIN. You'll be happier for it, believe me.

HERMAN. Guard the doors.

RUTH. All right, I'll do it.

MERVIN. She switches sides easily.

ALBERT. Take this. *[Albert hands Ruth the needle.]* It's ready.

MERVIN. Ruth? Do you want some more cake to give you confidence?

[Lights out}

Act Two

-

Scene Four

[Lights up.]
[Buford stands, staring at Ruth. The rope still hangs from his neck.]

RUTH. Why are you staring at me, Buford? Look somewhere else, would you? *[Buford remains motionless. Ruth avoids his stare.]* Please, don't look at me like a dog about to be put to sleep. Please, Buford, don't stare at me. *[she weeps]* This is so difficult for me. I'm not built for this sort of thing. Only a minute ago I was so sure of what I was doing, but now, suddenly there's nothing more important than my love for you.

BUFORD. Establish your loyalty, my buttercup.

RUTH. Yes, I must do that. Buford, I simply must live for once in the sunlight. Try to understand that, my husband. I find myself tongue tied, unable to express the horror of being controlled by an invisible and prodigious force hidden somewhere. I don't know who the enemy is really, don't have the vaguest notion of what is watching me, but it lurks everywhere, waiting to strangle me whenever I dare venture beyond my door. In the end there are no excuses for betraying you, Buford, other than my fear and the liberation that will come with never again being eavesdropped upon by those who judge me. Stick you with the needle, my darling, and free myself from the shackles that have fettered me for so long. *[Ruth hesitates.]* I wish so very much I didn't have to do this.

BUFORD. You're cold enough to kill me.

RUTH. I love you.

BUFORD. You've made other priorities.

RUTH. I have, yes.

BUFORD. Your safety has taken precedence.

Raymond J. Barry

Ruth. Look somewhere else, would you?

Buford. I'm a dog about to be put to sleep.

Ruth. Please, Buford, don't. This is our last conversation.

Buford. I was your friend and never would have betrayed you.

Ruth. This is so difficult for me.

Buford. I love you.

Ruth. Please, don't say that. I'm not built for this sort of thing. If only those men hadn't dropped in on us. This wouldn't have come to pass.

Buford. So do it.

Ruth. I can't.

Buford. You know, Ruth, there's nothing more important than love. Nothing else matters really. Killing our love is worse than killing me.

Ruth. I want to make love to you.

Buford. You know we can't do that.

Ruth. Nothing seems to matter without us.

Buford. Strange to hear you say that.

Ruth. Only a minute ago I was sure of what I was doing.

Buford. You forgot that people aren't replaceable.

Ruth. Make love to me.

Buford. We can't.

Ruth. It's the only thing we have left.

Buford. "The end justifies the means."

[RUTH puts her arms around him.]

Ruth. You're a sensual man, Buford. You want me now as you always have.

[RUTH bears her breasts.]

Buford. You're making me sweat.

Ruth. Are you hot?

Buford. Stick me with the needle.

Ruth. Stick me with your dick.

Buford. We shouldn't.

Ruth. At this point "shoulds" and "shouldn'ts" are irrelevant.

Buford. I won't, goddammit!

Ruth. I love you.

Buford. Get away from me.

Ruth. Take me! Take me! Take me!

Buford. Stop it!

Ruth. I'll make everything up to you. Here, I'll show you.

[RUTH sticks the needle into her breast, pushing the syringe plunger down so that all the virus enters her body.]

Ruth. Now will you believe me? I do love you.

Buford. My God.

Ruth. There is no God, Buford. There is only us and whatever God-like qualities we have to offer.

A Piece of Cake

BUFORD. What have you done to yourself?

RUTH. I'm infected, Buford.

BUFORD. What have you done?

RUTH. How long, I wonder, will it take?

BUFORD. Oh, my darling, I love you.

RUTH. Then make love to me, my darling, just once more.

BUFORD. I love you. I love you. I love you.

RUTH. Defy what they have done to us.

BUFORD. I love you.

RUTH. Make love to me, my dear, but first join me, my darling.

[While they passionately kiss and the lights dim, RUTH sticks the needle into BUFORD'S chest, pushing the syringe plunger down so the virus enters him. BUFORD falls to the floor.]

Act Two

-

Scene Five

[ALBERT, MERVIN and are in the room. BUFORD is dressing. They stand in scattered positions around HERMAN and RUTH, who are dancing a waltz together. There is no music. The syringe is on the floor.]

HERMAN. Dancing at my weight? I've done little more than eat cake for such a long time, for... years in fact.

MERVIN. Maybe you could change your ways.

ALBERT. We changed our ways.

MERVIN. When we saw what was happening to our kind we changed our ways.

ALBERT. We decided to stop drinking the water.

MERVIN. And we became less flamboyant.

ALBERT. Although we're still basically the same people.

MERVIN. A rash breaks out once in a while, but we're still basically the same.

RUTH. Couple of queers.

HERMAN. I should lose weight.

RUTH. So you can dance more easily?

[RUTH whirls HERMAN more intensely by the hand.]

HERMAN. *[Moving awkwardly.]* I've never done this.

ALBERT. He moves like a walrus.

MERVIN. A what?

ALBERT. One of those large mammals that walked the earth years ago.

MERVIN. What did you call it?

ALBERT. A walrus.

Raymond J. Barry

MERVIN. A walrus? Herman looks like a walrus?

HERMAN. What me? Looking like a walrus?

RUTH. A cute walrus.

[RUTH and HERMAN dance.]

HERMAN. There's no music.

ALBERT. I seldom hear music.

MERVIN. I heard music once, drifting out of a window as I passed by.

HERMAN. Shouldn't be wandering outside too often.

MERVIN. When I was working.

HERMAN. Oh, alone?

MERVIN. Albert usually comes with me but sometimes I wander outside by myself.

ALBERT. Why you little double crossing...

MERVIN. I can't always be with you.

ALBERT. But this is the first time I'm hearing about this.

MERVIN. Never mind; look at them dance.

[Herman and Ruth dance.]

RUTH. Buford never danced.

HERMAN. Buford isn't long for this world.

[Buford is feeling the effect of the injection, his torso bending all the way down to his ankles while standing on his feet.]

HERMAN. I'm feeling vulnerable moving around like this.

RUTH. You're enjoying yourself, you dancing fool.

HERMAN. No, really, I think we should stop, buttercup.

[Herman attempts to walk away from her, but Ruth stops him. They continue dancing.]

ALBERT. You sure are making a damned fool of yourself, Herman.

MERVIN. My rash has gotten worse from watching this spectacle.

HERMAN. Watch it.

ALBERT. Just joking.

HERMAN. Wasn't funny.

MERVIN. I'm feeling weaker.

ALBERT. Brace yourself, Mervin.

HERMAN. These two are getting too big for their britches.

ALBERT. Mervin, maybe we should go. Let them dance.

MERVIN. I'm so weak.

HERMAN. No stay.

[Herman and Ruth stop dancing.]

RUTH. Mean remarks by these men.

HERMAN. They were mean, weren't they?

RUTH. The big one over there broke into my unit.

HERMAN. They both enjoyed my awkwardness on the dance floor.

ALBERT. We're fans.

MERVIN. We liked your dancing.

HERMAN. You just stay for a while.

MERVIN. We'd prefer to leave.

RUTH. They want to run.

HERMAN. There's nowhere to run.

ALBERT. There's nowhere we can run.

MERVIN. My throat is sore.

HERMAN. You might be on your last legs, Mervin, from the way you carry on.

MERVIN. Albert, we're in trouble.

ALBERT. You wouldn't get rid of us now, would you?

RUTH. Mean remarks.

ALBERT. I merely said what came to my mind.

RUTH. Mean queers.

MERVIN. I'm kind.

ALBERT. We're not mean.

HERMAN. Made me feel self conscious about my dancing after eating my cake.

MERVIN. The cake helped my rash.

ALBERT. We're not mean people.

MERVIN. I'm too sick to be mean.

HERMAN. A man expressing himself by dancing, only to find himself made fun of by two pieces of scum.

RUTH. They never should have been spared.

HERMAN. I'm beginning to realize that.

RUTH. They know about us.

HERMAN. Believe me, I know they know only too well.

MERVIN. We'll keep it quiet.

ALBERT. We won't tell anyone.

RUTH. Don't trust them.

HERMAN. Dancing with my new girlfriend and you both turn me into a laughing stock.

[BUFORD falls dead.]

MERVIN. Albert, I need you suddenly.

ALBERT. I'm here. Goodness knows, I'm here.

[Herman approaches Albert and Mervin with the needle. Lights out.]

Act Two

-

Scene Six

[Lights up. Herman and Ruth standing. Buford, Albert and Mervin lay dead on the floor. The rope is still around dead Buford's neck. Bombs burst in the distance.]

Raymond J. Barry

RUTH. Those bombs.

HERMAN. You must be used to them by now.

RUTH. I'm never completely used to them.

HERMAN. You're safe with little old Herman, my little buttercup.

RUTH. I don't have much time left.

HERMAN. My little buttercup, why don't you lie down after you finish your cake?

RUTH. Maybe it would be good to lie down. I'm weakening.

HERMAN. The couch is at your disposal.

RUTH. So thoughtful; so very kind.

HERMAN. Think nothing of it.

RUTH. *[Herman leads her to the couch.]* I hate leaving my cake.

HERMAN. It'll be there after we've finished.

RUTH. After we've finished?

HERMAN. Yes, after we've finished our nap.

RUTH. We're taking a nap?

HERMAN. Oh, yes, that was understood, wasn't it?

RUTH. I had no intention of taking a nap.

HERMAN. Then why would you allow yourself to stop eating cake?

[Herman leads her to the couch and helps her to lie down.]

RUTH. I should rest a little just to relax my frayed nerves. I'm weakening.

HERMAN. And that's exactly what you are doing. Now rest, my buttercup.

RUTH. Yes, this feels so good.

HERMAN. I'm here to protect you.

RUTH. I feel safe during these last moments.

HERMAN. It's the manly part of me that comes to the fore whenever a woman is in distress. May I kiss you on the cheek?

RUTH. Later. I feel we've been taped. Have we been taped?

HERMAN. Yes, of course.

RUTH. I'm glad I'm here anyway with an abundant supply of cake.

HERMAN. Forget the cake. It's me I want you to love.

RUTH. "Love"? You said, "love".

HERMAN. Yes, I said it.

RUTH. And you meant it. I know you meant it.

HERMAN. It slipped out.

RUTH. Don't make excuses.

HERMAN. I can't help myself sometimes. I say the word in privacy just to hear it out loud. I say other words too like "loneliness" and "yearning" and "desire," words that bring me closer to myself when I think about their meaning. If only I could admit to my need for intimacy with another human being, admit to my need for you, my buttercup. My love for you is the life-giving force that propels me forward into the next hour, the next day, the next week. Love is what keeps me going.

RUTH. Careful. They could be listening.

A Piece of Cake

HERMAN. They? I am "they", my buttercup.

RUTH. There is something beyond you that could be listening. Surely they're listening. They're always listening. I do feel safer with you. I'm weakening. I feel faint.

HERMAN. Good, then let's take a nap, and afterwards, we'll have a piece of cake.

RUTH. No, I'm afraid there'll be no more cake for me, my friend.

[RUTH dies in HERMAN'S arms on the couch. Bombs burst in the distance, as the lights slowly dim.]

HERMAN. *Ruth? Ruth? Speak to me, Ruth. Don't leave me now. Speak to me. We could have such a wonderful time together with my influence. Please, Ruth, don't leave an old fat man now. Not now. I was almost happy with you, my buttercup. Please, Ruth, don't go from me. Please. Are you gone from me too along with everything else? Are you really gone from me? Nothing but cake left now, nothing but cake.*

End of Play

Raymond J. Barry